FEMALE, FELINE AND DANGEROUS

Half an hour from NewHome Grab the computer chimed.

"Good," Tatha nodded, and reached overhead to flip on one of the commiter transmitters. Jes glanced up curiously. When he looked down she held a small stunner pointed at his stomach.

"No," he said, searching her face for something beyond the silver fur and blue eyes.

"I'm sorry," she said.

He lunged toward the gun and she pulled the trigger.

After the first moment of blinding shock there was no pain; his body simply ceased to belong to him. He slumped onto the deck. Tatha picked him up and shoved him into the navigator's web. She strapped him in and turned his head so he could watch her.

"Comfortable, tauCaptain Kennerin?" she said, not smiling.

Jes could not close his eyes, and only his paralysis kept him from weeping.

Books by Marta Randall

Dangerous Games
Islands
Journey

Publshed by POCKET BOOKS

DANGEROUS GAMES

MARTA RANDALL

PUBLISHED BY POCKET BOOKS NEW YORK

A portion of this book has appeared in *The Magazine of Fantasy and Science Fiction*, April 1980.

Another *Original* publication of POCKET BOOKS

POCKET BOOKS, a Simon & Schuster division of
GULF & WESTERN CORPORATION
1230 Avenue of the Americas, New York, N.Y. 10020

ISBN: 0-671-82417-1

First Pocket Books printing September, 1980

10 9 8 7 6 5 4 3 2 1

POCKET and colophon are trademarks of Simon & Schuster.

Interior design by Catherine Carucci

Printed in the U.S.A.

Special thanks are due to Charles N. Brown and Elizabeth A. Lynn for bravura jobs of reading and criticism; Debbie Notkin for painstaking copy-editing; Dr. James Benford for not laughing; and David G. Hartwell for his limitless patience.

This one's for Lizzy.

THE KENNERINS

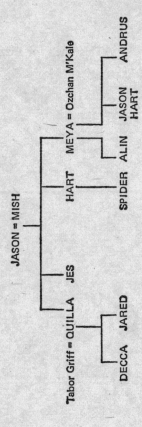

"For herein may be seen noble chivalry, courtesy, humanity, friendliness, hardiness, love, friendship, cowardice, murder, hate, virtue, and sin. Do after the good and leave the evil, and it shall bring you to good fame and fortune."

—Sir Thomas Malory
Le Morte d'Arthur, preface

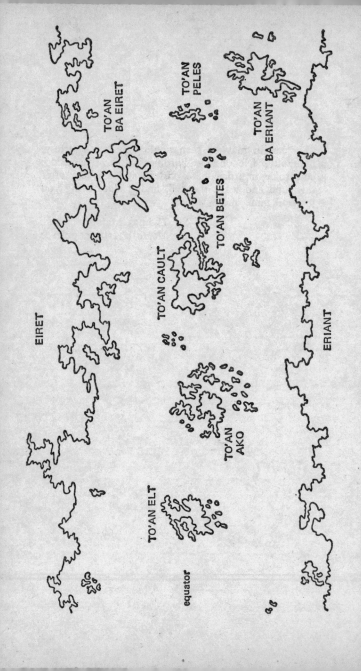

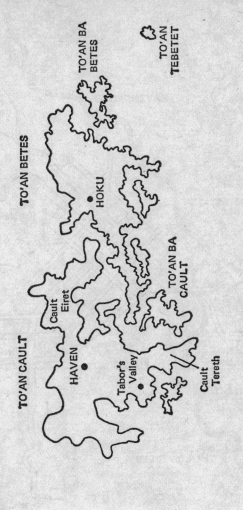

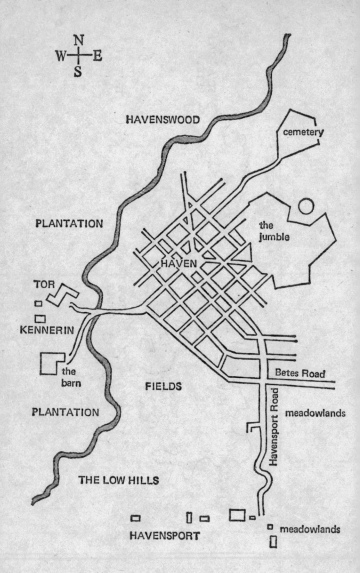

Part One

STRAYS
1242 new time

I came to the place of my birth and cried,
"The friends of my youth, where are they?"
And echo answered, "Where are they?"
—Arab saying

ALEJANDRO CRISTOBAL MARQUEZ PUT HIS hands behind his back and stood amid the dim lights and harsh noises of the portside bar. His palms were slippery with sweat and his chest tightened; he desperately hoped that his anxiety and hatred did not show in his face. Before him, the tall, dark-skinned tauCaptain rocked his chair back, put his feet on the table, and skimmed the contents of Sandro's Certificate. The blue light of the Certificate's readout flickered across the tauCaptain's face, imparting an almost demonic look to the high cheekbones and oriental eyes. The tauCaptain looked slightly interested and slightly bored; Sandro carefully relaxed his clenched hands and resisted the urge to look around, convinced that the other spacers were grinning and poking each other with their elbows. They had watched this scene before.

The tauCaptain tapped the Certificate with his finger and the blue light faded as he tossed the disk on the tabletop.

"It says here you're a Second, newly commissioned," he said.

"Yes, sir."

"And you want to ship with me?"

"Yes, sir."

"Why?"

Sandro's throat felt dry. "Rumor has it that you need a Second, sir. That you've been on MarketPort four days over schedule, looking for one. I'm a Second by paper, not promotion . . . it's hard to find a berth. I took my chances."

"Aerie-Kennerin does not ship neophytes."

"No sir. But A-K doesn't ship without Seconds either." Sandro held his breath, but the captain's lips tilted upward. He swung his feet from the table. The front legs of the chair made a sharp noise amid the cacophony of the bar.

"Get a chair . . . um . . ." He glanced at the Certificate. "Marquez. Am I pronouncing that right?"

"Yes, sir." Sandro pulled a chair to the table, feeling slightly relieved. The tauCaptain could still turn him down, or demand of him an evening of listening and companionship before casting him off, but could not, now, laugh and dismiss him in the publicity of the bar. The seven months since he'd received his commission had been full of such rejections; to be turned down by this man, this probable enemy, would especially hurt. Perhaps, he thought without much hope, this Kennerin was a minor one; a distant cousin or a second son. Sandro sat and looked at his Certificate lying on the table amid the collection of empty vibraglasses, then glanced at the captain. He didn't look like a monster.

The captain shouted an order at a passing shimmertray and gestured. Sandro ordered. The tray arrived with the fresh drinks, flashed a green acceptance of the tauCaptain's thumbprint, and hovered over the table. The empty vibraglasses snicked out of existence, and the tray floated into the smoky darkness.

The captain peered at Sandro's drink. "That's Jel-Watr," he said accusingly. "Don't you drink?"

"I do, sir. But not tonight."

"Huh." The tauCaptain adopted a serious expression. "My name is Jes Kennerin, and I am very, very drunk. Remember that. Also remember that I remember, if that makes any sense. Any conditions we bind tonight, we bind finally. I don't go back on my word. Is that understood?"

"Yes, sir."

"Stop that. This is a bar, not a ship. Call me Kennerin."

"Kennerin," Sandro said. The name didn't choke him. "Call me Marquez."

The tauCaptain nodded and raised his glass. "A society of families," he said. "Marquez. Sounds familiar."

"It's not uncommon," Sandro said, more casually than he felt. There was a Parallax agent dead on Marquez Landing, as much a part of Sandro as the paper Second, as his pride, as the memory of home. He evened his voice. "Not uncommon," he said again.

"You're probably right. Drink. I want to hear about paper training, Marquez. What in hell does a paper trainer know about Seconding a tauship?"

"Grab mechanics," Sandro said, relieved. "Astrogation and binary tauseep, pinpointing, controls maintenance, invalidation process, invoicing and documentation, controls port function and procedures, customs processes—"

Kennerin waved his long hand impatiently. "Fine. You know everything there is to know, except how to Second a tauship. Ever been on one?"

"I came in on one, sir. Nobody's native to Market-Port."

"I run a class 5b/14 merchant ship, basic 17 sub 5, reconditioned to a type G rating. Tell me about her."

Sandro talked for half an hour. Kennerin listened, blue eyes bright in his dark face. At times he drummed his fingers on the tabletop. Finally he waved at Sandro to stop.

"You're wrong on that," he said. "She's got seven four-gee holds, not five. But that's a custom change. Can you ship out tomorrow?"

"I can ship out now, sir."

"Eager, aren't you?"

Sandro's breath caught, but the tauCaptain took Sandro's Certificate, skimmed through the contracts section, and tapped the cassette for writing mode.

"Four-year contract, and I'm starting you as apprentice Second. Full Second after the first year, if you make it. Five hundred fremarks the run for the first year, with a twelve-fremark base for each month in space. We'll renegotiate after you reach full Second—you'll get crewgains then, too. You'll ship with me or any other A-K captain, on assignment. Standard duties, port leave, all the rest. Agreed?"

Sandro nodded and the tauCaptain pushed his thumb at the Certificate, then offered it to Sandro. Sandro unclenched his hands and carefully tapped in his personal code, thumbprinted the Certificate, and slipped it into his pocket. The captain twisted in his chair and waved at a passing tray.

Sandro took a deep breath. "I don't think you should do that, sir."

"What?"

"It's the duty of a Second to make sure that all officers

and crew are fit for space by end of leavetime, sir. As your Second, I think you've had enough."

Kennerin's face hardened. "You're not a full Second, Marquez."

"Nonetheless, sir."

"I have the feeling that I've made a very bad mistake."

"Still."

Kennerin stared at him, grinned, and pushed away from the table. Sandro's shoulders loosened, and as he followed the captain from the bar he made a rude gesture at the spacers watching him. Most of them laughed.

Spacers jostled and roared all along Dullard's Walk, spending freely, drinking copiously, smashing tables and heads with enthusiasm. Most of the light globes were broken and the Walk glowed dimly with the reflecting lights of the passing colorfloats. The tauCaptain paused at the bar's door, shook his head, and put his hand on Sandro's shoulder. Sandro looked at the hand, then glanced up at the captain's face.

"Not very tall, are you?" Kennerin said.

Sandro's face heated. "And you're not so short, captain. Where's the rest of the crew?"

"Somewhere. I'll find them. You have anything to pack?"

Sandro frowned. His small rented room contained a few extra pieces of clothing, a borrowed bookreel, the landlord's battered, stale-smelling furniture—nothing he needed, nothing he couldn't replace, nothing he ever wanted to see again. He touched his hip pouch; it seemed sufficient luggage for an exile. He shook his head and followed Kennerin down the crowded rowdiness of Dullard's Walk.

Pelican's Nest was stuffed to the doors; its walls seemed to bulge with the beat of music that shook the pavement but could not be heard over the rest of the noise. Spacers surrounded the Beard of Kaipha, Lizard's Revenge, the Frog King, and Scow's Folly. Seven different tunes met with a discordant jangle overhead and the colorfloats danced seductively, whispering enticements to lurid, fraudulent ecstacies. Jes Kennerin shoved his way down the Walk. Sandro, trailing in his wake, pondered the tauCaptain's broad shoulders and club of black hair, but they told him nothing. They reached a public caller; the tauCaptain banged his message into it and paid with his thumb, and soon Dullard's Walk glowed with colorfloats carrying the captain's insignia and flashing the boarding signal. Sandro looked at them dubiously.

"Will that be enough?"

"Yeah. They want to ship out as much as I do. Maybe as much as you do." The captain looked over the Walk, his expression unreadable, then shoved through the crowds again.

Dullard's Walk ended abruptly at the soundscreen which separate the shuttleport from the rest of the trading station. Sandro paused at the barrier and glanced back. The Walk seemed hazy and distant, already a part of his past. Kennerin strode toward the slidebelts, his hands in his pockets. Sandro heard his humming but could not place the tune. His lips tightened and he walked after his captain. The screen closed behind them.

Kennerin jumped from one slidebelt to another, turned a corner, and stepped off the belt. Sandro followed his gesture toward the sleek, winged shuttle resting on fat, battered landing gear. It was already pointed toward the runways. Kennerin rocked back on his heels, his hands still in his pockets, then reached for the port maintenance box. The door slid open and the tauCaptain extracted a form. He handed it to Sandro.

"Here, Second. See if we're spaceworthy."

Sandro moved closer to the box and peered at the form. Everything seemed in order. He nodded, glanced at the form again, and squinted at the nose of the shuttle. A merchant ship's shuttle generally bore only registry numbers, but this one had a name.

"*Spawn*, captain?"

"That's right."

"It's an unusual name, sir."

"It's a ridiculous name. The ship's called *Rabbit*."

Sandro looked blank. The tauCaptain tilted his head and looked at Sandro evenly. "The rabbit's a Terran original noted for producing lots of other rabbits in a very short time. I named it after my family."

"Your family, sir? I thought only owners could name tauships."

"That's right. You signed on with Aerie-Kennerin, Marquez. I own it."

I own it. Sandro stared at the ship and at the tau-
Captain. "I thought you might be a cousin," he said haltingly. When Kennerin didn't move, Sandro turned and
walked silently back to the open hatch. He closed his
eyes, feeling bitterness in his throat. Unwanted visions
danced across the screen of his eyelids; acres of green-
black zimania plantations, a tall, forbidding house set
amid gardens, the noisy bustle of town, port, island,
world—a mocking catalog of all the things that Sandro
could have owned. *I own it.* That, too? Sandro thought,
and when the captain touched his shoulder Sandro
jumped, startled and angry. He looked at Kennerin defensively, and the captain stared back at him with that
same infuriating, distant expression in his eyes.

"You want to back out?"

Sandro's lips tightened and he shook his head.

"Then you're a spacer, Marquez. You leave the past
right here, you don't take it with you. Not if it gets in
the way. You're my Second now, understand?"

Sandro nodded, confused, and looked away. The captain dropped his hand. Somebody shouted.

"Here's what passes for my crew," Kennerin said sarcastically. He smiled, and his face changed. "Haul yourself in, Second, and let's get out of here."

The crew were both drunk. Kennerin herded them
aboard with insults and curses; they laughed and cursed
back. One tried to hug the captain, but he pushed her
away. Her mouth pinched down. Kennerin ignored her
and swung the hatch shut behind them. Sandro's confusion doubled; he didn't know this man at all.

"The tall one is Beryl," Kennerin said, locking the
toggles around the hatch. "And the short bastard's
Greaves. This is Alejandro Marquez, new Second. You
should like him, Greaves, he's shorter than you are.
Anyone in condition to fly this drunktank?"

Beryl pushed red-brown hair from her dirty face and
looked at Sandro coldly. Her lips pinched down farther.
She turned on her side in the webbing and went to
sleep. Greaves shook his head and fumbled with his
straps. Kennerin sighed and dropped into the navigator's
web.

"Up to you, Marquez. First beam *Rabbit* and tell
Hetch that we're on our way, then get us out of here."

Sandro sat reluctantly in the pilot's web. Kennerin slumped in the web beside him and closed his eyes.

"Beam's thirteen, channel four. And *Rabbit* should be somewhere in sector five, level five, but check with Hetch. And, Marquez . . ."

"Sir?"

"Don't kill us."

Sandro didn't reply. It couldn't be any different from flying a simulator, he told himself without conviction. The board was standard and he easily found the commiter and toggled it to the proper channel. It wheezed and burped and the contact light glowed. The screen, presumably broken, remained dark.

"About time, Jes," a voice said grumpily. "Think I want to spend my life orbiting this junkheap?"

"This is Second Alejandro Marquez," Sandro said. To his relief, his voice didn't squeak. "I have tauCaptain Kennerin, Crew Beryl, and Crew Greaves. The tau-Captain wants to hit grab tomorrow. as soon as we get clearance. Can you give me *Rabbit*'s exact point?"

The commiter made a surprised noise. "Marquez?"

"That's right, spacer."

"Spacer, hell. I'm tauCaptain Manual Hetch, Second. You can call Kennerin anything you want, but you call me 'sir,' understand?"

Sandro flushed, knowing that he'd been set up and sure that Kennerin was repressing a smile. "Yes, sir. Can I have the point?"

"Open your board."

Sandro plugged into the board channel and let Hatch beam the point into *Spawn*'s routing tank, then read the point back to Hetch. Hetch confirmed and signed off. Sandro double-checked the controls, obtained leave clearance, and guided the shuttle to the start point. He thought an intense, brief prayer and fired the shuttle. It waddled down the short runway, bounced three times, and wallowed into the air.

"That," said Kennerin without opening his eyes, "will have to improve."

Sandro ignored him. He poised his hand over the second bank switches, anxiously waiting for the go-light. The acceleration pushed at his body. He fought it. MarketPort dropped away beneath them and Sandro's fingers went rigid.

"Don't poke it," Kennerin said sleepily. "Stroke it, Marquez. Nice and slow and gentle."

Sandro glared at him, assuming mockery, and the go-light winked. He set the second bank switches and *Spawn* rattled gently as she turned to the new heading. MarketPort slid out of sight; the sky turned black.

"Better," the tauCaptain said. "It seems your board scores were accurate, after all. Think you can synch with *Rabbit* without punching a gap in the hull?"

"Yes, sir."

"Fine. Wake me before we get there. I collect catastrophes."

This time the captain really did seem to fall asleep. *Spawn* would follow the routing until they approached *Rabbit;* until then there was nothing for Sandro to do. He watched the board intently anyway, rubbing his shoulders. The muffled roar of the donkey engines seemed far away. He checked the board again and turned in his webbing to look at Kennerin. The captain sprawled, utterly relaxed and utterly mysterious. Long slim body, elegant angular face, black hair tied at the nape of his neck with a bright ribbon. His eyelids twitched as he dreamed. Sandro remembered the amusement of the bar, the stiffness of Dullard's Walk, the calm and terrifying distance as they stood beside the shuttle, the sarcastic banter with the crew. He shook his head, falling deeper into confusion, and wondered when his captain would finally place his name.

Their families had been competitors, back when Sandro still had a family, but the competition had been a distant, impersonal thing. The Family Kennerin was far too small to threaten the Family Marquez. But now the Family Marquez was dead, or scattered, their home and planet wrenched from them, and a Parallax agent lay dead in Cuidad Garcia, by Sandro's hand. Our families were in competition, Sandro thought, looking at the captain. Did you arrange for this?

Jes Kennerin murmured indistinctly in his sleep and turned over. Sandro shook his head. If Kennerin had any hand in the death of Sandro's family, he'd have placed Sandro's name the moment he saw it. And he would not have turned his shuttle and his life over to someone who had reason to kill him. Would he? Kennerin's expressions tumbled through Sandro's memory, and he could not answer his own question.

I own it.

Sandro pushed the bitterness aside and turned to the controls again. There would be time enough in space, he thought, to consider who he was and where he was, and who slept beside him in the small lights of the shuttle's bridge.

When *Rabbit* clarified on the screen before him he woke the captain and brought the shuttle into the bay as smoothly as he could. Jes Kennerin rewarded him with a cool nod of approval, cracked the shuttle's hatch, and ushered Sandro Marquez into a complex, unknown future.

❧

THEY SLID THROUGH THE GRAB THE NEXT day, Beryl and Greaves riding the suits in the engine room, Jes guiding *Rabbit* through the grab's complexity of coils with smooth, practiced grace. Sandro expected and rode with the sudden feeling of disorientation and imbalance as the coils shimmered to life; he watched the screens as stars were replaced by blackness, and blackness by the chaotic glory of tauspace. *Rabbit* hummed solidly and the three men on the bridge were silent. Sandro looked at Hetch, to his right, and found the old tauCaptain staring intently at Jes Kennerin. Kennerin sat motionless in his webbing, gazing at the dizzying images of tauspace with an almost supernatural hunger. Sandro blinked and felt as though he had been given a glimpse into a labyrinth both familiar and infinitely strange.

Then Hetch freed his webbing and the snap of locks broke the moment. Sandro glanced at him and when he looked again Kennerin was relaxed and turned from the screen. He looked at Sandro distantly and his lips quirked.

"Think you can do that next time?"

"No, sir," Sandro said immediately. "Time after that, maybe. Not before."

"He's learning already," Hetch said. He passed his hand over his bald head, rose, and winced. His hand touched his hip and, part of the same movement, rose and patted his round belly with affection. "All that hard work makes me hungry."

"Anything makes you hungry," Kennerin said. Hetch looked indignant and left the bridge.

Kennerin touched the clasps of his own webbing. The cables slid into the seat and the tension locks opened. He swung the seat around to face Sandro.

"Does that bother you?" he said, waving a hand at the screens. Sandro glanced at them, watching the curious complexities of that alternate universe in which time had no meaning, in which all events happened simultaneously and never, and through which the tauships skipped and skimmed, launched from the grab at their startports, caught by grabs at their stopports and translated into realspace again. Tau seemed to him an insubstantial, never-ending light show, far too chaotic and fierce to be real. He shook his head.

"Good. This trip will take about four months standard, and you're going to be busy every second of that time. You'll learn to be a spacer first and a Second second. You'll start in the engine room under Greaves, then drive mechanics with Beryl, and finally controls with Hetch. Greaves and Beryl are damned good and Hetch is the best in the system. Remember that. If you have any questions or problems that they can't take care of, bring them to me. I'll answer the questions, but I expect a minimum of problems. Understood?"

Sandro nodded.

"Fine. You start now. Beryl has first shift, so Greaves should be unsuiting. You know how to find the engine room?"

"Yes, sir." Sandro rose and crossed to the round entrance of the passageway.

"Marquez."

"Sir?" He turned, his hand on the frame. Jes sat unmoving, his expression curiously relaxed.

"Do you have anything to tell me?"

Sandro's belly cramped. He stiffened and looked across the bridge, feeling the hatred build again.

"No, sir," he said coldly.

"All right. Get on with it."

Sandro got on with it. The first month in tau was exhausting. Greaves seemed eager to push the entirety of engine systems and controls into his head immediately, prodding him and exploding with impatience when Sandro lagged. Questions about the captain were treated with contempt. "Irrelevant," Greaves would snap, and proceed with the lesson. Sandro disciplined himself to learn and discovered an increasing fascination with the practicalities of taudrives, the beginning of a feel for the engines and their characters which, he knew, would never be as great as Greaves' feel, but which seemed to please the stocky, brown-haired spacer. One morning, peering into the speckled mirror above the clensor basin as he scraped depilatory from his face, he discovered a thin red line that would, eventually, become his first webscar, and surprised himself by feeling an enormous pride. He finished hurriedly and rushed down the passageway, grinning and fumbling with the clasp of his utility belt.

"Look what I've got," he said when he came into the engine room. Greaves put a test unit down and inspected Sandro's face, then grinned back at him.

"Another year and you won't look like a knocker at all," the spacer said. His own webscars curved over the planes of his face and disappeared into the collar of his suit. They came from working in the pit engines, and spacers carried them as a badge of professional pride. Sandro touched his cheek and felt the thin ridge of the scar under the pads of his fingers.

"The captain's got a lot of them," he said, and for once Greaves didn't glare at him.

"Captain's a good one," Greaves said, picking up the test unit. "You get some, they're too busy sitting in the bridge playing Tri-Captain to come along here, don't give a damn about the engines. You can always tell a good captain by the scarring, Sandro. Pick the ones with lots of it, it means they pay attention to stuff. Look at Hetch. He's got scars on the soles of his feet, and he's one of the best in the Federation."

"The captain spends a lot of time down here?"

"As much as he needs to, maybe more. Here, pick that up and follow me."

Sandro slung the toolkit over his shoulder and followed

Greaves into the donkey engine housings. "Does the captain do anything else? Aside from being a spacer, I mean?"

Greaves looked disgusted. "You are a goddamned long-nosed knocker. The captain's a spacer, understand? From one end to the other, and there's nothing to say about it. Now get your ass over here and pay attention."

Sandro bit his lip and hurried over. Greaves looked at him sideways, grinned suddenly, and touched Sandro's scar. "Big deal," the spacer muttered genially, and they bent their heads over the tattletales.

If Sandro got on well with Greaves, though, his relations with Beryl were disturbing. She treated him with a cold contempt which first alarmed, then angered, him; even their minimal contact was abrasive. She was the only person Sandro had ever met who could produce a silence as quick and vicious as her words, and he began to dread the ending of his time with Greaves.

On the fortieth day, Greaves buckled him into a drive suit and he filled his first engine shift, hooked between the controls of the bridge, the computer, and the huge, thrusting engines. The drive suits hung suspended over the silent intricacy of the engine room control banks; Sandro discovered that once fastened in place and secured the suits were entirely comfortable. He looked at Greaves standing on the deck below, looked across at Beryl hidden in the half opacity of her suit, and felt a growing excitement. Then Greaves touched a switch and the engine room disappeared. Sandro was overwhelmed by the vastness of the ship. He picked through the sensations carefully, recognizing them by their simulator counterparts and from Greaves' precise descriptions, and slid cautiously into his work. Slowly, delicately, the ship responded to his touch.

When Greaves brought him down at the end of the shift, he was at the point of collapse and too weary to feel surprise at the presence of Hetch, Jes, and Beryl in the engine room. He braced himself against the bulkhead and listened without comprehension to the voices around him.

"He's fast, then."

"Fast, and likely to be good. He'll take more when he gets used to it."

"First time I did engine shift they had to carry me out. You done with him yet?"

"Give me one more day. I need some help on a repair."

"Double-time it, Greaves."

"You'll get him, Beryl. Don't get too hungry too fast."

Sandro raised his head, but Beryl wasn't looking at him. She and the captain stared at each other, Beryl with her chin tilted defiantly, Kennerin wearing his expression of cool distance. Hetch, watching them from the side, touched his hip unhappily and Sandro felt suddenly insignificant. He shivered and let Greaves lead him from the engine room.

"She'll freeze you first," Greaves said the next day. "Then she'll needle, then she'll spite. And if you can take it all without breaking, she'll open and be a damned good mate. But don't break, Sandro. Don't lose your temper, don't plead, don't retaliate. Just take it cold and leave it cold, or she'll run you until you shatter."

They were down in the pit engines, amid the heat and stench of oil and metal. Sandro wiped his forehead and readjusted the sweatband, wondering briefly about scars.

"Is she the reason you lost your Second on Market-Port?"

Greaves shrugged. The gesture made lights run crazily down his scarred arms and stomach. "It's not the first time, and probably won't be the last. She was a full Second, too, and good at it, but Beryl broke her. Took her three runs, but she broke her."

"If she's that much trouble, why does Kennerin ship her?"

"She's good. She's reliable. If you can get through the ice, she's a damned good mate."

"Must be true of other spacers." A lock of curly brown hair escaped from Sandro's sweatband. He cursed briefly, put down his tools, and pushed the hair into place again. "That can't be the only reason. Kennerin must have more sense than—"

"One more thing," Greaves said, deliberately interrupting him.

"Yeah?"

"Don't sleep with the captain this trip. You're new, and Beryl's around."

Sandro took his hands away from the patch on the cooling tube and looked across it at Greaves. "Am I supposed to hear more than what you said?"

"About Beryl, maybe. What the captain does is his own business." Greaves gave a last twist to the patch jacket and gathered his tools. "Done, Sandro?"

"Almost." He let pressure seep into the cooling tube. The patch held. He stood and wiped his hands on his pants. "Any more good advice for me?"

"Yep. Get yourself a good night's sleep. You're going to need it."

As Second, Sandro had his own cabin but had to share the common clensor. He made sure that Beryl was on duty and not likely to bother him, stripped, and stepped into the sonics of the unit. The last time she had shared a clensor with him she stuck her head out of the unit, glanced between his legs, and laughed as though his penis was the funniest thing in the Federation. He felt too ambiguous in his position as apprentice Second to challenge her, and too new aboard to retaliate, so had controlled both temper and pride and pretended to ignore her. But he had no wish to repeat the experience. He finished quickly and returned to the privacy of his cabin.

Sleep evaded him. He dressed and prowled the small galley, picked out a tube of juice and a meatstick, and took them with him to the bridge. As he hoped, Hetch was alone on watch. The old man sat before the secondary bank, playing games with the ship's computer. He gestured Sandro to a seat and finished his move, watched intently, and cursed when the computer flanked his move and put his ship in jeopardy.

"Damned electronic smart ass," Hetch grumbled. He put the game in stasis while his eyes drifted over the tattletales on the main board. Satisfied, he began swinging his feet up on the bank, grimaced, and put them down again. He turned away and sat stiffly, holding his hip. Sandro wanted to ask what led to Hetch's occasional winces of pain and his increasingly pronounced limp, but felt that the questions would be unwelcome. He sipped his juice instead, wishing he could do something. After a time Hetch relaxed and turned back to the control bank.

Together the old captain and the new Second stared at the grid display that Hetch preferred to straight-vision mode. The sight of tauspace, Hetch claimed, gave him a headache.

"Greaves finished with you today, right?" Hetch said after a long pause. "You're pretty fast, Marquez. That's a good sign."

"Thank you, sir."

"And you're headed to Beryl tomorrow. Nervous?"

"Yes, sir."

The old man nodded and said "Beryl" dubiously. "One of the joys of being a useless old spacejock is I don't have to put up with her. But you do, at least for now. Greaves fill you in?"

"Yes. It didn't make me any happier."

"Not your business to be happy, Marquez. It's your business to learn. Do that, don't get scraped, and you'll be out of it by the end of the trip." Hetch grinned and faked a shudder. "Holy Mother, to have to go through training again. . . . How old are you, Marquez?"

"Eighteen standard."

"You look younger. I trained Jes when he was a year younger than you are. It was easy for him—he wanted to be a spacer so bad that he could taste it. Even stowed away with me once when he was just, what, eleven? That's right. I'll tell you the story someday, it's a good one." Sandro tried to envision Kennerin as a child and failed. Hetch leaned forward, took Sandro's juicetube and squirted juice into his mouth. "Took him on six years later," Hetch continued. "And he only had to put up with Tham, Merkit, and Bakar. Wonder he got trained at all. You, though . . ." Hetch looked at him speculatively and handed back the tube. "You're a spacer because you had to be, right?"

Sandro nodded and stared at his hands. "I had enough for a one-way flight and the farthest it took me was MarketPort. And from MarketPort, there's only one way out."

"You could have done it different. Could have taken a dirt job."

Sandro looked at him, and Hetch smiled.

"It's all right, Sandro. You chose the best, but you chose because you had to, not because you wanted it. It makes a difference. You'll be a good Second, maybe even a damned good Second, but you'll never be a great one. That bother you?"

"Yeah." Sandro put his feet on the ledge below the control bank and slumped back in the webbing. "Yeah. If it's pride to do your best, then it's pride to want to be the best, too, isn't it?" Hetch nodded. "And is it pride to feel mad because you'll never be the best?"

"That too. You won't get over it, but you'll get used to it."

Sandro licked the taste of the meatstick from his fingers and thought about that, then thought about Beryl. He frowned, trying to phrase a question.

"Captain?"

"Um?" Hetch was staring at the screen again, his eyes half closed.

"That day that I did my first engine shift, when everyone came into the control room?"

"I remember."

"I thought Beryl and Greaves were arguing over me. But when I looked, Beryl wasn't looking at me at all, or at Greaves. She and the captain—do you remember?" Hetch nodded, looking at Sandro. Sandro licked his lips quickly. "Today, when I was working with Greaves, he said that I shouldn't—he said not to sleep with the captain, because Beryl's around. He said that she lost him his first Second, the one before me. And when she looks at me, I feel like she's not looking at me at all, she's looking through me, or she's looking at what she can do to me, how she can use me." He took a deep breath and looked at Hetch. "I don't know why."

"Damn," Hetch said quietly, and put his hand over his eyes for a moment. "Sandro, forget about it. It's not your fight."

"But, that day in the engine room . . . I don't want to be a . . . a pawn in Beryl's fight."

"It's not Beryl's fight, either. It's Jes'. And as such, it's not your business," the old man said kindly. "Forget about it, Sandro. Do your job, get your training over. We've all got secrets, and you've no right to ask into this one."

"But if I get stuck in the middle—"

"Sandro," Hetch said sharply, and Sandro bit his lip. The old man looked at him with speculation and, for some reason, a hint of pity. "Marquez," he said quietly, as though to himself. "Enough for a one-way ticket to MarketPort. I'd like to hear about that, someday."

Sandro's belly went tight again. Secrets. Hetch watched him seriously, and Sandro remembered Jes saying, "Do you have anything to tell me?"

Jamás, Sandro thought. Instead he said, "How long am I under Beryl?"

"Until you learn what you need to know," Hetch said, accepting the change of subject. "She'll tell you when she's done with you."

"I'll bet."

Hetch grinned at Sandro's sarcasm. "Get some sleep, Second. It's almost tomorrow already."

Sandro nodded and walked to the doorway, expecting the old man to call him back. But Hetch leaned forward and resurrected his game, and Sandro moved quickly into his cabin.

It had been dangerously easy, these past four weeks, to forget who he was and who his captain was, to forget the reason that he, youngest son of Iberia Sector's most powerful family, had fled his homeworld with only enough fremarks for a ticket to a dingy, prefabricated trading station orbiting a barren star. *I own it. Do you have anything to tell me?* Logic argued that Kennerin was innocent of any part in Sandro's past; emotion kept the secret buried within him, and kept the suspicion alive. Besides, he thought suddenly, anything he could tell his captain would sound like the stilted ravings of an old Iberian tale: injured knight, banished heir, son of a dead father, disinherited princeling out to seek revenge on a power so big he could barely comprehend it. Safe in the belly of a rival's ship, it seemed that all his giants had turned into windmills. Fanged windmills, perhaps, but windmills all the same. He twisted in his hammock while images of Kennerin's face tumbled through his mind, each one different and none of them the truth, and it seemed to him that if he could only find the true face the answers would spill forth in neat, orderly rows, ready to solve his problems for him. Kennerin grinned and shook his head. Confused and dizzy, Sandro pulled the webbing of the hammock around him. The next morning he rose, dressed, muttered his family name like a talisman, and found Beryl.

She spent the first week pretending to ignore him, addressing her remarks to the bulkhead over his shoulder and making no effort to answer his questions. But she was quick and thorough, and Sandro absorbed her lessons hungrily, sometimes so caught up in the intricacy of Cohen-Albrecht Effect Drive mechanics that he forgot her coldness, his unhappiness, the captain's mystery. Purely out of self-defense he became almost supernaturally attuned to her, ready for the times when she turned on him unexpectedly and fired questions as though they were weapons. When he answered correctly she turned her back on him with no word of acknowledgment or praise and he learned not to permit himself the time to feel triumphant. When he made a mistake, the chill of her manner became an icy edge of contempt. He made increasingly few mistakes. He began to respect her knowledge and her abilities but refused to let it show, and she never treated him as anything other than a tool, a pawn. She's learning where my buttons are, he thought during that first week, and took pains to hide his emotions from her. She would not use him as she used a tool-drone, or a wrench.

The second week her tactics changed. Now she needled the information into him, accompanying each lecture with vitriolic comments about his performance, his abilities, his intelligence, his stature. Finding the buttons. He held grimly to his temper, using the knowledge that she herself taught him to play back her own contempt. Off shift he fled to *Rabbit*'s small gymnasium and worked his anger out, free-fall, on the bars and rungs until he verged on exhaustion and had energy enough only to scrub the day from his skin and collapse into his hammock. His worksuit and shorts tightened as his muscles grew.

One day he drifted, panting, from a high rung and looked over his shoulder to see her standing casually at the gym's lock, her green eyes glittering. A skinsuit barely covered her slim, muscular body. Caught in free-fall, her auburn hair drifted in heavy waves around her face, and her expression was, for once, relaxed. Sandro felt a brief disorientation: framed in her hair, beneath the thin web of scars, her face was almost beautiful.

"Pity you can't exercise your brains as well as your muscles," she said. She launched herself from the lock and caught a bar, curving her body sinuously around it. Sandro looked away from her, pushed himself from the rung, and slid weightlessly to the lock.

"I'll leave the gym to you," he said, deliberately polite.
"Is it easy to take the parallel bars with your tongue?"

She laughed, surprised. Sandro strolled down the corridor until he turned a bend, then ran to his cabin and
shut the door, shaking. He thought of her laughter and
her face and shook again, frightened. It's another button, he thought, remembering the planes of her face, the
curves of her sleek body. He felt sick.

Jes Kennerin appeared in the control room two days
later, coming in so silently that Sandro did not notice until
he turned and saw the captain leaning in the shadow of
a far bulkhead. Disconcerted, Sandro made a mistake.
Beryl turned on him and saw Kennerin; she pitched her
voice to carry and flooded the control room with venom,
looking always over Sandro's shoulder at the captain.
Sandro honed his anger in the sharpness of his response,
and when she abruptly turned her back to him he knew
that Kennerin was gone. She always wore skinsuits now,
and he thought he saw her shoulders shake under the
thin fabric. His breath caught. He wanted to touch her,
wanted to still the shaking and run his fingers along the
curve of her jaw. And knew that the moment he did, he
was lost.

In the gym afterwards he moved and twisted with
mindless intensity, hiding from the sound of her remembered voice, the planes of her remembered face, the terrible and fatal quivering of her body. Sweat coated his
fair skin, darkened his brown hair and left it plastered in
tight curls to his forehead and neck. I need sex, he
thought, and knew it for a lie. He spun among the
bars and rungs, driven by green eyes, until his muscles
locked and he fell through the flexible, brightly colored
bars. He tumbled slowly, unresisting, until he felt the
thick padding of the gym's side. His fingers locked around
a rung and he drifted, eyes closed, lost in the thudding of
his heart. She'd found the button, and his deepest terror
was that she knew it.

Eventually he forced himself to follow the padded
rungs to the lock and he fell through it. When he'd adjusted to the push of the ship's acceleration-gravity he
stood uncertainly and staggered toward the clensor, un-
seaming his shorts as he went. He stood in the unit, his
hands braced against its walls, while the sonics peeled
dirt, sweat, and dead skin from him.

Somebody shouted down the corridor and Beryl's voice, near the door of the clensor, said sullenly, "What do you want?" Sandro gasped; he'd left the door open. His hand drifted down to cover his genitals. He jerked it away angrily and stood quiet.

Hetch's voice, still indistinct, said something.

"I want to get clean," Beryl replied. "Talk about it later. Besides, I don't want to talk about it with *you*."

"You'll have to." Hetch's voice was clear now. Sandro peered cautiously around the edge of the unit but could see only Hetch's body, facing away from him. He leaned back against the unit's wall and clenched his hands. His discarded shorts lay in full view from the corridor; he tried not to think about them.

". . . bunch of dreck," Hetch was saying. "And damned close to insubordination."

"The hell it is," Beryl said defiantly. "I don't have to do—"

"You haven't a choice. You've a job to do and you'll do it. There's nothing more to discuss."

"I have a vote," Beryl said.

"Won't do you a damned bit of good. It's not something you can fluff, damn it. You'll finish what you started, and you'll finish it right. Without any more damned complaints, and without ripping things apart."

Beryl cursed. "Why won't *he* talk to me?" she demanded suddenly.

"Busy," Hetch replied coldly. "Leave him alone, Beryl. He keeps you on board, what more do you want from him?"

"You don't have to ask that," she said, her voice bitter. "Hetch, where's it gone?"

"You're assuming there was something to begin with, and you're wrong," the old man said, but his voice had gentled. "What name do you want to carry? You can't have them both."

"Manny—"

"Just do your job. You're going to hate anyone in Sandro's position. You know it, Jes knows it, I know it. Just do your job."

"I *am*—"

"You're not. Sure, you're teaching him, but you're also fucking him over. He's a kid, Beryl. Lay off him,"

Hetch's voice paused. "He took you out of a pit crew, and he can put you back there."

"He wouldn't."

"He could take you home."

"Oh, no," Beryl said, but her voice shook slightly.

"Beryl, *I* could take you home. Or bring Spider up to *Rabbit*. What name do you want?"

Beryl made a wordless sound, somewhere between anger and anguish, and Sandro buried his face in his hands. Footsteps ran down the passageway. Sandro opened his eyes and reached slowly for the unit's controls. As he closed down the sonics, the door of the unit swung fully open. Hetch looked at him, then held out Sandro's discarded shorts. The old man's expression was stony.

"Get out of here," Hetch said. He caught Sandro's glance and held it. "What did you hear?"

Sandro raised his chin, but words stuck in his throat. He looked down.

"Nothing," he muttered, and took his shorts.

THE TAUSHIP HAD A CREWROOM, BUT IT WAS rarely used. Instead the ship's complement tended to gather in the large bridge when off-shift, talking, working on small projects, playing games with the ship's computer. Two evenings later, when Sandro entered the bridge after his daily workout, he found everyone save Greaves seated near the secondary bank. They looked at him as he entered and he knew they'd been discussing him. He wanted to leave but Hetch beckoned him over. Sandro took a seat as far from Beryl as he could: it did no good. Beryl, smiling, went through her usual cutting insults, sprinkled now with taunting obscenities. She'd found the button, Sandro realized through his growing rage, and was using it now, in what on the *Rabbit* passed for public. Sandro felt the eyes of the two captains

on him and held his anger in check, clenching his hands
against the urge to hit, or touch, those quick, sarcastic
lips. Beryl smiled at him, sure of her power and his pain,
and he stood abruptly and left the bridge, refusing to let
his body shake until he was safely behind the locked
doors of his cabin. Furious and shamed, he hated not
only Beryl but the two captains who, it seemed, had
watched with an almost clinical detachment, as though
Sandro were nothing more than a laboratory animal to
be prodded and tested and written up as a series of
statistics in the journals of their minds. Footsteps moved
down the corridor, someone rattled about in the galley
nearby. Sandro gathered all his self-control and sought
out Greaves, standing silent before him, unable to speak
for fear of breaking. With wordless sympathy, Greaves
took him to the noisiest section of the engine hold and
Sandro turned his back to the spacer and screamed until
his lungs ached and the knot in his chest loosened.
Then Greaves took him first to the clensor, then to Sandro's cabin. Sandro put his hands over his face and began
crying. Greaves climbed into the hammock and held
him tightly until the sobs lessened, and Sandro could accept the simple comfort of Greaves' warm body.
Eventually he slept, lulled by the rise and fall of Greaves'
chest under his cheek, the sound of Greaves' heart. When
he woke, Greaves was gone.

He woke knowing what he would do. Dress, gather his
courage, find Kennerin, and request to be let off at the
nearest stop, be it planet, port, or grabstation Sal. Numb
with the force of his decision, he pulled on a clean suit,
scrubbed his face with the heels of his hands, and left his
cabin, holding his Certificate in his hand. Hetch stood in
the corridor outside the galley and Beryl, tea in hand,
stood in the doorway. She saw Sandro, smiled bril-
liantly, and said, "Well, knocker, how did you like your
little shipboard romance?"

Sandro carefully put his Certificate on the deck by her
feet, turned, and hit her as hard as he could. He felt a
brief satisfaction at her expression as she fell—she had
not expected that of him. Then he threw himself after
her. Beryl bounced up from the deck, twisted, and
kicked. He evaded the blow clumsily, catching the impact on hip rather than groin. He grabbed her foot and

brought her down with him, pinning her to the deck. She grinned at him maliciously and went for his throat.

Fat, bald Hetch was stronger than he looked. He hauled Sandro off Beryl and Jes ran in as she leaped up, her fist cocked.

"Damn it, Taine," he shouted. She cried out and twisted to swing at him, but he sidestepped and caught her about the waist, pinning her to the bulkhead while Sandro spit and cursed in the language of his home, and tried to break free of Hetch. Hetch's breath caught suddenly and Sandro, remembering the old man's pain, stopped fighting. Then Greaves appeared at the doorway, and Jes glared at him furiously.

"Who in hell is running this boat? You get your ass down to engines and keep it there!" The captain's dark face was purple with rage, and Greaves backed hastily from the small room. Sandro's breath hurt his throat. He remembered Beryl's expression, inches from his face, and shuddered. She stood motionless now, her eyes closed, body pressed against the length of Jes' body. Kennerin cursed and pushed her away.

"Hetch, get to the bridge," Kennerin said. "And put this one in detention." He pushed Beryl toward Hetch. She glared at him, shook auburn hair from her face, and followed Hetch from the galley.

Sandro looked defiantly at Kennerin's eyes. No mystery here: the captain looked simply and totally furious. Then the expression shifted; the fury remained, but Sandro was baffled by the difference. He breathed deeply and stiffened his shoulders. I don't care, he thought. Some shit I will not eat, not for you, not for your job, not for your ship. He stared at his captain evenly.

"Come with me," Kennerin said, his voice expressionless, and walked out of the galley. Sandro hesitated, then followed, stooping to pick up his Certificate and put it in his pocket. Jes led Sandro through the captain's quarters and palmed a lock along the hull of the ship. He stepped through and Sandro, bewildered, followed.

It seemed as though they had walked out of the ship into the astonishing craziness of tauspace. The room was a bubble tacked to *Rabbit*'s outer hull, connected only at the scant three meters around the hatch. The captain balanced easily on the curved permaglass and Sandro clung to the hatch frame, blinded by the colors and the light. Kennerin hauled him into the bubble and the hatch snapped shut.

It was like stepping into nothingness. Sandro lost his balance and sat hard on the permaglass, his fingers spread urgently. He looked infinitely down between his legs and closed his eyes. Kennerin stepped over him; he felt the movement of the captain's feet on the loose cloth of his suit legs. He tilted his head, eyes still closed, and waited for the captain to speak. The silence grew.

"Captain," Sandro said finally. It came out as a whisper. He licked his lips and opened his eyes cautiously. The captain leaned against the bubble's far wall, head turned away, and he stared unblinking into tau.

"Captain," he said again. "I want to know why she made me do that." Jes didn't move. "I have a right," Sandro said, and waited until he felt sure his voice wouldn't shake again. "She's been pushing for that since — She's a better fighter than I am, she knows that, you know that—I have a right to know why."

Kennerin closed his eyes. "No," he said quietly but firmly.

"Greaves said she's jealous," Sandro continued recklessly. "He said not to sleep with you because she's around. And she wasn't even fighting with *me*, captain, I was just a—a something, a tool, something instead of —and she swung at you, captain! I thought I was supposed to be the—but she tried to hit *you*, captain!"

"She had a right to," Kennerin said.

Sandro gaped at him. "That's insurrection," he whispered. "That's mutiny."

The captain's shoulders moved suddenly. "No."

Sandro let his breath out explosively. "All right! It's your ship, your crew, your business—but I still think I deserve an explanation. For what she's done to *me*, captain. For that."

"Fair enough," Kennerin said simply. He clasped his hands loosely in his lap and looked from them to Sandro, face calm. "You deserve an explanation, but I can't give you one."

"She wanted to kill me!"

Kennerin shook his head. Sandro stared at him, unbelieving and angry, and opened his mouth, but the captain reached forward swiftly. His hard fingers snapped Sandro's mouth closed.

"Shut up," Kennerin whispered. Sandro pulled back from the fury in the captain's voice and blue eyes. Kennerin moved his hand away contemptuously.

"Beryl will leave you alone. And you'll leave her alone, or I'll have you blackballed for insubordination, and you'll never see the inside of a ship again. Understand?"

"But she—"

"Do you understand!"

"Yes, sir," Sandro said, frightened.

Kennerin put his forehead against the transparent wall of the bubble and stared into tau. Sandro tried not to breathe. Finally the captain gestured wearily, without turning, and the simple movement brought Sandro's heart to his throat.

"I can't—I won't pass on secrets. Not Beryl's, not anyone's. You'll have to accept that." Sandro didn't reply. "I'm making a place for you," the captain continued. "I don't have to, Marquez. And that's as much as you're going to get. I won't break a confidence, not for you, not for anyone."

"Sir. Not even if she tries to kill me?"

"She won't."

Sandro licked his lips. "How do you know?"

The captain was silent. Sandro looked at his weary face, at his tense shoulders, and suddenly knew both the answer and part of the reason for Beryl's deliberate, escalating hostility. The captain would buy her cooperation, her sanity, with his body. Sandro remembered the curve of Beryl pressed between the bulkhead and the captain's belly and thighs, and felt dizzy. Kennerin, watching Sandro's face, nodded once.

"And now you know something of mine," he said quietly.

It seemed to Sandro as though the universe shifted; Beryl was suddenly as insignificant as Sandro himself had felt. The nub, the center, rested within the man who leaned against the curved permaglass across from him, the man with the exhausted eyes. Sandro had been given part of the secret, yes, but it only deepened the mystery, only added to the question. He gestured helplessly.

"I didn't know that— I—" he began. Kennerin

touched his cheek with lean, gentle fingers, pushing his head around to face the bubble's side.

"Look," the captain commanded. Obediently, defenselessly, Sandro looked.

Events without time, materiality without structure; the alternate universe of tauspace was not even chaotic, for chaos carries, implicit within it, order. If order existed in tau, it existed on a frequency that could not be grasped, that could not be comprehended, and the smeared and shattered brilliance of tauspace evaded thought.

"We're like newborns," Jes said quietly. "We don't even know how to look at it, we don't know how or what or when it means."

Sandro heard the words distantly. Beyond the thin, transparent shield provided by the Cohen-Albrecht Effect Drive engines, beyond their half-understood power, there moved such an incomprehensibility of energy, of force, of intensity, that *Rabbit* and all aboard seemed inconceivably petty. Sandro slid into tau, losing touch with his body, with any sense other than that of his eyes, lost in a world he didn't, and didn't want to, understand.

The touch of his captain's hand on his thigh brought him back, a persistent pressure. He turned reluctantly and looked at Kennerin's face, as Jes leaned away from him again and looked back from an unimaginable distance that, suddenly, Sandro began to comprehend. Sandro exhaled deeply and relaxed against the permaglass, brought back from tau by the knowledge that he had not voyaged alone. Words formed idly in his mind: she shall have his body, but I shall have his peace. He examined the words and let them slide away. The captain's face turned, and Sandro, imitating him, looked again at tau.

Patterns on patterns, order in chaos, colors and their absence, light and dark. Tau took on a new dimension, a seductive, constantly changing promise of smallness, of irrelevance. Tau did not care. And in that indifference lay freedom and the possibility of peace. Sandro felt a detached and grateful awe at the surcease of pain that tau granted, and understood that, as his own needs made this understanding possible, so must the captain's pain have made this peace necessary. Amid the captain's thousand faces, the one of hunger stood explained.

Sandro accepted the gift and, unprotesting, prepared a gift in return.

"I was born on Marquez Landing," Sandro said, and his voice seemed another face of tau. "My great-grandfather had the planet terraformed, years ago. Long time back. He thought it would make a good pleasure planet. Lots of water, islands, trees. It was a pretty place. Nobody came. Off in a backwash, off the main routes, an awkward journey, and no one made it. It seemed a lot of effort for nothing at all. But he was stubborn, my great-grandfather. He hired the Enchanter labs and they developed a plant. A bush. *Zimania rubiflora*. You know about it. Your family stole it from mine. It was something entirely new. We processed the sap and crystallized it to make a superconductive wire, and that was new, too. Enchanter set up the processing plant in a neighboring system, and sold it to a private company. Which was fine, because we were busy expanding the plantations. We covered every island on Marquez Landing, and people came to live there, to work on the plantations, to build the city. They did well, my grandfather, my father. So well that it was no tragedy when your family stole some of our seeds and started growing *Zimania*, and processing it, and selling it. There was plenty of market to go around. It seemed."

"We didn't steal the seeds," the captain said, his voice as expressionless as Sandro's. "They were given to us. It doesn't matter by whom."

"It doesn't matter," Sandro agreed. "My father inherited Marquez Landing and the plantations. We lived a good life, my parents, my sisters, my brother. A company came and offered to buy us out. We wouldn't sell. My father wouldn't sell. They bought the shipping line and raised the rates. We couldn't ship our sap, and profits fell. People started to leave. We imported most of our goods, and most of our land grew *Zimania* and not food. For the profits. We couldn't import food anymore. Then the company bought the processing plant, and refused our sap. Everything died." Sandro paused, and when he continued his voice held only traces of emotion. "People died. My father refused to sell. My mother died. My father—broke. He sold Marquez Landing, and went into the fields behind the town, into the oldest fields. He shot himself. My sisters went to North Wing, to friends. My brother . . ."

Sandro paused. Jes said nothing. Sandro splayed his fingers across the permaglass and watched tau move between them.

"My brother sold himself to the company and stayed on to manage Marquez Landing. I stayed too—there seemed nowhere else to go. Then the transition agent came, and he was all the company all at once. The one who killed my parents. The one who stole my world. He was arrogant, and cold, and I hated him."

Sandro stopped again, considering evasions. Jes stared unblinking into tau.

"I left Marquez Landing. I swore I wouldn't go back until I'd broken Parallax, until I'd seen it die the way my mother did. And went to MarketPort. And came here."

Finally Jes turned to look at Sandro, and said, "Parallax."

Sandro returned his gaze evenly. Jes swung about abruptly and irised the hatch again, and Sandro followed him into Jes' quarters. His mind seemed disconnected. The hatch snicked shut and he looked at the captain. Jes' face was cool and, for once, peaceful.

"There can be no fighting on my ship, no matter what the provocation."

Sandro nodded.

"I'm going to put you in detention and I'm going to let Beryl out. Because I need her more than I need you, and because you swung first. You won't be in for long. I'm changing course." Jes paused. "Sandro."

"Captain."

"Parallax tried to take over Aerie, my home, years ago. They didn't succeed that time. I want my family to hear your story." Jes paused. "Will you come home with me?"

"Do I have a choice?"

"Yes."

Sandro tilted his head to look up at his captain. "I'll come home with you. I don't have a home of my own anymore."

Jes turned and led the way to the detention cell.

THE CELL WAS THE SIZE OF HIS CABIN. A HAM-
mock stretched from a hook on one wall, across the
room to a hook on the far wall by the door, and during
the day was furled and hung from one hook only, leaving
the center of the room empty. A suspended slab of
round-milled plasteel served as a desk and table, with a
swivel chair bolted to the deck before it. Toilet, basin,
and a tiny cleanunit occupied the far corner of the room.
Sandro had seen cabins in passenger ships less well
appointed, but they hadn't been securely locked from
the outside.

Greaves brought him some bookreels at dinnertime,
pulling them from his pocket after setting Sandro's meal
on the table, and left after muttering a few indistinct
words. It set the tone for their few exchanges over the
next three days. The peaceful transcendence Sandro
had found in the captain's bubble melted swiftly, and
Sandro, falling deeper into depression, couldn't tell
whether Greaves was embarrassed, angry, guilty, or
simply contemptuous at Sandro's loss of control. He decided that he didn't care and, save for those times when
he sat at the table to eat meals, spent his time lying in
the hammock trying to read or, more often, staring at
the smooth, undecorated expanses of wall.

He hadn't seen Kennerin since the tauCaptain had
locked him into the detention cell, a fact which Sandro
could not interpret. He thought they had reached an understanding, thought that, given a glimpse at the captain's own obsessions, the rest of the mystery would un-
fold; instead Sandro found the mystery only deeper.
Each face he remembered stood contradicted by others;
blocked, he turned his attention elsewhere.

He thought about Beryl, about the hard edges of her
hatred and the smooth planes of her face under the web-

bing of scars. He wondered if she carried scars on her body, as Greaves did, and realized that he had never seen her naked. That, momentarily, surprised him. He had been raised to physical modesty and had not stopped to think about the lack of nakedness aboard *Rabbit*. But, he knew, nudity was the rule, not the exception, among spacers.

She's the only woman aboard, he thought, knowing the rationale as false. Her skinsuits were as revealing, and far more enticing, than nudity would have been.

"I have a vote," she'd told Hetch. Sandro couldn't begin to understand what she meant. "What name do you want to carry?" Hetch said coldly. Who was Spider? And the captain called her Taine.

"I won't pass on secrets," the captain had said. Sandro considered that, knowing that he wanted not Beryl's secret, but Kennerin's. That all his concentration on her was primarily an effort to see not Beryl herself, but the captain. The realization brought him up abruptly; he sat in the hammock, holding to the sides as it swung from the force of his movement. Using her to see him, just as she had used him to affect the captain; using each other as pawns. He hadn't realized that he and Beryl were so alike, and the thought did not please him. He scrambled out of the hammock and paced the three steps to the cleanunit, then paced back again, digging his fists into his pocket. She attracted him, yes, but more, he thought, for the revelations she might give into his captain, and that felt wrong. When she plunged into a complicated problem with the effect drives the world around her seemed to disappear; he remembered her single-minded concentration as she dove twisting through the rungs in the gym, the tremor in her voice when Hetch offered, bafflingly, to take her home. Her fear when Hetch threatened her with someone, or something, called Spider. He fell back into the hammock, remembering her body pressed against the captain's, remembering her closed eyes. The bookreel he'd dropped earlier poked a hard corner into his buttocks. Cursing, he fished it from under him and threw it across the cell.

The morning of the fourth day, Beryl came in. She leaned against the wall, the door open behind her, and put her empty hands along her belt.

"The captain says you can come out," she said. Sandro

rolled from the hammock and stood beside it, watching her. She didn't look at him. "Clean up the cell first. Your shift starts as soon as you get to the control room."

Sandro wet his lips. "As before?"

Beryl nodded. "You're still apprentice Second," she said, with only a hint of sarcasm. "We're not done with each other yet." She turned to leave, but stopped when Sandro said her name. She looked over her shoulder at him.

"Truce?" he said, holding his hand out.

She looked from his face to his hand and shrugged, but did not offer her hand in return. "Truce," she said. Sandro listened to her receding footsteps, then methodically began cleaning the cell.

Clad, as in the beginning, in a bulky worksuit, she picked up his lessons exactly where they'd left them. They moved as quickly as before, nor had she changed her coldness or lack of praise, but the overt hostility was gone. Instead she created a cool distance between them which Sandro was unwilling to bridge with aggression and unable to bridge with friendship. He wondered what she had said to the captain, what the captain had said to her, and knew that he could not ask. At the end of the shift he sought out Greaves and stood beside him in the roar of the engines. Greaves didn't notice him until he reached for a tool and Sandro handed it to him. The engineer looked uncomfortable but let Sandro continue to help him until the job was done and they gathered the tools into the case. Once in the relative silence of the passageway Greaves put the case down and faced Sandro.

"If you're mad at me, I can't blame you," Greaves said.

Sandro's eyebrows rose. "What for?"

"I should have left you alone, that night. I knew how she'd interpret it—I guess I hoped that she'd needle me with it, not you. I wasn't thinking."

Sandro considered that for a moment, then gestured. "It doesn't matter. We'd have fought over something else, if not that. Besides, I was getting ready to tell the captain that I wanted off."

Now Graves looked surprised. "Running away?"

"Yeah. Not very mature, is it? Anyway, it saved me from that, so I guess I can thank you for it."

Graves grinned suddenly. "Or Beryl." He reached for

the case. Sandro took its other end and helped carry it toward the toolroom.

"Tell me about her," Sandro said as they locked the case into its place. Greaves shrugged.

"Nothing much to tell, really. We'd pulled into Augustine Sal about three years back. One of the lateral vanes was loose, not enough to be a big problem, but the captain wanted it fixed. She was working on one of the pit crews." Greaves pulled his shirt off and used it to wipe grease from his arms. "The captain likes to supervise repairs, get his hands on things. He was down on one of the catwalks, talking with the pitboss about the vane and watching a waldo lift it off the ship. Then the waldo stopped in the middle of things and the captain looked up to where the operator stood. And then they just stood there, staring at each other." Greaves noticed a patch of graphite lubricant on his pants and cursed. "Anyway, the captain gets this funny thing, around some people, usually if he's down on Aerie, or if he's got one of his family aboard. Like his body shifts, like he's, oh, ten, fifteen years younger, and not sure of things. I don't know, maybe I'm wrong, but that's what it looks like to me. Anyway, he stood there looking up and his arms sort of went loose, like he wasn't sure of what to do with them anymore. Know what I mean?" Greaves tried to demonstrate, then gestured. "Then he walked out of the pit and spent the next day in a messhall, drinking everything in sight. And when the repairs were done and we were mustering to go, there she was, gear and all."

"Was she nasty, back then?"

Greaves made a specific gesture and locked the door of the toolroom. "She hasn't gotten any worse," he admitted. "But she's not any better either."

Sandro followed him to the clensor and stood leaning against the basin as Greaves stripped and turned on the unit.

"The day we fought," Sandro said, "the captain called her Taine. And she swung at him."

Greaves stuck his head out of the unit. "Captain's business," he said warningly.

"But you must have wondered."

Greaves turned off the unit. "Sure. But that's my problem. And I'm not going to wonder in company, understand?" He turned the unit back on.

"She said something about a vote," Sandro said, but this time Greaves didn't bother to answer.

Three days after that, Hetch called him to the bridge. He entered to find Jes and the old captain webbed in, and he accepted the seat Hetch indicated. The grid riding above his position showed the distinctive angular bends that signified a grabstation, and without instuction Sandro confirmed that Beryl and Greaves were riding the suits in the engine control room, synched the engines, and prepared the effect drives for closedown. Jes gave him clearance acknowledgment and ETA, and Sandro started the countdown. Hetch, watching, nodded and turned to his own board.

Kennerin slid *Rabbit* into the grab coils with an almost sinuous ease, the way someone putting on a familiar jacket never feels for the armholes. The coils shivered and shimmered, Sandro's belly flipped, and the grid displays dissolved to a backdrop of stars, one yellow sun, and four scattered planets. Kennerin reached forward to tap his board, and magnification pulled the image of one planet closer, until it filled the screen.

"Home," the tauCaptain said, and Sandro could not read his tone at all.

THE PLANET BELOW COULD HAVE BEEN MARquez Landing, swathed in clouds and ocean; a world of large icecaps and myriad islands set in a frame of blue sea. Sandro leaned forward in the webbing, peering from the shuttle's crystal port, almost as tense as the captain. But the world was too irregular, a natural world rather than a terraformed planet. The climate on each island along the equatorial belt would be slightly different from that of each other island; no one had carefully built the land and reefed the seas to create identical conditions along the center of the globe. The native flora would be different, the air smell odd, the stars at night be wholly unfamiliar. He repeated these things to himself but could not calm the pounding of his heart. It could have been home. From the corners of his eyes, quickly glanced, it could so easily have been home.

The shuttle angled steeply, propelled by the captain's hunger. Jes orbited only once and dove through the layer of cloud, punched out the other side, and they were so close to the islands that Sandro felt he could reach forward and touch them. He glanced nervously at the captain, then leaned back. Kennerin knew what he was doing, Sandro thought, and if Hetch could watch the landing without flinching, then so could Sandro.

Sandro looked over his shoulder at Hetch. The old man sat with his eyes closed, his fingers massaging his hip; the corners of his mouth pinched down. They would not, Kennerin had said, be on planet long, so Greaves and Beryl remained on the ship, using the time to catch up with a million minor maintenance chores. Aside from himself and the two captains, the shuttle carried only a small freightbox of goods, a minimum of personal luggage, and a padded crate marked "Souvenir from MarketPort" which the captain had carried from his cabin and, smiling, bolted securely to the shuttle's luggage rack. Sandro's pack, beside it, looked scruffy. Sandro turned back to the port in time to see high, white cliffs rise almost directly before him. He gasped and the shuttle skimmed the tops of the cliffs and fled through a corridor between flanks of forest. Treetops whipped by. Sandro refused to close his eyes, but his hands were white against the cables of the webbing.

For all his eagerness, Jes feathertouched the shuttle to the pad and closed down the systems carefully. Then he swung from his webbing to wrench the hatch open and leap from the shuttle, yelling. Sandro was overcome with envy, and ashamed of it. He sat staring at his hands until Hetch touched him on the shoulder and he rose. Jes was sprinting across the landing pad toward a woman. He swung her into the air, spun in place, and kissed her. She was most emphatically pregnant.

"The captain's wife?" Sandro said to Hetch.

"His sister, Meya. Come on, it's suppertime." Hetch's limp was even more pronounced as he led the way down the ramp.

"Shouldn't the shuttle be locked down?"

"No, port crew will do it. Don't worry about it, Sandro. It's safe enough. We're home."

Sandro glanced around the small port. A ground crew was already approaching—three humans and, towering over them, two strange, snouted, four-armed creatures that filled Sandro with apprehension.

Hetch, following his glance, said, "Kasirene. Come on."

Sandro hesitated. As Second, he really should supervise lockdown, but he wasn't completely sure that he was a Second anymore. He put his hands in his pockets and followed Hetch to the edge of the field.

Jes and his sister walked toward them, arm in arm.

"It's only one," she said, smiling.

"Doesn't look like it," Jes said grumpily, and peered at her. "You look tired."

"I'm fine, really. And you always forget how big I get, between times."

"I don't think there are any between times. Every time I see you, you're carrying a balloon under your shirt." The captain sounded unhappy, but his sister laughed and hugged his arm, then released him to kiss Hetch. Sandro wondered uneasily if she intended to kiss him, too, but she put her hand out to him.

"I'm Meya M'Kale Kennerin," she said. "Welcome to Aerie, Menet Marquez."

He bent over her hand and kissed it. "Your welcome honors me," he said, and rose in time to see the puzzled look she sent Jes, who raised his eyebrows. Sandro dropped her hand. Perhaps these people didn't understand manners, he thought hotly, but he did.

Meya grinned at him and tucked her hand under his elbow. "Don't mind us, Menet. We're a rough, uncouth bunch of dirt farmers who think welcome involves hot suppers and a place to take your boots off."

"I've had worse," Sandro admitted. Like the captain, the sister was tall, dark-skinned, black-haired, with the same intensely blue eyes set between epicanthic lids. She grinned at him until he smiled in return, then laughed briefly and guided him away from the port. "Are you coming, Manny?" she called over her shoulder.

"Not that way," Hetch replied. "I'll catch the flitter into Haven and see to the house. Want me up for supper?"

"If you don't come, Mish will kill you."

Hetch made a great show of being terrified and limped across the port to the shack. Meya stopped to look after him. She frowned as Jes came up and took her free arm.

"Is Manny getting worse?" she said.

"He says not. I've been after him to see Ozchan while we're home. Are you sure you should be hiking around like this?"

"You're hopeless. You always ask the same question, I always give you the same answer, and you always forget it as soon as I give it to you."

She looked very young. Sandro, thinking of the names of the captain's ships, asked how many children she had.

"Only two, and this will be the third. Don't let Jes mislead you. He thinks I'm a baby factory."

"You are," the captain said. "Who's home?"

"Me, Hart, and Quilla. Ozchan and Tabor are coming up by dinnertime. Mish should be home soon, and she should have one of the twins with her. We sent for her as soon as we got your message. The other kids are somewhere south with Palen, doing the spring hike. Will you be here long enough to see them?"

"I don't know," Jes said. "Perhaps."

The landing pad ended at the edge of a meadow, bright with grass and small flowers. Sandro paused, looking about. No town, no floaters or skimmers, just a dirt path meandering up the slope. Meya glanced at him as he caught step again.

"This is the way to the Tor, Menet. The main road's on the other side of the port and leads to Haven."

"And you walk this, every time you come here?"

"Of course," Meya said. "It's only a kilometer."

"Of course," Sandro muttered, and dropped behind to follow the captain and his sister up the narrow path. They bent their heads together, and Meya put her hand in the captain's pocket. It seemed an old, familiar gesture between them.

Sandro trudged behind, gazing about. Here was no resemblance at all to Marquez Landing, where the fields came right up to the edge of the landing field and marched in neat, orderly rows the length and breadth of Isla Ramon, where the broad warehouses made an unbroken line between the port and Cuidad Garcia, busy with cargo floaters and noise. Where a son of the family Marquez was met with pomp and dignity, and only the poor walked. Here they could have been the only humans on the island, on the planet, walking on a rich brown path between carpets of green. A flower popped near his foot and released a sweet, strange fragrance into the warm air. The captain and his sister were far ahead. Meya laughed, put her head on the captain's shoulder, and laughed again. Sandro bit his lip and hurried to catch up with them.

The view from the top of the hill surprised him. To the right, a town spilled across the foot of the hill to the edge of a dense forest; the bright thread of a stream circled it along one side and ran across the meadow directly before them. At the far side of the meadow another hill rose, taller than its neighbors, and crowned with an inelegant, sprawling, slapdash amazement of a house, looking as though it had been cobbled together entirely on whim. Someone on a flat, fenced section of roof waved and jumped and waved again, until Jes raised his hand and waved back.

"Go on," Meya said, pushing his shoulder. "We'll follow."

Jes ran toward the house, long-legged and eager. He took the stream in one bound and raced up the hillside. Sandro, staring after him, remembered Greaves' comment and nodded. The captain did look and act differently; younger, yes, but Sandro could not define the other particulars. The door of the house opened, spilling people onto the broad porch, and the figure on the roof disappeared.

"Prodigal son," Meya said, taking Sandro's arm again. "Do you mind, Menet? I'm rather tired, but I'd appreciate it if you wouldn't tell Jes."

Sandro smiled at her, feeling taller. Meya leaned against him lightly, and he guided the captain's sister across the stream and toward the captain's home.

FORMAL, COURTEOUS, AND DISTRUSTFUL, SAN-
dro sat at the Kennerin table and peered at the family
from behind his wineglass, striving to remember names
and apply them to the right faces. The laughter and talk
bewildered and, at first, shocked him. Talk at the Marquez family table had proceeded like the most stately of
oratorios, conducted by Sandro's father, Juan Luis, com-
pliantly performed by the low, civilized voices of his family. Here the Kennerins seemed entirely chaotic; laughing, talking, calling down the length of the table,
conducting a total anarchy over which Mish Kennerin
presided with calm strength. Sandro liked her, this tiny,
white-haired woman who had shaken his hand warmly,
welcomed him to her house, and turned her family loose
around him. Her children loomed over her, treating her
with a rough, affectionate deference which Sandro could
not comprehend and for which he felt vaguely called
upon to apologize.

"Mish, that's total nonsense," someone said. Sandro
hastily refilled his wineglass, poked at the food on his
plate, and inspected the others.

Quilla, the captain's older sister, took the foot of the
table opposite Mish and talked at length about a village
called Hoku which, he learned, she was in the process of
building. She planted her elbows on the table and tilted
her head as she talked. Her unruly black hair, dense and
frizzy, was streaked with gray and her body made crisp,
angular concessions to the world around her. Jes, before
landing, had described Quilla as being all brains and
angles, but Sandro caught a grace in that roughness, a
precision in her movements, a softness in her brown eyes.
She reminded him of Beryl, and he could not understand
why. He glanced around the table again; amid this collection of dark-skinned Kennerins, only Quilla's eyes, and

40

her mother's, were brown. The eyes of Mish's other children were the same intense blue as the captain's. From the father, Sandro thought. Who is—dead? Perhaps. No one mentioned him.

Hart, Jes' brother, disturbed Sandro. He seemed to spend the meal regarding Sandro as though he were an interesting specimen which Hart would like to pin to a dissecting board. Before dinner, coming into the room, Hart had collided with one of the kasirene servants and both had recoiled. It puzzled Sandro. Hart seemed to be the only Kennerin who didn't accept the natives, or who was not accepted by them. Now Hart gazed at him across the table, his eyes cold and speculative. Sandro tried to ignore him.

Halfway down the table sat Meya's husband, whose name Sandro could not remember. He did not sit with his wife and talked exclusively to Jes. His black skin glowed, contrasting with the copper skins of the Kennerins, and his fingers were long and tapered. Surgeon's fingers, Sandro thought, and remembered the man's name. Ozchan M'Kale, Haven's chief doctor. The only formality in the room, it seemed, came from M'Kale's stiff, frigid dealings with his wife. Sandro decided that he disliked the man.

"More wine, Menet Marquez?"

Sandro looked around quickly. The man next to him held the jug tilted over Sandro's glass. Tabor, Sandro thought, but could not remember the man's other name. Not Quilla's husband, but definitely the father of her son, Jared. Both pale-haired, gray-eyed people, although the father's skin was light tan, and the son's was golden. Sandro wished he could dislike them as immediately as he disliked Hart or M'Kale, but Tabor's friendliness made him hunger for warmth. He nodded, and Tabor smiled and poured wine.

"It's confusing at first," Tabor said. "I was confused too, and there were less of them, back then. Would you like some more stew?"

"Love some." Manny Hetch leaned in front of Sandro to hold out his plate. He winked. "Prerogatives of age," he said, and Sandro smiled at him. Hetch seemed relaxed here, at ease, at home. Quilla broke off her conversation with Mish to smile at Tabor and gesture toward the wine jug. Tabor passed it over, and their fingers touched briefly. Sandro politely refused another helping.

"I am not used to such families," he said quietly to Tabor. "At home we were very formal, and at school— well, that was school. Is it always like this, here?"

"Generally worse," Tabor said genially. "We're not all here yet."

Jared leaned forward to look around his father. "Where did you go to school?"

Sandro told him and they compared educations, finding various traveling professors in common. Tabor told a scandalous story about an itinerant scholar who had visited his own homeworld, and the entire family laughed as they left the table for the large, comfortable living room. They took chairs or pillows on the scattered rugs; Captain Hetch appropriated the seat nearest the fire and sat with his feet up and a wineglass in his hand, alternately beaming and dozing like some fat, beloved uncle. Jes detached himself from Ozchan and sat on the floor at his sister's feet. Meya leaned back and let her fingers tangle in her brother's hair. Hart put more wood on the fire. To Sandro's surprise, Mim the housekeeper came in after the table was cleared, poured herself a glass of wine, and sat on the couch beside Tabor, discussing household matters. Sandro wondered if they'd invite the gardeners and fieldhands in next. Jared produced a flute and began a low, sweet melody. After a moment Tabor picked up another flute and decorated the melody with inventions of his own. Jes, prodded, laughed and accepted a third flute, and the family listened to the music. It ended in a murmur of talk. Sandro smiled across the room at Hetch and felt his shoulders relaxing.

He had worried, since his talk with the captain, that when the time came he would be unable to keep his promise, unable to tell his story to his family's competitors. But Jes slid him into the story so casually that he didn't realize he'd begun until he found the room quiet, the eyes looking at him with interest or sympathy. When he told of his parents' deaths Mish cursed under her breath, and Hart, surprisingly, handed him a glass of brandy. Again Sandro did not tell them of the agent's murder; he no longer believed that the Kennerins had a hand in his family's demise, but he didn't entirely trust them either. When he finished Quilla nodded silently in thanks. He sat back in his chair, chest tight, and wondered what this unlikely bunch of people would do next.

Captain Hetch broke the silence. He rolled his glass between his palms and said reminiscently, "Parallax tried to take over West Wing, this sector, about twenty years ago. I'd had a run of bad luck, and they moved in and started undercutting my rates. I was about to go bust, but Quilla changed things."

"We'd have gone under if Hetch went bankrupt," Quilla said. "We had a full harvest of cured sap ready to go, and Hetch couldn't afford to lift it for us. Parallax was biding its sweet time, waiting for us to get so hungry that we'd have to sell out entirely to them, or die. So we bought Hetch's line on expected profits, merged it with our own plantations, and began running our own line."

"Later we bought the processing plant, too," Jes said. "That was Mish's doing. And we've always insisted that we produce enough foodstuffs for ourselves, at the least. So we're pretty safe from the sort of thing Parallax did to your family."

Mish made a skeptical noise. "The minute you start assuming safety," she said, "something's going to come along and catch you from the rear."

"I'd think Parallax would be content with Marquez Landing," Hart said lazily. "They've always been much bigger than we have. Why go after the little fry when you've got the whale?"

"Why just take the whale when you can have the whole damned ocean?" Quilla demanded. "I think Mish is right. Meya, the price change came about ten months ago standard, didn't it?"

"Yep." Meya pushed herself upright and Jes handed her a cushion for her back. "MarketPort prices for Z-line dropped by about twenty fremarks the kilo, then four months ago they dropped again. It takes about eight months to process the sap, from receipt at the plant to packaged export, so that puts things back about eighteen months ago, standard."

"About the time Parallax took over," Sandro said, and Meya nodded.

"So they could be undercutting our profits," Meya continued, "but it hasn't shown up as drastic, so far. They're probably still revamping Marquez Landing, cleaning up the mess. Sorry, Sandro."

He gestured, dismissing it.

"Another thing, though," Quilla said slowly. "Before I left for Hoku, I got a report from Processing. They said they'd had some slips, lost a couple of vats' worth. Said they'd solved the problem. I didn't like it, and I tagged it."

Mish nodded. "I looked into it. It's strange. Three months before that report, they'd had trouble. And again six months before that. Could be something, or nothing at all."

"I'd give a lot," Quilla muttered, "to see what's going on out there."

"I'm not going to look into it," Jes said. "I've got a shipping line to run, remember?"

Mish frowned and pulled her chair closer to the fire. "I've never liked having that plant in another sector. I'd rather it was here in Eagle System with us, but I suppose there's no help for it."

"If you don't like it where it is," Hart said, "move it."

"Come on, Hart." Jes looked across Meya's knees at his brother. "Be practical, for once."

"It's practical," Hart insisted. "Those things are modular. Take it apart, tow it through grab, put it together here. There's plenty of space between Aerie and Eagle, and they'd have the solar power they need."

Quilla tugged at her lower lip and stared at Hart. "There'd be a tax penalty for moving it out of its sector," she said slowly. "And the grab fees would be killers. But we could do it. It might eat into profits for the next couple of years, but, damn, Mish, we really could do it. At the least we'd have Processing here, under our eyes, instead of out where we can't supervise it." She turned to her sister. "Can you work me up a financial proposal on it? In time for the next Town Meeting?"

"If nothing else gets in the way," Meya said, patting her belly.

"Fine," Quilla said. She leaned forward, elbows on her knees, looking intent. Sandro watched firelight gild one side of her face. "Now, who's going to get up to Processing and see what's going on? No, I know you can't do it, Jes. Mish?"

"I won't leave Aerie," Mish said, brooking no discussion. "Not for any reason."

"I'll go," said Hart.

"You will not. Within two days you'd have a full-scale war going. I can't go," Quilla said. "I've Hoku to finish, and unless we get the fields in, the entire Betes colony will be back in Haven by winter. I don't think I can take time off for at least a year. Ozchan?"

"No way," the doctor said. "I've two interns, one resident, and a midwife, and I don't trust any of them on their own. Not yet."

Tabor simply looked at Quilla, raised his cane, and gestured expressively. She shook her head.

"Term starts in three weeks," Jared said. "But I can get back to Kroeber late, if you wanted me to—"

"No," said Tabor and Quilla simultaneously. Jared shrugged.

A frowning silence filled the room. Sandro, looking around, saw a smile grow on Meya's lips. She stretched and said, "I'll go."

"Don't be silly," Jes said immediately. "Walking to the port is one thing, but whizzing around in space—"

"The baby's due in two weeks. I could go a month after that."

"And abandon the baby?" Ozchan said sarcastically. Meya looked at his scowl and her smile faltered.

"I'll take the baby with me."

Ozchan gestured angrily and looked away from her. "Send someone from the village," he muttered, but Mish shook her head.

"I think it's a fine idea," she said. "Jes, can you have a ship for her here in six weeks or so? Whichever ship is passing both us and Processing, we shouldn't rearrange schedules any more than we have to."

"I suppose I could," Jes said. Sandro, amazed, heard the sullen quality of his captain's voice. "But I don't like the idea."

"You'll survive," said Quilla. "What time is it?"

"Nem'al," Hart said.

"Bedtime." Mish rose. "I don't know about the rest of you, but I rode for two days getting here and I'm tired."

The Kennerins rose from chairs, couches, pillows, and rugs, and talked themselves into the hallway and up the stairs. Manny Hetch protested that he could make it back to Haven, but was talked into spending the night at the Tor. Sandro remained in his seat, shaking his head in bewilderment.

"Menet Marquez?"

He looked up at Jared.

"I'll show you to your room," Jared said.

"Let me see if I have this straight," Sandro said without rising. "Since dinner you've listened to my story, given me a history of Aerie-Kennerin, considered the Parallax problem, talked about the Z-line market, proposed moving an entire processing plant, and appointed someone to go on a tour of inspection and someone else to get her there. Am I leaving anything out?"

Jared smiled. "Nothing important."

"What do you do for an encore?" Sandro demanded. "Revise the constitution before breakfast?"

Jared laughed and turned off the lights. "Not often. Come on, I'll bet you're tired."

"Quia Jared, you've no idea."

'Why don't you just call me Jared," Jared said over his shoulder as he led the way up the stairs. "We're about the same age. All this formality makes me nervous."

"Sure."

"Here's your room. Can I get you anything?"

Sandro shook his head and walked into the room, closing the door behind him. He reopened it immediately. "Jared?"

Jared, three steps down the hall, turned.

"Thanks."

"Sure," Jared said. "Sleep well."

Sandro closed the door, leaned against it, and rubbed his forehead wearily.

"MEYA?"

The hall was dark. At the far end, by the stairwell, a splash of light from one moon lit the wooden floor. Jes looked at the row of closed doors and knocked again.

"Meya? Can I come in?"

The door opened a crack and Meya slipped out, pulling a gown over her shoulders. She put her fingers to her lips.

"Ozchan's asleep," she whispered, and tugged at Jes' arm until he followed her down the stairs, through the dining room, and into the big kitchen at the back of the house. The huge windows were open and moonslight spilled into the room from west and east. Meya, without lighting a lamp, opened the pantry door.

"Hungry again," she said. "Want some pel? They're good this year."

"Sure."

She brought a basket of yellow berries from the pantry and put it on the table, then poured a large glass of cold water. Jes poked about in the berries until he found a ripe one and ate it. It tasted tart and fresh. Meya squinted at him, then lit a candle and set it on the table between them. She popped a berry into her mouth, spit the seed into her palm, and smiled.

"Don't leave any on the table or floor, or Mim'll get furious." She glanced at Jes and her smile disappeared. "You look miserable, Jessie. What's wrong?"

Jes put his finger in the basket and stirred the berries morosely, thinking of Beryl. "Problems on board. Not serious, you don't have to worry. But they're bothering me." He looked up at her. "I've been meaning to speak to Ozchan."

Her face tightened fractionally. Jes, used to reading the smallest emotions on her lips and eyes, reached across the table and touched her. "Really. Nothing important."

"Hetch?"

"Yes. And some other things. And I guess I want to talk with you about Ozchan, too."

Meya put another berry in her mouth. She looked at Jes and spit the seed out. "You don't have to."

"Does he always treat you this way?"

"What way? No, I'm sorry. I know what you mean." She paused. "It doesn't really matter."

"It does to me." When she didn't respond, he picked more berries from the basket, not looking at her. "I guess, normally, it wouldn't be any of my business. But we've never been—normal to each other. He didn't kiss you when he came in, he didn't talk to you during dinner, he paid no attention to you all evening. Is he mad at you? Are you mad at him? Is he making you unhappy?"

Meya sighed and shifted in the chair. "What can I tell you, Jessie? It's been getting worse—not actively bad, just not actively good. It's been uncomfortable the past five, six months." She shrugged. "He doesn't bother with a public mask anymore."

"What's he mad about?"

Meya smiled slightly. "Me. He's not happy about this." She put her arm across her bulging stomach protectively.

"I thought he wanted lots of children."

"He does."

"Then I don't understand it!" Jes stood abruptly and went to the counter. The stone top felt cold under his palms. "Why haven't you told me about this? It's been going on for—what, one year? More? You could have told me."

"Jessie, why should I? What would you have done about it, zipping around East Wing or Greengate Sector or wherever you've been recently? What can you do about it here?" Jes refused to answer, and after a moment she continued. "You flit off across the Federation and you think that we all stay the same here, that nothing changes while you're gone. But things do change, Jes. We don't stand still. We move, we grow, we develop. We come together and we fall apart, too. We can't stay forever the same, just because it makes it easier for you."

"That's not what I want," he said quietly. "Don't you think I've thought about this, too? I could fuzz the time regs, I could jump to Aerie so that no matter how long it's been, body-time, since I was here last, I was always here, once a month, once a week if I needed to. It's not even illegal, as long as I don't pop up *before* my last trip in. Believe me, I've thought about it. After you married Ozchan, I was set to do it. I'd lost you once because I wasn't here—I didn't want to lose you again."

"And?" Meya said into his abrupt silence.

Jes sighed and looked across the room at her. The candlelight gilded her face, shone in her long, loose hair; she looked fourteen again. "I thought of how it would be for you. For all of you. I'd be here, then take a five- or six-month trip, then be back the next day for you, or the next week. And sure, I'd watch things change, I'd always be with you. But between one day and the next, I'd be five months older, or eight, or two years. If I did it often enough, I'd be twenty years older in two standard years. I'd be dead by the time Jared and Decca finished school on Kroeber; I'd be dead by the time Jason Hart was old enough to vote. I'd be a curiosity," he said bitterly. "Crazy Jes, living at twice the rate of anybody else. So I could keep you by losing you, or I could lose you by keeping myself. Or something. And after I stopped wanting to kill Ozchan for having you, I thought that maybe what we had together, all of us, was strong enough so that I didn't really have to make a choice. That things would stay together for us, regardless of how long I was gone, or how often."

Meya sat very still, her hands in her lap under the table. Jes wondered if she was clenching them. "Is that my fault?" she said with careful slowness.

"I don't know. Is it mine?"

She shook her head and stood. He turned away from her. After a moment he felt her press against his back and her hands slipped into his pockets. "Jes, we change. We can't help it. Maybe Ozchan and I are just going through a bad time, maybe we'll be back together by the time you're here again. But it's our problem, Jes. Not yours. It's our lives, not your life. You care about us, and I cherish that. It helps me, but it can't change things."

He turned and put his arms around her, resting his chin on her hair. The baby kicked; he could feel it against his belly.

'Can you tell me what he's mad about?"

"No. He won't tell me. I think I know, but it's only a guess. It wouldn't be fair——"

"I know, to spread guesses." He kissed her hair, and the baby stopped kicking. "Can I talk with him?"

"If you want to. He's your friend too, Jes."

He felt the tension in her back, interpreted the angle of her shoulders, and pulled back slightly, forcing her to look up at him. "You're keeping something from me," he whispered. "Meya . . ."

She took his arms in her hands and opened them, went back to the table, and picked up the basket. "Don't," she said as she put the basket in the pantry. "Leave it alone, Jes." She put her glass in the sink and brushed the pel

seeds into the compost bin. Then she went to the kitchen
door, paused, and looked over her shoulder at him, sure,
he knew, of his attention.

"Marry a spacer, Jes," she said gently. "Marry someone you can be with all the time. Love something you
can take with you." She paused again, then turned and
disappeared into the dark dining room. Jes listened to
her quiet footsteps on the stairs. The candle flickered.
He retrieved the basket and sat at the table, morosely
eating berries until the basket was empty and the floor
scattered with seeds. Then, pinching the candle flame out
between thumb and forefinger, he went back to bed.

THE HAMMOCKS IN A STARSHIP, WOVEN OF
light, resilient material, wrap entirely around a sleeper and
are impossible to fall from. They will take any amount
of stretching and wriggling, hold fast during the worst
nightmares, and cradle the lightest sleep. They are often
used in hospitals, have been used in asylums, and are believed by many to be the best surface on which, or in
which, to make love. They are very, very easy to get
used to, and impossible to forget.

Sandro, having spent the past months of his life on a
starship, started the morning of his second day on Aerie
by falling out of bed.

The dream had been curiously wrought, a thing of
reality and fantasy which locked Sandro in terror. The
cool winter sun of Marquez Landing blistered his skin,
and the Parallax transition agent stood by the curing
shed, holding an invoice, detailing in a careless voice the
items of Marquez Landing's surrender. Sandro clenched
and unclenched his hands, and the invoice became his
father's head, dangling from the agent's hand, white hair
dripping blood. The head looked at Sandro, and the
mouth formed words. Sandro's hand wrapped around a

spar, while his father's head swung and smiled and
changed voices with the agent. Sandro raised his arm
and brought the spar down, and down, and down again,
until the agent twisted over him, bleeding into Sandro's
mouth, and raised the talking head like a mace against the
clear white sky. Sandro cried out and fell away from the
head, the blood, the ruined faces, onto a plank floor
which gained solidity under his scrabbling fingers. He
groaned and opened his eyes. Yellow sunlight poured
through the open window, highlighting the tangled knot
of bedclothes. He raised himself on an elbow and the
dream slipped from him, leaving a feeling of dread. He
stood and touched his side where he had fallen, and
walked to the window. The dread vanished, and Sandro
forgot that he had dreamed.

It couldn't have been very long after sunrise, yet the
fields and orchards bustled with workers. To Sandro's
right, a barn straddled the bottom of the hill. He blinked
at it, trying to make out the lines of the original structure,
and was surprised at its size, surprised that the family
had added even more to it. Quilla walked out of the
barn, deep in conversation with a six-limbed alien.
Sandro watched, curious. Marquez Landing had no natives of any type, sapient or otherwise, and Sandro was
puzzled by the Kennerins' seeming acceptance, respect,
and affection for these creatures. The kasir towered
above Quilla, looking vaguely threatening. Then a tiny
pup poked its head out of the kasir's pouch, looked
about, and dove inside again. The kasir put its hand in
the pouch, rummaged about, hauled out the pup, shook
it gently, and put it back. Sandro's eyes widened.

Quilla leaned against the barn's wall, gesturing toward
the fields. She had bound a bright scarf over her hair
and wore a blue jumpsuit with tools sticking out of the
pockets. Doing overseer's duty, Sandro thought. On this
planet, it seemed that housekeepers sat in the parlor
and the family's daughters worked the fields. It showed a
fatal lack of dignity, but the sight of Quilla in work
clothes held him fast. He wished he were close enough to
see the details of her face. Then she turned and walked
with the kasir toward the fields, and Sandro pushed himself away from the window.

After performing his morning rites in the bathroom,
Sandro dressed and went cautiously downstairs, drawn

by the sound of voices in the back of the house. He followed the sounds to the kitchen and stood at the door.

Two kasirene moved through the sunlit room, carrying pots and dishes. Their low voices made a constant murmur, like that of heavy insects in summer air, and they were not speaking Standard. They looked sinister: so tall, all those arms, the slightly snouted faces, the sleek gray fur. But their eyes were large and violet, and when one of them made a noise like laughter Sandro gathered his courage and walked into the kitchen.

"Mim," he said, slowly and carefully. "Where . . . is . . . Mim?" He gestured. The kasirene stopped working and watched him seriously.

"Mim," he repeated. He tried to sketch the housekeeper in the air and one of the kasirene laughed.

"You must be Sandro," it said. "We've kept your breakfast for you, but tomorrow you'll have to get up at some reasonable hour. Everyone's already working. Do you really want to see Mim?"

"No," Sandro said, blushing.

"Sit down, then. You're in the way. I'm Tapir and this lazy one is Dahl." The kasir pulled a chair away from the table and Sandro sat, feeling silly. The kasir called Dahl leaned sideways toward the counter, balanced on a thick tail, and snagged a teapot from the stove. Tapir rummaged in the oven and produced some steaming meat pies. They were both pouched: Sandro, lost in questions about pronouns, forgot his nervousness and began to eat. They worked around him as though he weren't there, resuming their alien chatter. He wondered if they were talking about him.

When he finished Dahl picked up his plate and cup, and Tapir gestured toward the front of the house. "Jes went into town, and Mish went back south this morning. But Jared's around somewhere, just listen for his flute."

In the hallway by the main door he listened for music and, not hearing any, went outside. Some strange, four-winged birds squabbled in a feathery tree in the yard before the house, and the air smelled rich. Sandro touched the dark, varnished timber of a porch pillar, then sat in a sunny corner, his legs dangling over the edge of the porch above a narrow bed of flowers. He tugged at the fringe of mustache he had grown since leaving

MarketPort, and pursued the thought that had come to him between bites of meat pie.

He was still thinking about it when Quilla came around the corner of the house, saw him, and waved. He felt a quick excitement, and the chaotic thoughts fell into place. He stood, waved back at her, and waited for her to come up the steps.

"Nice morning," she said in greeting. "Have you been fed?"

"Yes, thank you."

Quilla pushed strands of hair back under her scarf, and looked at her hands.

"I've got to wash," she said. "Paperwork to do. Is there anything you need?"

"Not really, Quia Quilla—"

"Don't do that! I've always hated that damned singsong. It's enough to make me want to immigrate to where I'll always be an offworlder, and be called Menet Kennerin like a civilized adult human being. Call me Quilla, but don't put that idiot honorific in front of it, all right?"

Sandro made a deep bow. *"Señora, yo soy a sus órdenes,"* he said gallantly.

Quilla laughed. "Should I curtsy?"

"It's the acceptable thing, back home. I wanted to speak with you about that, by the way."

Quilla raised her eyebrows, glanced at the sun, and nodded. "My office is the second door to your right after the living room. I'll be in as soon as I wash."

She cut through the dining room toward the kitchen. Sandro hesitated, then walked down the hall to the office.

A huge desk, some storage cabinets, and a battered terminal crowded the small room. An oil lamp stood on the terminal's dusty housing, and shelves along the walls were covered with tapereels, stacks of paper, ledgers, binders, and a miscellaneous assortment of dustcatchers. A large map hung on the wall beside the window. Sandro puzzled over it, finding Haven and the landing field, discovering that the name of Haven's island was To'an Cault, and its neighboring island was To'an Betes. Other islands dotted the planet along the equator, and two icecaps crept up and down the top and bottom of the map. Notes in various hands littered islands, oceans, and icecaps.

"Shaggies all north of here," said one at the tip of To'an

Cault. "Lousy wood—burning, not building." "Sour water,
safe." "Tabor's place." "Reefs—heading w/nw until
Spire sighted, bear s. sharp. Changing," "*Au* 14% survey
rpt. So?" "Good wheat lands here." "Note detail, map
413." "Floodplain." "Hoku."

Quilla pushed the door open with her hip and came
in, carrying a teapot and two mugs. She filled the mugs,
handed one to Sandro, and went around the desk. The
aroma of the hot tea tickled his nose.

"Now," Quilla said. She cleared a place on the desk
for her mug and sat down. "You wanted to talk to me?"

Sandro licked his lips and turned to face her. She put
her elbows on the desk amid the papers and cradled the
mug in her palms, obviously about to be busy, obviously
setting aside time for him. He ran through the opening
phrases he had created and discarded them all.

"Last night I told you about Parallax," he said bluntly.
"What are you going to do about it?"

Quilla smiled. "Without a director's vote, we don't do
anything at all. But I don't think that will be a problem."
She sipped at the tea, watching him through the steam.
"We'll run a check to see if they've affected us much, or
are likely to. Meya will take a look at Processing, make
sure everything's secure. If the figures work out right
we'll get a go-vote on moving the plant to Eagle System.
We might stockpile some import goods just in case we do
get into some kind of embargo situation, but frankly, I
don't think that's likely. And we'll sit back and see what
happens next."

"That's not enough," Sandro said passionately.

"I don't understand."

"Of course you do! My father, my mother—they died
just as if Parallax killed them personally. Everything's
gone, everyone's gone, and that simply wasn't fair!"

"Most of life isn't fair."

"That's no answer!"

"What kind of answer did you expect? Sit down and
drink your tea."

Sandro put his mug down sharply on a cabinet. "I'm
not a child!"

"That seems debatable," Quilla said. "Sit down.
You're in my office, not at a caraem game. I can hear
you when you don't shout."

"I wasn't . . ." Sandro yelled, and stopped. He marched

back to the map and turned around again. Quilla didn't look angry. He thrust his shaking hands into his pockets.

"Please," Sandro said. "Don't be—haughty with me. The Federation didn't give a damn about what happened to us. Parallax just moved in on us and no one did anything to stop them. Someone, *anyone,* should do something, not just let them get away with it. They've got to be stopped, they've got to pay for what they did." He drew in his breath. "I don't think that's unreasonable."

Quilla put her cup down, folded her hands, and looked at him. "Sandro, you've been to college. The Federation's a glorified regulatory agency, and that's it. They're not in business to stop people from doing things, unless it cuts into their monopoly on tauspace or on communications. As for what Parallax did to your planet and your family, it's perfectly legal, so far as the Federation is concerned." She put up her hand to forestall his shouting. "I'm not saying that it's right, or moral, or proper. That's simply the way it is. And we're trying to run a planet here. It's a business bigger than what we expected or wanted, but we've got it and I'm not sorry about it. Compared to what your family had, we're laughably small. I don't care. We're trying to make a good life here, for ourselves, for our people. We'll learn as much as we can, we'll protect ourselves as much as we can. We'll give you a home, if you want one. But I think that's all we can reasonably be asked to do."

"God, you *are* reasonable, aren't you?" Sandro put his forehead against the map and closed his eyes. When she put her hand on his shoulder he whipped around, startled and frightened.

"Sandro," she said gently, pulling him around to face her. "What do you want?"

"Revenge!" he shouted.

Quilla's eyes widened. "Whatever for?"

"Oh, you wouldn't understand," he said, jerking away from her. "You've never suffered, any of you. It's beyond you."

"I think you underestimate us. You know nothing about us."

Something in her quiet voice reached him and this time, when she urged him toward a chair, he sat. She perched on a corner of the desk and leaned over to reach for her tea.

"Do you know about the landslave system on Terra?" she said.

Sandro thought it an irrelevant question, but he nodded. "Something about failed colonists, when they return they have to work for the Four Families."

"Four Hundred Families, and it's more unpleasant than simple work. Returned colonists are forcibly apportioned to the various Family holdings, forced to accept work which may or may not have anything to do with their backgrounds, watch their families broken up. They're under the control of the Family that owns them from the moment they land to the moment they die. And their children are landslaves, and their grandchildren, for as long as children come. If a landslave wants out, she can die or buy passage out, and the Families make it damned hard to buy passage out. Think of what that must be like, Sandro. To watch your chosen world fail around you, to have to return to Terra, and to be caught in a web like that." Quilla paused and sipped her tea, watching Sandro. "My mother was a landslave on Terra. That's where I was born."

Tiny, straightbacked Mish a landslave? Sandro shook his head, unable to accept it.

"Oh, it's true," Quilla said. "Her parents died when her birthworld went bad. She was about sixteen when she landed on Terra. She wasn't even given a choice."

"Did she have to go to Terra?"

Quilla shrugged. "The Families keep an eye on failing worlds. They send out transports, offer to take people back free. When it's that or die . . ."

"How did she get out?"

"My father was a member of one of the Families."

"So he bought her out," Sandro said dismissively. "Money and power. I think that proves my point."

"Not quite. When my parents married, his Family banished them, and me. They gave him just enough money for passage out, and when he threatened them, they gave him enough to buy Aerie. Just before Jason and Mish left Terra, his father struck Jason's name from the Family list. Jason could have owned a four-hundredth of Terra, Sandro. A hunk of the motherworld, a hunk of one of the richest planets in the Federation. Should he have sought revenge for that?"

Sandro moved uncomfortably in his chair. "But he had

your mother, and you, and Aerie. He didn't lose everything."

"That's the way he saw it," Quilla agreed. "He made
his choice and he lived with it."

"But I didn't choose this," Sandro shouted. Quilla
looked at him, and he lowered his voice. "My parents
didn't choose to die, they were forced to it. My father
didn't choose to sell. I didn't choose exile, or poverty, it
was chosen for me. Don't I have a right to feel angry
about that?"

"Certainly. But Parallax, from what I hear, is fairly
generous with the companies they swallow. Surely they
didn't get Marquez Landing for free."

Sandro looked away. Perhaps his brother Enrique still
held Sandro's share of the money, or perhaps, hoping to
save face, he had loyally returned the money to Parallax
in payment for the agent's life. Or had kept it himself—it
was irrelevant. Sandro had not taken the money, and
would not, and, now, could not. Quilla looked at him with
the same "tell me something" expression that Jes wore so
often, and Sandro closed his lips stubbornly. After a while
Quilla sighed and moved around to the far side of the
desk.

"There's another thing," Sandro said, breaking the
quiet. Quilla looked up from the papers on her desk.
"There's a woman called Beryl aboard ship. Do you
know her?"

Quilla frowned and shook her head. "Should I?"

"I don't know. Captain Hetch knows her—there's
something strange going on between her and Captain
Kennerin."

"I haven't heard about it," Quilla said. "Jes lives two
lives, Sandro, and they very rarely touch."

Sandro gestured. "What about Spider? Who's he?"

"Hart's son." Quilla leaned back. "Where did you hear
about him?"

"Hetch mentioned him once. To Beryl. It seemed to
frighten her."

Quilla smiled widely. "Spider is a fairly awesome
specimen but I wouldn't call him frightening. Hetch did
mention something about trouble with the crew but that's
Jes' problem, Sandro." She picked up her teacup and the
smile slid from her face. "Sandro, I don't want to know
about the ship, not unless Jes tells me about it. It's not my

business, and it's probably not yours either. He has a hard enough time without people snooping into his life."

"I'm not snooping," Sandro began indignantly. Quilla waved her cup.

"Yes you are. Not that I can blame you, but I won't be part of it."

Sandro tightened his lips. "And Parallax?"

Quilla sighed. "We're not bookreel heroes, Sandro. There's nobody on Aerie to play Tri-Captain Delta Three."

Sandro remained silent, trying to quell his rising fury.

"We count our profits in fremarks. Parallax counts its profits in worlds. If we set out to fight Parallax, we'd be dead within a year, and Parallax would be hysterical with laughter. If they bothered to notice."

"Cowardice," he muttered.

"No, reality."

Sandro glared at her. "I should not have expected honor from a woman."

Quilla looked at him with calm, unjudging compassion. He stood abruptly and walked out of the room, down the hall, and to the porch. A stand of trees grew to his left, along the top of the hill, and he ran toward it.

Quilla didn't follow him. He hadn't expected that she would. By the time he reached the trees the anger had burned itself down. He wandered amid smooth and scaly trunks, touching them with his fingers, thinking about what Quilla had said and how foreign it sounded.

He had been taught that a man stood up for what was right, regardless of the odds. That one sought revenge against one's enemies, and that should a man not seek such a revenge, his honor was irreparably and forever damaged. He would lose his manhood, and without manhood there was no longer reason to live.

But he had not been taught how to fight star-tides, or fate, or a combine as large as Parallax. The enemy of a friend was the enemy of oneself—were the Kennerins his friends? Surely they had a common enemy, but it seemed to him suddenly that no relationship was thereby established. They would protect themselves, that was right. They would offer him shelter, and that was right. But they could not, would not, offer him the tools of his revenge, and, with Quilla's calm words echoing through his mind, he was no longer sure that they were wrong.

Baffled and beset, he resolutely pushed the conflict into the back of his mind and marched down the hill toward Haven.

It seemed to be market day in Haven. The square in the middle of the village was crowded with vendors and shoppers, terran and kasirene, and what appeared, at first glance, to be a thousand children. Sandro hesitated, listening to the babble of languages, then cautiously moved along the edge of the square to a beerhall. A short, buxom woman grinned at him, offered him a beer, and told him that Jes was up at Haven hospital. Sandro politely declined the beer and asked directions. She gave them, laughed, slapped his ass, and wiped her hands on her apron before going into the public room again. Sandro blushed, then blushed harder at the grins of those who sat at tables on the beerhall's broad porch. He shoved his fists in his pockets, ducked his head, and followed the woman's directions out of Haven toward the hospital.

JES RINSED HIS HANDS, INSPECTED THEM carefully, and scrubbed at them again until they tingled and ached. He stuck them under the blower and glanced up to see Ozchan entering, pulling at his operating greens.

"Think you can remember how to do that, captain?" Ozchan said.

"If I have to, and I hope I never have to." He thought about the compound fracture he'd just helped Ozchan set; white bone puncturing muscle and skin, the blood. "How did she do it?"

"Playing on a roof. Lost her balance and fell, forgot how to land." Ozchan peeled the rest of the greens from his body and tossed them into a bin. The nine years since his marriage to Meya had thickened his waist slightly, but had not otherwise changed his lithe, dark body. Jes saw Ozchan glance back at him and he sucked his stomach in. Ozchan grinned and walked into the shower.

"They brought her in from Hoku," Ozchan called over the sound of water. "They've a good nurse there, but he can't handle this sort of thing. Her name's Anye Olet."

Jes looked at his hands again and reached for his clean clothes. "I didn't recognize her," he said. "She's grown."

"Children do, generally." The water stopped. "You ask about her, though. And her brothers. I've heard you."

Jes shrugged into his shirt, his back to the doctor. "I knew her mother well. Will you cite my Certificate?"

"Later." Ozchan pulled on fresh clothing. "If it were just you asking, I wouldn't think it strange. You almost married her mother once, didn't you?"

"Ozchan—"

"But Hetch asks, too. Not directly, but casually. Each time he's on planet." Ozchan slid his feet into his shoes and stood up. "I'm not letting him back into space, Jes. The bones in his hips are almost gone. I can retard the deterioration if he stays on planet. But once he goes up again, or once he gets away from me—you know him. He won't take medicine unless you cram it down his throat."

"I could—"

"And a few more takeoffs and entrys are going to collapse the pelvic girdle completely." Ozchan put his hand on Jes' cheek. "I'm sorry. I know he's special—he is for a lot of us." The doctor paused and Jes angrily seamed his shirt together. "That's another odd thing," Ozchan went on. "Hetch was spending most of his time here, until about, what, three years ago? A little less? And the next thing I know, he's off whizzing around space with you."

"He didn't tell me he'd been feeling unwell," Jes said defensively.

"I don't imagine that he would. I'm not blaming you for anything, Jes. Just being curious."

"Yeah." Jes finished with his clothing and looked over at Ozchan. "You're full of interesting speculation today."

"Make you a deal," the doctor said lightly. "Answer my questions and I'll answer yours."

Jes shrugged, nodded, and followed Ozchan down the short hallway to the ward. Anye was still groggy but she slid her hand into the doctor's and listened gravely while Ozchan told her that she was a brave girl, but a little incautious. She giggled when he said that he'd be pleased to set her broken legs any time she wanted, but that too much would get monotonous.

"I had a special assistant," Ozchan said, and beckoned Jes over to the bed. When he introduced them, Anye's eyes widened with awe. Jes said something meant to be light which came out awkward, kissed the child swiftly on her forehead, and left the room. After a moment Ozchan joined him.

"Big hero," the doctor said, smiling uncomfortably, and opened the door of his office. Kayman Olet rose from a chair by the desk. Jes froze at the door, but Ozchan walked to his desk, sat, and began telling Olet that his daughter was doing well, would be out of the hospital in a week and running in four to five months, if she took care of herself. Jes closed the door, feeling trapped, and walked to the window. He put his hands in his pockets and closed his eyes.

Kayman Olet touched his arm. Jes turned and looked down at the preacher. Age had only intensified the blandness of the man's face; even his wrinkles seemed indistinct and soft. Secondhand weariness, Jes thought.

"Ozchan tells me that you helped with Anye," the preacher said. "I'm grateful."

"I'm glad I could help."

"Thank you. She's thrilled, I know. You're one of her heroes."

Jes glanced at Ozchan helplessly, but the doctor's expression was neutral.

"Her mother spoke quite a bit about you," Kayman continued. "Before she left. The children miss her."

"It's been three years," Jes said. "Surely they're used to it."

"I doubt whether anyone gets used to being abandoned," Kayman said. "Or forgotten."

"She hasn't been in touch?"

Kayman looked at him. "Please don't bait me, tau-Captain. I think you know the answer to that."

Jes looked at the pale, sad-faced man, feeling both anger and relief. He sat in the one vacant chair, stretched his legs before him, and looked at the preacher over his clasped hands. "How did you trace her?" he said.

"With Doctor M'Kale's help." Kayman took his seat again and looked down at his fingernails. "We knew when she'd left Aerie, and the destination of the ship. The name change was a bit awkward, but once we figured it out . . . She went straight from here to Augustine Sal, and from there straight to you."

Jes shook his head. "Not entirely, Kayman. How much do you know about tau?"

The preacher looked up. "Not much. Basic stuff."

Jes looked at Ozchan, who spread his hands.

"You know that tau is a different universe? Okay, you might call ours a time-frequency universe, and things take place in terms of time, one after the other. We measure distance, measure space, in terms of time. Light-years. Parsecs. It's so basic that we don't even question it." He waited for the others to nod before continuing. "Tau is not a time-universe. There is space, if you want to call it that, although location is a better term to use. The locations are congruent with locations in our universe, but time has nothing to do with it, and time is so much a part of how we see things that we can't understand the tau-universe when we do see it. It looks like chaos to us. It makes no sense."

"Is any of this relevant?" Ozchan said.

"Yes." Jes leaned forward, gesturing. "If we can get from our universe into tau, we can move from point A to point B without worrying about the speed of light, because that's a time-based factor and in tau you don't have to cope with time. You simply have to get into tau, move from one point to another, and move out again. But when you do get to point B, you're likely to get there at any time at all; that is, at any time in *our* universe at all. The grab can flip you out of tau, but it will flip you out randomly. You could end up orbiting a star that doesn't exist yet. You could pop out at the end of the universe. So part of a grab is something called a coil, a time-coil. You tell it when you want to be, and it takes you there."

"I still don't see—" Kayman said, and someone knocked loudly on the door. Ozchan stood and opened the door, and over his shoulder Jes could see Sandro's face.

"I'm in conference—"

"Wait," Kayman said. He stood and walked over to Ozchan. "Young man? You're from Captain Kennerin's ship? From *Rabbit*?"

"Yes, sir," Sandro said, fingering the collar of his uniform. He looked over Ozchan's other shoulder at Jes, who looked down uncomfortably.

"Let him in," Kayman said, and went back to his chair.

"You don't trust me?" Jes said, a trace of bitterness in his voice. "Kayman, I don't think this should get out anymore . . ."

The preacher folded his hands. "We are three emotional men dealing with an emotional situation. I think that some impartial person would help."

Jes glanced at Sandro, his expression sarcastic, and gestured an assent. Ozchan let Sandro step into the room and closed the door behind him.

"I didn't mean to interrupt, sir," Sandro said to Jes. "I just wanted to—"

"Never mind," Jes said wearily. "Sit down somewhere and listen. You asked me a question once, and I wouldn't answer."

Sandro looked puzzled and opened his mouth. Jes glared at him. He closed his lips abruptly and, seeing no vacant chairs, sat on the windowsill. Jes waited until Ozchan was behind his desk again.

"Coils. I don't know how they work. You could look up the physics somewhere, but I doubt whether you'd understand it any more than I do. In some grabstation facilities, spacers occasionally set up an illegal coil and use it for kicks. Augustine Sal has an illegal coil."

Kayman fidgeted. "I don't want to talk about tau," he said. "I want to talk about—"

"Give me time. Three years ago, I came into Augustine Grab with a loose vane and looked for a good pit on the Sal to get the repairs done. I met someone in the pit crew who looked almost identical to Taine. Older, and scarred, and harder than Taine was. A good pit worker and an excellent drive jockey. She said her name was Beryl, that she'd been a spacer since twelve thirty-two and got her registry license in twelve thirty-five. The number is a twelve thirty-nine number, but she said they'd made a mistake. They do, sometimes." Jes shrugged. "She's got enough experience, enough webscarring, to have been a spacer that long. I met her after her shift, bought her a drink, asked some questions." He stood quickly. "She hinted some, just enough to make me curious. I needed another drive jockey, so I took her on." He paused, staring oùt the window without seeing anything, oblivious to Sandro beside him.

"Go on," Kayman said.

"When we were back in tau, she told me that she was Taine. That she'd left you, that you'd been cruel to her —she has scars, Kayman, they're pretty convincing."

"I never—"

"I know that now. I didn't, then. She said she'd come to space to join me. That she loved me. That if I didn't keep her on, she'd kill herself. She told horror stories— I'd been away a long time, for all I knew she was telling the truth. She made me swear that I'd keep her secret, and like a fool I swore. I figured that she'd come to Augustine, gone coiling, picked up years of experience and a registry, then jumped back to the day after she'd left and sat there waiting for me."

"How could she know you were coming?" Ozchan said.

"You can coil forward, doctor," Sandro said quietly. "It wouldn't have been hard. Jump up the line a year or two, look in the records to see if *Rabbit* had come through, then jump back and wait for it. Captain?"

Jes nodded. "She'd been on the pit crew for about three months standard when I got there. They don't ask your background when you work pits, or generally when you work space unless you're an officer. After a month or so I finally realized that she was . . . lying about some things. That a lot of her story didn't make sense. I tried to talk her into coming back to Aerie."

"Did you?" Kayman said.

Jes looked at him, then paced around the room unhappily. "She said she'd never been on Aerie in her life. Asked what sector it was in. I told her your name, the kids' names. She shrugged and made a joke. She was pretty convincing. And I figured that, maybe, you wouldn't want her back, once you saw what she'd become. She's . . . she's not a nice woman, Kayman."

Sandro laughed and the preacher whipped around to stare at him. Sandro gestured angrily.

"She's a bitch," he said simply. "She's a mean, hard, games-playing, stony-assed bitch. She needles and drives

and doesn't stop until you break. I wanted to kill her."
Sandro paused. "Then."

"The only one she doesn't assault is Hetch," Jes said.
"That's why I asked him to ship out with me again. That's
why he came. But she says she's never been Taine, that
she plays the game because I force her to. And she
throws my words back at me. She either knows enough
about Aerie, or remembers enough, so that sometimes I
can't remember whether I'm right, whether she is Taine,
or whether she's right and is really Beryl playing at Taine.
Whoever she is, she's crazy, Kayman."

"Then why do you keep her on?" Ozchan demanded.

"Guilt," Jes said calmly, looking at Kayman. "I fired
her once, figuring that she'd be forced to come home. She
took a knife to herself. That's where the original scars
came from, too—I talked to someone who knew her during the coiling years. She doesn't make empty threats."

Olet looked as though he'd been struck. Jes turned
away, sickened, and stared at the wall.

"I know she'd always loved you," the preacher said
finally. Jes closed his eyes. "She told me that, when I
asked her to marry me. She said that you loved her."

'I did, then," Jes said into the darkness behind his eyelids. "She turned me down. Said she didn't want to be a
spacer's wife."

"She didn't want to be a preacher's wife either, after a
while." Kayman's voice paused. "She used to taunt me.
She told me that you were her lover."

"Not after she married. I didn't touch her."

"Why not?"

"She didn't want me, really. She wanted to hurt you, to
play games. I wouldn't do it."

There was a brief silence. "She was often untruthful,"
Kayman said. "I couldn't make her happy and she punished me for it. Punished the children."

"She's punishing me," Jes whispered. He sat and
looked at Kayman hopelessly. "Maybe she's right, maybe
it is all my fault. I don't know. I'm half convinced that if
I hadn't loved her once, if I hadn't turned her down, this
wouldn't be happening—"

"Nonsense," Ozchan said crisply. Jes ignored him.

"Kayman, what do I do now? Force her to come down?
You don't know what she's like now. What good would it

do? I don't want her—whatever it is that I want, she's not it. But she won't believe that."

Sandro looked up abruptly. "I heard Hetch threaten to bring her home once. It frightened her."

"That doesn't prove anything," Jes said.

"Then he said he'd bring Spider up, and that frightened her more."

Jes and Ozchan stared at him. Sandro spread his hands. "I don't know why."

"Spider's telepathic," Ozchan said. "She wouldn't even know enough to be afraid of him, if she wasn't Taine."

"Wonderful," Jes said with an edge of sarcasm. "That proves that I'm not crazy. What about her?"

Kayman jumped out of his chair and turned to Sandro, hands spread. "Young man, you've heard what the captain said. You've spent time around my wife. Is it true?"

Sandro nodded slowly, his face expressionless.

"Believe him," Jes said. "He's half in love with her, aren't you?"

Sandro looked across the room to the captain, stood, and walked to the door. "Not with Taine," he said over his shoulder, and went out, closing the door firmly behind him.

Jes gestured hopelessly. "Kayman?" he said, pleading.

"Do you want absolution?" the preacher said. "For what? For not telling me three years ago? Yes, yes, I forgive you. For what else? You've behaved admirably, we've all behaved admirably. There's nothing left to say, is there? There's nothing . . ." He passed his hands over his wispy hair, touched the collar of his shirt, and half bowed with awkward formality. "Doctor, tauCaptain, thank you for your time. Your trouble. I'm sorry I—I must see my daughter. I should have been there immediately, thank you, I must be—yes."

Ozchan, giving Jes a stern look, followed the preacher from the room and came back a few minutes later. Jes remained standing by the wall, hands at sides, staring at nothing. Ozchan took his arm and guided him firmly to a chair.

"Will he be all right?" Jes said.

"Yes. I have someone watching him. When he's finished visiting Anye he'll be given a sedative. There's room for him."

Jes put his head in his hands. "Can I have one, too?"

"Different prescription," Ozchan said. The glass he forced into Jes' hand was filled with kaea, the strong kasirene drink. Jes took a swallow and coughed.

"Sweet Mother, I knew it would be hard when it happened. I didn't know it would be that hard," Jes said. He took another swallow. He looked across the desk at Ozchan and managed a smile. "Now you want to tell me your troubles, doctor?"

"After that, they're pretty anticlimactic," Ozchan said, and smiled back. "I've only got one problem, captain. My wife is pregnant by someone else. I thought it might be you."

A HALAEA GREW AT THE HEAD OF JASON'S grave, grown from seeds off the halaea in front of the Tor. Mish had planted a *Zimania* bush at the foot of the grave. Buds covered the plant. Jes picked one and held it loosely, looking down at the small stone plaque on which were engraved his father's name and the dates of his birth and death. He sat beside the stone and stared through the line of trees toward Haven and the Tor. His fingers began shredding the bud. He closed his eyes and tried to see tau.

"Bucolic reveries, older brother?"

Jason looked up. Hart stood across the grave from him.

"I saw you leave the hospital," Hart said. "I assume you talked with Ozchan."

"You know what he thinks?" Jes said. Hart stood with his back to the sun and Jes could not see his face.

"Yes. He's wrong, of course, but the good doctor is not going to listen to me."

Jes drew his knees up. "It couldn't be his child. He had a capsule put in after Andrus' birth. He checked it— it's not defective, and it's still working. So if it isn't Ozchan's baby, whose is it?"

Hart sat. "Immaculate conception?" he suggested. Jes

looked at him, disgusted. Hart gestured lightly. "It is a thought. On the other hand, does it matter?"

"Ozchan thinks so. So do I. Sleeping around is one thing, we all do it. But children are important. It's basic, Hart. How would you feel if you thought Spider wasn't your child?"

Hart smiled. He leaned forward and took a bud from the *Zimania*. "Totally impossible, older brother. Spider's mine, and I share him with no one. Meya's baby is Meya's, and I don't see what's wrong with that. After all, we know who the child's mother is, don't we?"

"Hart, you've no social conscience."

"True. But we can't all be paragons." Hart's skilled fingers carefully dissected the bud, removing the tight layers one by one and placing them delicately along the top of Jason's headstone. Jes looked at his own bud, lying clumsily shredded in the palm of his hand. He closed his fingers over it. "Look at yourself, for example," Hart continued. "Playing Tri-Captain, bringing home worthy cases. Sandro's your second stray, isn't he? Have you even tried to see Chiba, find out how he's doing?"

"I haven't had—"

"Time. Sure. None of us do. What's on your mind, Jes? What do you want from us?" Hart said sympathetically. Jes looked at him with distrust.

"What does anyone want? Love, stability, kindness, warmth—I don't see that those are impossible. Are they?"

"I don't know," Hart said. He had peeled the bud down to its intricate inner core; now he unclasped the brooch from his shoulder and used its pin to tease the final petals away from the bud, working to preserve their structure intact. His eyes narrowed with concentration. Jes contemplated his brother's face, envying the smooth, strong lines of cheek and jaw, the thick lashes, the wings of deep black hair. Everything had come together in Hart, he thought; those stray pieces of family beauty, the wit, the strength—and all the darknesses. He found himself wishing that he could pursue the center of his brother as his brother pursued the center of the bud, and knew that he was far too clumsy a surgeon for the task. Hart, as though sensing his thoughts, glanced up at him, a sardonic twinkle of blue eyes glimpsed through a screen of dark, smooth skin and long hair.

"Tell me about it, Jes," he said, and returned to his dissection.

Jes sighed and lay back along the grave. He put his hands under his head and stared into the branches of the halaea. "I sometimes wonder whether it's not a translation thing," he said. "I wonder if you can even comprehend my life. Planet-bound, living on one world. Day by day, watching the seasons come and go, watching people change. The changes must seem smaller to you because they're so tiny, so constant; they hit me every time I come back. For you, children grow. For me, they jump. Everything jumps, and I can barely keep track of it." He paused. "I can barely keep track of myself, Hart. I can barely understand what's going on."

His brother did not reply. Jes closed his eyes. How did one explain twenty-one years of a spacer's life to someone who could barely comprehend space at all? Long after the romantic notion of being a starship captain had been driven from him, Jes clung to the terrifying, majestic glory of tau, the feeling of insignificance which transmuted into a sense of immensity, the satori of tau. It worked in him like a drug, heightening and sharpening his senses, removing him from the confines of his skin and hurling him into a universe of pure energy. He knew that tau rarely had this effect on spacers, knew it for a specialness almost entirely his own, and could no more relinquish it than he could relinquish breathing.

But the price of this intoxication was a lessening of what he had, once, thought the strongest ties of his life: the love of his family, the smell and touch and taste of his home, the complicated web of past, present, and future caught in a glimpse of Meya's hair reflecting firelight, of Quilla tall amid the fields, of Mish surrounded by her grandchildren. Even Hart, dark-visioned, caught the flow and held it. At fifteen, Jes had not even thought about these ties; Aerie would always be Aerie, his family would remain constant, and he himself be as tightly embedded in the flow as the others. At seventeen the flow seemed more tenuous, harder to grasp. At thirty-eight, it seemed that the flow had spit him out, left him wandering a complicated maze which afforded only frustrating glimpses of his family's life; all his anchors were gone. Meya made a secret of herself and would not even give him the solace of a promised revelation. Ozchan, lover and friend, was too lost in his own pain to comprehend Jes' needs. Jes thought, suddenly, that he had more in common with Beryl than he had with his own family, and the thought made him snap upright, shaking his head in negation.

"Older brother," Hart said, "you're crying."

Jes hid his face in his hands. "Don't mock me."

"Who am I to mock? I've fucked things up at least as badly as you have, probably worse. I am constantly on probation. You are greeted with kisses and exclamations; I'm barely tolerated."

Jes looked across the grave at him. "And the kasirene?"

"And the kasirene," Hart agreed.

"I don't suppose you want to tell me about that?"

"I do not." Hart smiled. "Some secrets I reserve, captain. That's one."

"At least you have Spider," Jes said, and Hart nodded.

"Spider," he repeated. Jes recognized the tone of his voice; it was the same tone that Jes, planet-bound, used when he thought of tau. "Were it not for Spider," Hart continued, "I'd not be here. You know that. I'd be the cheerful, unreformed villain, mucking about in people's lives on distant planets. You've heard the rumors—I wish I could say that all of them are true, but they're probably not," Hart said regretfully. He was working on the heart of the bud now, laying pieces almost microscopically small along the headstone. Jes shivered and looked away.

"That's a burden to put on your son," he said. "Aren't you afraid that you'll resent him? Or that he'll resent you?"

"No." Hart finished with the bud, dusted his hands, and looked at the results of his labor. "We're all passionate people, older brother. You for space, Mish for security, Meya for . . . her secret. And I for Spider."

"And when Spider goes away?"

"He won't," Hart said coldly. He leaned forward and blew at the line of petals, watching them lift and swirl and disappear into the grass.

"Ozchan says that Spider's definitely telepathic."

"He is."

"That doesn't bother you?"

Hart shrugged. "I can control my thoughts. I don't

think he can read that deeply anyway. Besides, Decca and Jared are telepathic, too, and it doesn't seem to bother anyone."

"But they can only read each other."

Hart shrugged. "Minor quibbles. Spider's not a monster. Unlike his parent." Hart grinned suddenly. "We're not that different, Jes. I built Spider, and you built your ship. At least we both have solid obsessions."

"Sure," Jes said bitterly. He turned over onto his stomach. "Up there, I'm competent and intelligent and one of the best captains in the Federation. And down here, I'm an adolescent fool. I shed twenty years every time I come through Eagle Grab. I stop understanding things. I fuck things up."

"You don't have to," Hart said mildly.

"Fuck things up?"

"Come through the grab."

Jes sat up and stared at his brother. Hart shrugged. "There's no law forcing you to come home. There's no law forcing you to be a spacer either. If you don't like a situation, you can walk away from it. That's not a choice that the rest of us can make."

"Are you telling me to stay away?"

"I'm merely pointing out options, Jes." Hart laughed abruptly. "I'm very good at other people's problems, even if I can't seem to do a damned thing about my own."

"You want to tell me about them?"

"Why? You'll just pop off into space, and when you come back they'll all have changed again, and you'll be working on obsolete information. What good would it do?" He stood and brushed the seat of his pants. "It's almost suppertime. Coming home?"

"No. Will you tell them I'll be late?"

"Sorry. I'm staying in Haven tonight." Hart smiled down at Jes. "Remember Mertika? Meya's friend, Ped Kohl's daughter? She wants to marry me. And she's the only one who can't see the absurdity of it."

"And you'll sleep with her anyway? You have no conscience."

"Nonsense. I have quite a bit of conscience. It's simply selective." He turned to go.

"Hart?"

Hart turned around and looked at him.

"Do you want me to go away? Permanently?"

"No." For a moment Hart's smooth, handsome face looked troubled. "I'm trying to build a family too, Jes. But I have to make and pick my own options. So do you."

Jes watched his brother walk through the trees of the cemetery and out of sight. He rolled onto his back again and listened to the arguments in his head while the sun set and pallid stars appeared overhead. After a while he saw the moving dot that was *Rabbit*, patiently waiting for his return.

Time to go home, he thought, and tracked the light until it fell below the horizon. He stood, scrubbed his hands across his face, and went to tell Sandro that it was time to leave.

SANDRO WALKED CAREFULLY AND SLOWLY down the road from Haven hospital toward the town. To his left, behind the brow of the hill, he heard the sound of shuttle engines alternately roaring and choking; someone tuning the engines. He thought about the ride down to Aerie, then thought about the ride back. Beryl, who was Taine and wife to the quiet, desperate little man in the doctor's office, spun somewhere overhead, engaged in domesticity. Scrubbing the corridors of the tauship, mending the myriad little things that always became frayed during a run and were too small to worry about until the trip's end. Replacing dead light discs. Sponging scum from the curved screens in the bridge. He wondered if she paused to set the screens to Aerie, whether she watched for To'an Cault, whether she magnified to spot Haven, or the Tor, or her husband's wispy head. Sandro shook his head; he could no more imagine Beryl homesick, Beryl compassionate, than he could imagine himself, now, tilting at Parallax's windmills.

Market-day sounds reached him by the time he neared
the first houses. He turned away and walked through the
meadow skirting the edge of town. He wondered if the
captain had deliberately called that meeting at the hospital, and doubted it. If the story were Beryl's, it was also
her husband's; they must have forced Kennerin to it.

On Marquez Landing, a woman who ran away from
her husband was a disgrace; people who aided her were
a disgrace; the husband who did not force her to return
was, equally, a disgrace. Sandro shook his head again,
bewildered.

If Beryl were old enough to be that preacher's wife, if
she had taken years through the coil, she'd be . . . older
than the captain? Much older? Certainly years older
than Sandro. A man should not lust after older women,
and Sandro, after a moment's consideration, admitted
that he did lust after Beryl; that he wanted to touch her
body, that he also wanted to touch her mind. He had
walked into the small ward after leaving preacher, doctor,
captain; bent over the bed and contemplated Beryl's sleeping child. They looked much alike, and now he tried to
put all three together in his head, Beryl, Kayman, Anye,
a family grouping so wrong that he could not make the
images stabilize. He should, he told himself, feel contempt
for the woman who had abandoned husband and family,
the woman who publicly and disgracefully forced herself
on a man who did not want her. The contempt, too,
would not stabilize, and instead he felt a growing sadness, a desire to soothe and protect that harsh woman
until she no longer needed her hatred, until she could
move toward sanity herself. He examined the feeling,
knowing that Beryl would use it against him, and knowing that he didn't care. He couldn't fight Parallax, he
couldn't regain his homeland; he could, at the least, offer
friendship. The more he thought about the idea, the more
he liked it. He tucked his thumbs under his belt, feeling
less impotent, and looked around.

The aspect of the town had changed. Instead of neat,
separate houses, Sandro skirted a section where the
buildings were crowded together, pasted one atop the
other, connected by corridors or balconies. The entire
thing was painted in bright, chaotic colors. He paused
and stared. A kasir popped out of a door, yelled angrily

along a balcony, and went inside again. Sandro raised his eyebrows and kept walking.

The kasirene section of town dwindled away, replaced by a broad dirt field. Young people scuffled in the dirt, playing a game with balls, bats, some sort of scoop, and baskets at either end of the field. They laughed and shouted angrily. Off to the side some younger children were imitating the game with makeshift equipment of their own. Sandro stopped to watch. Half the players were terran and half were kasirene; the teams seemed integrated. Someone threw the ball at him and he caught it awkwardly, amid laughter. He cocked his arm back and flung the ball hard across the field, grinned, declined to continue playing, walked away. As soon as his back was to the game, he stopped smiling.

Fields edged up to the town. The sun had passed the meridian and sat midway down in the western sky. Sandro shrugged, picked a road, and walked along the edge of the fields and up the hill.

Jared stood in the yard under the tree, talking with someone. Sandro skirted the yard, walked around the house, and found the kitchen door fronting on a garden. He walked through rows of strange vegetation and pushed open the kitchen door.

"Good, another pair of hands," Mim said. She put a load of dishes in his arms.

"But—" Sandro protested.

Mim snatched the plates back and inspected his hands. "Oh, Mother," she said, exasperated. "Go wash first. Is that mud or grease under your fingernails?"

"Neither," Sandro said defensively and washed his hands in the sink. Mim took the dishes into the next room.

Dahl handed him a bowl. "On the table," the kasir said, "then come back and get some more. It's always harder when the children are gone."

Sandro looked from the kasir to the bowl and shrugged. He put the bowl on the dining room table, evaded Mim's attention, and went back to the kitchen.

"I just wanted some water," he said as Dahl put another steaming bowl into his hands. The contents of this one smelled delicious.

"I'll get you a glass while you're gone."

This time, Mim caught him in the dining room and

bullied him into arranging glasses around the table. When he returned to the kitchen, Tabor handed him the glass of water and smiled.

"Glad you're helping," he said, and gestured with his cane. "I can carry the small stuff—wish I had four hands, like the kasirene."

"Biological superiority," Dahl said loftily, then grimaced and put one of those hands into its pouch. "That child damn near chewed off my nipple today."

"Hah," Tabor said genially. "Biological superiority, indeed. Sandro, would you take that platter? I'll show you where it goes."

As they entered the dining room, Sandro said, "She's very tall, isn't she?"

"She?" Tabor said, inspecting the table. "Oh, Dahl. He's not that tall—his womb-mother is taller. Mim, did you find those—oh. Good. I guess we're ready to eat, then." Tabor counted the places at the table. "Who's not going to be here tonight?"

"Hart's staying in Haven with Mertika," Mim said. "Jes didn't say anything about coming in late—" She looked quizzically at Sandro.

"I don't know," Sandro said, and paused. "He might be late. He was busy, last I saw him."

Mim made a face and loaded a plate with food, which she took into the kitchen and put into an oven. Sandro, coming in after her, finished his glass of water and put it in the sink. When he came back to the dining room the Kennerins, the housekeeper, and the kasirene cooks were gathered around the table. Sandro, too tired to be any more surprised, sat amid them and ate his supper.

Jes came in late. When Mim grumpily offered to fetch his supper, he shook his head and put his hand on Sandro's shoulder.

"Time to go," he said quietly. His eyes looked puffy. Meya came around to them and put her hand on the captain's arm.

"Sandro, get your stuff together," the captain said and, taking his sister's hand, took her onto the porch with him. Sandro ran up the stairs and stuffed his few belongings into his pack. As he came out of his room he saw the box labeled "Souvenir of MarketPort" sitting in the hallway outside of the captain's door. He paused, then shrugged and hurried down the stairs.

"Come back," Quilla said, offering her hand. "We can't offer you more than a home . . ."

"It's enough," Sandro said. He smiled uncomfortably before pulling his hand away. Tabor and Jared shook his hand, and Ozchan looked up from his bookreel, nodded unhappily, and looked down again.

On the porch, the captain stood holding his sister; Sandro could hear her muffled crying. Jes patted her on the head, said something indistinct, and pulled away. Sandro felt her eyes on them as they walked down the darkened hillside. The silence grew.

"Will Hetch meet us at the port?" Sandro said, desperate to break the quiet.

"Hetch isn't coming anymore," Jes said. "He's ill."

Sandro stopped. "I'd like to say good-bye to him."

"Not necessary. You'll be back."

"When?"

"Sooner than I will," his captain said, and moved off toward the port. Sandro hesitated a moment longer, caught in a rush of things he barely understood, and hurried after his captain down the dark hill.

SPIDER

WE CAME BACK UP THE HILL TO THE TOR, tired, dirty, sweaty, happy to be home. Decca, sitting on the lead dray with Andrus asleep in her lap, said something to Palen which I didn't hear: my mind was busy in the Tor, finding out who was home and how they felt about it. Mim in the kitchen, fussing over the biscuits; Tabor worried about the price of wheat and the quality of beer; Meya napping in her room, curtains closed against the late afternoon sunlight. My father in his laboratory, straining his hearing to detect our approach. He seemed well, worried about Meya, anxious for my presence, and with half his conscious mind and all of his unconscious one monitored the blinking panels of the keeper before him. Curious, I went in a little deeper. He'd perfected the running drays that he'd started work on before we left the Tor; the first batch were gestating in the warm keepers before him. I'd let him tell me about them, I knew how pleased he was when he could tell me something that I didn't know.

Mish, on the dray ahead of Decca's, stood upright in the stirrups and shouted toward the Tor. The dray shifted all of its feet, upset by the noise, and I enjoyed the sudden excitement from the house. The door opened and Quilla came out, saw Decca, ran down the hill with her arms open. Decca handed Andrus down to Palen before jumping off her dray and running uphill toward her mother. Andrus woke and whimpered unhappily, and Palen tucked him into her pouch. Jason Hart said something unpleasant about his younger brother. I leaned over and hit his shoulder hard.

"Leave him alone," I said. "Or I won't let you into the club."

His thoughts were still angry, but he rubbed his shoulder and didn't say anything further. Palenka and

Paen swerved around Decca's abandoned dray on their way to the house, scaring it. It mooed wildly and took off down the hill—by the time Mish's shouts brought it back, the entire Tor had emptied.

Decca, Jared, and Quilla stood in a huddle together, hugging each other. When Tabor came down to them the circle opened and swallowed him. Hart glanced at the keeper lights, punched something into stasis, and watched a moment longer before flinging the door open and running around the side of the house. I saw him skid through the vegetable garden and bound down the hill, waving his arms wildly. Meya waddled onto the porch. Jason Hart jumped down from before me and started to run, but when I shouted he swerved over to Palen, took Andrus from her, and held his brother by the hand while they ran up to Meya. She sat abruptly on the lowest porch step and hugged them. Then Ozchan came out of the house. Meya opened her arms and let the children run to their father, while she stood slowly, her hand on her stomach, and watched. My father was halfway down the hill by now, and I slid off my dray. Quilla and Palen hugged hard, everybody started to hug Mish, and then I was safe in my father's arms and forgot the rest of them entirely.

That night I sat cross-legged on my bed in the dark room, listening to the sleepers. In the adjacent room my father slept uneasily, pursued by a dream of goats and archbishops and dead kasirene pups. Quilla and Mish would have recognized part of the dream, and Palen would have turned from it in hatred and fear. My father kept it from his waking thoughts, not knowing how deeply I could read him, just as he controlled his own terror of losing me so that I would not be frightened by his fear. But he didn't know how well I knew him, how easily I could move beyond his careful blocking to his fear and the love which generated the fear. He thought of me not as part of Hart, but as Spider, individual, unbound, and sought to protect me from himself; to make of himself, for me, an image compounded entirely of love and wisdom. But I knew all there was to know of him, I thought. Parts of my memories, parts of his; the layers of knowledge that we both knew and that I shared with him. He would not have believed that I loved him, despite that knowledge and those fears.

How could I not have loved him? We were the same, I entirely the flesh of his flesh and no others. My father built me alone, as much as if I had been a sculpture, or a song, or a dream. Tinkering with more primitive versions of those present machines which the family so distrusted, he picked components of himself and melded them into the broth that would, eventually, form me. And lost me before he knew he had me, told by the old man who helped him that my exo-uterus, my metallic mother, had aborted me. The old man hid me, raised me, eventually lost me to people who used me as the price of my father's cooperation. And cooperate he did, for a child he did not know he had, paying a strange and complicated tithe not only for myself but for his soul. He loved me as I loved him, but I did not dream of goats and archbishops, save when I dreamed with him.

Growing up in other people's minds, my grandmother once thought, looking at me. I glanced at her and nodded, and she repeated the thought deliberately, as though in warning or, possibly, supplication. She didn't know which, and I don't know either. I can't form resolutions that don't exist.

Mish, as I touched her that night, didn't dream. Her sleep was a sweet darkness which would later curve into labyrinths of images, or a vision of Jason, my dead grandfather. She didn't entirely trust me, because she didn't entirely trust my father. And she was wise in this, for my father twisted like an eel beneath her memory, and hid himself from her, from the rest of his family; tried to hide himself from me. My father's dark and private battles had not, as yet, been won. She would, I thought, learn to trust me, for I had grown in her mind, learning from the books of her history and her thoughts. It would frighten her, and I didn't tell her. But I did try to tell her how much I cherished her, if I could not tell her how much I cherished what, in her, I found.

Tabor dreamed of the mountains, remembering them as taller, cleaner, crisper than his memory told me they were. It had been years since he'd lived in the Cault, and he doubted that he'd ever return. So did I. He was too much a part of the Tor now, too much a part of the daily tides of the family. And over the years the scars of the burn on his leg had tightened, crippling him even further; he could not walk the mountains now. So he

moved about the Tor, ordering the house, consulting with
Mim, sitting in the living room before the fire with children piled in his lap while his own children, light-years
away, pursued the strange paths of learning on a distant
planet. And while his children's mother flitted from island
to island, building towns, laying out fields, planning irrigation canals, bullying and advising and shaping and
planning, and coming home, exhausted, to seek a quiet
shelter in his arms. He'd fought against it, once. Now
he accepted it, and dreamed of owning all of Quilla's
love in the same way he dreamed of walking the mountains.

Quilla, restless against the curve of his body, struggled to escape from a clinging meadow which resisted her
every movement. She thrashed angrily, furiously, then
twisted about herself and broke free, rising high over the
meadowlands, tilting and banking through a clear,
boundless sky. Below her, meadow, fences, fields,
town, and Tor dwindled and fell away, and she sparkled
above the ocean like a bird. Then Tabor muttered in his
sleep and put his arms around her. He buried his face in
her hair and, as she automatically curved her body more
snugly to his, her dream fled.

In the next wing Decca and Jared slept wrapped about
each other, as always, in their wide bed. I lingered over
their linked minds, still puzzled that they, not genetically
identical, could share a link which I did not share with
my almost genetically identical father. Hart had explained to me that I was not a clone, that I had come
from a mixture of gametes rather than from a fully
developed cell; the arrangements of our genes were
different. But, rearranged or not, my genes still came
only from Hart, and we were further apart than my twin
and twineing cousins, who, that night, shared a dream
of complex simplicity. I could barely imagine a trust so
great that I would willingly share my dreams.

Jason Hart dreamed of ruling the world from the
warmth of a kasirene pouch. Infantile dream. Jason
Hart hurt things, hurt people, strutted himself about our
shared world refusing to see that it was shared. Demanding love, and seeing obedience as love. Yet I could
not hate him, this awkward younger cousin, if only
because, at least in dreams, the warmth was always

there. He would learn, if the lesson had to be driven into him with sticks. As it probably would be.

Andrus, Jason Hart's young brother, dreamed not at all. I felt relief. Andrus was subject to nightmares, and I hated being a spectator to that darkness, unable to dispel or lighten the dreams. My gift was not that of projection, save in one special case. But Jared and Decca could project, if only to each other. It puzzled me, a limit to what I saw as an otherwise limitless world. Then Andrus' mind called forth the image of a tree-ghoul, and I fled.

Ozchan was still awake, sitting in the darkness by his bedroom window, watching Meya sleeping. The month that I'd been gone had not substantially changed his thoughts. He wanted to touch her, but her belly stood between them like an unanswered question, and my uncle's mind filled with a list of every male that he knew, trying to puzzle out the father of his wife's child. My uncle Jes' name was absent from the list this time—when Ozchan was less obsessed, when I was less hurried, I'd slip into his mind and find out why. But now the list repeated itself, monotonously, from the most to least likely, and never once hit upon the truth. I slid out of his mind and into Meya's.

She, too, slept dreamlessly; rather, she slept in a dream without images, a dream of earth-warmth and sunlight, diffuse and restful. Then, finally, I let my mind slide into the tiny girl-child in Meya's womb. The barely wakened mind reached for me eagerly and I worked to gentle my excitement, to soothe and please and cradle her. Loving, frightened, jealous Ozchan had missed the obvious, missed the truth: if Meya's child had a father at all, it was my father, and then only by courtesy. For Meya's child, at last and finally, was like me. Almost exactly, entirely, like me.

THREE DAYS LATER SOMETHING WOKE ME before dawn. I lay still, questing through the house, and found Meya in the bathroom, mopping water from between her legs. It was time, then. The baby was quiet, fearless, prepared; Meya happy and apprehensive. She'd done this twice before; she knew that it would hurt. I kicked out of bed and pulled on my clothing, crept to my father's room and, not bothering to look into his dreams, touched his shoulder. He mumbled and frowned terrifically. I shook him again.

"Hart. Wake up. It's time."

He opened his eyes, looked at me, and reached for his clothes. I watched his body, enjoying it, knowing that in time it would be mine, the light, slender frame, the sleek muscles. But our faces would be different, or different expressions of the same man. He seamed his pants closed and pulled his shirt over his head.

"Where is she?"

"In the bathroom. The contractions haven't started yet, but they will soon. The baby's ready."

Hart knelt before me and held my shoulders. His skin was warm from sleep, and I stepped into his arms.

"Are you ready, Spider? It won't be easy."

"I know. I was there for Andrus."

He was surprised; he didn't know I'd done that. He didn't know that I'd have been there in any event. Andrus' birth was not easy, and I could not touch him as I could this child. Hart nodded suddenly. I kissed him and he hugged me, hard and warm, before we went to wait for Meya.

The contractions started an hour later. By then the family was in full hue and cry. Mim pragmatically insisted that everyone carry on as usual, that babies were born all the time, that there was no reason to get excited.

She set Dahl and Tapir to baking bread, then began boiling sheets and towels. It seemed, she said indignantly, a reasonable thing to do. The baby was still closed, involved entirely within herself, and would not need me for a while. I sampled the tensions and expectations that ran through my family.

Hart, worried and hiding it, moved about the bedroom. He was Meya's doctor, since Ozchan firmly believed it unwise to treat one's own family. He bent his principles when it came to the rest of us, but his wife and children were under my father's competent care. Hart checked pulse, respiration, and dilation, affixed a monitor to Meya's stomach, made a joke, Meya grinned. Mish sat by Meya's bed, holding my aunt's hand. She looked at me strangely, shrugged, and did not ask me to leave. Quilla came in and out, bringing water and offering good advice. Meya laughed at her, telling her that she'd only been through labor once, while Meya had done it twice already. Quilla told her not to give herself airs. Decca and Jared took over the children, keeping them quiet, sending progress reports to them from Meya's room once Hart kicked them out. Andrus was confused and frightened, but Jason Hart was terrified, convinced that something was going to take his mother from him, in punishment for his many sins. Decca and Jared finally gathered the cousins into their arms and held them, crooning songs and stories until most of the terror went away.

Ozchan called the hospital, told them that he wouldn't be in, and paced about the living room, desperate to be upstairs and afraid of what he'd find there. He finally came up, kissed Meya, and sat in a corner, trying to look as professional as Hart, and radiating fear and supplication. Tabor played on his flute, remembering that he'd missed the birth of his own children. But the sorrow was an old one, and well blunted. Quilla, passing by him with water for Meya, paused and brushed his forehead with her fingertips.

The contractions strengthened, and the child reached out for me. I created a large block against the world. There was no resistance and no fear, not until the very end, and then it was easily dissipated. Meya grunted and pushed and the baby popped free. She drew a deep breath but gave no cry, content to rest in her grandmother's arms. I relaxed, released the blocks, and almost panicked at the emotions in the room.

Mish stared at the infant, stared at Meya, stared accusingly at Hart. Tumblers turned in her mind, arriving at the answer which I had known for months. She was too startled to praise or condemn, but Ozchan, looking from the baby to Mish's face, turned to grab Hart by his arm.

"Yours?" he whispered.

"Don't be an idiot," my father replied, busy with the afterbirth.

"That's not my child," Ozchan shouted in anguish. "I want to know——" He burst into tears and ran out of the room, his thoughts chaotic. The baby shrieked and I rushed into her mind, soothing her, making blocks that she could not, yet, make herself. When I looked for Ozchan he was stumbling down the hillside, carrying one of Jason's old flashguns in his hand.

"Hart, you'd better get to him," I said. Hart looked at me with annoyance. "Please. He's going to hurt himself."

"Let him," my father said shortly.

"I mean it. And so does he."

Meya began to cry, holding her baby to her breast. Hart made an exasperated noise, gave some rapid instructions to Quilla, and ran out of the room. He swung down the stairs, leaped over the banister, and ran out the front door. The baby's distress fell away; she was too young to read at any distance. I relaxed my concentration to follow my father and my uncle down the hill. Hatred, rage, confusion, pain, determination—it suddenly came to me that one of them might die, or both; that I'd read only the surfaces of emotions, and never the emotions themselves. I hadn't grown at all—the reality of Ozchan's pain and my father's anger was as new to me as though I'd never read either of them before.

Mish grabbed me and held me tightly, whispering, "Don't watch, Spider," while her own mind filled with fear. I was suddenly lost, unable to track, unable to interpret; so full of seeing that I could not see. I clung to Mish and wept helplessly, feeling like the ten-year-old boy that I was, while she held me and rocked me and murmured baseless comforts from her own fears. And that, too, was something I had never learned to do.

Then the emotions muted, clarified. I opened timidly,

searching for my father's mind. His knuckles hurt and he sucked at them, cursing.

"What happened?" my grandmother said.

"Nothing. Ozchan was crying so much he couldn't see. Hart tried to take the gun away and Ozchan tried to shoot him. So Hart took the gun away anyway and knocked him out." I looked over at Meya, who lay in the bed looking at me strangely and holding the baby. "He's all right," I assured her. "Hart's going to explain it all when Ozchan wakes up." I giggled suddenly. "All that shouting and boiling over, for nothing much at all."

"That's not the point," my grandmother said sternly. "What were you feeling, before you looked this time? Before Hart knocked him out, what was going on?"

I sobered instantly and sat down, clinging to her hand, ready to cry and wondering how in the world she'd known. She looked hard at me, willing me to remember the lesson, then sat on the bed by Meya and touched the baby with her fingertips. Quilla, standing on the other side of the bed, watched them both as though from a great distance, but I was unwilling to go into anybody's head just then.

"You should have told us," Mish said.

"I couldn't," Meya whispered. "This one is *my* child. I wanted her, I planned her. Hart made her for me. I didn't want to give anyone a chance to take her away from me. She's *mine*, Mish."

"I know," Mish said. "She looks like a memory."

Quilla, still from her distance, took the baby gently and wrapped her in a blanket. I stood and the three women looked at me, knowing me now. I was surprised to realize that not one of them was really surprised. Quilla drew me to her side and put her arm around my shoulders. But I knew that if I asked to hold my cousin, Meya would not let me. Not yet.

"What's her name?" I said.

"Alin," Meya said, and I nodded. Alin is the kasiri word of light.

Part
Two

DANGEROUS GAMES

1244 new time

"Will he never come back from Barnegat,
With thunder in his eyes,
Treading as soft as a tiger cat,
To tell me terrible lies?"

—Elinor Wylie
The Puritan Ballad

THE LOOSENING OF THE FOURTH-QUADRANT stabilizer leads plate was more of an annoyance than a crisis, but it could not be fixed in tau. EVA in the dense strangeness of tauspace was dangerous at best and to be contemplated only in the event of a catastrophe: certainly the breakdown in the leads plate did not so qualify. The backup stabilizer, whining in protest, took most of the strain. Jes slapped temporary patches on the inner hull beneath the loose plate, magnetized the patches, confirmed that they held the plate tightly to the hull and, cursing, instructed the navigational computer to home for the nearest grabstation. And so, two weeks out of Estremadura on a solitary flight to MarketPort to meet his ship, tauCaptain Jes Kennerin brought his limping sloop to Priory Main Grab and requested entry.

The Grabmaster himself, squinting with anticipation and delight, appeared on the comscreen and crowed happily when Jes outlined the nature of his problem. Tiny jewels danced beside the 'master's plump cheeks. He swatted them away from his eyes as he cheerfully announced that his station had no facilities to handle repairs, that the repair docks for the station were closed, and that he would not open them for Jes' use. And, when Jes said angry things about backwash spit-stops manned by incompetent ninnies and taking up perfectly good vacuum that was best used for something of some value, the Grabmaster glared in wry and superficial irritation.

"We," he said importantly, "are a full Alpha-Class grabstation, with complete facilities. We are the main-station for one of the largest sectors in the Federation, I'll have you know. We happen to be nonoperational, my dear, but that doesn't affect our size at all." The 'master smiled suggestively. "Is that simple enough for you to understand?"

Jes put his head in his hands. His fingers tangled in his black hair. "Look," he said, "all I want is space to fix my sloop. Or is your freespace nonfunctional, too?"

"Of course not," the 'master said, and leaned forward to do something to the control board. "There you are, my dear, Priory Main Grab warming itself up, and all for your sweet benefit." The Grabmaster grinned through his cloud of jewels and signed off.

Jes glanced at the control bank. The grab coils showed close and clear on the screen. The onboard computer locked into the grabstation net and guided the ship through tau and into the loops of the time-coil.

It was immense, larger than the shipping coils outside MarketPort; within the heavy bands the tausloop seemed no bigger than a gnat on a wine barrel. The coils glowed sedately, in no great hurry to increase their pull until they affected his ship. Jes watched them impatiently and tapped his readout screen, requesting whatever information the ship's computer held about Priory Sector.

The general information log was concise but limited. It told him the tau and realspace coordinates for Priory Sector, mentioned the names of the major planets and gave their intrasector coordinates, provided a date of colonization and a date of Federation entry, and left it at that.

Jes tapped the screen thoughtfully and, almost unwillingly, requested a readout of properties and planets currently owned by Parallax Combine. The list was long and he scanned it quickly. Priory did not appear on the list, nor were any of Parallax's properties noted as being in Priory Sector. Jes cleared the screen, annoyed that he'd bothered with what was, after all, only family programming. He thought that, after two years, he'd managed to divorce himself from their concerns and problems, yet still found himself automatically reflecting their worries, following their constant suggestions, awkwardly longing for their comfort and assistance even as he fought to keep his distance. He took this as a sign of his own weakness and it was therefore with a fair amount of free-floating hostility that he watched as the coils shimmered and the ship flipped through time. He guided the sloop out of the coils and into the stable lights of realspace.

"Good," said the Grabmaster, reappearing on the

screen. "Now what are we going to do with you?" The jewels glittered before his eyes and he batted at them.

Jes glanced from the Grabmaster's beaming face to the forward screens. Priory Main Grab hung in space, an immense, gilded complexity of struts and bars and rings, attached to the coils of the grab by a delicate network of light.

"I don't understand," Jes said. "You do have an Alpha-class grabstation, but . . ."

"Oh, very simple," the Grabmaster said. The jewels tangled in his carefully curled hair. "Priory Sector is the second largest sector in the Federation: hence this totally preposterous station. It's not needed, of course—Priory is big enough so it doesn't need outside trade and doesn't want any, thank you. Three separate systems, you know, and tens of inhabitable planets, not counting the Labyrinth, and nobody much counts the Labyrinth anyway." The 'master made an airy gesture, brushing jewels from his hair. His curls sprang rigidly back into place. The jewels twinkled down to collar level, save for one small blue gem which nestled just above the 'master's left eyebrow. Jes stared at it.

"So almost no traffic through the grab," the 'master continued, "and I'm simply dying of boredom. Not, of course, that you'd care a flip about that; parties like yourself seldom do. Well, sweetling, just set your drives and head twenty even, four cross. You can sit there nice and tidy while you play with your . . . little ship." The Grabmaster signed off.

Jes shrugged. He'd met stranger folk in the channels of space, and Priory's Grabmaster would be good for some laughs and a couple of beers in the saloons on MarketPort. He entered coordinates, slapped the forward thrust slides, and the tattletales for the backup stabilizer went scarlet. The sloop shuddered, the bridge filled with the scream of tortured metal, and the entire leads plate ripped from the hull and sailed majestically, and irretrievably, through the still-shimmering coils of the grab. The plate flared once and disappeared from realspace.

Jes raced to the injured hull. The skin bulged under the missing plate and stress lines crept along the metal. He layered an emergency seal over the bulge, locked it in place, kicked the defective backup stabilizer, and retreated from the access hold, double-sealing the hatches behind him. The ship needed a repair dock immediately, for while she had been slightly crippled by the loose leads plate, the stress on her hull was an active emergency. His anger refueled, Jes slapped at the commiter and bellowed until the Grabmaster's bland face appeared on the screen again.

The Grabmaster regretted the accident, tendered condolences, and firmly refused to open one of his repair docks, even when Jes threatened a report to the Federation. The man smiled and shrugged and pointed out that opening a dock would do no good whatsoever, as there were no tools in the dock, no replacement leads plates or stabilizers, and that no amount of furious shouting on Jes' part would cause these items to appear. However, the 'master reluctantly said that Jes might use the docks of Gensco Station, provided that Gensco agreed. Jes collected the tattered remains of his patience and cajoled the Grabmaster into admitting that Gensco Station was the headquarters for Priory's main transport agency; that the Station, in its continual circuit of Priory Sector, was conveniently close by; that they would be very likely to provide Jes with replacement parts, a repair dock, and a repairs jockey to do the work. For a price, of course. The 'master finally produced Gensco's current coordinates, and smiled, and tapped the face of his screen with a manicured finger, as though he were trying to put his finger through the fabric of space directly into Jes' dark, impatient face.

"Mind you," the 'master said, "I'm not promising that Gensco will lift a finger for you. They're an odd lot down there. Mind your sweet self, and for heaven's sake be polite. They don't take kindly to strangers in Priory, my dear. Not even wounded ones." The Grabmaster, for the last time, broke the connection.

Jes nursed his sloop down the coordinates given him by the Grabmaster of Priory Main. His hands flickered between the pressure gauges and the correction keys, his eyes between the sensors and the directional screens, and his mind, between curses and computations, considered the strangeness of Priory's Grabmaster. Of the 'master's oblique warning about Gensco, Jes thought not at all. Any station would help a ship in distress. It would be unthinkable not to.

GENSCO PERIPHERAL WOULD NOT BELIEVE that Jes was who he said he was. He held his ship steady amid the crowded skies, praying that no one would hit him. The accented voice on the commiter, alternately angry and exasperated, at last ran a scan on his ship and immediately signed off, leaving Jes shouting into a dead microphone. His eyes ached. He rubbed them with the balls of his thumbs and cursed Priory Sector and everyone in it.

"That's quite enough," said the commiter in light, slurred Priory accents. The screen shivered and cleared to show a fat, sharp-eyed woman who looked at Jes with disapproval. All the lines of her face angled toward her excess of chins. Her hair, thick and richly auburn, curved over her brow and around her cheeks; Jes, forgetting his curses, wondered if all those shades of red and gold were natural. His own thick black hair felt limp and dirty, and he resisted the urge to brush it back.

"I'm sorry," he said. "I'm not used to being treated as a pirate." She didn't return his smile. "I've a crippled ship. I need a repair dock and a good jockey, and I'll pay for repair fees, rentals, parts, and anything else. I beamed you my identification codes—"

"Codes can be forged, Menet . . ." She paused, glancing down. "Kennerin. We have our own security to worry about. And we're a very busy station, we can't take in every cripple that comes along demanding dock time."

"I believe you can't refuse," Jes retorted. "According to Federation regulations, and I can quote you section and paragraph if you want, it's a major offense to refuse aid to a ship in space." The woman opened her mouth, but Jes overrode her. "I don't think you have a choice, Quia. Refuse me and I'll beam a priority complaint to

Priory Main. And even your tame monkey up there wouldn't dare ignore it."

The woman looked even more sour. "You, Menet Kennerin, are a good example of why we don't care for strangers here."

"Quia, if you don't give me dock time, and pretty damned quick, you're going to have more strangers in your system than you've ever seen before. I'll have every investigator and agent in the Federation on your ass."

The woman pressed her lips together and disappeared. Jes checked the pressure sensors; the patch was holding, but barely.

The woman reappeared. "We've dispatched a pilot drone to take you to a repair dock. You'll be issued a restricted visitor's pass, which you must carry at all times, and we expect you to leave as soon as the repairs are completed. You'll be billed for that, and for your room and board, and we want payment in fremarks before you'll be allowed to leave."

"Your charity should be the basis for a thousand songs," Jes said. The woman's face pruned with disapproval and she signed off.

The pilot drone hooked onto the sloops's guidance system and the flight bank went dead. Jes sat back, his fingers resting on the pressure controls, and watched the vision screens.

Gensco Station was spherical, an enormous silver orange whose exterior was a maze of metal valleys and square metal mountains, overlaid with the bars and graphs of the flight directors. The space around it bristled with commerce. Small, powerful freight donkeys hauled pod upon pod of goods carriers; a fat, strangely shaped spacebus passed overhead; innumerable small ships darted between the larger vessels and the thick sprinkle of auxiliary satellites. Jes watched space and tattletales, and fretted. The drone led the sloop in a direction counter to the rotation of the Station, then veered north before beginning its descent. An aperture irised open in the skin of the Station and the drone dropped toward it. Jes concentrated on balancing the pressure in the sloop's access hold against the changing pressure of the various airlocks. The drone guided the sloop to a resting place in a large, dimly lit bay and slid back through the locks. Jes cracked the sloop's entry hatch and looked out.

To his left lay the skeleton of a small freighter, its curving struts dull with oxidation. On the right a skip-sloop lay gutted; a large, angry gash ran up the ship's forward hull and burn marks darkened the lateral fins. Before him stretched other dead ships, all Delta-class or smaller, all decayed or in the process of being cannibalized for parts. The air smelled of old oil and ancient burns, and tasted stale. Jes climbed the hull of his sloop and peered at the damage; the plate had taken most of the leads wires with it, and those remaining were scarred beyond redemption. He touched the wires briefly, as though in apology, locked the sloop, and went in search of the jockey.

A light glimmered at the far end of the bay and he heard someone singing in an alien language. He paused, listening to the smooth, slippery melody. The voice slid from major to minor keys, exploring variations in a rich, controlled contralto. Then Jes stepped around the last dead ship into the light and the singing stopped.

"Hello," he called. No one answered. Jes put out a hand to touch the hull of the ship behind him, reluctant to move forward. "Hello," he shouted, and his voice echoed back from the distant sides of the bay.

"Why, welcome to my parlor, said the spider to the fly." The voice was soft, amused, unaccented, and close by. "Let me guess. We have here an incompetent ore-jockey who bothered someone, and has been sent to me? No, you don't have the look of one of our outstanding humpers. A private pilot for a disliked minor manager, come with dented chrome? I think not—you look far too fierce to be a tame captain. Whatever you are, my curious fly, you are certainly unpopular. And for that mystic deduction you will not be charged at all." The voice slid into song again. Jes glanced overhead to see a dark shape seated casually on a swing dangling below a suspended hull. The harsh lights behind the swing dazzled his eyes.

The singing became laughter. "Discovered, by all that's cross and holy. State your business, please. I am, as you can see, a very busy person."

Jes shaded his eyes with his hand. "My name is Jes Kennerin. My tausloop pulled a leads plate in tau and lost it entirely after I came through grab. Your managers sent me here for repairs."

"Not *my* managers, my outlandish friend. Nor am I theirs, much to my dismay. I'm surprised they offered to help you at all."

"They didn't offer anything. I had to threaten them with a Federation complaint."

"Did you?" The voice was delighted. "My admiration for you increases by the second." The voice began humming.

"I'm in a hurry," Jes said evenly. "I'll be late as it is, and if you could——"

"Rush to your repairs, forsaking all others? Ah, but I've work and much work, to fill the days and ways of hands." As if in proof, Jes heard the sound of metal on metal and some flakes of rust drifted into the light. He wondered if everyone in Priory Sector was crazy. "Still, I should endeavor to leave you with at least one good impression of Gensco Station, may its wane wax and its decrease increase."

The swing arched away from the light. A dark figure leaped to grab a dangling line and within a moment the jockey stood before Jes, grinning.

She was slightly smaller than himself, with long, silvery gray hair pulled into a messy knot at the nape of her neck. Her eyes, oval and sardonic, were of a blue cooler and deeper than his, and her face was delicately furred from the neck of her suit to her hairline. Jes glanced at her hands and she obligingly raised them for his inspection. Small, curved claws slid from the silver fur and slid into hiding again.

"You're a . . ." Jes began, and stopped in confusion.

"Santa Theresan," she said. "Or Tabby, if you prefer speaking in the present tense offensive." She gestured and her claws flashed briefly. "Why don't you show me your ship, captain mine, and we can discuss philosophy and biology and anthropology and, perhaps, apology. You may stop staring now."

Jes flushed, then marched toward the ship, hearing her footsteps behind him. The humming resumed, sweetly competent. Jes put his hands in his pockets and clenched his fists.

She swung up the side of his sloop and probed the wound, still humming, before insisting that he open the ship so she could inspect the damage on the inside. She peeked into the cabins, ran her fingers lightly over the control board, and gave a nod of approval when Jes unsealed the last lock. Removing a probe from the pocket of her blue suit, she stepped into the access hold and tested the emergency seal, twisted the magnetic clamps, and lowered them. Jes stared at her trim backside.

"No tail," she said without turning around. "And no pointy ears, and we don't go into heat and we don't bear in litters. Any other scurrilous myths you want quashed; Menet Curiosity?"

Jes flushed again. "I'm sorry," he said stiffly. "I've never met a Theresan before, and I've only heard a little."

"And all of it false. I live," she remarked, "constantly surrounded by lies and liars. Beware of them, Menet. They will only lead you into sin." She slapped the bulkhead and turned to him. "It will take some time, and I'll have to order the part from main, but I should be able to get you spacebound again."

"How long?" Jes said eagerly.

She shrugged. "Depends. On supplies in main, and the mood of their keepers. It's rarely easy to get supplies, and for me it's never easy. It might take weeks."

"Weeks!"

"At least," she said calmly and jumped out of his ship. "Don't bother to lock it, Menet. I'll need to get inside to repair it, and you may not want to be hauled away from your diversions and delights."

"I don't see that I'll have much to do . . ."

"Ah, but I've yet to introduce you to the wonders of Gensco Station, Peripheral Sector, Repairs Bay Colony. You've much and much to learn, my fly. You've yet to find either flowers or nectar. And you'll need a cabin. Come along, Menet Outworlder. We'll secure you a parlor of your own, to which you can invite any number of succulent little insects."

"I thought I'd sleep in my ship," Jes said.

The jockey pruned her face into a devastating, silvery imitation of the red-haired woman's scowl. "Regulations," she intoned in Priory accents. "No sleeping aboard disfunctional vessels. You will stay, Menet, in transient quarters, and no arguments."

"But—"

"On pain," the jockey said with positive relish, "of dismemberment." She grinned suddenly, and Jes, bemused out of anger, collected his gear and followed her swaying hair and lithe walk out of the bay and into the corridors of Gensco Station.

HER NAME, SHE TOLD HIM, WAS TATHA, AND she'd been on Gensco Station for six standard months, working as a repairs jockey. That she didn't care for Gensco was obvious; that she, in turn, was disliked became apparent as they negotiated the corridors and cramped public spaces of Repairs Bay Colony. She ignored the "meows" and occasional murmurs of "Here, kitty," and arriving at Transient Registry, she arranged a cabin for him, slicing through a maze of regulations and bureaucratic confusion. When they left the air was thick with Tatha's sarcasm, and she allowed herself one triumphant glance at Jes before schooling her face to calm irony. She pointed out mess halls, restaurants, bars, and shops, and told him that transient quarters were divided into a section for visiting Gensco employees and a section for non-Gensco transients, mostly Labbers in on business. His cabin was in the Labber section.

"Gennys are taught hatred with their first breaths," she explained. "For Labbers, for outworlders, for aliens, for any strangers. For themselves. You'd perhaps not be in danger staying in the Genny section, but it's best to avoid the problem entirely. If possible. And, of course, you're blessed in not having fur."

She swayed on the slidebelt and a gobbet of something smelling strongly of fish just missed her shoulder. It didn't break the flow of her conversation. Once they reached the small cabin she had secured for him, though, Jes noticed that her claws were half extended.

"Does that happen all the time?" he said.

"Yes." She ran her fingers over the comscreen. "This will give you general information, but it won't tell you the important things. Such as that eating in the company mess halls is guaranteed death, and kevefah, the local brew, will give you a twenty-day hangover and cure your warts. Or possibly you don't drink?" Jes shook his head. "Good. I don't trust the totally innocent."

The ·chute bleeped and coughed out a small packet. Tatha scooped it up before Jes could reach it. She unseamed it with one claw.

"Your symbols of existence, blue eyes," she said, flicking through the contents of the packet. "A restricted greenpass, you won't like that. Or possibly you won't be around long enough to learn not to like it. A room credit plate. Every day billing? Oh, they do indeed dislike you. This has the reek of an insulted Maigret about it. Did you have contact with a small, fat woman of incontinent tongue and quick temper? Reeking of the blood of children and small mammals? Red hair and eyes to match?"

Jes, grinning, sat on the bed. "Or someone very like," he agreed.

"Our sweet Maigret, in charge of making life interesting for the likes of you and me. It's a means of checking up on you, mysterious and dangerous unfurred alien. Maigret is very interested in strangers, right about now. She asked me to check out your accident."

"My accident?" Jes said, startled. "Why?"

"Accidents can be faked, plates can be lifted. I'm giving you a clean bill."

"Does she really think I'd damage my own ship? Who does she think I am?" Tatha simply looked at him. "Listen, I'm a tauCaptain trying to join my ship in Market-Port. That's all. And all I want is my ship fixed. Sweet Mother! Is everyone on this station crazy?"

"Not totally," Tatha said. She sat on the table and swung her legs idly. "I, for one, am entirely sane. And Maigret has her reasons . . . you've come at a bad time, tauCaptain. But you'll manage." She went on to suggest which mess halls to avoid, which to patronize with caution ("Don't eat anything yellow, please"), and told him to speak in public as little as possible ("You have an accent, you know"). She further suggested that he pack away his own clothing and buy some company issue. It would serve to keep him inconspicuous and harder to follow.

"Should I worry about being followed?" he said.

She shrugged. "What's your opinion? Never mind, you haven't been here long enough to have one. I've business, tauCaptain, among which is the ordering of your leads plate. Take a care." She swung off the table and out the door.

"Tatha—" he said. The door closed behind her.

He opened his sack and looked at the clothes niche uncertainly, decided that he wouldn't be on Gensco long enough to unpack, and, sliding his Certificate among the folds of his clean suits, he closed the sack again. He secured a line on the commiter to the communications center and, after a great deal of shouting and nonsense, sent a message direct-line to Sandro in MarketPort. Then, taking Tatha's suggestion, he ordered a standard blue company-issue suit and used the clensor while waiting for it. It popped through the chute as he came out of the clensor, drying himself. It was poorly made and scratched his skin at the seams. He took it off, put on his light-weather underclothes, and put the company suit on again, stowing the greenpass and credit plate in his hip pocket. Sitting at the commiter, he secured a line to the main library computer and requested information on Santa Theresa.

There wasn't much of it, and what there was seemed vague and far too general, as though it had been programmed directly from a second-level text.

Santa Theresa was one of the earliest colony planets, settled so far back that the dates were still reckoned by the old calendar. Before the discovery of tau and the invention of coils and taudrive, colonists had been sent in large, big-bellied ships to eight systems: Santa Theresa, the last planet colonized and the farthest from Terra, was a large, dense, cold world, rich in rare and costly minerals and miserly of its heat. Not fit for normal human habitation, the colony-masters declared, and in those days of slowdrives and limited xenotechnology they created Theresans to serve the climate of their planet. Fur, to protect from the cold. An extra layer of subcutaneous fat, for the same reason, layered over a musculature slightly more powerful than that of unchanged Terrans. More sensitive eyesight, to cope with the long, dark winters. A metabolic system slightly altered to extract the maximum protein from foodstuffs. And claws replacing fingernails, retractable to facilitate the use of the hands. Claws to capture and kill, for the colony-masters, taking into account the roughness of a new world, the distances between Santa Theresa and the mother world, the long cold winters and the short growing season, had decreed that Theresans be, when necessary, predators.

Yet the changes were small. Theresans had hips and joints and sockets and limbs, curves and angles, that were distinctly human. Had features and expressions that were human. Had brains, minds, souls, as human as those of the race from which they sprang.

Two centuries after Santa Theresa's colonization, Terra and her three closest colony worlds disagreed about levies and tax rights, and the disagreement quickly escalated into the Last Great War, which left two worlds in cinders and Terra herself badly scarred. War, always the parent of innovation, this time produced the discovery of tau and the invention of the grabcoils and taudrives. The universe opened, not to Terra, still sullenly rebuilding herself, but to Reba, Ha Olam, and Jirusan, three untouched colonies. Santa Theresa, the youngest and most distant, was misplaced during the war years and lay forgotten for twelve centuries.

Twelve hundred years of tau changed humanity and changed its nature. Santa Theresa had been born during a time when the complexity and cost of space travel dictated a stable colony population: tau created a mobile workforce, independent of the need for special adaptation to any one planetary condition. Gene engineering, since the days of Santa Theresa's foundation, had become a cosmetic art and nothing more. Most importantly, Santa Theresa had sprung from a time when humanity had yet to meet any sapient aliens at all and re-emerged into a universe where alien races were known, and regarded as, at best, the results of an inferior creation. The unchanged humans of the Federation were bewildered by the furred Theresans, tempted to see them as alien yet forced to recognize their human stock, to grant them citizenship and full rights in the Federation. For Theresans and humans could, together, produce fertile offspring, thereby meeting the most basic definition of shared species.

The computer could provide Jes with little else. Santa Theresa was a one-country planet, had a quasi-feudal system of government, spoke a language as different from Standard as Standard was different from any original Terran tongue. Santa Theresa had a short growing season and long, fiercely cold winters. Mined and exported ores, had a stable population, and was the only colonized or colonizable planet in its Sector. According to the Theresans, there had been no regression of culture in the twelve centuries between its loss and rediscovery; they remembered, adapted, and flourished. The tape ended. Jes envisioned a frigid, lonely world and could not picture Tatha's quick tongue and lithe songs set in such a dim, unfriendly place. He closed the computer link and allowed himself exactly two hours of sleep before going in search of food.

He returned to find Tatha curled on his bed, scanning through his Certificate. He slammed the door, out of temper with bad-mannered waiters, badly cooked food, and exorbitant prices, and glared at her. She gave him a crooked smile, supremely unembarrassed, tossed his Certificate on the table, and rolled off the bed. She wore a brown jumpsuit and her silver face gleamed from the darkness of its hood.

"I've come to take you adventuring, my friend. And you had the discourtesy not to be here."

"I locked the door," Jes said, putting the Certificate back in his sack. "And I don't remember leaving this out either."

"You had, and you hadn't. Locked doors are a specialty of mine, and if you thought you were hiding your record, you did a poor job of it. It's obvious that I've more to teach you than the ins and outs of Gensco Station." She leaned against the wall. "I've ordered your leads plate."

Jes grunted unpleasantly. Her eyes gleamed with laughter and she crossed her arms, as though ready to spend all night, if need be, outlasting his anger. He found himself smiling back.

"Good. When will it arrive?"

"Having engineered your good humor, I'm loath to lose it again. I won't tell you. It's evening, by the dictates of the Lords of Gensco Station. Let's use it—and not for business." She laughed at his expression. "Drinking, tauCaptain. Deep and philosophical discussion. I've an urge to introduce you to the finer elements of Repairs Bay Colony. Will you come?"

He hesitated, feeling tired and still a little angry. But Tatha had suggested that something out of the ordinary was afoot, and had also insinuated that Jes himself was under suspicion. The more he learned about Gensco, and about Tatha, the safer he would feel.

"All right," he said. "Bring on your wonders, and I'll be properly impressed."

She slipped around him, lifted his sack, and extracted his Certificate.

"This first," she said. "When in Rome, Menet, do as do the Romans, but hide your gold. Come along." She walked into the clensing unit.

"If everyone here is as nosy as you are . . ."

"Correction. I'm healthily inquisitive. With some others the adjective does not apply." She glanced around the room, swung herself atop the box of the clensor, and leaned toward the light panel. She ran one extended claw under the clips, slid the panel away, and tucked Jes' Certificate between the ceiling and the drop panels before snapping the panel back into place and dropping to his side.

"When you get back, change the angle of the panel clips and remember the change. I doubt if our hosts, or others, are subtle enough to find the Certificate or if, finding it, they remember to reset the clip. Come along."

As they reached the door she looked at it sadly and shook her head. "Nothing you can do about this, though. Junk."

Jes followed her out, locking the door behind him.

"Why?" he said. "I mean, why the lessons in being sneaky, and why the invitation tonight?"

"Simple. You're the only one on this station who even approaches being as alien as I am. And if I don't mind the onus of your suspect company, why should you mind mine?"

"I don't," he said, remembering the hostilities of the afternoon. "I can handle it . . . you must be used to it."

"One never gets used to it," she said quietly. "We hop on here."

The slidebelt moved across the main public squares of Repairs Bay Colony, through areas of after-work merry-making and along the lit and flashing fronts of entertainment halls. Tatha leaned against the slidebelt railing, her back to the crowds and her face to Jes. In her dark suit with the hood pulled over her bright hair she was, from behind, effectively disguised. Jes tried to watch her without obviously watching her and thought he was successful until she suddenly crossed her eyes and stuck her tongue out. Jes bit his lip and looked away, and Tatha swung off the slidebelt so unexpectedly that it took him a moment to realize she was gone. He hopped off and walked back to her. She was strolling down a side alley, her hands in her pockets, humming. She glanced at him, eyes amused, when he matched her pace.

"Do you fancy beer?" she said, pausing by an unmarked door.

Jes nodded.

"Good. Welcome to Tammas' Hopyard, captain."

"Another parlor," Jes said as he stepped inside. She laughed behind him.

The crowded room was small and dark. People looked up briefly and went back to their drinks and conversations. The barkeep nodded and turned to fill two steins with beer. Tatha guided Jes to a table in the back of the room.

"Tammas' father came from The Lab, and it makes him bearable, if not adorable."

"The Grabmaster mentioned The Lab—the Labyrinth? I don't know what it is." Jes sat.

"An asteroid belt in one of the neighboring systems, same Sector. The Labbers live in hollowed asteroids called 'holes' and bump about being immune to domestication. Gensco's been trying to wipe them out for decades."

"Why?"

"Because they don't fit." Tammas put two steins on the table and rocked back on his heels. He was a tiny, sour-looking man, and he looked at Jes curiously. "Gensco wants everything to fit nice and simple and easy. Labbers have never worked that way, and aren't about to. Did you tell him," he said to Tatha, "about my Da?"

"I will, Tammas. We'll want another two soon."

Tammas nodded, unperturbed, and went back to his bar.

Jes sipped his beer. It was cold and tasted slightly flat. He made a face and Tatha nodded.

"But it's the best you'll find, this side of Gem Sphere, or The Lab."

"What's Gem Sphere? And what about Tammas' father?"

Tatha put her stein down. "Gem Sphere is manager's country, my innocent. Gem Sphere is the heart and center of civilized living on Gensco Station. Parklands, fountains, mansions, finesse and richesse. I'll take you there, if you like. It will impress your impoverished provincial soul. And Tammas' father was a Labber brewmaster who responded to a Gensco attack by flying his chunk of rock into a Master Craft and crippling it. Unfortunately, Tammas survived. He was raised in the bosom of Gensco's love, and when they found that he didn't know anything of any use to them, and couldn't be made to like them, they sent him here. Very careful of its resources, Gensco is. Tammas makes a good barkeep, and as long as he's here the managers know where to find pilots come in from The Lab on business. They don't mind that our bitter friend spreads sedition and sows the seeds of rebellion. The seeds fall on hard ground." She tapped her foot against the metal floor. "Tammas, of course, hates the entire business."

"Then why doesn't he leave? Why don't you leave, for that matter?"

Tatha, her mouth full of beer, looked at him over the rim of the stein. The hum of conversation in the room rose and fell, and Jes caught a brief scent of hot stew and what might be fresh bread.

"Tammas can't leave," Tatha said finally, "because he's nowhere to go. The Labbers that come to Gensco are here on sufferance. If they smuggled him off they'd be open to charges of kidnapping or suborning a Gensco employee. If he leaves by himself, Gensco would suspect the same thing. An incident like that could start active warfare again, and the Lab's still recovering from the last bout. And Tammas, bless his twisted heart, is enough of a patriot to refuse to jeopardize The Lab for the sake of his freedom."

She turned in her seat and waved an arm at Tammas, who nodded and reached for two more steins.

"What about you?" Jes said. "It's not patriotism that's keeping you here."

"Not likely," Tatha said wryly. "Gensco's got a charming policy about outsystem workers. They take something you need and don't give it back. It's surprisingly effective."

"It's coercion," Jes said angrily.

Tatha shrugged. "I've told him, Tammas, about your Da." Tammas deposited full steins, collected empty ones, nodded gravely, and retreated.

Jes watched Tatha, and Tatha, leaning comfortably in her chair, watched the room. She fascinated him: the sleek silvery body, the expressive eyes, the quick, complicated mind. He wondered how she saw the room's collection of Labbers, wondered what, beneath the wit and chatter, she thought of the universe around her, the Station, herself. He'd dealt with spacers before and was confident that he could extract information. A little delicate probing, he thought, was in order.

She obliged. No, she hadn't known about Gensco before she entered the Station. Yes, Gensco had made it hard for her to leave. No, she did not learn jockeying on Santa Theresa. When he asked her why she'd left her homeworld, she put the stein down and looked at him pleasantly.

"Your Certificate says that you were born on Aerie, tauCaptain. You'd go back at least thrice a year, but for the past two years you haven't been back at all. Why is that?"

Jes glared at her. "That's none of your damned business."

"Exactly," she said, standing. "Come exploring, Menet? I promised you the wonders of Gem Sphere, and my promises, you'll learn, are always kept."

Jes rose, embarrassed. A little delicate probing, indeed. He followed her from the bar but she gave him no chance to apologize, merely strode down the alley ahead of him. Jes decided that she was too prickly for her own good and hurried to catch up with her.

But her face, lit quickly as she passed a lamp, seemed unconcerned. She led him around three corners in quick succession and into a maze of empty supply lines. The lights were off; Tatha, in her dark hooded suit, was a denser darkness and a melody in front of him. When she touched his chest he halted, and she pointed out the far glow of a tubegate. Not one of the main gates, she explained, but an auxiliary one maintained for the passage of freight.

"Gateway to heaven," she said sarcastically. "Feeling adventurous? Good. Mind, we're not welcome in Gem Sphere, we lack the odor of jewels and high living. Keep your shining head down and your ringing voice low, my dove, and do as you're told. Ready? Then boldly forward. It gets darker before the gate, so mind your step —the pavement's uneven."

He walked forward, feeling her warm hand resting on his shoulder. It did indeed get darker before the gate, and within two meters he stumbled over a ragged edge in the pavement and fell, taking her with him. She twisted nimbly to her feet, found his hand, and helped him up. Then she raised her hand, ran her fingers along a ledge high on the wall, and rubbed her fingers against his palm. They felt gritty.

"The Lords and Masters don't believe in changing the filters regularly, at least, not in the warrens. Or in maintaining the pavements." She put her hand back on his shoulder and resumed humming. The melody sounded contemptuous.

Just beyond the lights from the gates she halted again. "Do me a favor? Pop through and see if there's anyone around. Some louts I want to avoid."

Jes nodded and walked to the gate, wondering if Tatha was as hard as she let on. Feeling protective, he surveyed the empty gate area thoroughly before gesturing to her. She ran past him, grabbing his hand and propelling him down a smoothly cushioned drop-tube. They scampered through the brightly lit space at the foot of the drop and into a dark side corridor. Once away from the light, she leaned against the wall and laughed quietly. Her hood had fallen back. She twisted thick handsful of silver hair into place and pulled the hood low over her forehead.

"And again the slip! Come, master mariner of space, and I'll show you the glittering byways of Gem Sphere."

GEM SPHERE DID INDEED GLITTER. LAYERED between the outer service areas of the Station and the inner power cores, it filled the entire center stratum of the Station. The tall vault of ceiling reflected pinpoints of starlike lights, the fresh air smelled of flowers, and somewhere in the darkness a fountain burbled gently. Tatha led him between high white buildings whose windows glowed with light. They moved along the edge of a park, peering from the bushes at finely clothed people strolling beneath trees in the amber light of floating lamps. Someone played a twelve-tone tairene expertly; Tatha, eyes closed, listened intently to the subtle chiming music. A child laughed. Jes gaped and stared. At a silk-draped stand, crystal goblets of wine stood ready for sale. Jes told himself firmly that the denizens of Gem Sphere couldn't possibly live this way all the time, that during the daylight hours they had jobs to do, work to be done, but he didn't really believe it.

Tatha scanned the passing faces and touched Jes to stillness. Three people sat on a bench by a fountain; an older man with polished gray hair, a tiny, dun-colored woman in rich brocades, and the red-haired woman who had talked with him when he arrived at Gensco in his crippled sloop, and whom Tatha had later identified as Maigret. The three leaned together, talking. Tatha moved forward cautiously. Maigret, after a time, rose, shook out the folds of her robes, and walked away. Tatha slid back through the bushes to Jes and led the way out of the park.

She moved faster now, leading him through a maze of alleys and dark streets. They ran up a flight of shallow stairs to a wide stone balcony. Tatha put her hand on the rail and vaulted into the blackness below. Overcome with a joyous recklessness, Jes followed her. The ground was closer than he'd thought and he gasped slightly as he landed.

Tatha put her hand on his arm. "We're being followed. Can you keep up with me?"

Jes heard the challenge in her tone and would have replied, but she put her finger over his lips and raced away. He leaped to his feet to follow. Someone landed under the balcony with a thud and a muttered curse. Jes didn't bother to look back.

Jes discovered that keeping up with Tatha would not be as easy as he'd assumed. She moved swiftly and economically, and he envied the quick precision of her body as he followed her around a pool and over a hedge. They fled down a street of shops. In the light of one of the few glowlamps, Jes saw a pile of fruit, left by an over-trusting grocer in the street before the shop. Tatha grabbed two globes from the bottom of the pyramid. The rest of the fruit trembled and the pyramid collapsed onto the street. The footsteps behind them became awkward thuds as their pursuer tried to dodge the rolling fruit. Tatha glanced over her shoulder and tossed a fruit to Jes. Tart juice flooded his mouth. At the next corner he paused, aimed, and flung the fruit back down the street. Tatha grinned and ducked into a stand of trees. Jes followed her into darkness. She put her hand in his and guided him around the trees.

"Can you fit through here?" she whispered.

The open pipe mouth was a black patch against the paler darkness of the trees. He dropped on his belly, scooted inside, and kept going until he felt Tatha's touch on his ankle.

"Next right," she said, her voice choked with laughter. He followed her signals until the tube opened before him and he looked down at the bright area before the supplies gate. He made sure the area was deserted, pulled himself half out of the tube, twisted, dropped, and landed on his feet. In a second Tatha was beside him and a moment later they were up the droptube again and sprinting down the dark supply line. Tatha slowed to run her fingers over the ledge, then raced him to the alley in front of Tammas' Hopyard.

Light spilled from Tammas' open door. Jes, catching his breath, looked at Tatha and doubled with laughter. Her brown jumpsuit was filthy and her hair had come loose and lay tangled on her shoulders. A leaf had caught in it. He pulled the leaf from her hair and presented it to her. She took it, gravely, and in turn handed him his greenpass.

Jes looked at the pass and stopped laughing. He stuck his other hand in his pocket and felt around.

"Where did you get this?" he said.

"From your pocket, when you fell before we reached the gate. They trigger alarms and I decided that you wouldn't miss it."

Jes looked at her, confused. She looked back at him with patient expectation. He put the greenpass in his pocket, beside the credit plate.

"You've quite a few skills," he said finally. "Who was following us? Maigret?"

"Hardly. Our red-haired friend owes us a favor—whoever followed you was, originally, following her."

"Followed *me?* We were both trespassing."

"We weren't followed by Gensco, tauCaptain. If we had been, they'd have raised alarms and closed down the gates."

"Then who . . . ?"

Tatha shrugged and walked past Tamma's bar. "I was rather hoping you knew."

The slidebelt was off for the night, the lights dimmed, the crowds dispersed. Tatha didn't speak as they crossed the square and moved down the corridor toward Jes' cabin, but when they reached his door she put her hand over his mouth, forestalling his questions.

"As me tomorrow," she said quietly. "But before you go to bed, request the file I've noted on the back of your greenpass. And sleep well, my fly." She turned swiftly and disappeared around a bend in the corridor.

Jes stood in the clensor, wishing the water would clear away his weariness as easily as it cleared away the dirt. His mind kept asking questions that he couldn't answer. Clean, dressed, and desperate for sleep, he sat before the commiter and punched in the file number. The screen presented him with a reproduction of a months-old fax sheet.

Gensco, the fax reported, had received a takeover bid of surprising size and, after due consideration, had turned it down. A second offer was made and also rejected. No further offers were pending. The managers assured all

residents and employees that they would never sell Gensco to any agency, no matter how big, and urged confidence in slightly hysterical tones.

The bidding party was Parallax.

By first light, Jes felt the effects of the wake-up he'd
taken begin to wear off. He dialed another dose and resumed pacing the cabin.

There were no further public reports on the bids, although Jes tried to key information under every heading
he could imagine. He found nothing further on Santa
Theresa either, but that proved nothing.

A combine as large as Parrallax could pick its
agents from any part of the Federation; but if Tatha was
a Parallax agent, why would she take him on that mid-
night trespass? And certainly Gensco was not interested in Aerie-Kennerin, although Parallax would be.
Parallax wanted Aerie-Kennerin, Jes knew that; in Parallax's hands Jes would serve as a hostage against his
family's quiet capitulation. But he couldn't see how his
presence would aid or hinder the Parallax-Gensco bid at all.

Yet if Tatha was not a Parallax agent, why had she assumed that a stray tauCaptain named Jes Kennerin
would have any interest in the bid?

If she was a Gensco agent, then why trespass? And if
their pursuer had been a Parallax agent, why was the
agent following a stray Theresan and a stranded tau-
Captain?

"Whoever followed *you* . . ." Tatha had said.

But she'd broken into his room, read his Certificate,
and neatly picked his pocket, all in the course of one
evening.

Faced with an unsettling conundrum, Jes reacted in
the time-honored manner of all blunt, square-seeing
Kennerins. He marched down to the repairs bay to con-
front Tatha.

His sloop hung suspended high over the floor of the
bay. Jes walked under it, shouting Tatha's name, until
her face appeared over the side of the ship.

"Come on up," she said, and disappeared.

There seemed no way up save the dangling, knotted
rope that hung from a high beam. He flexed his hands,

remembering the hours he'd put in on his ship's swing-gym, and started up the rope.

He'd conveniently forgotten that a ship's gym functions in free-fall; by the time he reached the sloop his hands felt permanently cramped and the muscles in his shoulders burned. He sat near Tatha and rubbed his shoulders. The burned leads were scattered around her and her laserpencil glowed as she soldered new leads into place.

"You haven't slept," she said. "That stunts the growth, you know."

"I'm used to sleeping in hammocks. I haven't been able to sleep in a regular bed since I went to space."

"Flexibility is a virtue," she said severely, and reached for the wires. Jes picked one out and handed it to her.

"Why did you want me to look at that file?"

Tatha, the wire between her teeth, didn't answer. The connection was smoothly made. She released the wire and pressed it into its groove.

"I thought you might be interested."

"Why?"

"Why not?"

"Tatha," he said, annoyed, and she smiled.

"It's the reason Gensco's edgy right now. Not that they're friendly at the best of times, but you came in the middle of a big scare. Another wire, please."

Jes complied. He lay on his belly and propped his chin in his hand.

"I don't see why they're so worried," he said. "Surely it's not the first time someone's tried to buy them out."

"For these folk, it is. And Parallax is not your all-around good guy."

"Why not?"

"Oh, come now, you're not that innocent. You've heard of Parallax—everyone has."

Jes raised his eyebrows. "They're just a large combine. I don't know why they want to buy Gensco, but if they've been refused they'll go away."

Tatha glanced at him. "Parallax is a stubborn bunch, captain. They don't make offers lightly and they don't accept negatives. Gensco has no intention of being bought, and knows Parallax's reputation, and is running scared."

"So?"

"Parallax is looking for a lever, something they can use as a hostage to force Gensco's capitulation." She put down her laserpencil and opened her collar. "A hostage," she repeated bitterly. She looked at Jes and the corners of her mouth twitched. "Think they'll find it?"

"How should I know?"

"Exercise your imagination, tauCaptain. If you were a lone agent for a big company, under orders to find a lever for a takeover bid, a lever that won't damage the company such that it's rendered worthless, where would you look? What sort of thing would you aim for? How would you go about finding it? And how would you go about obtaining it?"

"And why would a stray Theresan want to know?"

"Meow," Tatha said.

Play along, Jes thought. Information runs two ways. He frowned.

It had to be something that Gensco could not easily replace but that Parallax did not particularly need; if Gensco decided to sacrifice the hostage, Parallax would have to be able to destroy it without destroying the company. And that immediately cut out most of the technical aspects of the stations, the power cores, life-support systems, communications net. Tatha pointed out that an individual manager would also not serve the purpose; Gensco's owners lived in well-protected seclusion on a distant planet, and the managers themselves, despite their individual talents, were interchangeable and hence easily replaceable. Any attempt to capture the Station by siege or attack would also be impracticable: Parallax would either have to bring warships in through Federation tau, which was illegal and bound to incur Federation discipline, or would have to assemble the ships in Priory Sector. But the Sector was well patrolled, Tatha said, and any such shipbuilding operation would be soon discovered and destroyed.

Tatha began humming, the same slippery tune Jes had heard when he met her. Jes shrugged.

"I don't know what an agent would look for," he said finally. "If it were my job, I suppose I'd creep about poking into things and take what came. Watch out for anything secretive. Keep alert."

Tatha nodded. "Especially to unexpected occurrences.

Like people sneaking about in the bushes in Gem Sphere."

"If I were an agent for Gensco, I'd be interested in the same thing."

"Indeed you would."

Jes took a deep breath. "All right. Why were we creeping about in the bushes last night?"

"You wanted to see Gem Sphere, didn't you?"

"That's not responsive. You were looking for something, weren't you? When you eavesdropped on Maigret —what were you looking for?"

"Why, I'm incurably curious. I told you that before."

"Will you answer my questions?" Jes demanded. He stood up. Tatha didn't break the rhythm of her work.

"The ones you've asked, or the ones you haven't? I gave you the Parallax file code because, Menet, that's who Maigret thinks you are. She was telling the others last night. Dear me, you do look astounded. Surely it's not that surprising—"

"It's absurd! Me? Sweet Mother—I'll tell her. That's what's holding everything up, isn't it?" Jes laughed a bit wildly. "All I have to do is tell Maigret that I'm not, and we'll have all the parts we need immediately."

"And how, friend, are you going to convince her that you're not a Parallax agent?"

Jes stared at her. What, indeed, would he say to Maigret? That Parallax had tried to take over his home-world once? That the indications were that they were gearing up to do it again? How could he prove that to Maigret's satisfaction? Worse, what if Parallax made its attempt against the Station while Jes was still aboard? And Maigret survived? Would she curry favor with her new masters by bringing them tauCaptain Jes Kennerin, head on platter?

Maigret, he remembered, seemed very easy to spy upon.

And Tatha said, echoing his thoughts, "There *is* a Parallax agent on Gensco, Jes. The agent's been here for at least a month. And is as capable of eavesdropping as I am. Another thing—we've no guarantee that the agent is an outsider. It could be a member of management, or the staff. It could even be Maigret."

"It could even," Jes said slowly, "be you."

"It could," Tatha agreed. "But it isn't."

"Am I to believe that?"

"I've never lied to you," she said easily. "And, you'll notice, I've no interest in learning just how you would go about convincing Gensco that you're not the agent, because I think your argument would interest Parallax intensely. I don't want you to tell me."

"Because you know already?"

Tatha shook her head.

"I don't believe you," he said, his temper rising. He made no effort to control it. "All I know of any of this has come from you, and you may be the best liar in the Federation. I don't even know who the hell you are. Who are you?"

"I've already told you," she said. "You simply have to arrange to believe it."

Jes lost his temper entirely. "All right. No more games. I don't like webs and I don't like plots and I don't particularly like you either. You and Gensco and Parallax and this entire damned Sector can go to hell. All I want is to have my ship fixed. Now. *And no more games!*"

"Linear thinking is not only boring, it's unproductive," Tatha remarked.

Jes cursed. "You can call me when the job's done," he said, grabbing the rope. Tatha dropped the leads wires and put her hands in her lap. She looked at Jes expectantly.

"And I won't be coerced," he shouted before swarming down the rope. As he marched out of the bay, he heard Tatha's voice above him, raised cheerfully in song.

HIS DAILY BILLING WAS WAITING FOR HIM when he returned to his cabin. He paid it, cursing, and yawned. The effects of the second wake-up had worn off, and his muscles felt slack and heavy. Except for his two-hour nap the day before, he'd been without sleep for three standard days. He sat on the bunk and rubbed his eyes, and, seeking nothing more than a moment's rest, he lay back and slept for ten hours.

He woke refreshed and ravenously hungry, and it seemed that the problems he'd taken with him to sleep has smoothed themselves. Feeling that, with some deplorably linear thinking, he could easily clear up any and all misunderstandings, he showered, dressed, and made his way to Tammas' Hopyard.

Save for Tammas and a small woman in an odd green spacer's suit, the place was empty. Jes entered and sat at the bar, and Tammas came over to scowl and flap his traditional cleaning rag on the counter.

"Tatha said you serve food," Jes said. "I could use some."

"Stew," Tammas muttered, glaring.

"Fine. Do you have any juice?"

Tammas' brows nearly met and he straightened his shoulders. "I run a saloon, Menet. Not a bloody nursery."

"A beer then," Jes said, resigned.

Tammas nodded, still scowling, and disappeared through a door behind the bar. Jes saw the small woman looking at him.

"Well, you're obviously not a Genny," she said amiably. "Your accent is thick as curds."

"And you're not one either," he replied. "My ship blew a leads plate in tau and I had to come in for repairs."

She hooted. "You sure picked the wrong place to look for help. Are you getting any?"

"After a fashion. They sent me to some crazy Theresan."

"Tatha? I've heard about her." The woman stuck out her hand. "Name's Min Calder, bumpcaptain from East Lab."

"Jes Kennerin." Jes shook her hand. "You're here on business?"

"Such as it is. We had to make a run in and I pulled the short straw. Gensco makes me twitchy."

Jes rolled his eyes in agreement. Tammas came backwards through the door, turned, and put a bowl on the counter before Jes. Steam rose from hunks of meat and vegetables. Tammas provided spoon, beer, and bread, and Jes ate hungrily.

"You going to be here long?" Min said.

Jes shrugged and swallowed. "As long as it takes to fix my sloop. And for all I know, that may take forever."

"Me, I'm stuck here for another two, three days. The idiots don't have the return cargo ready. So here I am with nothing to do but hang around Tammas', and I'm getting prettty tired of watching beer drinkers."

Jes paused with a spoonful of stew halfway to his mouth. It was as obvious an effort to pick him up as any he'd encountered. He glanced at her obliquely. Trim, tiny woman, brown hair, brown eyes, laugh-lines grooved about the mouth. She smiled back at him and turned to call an order to Tammas, letting Jes take his time.

She's a Labber, Jes thought. Labbers have no love for Gensco—one could easily be spying for Parallax. He shook his head, annoyed. Gensco had no love for the Lab, either, and would be doubly suspicious of any Labbers come aboard. Getting as bad as Tatha, he told himself. When Min finished placing her order, Jes smiled at her.

"What's to do on Gensco Station, aside from drinking beer?"

"Oh, I think we could manage to come up with something."

"Something," with Min, became spending the rest of the day wandering through the public areas of Repairs Bay Colony, peering in the shops and gossiping maliciously about the inhabitants. Min had a quick, sharp tongue and used it lavishly; her gripes about Gensco were all solid, realistic, and devoid of plots, counterplots, and subtle intricacies. Jes found it refreshing, and during the course of the afternoon he learned quite a lot about Gensco, from an enemy's point of view.

"Of course they're bloody-minded bastards," Min said at one point. They were leaning over the railing of an overpass, watching the movement of cargo cubes through a transparent supply line. "You know that one of the first things they attack in The Lab are the children's worlds? They try to capture them, to raise our kids as stinking Gennys, and if they can't capture, they kill. We've had to move the worlds time and again, lying about where they are—we'll get as bad as they are, eventually. You got any kids?"

Jes shook his head. "Nieces and nephews until hell won't have it, but none of my own."

"Me neither. I've been thinking of it, though. It'd be nice to have a kid around the hole, keep me from getting lonely. My lover's got a kid—I kind of envy her, having someone brand new to bring up. You know what the Genny bastards do with theirs?"

"What?"

"Freeze them. You come to work on Gensco and you've got kids, they take them somewhere and put them on hold until you can get them out of hock again."

"Mother! Wouldn't it be simpler to control births? Or to abort?"

Min looked at him. "Come on, tauCaptain, you can do better than that. Gensco's got two aims." She ticked them off on her fingers. "Keep the population steady and, second, keep the population quiet. They rotate workers for five-year terms, and if they have kids, they take them. Behave yourself, you get your kids back. Don't behave yourself, and . . ." She gestured expressively. "Is it any wonder that every Genny's a bloodpicker? If your own folk can do that to you, you've got to believe that outsiders will be even worse."

"Sweet Mother." Jes looked at her with amazement. "The parents must object. Hell, if they did that with a kid of mine—"

"You'd have no choice. Whip away goes the kid while you're not looking and if you don't behave yourself, they off the kid."

"I don't believe you."

"It's the truth. Rumor is that they keep the cold creche somewhere well hidden, along with anything else they want to keep safe. You know how they keep outsystem workers here?"

"Yeah. Take something they need and don't give it back."

"There was an old fellow here once, they took away his spare lung. Real effective. Or they take any money you've got, and the wages they pay all go toward keeping you alive here. Room, board, rental space in the yards— hell, they even regulate the air, call it a sanitation tax. You can't pay your way off, and you can't save enough to get off, and you can't get your hands on anything you brought with you. Outsystem workers aren't rotated—

it's a life sentence. And they claim that *we're* barbarians."

"Then why bother with them at all?"

"We have to. They want our ores, and they've closed all our other markets. We *have* to sell to Gensco, at Gensco's prices. But they want us offed, too. We're anarchistic, we don't come prepackaged and we don't fit into boxes. And that offends them." Min looked up at Jes and shook her head. "You want my advice, Kennerin, you'll raise hell until your ship's fixed, and you'll lam it out of Priory as fast as you can. Whoever you are and whatever you want and wherever you're from, you sure as hell don't need this."

Jes silently agreed. The light had paled to evening. They left the bridge and bounced from one entertainment hall to another, playing the games, gambling, watching the shows. They were constantly surrounded by the quick, slurred accents of Priory speech, and Min kept her voice low, touching Jes' arm whenever he spoke too loudly. He didn't understand why until, backed against the bar in a crowded cabaret, someone jostled his elbow sharply, sending his drink flying out of his hand to drench the Genny on his other side. The Genny spun around, glowering.

"I'm sorry," Jes said. "Someone hit my arm. Here, let me help you clean up."

The Genny tensed his shoulders and glared at Jes. "Hey, folks, we've got us a pigeon," he said unpleasantly. "You keep your pigeon hands off me. I've heard that story before."

"It was an accident," Jes said firmly. "I said I'm sorry." Min was tugging at his arm. Jes tried to shake her off. The crowd had moved back, leaving a small clearing around them.

"Not only am I wet," the Genny said, "not only is my evening fucked, but I'm probably covered with alcoholic pigeon germs." The people laughed.

Jes shook Min away and clenched his hands. "Back where I come from, we teach people to be polite to strangers. Some folk need to have the lesson beat into them."

The Genny obligingly raised his fists. Min glanced at the doorway and yelled, "Pols!"

Immediately the Genny swung away and disappeared

into the crowd, which just as quickly went back to drinking and conversations. Jes stood alone, bewildered, his fists raised foolishly before him. Min grabbed his arm and pushed him to the door. There were no pols in sight.

"You idiot," she said, when they were on the street again. Jes looked at her with surprise. She was shaking.

"Haven't you been in a barroom fight before?" he said.

"That's not the point. You know how the Gennys hate us. One barroom fight could spread until every Labber on the Station is dead. And it wouldn't stop there."

"Oh, come on. A fight between a Genny and an outworlder?"

"And me, Kennerin." She took a deep breath. "We've barely recovered from the last battle—if they chose to come at us now, we're lost. That last bout was started by a Labber who accused a Genny of cheating on a cargo load. And got strung up for it." Min paused. "We lost four hundred people in ten days, including a whole lot of my family. I like you, Kennerin, but I swear to God, do that again and I'll kill you myself."

She was still shaking. Jes put his hand on her shoulder. "I'm sorry, Min. The more I learn about this Sector—"

"The happier you'll be to be off it. You won't be the only one. Someone bumped you deliberately."

Jes stared at her. She nodded. "Don't ask me why, and don't ask me who. I was standing next to you and someone stuck a hand between us and hit your elbow. Next thing, you were getting ready to be creamed. You're dangerous company, Kennerin."

Jes slid his arm around her shoulders and resisted the impulse to shiver.

"If I promise to behave myself, will you put up with me awhile longer?"

Min silently put her arm around his waist and fit her tiny body into the curves of his tall one. By the time they reached Tammas', though, her ebullience reasserted itself, and Jes began to think he had imagined the entire thing. They ate, drank, talked, laughed, and, entering Min's cabin at the end of the evening, took an amiable, easy pleasure of each other.

When he woke, Min was gone. A note, propped on the table, said that she'd left to cope with cargo handlers and she'd be at Tammas' later in the day. Jes tossed the note in the disposer, showered, and returned to his own cabin through the purposeful bustle of the morning. He kept his head well down and didn't speak. Reaching his own cabin without incident, he let the muscles of his chest relax and opened the door to chaos.

The room had been thoroughly ransacked: bedding ripped apart, the contents of his sack scattered on the floor, the clothes niche flung open, the empty drawers of the desk upside down amid the wreckage on the floor. Jes snapped the door closed behind him and stared at the mess in shock. He ran to the clensor unit and reached for the light panel. The clips were angled as he'd left them, and the Certificate, untouched, rested in its hiding place. He reset the clips and quickly repaired the damage to the room. Nothing had been taken and nothing, save his own peace of mind, had been destroyed.

Not Tatha, he thought as he worked. She'd have made a far neater job of it, for one. And she couldn't have been the one who jostled him the night before, not a Theresan in a crowd of xenophobic Gennys. He finished cleaning up, wolfed down the unpleasant breakfast provided by the chute, and marched off to Tatha's repairs bay.

His sloop remained suspended overhead, but the lights around it were dark. He swarmed up the rope, switched on his pocket light, and swore as he looked at the damaged area. Tatha had left it exactly as it had been the day before: new wires scattered around the gap, a few wires half connected, a couple of tools lying on the metal hull.

Jes let himself get furious. He slid down the rope, slammed out of the bay, and, reaching his room, demanded of the commiter that it connect him with Maigret. Instead he found himself shunted from one bureaucrat to another, each of whom listened to his complaint with distaste and passed him along the line until he found himself faced with the person who had originally taken his call. And: "I'm sorry," he was told. "We're far too busy to deal with this. You've been assigned a jockey and we've no time to disrupt the entire work schedule of the Station because you can't get along with her. You're being done a favor, Menet Kennerin. Please remember that."

Jes cursed at length in Standard and in Kasiri, with all the righteous indignation of a reasonable being faced with irrational nonsense. Then, deliberately calming himself, he sat at the desk and did some heavy-duty thinking.

He couldn't take his sloop out until she'd been repaired. He could resolder the leads wires himself, but could not obtain a leads plate without Tatha's help. Tatha, though, had made it quite clear that she would not help him unless he helped her. With what? Jes shook his head and left the question for later.

Think elliptically, he told himself. Suppose that there was a Parallax agent on Gensco, that the agent had followed them in Gem Sphere, that the agent had overheard Maigret's suspicions about Jes. The agent would have followed Jes to find out who, in fact, he was. And would attempt to divert Gensco's suspicions on to Jes, thereby taking the pressure off himself. In which case the ransacking of Jes' cabin would have happened before the incident in the entertainment hall.

Further: it was entirely likely that the agent would know nothing about Aerie-Kennerin. True, if the agent reported to Parallax and Parallax ran a search on the report, Jes Kennerin's name would set off bells. But the agent wasn't likely to beam a report, and thereby jeopardize cover, before the mission was completed. And Parallax was not likely to blow *its* plans by making any special effort to capture Jes while Gensco remained free.

He could protect himself, he decided, by keeping his head down and his temper in check, by staying out of trouble, and by making sure that Tatha fixed his ship as soon as possible. And if that meant playing her game, or pretending to, it was a price he'd be prepared to pay for his freedom.

He returned to the repair bay and, picking up Tatha's laserpencil, began soldering the leads himself. He finished the work, put down the pencil, and rubbed his eyes. The next stage needed a larger laser, but he didn't know where Tatha kept her tools. He left the tools he'd used stacked neatly at the rope's end and, after cleaning up, when to Tammas' Hopyard and ordered a beer.

Tatha was not there, and Tammas said he hadn't seen her since breakfast that morning. But Min came in a few minutes later and detailed the day's mishaps with Gensco Cargo. Jes leaned back in his chair until he had a clear view of the doorway. The bar filled during the course of the evening; the air grew dim and stale. Tammas, catching his eye, shrugged sourly and brought more beer.

"If she comes in," Jes said to him, "will you tell her that I was looking for her? And would you tell her—?"

"That you're sorry? She said you'd say that. I'll tell her."

Jes glared at Tammas' retreating back, then turned to answer the question in Min's expression.

"Tatha's disappeared," he said. "I think she thinks I insulted her, and I want to apologize so she'll finish work on my ship."

Min raised her eyebrows. "She doesn't sound like the type to get huffy over an insult."

"Oh, fuck her," Jes said. "You want to leave?"

Min nodded and pushed her beer away. "For you, any time."

❧

THEY WERE ASLEEP, PRESSED TOGETHER IN Jes' narrow bed, when Jes woke to the sound of the door closing softly. He reached for the light switch beside the bed.

"It's okay," Tatha's voice whispered. She sounded tired. "It's me, don't panic. Turn it on low."

"I'm not alone," Jes whispered back.

"I know." There was a soft rustling; Tatha crossing the room to sit, Jes presumed, on the edge of the table. "Tammas said you were looking for me."

"Surely you expected that." When Tatha did not reply, he said, "Look, I'm sorry. I didn't mean to yell at you. All I want is my ship fixed so I can get out of this crazy Sector."

"A consummation devoutly to be wished," Tatha said. "I know who's with you, and I know she's not asleep. Turn on the light, Jes. I need help."

"Min?"

"Go on," Min said. "I'm awash with curiosity."

Jes sat and pressed the switch gently. A faint glow filled the cabin. Tatha was indeed perched on the edge of the table.

"More," she said. Jes turned the light higher, gasped, and jumped from the bed.

Tatha's brown suit was in tatters, her hair crusted with dirt, and one hand held her shoulder tightly. Between her fingers, blood welled slowly to trickle down the fur of her bare arm. Her eyes were heavy with pain and exhaustion.

Min rolled from the bed, crossed to Tatha, and pulled her hand away from her shoulder. A dirty wound showed beneath the blood-soaked fur.

"What else?" Min demanded.

"Bumps and bruises, but this is the worst." Tatha put her hand over the wound again and grimaced sharply. "You'd better leave."

"But you need help—"

"Kennerin has surgeon's citations. You don't want to get involved—you've yourself and The Lab to protect."

Min reached for her clothing. "Is it that bad?"

"I don't know. It may be. You don't want to know about it."

Min bit her lip, nodded, and dressed swiftly. She paused at the door, fumbled in her belt pouch, and tossed something to Jes. "This might help," she said. "You won't want to order supplies." She slid through the door and closed it behind her.

Jes looked from the emergency medical packet in his hand to Tatha.

"Do you want a full-scale explanation now or later?" she said.

"Sweet Mother," Jes said, exasperated. "Lie on the bed."

Tatha slid from the table and swayed. Jes caught her and carried her to the bed, stripped the jumpsuit from her, and threw it in the disposer. He began cleaning the area of the wound with water. Tatha clenched her teeth.

The incision was not as deep as he'd feared, but it was wide and long and filthy. He stared at it, tapping his lip with his finger.

"It needs stitching," he said. "We'll have to find a doctor."

"We can't. You've enough citations, you can handle this."

"God, Tatha. I don't have any anesthetic—"

"If you call a medic, they'll kill me. I swear it, Jes." She grinned pallidly. "It's up to you, brave one. I may faint, but I trust that you won't."

Jes quelled a moment of sickness. He'd done his share of stitching before, but never on an unanesthetized patient. Tatha looked at him, dirty gray face, tangled silver hair, her bloodshot eyes calmly expectant. Jes took a deep breath, nodded, and opened the kit.

She fainted when he began cleaning the wound. He worked faster, trying to get most of it done before she woke. When the needle entered her skin she moaned and stirred, and he bound her body to the bed, placed his fingers briefly on her throat and determined that her pulse was steady, and continued grimly with the stitching. Finished, he looked critically at the job, decided that it would hold, and layered strips of protective absorbent and clingtape over the wound. Finally he checked her pulse again, peeled back her lids to look at her eyes, released her bindings, and bound her arm tightly to her waist. He covered her with a blanket and sat back in the cabin's one chair. After a while, unexpectedly, he slept.

He woke a few hours later, muscles stiff, and went to the bed. Tatha lay still, breathing evenly and deeply. He checked her pulse again, relying, as before, on its steadiness and not on its speed. He had no idea what the normal pulse rate of a Theresan was, nor of normal temperature. She showed no signs of waking. He pulled on his suit and went to the repairs bay, where he shimmied up the rope and into his ship. He removed a range of antibiotics and analgesics from the medical supply rack and put them in his pocket, added an extra roll of absorbent and tape, and slid down the rope again. Tatha was awake when he returned.

"I don't know which antibiotics you can take," he said, emptying his pockets. "Or painkillers. So I brought a range of them. I cleaned the wound as thoroughly as I could, but without a diagnostat—the stuff's from my sloop."

"I thought so. You're stubborn, but you're not stupid." She tried to sit up, and Jes came to help her. "I'm filthy," she said with distaste.

"I'll give you a bath."

Tatha laughed. "I'm not paralyzed, Kennerin. I can clean myself."

Jes looked at her dubiously but helped her to the clensor. While she bathed he stripped the dirty sheets from the bed, dumped them, and ordered a new set. He collected stray bits of matted fur and pushed them in the disposer, brushed his hands, and remade the bed. Tatha came dripping from the unit.

"I can't dry myself," she said ruefully. Jes accepted the towel and passed it over her soft fur, and when she gave him the name of an antibiotic he picked it from the litter of drugs on the table and gave it to her. She refused a painkiller.

"You're being remarkably silent," she said, once back in bed. "Aren't you anxious to yell questions?"

"I'm not sure I want to know the answers," Jes said. "But I guess you'd better tell me what this is all about."

"Water?"

Jes brought her a cup, then sat at the table. Tatha stared into the cup.

"Santa Theresa," she said finally. "My name is Tatha Al'Okelough preParian, which doesn't mean a thing to you. I'm Tatha, the second child of the clan Okelough, of the province of Parian. Parian's the fiefdom of clan Okelough, my parents rule it. It's a productive province, wealthy, influential. It bored me. I left fairly young to work as a jockey at the local Sal. It was the only job they'd let me have, family or no. And when I found, after a couple of years, that they'd no intention of letting me move up to taujockey and ride the ships, I went home. My clan took me back. I suppose they were used to me, by then. They sent me off to Egliesa, the capital, to university. That bored me too, and I spiced things up. Extracurricular activities. *Tempus est jocondum.* The last prank went sour, my lover died, I became very unwelcome on Santa Theresa. My father gave me what little money he could and some jewelry that was to come to me anyway. And he told me to get off Santa Theresa and not come back." She paused. "I had something of my own by then, too. The money was enough to buy passage to Priory, the only jobs were on the Station, and when I came here they took what my father had given me, and what I had myself, and I can't leave until I get it back."

She stopped, drank some water, and sat staring into the cup. Her eyes were downcast and Jes could not read her expression.

"Go on," he said.

She went on without looking up. She had deduced that Maigret knew the location of the confiscated goods, and Tatha had set herself, over the past months, to follow Maigret, trying to learn where the hiding place might be. When she learned that Parallax too was interested, her search quickened, became a complex game of following the Parallax agent while trying not to be followed herself, for if Parallax learned the location and captured it, Tatha would lose all chance of regaining that which was hers. Last night, in the cool fastness of Maigret's deserted office, Tatha had learned the location of her possessions. The Parallax agent had found her there and tried to kill her.

"He had the benefit of surprise, and I think he damaged me more than I damaged him," she said with regret. "A sorry blow to the ego. And I came here."

"And now that I've patched you up, you can march off and rescue your jewels," Jes said curtly.

Tatha shook her head. "I know where they are, but not where that is."

"And you want me to help you get it." Jes stood, kicking the chair aside, and shoved his hands angrily into his pockets. "Doesn't it strike you that all this is a lot of trouble for a bunch of jewelry? You can leave with me, I'll take you. And you can make up your loss. It's not as important as your freedom, is it?"

"I think it is. It's not easily replaceable, you know."

"Of all the cross-grained, idiotic, bull-headed, greedy nonsense," Jes shouted. "You can risk your own ass for a bunch of glitter, but I'm damned if I'll let you risk mine."

Tatha sipped from the cup. "I assume you tried to get another jockey. And I assume they told you to be happy with what you had."

Jes stood at the edge of the bed and glared at her. "I don't like being bullied and I don't like being coerced."

"Then how about moral blackmail?" she replied. "Our shadow is a Parallax agent and what I know, he knows. If he finds the location of the place before I do, or before Gensco is warned, he'll have the leverage he needs for the takeover."

"I don't care. Gensco and Parallax deserve each other. All I want is to get the hell out of here, and soon."

Tatha didn't look up. "The hiding place is in the cold creche. And we've found out what the cold creche is."

Jes put his hand on the table. By all the criteria he and Tatha had discussed that day in the repairs bay, the cold creche was the perfect lever.

"Not fair," he said. "Oh, that's totally dirty, Tatha. I'm not responsible for those children." Tatha didn't reply. "Besides, how could my helping you help them? Why don't you just tell Gensco? Take the commiter, call Maigret, and tell her. Let Gensco handle it."

"If Gensco sets up a quickwatch on the creche, it will be impossible for me to get in. And they won't give me what's mine as thanks for uncovering Parallax, either." She balanced the cup on her lap. "Gensco won't be told until I've what I want and am on my way out of the system."

"Moral blackmail," Jes said with revulsion. "You're immune to it, aren't you? Your heap of treasure is far more important than those lives."

"The children won't suffer. They're in stasis, they'll never know what hit them."

"Holy Mother, you're a bitch."

"Perhaps. Help me, and I'll fix your ship."

Jes made a sharp gesture. "What makes you think the agent isn't there already? It's been seven hours since you came here."

"Because he's busy looking for me. To kill me. I'm as much a threat to him as he is to me, and until he offs me he can't do anything else." She looked up. "The cold creche is in an orbiting satellite. There are fifty-eight of them. I don't know which is the right one, but I think that, by now, the agent does. I wiped the bank of tapes in the office before the fight, so Gensco knows we found something, but they don't know what. And they'll soon know for sure that I was one of the finders."

"Why?"

"Because Maigret's pretty office is fairly well splattered with my blood. All they have to do is type it—the differences are subtle, but conclusive. And there's only one Theresan on the Station."

Jes stared at her. Both Parallax and Gensco were following her, and the trail led directly to his cabin, to himself.

"There's another choice," he said. "I could call Maigret myself, tell her what you've been doing, what condition you're in. If necessary, I could even hurt you."

"The moment Parallax knows that Gensco's on to him, he'll head for the creche immediately, without waiting to finish with me. And you could hurt me, if necessary." She lay still, the bandage thick and stark on her shoulder, her arm strapped tightly to her waist under her full breasts. She looked totally unafraid.

"All right," Jes said angrily. "Fix my ship and I'll get you to the cold creche. I'll even take you out of Priory. And then I never want to see you again."

"Why is it," Tatha murmured, "that people keep saying that to me?" She swung her legs out of the bed and stood carefully. "You'd best order something for me to wear, tauCaptain. And a jacket or cloak to cover the shoulder. We've another four hours, I'd guess, before things get hot."

Jes, on his way to the clensor to retrieve his Certificate, stopped. "Four hours? How are you going to get my leads plate in four hours?"

"I had your plate yesterday, I stole it from another bay before I went into Gem Sphere. And it's four hours before any blood tests come up conclusive, if they haven't screwed things up. We haven't much time."

When the suit arrived, Jes ungently helped her put it on. With a short jacket covering her sling, Jes' sack cradled in her good arm, and her hair covered by a hood, she led the way to the repairs bay.

She couldn't climb the rope to the sloop, so Jes lowered the ship to within a few meters of the floor of the bay. She sat on the hull giving directions while Jes soldered and positioned and sealed, and she ran the checks with professional ease. Two and a half hours after they began, the job was finished. Tatha reached for Jes' chronometer, then suddenly flicked off the pocket light. Jes listened intently.

The noise was slight but definite. Someone, walking through the far side of the bay, knocked against a piece of loose metal. Tatha silently collected her tools and dropped them into her pouch, touched Jes, and slid down the hull of the sloop. When Jes landed beside her, she pulled his head down and whispered, her lips brushing his ear.

"Parallax. I have to take care of him, find out where the creche satellite is." She put her fingers over his mouth. "Go inside. If I'm not back in an hour, get out of Priory, fast." She disappeared into the darkness of the repairs bay. Jes barely hesitated before sliding into the darkness after her.

Another clink of metal sounded from the far side of the bay. The agent was either inept, which Jes doubted, or wounded, which was possible, or as eager to find Tatha as she was to find him, and deliberately letting her spot his location. Jes turned and crept in the direction of the sound.

Another scrape of sound, closer this time. Jes paused, wondering if the agent was armed. The glow from the commiter bank lit the space before him. He stepped back from the light and someone grabbed him and locked a hard, unfurred arm around his neck.

Jes had fought in the crowded back alleys of Market-Port, and his response was smooth and immediate. In two movements he was free of the hold and attacking. His assailant made a small, surprised noise before silencing into battle.

Jes fought almost automatically. His movements were economical, engrained, and dictated on a level above that of conscious thought. He judged moves, circled, retreated, engaged with sudden ferocity. The agent carried a knife; small, silent, ancient, and efficient. Jes feinted, reversed, and kicked the knife from the agent's hand. Within the intensity of the moment he was aware of Tatha poised by the commiter, her good arm upraised, hand hard and flat. Jes edged his opponent around until the agent's back was to the Theresan, and unexpectedly shoved him backwards. Tatha brought her arm down efficiently across the agent's neck, and the man staggered. Then Jes had him in a firm grip, pinned to the dirty floor of the bay, and Tatha stood above them both.

"You fight as dirty as I do," she said to Jes, and knelt beside the agent.

"Gensco knows," the agent said. "Or will." His voice was surprisingly pleasant, despite the harshness of his breathing. "Take me with you. I'll let you take what you want, and you can leave me there."

"No," Tatha said. "Tell me where the creche is."

The agent shook his head.

"Tatha, listen to him. It makes sense."

She rocked back on ther heels, looking at Jes. "Our friend here said something very interesting yesterday, before he knifed me."

Jes felt the muscles below him tense, and he shifted his grip. The agent went limp again.

"He said," Tatha continued calmly. " 'Where's your friend from Aerie?' Does that mean anything to you?"

"Idiot," the agent said. "He doesn't mean anything to you. I'd have bought him from you—" He gasped as Tatha ran a claw down his leg.

"Where is it?" she said.

"I'm not going to tell you," the agent said in his pleasant voice.

"I think I owe you something," Tatha replied, and her voice was not pleasant at all.

Neither was what followed. Jes held on and turned his face away, bracing his hands against the movement between them, trying not to listen as the agent's breath caught, moaned, sobbed.

"Tatha," Jes muttered, but she ignored him. The agent's back arched. He said a string of numbers, and went limp. Jes looked. Even one-handed, Tatha was remarkably efficient.

"Is he dead?"

"No." Tatha wiped her claws on her pants leg. When she looked at Jes her eyes were wide and clear and cold. "Do you want to do that?"

"God, Tatha."

"Then I will." She unsheathed her claws again.

"No!" Jes stood, breathing unevenly. "No. I'll do it."

Tatha looked at him, considering. The agent moaned. Without changing her expression, Tatha bent down and sliced open his throat. "Come along, captain," she said. "We haven't much time."

Jes lingered a moment longer, still in shock, and ran after Tatha.

She leaped into the sloop ahead of him and settled in the navigator's web. He locked the hatch and stood behind her.

"Tatha—"

"I said, we haven't much time." She slipped her arm

from the sling and swung it carefully back and forth. "I've programmed your navigator. The creche is about an hour from here, nearing the northern pole. I don't think you should wait for takeoff clearance."

Jes webbed himself in, fighting nausea, and flicked through a first check before warming the engines. As soon as the tattletales turned green, he lifted the sloop over the dead ships in the bay. The cables which held it snapped and fell free. Tatha leaned in front of him and did something with the call beam, and the gates of the first airlock swung open.

"They'll track us, but I've set your identity beamer to a standard Gensco code. They won't bother us until we approach the creche. We'll have to move fast, then." Tatha fell uncharacteristically silent. Jes looked at her; she swung her arm back and forth, her forehead creased. The bloodstains on her thigh dried and darkened. He turned back to his screens.

The tracking screen glittered with a multitude of points. Tatha rotated her shoulder and made a small noise. The tattletales for the new leads plate were comfortably steady; the pressure in the ship was constant. The rind of Gensco station passed below, monotonously irregular. Tatha kept working her arm. A brittle, tense silence filled the sloop's small bridge. Jes relaxed his shoulders and wondered if this howling silence would last until he had finally deposited Tatha and her precious fortune on some distant planet. His hands ached, remembering the agent's body twisting between them. He wished, desperately, that she would at least hum, and it was as much to silence the running of his memory as to break the silence that he finally spoke.

"What will happen to Tammas?" he said, peering at the tracking screen.

"Nothing. He'll pour beer and cook stew until he dies, or until The Lab decides its time to fight again. Then either someone will remember to come get him, or Gensco will kill him."

"He knows this?"

"He knows it." Her voice was without expression. The dreadful silence threatened to fall again.

"And Min?"

"Your bedmate? She's a Labber. She'll carry her cargo

back to The Lab and spend time until the next run planning warfare. If she's lucky, she'll live to see her old age."

"You don't care about any of them, do you?"

"Why should I? I didn't ask to be part of their lives or part of their problems." She swung her arm in wider arcs.

"Why don't you take a painkiller?"

"Later."

He bit back a rude comment and watched his screens. Better silence than this abrupt, abrasive conversation.

"You wouldn't have killed him," Tatha said. Jes tightened his grip on the thrust slide and the ship spurted forward. He carefully eased it back to cruising speed.

"You didn't expect me to, did you?"

"I was hoping," she said conversationally. "Do you know what would have happened to him, if I'd left you to it?"

"He'd still be dead. Your session with him was more than enough."

"If Gensco had him, and they probably would, they'd have patched him together enough to get him to talk, then killed him far more unpleasantly than I did." She let that sink in. "Be grateful for my bloodthirsty instincts, captain. Because if Gensco had him and he talked, we'd be met with fire when we approach the creche. We'd be killed. And that, I think, is a fairly high price to pay for a misplaced humanitarian gesture."

Jes turned to her, shaking with anger. "You are a bloodthirsty, inhuman, soulless bitch."

"Oh, come. You refused to kill a man who would have taken you and, presumably, used you against your own people, for evil ends. And with no more concern than you think I've shown toward the Labbers. I'm not an inhuman bitch, tauCaptain. I'm a predator. And what does that make you?"

She rose and paced about the bridge. Jes, unable to think of a reply of sufficient power, turned his back on her. He remembered that he'd once found her attractive and his stomach turned again. After a while, she started humming.

"What in hell is that tune?" he demanded.

She came out of his cabin and walked along the supply racks, peering into them. "It's a love song, tauCaptain. An old one.

> *Western wind, when wilt thou blow*
> *The small rain down can rain?*
> *Christ, that my love were in my arms,*
> *And I in my bed again."*

The words were not in Standard, and Jes did not understand them.

"Prewar terran lit was the most useless major they offered at Egliesa," she said. "So I took it."

"I'm not surprised."

"Oh, and I loved it, tauCaptain. Not all my urges are black and complicated." She found an insulation sheet and a carry pack, and was busy stuffing one into the other with one hand. She managed to do it gracefully. Jes looked to his board again.

There were fewer blips on the tracking screen now. Jes checked the bridge chronometer.

"We're approaching the pole," he said.

Tatha tucked her carry pack under her seat and webbed herself in again. "It's a Beta-class satellite, probably with an open space landing grid, probably with at least three alarm buggies. Following a steady course; they ought to be at four down, twelve across relative to the pole. Priory warehouse markings, look for three letters, three numbers, two letters, one number. They should have a standard codebeam." She stared at the tracking screen. "If they've changed orbit, we're lost."

Jes spotted three likely blips on the screen and flashed code demands to them. One was an inbound freighter, another was a hulk. The third answered in the proper letter and number sequence. Jes slid his ship into a new heading and approached.

"We don't want the main grid," Tatha said. "It's probably watched. Tuck around the side."

As he did so, the commiter beeped urgently. Tatha reached over his shoulder and turned it off. She touched the vision screen. "There. That's perfect."

It was a small grid, almost invisible under the satellite's markings. Jes dropped the sloop and felt the clamps lock in as Tatha left her seat and slid into the harness of a Barre suit. She slung her carrypack on her back and her toolcase about her waist before activating the suit's field. Jes stood while she walked to the airlock and slammed the hatch behind her. With a helpless oath, he grabbed a second Barre harness, pulled a handlance from its hiding place below the control board, and followed her out of the ship.

The field of her suit glimmered in the starlight. Jes followed the shimmer of it and found her kneeling by a thick metal hatch. She leaned forward until the suit's field covered the locking area and began probing with her tools. Jes looked up and around, but nothing moved in the cold silence.

The hatch swung open. They moved inside and clamped the outer door shut. The airlock cycled through and they stepped into a corridor.

The corridor was lit only by direction signs. Tatha moved down it without hesitation. Jes drew the handlance and followed, peering around. The silence unnerved him.

Tatha hesitated at a branching of the corridor and took two steps down one hall. Nothing happened. She turned and took the other hall. Alarms shrieked, filling the corridor with noise and flashing lights. Tatha ran and Jes hurried behind her. At a second corridor she again took the path of least quiet.

The corridor was lined with doors. Tatha opened them quickly until one resisted her hand. She probed the lock and the door opened with a further blast of alarms. Jes stood in the open doorway while Tatha raced down the rows of locked cabinets, peering at the markings on the doors. Jes was unable to make out the words. Tatha stopped, read a label again, and broke the lock on the door. She pulled out a plain gray cylinder, closed off the wires leading to it, and wrapped it in an insulation sheet. The cylinder filled her arms. She ran back into the corridor, with Jes at her heels.

People appeared around the far bend; Jes could hear their voices shouting over the sound of the alarms. Tatha glanced back at Jes. He ran ahead of her and pointed the handlance. A traceburn appeared on the floor before the pursuers and they jumped back. Tatha dodged into a flashing corridor and Jes spun to follow.

He didn't understand why the guards weren't armed until he remembered that they were probably in the area of the cold creche itself, and that a misaimed bolt would puncture the walls and kill the frozen children. The pursuers appeared at the far end of the hall. Jes waved the lance at them menacingly and they faded back. He saw medical smocks among them—not guards, then, but staff. He ran faster, afraid that if they didn't reach the lock soon, he'd have to kill someone.

The lock's codeplate glowed scarlet; it had been automatically locked when the alarms went off. Tatha pushed a door open and glanced at Jes. Within the room were the pumps and tubing and regulators that maintained the creches. He nodded. She put her cylinder on the floor by the airlock and fumbled with her tools. When the pursuers appeared, Jes aimed his lance into the regulator room and waited. They stopped and made supplicating gestures, their words lost in the howling of alarms.

Tatha threw her tools down, pulled open the airlock door, and ran inside. Jes followed, grabbed the door, and slammed it shut, throwing the emergency lock on the inside. The outer door opened and he took a moment to prop it open before following Tatha to the sloop. The inner door would not open with the outer door unsealed; perhaps they had bought a little time.

They slid into the webbing without removing the Barre harnesses.

"Go," Tatha said urgently. "Go, go, *go!*"

Jes went. The sloop shuddered and flung itself away from the satellite. As soon as its flight smoothed, Tatha was out of the seat, the cylinder in her arms, and heading for Jes' cabin. He leaped up, grabbed her wounded shoulder, and turned her around. She almost dropped the cylinder, and Jes grabbed it from her.

"You call Gensco. That was the deal, remember?"

"For God's sake." She reached for the cylinder. He held it away from her. "Give it to me," she said desperately.

Jes shook his head. "You call now, or I'll jettison this. I swear it."

Tatha grabbed the commiter mike, punched the all-bands transmitter, sent her message twice, and banged the mike down on the control board. She grabbed the cylinder from Jes and ran into the cabin. The bolt snicked shut behind her.

Jes turned to the commiter. Maigret's voice cut across the shouting; she ordered quickguards and seals around the cold creche, and sent out flights of interceptors. But the tausloop had been built for speed, and Jes pushed it to its limits. The interceptors dropped farther and farther behind. The sloop's navigational computer locked into the grab's coordinates. And when the Grabmaster's face, puffy with sleep, appeared on the screen, Jes demanded grab clearance before the 'master had a chance to talk.

"Why all the hurry, dear?" the 'master said. "Surely you've a moment to chat."

"I don't have a moment for anything," Jes said nastily. "I'm interested in getting the hell out of this fucking sector, forgetting it exists, and not hearing another word out of you or anyone else in Priory from now until doomsday. Do I have my clearance?"

"Oh, dear. You were impolite down there, weren't you? And after all my warnings. The commiters have been simply frantic for the past hour. Well, you can't blame others for your own lack of manners, my dear. Yes, yes, don't carry on so. It's not a Federation complaint they have against you, so my hands are tied. Pity. You have your clearance, sweetling. 'Bye." The 'master signed off in a flutter of jewels and fingers, and Jes dropped the sloop into the embrace of the coils.

HE'D TAKE HER TO MARKETPORT AND DUMP her there, he decided. And he'd tell her, if she ever came out of his cabin. They had been in tau for three hours and the door remained bolted; by putting his ear against it he could hear her moving about within the cabin, and the sharp clatter of metal on metal. No singing, no humming, no quick spill of words. He pounded on the door but she didn't answer, and eventually he returned to the control board and slumped before it, thinking angry thoughts.

Half an hour later, the gauges on the power grid jumped to full, and stayed there. Jes' stomach felt cold. He ran through every tattletale on the board, then through every sensor, but found nothing. The drain remained high. Cursing, he strode through the ship, checking everything manually, and still could not find the drain. He beat on the cabin door.

"Tatha! Come out of there! Something's broken again."

She didn't answer. He put his ear to the door. The metallic sounds were gone; now he heard her voice indistinctly. It sounded as though she were pleading: the words became melody, and the melody became words.

"Tatha! Damn it, get your ass out of there!"

She ignored him. Suddenly suspicious, he ran to the board and retraced the drain. It stemmed from his cabin. He pounded the cutoff switch and the grid didn't so much as twitch—she must have opened the paneling and bypassed the cutoff. He cursed and made a series of calculations. If she kept up the drain, they wouldn't have the power to make MarketPort. He fetched a laser and prepared to cut through the cabin door.

As suddenly as it had risen, the grid dropped to normal again. Jes put his ear to the door and listened to total silence. Setting his jaw, he activated the laser and sliced through the door.

The cabin was a catastrophe. Panels along one side had been ripped open and wires trailed from the conduits across the floor. The desk and table were invisible under a complicated arrangement of wires and resistors, all created from the ruins of the wall conduits. He recognized component parts of his tape scanner, decorating the edges of the cylinder that Tatha had stolen from the cold creche. The cylinder itself was open along the top. The room was unbearably warm.

He turned to the rest of the room and found Tatha. She lay sideways in the wide hammock, her eyes closed, blood seeping from her wounded shoulder. The fur along her arms was singed; her Barre harness and suit had disappeared. Held close to her body, cradled in her arms, a small, gray-furred infant sucked at her breast.

Jes lowered the laser and leaned against the door, staring. "Something of my own," she had said. "Not easily replaceable." "My lover died." The infant's tiny hand curled in the fur of her breast.

Of course, she would not have told him. For he would have mounted a holy war and they would all have died. The child first. Gensco policy. He pulled himself away from the wall, walked to the hammock, and looked down at Tatha and her jewel. A trickle of blood touched the small fingers, and Jes cleaned them gently with his fingertips. Tatha opened her eyes and looked at him without expression.

"I think," Jes said unevenly, "that I'd better tend your shoulder again."

Tatha closed her eyes, and the ghost of a smile played about her lips.

JES

SHE COULDN'T RETURN TO SANTA THERESA; she'd made that abundantly clear already. And Market-Port is no place to raise a child—filthy, noisy, dangerous, a place of no trees, no grass or flowers or sunlight or joy at all. She didn't know MarketPort, but I did, and did not even suggest it to her.

Those first four days out of Priory, in fact, I barely saw her. She fed the child: I could imagine her, in the grim darkness of her repairs bay, teasing and stroking her breasts to keep their milk as she planned the abduction of the boy. I wondered if there was anything that she did not plan, but when I asked I found that she had no plans beyond the escape from Priory at all. She would go where I took her and remain where I left her, sure of finding work, sure of making a life for herself and her son. I never doubted that surety, but she could not return to Santa Theresa. And MarketPort is no place to raise a child.

I offered her money. She simply looked at me, said something lightly in an alien tongue, and went back to her son.

How could I not hate her? I'd seen the workings of that quick mind and the workings of those clawed fingers; she was not to be trusted. But there was the child, always the child—and no child should suffer for its parent's sins.

So I offered to take her to Aerie, for the child's sake, and she accepted. I could not see why she saw money as charity, but not the offered sanctuary. Another of her small madnesses, perhaps. On Aerie the child, at least, would be safe.

Rabbit was as I'd left her two standard months before. Sandro had taken the slack time of my absence to have the ship scoured and repainted inside; the passageways and cabins almost glittered. Greaves had tuned and retuned

145

the engines; pits, donkeys, stabilizers, even the Cohen-Albrecht Effect Drives purred when he put them through demonstration runs. Beryl, looking sullenly over my shoulder at Tatha, told me that she'd rewired some of the engine controls and transposed some others to simplify operations, and where did the cat and kitten come from. Tatha smiled at her, said nothing, and disappeared into the cabin I'd given her. Sandro, wildly curious, restrained his questions and got us through the grab and into tau.

I didn't know where Tatha found the bright length of cloth she appeared in the next day. She twisted it about her body to form a sling for Daren, the child, and from that day forward she moved about my ship, amid my crew, fixing things. Under her ministrations the projector in the crewroom glowed for the first time in years; Greaves' tooldrone coughed to life again; the irritating whine in the tauband receiver disappeared. Paying her passage in competence. Greaves spent a morning watching her work and listening to the ceaseless murmur of her voice; I could hear them laughing together as I passed the pits and wondered, suddenly, if she carried webscars beneath her sleek fur. Sandro, attempting to impress her with his knowledge, found himself the object of such gentle derision that, for once, he minded it not at all. Beryl she treated with a profound courtesy tinged with irony, and for the first time I saw Beryl flounder. And, because I am a slow man, a stupid man, the first to admit personal catastrophe and the last to perceive it, I finally saw the ways in which my crew had changed over the past three years, while I was so involved in my own self-made miseries that I did not see.

My crew was running like a well-oiled machine, all the cogs and gears functioning together, all the linkages smooth, all the flip-flops flipping and flopping in tune and in time. Or so it seemed to me. Beryl, from the control room, called the bridge with some minor complaint and said vicious things to Sandro about Sandro. Sandro grinned and said vicious things back, and Beryl laughed and closed the connection. When had that change happened? Greaves and Beryl locked themselves into the crewroom during one shift and emerged after hours, smiling sleepily; later Sandro and Beryl tried the same trick, but Greaves wanted to watch the projector and chased them out, and Beryl's muttered imprecations were almost affectionate. I tried to ask Sandro about it but he gestured uncomfortably. "We're friends," is all he said before turning back to his board, and I had to leave it at that. But if a miracle had taken place, it was only a relative miracle; those first days aboard *Rabbit*, Beryl watched with unsmiling discourtesy each time she and I were together, or each time Tatha and I, uncomfortably, shared a corridor, crewroom, control room, bridge. Tatha now treated me with a cool politeness which I could neither fault nor forgive and Beryl, seeing it, relaxed her shoulders and relaxed her animosity. Beryl began to look at me with an expression which I could not read at all. The fifth evening aboard, tense to the point of cracking, I invited Beryl to share my hammock, and couldn't understand why she didn't seem surprised. She took my body and drained it, murmured a few sarcastic endearments, and did not once mention love. I felt as though I'd been cast into the company of strangers, of folk who barely shared my language; cast adrift. The crew no longer congregated on the bridge during moments of rest. Instead I heard them in the crewroom, laughing in counterpoint to the dry lilt of Tatha's voice. She knew the lyrics to more bawdy songs than I knew existed, but she sang none of them for me.

I didn't know the extent of my own anger until the day I found them in the gym. I'd come to silence the voices in my head with exhaustion, but as I approached I heard voices and cautiously peered through the hatch. Tatha, silvery-naked, her hair a cloud around her, danced in free-fall. She seemed barely to touch the bars and rungs, and her body spun and stretched like an acrobat's, perfectly in tune. She no longer favored her wounded shoulder. I watched, stupefied, not understanding the source of the music to which she danced. Then something at the far end of the gym caught my eye. Beryl straddled one of the bars, ankle locked around knee, and held Daren loosely in her arms. The baby's hands were lost in her hair. She untangled her fingers gently, but her eyes were on Tatha and both women were singing. I'd never heard Beryl sing before. I'd never seen her so calmly satisfied.

Neither of them saw me and I slunk back to my own quarters, through the passageways of my own ship, consumed with fury and a blind, envious rage. After that I spent more and more time in the bubble, but the tran-

scendence of tau filled with silver fur and a cutting edge
of laughter. The woman infested my ship, seduced my
crew, stole my peace. Even sitting in the bridge, deep in
work, the quiet sound of her footsteps would cut through
everything else and set my teeth together.

When I first thought of offering her Aerie, I planned
to put her on one of my other ships while I went about my
own business. Reaching MarketPort, I found myself rearranging cargo schedules; *Rabbit* could well afford to sweep
through West Wing and by Eagle System, it wasn't out of
the way. Sandro could take Tatha and her son to Havensport, I need not go myself. But when I propped *Rabbit* out
of tau and saw the sweet blue and green planet, I knew
that I was going down, and knew that, somehow, I had
always planned this.

Greaves gave Tatha a tiny mechanical toy he had
made for Daren. Beryl formally presented her with the
bright cloth: neither ownership nor gifts were things I
would have expected of her. And Sandro grinned at me
as we boarded the shuttle, as though he carried a great
secret. By the time I realized that I didn't want to go we
were passing above the southern pole; by the time I accepted my dread we were almost home.

Sandro slapped the engines down and released the
locks. The hatch swung out and down, and all my family
stood around the ship, waiting. I hadn't told them I was
coming, hadn't known myself until six hours before,
sliding through the grab. Beside me, Sandro grinned and
Tatha's expression of calm interest didn't waver. I felt so
many things that I felt nothing at all, and stepped uncertainly onto the pad.

"We decided against a marching band," Quilla said,
and kissed me. It was as simple as that. They made it
casually and lovingly obvious that they were glad to see
me, that they had always expected my return. Hetch, on
crutches, asked endless questions about the ship, and
Meya held a strange child out to me; a two-year-old
memory of herself. We trailed out along the path to the
Tor, and I let them walk farther and farther ahead.

Tatha, too, lagged, looking with speculation at the
world around her. When she fell into step beside me I
waited for questions about the place I had brought her,
but she remained silent, walking with an easy, loose-

limbed gait. I expected her to start loping across the
greenlands, looking for prey.

"I told them," she said unexpectedly.

I looked at her, and she shrugged. "It was fairly obvious," she said. "I had Sandro com them a few days out
of MarketPort."

Then Meya came back to us, put her hand in my
pocket as though she'd never taken it out, and talked
across me to Tatha about children and ages and how
Theresans grew. I put my hands behind my back and
scowled at the meadow.

During dinner Hart stared impolitely at Tatha. If it
bothered her she didn't show it. She fit easily into the
conversation, rarely at a loss for topic or expression,
totally charming. I answered Hetch's questions curtly,
listening to the rise and fall of Tatha's voice as though, if
I listened carefully enough, I'd find a way into her soul.

She discussed agriculture with Mish, politics with Quilla,
economics with Ozchan and, with Tabor, talked about
music.

"Jes plays," Tabor said. "Quite well, too. I taught him."
He laughed. "Hasn't he played for you?"

"No," Tatha said, looking down the table at me. "I
didn't know."

"I had better things to do," I muttered, and turned to
Ozchan. An awkward gap in the conversation disappeared
behind Mish's call for dessert.

After dinner, sitting on the broad porch in the cooling
heat, Tatha told them about Parallax and Gensco. She sat
relaxed against a pillar of the porch, cradling a glass of
brandy; Alin and Daren slept together between her knees.
The story was told without witticisms and the amber lights
from the living room window gilded her silver hair. I
stopped listening to the sense of her words, lost in the
music of her voice, in the shifting inflections. She said
something and my family laughed; the words became real
again. She didn't tell them about her child, herself, the
Parallax agent—leaving that to me, I supposed, to color
any way that I wished. My palms tingled. Spider, sitting
on the floor near me, looked up quickly. I made my face
blank and stared at the dark halaea in the yard.

Then: "Captain?" Tatha said. "Do you have anything
to add?"

I looked at the baby and shook my head. Later, when

she wasn't around, I'd tell Mish and Quilla. But not with Tatha's eyes on me, not in the presence of her son.

Tatha put her glass down and carefully separated her son from my niece. "Can someone show me my room? It's been a long day."

Spider stood and walked to the door. As Tatha followed him she smiled at us and said to Hart, lightly, "No, you can't dissect me. Goodnight."

Hart laughed, startled, and Tatha left the room. The family looked expectantly at me and I spread my hands.

"Another of Jes' strays," Meya said, smiling. "Am I right?"

"Sure," I said, accepting the evasion, grateful that Spider wasn't there.

Mish moved her shoulders. Ozchan went behind her and began massaging her neck. Her head drooped forward. "Quilla?" she said indistinctly.

Quilla glanced into the house before turning to face me.

"We got a com from Parallax," she said. "We tried to reach you, but you'd just gone into Priory and I couldn't trust a safebeam there. And after, we thought it would be simpler to wait until you came home."

I made a noncommittal sound. Sandro had already left with Hetch. "What did they want?"

"Standard buy-out offer. Estimated Althing Green price for Aerie, shipping line, processing plant, the whole works. Plus a sweetener for us, personally; a few million fremarks on the side. They obviously hadn't done their homework. I told them that we didn't own Aerie-Kennerin, and that even if we did, their offer would be unacceptable." She shrugged. "We haven't received a reply, so either they've taken their burned fingers and gone home, which isn't too likely, or they're planning something else."

"Like what?"

"We'll have to wait and see," Mish said, her voice muffled. Ozchan's fingers moved over her shoulders, and she grunted a bit. "They've a limited number of options as I see it—"

"We all think that," Meya said. "But we've each got a different opinion of what those options are."

"Have you taken it to Meeting?"

"No." Quilla stood and reached inside the window for the brandy bottle. "It was an offer to the family, not the shareholders. I didn't see a need to."

"You're probably right," I muttered, suddenly eager to get away from them all. "After all, we're not big, not Priory or Gensco or even Marquez Landing. They'll leave us alone."

"Simplistic nonsense," Hart said. I looked at him, surprised by his anger, but he went inside and closed the door behind him. I grabbed the opportunity and stood myself.

"Going to take a walk," I said. "It's still midafternoon, ship's time." And walked away before they had a chance to protest.

The barn glowed dimly. Someone had left a broken sap-barrel leaning against one of the walls, and I hit my leg against it and stood in the shadows, cursing and nursing my shin. The air smelled right, the sounds of the night were familiar, all the darknesses against the moonlight held the outlines of my home. But a thick anger rose in me, an anger at loving this place, an anger at my family, an anger most of all at the silver Theresan who so easily, so knowledgeably, guessed at my mind and knew my desires before I knew them myself. While I did not, could not, know her at all.

When Ozchan touched me on the shoulder I jumped, hitting my shin again and cursing.

"You feel like a spring," he said. "Come one." He turned and walked up the hill toward the stand of trees that held the hot tub. After a moment, I followed.

He flipped the cover from the tub and glanced at me.

"I'm not going to undress you, captain," he said, and took his clothes off. Steam rose, pale in the light of the moons. My fingers felt stiff against the fabric of my suit. The water was so hot that I gasped as I stepped into it.

The trees rustled overhead and sprinkled cool droplets of condensed steam against my skin. A few nightbirds called. I leaned back, letting the heat lick along my body, but could not relax. Everything I looked at was a question.

"Spider caught a shaggy," Ozchan said conversationally.

"What?"

"A pup, really. He and Hart had gone north, walking, and came back with this ugly pup. Hart had killed the mother, he's got some strange story about being attacked. When they turned her over, they found the pup in her pouch, and Spider begged until Hart brought him home."

"What's Spider want a shaggy for? They're vicious."

"He says it's a pet. It doesn't seem very wild; it's about a year old now, half grown. Hasn't bit anyone yet. The kids have made it part of that club of theirs; they sit in their shack telling each other dark secrets, and yelling shaggy-shouts for some reason."

"Shouts?" I said, mostly to keep Ozchan talking, to keep my own thoughts busy.

Ozchan tipped his head back and yelled "AAAAAAA —ROOOOOO!" and I almost leaped out of the tub. He doubled with laughter.

"You *are* tense," he said, and, taking my shoulder, turned me around. His fingers dug into my back, hard but good.

"Come on, loosen up." He shook me.

I let my head fall forward. "Why are you still here?" I said to the water. "Last time I was home, you were ready to leave Meya, move to Hoku, get off planet. I didn't think anything could stop you." I paused. "Alin?"

Ozchan didn't say anything. I turned to look at him, but he pushed me around again.

"Quilla," he said finally. "And Hart, to a certain extent. Have you looked at her?"

I didn't have to ask who he meant. "She's all Meya's, isn't she?"

"Hart tailored her. It should have been easier for me, knowing she was Meya's, that she wasn't the daughter of some other man. It wasn't, though. After Alin came, I wasn't entirely sane." His fingers didn't falter. "Quilla got tired of it, I guess. She dragged me out of Haven as soon as her fields were in and spent two weeks marching me up and down the island."

I thought about that. "And?"

Ozchan laughed again, and his fingers moved farther down my back. "She didn't say a word to me the entire time. She walked, and cooked, and slept at the far side of the fire, and ignored everything I said. So eventually I learned to shut up and listen to myself. And when we got home, she dropped her pack, put her hands on her hips, and said, 'Now will you behave yourself?' I didn't really have a choice."

I moved away from him, feeling jealous. His hands slipped off my back. "What did you learn?" I muttered.

"That sometimes the love we're given is better than the love we think we want."

"Table scraps."

"No," Ozchan said. He took a handful of my hair, pulled my head back, and kissed me.

I'd remembered the clean precision of his body, but I'd forgotten the tiny details, the sweetness, the way he concentrated so entirely that the rest of the world was superfluous. All the voices in my head went away.

I fell asleep against his shoulder, and eventually he woke me, got me out of the tub, and handed me a towel before he snapped the cover over the tub again. I dried one arm, decided not to finish, and tied the towel around my waist. I put my dirty suit over my shoulder. We didn't touch as we walked back to the Tor. The house was dark and still. I looked at the window of the room they'd given Tatha and Ozchan followed my glance.

"When you feel ready," he said, and did not ask again. I nodded, tired and grateful, and when I crawled into the hammock in my room I fell instantly asleep.

I woke late. Tatha had already left, with Quilla, to find a place to live in Haven. Mim, handing me breakfast, made disparaging comments about Theresans. I lectured her on the virtues of tolerance and the definition of humanity. She banged pots together in the sink and ignored me, so I took my tea into the office.

The office window faced the vegetable garden. Meya sat in the sunlight, weeding; nearby, Alin and Daren played with their respective toys: Alin with a battered doll, Daren with his toes. Mish, watching me watch them, came around the desk and pulled the curtains closed.

"Pay attention," she said. "I don't imagine that you're going to be here long, and there are things to talk about."

I put my hands in my pockets. "So talk."

She frowned up at me and sat behind the desk. "Now that we know about Gensco and how Parallax operated there, we can expect them to try us again. And this time, they'll have done some research. I've accumulated some background on them." She tapped a pile of tapes and papers. "I want you to read it."

"Why? You and Quilla take care of that end of things. I just run ships."

"Don't be foolish. There are three parts to Aerie-

Kennerin. We can keep a close watch on Processing and a fairly close watch on the planet. But the shipping line's the most vulnerable part of the operation."

"The hell it is," I said, offended.

"Shut up and listen. There are twenty-seven ships on the line—"

"Thirty-four, counting sloops. One-fifteen, counting sloops and shuttles."

"I'm not counting them, they keep to the ships. We have twenty-seven separate merchant ships, twenty-seven separate crews, and twenty-seven separate runs. We simply can't monitor each and every one of them. How trustworthy are your captains?"

"They're as dependable as Hetch and I could find."

Mish grimaced. "I trust you. I trust Hetch. I don't know how much I trust the others, or how much we should trust the others."

"They're safe."

"Balls. Listen, here's what we've found out so far. Parallax began as a shipping concern, a one-person operation out of Barian Sector. It bought a few manufacturing concerns, expanded the shipping lines, took control of some planets. Grew pretty fast, considering. By the time its founder died, it controlled shipping in Barian and neighboring sectors, owned a system of agricultural planets, a handful of general manufacturing and processing plants, some die-making businesses, and some other odds and ends. It also put together a private communications net, which worked as well as the Federation net and cost less to enter and less to use. They kept the comsystem intrasector strictly, and stayed within GalFed regulations."

"Sweet Mother, Mish, what do I care?"

"You'd better care," she said angrily. "Knowledge is a weapon, Jes. If you don't use it, someone else will. Against you."

I took my hands out of my pockets and sat down, prepared to be bored. But my mother glared at me until I looked like I was listening carefully, and after a while, I was.

Parallax Corporation, duly chartered by Althing Green, remained a Barian Sector corporation at about the level it had reached when its founder died. Parallax Combine, though, was something else again. Run by its board of directors in tandem with the corporation, it collected monopolies, and if they didn't exist, Parallax created them. The monopolies could be relatively innocuous, such as control of all shipping within a certain sector, or could be complete: control of all maraeasilk production was an example here. They were trying to make control of all *Zimania* and Z-line production another. They acquired diversified systems, built and maintained their own multi-purpose, open-entry processing plants, maintained a private grabstation network and a private communications net, which they managed to keep, as far as could be told, just within GalFed law. That is to say, they never went into direct competition with the Federation's monopoly on intersector tau or communications, but they were getting uncomfortably close. Parallax maintained its own policing agency to assure that its own company laws were kept. The more Mish talked, the more Parallax appeared as a totalitarian quasigovernment, and the "quasi" was only a relative term. Within another one or two centuries, it was estimated that the range of Parallax influence and interest would exceed that of the Federation itself.

There were some signs that Althing Green was beginning to worry about Parallax, but, so far, the worry was diffuse and ineffectual. There were currently 478 members in the Federation; the number of Parallax-controlled or owned worlds was 321 and growing. A goodly number of Parallax worlds were not Federation members: they dealt only with other Parallax worlds, used only Parallax grabstations and comnets, and paid fees only to Parallax. Parallax claimed that it exercised no control whatsoever over its own memberworlds, despite the fact that some of those members had been members of the Federation but had dropped out. And for each dropout, or each new world that came under Parallax control, the Federation lost revenues. So the Federation was beginning to worry but would, more than likely, only act once Parallax made a definite move toward secession—in other words, until it was already too late.

I reached over Mish's shoulder, secured the teapot, and filled my cup while Mish watched me, waiting for some reaction. I cradled the cup between my palms and looked at her through the steam.

"Who's behind it? Who runs Parallax?"

"No one," she said. "It's so damned large that it doesn't need a controller. It's board seems to be along for the ride, and they never know the details anyway. Hell, Jes, it's so big that it runs on growth, because if it doesn't keep growing, if it loses its own momentum, it'll fall apart. It eats the way any predator eats, to keep alive. If you want to stretch the point, it's not even malign, no more than a nova is malign—it just is. So we're not going to save the universe by subverting the evil genius behind Parallax Combine, because there isn't one."

"It begins to look like we won't even be able to save ourselves," I muttered. "Lord, Mish, I didn't sign on to fight fate."

"It's not fate," she said fiercely. "We'll do it. I'm frankly damned if I know how, but we'll do it. Are you going to read this stuff?"

I took a box from the floor and filled it with tapes and papers. "You want me to do it all before I leave?"

"Nope," she said, and smiled. "Those are copies for you."

"Sure of yourself, aren't you?" I said, but smiled back.

She opened the top of the teapot and looked inside, then poured the last of the tea into her cup. I'd never understood how she could drink the harsh stuff at the bottom, but it never seemed to bother her at all. She claimed she was tanning herself from the inside and would therefore live forever.

"Okay," she said, putting her feet on the desk. "Now tell me about Tatha."

"She's just another stray," I said, looking at the stuff I put into the box. "A Theresan I found on Gensco. I'm always bringing people home, Mish."

"True. But generally you like them. I want to know why you don't like her, and why, not liking her, you brought her home. I think I've a right to know that."

I fiddled with the stuff in the box. "It's not that I dislike her," I said slowly, and caught Mish's raised eyebrows. "Or not primarily," I amended. "It's that I don't trust her."

Mish kept her eyebrows up and tilted her head to one side. I sighed and picked up my teacup.

Mish waited patiently as I tried to find a suitable beginning to the story. Finally I simply told her what had happened, trying to be fair. Trying not to color things, and by not coloring them, keeping my temper. When I finished Mish opened the curtains again and looked outside for a while, then came back and sat. My tea was cold.

"Could you kill someone?" she said finally.

"I didn't. I don't know."

"I have."

I remembered the incident, years ago, during New-Home's attempted takeover of Aerie. Hetch's ship, with Mish and myself aboard, had been captured and in effecting our escape, Mish had pushed two NewHome soldiers into the cargo hold and decompressed it, and them. My nonviolent mother, with strict ideas about the sanctity of life, had paid for those deaths with endless remorse.

"That was different," I said. "You had to, or we'd have been killed. But Tatha did it coldly, because she wanted to."

"Because she had to," Mish said, and turned toward me again. "Because it was necessary, and she did what was necessary. If there's a difference, it's one of quality and not of kind. But I couldn't do it now. I couldn't even order someone else to do it. Quilla might, but she'd hesitate. Meya wouldn't." She paused. "I don't know about Hart. I wouldn't want to give him a chance. We need Tatha, Jessie. Theresans are predators, and we may find a predator useful."

"Sweet Mother! That's like keeping a slagbomb because it might come in handy someday."

"No. Not quite. I don't think she's vicious, Jes. I think she's intelligent, and practical, and tough, and I think we can use her. If we help her, she might feel obligated to help us."

"I'm sorry I brought her home," I said, standing. "If I'd known this—"

"That's irrelevant. You did bring her home, and she'll be needed here." Mish frowned at me. "Why did you bring her home, Jessie?"

"I didn't know any better," I said sharply. "And there's the kid. I couldn't leave her on MarketPort, with the kid."

Mish raised her eyebrows again, infuriatingly. I picked up the box and walked out of the room.

The tapes and papers fit neatly into my small pack. I wouldn't be here long enough to read any of them; I'd be gone, I hoped, by nightfall. Tabor's small workroom was empty. I sat at his desk and got a line through to Hetch's house, where Sandro habitually stayed when on planet, and curtly told Sandro to meet me at the port at the end of jev'al, just before sundown. He wasn't happy about it, but he didn't argue.

Meya had finished gardening and sat under the halaea, playing with the two children. I watched them from the window of Tabor's office. After a while I went outside and sat with them, chattering aimlessly with Meya and watching Daren. Eventually she looked at me and put Daren in my arms. Involuntarily, I thought about Beryl in the gym.

I hadn't held him before. He was tiny, no more than six months old, and his hands floated between his mouth and my face. He grabbed my nose and pulled it, drooling. Meya's children had been larger at his age. He grinned and gurgled and twisted his head to peer around him, eagerly drinking in the world. He wet on my shirt. Meya wanted to change him but I still remembered how, and when I had him freshly diapered he grabbed my finger, stuck it in his mouth, and gummed it fiercely. His claws were soft, and his eyes looked the way Tatha's did when she laughed. He made me feel helpless.

"I told Tatha I'd take him down to her before lunch," Meya said. "I should be going."

"I'll take him," I said. "I want to look into the village anyway."

Meya said something grateful about time to do some of the bookkeeping before the meal. She picked Alin off the grass, wiped the dirt from her cheeks, and took her inside, leaving me with the baby and a pack of clothing. I slung the pack over my shoulder, cradled the child in my arms, and walked down the hill toward Haven.

The last airflowers of the season poked through the grass of the hillside and the air was heavy with late autumn warmth. Soon winter and the unending rains would take over the island, but I could not smell them in the breeze. The baby turned his head toward my chest and fell asleep. I opened my shirt and pulled it over him to cover his eyes from the sunlight.

Haven hadn't grown much in the two years since I left. Most of the newer people were settling in Hoku, and my family had worked to keep Haven small. A couple of flitters scooted along the dirt track around the town; a dray drew a fishcart along the road from the shore. The kasirene section was freshly painted; someone had imported the new liquid crystal paints, and sections of The Jumble glowed and shifted colors and danced about, betraying vision. The kites danced overhead and windmills turned slowly, their gaudy vanes spread flat against the sky.

Ved Hirem, ancient irascible lawyer and Haven's only judge, sat on the porch of Kohl's Beerhall, haranguing the passersby. He thumped with his cane's end on the wooden floor and leaned forward, lost in the ferocity of his argument. I skirted the building and entered through the kitchen door, surprising Mertika at the stoves. She whooped, put down her ladle, and kissed me. The kitchen was hot and smelled of baking meat. Mertika was still curved, plump, and did wicked things with her tongue and teeth.

"I don't want Ved to know I'm here," I said when she let me have my mouth again.

Mertika rolled her eyes and reached into the cooler. "He's lecturing on Theresan law," she said, pouring me a glass of juice. "Been at it all morning."

"Is he right?"

She gestured. "Ask your furry friend. She's rented Avatar's house. Quilla went surety for her."

I didn't have to ask how she knew. Kohl's functioned, always, as Haven's instant and unimpeachable switchboard. Daren woke up and whimpered. Mertika plucked him from my arms and put him against her shoulder. He quieted and I finished my juice.

"Chiba's due back in the spring," she said.

"Where'd he go?" I said, surprised, and she looked at me oddly.

"You don't keep in touch, do you?" she murmured. "Remember that hot-air balloon he was building? Well, he filled it up one bright morning and took off. Said he was going to circumnavigate Aerie at the equator."

"Sweet Mother."

"We haven't heard from him since, but the kasirene say he's been sighted here and there among the islands." She sniffed. "It took almost all our spare solar sheeting to build that damned balloon—I still can't figure out how Quilla talked us all into it."

"She's persuasive," I said, taking Daren and standing up.

"Are you going to keep a closer watch on *these* strays?" she said, and grinned. Without waiting for my answer, she pushed through the doors to the common room, her hips swinging. Ved yelled something about the quality of the service and I went out the back door.

Avatar's house was on the edge of Haven nearest the landing field. I remembered helping build it, back when we were all busy reinventing carpentry and architecture. The boards on the step still creaked but the knot in the wood by the doorknob had been planed smooth. When no one answered my knock, I opened the door and went in.

The rooms were empty save for Tatha's pack resting against a wall in the front room. The windows were opened, but the house still smelled musty and closed-up; stains decorated the walls and floors, and paint blistered and peeled. Daren started to whimper again, hungry. I put my finger in his mouth and he quieted. The windows were filthy. I went back onto the porch and sat on the steps.

Tatha, Quilla and a handful of townspeople came down the street, followed by a dray and a cart loaded with furniture. Tatha walked with her hand on the side of the cart, her face turned up to talk with someone seated atop a crazy pile of chairs. Quilla said something and Tatha laughed. Daren started crying lustily. Tatha saw us, sprinted down the street, took Daren, and opened her shirt. The baby homed in on her nipple and sucked hungrily. I went down the steps to help with the furniture.

The beds and tables and chairs were as depressing as the house. Quilla talked about paint and someone came from the market with a basket of food and a small keg of beer—the standard Aerite housewarming presents. Tatha put the baby on the bed and poured the beer, still supervising the placement of things.

"That, I think," she said appraisingly, "should go in a very dark place. A cesspool, preferably. Barring that, in the back room, against the far wall." She thrust a glass of beer into the kasir's hand. "Could you arrange to sit on it, maybe? Hard?"

The kasir laughed and took the glass. Quilla started explaining the fairshare system: when Tatha had been on Aerie for three years, and if she wanted it and decided to stay, she'd be issued her one voting share in Aerie-Kennerin. And she could, if she wished, buy any number of common shares; they'd provide her with dividends from total Aerie-Kennerin profits during the year, but would not increase her vote from the original one. And Daren, were he still here at age sixteen, would be issued his one voting share, too. Tatha listened and I wanted to tell my sister to shut up, not to make this predator any more welcome than she was. But Tatha moved among the folk of the room, offering beer, her voice light and constant and, always, attended by laughter. Tomorrow, the people said, they would come and help wash the walls; the kasirene had already agreed to paint the house, inside and out, in return for a certain number of repair jobs. Here, as on my ship, she would pay her way with her skills. I leaned against a wall in a corner, out of the way, watching her and hearing her. Somebody said something about the fields, somebody else said something about lunch, and people trailed out of the house. I looked up into the silence. Tatha stood against the far wall, holding an empty glass. Watching me.

I had prepared speeches in my head, telling her to leave Aerie, telling her that I didn't trust her, telling her to leave my family alone. But I looked at her and it seemed that my heart stopped then started again, beating to a different rhythm.

Tatha watched me with her wide, clear, cool eyes, endlessly patient, and I could not read her at all.

I put the beer down and walked out of the house, through Haven, and up the hill to the cemetery. When I reached my father's grave I sat carefully and put my arms around my knees. My ears seemed cottoned shut with air.

Untrustworthy, yes. Devious, manipulative, predatory, selfish—I clung to the words, trying to make of them an impermeable barrier. But something in my chest spoke a terrible, alien language, and I put my head on my knees and wept.

Part
Three

CROSSROADS
1245 new time

"Every body continues in its state of rest, or of uniform motion in a right line, unless it is compelled to change that state by forces impressed upon it."

—Sir Isaac Newton
Philosophiae Naturalis Principia Mathematica

THE ENTIRE POPULATION OF HAVEN SCHOOL, plus some dragooned adults, straggled over the foothills north of Haven. The day was fair and clear, and behind them Palen could see the light smudge of pale smoke over Haven Valley. Squinting, she made out the gaudy vanes of the windmills standing on the brows of the hills —they were almost invisible with distance. Palen looked east again, counting heads.

Headmaster Simit sat on a plodding dray, leaning down to talk to the children who surrounded the animal. Most of them were paying him only the scantest attention; they preferred to make sudden forays off to the side, yell at each other, sing, fight, and come running to the adults with an endless stream of questions, comments, complaints, and observations. Palen shook her head—the children had been up late the night before, too excited by the campfire and the stars to sleep, and she thought grumpily about the energy they expended. By afternoon, with any luck, they woud have worn themselves down and would crowd docilely atop the drays.

Paen and Palenka, children of one of Palen's own womb-children, grabbed one hand on either side of her and made bitter complaints about each other. Palen clouted them both with her upper arms and sent them running toward a crowd of children. Andrus, intent on proving his maturity, insisted on walking with the adults. Even for a terran he was tiny; his legs scurried to keep up, but when Palen offered him a ride in her pouch he refused indignantly. The drays plodded on, their six legs moving in strange counterpoint, and they managed to cover the ground efficiently, if not gracefully. Hart had complained that he could provide far more suitable riding animals, and tried to convince his family to let him reconstruct Aerie's beasts of burden. Meya had refused on

165

fiscal grounds, Mish on emotional ones: she and Jason had not had the capital to hire the expensive Enchanter Labs, and made do with one of the tinkerlabs that meandered through the backwash systems of the Federation. The awkward beasts were part of Mish's history, and she would not allow them to be changed.

But the cattle-rangers of Cault Eiret's foothills were receptive to the idea. The drays were almost useless to them, moving far too slow to cover the rolling kilometers of grazing lands, or to help herd the droves of cattle. The rangers hired Hart to produce running drays and provided financial backing, and now the school-age population of Haven journeyed north to see the results of Hart's obvious talents.

Hart's obvious talents. Palen buried her lower hands in her pouch, uneasy. The kasirene had learned of Hart's talents far earlier than had the human population of Aerie, and learned to their grief. An unwilled memory of dead pups flashed through her mind. Sometimes she dreamed of the pup she herself had lost to Hart's youthful laboratory, and in the dreams she hunted through labyrinths of unseen dangers, trying to remember the name of her child. She shook her head quickly, imitating the terran gesture, and looked out at the children again.

Decca, walking beside Keleh, leaned toward him and poked his upper shoulder. Telling him, undoubtedly, the tale of his problems with her family, telling him that despite her extensive and expensive education, her family would not give her a definite job, that she was dying of boredom. Palen had heard the story before and, despite her sympathy for Decca's plight, did not want to hear the story again. Beyond Decca, Jared sat astride a dray with tired children of both species clinging to him. He was singing a song in Kasiri to them. A few of them giggled when he came to the chorus. Palen found Simit, striding along at the head of the group, pointing with his stick and lecturing; Kerelet and Taraean walked hand in hand, and Palen noted, from the flatness of Kerelet's pouch and the small bulge in Taraean's, that they had finally exchanged the pup. The two of them and Simit made up the entirety of the school's teaching staff, with occasional help, as now, from other adults in Haven. Palen wiped a few noses and made Jason Hart stop riding a dray's trail. The dray hadn't noticed yet, but when it did, it would kick. Drays kicked hard. Sullenly, Jason Hart released the coarse tailhairs and went in search of Spider. Palen slid into thought again.

In the years since the discovery of Hart's laboratory and his subsequent banishment from Aerie, the knowledge of his experiments had not died, despite Palen's intercessions. When Hart returned permanently to Aerie feelings in the kasirene community had steadily increased, steadily darkened. Palen found herself uneasily balanced between her love for her own people and her love for the Kennerins, particularly Quilla, excluding Hart. The Kennerins shared a sense of community as strong as that of the kasirene, although the Kennerin sense was bounded by their family ties, while the kasirene, if they thought in terms of family at all, thought in terms of the entire planet. To damage Hart, to allow Hart to be damaged, would be to damage all Kennerins. And Hart, according to a growing number of kasirene, should be damaged.

A good-natured commotion broke out ahead. Spider, with Belshazar the shaggy beside him, led a group of kasirene pups and terran children in an ear-splitting rendition of his club's theme song. The young ones tilted their heads back and capered about the grasses, yelling the two-toned shaggy howl. Belshazar, excited beyond control, capered with them, leaping into the air with all six hairy legs extended, and added his discordant yowl to the noise. His predator's teeth flashed in the sunlight. Belshazar had the unfortunate habit of sneaking into the Tor's kitchens and eating the family dinner. Tabor, surveying the ruins of that first shaggy-consumed meal, had given the creature its name: "Not our dinner anymore," he had said sourly. "It's obviously Belshazar's feast, after the advent of the finger." The reference was arcane and its explanation quickly forgotten, but the name stuck.

Palen suspected that Belshazar the shaggy was on his way out of Kennerin affections and the Kennerin house. Too many feasts had been consumed in the kitchen, too many nights disrupted by Belshazar wanting either in or out, and howling about it. Jes' latest stray, the Theresan, had expressed willingness to take Belshazar and the shaggy seemed to like her. One displaced predator getting along with another, Palen thought. Under Simit's anguished pleas, the howling died down. Jared and Decca, walking side by side now, laughed.

Strange what these albiana bring us, Palen thought. Kasirene do not give multiple birth, yet here are Quilla's children, identical and separate. Double-creatures. They deal with conception and gestation and birth as one continuous process, entirely unshared save for that brief spasm of the male at the beginning. Strange, and sad. Simpler, and warmer, to make children the kasirene way; conception followed by shared gestation, passing pups from male to female, from lover to friend to stranger, making ties of kinship with an entire tribe, an entire island. How many womb-siblings do I have? Palen thought. How many pouch-siblings? As many as there are on To'an Cault—how could I think of owning any of them? How could they think of owning me? Yet terran children *belong* to someone, are someone's children; specific ownership. And when the ties are that tight, how to deal with one member without affecting all?

Yet the terran family was not all that strange to Palen. She loved Quilla and, provided always that Quilla could love anyone, Palen was convinced that Quilla returned that love. For almost three decades she and Quilla had shared their lives, borne each other's sorrows, created each other's laughter. Had wandered the island together in silence or speech, had passed their children back and forth. Had fought, reconciled, fought again, had held and cherished each other's souls. Uncomfortably, Palen felt the ownership of that close a friendship, and remained caught between the pulls of her nature and the snares of her experiences. She could no more repudiate one than she could repudiate the other.

The problem was without solution, Palen told herself, and looked about again at the children and pups. The group of singers had expanded and Jared accompanied them on his flute. Andrus was asleep amid the bundles of supplies on a dray's broad back, with his shirt pulled over his head. Paen and Palenka, having temporarily solved their differences, were trying to ride on Belshazar's back. He growled at them and loped away, floppy ears bouncing. Jason Hart walked beside Simit, listening to the headmaster.

Spider now rode alone, behind the rest, intent on something in his hands. Feeling queasy, Palen dropped quietly behind to watch, and saw that he was merely plaiting some of the grasses into a complicated structure of struts

and air. His skilled fingers worked to a carefully con-
ceived pattern, but Palen could not make out what he
was shaping. Hart, at his age, would have been vivisect-
ing a lizard. Palen reminded herself sharply that despite
Spider's uncanny resemblance to his father, despite her
own hatred for Hart, the boy was an entirely separate
creature, innocent of his father's sins.

Spider, she thought forcefully, but the boy did not look
up. She had seen him anticipate his family's need, produce the answer before the question was asked, but
whatever it was in him that read his fellow humans, he
did not seem able to read the kasirene. Palen deliberately
moved closer. Spider glanced at her, smiled, and held out
his construction. Palen peered into a maze of cubes within
cubes. Spider touched one of the inner cubes and the
toy turned over on itself, twisting and spinning from a
series of parted grasses, the thickness of thread.

"You can keep it, if you like," Spider said.

Palen touched the cube, watching its complicated motions. "Why don't you come to The Jumble?" she said,
not looking at him.

"My father doesn't want me to." Spider spoke without
apology, and without arrogance.

"Do you know why?"

Spider nodded and set his lips together firmly. Palen
handed back the cubes.

"No, please keep them," he said. "I can make others."

Palen hesitated, not knowing how to refuse him.

"Please," Spider said. "I'm not my father."

Palen put the cubes in her pouch. "I'm not sure I know
what you are," she said, and moved up the line toward
the other children.

SHOSEI CHIBA SIGHTED THE SPIRES OF CAULT
Tereth in midafternoon and nodded, pleased with himself.
He rummaged through the small locker at his feet, produced his log book, and entered the sighting. The gondola
creaked under his feet and the shadow of the sleek-delta-
winged airship floated on the waves below. Fourteen
months earlier he had lifted the airship from Havensport
field, nosed it into the prevailing westerlies, and proceed
to circumnavigate Aerie at the equator in his improbable
ship, navigating by the stars and the undetailed orbital
maps taken so many years ago. Now, with To'an Cault
rising from the sea before him, he shook his head at the
thought that, ignorant as he'd been, he'd even considered
making the trip. His log book, and its companion rutter
and sketch pad, were filled with his carefully detailed
notes and drawings of Aerie's equatorial islands; his gift
to the Kennerins, his most profound pleasure, and the details of a fourteen-month solitude that had finally re-
stored his serenity, his sanity, and his self-confidence.
The trembling, broken geographer that Jes had brought
home seemed an entirely different person, and Chiba
could barely encompass the thought of what he'd once
been.

Federation survey work ate people; he'd known that
before he'd ever signed on. Robot seekers, sent out from
survey bases, established small grabs wherever the para-
meters of their programming were met; the grabs extended lines into tau, lines which the survey ships
followed. Squat, uncomfortable, insulated against almost
everything the universe could throw at them, the survey
ships reached the new grabs and coiled through, never
knowing what they would find on the other side of the
time journey. Chiba had seen the blackness of grab transition give way to novae, to unformed dust, to total empti-

ness, to collisions of worlds. The ship could survive almost everything; but in an infinite universe, "everything" was an infinite concept. Ships disappeared. Ships died. If luck rode with one, the ship could jump into catastrophe and jump immediately out again, to seek another time for entry. Luck, though, was an undependable phenomenon. Until a safe-time was found the ships continued to jump from tau to realspace and back again; only after a safe-time was established could the grabs and coils be refined, their timers set, durators installed. And until then a survey crew lived on the thin edge between the dictates of their jobs, and terror.

Some went quietly crazy; some went loudly crazy. Some killed themselves. Some hid their terror behind apathy, until the apathy was no longer a mask. Some fucked everyone and everything in sight. Some fought. Some drank. Some took drugs.

Chiba took drugs. To calm himself, he'd said originally. To deal with the terror, subvert it, slip around it so that he could continue to do his job. Like his scanners, his magnifiers, his programs, the drugs were a tool of his profession. He claimed. But this tool grew, this tool demanded. Terror slipped around the edges and Chiba increased his dosage; fear sprang up between one moment and the next and Chiba reached for another hypogun. Eventually he left the survey team, kicked out on a barren mining planet where he could barely make enough money to feed and clothe himself, and where his habit rode him like a tenacious, poisonous spider. He took to theft, telling himself always that the proceeds would get him off planet, get him to Solon or Gates where the doctors could cure his habit, make him whole again. But the money went for drugs and the drug demanded more of him, and more again. He grew weaker as the drug grew stronger and, welcoming the prospect of death, nonetheless pushed his disintegrating body to one more theft, one more burglary, one more taste of oblivion. The drug had never given him pleasure, had only promised a surcease of pain; now the pain rode with him all the time.

Jes had found him in the midst of an inept attempt to steal from *Rabbit*'s cargo hold, beat him unconscious, and tied him to a bunk in sickbay, where Chiba awakened two days later. Jes filled him with food and medicines, and gave him just enough of his drug to keep the

pain at bay while Chiba's body struggled to rebuild itself. Then Jes had withdrawn the drug completely. Chiba
had no memory of the following weeks; Hetch told him,
later, that Jes had been with him the entire time, but
no one would tell the geographer what he had been like,
what he had done. Chiba had sufficient knowledge of
his own addiction to make guesses but declined to do so.
When Jes helped him out of the shuttle at Havensport,
Chiba could barely walk and his skin hung in folds
around his bones. But his mind was his own again, and
the fourteen month journey around Aerie had cemented
that possession. It had been three years, now, since Jes
brought him home; when he came to Haven, he'd register,
receive his voting share, tie himself permanently to the
life of this planet. Aerie was, entirely and completely, his
home.

He put the log book back in the locker, nudged the airship into a new heading, and recalculated the time it
would take to reach Tabor's Valley. The shadow of the
airship's nose touched To'an Cault's shoreline and Chiba
angled the vanes. The nose tilted and the ship gained
altitude. He checked the heater, opened it fractionally,
and prepared for the mountains.

By now, riding the air currents seemed as familiar as
walking. He teased and angled the ship through the
Cault's passes, flying by touch as much as by sight, by
the taste and smell of the wind. It was late spring and the
air grew crisper as the ship rose. He boosted the heater's
output and skimmed the highest passes, using the auxiliary engines only at the end, when the crosswinds in
Tabor's Valley prevented him from angling precisely into
the meadow by the house. The house looked deserted
and the corrals were empty. This, too, pleased Chiba.

The three hours to sunset left plenty of time to batten
the airship securely. He closed the heater and, as the dark,
energy-absorbing fabric of the ship settled around its
internal framework, he carefully pleated it for the morning's rising. The skin of his ship was sleek and warm under his hands; he felt a quick affection for the ship, object
of such debate and derision in Haven when he and old
Dene Beletes had finally turned their plans into actuality
and the ship had risen from Havensport. But she had held
together, fulfilled all the expectations they'd had of her,
taken him there and brought him back again. He secured

the fabric, put the spare batteries atop his locker, and took them into the house.

A pile of logs and kindling filled the woodshed, and Chiba found dried vegetables and meat in the pantry. Although Tabor had not lived in the valley for years, the Aerites kept the cabin well stocked and in repair; both species used it as a resting station on trips through Cault Tereth. Chiba lit the woodstove, filled a pan with water from the pump, and started a soup. He found the wooden bathtub and dragged it into the parlor, and, after supper, relaxed into the luxury of the first hot bath he'd taken in over a year.

The next morning, as the airship slowly filled, he took the ax, found an old stump in the woods behind the cabin, and replaced the wood he'd used the night before. Then he walked through the house, unplugged the batteries from the recharger, and made sure that the kitchen was neat and clean, the parlor tidied, all the fires cold. He put his name to the list kept by the main door and hesitated, trying to find words of gratitude. Not finding any of sufficient warmth and brevity, he closed the door behind him and left the valley.

A few kasirene on the savannah waved to him, as casually as kasirene on the distant islands had greeted his arrival. He began to think of Haven, of settling the ship at the port, gathering his things together. He supposed that he could stay at Kohl's the first night and would find a house after that. He thought with pleasure of a quiet meal and a glass of dark wine, of fresh sheets and a real bed. He wondered if Haven would remember him and decided that it didn't matter. The savannah dropped behind him and he spotted the patchwork of Haven's fields in the distance.

People in the fields looked up, threw their tools to the ground, and raced toward the small port. He leaned from the gondola window, baffled, then withdrew hastily when he realized that they were cheering. The gaudy kites and windmills of Haven decorated the sky, first below him, then above as he dropped the ship toward the pad. Dozens of hands reached to steady the gondola. The crowd frightened him. He forced himself to tuck the locker under his arm and slide out. Faces beamed, voices laughed and shouted. A tall kasir scooped him up and settled him on broad, furred shoulders. He was suddenly

grateful that he'd bathed. He was embarrassingly close
to tears. They carried him in triumph into Haven and sat
him down in the best seat at Kohl's. He put his locker
under his feet, blinked at them, and hid his face behind
a glass of wine.

They filled his glass and asked endless questions; filled
his glass again and listened in silent fascination to his
answers. His voice sounded strange to him, but they
nodded and leaned intently forward, and kept his cup
brimming. The Kennerins came to the beerhall and clapped
him on the back. Dene Beletes stumped into the room,
her wooden leg making a loud, staccato noise on the bare
floor, and kissed him. He laughed. Someone gave him
more wine.

The celebration lasted well past sebet'al, but by then
he was alseep, tucked warmly into a bed above the public
room, his locker by his side. Mertika chased the last
celebrants out, turned off the lights, and opened the
door of his room, He burrowed farther under the covers
and mumbled something in his sleep. He looked so ordinary, she thought. So ugly. Rough-cut black hair; ugly,
defenseless face; squat, muscular body—he could have
spent the past five seasons farming rather than exploring,
in solitude, uncharted lands. She rearranged the covers
around his shoulders, touched his forehead, and went
down the hall to the room where Hart waited.

MERTIKA SAT ON THE EDGE OF THE BED, HER
head bent to one side, and ran the comb through her hair.
Watching her, Hart felt an unexpected stab of affection;
not, he thought wryly, for Mertika herself, but for what she
represented to him at moments like these. Warmth, friendship, convenience; the comfort of his body and, save for
her occasional importunate demands for something more
stable, the comfort of his mind. He reached across the

pillows and took a lock of her hair in his fingers, tugging it slightly.

"Don't," she said, and smiled at him. "Let me finish."

He put his arms under his head and contemplated the ceiling. She took pains to please him, always coming to him warm and scented from her bath, always open to his smallest suggestions, studying him for the sake of his pleasure. Her assiduous courtship amused him, when he bothered to think of it at all, nor did he find anything inappropriate in his acceptance of her favors. She had his body, his presence, was the recipient of his monogamous attentions, and if she refused to believe that he was monogamous through convenience rather than love, that was her problem. All his love was already taken, already invested in the person of his son; he had not told her that there might be some love to spare, and refused to hold himself responsible for her own misconceptions.

"What do you think of him?" she said, putting her comb aside and nodding her head at the door.

"Who? Oh, Chiba?" Hart rolled onto his side and gestured. "Hasn't it all been said already? Incredible adventure, astonishing success, immense courage, racka-racka-racka. He seems a nice enough man, although why anyone would want to go puffing about in that balloon is beyond me."

"You've no sense of adventure," Mertika said. She stood and crossed the room to rummage about on the dresser. Hart watched her bottom appreciatively.

"You've put on some weight," he said, and her back stiffened.

"I thought you didn't like skinny women."

"I don't. Don't be prickly, Tika."

She gestured without turning around. "You always find something like that to say to me."

Hart rolled his eyes and got off the bed. He didn't want to walk all the way back to the Tor tonight. He stood behind her and put his hands over her hips, pressing her back against him.

"You're being foolish," he said into her ear. Her plump body remained stiff under his hands. He sighed inwardly; he would either have to cajole her into a better humor or leave, and neither prospect pleased him. Neither did the prospect of an argument, though, and he put his lips to her ear again.

"No." She twisted away from him. "I want to talk with you," she said, and put on her robe. Hart sat on the stool before the dresser and put his hands between his thighs.

"It's almost dawn," he said without much hope, but she dismissed that with a gesture and sat at the foot of the bed, her expression determined. "Well, what is it this time?"

"I think it's time you moved down here," she said. "Permanently." He shook his head, but she continued before he could speak. "Hart, listen, it makes sense. There's room for your lab here, I could build another room onto the inn. You'd have your privacy, and it would be more convenient, too—you do most of your business with people in the town anyway, and your supplies come from Haven. You already spend as many nights here as you do at the Tor, wouldn't it make sense to move in formally? No, please, let me finish." She took a deep breath and clasped her hands in her lap. "I'm not asking you to marry me," she said carefully. "I know that you don't want to. I can live with that. It's—it's a practical arrangement, that's all."

"But it's not," Hart said patiently. "What about Spider? I want him to grow up at the Tor, not here in Haven. Besides, there's no room for him here."

"He could stay at the Tor," Mertika said, and Hart jumped to his feet.

"While I live here? That's totally absurd."

"Hart, he's not going to stay a child forever," Mertika said desperately. "He'll leave someday, you know that— you can't tie your whole life to him."

"I don't want to hear another word about it," Hart shouted. Mertika made quick, shushing motions with her hands and Hart stalked toward the windows. He turned and put his hands against the sill behind him. "That subject is not open to discussion," he said clearly. "Not now and not ever, not by you and not by anyone else. I thought you understood that."

"But it's not natural," she said, pleading. "Hart, you must understand that. It can't be good for Spider, to have you this dependent on him."

"I'm not."

"Then prove it! You'll feel different if you have other children, if you—"

"That's what you want?" Hart said savagely. "Squalling brats? That's your recipe for happiness? Go ahead and have them, have millions of them. But they won't be mine, lady. I'm not here to provide you with a clutch of offspring."

"But I want to have your children," she said, her eyes bright with tears.

"That's understandable. I, however, do not want to be the father of *your* children." He grinned suddenly. "Stalemate, Mertika. Why don't you push your favors on Chiba? You admire him—you can have a cuntful of bandy-legged little geographers all your own." He reached for his pants and put them on quickly. "I'll even be godfather to them all; would that please you?"

"Hart—"

"Hart," he said, mimicking her, and pulled his shirt over his arms. She put her face in her hands. He ignored her as he finished dressing and went into the hallway, closing the door quietly behind him.

As he expected, she caught up with him by the time he reached the kitchen door. He allowed her tears and supplications to go on longer than usual before letting himself be cajoled back up the stairs and into bed. Once in bed he relented slightly, stroking and kissing her to orgasm before seeking his own release: after all, she was a convenient, cozy little thing, and even their arguments served to inject some passion into his otherwise tightly controlled life.

"I love you," she whispered, her lips against his shoulder. Hart patted her head with absentminded fondness and drifted into sleep.

∾

QUILLA PUT DOWN THE SKETCHBOOK AND formed an expression of rueful astonishment.

"It's so much more than I expected," she said. "The detail, the observations—not simply that you did it, but that you brought this back, as well."

"But that's why I went," Chiba said. Quilla leaned forward and filled his cup with hot tea.

"I know. It's the multiplicity of talents that amazes me. These are invaluable. I don't know how we could repay you."

Chiba smiled. His square face was dark with sun and wind, and new lines etched the corners of his eyes. But something deeper had changed, and Quilla, watching him, realized that he looked somehow centered, serene. At peace.

"You're the one who told me that Aerie was a planet of generalists," Shosei was saying. "And I've been paid. Jes brought me here, for one. You helped me along, financed the expedition—believed that I could do it. That's not the sort of thing that can be repaid easily. If this"—he lifted the sketchbook fractionally—"even begins to pay my debt, then it was worth it. It would have been worth it in any event."

"Was it very hard?"

"Of course," Chiba said. "That's why I went."

"Tell me about it."

Chiba leaned back and closed his eyes, cradling the teacup in his hands. Somehow he knew what she wanted: not the practical details, the tales of danger and escape —instead he told her about sunset over Mother Sea, with no land in sight. The brilliant colors of sky and water, the murmur of wind in the rigging, the parti-colored reflection of the airship dancing along the skin of the sea. He talked about drifting above thick forests in a stillness so deep that the sudden call of a bird seemed to pierce the universe. Talked of skimming the peaks of mountains, the heater opened to full and snow crags looming beside him. Talked of the terror and exhilaration of riding the storms, and the profound peace of a midday silence. Quilla stopped watching his face and traveled with him, feeling a familiar ache fill her chest. The squat, ugly little man before her had lived adventures, had tasted of the new and strange, while she spent the months, as she had spent her life, surrounded by the urgent, irritating, important trivia of the commonplace. The bitterness threatened to choke her. She stared at her folded hands, willing the emotion to pass, and when she looked up she realized that Chiba had fallen silent and was looking at her with an expression she could not read.

"I'm sorry," she said. "I guess I went traveling, too."

He nodded and started to say something, then leaned forward and tapped the log book. "I took along an analyzer, you know," he said. "You could mine the far islands—iron, tin, other stuff. And helium, there's a natural gas bank on To'an Elt, almost ten percent helium." He paused. "I'd like to use helium. Hot air has disadvantages."

"I'll look into it," Quilla said. "But some things have changed in the past year, you'll hear about them. I can't promise, but I'll see what I can do." She stacked the log book, rutter, and sketches on a corner of her desk. "Shosei, you know you have our thanks. You've a place to stay?"

"Yes, at Kohl's. Mertika's offered me a permanent room. She won't take payment." He paused. "I don't really understand it. All I did was take a trip. But the way people treat me—"

"You're a hero," Quilla said, smiling. "You spent fourteen months by yourself, in an untried airship, circumnavigating the globe—and you made it back in one piece, in good health. Sweet Mother, Shosei, you did a wonderful, adventurous thing. Of course people feel in awe of you, and proud of you."

"But Jes takes longer trips than that, and—"

"That has nothing to do with it. The only drawback is that Ved will find some way of fitting you into the Beginning Day program."

"Speeches?" Chiba laughed and rose. "I don't know. Maybe I'll plan to be away that time of year."

Quilla, too, laughed and stood. "Not a bad idea. But if there's anything at all we can do for you, Shosei, just ask."

"All right. Finance my next trip."

"You've barely returned from the last one!"

"I know. It'll take at least another year to prepare for the next one. I want to do a north-south voyage," he said, excited. "Circumnavigate at the axis. But until then, there are shorter trips. The east coast of Betes—it's impassable by land and the seas are pretty rough along there. But I could map it easily, take a month or two, come back with a coast map, analyzer readings, even seabed readings. It wouldn't cost much."

Quilla grinned. "I'd have to talk it over with Mish," she said, caution competing with humor. "Can you wait a week or so for the answer?"

Chiba smiled and took her hand. "Of course." He paused. "You could . . ."

"Could what, Shosei?"

But he shook his head, thanked her again, and left the Tor. Quilla stood at her office window and watched him go, then stared at her hands. The nails were cut short and square, a scab decorated one knuckle, and the calluses along her palms were scored with ingrained dirt. Suddenly annoyed, she marched into the washroom and scrubbed at her hands until they ached.

The feeling of bitterness rode with her for the rest of the day and she was annoyed at the irrationality of her envy. When Meya went up to Processing for her semi-annual inspection, Quilla envied her the trip, although she knew it always left Meya exhausted and irritable. She envied Jes his trips through tau, despite the fact that the one time he'd taken her up to his ship she'd become thoroughly claustrophobic and knew she'd go crazy if she had to spend so much as a week in space. She envied her children their distant, exotic lives on Kroeber, the lives they had abandoned with such eagerness whenever it was possible to come home, and which they discounted, shrugging, now that they were home for good. Even Hart had lived adventures in alien lands; even Mish had seen more than one small corner of one small planet. Since the age of fourteen Quilla had worked the land, run the plantations, participated in and eventually directed the casual governing of Aerie. Built towns, created irrigation systems, arbitrated disputes—all important, rewarding things which nonetheless left her with a feeling of loss, a sense that her life was sliding through her fingers on a strong tide of trivia, even and unremittingly gray. It did no good to tell herself that a forty-three-year-old woman with grown children and a planet to run should not go chasing after romantic dreams of adventure. The dreams persisted, as did the unhappy jealousy of those who had, at the least, an opportunity to live those dreams.

She was quiet throughout dinner. The others assumed that she was busy pondering important things, as indeed she should have been. She didn't care. She pushed her food around her plate, left the table abruptly, and went to the widow's walk atop the house. The night air chilled, but the last clouds of spring had blown away, and the sky was crisp and decorated with stars. She lay back in one of the reclining chairs, looking at the sky and trying not to think. Both moons were up tonight; Pigeon midway through the sky, Dove already touching the western horizon. After a while she noticed a new light overhead and aimed the telescope at it. The unmistakable configuration of *Rabbit*'s struts and orbiting lights filled the view-finder. She turned off the scope and lay down. Eventually, when the house was quiet and the angry yearning within her had abated, she went to bed, woke Tabor, and made love. That, at least, was always good.

THE KASIRENE SECTION OF HAVEN WAS NOT so much a collection of structures as one vast, interconnected house, each section tied to the others by a series of roofed walks, corridors, mutual walls, interior and exterior stairways, sprawling verandahs, and garden paths. Within the secure webbing of their extended families, the kasirene were both individualistic and playful; sections of the vast house were as different as their inhabitants. Gables, false fronts, porticos, towers, gargoyles, false doors, extraneous stairways leading nowhere in particular, swaying rope ladders quivering precariously high over the streets, trap doors, tunnels, and elaborate rooftops were painted an assortment of startling colors. Murals decorated some walls, others were solid, or abstract, or held long dissertations, either in Kasiri or Standard, which identified, praised, joked, or made complaint. Finding an address in the kasirene section, in The

Jumble, was, to newer Aerites, a source of frustration. Where in the devil would one find Kabit's house, next door to the great flood, around the corner from Havaea's dissertation on the nature of wind (internal), just under the shaggy in plaster, second floor?

The kasirene had a much simpler method of locating people, since whoever they sought would be as likely to be visiting as at home. They marched through the twisting corridors of The Jumble shouting names.

Only one structure stood apart from The Jumble, at the far side from terran Haven; a mound of curving, thickly plastered walls, painted white, with a single door facing south and a smoke hole in the middle. The building was not sacred, nor were the activities which took place within it. The kasirene referred to it, casually, as The Meeting, and it functioned as meeting hall, social center, sanctuary, theatre, and center from which the complicated ethics of kasirene life were debated and clarified.

The day after the outing to Cault Eiret, Palen sat in The Meeting, nursing a cup of kaea and staring with dissatisfaction at the firepit. A narrow band of light fell through the open doorway and pinked the far wall, and voices floated in from the square outside as kasirene straggled back to The Jumble at the end of the day. Palen listened morosely to plans for the evening: a quick game of caraem, beer at Kohl's, gossip about the little man who had returned from floating his inflated bladder around the world. She drank some more kaea and shifted her position slightly, glanced at the edge of light against the wall, and waited for Beriant. It was his week to maintain The Meeting, a task he usually completed at the end of the day. Palen wished he'd hurry up.

He came in from the sunlight, blinked, and started across the hall toward the firepit. Palen leaned back in the shadows and watched him. They had spent a winter together, years back, producing a fair amount of personal knowledge and one pup, who was now father to pups in turn. Since then they'd not had much to do with each other: Palen respected Beriant's intelligence, still found him attractive, and didn't like him very much. The feeling, she suspected, was mutual.

He hunkered down by the firepit, balanced gracefully on his tail, and laid some twigs on the small fire while his upper arms stretched to arrange the rake and stone bowl. Then, leaning forward, he began raking around the fire, scooping the ashes and embers into the bowl held by his lower hands. He worked quickly. When the ashes and embers were cleared away and a complicated pattern had been raked into the sand of the pit, he layered twigs and small logs over the fire, building the radiating sun pattern which was the primary symbol of kasirene thought. Then he sat back and stared into the fire. The shaft of sunlight had disappeared and fire light flickered at the corners of the room. Palen called his name.

He turned, surprised, and looked around The Meeting.

"Oh, Palen." He stood, brushed ashes from his pelt, and came over to her. "Do you make a habit of hiding in deserted places? I didn't see you."

She moved over to give him a place to sit against the wall. "I want to talk with you."

"About Belen? Is he all right?"

"Belen's fine, as far as I know. You hear more from him than I do."

Beriant took Palen's cup and drank some of the kaea. "Then it's about the Calling."

Palen put all her arms around her legs. "You can still call it off. You haven't made a firm request yet."

He moved his shoulders in negation. "Things have to have an ending, have to have a resolution."

"It's been almost twenty years," Palen said. "Besides, he was banished."

"He's back again," Beriant pointed out. "And the twenty years only make it worse. That banishment may have been some sort of restitution to his family, but he's never made any restitution to us."

Palen took the cup back. "What sort of restitution do you want? You can't bring those pups back, and neither can he." She drank the last of the kaea and rummaged about in her pouch for the flask. It was almost empty. "Things are tense enough already, Beriant. This whole Parallax problem is growing again, and I suspect that it's going to get a lot worse before it gets better. You're just complicating things by bringing Hart up now."

"That argument won't change things, Palen. We've never been a people to put things off for convenience's

sake." He rocked back onto his tail. "We've lived by
their laws, and I won't say that they're bad ones. But
we've laws of our own, too. Don't you think that some
of our younger ones think about that? If Hart had done
those things to terran children—"

"Beriant—"

"You know it as well as I do," he said, and his lower
shoulders tensed angrily. "If one of our people had
done it to terran children, how many of us do you think
there would be left?"

"The Kennerins have always dealt fairly with us,"
Palen said, working to keep her voice even. "They've
protected us, they've made us part of their culture.
They've respected us, and what we think, and the way
we do things. This sort of speculation is worse than useless—it's dangerous, and you know it. It's over with,
Beriant. It's in the past, let it stay there."

He rocked forward and drew a circle in the dust. "It
may be in the past, but it's not finished," he said, and
broke the circle with a thick line. "We live by circles,
any pup knows that. Things have to have a resolution.
The business of Hart has no resolution at all. And
neither, Palen, do you."

She straightened her back. "By what right do you
say that?"

Not looking at her, he erased the broken circle and
in its place drew two more, side by side and overlapping
slightly. Through the points of overlap, he drew another
thick straight line. "You were born one thing and you
chose another," he said. "You try to keep two circles
where you should only keep one." He leaned back, rested
his lower arms on his knees, and looked at her. "Things
come in circles, Palen. Perhaps your circles have come to
this, too."

"I can manage both," she said stiffly.

"Can you? Is there any peace in your house?"

She stood abruptly and gathered the cup and flask.
Beriant smoothed a palm over his drawings and rose.

"I'll oppose the Calling, Beriant. I'll not let you speak
in Meeting without my opposition."

Beriant dismissed this with a shrug. "And your circles?"

Palen turned, distressed, and left The Meeting.

SANDRO LUGGED A HUGE BOX OUT OF THE shuttle. He dumped it on a wagon and grinned over his shoulder at Jes. Jes scowled back.

"I'll walk," the tauCaptain said. He marched across the field toward the path. The captain was in one of his foul moods again; there was nothing to do save lay low and wait for it to blow over.

The captain's moods always darkened now when they came through Eagle Grab, while Beryl's lightened. She even made jokes about the captain's towering rages, jokes which baffled Sandro slightly, but he did not yet feel close enough to Beryl to ask for an explanation. A year ago, and with a great deal of foreboding, he had obtained holos of Taine's three children and brought them up to *Rabbit* with him. Instead of trying to kill him, Beryl accepted the presents silently and Greaves said that she had hezed them to the walls of her cabin, above her desk. She never mentioned them to Sandro, but as he and the captain entered the shuttle earlier in the day, she had pressed upon him two message cubes, one addressed to Captain Hetch and the other, surprisingly, to Kayman Olet. And, loudly enough for the captain to overhear, she had asked Sandro to convey her regards to Tatha. It was a deliberate dig; everyone aboard *Rabbit* knew of the captain's animosity toward the Theresan.

Sandro uneasily slipped the message cubes into his pocket and entered the shuttle, where Jes' warning stare advised him to keep his mouth securely closed. As they approached Aerie, though, Sandro's own cheerful mood reasserted itself. He sang to himself as he oversaw the unloading of the shuttle, closed down the ship, and climbed aboard the loaded wagon. It coughed to life and bumped down the paved road to Haven. The halaeas were still blooming and someone had planted flowering bushes along the road. He approved.

His business on Althing Green in behalf of the planetary company of Aerie-Kennerin had been long, sticky, and unpleasant, but he had, at least, secured permission for a representative of the company to speak before the next Joint Session, and that, as Mish had said, was all that was really important. And coming home to Aerie always made him feel better. The message cubes rode securely in his pocket, proof that his long campaign in behalf of Beryl's sanity was finally, albeit slowly, paying off; he had filled the list of commissions that the family and various friends heaped on him. Most important, this trip home coincided with the end of his three-year waiting period and he would, finally, go into Haven's town hall, set his name to the register, and become a full citizen of Aerie and a voting shareholder in Aerie-Kennerin. Over the past three years he had bought enough A-K common stock so the dividends now gave him a pleasing extra income—within another year or two he would be able to buy a house in Haven and, if he wished, give up space entirely. But that was a decision he did not yet feel ready to make. It was enough, for now, to be coming home.

He stopped first at Tatha's house. The wagon backfired twice before expiring; he grimaced as he swung from the high seat and delved into his large box. The exterior of the house had been painted light brown and dark brown, with thin traces of burnt orange around the door and window frames. The colors looked good together. A few plants flowered in the yard, deliberately placed to counter the lines of the porch supports. Sandro pulled a sack from the box and took it around the house to the separate workshop.

Tatha, bent over a small piece of machinery on a high counter, looked up, smiled, and put a tool down before coming across the room to take Sandro's hand.

"Home from the sea," she said. "You're looking fit."

"I should be. Jes has been running us through the gym as though we were in training for something."

"You are," she said, leading the way toward the house. "And you've me to thank, or curse, for that. I suggested it to Hetch."

'Whatever for?" Sandro demanded, remembering kinked muscles and disappearing free-time.

"None of you is strong enough, or fast enough, on planet. You're fine in space, sure, but down here you're almost useless. Oh, graceful," she said, raising a hand to still his objection. "But still too slow."

"Hell, we're not going to start a circus, are we?"

"No. But Parallax might."

Sandro shook his head and followed her through the doorway. "Knowing you, that's from fact and not supposition."

"I know where to listen and what to ask. Do you want a beer? And I expect those are my micro-waldoes, were they hard to find?"

"Yes, and yes, and what have you done in here?" Sandro looked around the room in amazement. The stained walls had disappeared behind brightly patterned kasirene rugs, the dingy floor was thickly carpeted. Furniture had been repaired and recovered and some pieces were new. The overall effect was one of warmth, charm, and elegance, and Sandro made a gesture of appreciation. "It's stunning."

"Addicted to luxury, I am." She went into the kitchen.

Sandro wandered about, touching things. He picked up a small carving, recognizing kasirene work. They could be bought for little in the market, but this one was perfectly done, and perfectly set amid the room. Sandro's experience of elegance was limited to the large, overfurnished, dignified house his parents had maintained on Marquez Landing—it had not prepared him for the smooth beauty of this room. He put the carving down, puckered his lips appreciatively, and accepted the mug of beer from Tatha.

"I'm impressed," he said.

"You're meant to be comfortable. Sit down and tell me about Althing Green."

Sandro sank into one of the chairs and sipped the beer. "I still think that they should have sent someone else," he said. "I'm not used to all of that, all the lobbying and meetings and being nice to awful people. There are a lot of awful people up on Althing Green—politicians. I guess I should have expected that. And not one of them will admit that they, or their staffs, can do anything at all. I kept trying not to lose my temper."

"Probably a good thing. That was a stroke of genius, actually, Mish asking you to go. After all, you've been harmed by Parallax; we've only been threatened. Althing Green was more likely to listen to you than to one of the Kennerins. I take it that you got what you went for?"

"I suppose. A representative of Aerie-Kennerin is supposed to present something to the Joint Session when they next convene, and I guess that's a couple of months from now. It's the best I could do. I tried to get something earlier, but . . ." He shrugged. "Why didn't they send you? You'd probably have had everything done in two days, and no delays at all."

"I'm not an Aerite, Sandro. And Althing Green's not too likely to take to Theresans."

"Um." Sandro finished his beer. "Is Decca around?"

"Yes. We're all invited to dinner tonight, by the way. You, me, Hetch, Chiba, the whole crew."

"How is Hetch?" Sandro said, standing as Tatha rose. She shrugged. "Holding out. You didn't expect him to last forever, did you?" Sandro frowned. "I'm sorry, Sandro. But he's an old man. Ozchan's kept him going and pretty much out of pain, but he can't take it much longer." She paused, looking out her front window at the small garden. "It's not the body's collapse so much. He's dying of being planetbound, though he won't say so. He wants space so much it hurts to watch him."

"And going into space will kill him," Sandro said.

Tatha nodded. "Not an enviable position. But it's his life. The most we can do is watch—and sympathize."

Sandro looked at her. "You're cold, aren't you?"

"I suppose so. Does it matter?" She opened the sack he had brought and took out the micro-waldoes. "How's Jes?" she said as she inspected the equipment.

"In a foul mood most of the time, but that's nothing new. You'll see him at dinner tonight."

"I'm willing to bet against it," Tatha said, and walked him to the door. Sandro wanted to ask why but she fed him stray, hilarious bits of gossip about the citizens of Haven, and by the time he remembered his question the wagon was in motion and Tatha had gone back to her shop. He shook his head and concentrated on guiding the balky wagon around the curves of the street, through the marketplace, and toward Hetch's house. Hetch himself occupied a chair on Kohl's porch, deep in animated talk with someone Sandro didn't recognize. Suddenly unwilling to face the old man, Sandro took the wagon down to

Hetch's house, lugged his box into his own room, and returned the wagon to the public garage before setting out for Kohl's.

Hetch looked worn and gray, especially around the corners of his mouth, and his robust fatness had slackened. He looked deflated, Sandro thought, as he hurried up the porch. Hetch hugged him briefly, then gestured at himself.

"You see what they're doing to me," he said gloomily. "Starving me to death. Never let the doctors get their hands on you, Sandro, you'll just end up worse than before. Sit down, here's another of Jes' strays. Mertika!"

The other stray was a small, ugly man called Shosei Chiba, a geographer who had just circumnavigated Aerie at the equator in an unpowered, hot-air ship and had returned only three days before. The geographer, slightly surprised, answered Sandro's eager questions and asked some of his own. It appeared that, to him, sailing through tau was as great an adventure as circumnavigating the globe alone. Mertika came out onto the porch, holding a glass of beer.

"Stand up," she said to Sandro. When he did she whapped him suggestively on the ass and went back inside, evading his answering slap. Chiba grinned.

"But you must have been through tau before," Sandro said.

"A few times," Chiba replied. Hetch snorted.

"He was on the survey team," the old man said, and nodded in satisfaction as Sandro gaped and Chiba looked uncomfortable.

'It was a long time ago," the geographer said, looking at his beer. "I don't think about it much anymore."

Sandro started to say something, and Hetch kicked him under the table. "I don't like false modesty," the captain grumbled. "Finish your beer. I'm hungry."

Chiba jumped up. "I'm done," he said. "I'll get it." He disappeared into the beerhall and came out a moment later with a contraption Sandro didn't recognize, and at which he stared in bewilderment. It seemed to be a chair, with two large wheels in front and a number of smaller ones in back, powered by a motor balanced under the seat. Chiba bumped it down the stairs, and came back to offer Hetch his arm. Hetch stared at the chair with something more than distaste, but let Chiba walk him down the stairs and deposit him in the chair.

"I can walk, but not too far," he said. He spun the chair around and up the street. Sandro and Chiba exchanged glances, then followed.

"Where did it come from?" Sandro said.

"It was Jason Kennerin's," Chiba said. "Mish's husband. He had an accident before he died, he was working with Hetch on the ships and something happened on one of the mining planets. Ship hatch failure or something. They made this for him but he died before he could use it much." Chiba paused. "Hetch doesn't like to talk about it. I don't think any of them do."

Sandro, taking the hint, nodded. The two hurried to catch up with Hetch. They paused at the captain's house while Sandro ran inside and emerged with a sack over his shoulder. Hetch raised his eyebrows questioningly.

"It's not every day that I get to Althing Green," Sandro said, and refused to elaborate.

The crest of the hill welcomed them with scents of dinner. Sandro sniffed appreciatively. Even Hetch, ever conscious of the state of his stomach, managed a grimace of anticipation and speeded up. The two younger men hurried to keep pace.

JES' SOUR MOOD WAS NOT IMPROVED BY THE announcement that Meya had planned a large dinner party for the evening, but his displeasure became alarm when he heard the guest list. He paced Meya's office while his sister, the list in her hand, perched on the edge of the desk and watched him.

"I'll eat at Kohl's," he said. "Hell, I didn't come home to get prettied up and play host to a million people. Let Hart take care of it. I'm tired."

"It's not a formal dinner, Jessie. You won't have to play host at all. Just a gathering of friends."

"Friends!"

Meya put the paper down and folded her hands in her lap. "I don't see why you dislike Tatha so much," she said reasonably. "Granted she may have been a bit rough with you, but she had her reasons. Even you concede that."

Jes shook his head stubbornly. "I'm not comfortable around her, that's all. I don't see why you have to make such a bloody big thing about it."

"I'm not making anything of it, you are. Come on, Jes, I'm not asking you to love her, I just want you to be polite."

Jes stared at her suspiciously. She crossed her arms, looking exasperated. He repressed a curse, made a gesture of grudging assent, and left the house.

It was still early afternoon. Peering toward the port, he saw Sandro's wagon move up the road toward Haven. Workers moved through the newest fields and beyond them dark rows of *Zimania* gleamed in the sunlight. At the other side of the hill, people rolled empty sap barrels into the yard in front of the barn while others recaulked, inspected, tore apart, and built them again. He put his hands in his pockets and thought of knocking on Hart's laboratory door, then walked away from the Tor.

He skirted the town, hopped over the stream behind the schoolhouse, and climbed up the hill to the cemetery. Jason's grave was covered with tender shoots of grass and budding airflowers, and the leaves of the halaea and *Zimania* stirred lightly in the breeze. He sat down, his back against the halaea trunk, and took a smooth stone from his pocket. Rubbing it aimlessly, he leaned his head against the trunk and closed his eyes.

It surprised him that Meya, whom he thought the closest to him of anyone, could not read him. But he was sure that Tatha could, and would the moment she saw his face. She wouldn't ridicule him, wouldn't sharpen her tongue on his discomfort—there was, he thought, a well of compassion behind her cold blue eyes and smooth silver fur that was little in evidence. No, she would pity him, and that above all he could not take. The history of Jes in love was enough of a farce without that.

He'd been home twice since bringing Tatha to Aerie

and had, he thought now, spent each visit running away from her. Refusing to go to Haven when she was in Haven, refusing to appear at the Tor when he knew she was there—his family was fond of her, making chance encounters even more likely. He wished savagely that she'd decided to live in Hoku.

He still didn't trust her.

An early airflower popped on Jason's grave. Jes looked around quickly. No one appeared, and eventually he leaned his head against the tree again and stared at his father's grave. He wondered if he wasn't making a huge noise about a small problem and decided that he probably was. Tatha was coming to dinner. Very well. Given the circumstances, he could behave with polite distance, hope that she didn't see through him, and school himself to a civilized quiet no matter what happened. Surely Tatha, of all people, could appreciate civilized quiet, and pay him the compliment of not letting him know whether she knew.

And if she really didn't know? If she could not read him as well as he thought she could? He contemplated the idea with a mixture of relief and dread, and fled into the precise solace of his flute.

Alin and Spider, in the midst of battle, kept the kitchen in an uproar until Mim declared angrily that they had much better things to do. She grabbed each child by an arm and flung them out the back door, then paused and listened, shaking her head.

At three, Alin still refused to talk, relying on Spider to transmit her messages to her family. A week ago Spider had decided that he wouldn't play messenger anymore. He and Meya together made it clear to the rest of the household why the step had had to be taken and everyone agreed that Alin should learn to communicate on her own. What they had not expected was the extent of Alin's resistance to the change. She stubbornly refused to do anything; refused to play with the other children, refused to laugh, refused even to point out her needs or demands to the adults. Instead she sulked about the house, yelling in her head until Spider, shouting angrily, left the Tor and took up temporary residence with Simit, the headmaster. Alin's immediate apathy so frightened Meya that she demanded Spider's return, and since that morning a strange argument had filled the Tor, consisting mostly of Alin's glares and Spider's shouts.

"The hell you can't," he yelled now. Mim shook her head again. "What? Dreck. I never signed on to be your caretaker forever, and you know it. Of course I love you, you stupid treffik. Everyone does, that's why—you *what?* You can talk as well as anyone and you know it. Well, you just go ahead, then. You'll just pass out, and I don't give a damn. You're a great big overgrown baby. Even if you could talk, I'll bet you couldn't think of anything interesting to say. You could not—just think of all the crap *I've* been getting from you all morning. Oh, Sweet Mother. Alin, come on, baby, come on, don't cry. I was angry, is all. No, I won't let you into my head again, not until you learn to talk. It's for your own good—*don't scream like that!* Please, come on, Alin, come on—you want a pastry? Okay, just wait, and stop yelling, just for a minute, okay? Please? I'll be right back—"

Mim stepped back from the door as Spider came into the kitchen. He took a fruit tart and looked at the housekeeper wildly.

"I'm going out of my mind," he said with ragged calm, and took the tart outside to Alin.

Mim, sighing, went back to the roast being prepared for that night's dinner.

Jes saw Hetch sitting in Jason's chair and started. The old man looked up at him and gestured bitterly.

"I know," he said. "I don't like it any more than you do, but someone found it in a storeroom and I needed something like it. We can't waste things, even if they have—uncomfortable associations." Hetch spat. "According to Quilla. Tell me of the run."

Jes sat with the captain on the porch, obligingly feeding the old man's hunger for space, and watched the road to Haven. Sandro took his sack into the living room and threatened the children with instant death if they so much as touched it. They laughed and climbed onto his lap, demanding caresses. Jes listened to their laughter. Chiba stood talking with Quilla by the fireplace. Mish marched in, dusting her hands on her thighs, and demanded a drink. Jared gave her one and said something. Mish laughed. Jes went inside when Ozchan arrived, fixed drinks for himself and Hetch, and went back onto the porch. Tabor entered with Decca; Sandro stood, spilling children from his lap, to say something gallant. Their voices sounded unreal behind Jes; he kept turning to look through the open window, as though expecting the room to be populated by ghosts. Hetch put his hand on Jes' arm and asked a question about the older ships. Jes answered absently. When he saw the unmistakable gleam of Tatha's silver hair in the fading light he stood quickly and wheeled Hetch inside.

Hart, coming around the side of the house, called a greeting to Tatha, who replied with a line which brought surprised laughter from Hart. Jes angrily wrenched his attention from their voices and immersed himself in conversation with Chiba. Tatha came into the room.

Cas Hevant, the weaver, made a supple, silky cloth which she dyed a number of dark colors. Tatha had chosen blue and made it into a simple shift which covered her with a minimum of fuss. She wore elegance as though born to it. Jes double-checked his expression, offered her a drink, and introduced her to Chiba before escaping to the far side of the room. Spider and Alin stood uneasily together by the fireplace, Alin holding on to Spider's shirt with clenched, chubby, dirty hands. Spider looked at Jes, looked at Alin, shrugged, then winced. Jes looked Spider full in the face and thought, as clearly as he could, Don't you dare tell anyone. Spider shook his head and said to Alin, "You'll just have to get it for yourself." She marched away from him angrily.

"I've troubles enough of my own," Spider said. "It's like having somebody else's headache." He brightened. "Have you met Belshazar?"

"The shaggy? No, is he around?"

"Not today. Mim insisted that we lock him up somewhere. She said that this feast was one he was not going to get to." Spider grinned. "Did I tell you about the night he ate Tabor's duck?"

Jes shook his head. "Tabor had a duck?"

"Well, that's what he called it," Spider said. He launched into a story about the epic conflict between the tame shaggy and a four-winged bird that Tabor insisted on calling a duck, although not even by courtesy did it deserve the name. Tabor was raising the duck to serve for dinner; Belshazar had dinner plans of his own; the duck seemed to suspect that something unpleasant was happening, and the story, as Spider told it, soon had Jes gasping with laughter. His shoulders relaxed and he breathed more easily, although his awareness of Tatha never left him.

By the end of dinner he was congratulating himself on his self-command. The meal passed without incident, he had been unfailingly, albeit coolly, polite to Tatha, and she concentrated her conversation on Hart and Quilla, sitting at the far end of the table. Jes accepted a second glass of wine and joked across the table with Tabor. Alin, on her good behavior, didn't spill a single thing and Spider stopped looking as though he had a brass band locked in his skull.

Sandro announced that he was prepared to reveal the contents of his sack, and was pursued into the living room with eagerness and laughter. He appropriated a chair at the center of the room and waited, bouncing and grinning, while the family arranged themselves around the room. Jes, who knew what was in the sack, lounged against the mantelpiece and prepared to be amused.

"Tomorrow I'm going down to the town hall and register," Sandro said. "Anyway, I thought it would be a good excuse to celebrate."

Sandro had brought presents. He's been saving money since he learned that he'd be sent to Althing Green, and once there had gone on an epic shopping spree. He opened the sack and out came wonderful frivolities.

For Mish, a jeweled hair ornament that glistened in her thick white hair. For Tabor, a cane whose head was sphere within sphere of carved white stone. A thin, crystalline necklace for Meya, which changed color with her pulse and breath. Intricate, three-dimensional puzzles for the children, who immediately took them apart, then stared at them with dismay, wondering how to put them together again. For Jared a new flute, and for Decca an alien instrument called a jeverah, an egg-shaped metal device with holes and stops. Sandro tried to demonstrate it and produced a series of awful noises, but after a few moments Decca managed a simple melody. It sounded like water running over stones. He gave Ozchan a single earring, made of an alien stone. And for Quilla, a wrapped package which he put in her lap and urged her to open. Quilla laughed and undid the strings, then stopped laughing. Within the folds of wrapping lay a shimmering gown, the color of *Zimania* berries, of a material so delicate it seemed to float off her lap. She looked at it, astonished.

"Oh, Sandro! Whatever for?"

"Beginning Day, or your birthday, or doing dishes, or something. Anything you like. The color reminded me of you."

She smiled and lifted the dress carefully. Jes had doubted Sandro's taste in this purchase, but Quilla's expression was one of rapture. Sandro, looking at her, glowed as though he'd been given the universe as thanks. And Tatha, seated comfortably on a floor cushion, cradled a sleeping child in her lap and looked at them all with cool, tolerant eyes. She turned her head as he watched her and caught his glance. Jes looked down. When her attention was elsewhere he walked out of the room.

Most of the porch was in darkness. He leaned against a wooden column. Light spilled from the living room window, a sharp-edged slash of brilliance that ended abruptly at the line of potted plants along the edge of the porch. The flowers looked magical, conjured by light from darkness. Jes stared at them. Someone laughed inside the house. Patiently, he pared away his perception of sound, letting the luminous flowers fill his mind until only they in the world seemed real. Petals, stamen, the heart of the flower, and beyond that into a place where even the flower didn't exist. He floated in a timeless serenity that gradually readmitted the world, sense by sense. The colors withdrew, dwindling gently into the shape of petals against darkness. The night air smelled crisp and sweet; the hard line of the porch was solid and clean against his shoulder and hip. The sounds from within the house were those of a distant, alien contentment.

Something flickered at the edge of his vision. He turned his head and saw a pale dissonance in the darkness beyond the shaft of light. Tatha stood in the shadow, leaning against a porch column; they looked at each other from their posts of darkness. She seemed as distant and immaterial as the flowers, and he watched her with the same detached appreciation.

"I'm sorry I interrupted you," she said at last. Jes listened to the echo of her words in his head and nodded. "I came out to ask for a truce."

"A truce," he repeated. The world became real again. "Why?"

She turned, put her hands on the porch rail, and looked over the slope of the hill. Haven's lights glowed in the bowl of the valley below. A fold of her sleeve caught the light, a brief flash of blue. Jes looked away from it.

"I can't apologize for Gensco," she said. "I'd do it again. If I had to, I'd be even harder."

"Or more deceptive."

"Deceit is a tool," she said to the lights in the valley. "I use whatever tools I find to hand."

"The end justifies the means?"

"Do you think I think that?"

Jes considered, remembering her refusal to give him to the Parallax agent, remembering her care for the frozen infants in the creche. Remembering the gleam of her claws along the agent's throat.

"I don't know," he said finally. "My perceptions are ... colored."

She accepted that with a brief swing of her hand, silver against blue. The gesture hurt him.

"Why a truce?"

"Mish told me about the Parallax bid. I've done some research on my own. I think Parallax is going to move against Aerie soon and I don't think it will be as subtle as what they tried to do in Priory. Do you want my reasoning?"

"No. I agree with you." He paused. "Do you want me to take you away?"

She shook her head. "I owe you, Jes."

He made a small noise of surprise.

"You needn't have brought me here, but you did. Quilla needn't have set me up here, but she did. I've good work to do, I'm accepted. I can raise my child here." She paused. "It's been a long time since I had a home. I didn't think I'd find another, but I have. I'm in your debt for it. Aerie may need me—Aerie will need all of us. We'll work together better if we can put aside our hostilities for a while." She stepped into the light and extended her hand. "I'm not asking that you like me, Jes.

I don't think I've a right to ask that. I'm simply asking for a truce."

Tatha standing in the light, offering her hand, asking for toleration. Not understanding him at all. He took a deep breath.

"You don't—" he said, and stopped. Tatha didn't move. He reached out quickly, took her hand, and nodded. She nodded back and went into the house. Sparing him her company, he thought, for all the wrong reasons. He leaned against the porch railing, taken with a profound relief. This act of the interminable comedy, at least, could be conducted in dignified privacy.

He put his hand briefly to his cheek, then went into the house to bid the children good night.

QUILLA WAITED UNTIL EVERYONE HAD GONE to bed before, feeling very silly, she took her dress into the mirrored robing room by the bathroom and locked the door. Her skin prickled in the coolness. She held the dress before her, watching the colors flow and change as the lamplight moved over it. It seemed to embody all the forgotten promises of her dreams, all the elegance and grace which had never touched her life; the promise of enchantment, of excitement, the breath of the exotic. She tried to drive the delight from her with hardheaded practicality, but she held the fabric of dreams rippling and soft in her hands. She slid the gown over her head and settled it along her shoulders and hips. The sleeves widened from shoulders to fingertips, the fabric felt cool and soft across her belly and down her legs. She gathered her frizzy hair into a bunch and pulled the hood of the gown over her head, arranging its folds by her throat. And, catching sight of herself in the mirror, stared. Clothed in the shimmering fabric, the harsh angularity of her bones became graceful, and in the delicate shadow

of the hood her cheekbones gleamed and her eyes seemed
enlarged and mysterious. She turned her head cautiously,
waiting for the image in the mirror to laugh and disappear, but it stared at her with wide-eyed distrust. Not
beautiful, by no description beautiful—but alien, yes,
and secretive: a mysterious, tall, elegant woman both
mantled and revealed by the smooth folds of the gown.

It's a fraud, she thought from her own bemusement. I
can't wear this dress. I'm not—but the words would not
frame themselves in her mind. Pitchforks and loaded
carts, the glittering summer sun and a cold winter wind
that chapped and blistered her lips; the swift efficiency of
her office, hardheaded arguments during town meetings.
Standing spraddle-legged and flat-footed, hands on hips,
bawling out orders to the fieldworkers, pushing sweat-
soaked hair from her face as she took inventory in the
curing sheds. All of that, yes, but not this strange woman
in the mirror. And, above all, not the knowledge that
through all the years of bitterness, this elegance waited
only on a curve of fabric, a trick of light, a willingness to
see it. Quilla pushed the hood back, and her hands
shook. Willing accomplice, she said inaudibly, and the
mirror lips framed the words at her. I have robbed myself.

The time had passed; too late, now, to make acceptance of this stranger, too late to redefine. She did not
know how the woman in the mirror would talk, would
think, would move her body; did not know how the illu-
sion could begin to enter her life. Dressed in splendor,
pitching hay. Robed in beauty, behind a mask; play-
acting, untrue, not right, and no time to grow toward
rightness. I am Quilla Kennerin, and Quilla Kennerin is
not this.

Of my own free, blinded will.

Ignorance is no excuse.

As if in confirmation, she felt her nose stuff up as her
eyes filled with tears. She pulled the dress over her head
impatiently, scrubbed at her eyes with her wrist, and,
folding the dress with care, put it back in its package and
retied the strings. She jerked her jeans and shirt on, blew
her nose, and took the dress back to her room, where she
put it on the top shelf of the closet, behind her carefully stored raingear.

I won't borrow fraudulent elegance, she thought with angry sorrow, stripped, and slid into bed beside Tabor. He murmured and put his arm over her and, unable to help herself, she rolled tight against the curve of his body and wept.

ALIN, MUCH AGAINST HER WILL, SPENT THE next day at home, where her mother scrubbed her down, clipped the ragged ends of her hair, and made her stand still while she and Cas Hevant involved themselves in meters of cloth. Alin's current wardrobe consisted primarily of clothes which had passed from Spider to Jason Hart to Andrus and were, Meya declared, held together only by hope and dirt. Eventually, interested in spite of herself, Alin began fingering the cloth and making known her preferences in colors. Meya, relieved, smiled and took the cloth from Alin's fingers.

"That would be fine for a shirt, lovey, but you need something more practical for every day. How about this? In blue? The yellow's nice, too."

Alin grabbed the yellow and looked fierce. Spider, standing in the hallway outside and watching things through Meya's eyes, felt relieved. He tiptoed down the stairwell, stopped in the kitchen for a bun stuffed with sauced meat and, putting it in his pocket, ventured outside.

The morning was crisp and new-made, and Spider decided to give himself a vacation. He carefully closed his mind, creating blocks against the thoughts around him, and wandered cheerfully down the hillside. There was some major activity going on at the barn and it had the unmistakable flavor of work. He veered through a line of bushes until he reached the stand of trees that concealed the hot-tub and stood under the branches, considering what to do next. There would be caraem games going on in the schoolyard but Spider didn't feel like playing today. Besides, he always knew what the other terran players were planning and a game was no fun if one always knew what was going to happen next. It was too fine a day to spend in the laboratory with his father, and if he went down to Tatha's he'd get stuck baby-sitting, as usual. Sandro's registration would not take place until late afternoon. Spider decided that he'd find Belshazar and take the shaggy running through the meadow on the far side of Havensport; Belshazar would appreciate the exercise and it might recompense the shaggy for having been tied up the night before. He'd left Belshazar in the hut which he and the other children maintained as a clubhouse, down by the stream behind the school. Whistling, Spider strolled down the far side of the hill.

To reach the hut, he crossed the stream well before reaching Haven and proceeded through the trees, occasionally hopping from stone to stone when the bank fell away too steeply into the water. Small insects chittered, and a stir in the stream betrayed the fish lying underneath. Spider paused to watch them through the clear water, wondering whether Hart might be free again, in a couple of weeks, for another trip north. Some camping out, some fishing, mostly just days of walking beside his father, talking aimlessly—the memory of past trips pleased Spider and he looked forward to another one. Three weeks, perhaps; after the fields were all in. Perhaps, this time, they could take Andrus.

The hut seemed to be occupied. Something crept through the edges of Spider's block. He frowned and moved more deeply into the trees, still unwilling to open himself. The hut faced the stream, with one window toward the back. Spider crept up to the window, peered inside, and stared in shock.

Jason Hart crouched in the center of the hut by the rickety table. He'd taken a lantern, probably from the barn, and hooked it to the support beam overhead; it threw a strong, clear light down on the table. Pinned to the table, upside down, a small, six-legged lizard still struggled as Jason Hart carefully sliced into its body. Belshazar, muzzled, huddled in a corner, his tail between three of his legs; Spider could hear his muffled whimpering.

Spider jumped in through the window, yanked Jason

Hart upright, and grabbed the small knife from his hand. He turned and decapitated the lizard quickly; the reptile shivered and was still. Then, still shaking with anger, Spider turned to his cousin and shook him hard.

"That's the last time," Spider shouted. "I've told you, I've warned you, I won't have this. Damn it, this time you've really blown it."

"It was just a lizard," Jason Hart shouted, afraid but still defiant. "Leave me alone! I just wanted to see what's inside—"

"Then pick on a dead one," Spider said. "You don't have to chop things up like that—and what have you done to Belshazar?"

"Nothing. He was making noise, is all. I just wanted to keep him quiet."

Spider shoved Jason Hart toward the wall and went to the shaggy. Belshazar tried to yelp. He was roped thoroughly, the thin lines cutting through his thick pelt and into his skin. His pouch was filled with lizards, most of them dead from the shaggy's high body heat. Spider kept his fingers from trembling as he untied the shaggy, petting and soothing him. Belshazar put his head on Spider's knee and whimpered mournfully.

Jason Hart, thoroughly afraid, remained against the wall. He put his hands up as Spider turned toward him again.

"Don't hurt me," Jason Hart begged. "Please, Spider, I promise, I'll never do it again."

Spider threw the handful of dead lizards onto the table and put his hand on his hips.

"You like killing things, don't you?" he said coldly. "I've watched you, I've listened in. You really like it, but you don't know what it's about at all. You haven't got the slightest idea." Spider paused, then nodded. "Okay. You want to kill things, you come with me."

Jason Hart shrank back, completely terrified. Spider threw all the lizards out of the hut, untied Belshazar, grabbed Jason Hart's arm, and dragged him into the sunlight.

"A good lesson," Spider muttered as he marched his cousin along. "We'll see what you really like."

Jason Hart stumbled and wept.

Haven's slaughterhouse stood well outside of town, attended by its own disposal unit and a small corral which was, this day, crowded with complacent six-limbed cattle. Slaughtering took place twice a week, the other days being devoted to turning the carcasses into chops, roasts, steaks, filets; achieving the translation from animals to food. Jason Hart had run out of tears by the time they reached the slaughterhouse, but he dug his heels into the ground and grimly tried to fight away from Spider.

"Don't be an ass," Spider said impatiently. "I'm not going to slaughter you, although sometimes I wonder why not. You like killing things, don't you? Well, don't you?"

Jason Hart nodded reluctantly.

"Good," Spider said dragging him forward again. The slaughterhouse was gearing up for the day's work; Spider had no trouble finding Cerval, the tall kasir in charge of the operation.

"I've a favor to ask," Spider said grimly. Cerval listened, pulling at his ears, and finally assented.

When Jason Hart understood what he was to do, he went at it with gleeful vengeance. He stood with butchers as each beast came through the line, and swung his stunner, set to maximum, with enthusiasm. Cerval finally had to clout him to make him understand that the stunner must be used with some care, that the object was to give the animals as little pain as possible; Jason Hart did not take readily to the lesson, but another clout from Cerval convinced him that he'd best abide by the rules. Spider, feeling sick and angry, sat outside the slaughterhouse, waiting for Jason Hart's interest to slacken.

Properly used, the stunners killed the beasts immediately. The carcasses were then hoisted swiftly to hooks running along the ceiling of the slaughterhouse, where they were bled, skinned, and gutted. The slaughterhouse soon filled with the scent of hot blood, and Jason Hart's borrowed coversuit dripped. The temperature rose. The dressed carcasses were shunted into refrigeration units for the next day's work, high-pressure hoses pushed guts and blood toward the huge stone gutters, and still the work went on. Jason Hart's arms ached, and his stomach started to rebel. But before he could turn to Cerval and demand to be sent home, Spider appeared at his elbow.

"You're not done yet," Spider said coldly. Jason Hart cringed and went back to work.

He was offered somthing to eat at lunchtime but could not keep it down. Spider took his own meat bun from his pocket, looked at it, and threw it away.

"Now?" Jason Hart begged, and Spider shook his head. The slaughter continued.

By the time the holding pens were empty and losh'al had come, Jason Hart could barely stand upright. Cerval, his saucer-sized violet eyes compassionate, held the boy up while filth was hosed from their suits, and handed him to one of the other workers who helped him strip away the coversuit. Spider leaned against a wall, fighting his own sickness, and watched the tall kasir cross to him.

"That was a hard lesson," Cerval said.

"I know," Spider whispered. He pulled himself upright. "I couldn't think of any other way. He had to learn about—about killing things."

Cerval nodded and dropped his hand to Spider's shoulder.

"Will you come to The Jumble?"

Spider met his eyes. "I can't," he said. Cerval nodded and turned away to supervise the cleanup.

They had to stop twice on the way home, while Jason Hart vomited, then the boy refused to enter the house, claiming hysterically that he was still covered with gore. Spider took him to the hot-tub and scrubbed him in the shower, then scrubbed him again, and finally helped him back to the house. The family was sitting down to dinner when they came in. Meya leaped up from the table when she saw them.

"Later," Spider said wearily, took Jason Hart upstairs, and put him to bed. The urge to fall into bed himself was almost overpowering. He pushed it away and went back downstairs, to refuse dinner and tell the family what he'd done.

They accepted it, when he'd explained it sufficiently. Meya went upstairs to sit with her son, but Hart looked across the room at Spider with bewilderment. Spider caught, just for a moment, his father's chaotic wondering about his own past, before the boy firmly locked down his mind and went upstairs to bed.

HART COULDN'T SLEEP. THE HOUSE WAS SI-
lent, save for the occasional sigh of settling wood, the
small creaks and groans that were the ramshackle Tor's
nocturnal voice. Hart pulled the thin blanket up to his
shoulders and lay with his hands under his head, staring
at the dark ceiling and seeing the weariness in Spider's
face. After a moment he climbed out of bed and walked
silently down the hall to his son's room. The boy was
sleeping soundly, his limbs sprawled half in and half
out of the covers with the total abandon of childhood.
Hart tucked arms and legs under the blanket, brushed
Spider's forehead with his lips, and, assured that his son
would not waken before dawn, went back to his own
room. He looked at his bed, then pulled on pants and a
warm sweater and climbed the stairs to the widow's walk
at the peak of the house.

The world was a study in black and white and gray,
indistinct in the dim light of the moons. Hart pulled his
chair to the edge of the railing and sat, his arms along
the railing and his chin on his hands. He tilted his head to
look at The Spiral, resting on the western horizon, and
let his mind slide back to Spider again. Thoughts chased
each other around his head. He could not make sense of
any of them.

The sound of the roof door startled him. He turned
to see Tabor close the door quietly behind him.

"I thought I was the only insomniac around," Tabor
said genially. "Mind if I join you?"

Hart gestured toward the other chair. Tabor sat in it,
put his cane between his thighs, and stretched his bad
leg out, resting his heel on the railing. They sat quietly
for a while, each occupied with his own thoughts. Then
Hart sat back abruptly and looked at Tabor.

"I didn't know you had trouble sleeping," he said.

"Normally I don't." Tabor shifted his leg. "Quilla's brewing something again and, as usual, I don't know what it is. Tends to keep me awake nights."

"Trying to figure out what she's up to?"

Tabor laughed quietly. "No, I gave that up years ago. Quilla does as she pleases—she always has, and I don't expect her to change. It's just that I forget how to accept that, and have to learn it all over again, each time." He gestured. "You'd think I'd do it automatically, by now. I've certainly had enough practice."

"If you don't like it," Hart said, "why do you keep putting up with it?"

"Because often the only way of keeping something is to let it go."

Hart looked at him distrustfully and put his chin on his fists again. "That doesn't make sense," he said.

"Makes perfect sense," Tabor replied. "I don't own Quilla, any more than she owns me." He paused. "She's far stronger than I am. She always has been. If I tried to force her, if I tried to make her live the way I wanted her to . . . I'd rather not take that chance."

Hart considered that. "Well, Quilla's special, I guess. Maybe that is the only way to deal with her."

"No, it's not just Quilla. Ozchan had to learn that, too, when Alin was born. I had to learn it again, with the twins." He smiled suddenly. "I think our womenfolk learn that lesson easier than we do, and earlier."

"Or maybe they're just more selfish."

"Maybe. It's not always easy to understand that everyone else isn't simply an extension of yourself."

Hart looked at his hands, turning them over in the dim light. "For a while, I thought that. Thought that there was me, and there was everyone else, no ties, nothing to join us at all. I wanted it that way. Then Spider came along and suddenly it was me and Spider, and everyone else. I didn't know that I could feel that way about someone, the way I felt about Spider."

"What way?"

Hart shrugged. "Love. Redemption. Resurrection. Someone I had to work to deserve. There were so many things that I thought were nonsense, and he made them all real. I thought I knew him—and tonight I realized that I don't know him at all."

Tabor sighed. "Children do that to you. Turn into people of their own while your back is turned. And you have to let them do it; the more you try to hold on to them, the less you can keep them."

"But what's to hold me when Spider's gone?" Hart whispered. "When I don't have to deserve him anymore, what's to keep me?"

"Aren't you being a bit simplistic about that? No, listen to me. Spider's not the only reason you do things—you didn't make Alin for Spider's sake, did you? When you tried to help Jason, before he died, Spider had nothing to do with it. Do you really believe that if it weren't for Spider, you'd be totally black-hearted?"

Hart looked at him dubiously. "You don't know me very well."

"Nobody does, and you've made it that way deliberately. Hart, loosen up. You've tied yourself into things that simply aren't true, you've turned Spider into your only reason for not doing evil. That's merely another way of avoiding responsibility. Mother, Hart, you're not a stupid man. Use half as much intelligence on this as you do working in your lab. You said that you don't know Spider—I think that you don't know yourself either."

"Do you?"

"I know you well enough to believe that you won't pitch me over the edge of the railing, Spider or no Spider." Hart's clenched hand rested on the arm of his chair. Leaning forward, Tabor took it into his own hands and massaged Hart's wrist until his fingers loosened. "There, that's better," Tabor said. He put Hart's hand on the chair arm again. He stood, leaning on his cane, and stretched. "Best get some sleep," he said. Hart remained in his chair, staring at his hand long after the sound of Tabor's footsteps faded into silence.

PALEN STOOD IN THE PACKED, FIRELIT MEET-
ing and looked around. Kasirene were crammed from
wall to wall; the speaker's circle by the fire was barely
maintained. The kasirene swayed and muttered. One
kasir, shoved too far into the speaker's circle, turned and
shouted angrily. Palen shook her head, realized that it
was a terran gesture, and defiantly did it again. This
should never have been called, she thought in anger
and apprehension. We are too close together to think.

Old Altemet pushed his way into the speaker's circle.
The hut quieted. Palen watched him, recognizing the tension in his stance; he did not like this any more than she
did, but the laws of the tribe would force the TribesRite
through to its conclusion, just as the laws of the tribe had
forced the Rite to be called in the first place, after Beriant's demand. Palen looked around the hut again, wondering how many of the young faces knew all the permu-
tations of what they were about to do, and felt a slight
prickling along the fur of her spine. She hooded her eyes
and turned her attention to the speaker's circle.

Altemet spoke in High Kasiri, the ancient ritual language. Palen sat back and waited through the responses
of the opening, until Altemet made the ritual demand for
any who objected to the Calling. Then she stood and entered the circle.

She spoke her names and her ties, the names of her
womb- and pouch-family, setting herself within the fabric
of kasirene society. When she mentioned her blood-
friendship with Quilla, the younger kasirene moved, but
did not interrupt.

"I object to the calling of this TribesRite," Palen said,
the harsh tones of the old language strange in her mouth.
"The calling is of fear and not of thought; the deliberation is of emotion and not of reason; the outcome is

of danger and not of peace; the calling is of vengeance, on which there is no light shed, and the circle may be broken. I speak as conscience for all the tribes."

The ritual words echoed faintly about The Meeting as she stepped out of the circle. The position of conscience was one of power and she knew that her assumption of it would be questioned. It was.

"I am Taeleon the pouch-brother of Kalen, whose death is in the scope of this calling. Palen is blood-sister to the birth-sister of the one who is the subject of this calling. She has spent her life among those whom we judge. She cannot speak as conscience, her loyalties lie without the tribe."

Palen shifted to balance more squarely on her tail. "I have sworn the blood-friendship with Quilla Kennerin; her life is my life, there is no secret there. But I lost a pup to the birth-brother of my sister Quilla, and for this reason I stand balanced in light and shadow, and can perceive with clarity on both sides. I request the silent deliberation, and claim conscience."

As she sat, the kasirene fell into the requested silence. She closed her eyes, feeling her spine prickling again. The terrans and the Kennerins had other friends among those gathered at The Meeting, but Palen knew that none could speak as strongly, nor with as much knowledge, as she. She tried to consider disaster with detachment, but when Altemet called the question again and no one objected, she allowed herself an intense moment of relief.

Beriant entered the speaker's circle, paused, and looked into the fire, as though seeking inspiration. Actor, Palen thought with scorn. He clasped his upper arms behind his back, his lower ones over his pouch and, rocking back, began speaking in a quiet voice.

"Before the coming of the albiana," he said, "all the tribes of the kasirene lived in freedom among the to'anet. All the land was ours, and all things on it. We kept to the ways of the tribe, we kept to the circle, and were served and protected. But the albiana came to To'an Cault and the ways of the tribes changed. Their goods entered our villages and their words entered our minds. Our circles were not their circles, nor were their circles ours. They changed the paths of our lives and took from us the freedom of our world. We are lessened," he said, his voice strong. "We are diminished, and our freedom was stolen from us while we did not look."

Palen scooted forward until she sat within the speaker's circle. When Beriant paused to draw a breath, she crossed all her arms and grimaced.

"Well, that's all wonderfully vague," she said easily. "but not to the point. We've lived well among the albiana. We've worked for them and they've worked for us. We still hunt and fish as we please, come and go as we wish. Our huts are warmer, our fields richer. They respect us, and always have. Teloret sits on the council in Haven, we all vote. Of the three teachers at Haven School, two are kasirene. Jes Kennerin has taken five of our pups in his ships, and they are pleased with their choice. It's true that things have changed, and it's equally true that not all of the changes are for the better. But it's also true that we cannot change what is past. We prosper, and we live in respect and dignity. Remember the balance. Our lives are good."

Beriant glared at her, but Altemet banged his staff against the floor.

"We're not here to talk generalities," the old kasir said, glaring at both Beriant and Palen. "We are here for one cause only. Beriant, you are not to stir up nonsense with nonsense. Palen, you are not to evade the issue. This will be a long calling no matter how we do things, so stick to the point." Altemet glanced around the room, collecting signs of affirmation, and sat again. He had spoken in low Kasiri and The Meeting relaxed slightly, now that the rituals were over and they were in, with luck, for a good, long argument. Beriant clasped all his hands together and bowed to Altemet, then turned to address the meeting again.

"Palen has talked about mutual respect," he began. "And for the most part, this is correct. There have been times of misunderstanding, and there have been times of hostility—"

"Not active," Palen said.

"Granted. Let me say, then, that there have been times of promised hostility. But the Kennerins have done much for us, protected us from the new albiana until the new ones learned better. They have been our friends and supporters. Save once."

Palen carefully flexed her arms. Her mouth went dry.

"We speak," Beriant said with terrible gentleness, "of Hart Kennerin, who killed and walks free, who took our children from us and has not spoken for his crimes."

Palen wet her lips. "It's a little late, isn't it?" she said. "That happened twenty years ago."

"It makes no difference. There was death, and the deaths were not spoken for. There was no atonement."

"Hart was sent away," Palen said.

"Without council," someone called from the back of the room. "We were not approached."

"Nor were his own people," Beriant said. "Hart was dealt with by his own family, and while that is fitting for crimes within a tribe, crimes outside the tribe are a council matter."

"His banishment was sufficient," Palen said. She tried to relax her four shoulders. "He was deprived of his world and it sat bitter on him. Can't we accept that punishment as enough?"

The room echoed with negatives, shouted and angry. Palen bowed her head.

"I am conscience, and I acquiesce. The crime is not spoken for in proper council. But he hasn't damaged us since his return, and I believe that he will never again damage us. The counsel of his family is strong."

Puti pushed her way through the crowd. "He may not damage us," she said angrily, "but he doesn't care for us. Granted that we can't force his liking, but he is actively rude to us, he makes his hatred and his fear obvious. He teaches his son against us."

"Not true," said Palen, and was relieved to hear other voices supporting her. "You haven't been around Spider, as I have. Ask Cerval, or Dahl, or Kerelet, or Taraean, or Tapir. The child is uncomfortable around us, that's true. But there is no hatred in him, I swear it."

"And Hart?" Puti demanded.

"He fears us," Palen said uncomfortably. "But he will not harm us. His circle is closed, let him be."

Altemet pounded his staff again. "Palen, you are blood-sister to Quilla. It's been said that you are so near her that your eyes are filled only with her. There is truth to that, and you must realize the limits of your perception. Surely I should not have to instruct the conscience of the council."

Palen took a deep breath. "I am corrected, and I

thank you. But about the child Spider. I am correct myself."

Altemet fingered his staff. "Does Spider know of his father's past?"

"I don't know," Palen said, frowning. "But I believe that he does. I believe that, except for ourselves, he can read anyone."

Puti, sitting near Palen, nodded. "I have spoken to Meya about this," she said. "She says that Spider can read the souls of other albiana, and I've watched him, and I believe it."

A few voices rose in confirmation.

"If Hart remembers his crimes," Puti said firmly, "then Spider knows about it."

"What other albiana know?" Altemet said.

Palen took her hands from her pouch and spread them. "Mish, certainly. And Quilla. I think the other Kennerins suspect something but are unwilling to find out."

"And none of the other terrans know at all," Puti said. "Hoku knew, but she is dead. Meya does not know, and I believe that Jes does not know, nor do any of their spouses or children or friends. So you see," she concluded, looking across the fire at Beriant, "his crime was not even a matter for his own small tribe, for much was kept even from them. I don't think it fitting that this knowledge remain buried."

Palen leaned over and touched Puti's thigh. "You are Meya's friend," she said. "Would you cause her that pain?"

"You are Quilla's blood-sister," Puti said coldly. "Does that mean you have to love her brother?"

Palen looked away silently.

Beriant bounded up. "I call the resolution," he said, glancing at Palen. "Hart Kennerin committed crimes and has not spoken for them. His crimes are hidden even from those closest to him. It's fitting that he speak for his crimes, and fitting that he speak before all of To'an Cault."

"No," Palen cried, aghast. She leaped up and confronted Beriant across the heat of the fire. "Would you punish all the Kennerins in order to punish one? You've said that they are our friends, our equals, our protectors. Don't you realize that they can only protect us as long as they hold the respect of the other albiana? They would lose that respect the moment Hart's crimes became common knowledge. You'd destroy them, and all that they and we have accomplished together. Remember the difference, Beriant, between punishment and vengeance."

Altemet stilled the resulting furor by pounding his staff violently against the floor and glaring until the room silenced.

"There are points on both sides," he said. "Vengeance is not within the circle, but a crime must be spoken or it will not pass. We seek compromise."

Palen and Beriant stood across the fire, each tense, staring into each other's eyes.

Beriant spoke slowly. "Palen has said that we hold greater freedoms now, and of a different kind. She's right. Had we called Hart Kennerin to a speaking five years ago, or ten, or twenty, we would have been ignored. But we call him to a speaking now, when we are part of the life of this to'an, when our council is sought and our opinions considered. Now, our calling will be answered by all the lives on To'an Cault and To'an Betes, kasirene and albiana, and we shall be believed."

"Beriant," Palen said, almost pleading.

"Palen has said that without the support of the Kennerins, we may lose all that we have gained." Beriant paused. "Here, too, she is right. It is therefore not to our advantage to call Hart to a free speaking."

Palen closed her eyes in thankfulness, then snapped them open again at Beriant's next words.

"But it is not fitting that the Kennerins should lack knowledge of his crime. I call the council to decision, that all the Kennerins of this to'an, without exception, be called to a speaking in our tribe, and further that should they refuse, or should any of them be absent, the speaking be opened to all who live on these to'anet." Beriant clapped all his hands together, bowed, and sat.

Palen raised her head in the silence and stared at him across the fire. "You would bring them to a speaking with threats?"

"I would bring them to a speaking," Beriant said calmly.

"They would come for friendship." Palen said quietly, but Beriant merely shook his head.

Altemet stood again, leaning on his staff, and looked

around the crowded Meeting. "Beriant has spoken. The council may decide."

Palen leaped up. "I would speak first," she said desperately.

Altemet turned to her. "It is your right, as conscience. But Palen . . ." She looked at him. "Remember that you had a pup."

She put her upper hands over her face and stood in silence for a moment, then lowered her hands to her sides and looked around the room.

"I grant to Beriant," she said. The kasirene sighed gently. "But as conscience of this calling, and as bloodsister to Quilla, I request the right to deliver the council's message myself."

"In delegation," Beriant insisted, and Palen, with a weary gesture of consent, lowered herself to the floor. The assent of the council made a thick, painful thunder in her ears, and she wished desperately for a drink.

∿

SANDRO HAD ASKED DECCA TO WITNESS FOR him during his registry. Now she stood beside him in the small office tacked to the side of the town hall and watched with a mixture of amusement and pride as Sandro affirmed that the planet of Aerie was his chosen home, that he would abide by the laws and regulations of Aerie and of Aerie-Kennerin, and that should he ever move permanently out of Eagle System, he would forfeit his voting share back to the company. He put his name on the registry just below that of Shosei Chiba, and grinned at Decca.

"Two strays in a row," he said. "Jes could repopulate To'an Cault with mongrels if he wanted to."

"I don't know if mongrels is the right word," Decca said, slipping her arm through his. They walked out of the town hall and blinked in the sunlight.

"You're going straight to the port, aren't you?" she said wistfully. "Can I come down with you?"

"Sure," Sandro said, flattered in turn. "Jes has been yelling about his schedules all morning." He started to swing up onto the wagon, then said, "Oh, damnation," and put his hand in his pocket.

"I almost forgot," he said, taking out a slender cassette. "It's for Kayman Olet, and I promised that I'd deliver it."

"I'll take care of it," Decca said. She took the cassette and looked at it curiously. "Who's it from?"

"A friend," Sandro said, uneasy with the lie, and swung himself into the wagon. "Coming?"

Decca put the cassette in her pocket and swung up beside him. She listened absently as they moved down the streets of Haven, while Sandro talked about space, and ports, and cargoes, and tau, and it was only when they reached the port that she realized that Sandro was desperately filling the emptiness, that he was, in fact, extremely nervous. When she looked at him, curious, he blushed violently. She couldn't understand why, so ignored it.

"I wish I could come with you, sort of," she said. Sandro blushed even more.

"Why?"

"Because I've nothing to do here," she said. "Lord, I'm beginning to sound like a tape loop. At least you have a job to do, something that helps. Me, I'm stuck lurking around, and every time I ask Quilla to give me a job, she just shrugs it off. She says," Decca continued indignantly, "that I should enjoy leisure while I have the time, that she never had any and she wants to make sure that I'm not pushed into things. Damnation, Sandro, she's pushing me into things right now, she's pushing me into going crazy. Years they had Jared and me at Kroeber, learning all sorts of shit, and now you'd think they'd find some kind of use for it."

"But you don't really want to become a spacer, do you?" Sandro said, not looking at her.

"No, not really," she said. "I love it here too much, I wouldn't want to be like Jes, always rushing about with never enough time to be home much."

Sandro chugged the wagon to a stop before the shuttle, gritted his teeth against the expected double backfire, and swung down from the seat.

"It's not a bad life," he offered, speaking to the box he was dragging from the back of the wagon. "It pays well, and there's always something to do. And you can arrange your schedules, if you work it right. There's no reason that a spacer has to be gone for very long."

"Perhaps," Decca said, dismissing the subject. Jes appeared at the hatch of the ship and looked down at Sandro sourly.

"And what kept you?" he said sarcastically.

"He was registering," Decca said. She came up the ramp and kissed her uncle. "Now he's really one of us."

"Whoopee," Jes said with no enthusiasm at all. He kissed Decca back and shooed her down the ramp. "We're late as it is. Come on, Sandro, get it in gear."

Sandro hastily pushed his box up the cargo ramp, where it bounced awkwardly before disappearing into the hold of the shuttle. He turned to Decca and held out his hand.

"We should be back fairly soon," he said uneasily. "Will you be around?"

"Sure. No where else to go," she said. She ignored his hand, kissed his cheek lightly, and jumped into the wagon. Sandro watched her drive it off the field, then, when Jes shouted, he ran up the ramp and slid into his webbing. When he peered from the shuttle's port, Decca and the wagon had already disappeared.

CHIBA WANTED A NEW VALVE FOR HIS heater, something he could control with greater accuracy, something guaranteed not to jam. Dene Beletes designed it for him, shaping an image of it on the tri-planer in her shop, then snapped the image to steadiness and handed the cube to him.

"Take it to Tatha," she said. "She'll make it for you. She can make damned near anything."

Tatha, after inspecting the cube closely, agreed that she could fashion the valve and named an unexpected price for it: she wanted a copy of Chiba's new map of Aerie. He agreed, and now stood in Tatha's workshop, holding Daren on his hip and watching Tatha's fingers as they fashioned a small thermocouple linkage. They were talking about survey work. Chiba had just discovered that he did not mind telling Tatha about it at all when Quilla walked in and blinked, adjusting to the interior dimness after the bright daylight outside.

"If you've come for Tabor's receiver, it's still curing," Tatha said in greeting.

Quilla shook her head and took Daren from Chiba. "No. Dene told me that Shosei would be here." She put Daren against her shoulder. He immediately tangled his silver fingers in her hair and gurgled. "Shosei, I've the authorization for your Betes trip. We found some extra chargers, enough for a round trip, I think, and some left over. I've already told Cas to start new panels for the frame, she found enough sheeting somewhere to mend that lower section. When do you want to leave?"

Chiba laughed and turned to Tatha, spreading his hands. "These people," he said happily, "are totally astounding. I ask for something, prepare to wait forever for a reply, and within five days not only do I have permission, but everything's half finished. Leave? When do you think the valve will be ready?"

"Tomorrow," Tatha said, not looking up.

"And is Cas working on the panels now?" he asked Quilla.

She nodded. "She should have them ready in about two days, she's got all her spare tailors working on them."

"Fine," Chiba said, and grinned. "Four days? Three? I'd leave now, if I could."

"Four days," Quilla said. "Give me a list of what you need and I'll have it ready for you." She paused and busied herself with Daren's fingers. The baby mouthed the collar of her shirt. "Can I speak with you a moment? Alone?"

Chiba glanced at Tatha, but the Theresan was bent

over her workbench, deliberately busy. Puzzled, he followed Quilla from the workshop.

Quilla walked into the garden and stood staring at the neatly hoed rows of vegetables. Daren yelped, and she bent and plucked a peapod for him. She rubbed it clean on her shirt. He grabbed it with both hands and mouthed it happily.

"Quilla?" Chiba said.

"I'd like to go with you," she muttered.

"I beg your—"

"I'd like to go with you," she said, louder, and turned to face him. "I know you prefer going alone, and if you don't want to take me, that's all right. It won't affect anything. But if you'll take me, I'd like to go. As a favor."

Chiba gestured uncertainly. "It's not an easy trip," he said. "Not luxurious." Quilla looked at him from the corners of her eyes. "I travel light, and at the dictates of the wind. The gondola's not warm, and it will be crowded."

"If there's no room—"

"There's room. I just want you to know what you'd be getting into." She looked at him again, quickly, but he didn't give her a chance to speak. "It may be an adventure, but mostly it's cold, and muddy, and uncomfortable. And you'd have to work, you wouldn't just be a passenger. Do you know anything about airships at all? Or flying?"

"I can learn," Quilla said. "I'm used to living hard and working hard. I can hunt and fish and cook, I can mend things. I'm a good general mechanic. And I can take orders," she said, smiling for the first time. "I remember how."

"Under those conditions . . ." Chiba paused, frowning. "All right. I want to leave at dawn four days from now, to catch the wind. You'll need heavy boots, two shirts, two thick pants . . ." he went on, detailing the list while Quilla nodded. "Can you remember all of that?"

"Sure. Do you want me to take care of provisions?"

"No, I'll handle that. Do you hunt?"

"Fairly well."

"With what?"

"Bow."

"Fine. Bring it, and a rod if you have one. Remember that every gram counts."

"Will do." Quilla put Daren in his arms and went around the side of the house. Chiba looked down at the child, shook his head, and went into the workshop.

"She wants to come with me," he told Tatha.

She stood back from the bench, squinting at the finished coupling, and moved toward a bank of testers. "What did you say?"

"I said yes. Was that a mistake?"

"Probably not." The unit tested to Tatha's satisfaction. She took it back to the workbench and put it aside while she turned her attention to the valve body. "If Sandro's reports from Althing Green are any indication, and our guesses are right, I'd imagine that we have a year to fuck around playing explorer before we begin to regret it."

Daren started to cry. Tatha slid a sling over her shoulders, put Daren in it, opened her shirt, and went back to the valve as he started nursing. His silver hair shone from the side of the sling and one tiny hand held the open front of her shirt.

"I don't understand," Chiba said.

"It's very simple," Tatha said, her voice still light. "Aerie-Kennerin is about to be eaten by a big, nasty, immense combine with no scruples whatsoever, and the Kennerins are doing nothing save keep an eye out and watch the big nasty bad guy get closer and closer. And hope that a heart-wrenching appeal to the incompetent ninnies at Althing Green will work a miracle." She sounded amused. "I suppose that when the time comes, they'll politely ask the bad guy to go home, and he'll say, 'Oh, gee, is this your part of the universe? Sorry about that.' And disappear." She made a rude noise. All the amusement fled her voice. "Don't tell me this is news to you."

Chris gestured apologetically. "I've heard people talking, but I don't really pay attention. I'm not too interested in politics."

"God Almighty," Tatha said. She swung Daren around to work on her other breast. "Are you interested in living?" she said sweetly.

"Of course. But I'm not very good at politics, or anything like that. I'm just a geographer, Tatha."

"You're an asset, Chiba. You've got a craft which can't be detected from space and you know more about the rest of this planet than anyone else does."

"I don't see what good that does," he protested.

"Neither do I." Tatha turned to her workbench. "But you're still an asset. We don't yet know what will help, and we've got to keep everything in mind."

Chiba hooked an ankle around a stool, pulled it to him, and sat, putting his arms around his knees. "It all sounds rather melodramatic."

Tatha didn't bother to reply.

"I mean, first of all, Aerie's a nice planet, and A-K is successful in a small way, but neither is anything special. Oh, they're special to us, because we live here, but I don't see why anyone else would take them over. Even if they did, even if they made some kind of offer, the Kennerins would turn them down and they'd have to go away, wouldn't they? What else could they do?" Tatha looked at him over her shoulder, but he continued doggedly. "And even if worse comes to worse, I don't think a big company buying the Kennerins out would change anything much. I mean, the Kennerins would stay around, right? To run things. And with Mish and Quilla in charge, things wouldn't change. I don't see what all the fuss is about."

"You really don't think about politics, do you?" she said without inflection.

"Oh, it's not just *my* thinking. I've heard folk talking at Kohl's and that's basically what it boils down to. The Kennerins have taken care of things before, they'll do the right thing."

Tatha put down her soldering laser. Daren had fallen asleep. She put him in his cradle, removed the sling from her shoulders and closed her shirt, then picked up the valve body and balanced it thoughtfully.

"I'll be finished with this tomorrow morning, and I'll bring it to Kohl's for you," she said. "I want to be alone now, all right?"

"Okay." Chiba slid from the stool. "I wouldn't worry too much about things, if I were you. It'll work out all right."

"Sure," Tatha said distantly.

Chiba walked around the edge of the garden. The sun flashed on a shuttle rising from the port, just over the

crest of the hill. He hesitated for a moment, turned, and
walked toward the port. If there were to be two people
in the gondola, things would have to be rearranged to
make slightly more space. He began thinking of where
things would fit and swung down the road, the conversation with Tatha already forgotten.

THAT NIGHT TATHA LEFT DAREN WITH A
neighbor and sat for a few hours at Kohl's, listening. Ved
Hirem, purple with the intensity of his argument, was of
the opinion that the Federation should be called in to
blow Parallax from space once and for all, but nobody
paid attention to him. Ved was always calling for the total destruction of something, and Parallax meant as little
to him as it did to the other Aerites. Most opinions
paralleled those Chiba held, and Tatha listened with increasing disgust. Finally she paid for her beer, compli-
mented Mertika on the quality of that night's sausages,
and went up the hill to the Tor.

She arrived in the middle of a flaming row. Decca
came to the door, rolled her eyes heavenward, took
Tatha's arm, and led her to the garden in front of the
house.

"Death and destruction, thunder and lightning," Decca
said, sitting on a bench under the halaea tree. "You
might as well sit, they're going to be at it for quite a
while. Quilla told Mish that she's going with Chiba to
Betes, and it's been a madhouse ever since."

"Why?"

"Well," Decca said, considering, "Mish does have a
point. She's got stuff of her own to do, and with Quilla
gone for a month everyone's schedules will have to be
rearranged. The minute she said that, Quilla hit the roof.
She said," Decca recounted, eyes wide, "that it's about
time people started arranging their schedules around her,

instead of vice versa. She said she'd had it with running everybody's everything, and everybody had better start running their everything for themselves. Then she said she'd put in thirty-nine years for everyone else, and she was going to start putting in time for herself, and if Mish didn't like it, Mish could shove it." Decca paused. "It went downhill from there."

"Sounds exciting," Tatha said dryly. Decca rolled her eyes.

"Of course, part of the problem is that Mish simply won't believe that Jared and I can manage the plantations while Quilla's gone. Quilla doesn't believe it, either. We're getting a little tired of being treated like children around here."

The porch lights were on, spilling brightness into the yard. Tatha turned to look at Decca. She had her mother's height and father's coloring: a pale Kennerin, with light, silky brown hair, high cheekbones, and the oriental Kennerin eyelids, set about unholy blue eyes. The twins had arrived home to stay a few months after Tatha's arrival on Aerie, and she had watched them darken under the sun, watched them at play and, increasingly, watched them trying to work. They looked almost identical and rarely spoke to each other, depending instead on a complex system which seemed part shared knowledge, part a similarity of expression and gesture, and part pure telepathy. Tatha stretched her legs before her and contemplated the toes of her boots.

"Is that why Jared took off?" she said.

"Pretty much." Decca glanced at Tatha, then settled herself more comfortably on the bench. Tatha recognized the signs of impending confidences.

"They sent us all the way to Kroeber," Decca said, as though launching into a prepared speech, "they paid for our schooling, and it wasn't cheap. They let us come home twice a year, and even using our own ships, it was expensive. So we've finished school and come home to stay, with our heads stuffed full of useful junk, desperate to put it all to some use, to get things done, to *work*— and we get treated like kids. Run off and play. Here are your chores for the week, and have some pocket money. The trouble is," Decca said, turning on the bench to face the Theresan, "that both of them, Mish and Quilla, have spent their lives managing things, and now they can't believe that anyone else can do it. *That's* what they're really fighting about in there. Not whether Quilla should go or not, but who's going to run things while she's gone. They both of them believe that they've got some kind of monopoly on competence, the only difference is that Quilla's too furious right now to care." Decca moaned, exasperated. "So right now, nothing's being done at all because they're too busy fighting about who's going to do the things that they're not doing anyway. Sweet Mother."

"Then why don't you do those things?" Tatha suggested casually.

"Me?" Decca looked surprised. "But they'll both blow at me, and—"

"If they're too busy fighting to work, they're too busy fighting to notice."

"Do you think so?" Decca said with interest.

A door slammed hard inside the house, but the shouting continued unabated. Decca winced. "They're both berserk. Lady Mother, Quilla could at least have been a bit more politic about it, couldn't she?"

"Comes a time when the last thing you want to be is politic." Tatha crossed one leg over the other and glanced at Decca. "Is Mish worried that Parallax might do something again, and wants Quilla around to help cope?"

"She hasn't said so," Decca said. "Should she? No, she's worried about the end of harvest, and the general meeting coming up, and all that. You know, the regular stuff. Besides, we don't have to send anyone to Althing Green for two months or so, and nothing's going to happen between now and then."

Tatha gazed with great interest at her boot tips. "What do you think about Parallax?"

Decca shrugged. "What's to think? They'll make another offer, we'll turn them down again, they'll make another one, we'll turn them down again." She grinned suddenly. "We can make it a yearly occasion, like Beginning Day or YearsEnd. Ved can make a speech and everyone can get drunk and dance. We'll call it, um, No-Day. The Celebration of Graceful Refusal." She laughed.

Tatha stood suddenly and brushed the seat of her pants. "Is Jes around?"

"No," Decca said, surprised. "He left this afternoon."

Tatha stared into the darkness of the halaea branches, frowning. Quilla and Mish wouldn't do, not if they were engaged in a raging argument. Tabor? No. Tabor may once have been a bright, energetic, colorful man, ready for adventures and great deeds, but the years had turned him gentle, gray, and placid, content to manage the domestic arrangements of Tor Kennerin and play his flute. Meya? Perhaps, but upon questioning Decca, Tatha learned that Meya and Ozchan were closeted with their two difficult offspring: Alin still refused to talk, and Jason Hart, since his adventures of the day before, had kept to his room and refused to eat anything that even smelled remotely like meat. Tatha listened to the story with interest, then thought for a moment. She extended her claws slightly, retracted them, smiled, and turned to Decca.

"Where's Hart?" she said.

"In his lab, I guess. You know where it is?"

"Yes. Are you going back to the house?"

"Sure. Someone's got to put the pieces back together when they finish ripping each other apart. You want me to come tell you when it's safe to come in?"

"No," Tatha said slowly. "No, I can talk with Hart."

"Okay," Decca said cheerfully. "Oh, Tatha? Thanks." She strode toward the front of the house. Tatha watched her go, then went around the side of the house and knocked on the door of Hart's laboratory.

"Who?" Hart shouted.

"Tatha," she shouted back.

The door opened quickly, and Hart's eyebrows rose. He stepped back, holding the door for her. "Menet pre-Parian. I wasn't expecting you."

"I wasn't expecting to be here," she said, and walked into the laboratory. "Do I have to call you Quia Hart, or will you call me Tatha?"

He smiled slightly. "I try to be polite, if nothing else." He led the way to a corner where two easy chairs and a small table were crammed in amid the lab benches and boxed supplies.

"Then politely call me Tatha. Family names are used only formally, on Santa Theresa."

"As on Aerie." Hart put his head to one side. "Would you like something to drink? Some brandy?"

"Yes, thank you," she said, resisting the urge to bow.

Hart went into the side room. He was, Tatha thought, certainly the handsomest of the Kennerins, perhaps even the most beautiful. She looked around the laboratory. What appeared at first glance to be scientific pandemonium became, upon consideration, the neat and rigorous clutter of a working lab. Tatha recognized an expensive multichamber stasis unit along one wall, but before she could explore it Hart returned, carrying two wide-mouth specimen jars and a bottle of brandy. He put jars and bottle on the small table.

"Mim throws a fit if I take any glassware from the house, so I make do." He gestured her to a chair and poured the brandy. Pale amber filled the jars, and when he handed one to Tatha, she sniffed it appreciatively and nodded her approval.

"I'm interrupting you," she said. "I won't apologize for it. I need to talk to one of you, and you're the only one who seems fit right now."

"Quilla and Mish are still at it, then?" Hart settled back in his seat and balanced the jar between his long fingers. "Not all sunlight and merriment on the Tor, I'm afraid. Doubly a sin when they could be enjoying your company rather than each other's blood. I do apologize, Tatha. Perhaps I can make it up." He smiled at her through the curved sides of the glass.

She smiled back at the smooth, sculpted face, the deep blue eyes, thick wing of hair, lazy grin. "You can begin," she said, "by turning off the charm. I can do it at least as well as you, if not better. And it won't help, you know—you still can't dissect me."

"I wouldn't dare," Hart said seriously. "I'd start by arguing with you and end by dissecting myself."

Smiling, they half bowed toward each other. Tatha sipped the brandy, still smiling, then put the jar down on the table and leaned forward. "I want to talk about Parallax."

Hart's eyebrows rose again. "I'm glad somebody does," he said. "Why?"

"You've seen Mish's reports?"

"Yes. And listened to Jes talk about Gensco, and listened to Sandro talk about Marquez Landing."

"I don't know all of that story," she said. "Tell me."

Hart outlined Sandro's story concisely, waving his

brandy jar in emphasis. When he finished, she looked at him and said, "You take it seriously."

"Of course I do." Hart rose and paced down an aisle lined with equipment. "I've a reputation around here, you know. My family thinks I'm some sort of backwash Machiavelli, ready to make a complicated muck of everything. But I've lived politics, I've watched people playing power games, I've played them myself. Without a great deal of success, I might add, but nonetheless. But my family and the people on Aerie are so damned—" He paused, searching for a word. "They're so damned innocent! They're decent, hardworking, open people who think that all conflicts are as small as theirs, and as easily resolved with a little common sense and honesty. Sure, they listened to Sandro's story, and shook their heads, and sympathized, and took him in. Another of Jes' strays, like most of the refugees were Jason's strays. Evil is some sort of disease, to them. You isolate it, you stay away from it, and you're safe. They don't really understand that it doesn't respect their petty little constructs, that if it wants to, it will come in after them whether they're ready for it or not, and it won't go away because they ask it politely." He stopped suddenly. "Lady Mother, I'm ranting, aren't I?"

"Yes, but it's interesting. Why are they so innocent? They're sensible adults, they ought to be able to see danger when it comes at them."

"It's not a question of seeing, it's a question of interpretation." Hart's pacing had brought him back to the brandy. He offered some to Tatha, and when she shook her head he refilled his own jar, put the bottle on the table, and stared at it thoughtfully.

"You know that we, the family, lived here alone for twelve years before the rest of them came? Okay, most of the Aerites come from a place called NewHome. Nearest system to Eagle. It's not around anymore, its primary went nova years ago. That was the problem, of course. The weather on NewHome changed, crops failed—they knew it was going to blow, they had plenty of warning. But instead of evacuating, the people in charge backflipped. Started holy wars, blamed each other, did land-grabs, put people in concentration camps. Lots of killing, lots of ugly. When Jason and Mish heard about it, Jason and Hetch went off to NewHome and rescued a bunch of them, about two hundred fifty all told." He paused. "I hated them, but that's not the point. The point is that all these people were in concentration camps and hadn't made any serious effort to get out. They were so shocked by what had been done to them that they couldn't cope at all, just fell apart. So Jason brought these examples of self-determination back to Aerie and set them up in a new life."

Hart made a gesture of extreme disgust and paced back down the aisle.

"All right. A population of people whose first response to danger is to go into shock. Bad enough. But some years later, when NewHome was on the verge of blowing, New-Home tried to invade Aerie. Oh, Sweet Mother! Mish and Hetch went off to spy on the NewHome fleet, while Jason and everyone else took to the woods with pitchforks, scythes, broomsticks, rocks—against a fleet that could slag the entire island from as far out as one of the moons. Jes stowed away on Hetch's ship, Mish and Hetch found him, they got to NewHome, and the fleet detected Hetch's ship and boarded. Jes was captured and taken to one of the NewHome ships, and Hetch was forced to come back through to Eagle System, pretty much leading the New-Home fleet. Anyway, Jes escaped, stole a lifeboat, brought it through Eagle Grab just behind Hetch's ship, and brought it in so fast that it blew the grab entirely and locked NewHome's fleet in tau. A few weeks later, New-Home's primary went nova and finished them all off." Hart paused to sip his brandy.

"How old was Jes?"

"Eleven," Hart said. "So on top of a population of muffins, you've got a boy hero who saved the world without a shot being fired. Then the first time Parallax made a bid in West Wing, Hetch had had a run of bad luck and was about busted. Quilla arranged to buy his shipping line, refurbish it, run our own sap to the processing plant, and by the time Parallax got to Eagle System we were sitting so tight, and so pretty, that they didn't have a chance. Not then, at any rate, and they just weren't that bloody interested. They packed it up and went home. Another great victory for the cause of good, truth, and pudding. Shit, Tatha, the history of the whole damned planet has been like that. These people's idea of aggression is arguing over who's going to win the caraem championship this year."

"It makes for a pleasant life," she said mildly.

"Oh, sure, until something comes in and offers to eat you whole. And then you put a bag over your head and hope that it doesn't notice you and goes away by itself." Hart sat abruptly. "You know how to pick the vocal points, don't you?"

"It's a talent," she said, and sipped at the brandy. "So what about Parallax?"

"I don't know. They'll make a move or they won't make a move. It will be terrible or it won't be terrible. We'll pretty please ask the Federation to save our asses, and either they won't or they will, which isn't too damned likely." He slumped in his chair, putting his feet up on a box of supplies. "What galls me is everyone mooching around being complaisant."

Tatha reached for the brandy bottle and refilled her jar. "Are you worried about Parallax, or do you just want to liven things up a bit? There's a difference, you know."

Hart smiled crookedly. "I do have a reputation to maintain," he admitted.

Tatha raised her jar in acknowledgment. "I think we want the same thing for two different reasons, but we can work together, if you're willing. I need a Kennerin to make things legitimate, and you need me because I know what I'm doing."

"Modesty," Hart said.

"To match your humility. Will you consider my plans, Quia Kennerin?"

Hart smiled a smile of pure pleasure, poured himself another brandy, and listened.

QUILLA STORMED INTO THE LIVING ROOM AND confronted Tabor, who sat with his head bent over a bookreel.

"And you, I suppose, are going to tell me the same damned thing," she shouted.

"I wouldn't venture to tell you anything," Tabor said without looking up. Quilla paused, torn between the desire to throw something at him and the desire to hide in his arms. Finally she muttered a curse, grabbed her jacket from the hall closet, and strode out of the house. Tatha came out of the laboratory, deep in conversation with Hart, and Quilla detoured around them and plunged down the hill, skirted Haven, and marched into The Jumble. No one called a greeting, but she was too angry to notice.

Palen was home; her walking staff rested above the high lintel of her door. Quilla pounded on the door frame until the kasir shouted and stuck her head outside.

"I need to talk with you," Quilla said, ignoring Palen's expression of distress. She shouldered past the kasir and walked into the room.

Puti, Beriant, and Altemet sat before the fire. They looked at Quilla, then looked beyond her to Palen and rose.

"Have you spoken . . . ?" Beriant said in Kasiri. Palen made a gesture of extreme negation and Altemet nodded at Quilla as he left. She barely remembered to bow back. Puti muttered "Just leaving," and slipped from the room. Beriant paused at the doorway, his hand on Palen's shoulder, and said something. Palen shook his hand away and closed the door behind them. Quilla ignored the entire business. She unhooked the jug of kaea from a beam and took a deep swallow. The stuff was new and harsh. She grimaced and took another drink.

"It's not ready yet," Palen said. "I could have told you, if you'd bothered to ask."

Quilla didn't reply. She marched about the room, poking at things, then threw herself down on a pile of cushions by the fire and glared into the flames. Palen reached over and put a different jug in front of her.

"Want to get drunk?" the kasir said.

"I would rather," Quilla said clearly, "kill somebody."

The cushions rustled abruptly as Palen moved. Quilla looked in her direction, but the light from the fire dazzled her eyes. She unstoppered the jug, tilted her head back, and let the liquor run down her throat.

"Then," she continued, stoppering the jug and putting it in her lap, "I would like to dismember somebody, and to finish it off, I think I'd like to commit a touch of civic mayhem. Serially, I think. I don't want to be so busy that I can't enjoy it." She flopped over on her belly. "Fuck," she said feelingly, and put her arms over her head.

Instead of coming around to cradle her, Palen said with cautious formality, "Maybe you'd better tell me what this is all about."

"Oh, Sweet Mother. It's ancient history, that's what it's about. You've known about it for years, Palen. Do I have to tell you everything?"

"Sometimes it might be a good idea."

"Don't get elliptical with me, damn it. You really are just like the rest of them, aren't you?" Quilla drank some more kaea, remembered that she hadn't eaten yet that day, and decided that she didn't care. "If it's not one damned thing, it's another. Does everyone have to make a Federation case of it? Just let the damned thing drop. I'm not asking for moons, am I?" She sat and glared belligerently across the fire. "Am I?"

Palen lost her temper. "You're asking for a good chop across your dripping nose. Drunk is no way to talk about this. Stupid albiana melodramatics again. Here, give me that." Palen grabbed for the jug, Quilla snatched it out of reach and, standing, held it over her head. Palen lunged for it and Quilla went over backwards, hitting her head against the stone side of the jug.

"And that," said Palen, "serves you right." She took the jug away, put Quilla's head on her lap, and smoothed the wild hair.

Quilla turned her face toward Palen's pouch.

"Fuck the whole business," she said wearily. "I'm sorry, Palen. It's been a rough couple of days."

Palen nodded in silent agreement. Quilla caught one of Palen's hands with her own and pulled it over her eyes.

"Remember walking?" Quilla said into the darkness. "All those weeks and months we'd spend together, whenever I could escape from the Tor. Walking all over the island, talking."

"And sometimes trying to kill each other," Palen said dryly.

Quilla smiled. "That too. But remember, Palen, in the savannah, talking about all the things we wanted to have happen, all the different things we wanted to be, to do, the places to go, the things to see. All the adventures."

"Those were your dreams," Palen said. She moved her thumb along Quilla's cheekbone. "I had my own."

"We tried to share them."

Palen was silent for a moment. "I think sometimes that we were too early to share them, Quil. I think, used to think, that only our children, growing up always around each other, could share that way. We were too different, even being so alike."

"But you've changed your mind?"

"Yes," Palen said, and did not elaborate.

Quilla sat up and found the kaea jug. She offered it to Palen, who shook her head.

"I'm so tired of the whole damned business," Quilla said. "I'm so tired of coping with other people's problems, of letting other people's messes run my life. Can't it just drop?"

"I don't think so." Palen took the jug away and drank some, after all. "It generally gets worse."

"Yeah. And never gets better." Quilla took the jug back and drank. "We're going to need the new stuff, you're almost out of this." She took another swallow. "Have any of your dreams come out?"

"Some," Palen said after a moment. "Not all. Some came, and are going away again."

"At least you had some use of them," Quilla said bitterly. "Oh, Palen, it's not that things change, it's that some things have never been any different. And I'm too damned slow to see them, too stupid to understand them. And when finally I do see them, I'm too damned stupid not to get mad."

Palen took the jug away and captured Quilla's hands with some of her own.

"I think you'd better tell me what you're talking about," she said seriously. "I keep thinking I know, but I'm not sure. So tell me in simple words. Please."

Quilla pulled her hands away and put them in her armpits. "You know Chiba, the balloonist?" she said, and without waiting for Palen's nod she talked about his solitary voyage, talked about the adventure, the yearning for strange places. Palen sat with her hands in her pouch, frowning with concentration as though trying to punch her way through Quilla's words to their meaning. Quilla stared into the fire and told Palen about Sandro's gift. She gestured, trying to find the right words in Standard and in Kasiri to convey what she had felt in the quiet robing room, surrounded by her sleeping responsibilities, staring at a strange, seductive woman in the mirror.

"I thought I could handle it, but I can't," Quilla said, and tucked her hands in her armpits again. "I thought I could treat it as an interesting insight and forget about it, but I can't. It's as though everything around me is waiting to freeze, waiting to lock up, and if I don't grab for something now, I'll never get the chance to do it again."

"I'm not sure what you're trying to say," Palen said cautiously. Quilla shrugged.

"If everything's going to freeze up, then I'm going to do a little grabbing beforehand, if only so I can remember that I did. Chiba's going to scout Betes' east coast, and I asked him if I could go along. He said I could. Then I told Mish, and she damned near took my head off." Quilla looked around for the kaea, caught Palen's glance, grimaced, and put her hands in her lap. "We argued about it for hours—since before sundown, and only stopped when I marched out and came down here. Hell, Palen, even Tabor refuses to understand."

"I'm not sure that I do either," Palen said, but her voice sounded oddly relieved. "After all, they're not my dreams. To tuck yourself in a bag of hot air and go sailing out over water and rocks and mountains . . ." The kasir shook her head. "No, I don't understand that dream at all. But I can understand why you want to do it."

Quilla closed her eyes and leaned sideways until she fell against Palen's side.

"I am once again grateful," she said, "that I didn't push you into that river, back on the first walk."

Palen snorted. "Much good it would have done you. I can swim."

"Sure, like a dray can fly."

Palen laughed and rearranged her arms until Quilla's head felt comfortable on her shoulder.

"Don't sleep," Palen said. "You've still got to get home tonight."

"Screw home. Later." Quilla giggled. "Remember that camp we made in the Cault, near those caves? The ones you said were safe?"

"With the shaggies in them? Do you know that you almost kept pace with me, running away? I didn't know albiana could move that fast."

"I didn't know kasirene could make a noise like that."

Palen laughed. "We've had adventures, Quil. That time, and others. It hasn't all been dry."

"But that was just us," Quilla objected sleepily. "That's not what I meant at all."

Palen was silent and Quilla, misinterpreting the quiet, grinned. "At least it hasn't all been terrible."

"Matter of definition," Palen said eventually, in a voice deliberately light. "I had to put up with you."

Quilla said something insulting in Kaseri and Palen tilted the jug threateningly over her head until she apologized. Then Quilla took the jug and drained it.

"Come on," Palen said. "Time to go home."

"Why? I want to spend the night here. Fuck home."

"Quilla." Palen paused. "You spend the night here and Mish will really be furious. Besides, you don't want to miss the morning battle, do you?" She heaved Quilla to her feet.

"Oh, I guess not." Quilla stumbled and put her arms around Palen.

"Come on, I'll walk you part way. By then you should be sober enough to make it up the hill yourself."

"Have you ever known me to be incapable of walking?"

"Yes." Palen held the door open. Quilla grinned and walked out, swaying. The Jumble was dark and they shushed each other as they moved through the narrow corridors. In the moonlit meadow beyond, Quilla sat to rebuckle her boot and Palen stood looking at Haven, the spot of light above it from the Tor, and the dark rows of fields stretching up the sides of the valley. The earth felt good beneath her broad feet, and for the first time in days she began to feel cautiously optimistic, to believe that between them the kasirene and the Kennerins would work things out. She reached a hand to help Quilla to her feet and they walked side by side through the grasses.

"Chiba is going to Betes?" Palen said.

"Yes. He's planning a longer trip for later, but Betes comes first. We can do a thorough job on the east coast of the to'an, and if the weather holds, we can swing north and take a look at the cliffs."

"Weather in summer's pretty steady," Palen said. "You shouldn't have any problems, even in that ridiculous bladder he's got."

"Summer would be easier," Quilla agreed. "But Chiba wants to get the trip finished before Turning, and he'll do the big trip starting next summer, if things work out."

Palen stopped abruptly. "Turning? Turning this year?"

Quilla stopped too and looked at Palen, frowning. "Of course, Turning this year. We'll leave in three days, sooner if we can manage. The trip should take a month, maybe more, and we'll need all the leeway we can get."

Palen raised her upper arms and massaged the sides of her head with her palms.

"I know that gesture," Quilla said accusingly. "What is it?"

"I don't think it's a good idea," Palen said, hearing how weak it sounded. She put her hands down. "I don't think you should go now. Maybe in the spring, after planting."

"Why the sudden about-face?" Quilla demanded, coming closer. "What's wrong with going now?"

"There's a lot to do," Palen said desperately. "There's harvest, and you'll miss Beginning Day—besides, the weather might turn early, and you'd be stranded on Betes' coast, if you're not killed outright. No, I don't think you should go."

"Shit," Quilla shouted. "A minute ago you were telling me it's a great idea, and now—Sweet Mother, Palen, what's riding your tail anyway?"

"Quil, please." Palen put her hand out but Quilla jerked away. "Please, trust me. Don't go now. I think you should go, I think it's a great idea, but not now. It's just not the right time. Please."

"Why in hell should I trust you? Yes, go; no, don't. You're no better than the rest of them. Why shouldn't I go? I know, I know, there's work to do and Quilla's the one to do it, right? Well, fuck you, and fuck every damned one of them!"

"Quilla," Palen cried. "Don't make me choose!"

But Quilla was already marching across the dark meadow and would not turn back when Palen called again. The kasir eventually stopped crying Quilla's name, put her arms at her sides, and watched until Quilla disappeared into the hill's darkness. Then Palen turned round and round in the meadow, facing fields, town, Tor, fields again, trying to find some answer or some solace in a night bereft of them both.

QUILLA DIDN'T MAKE IT TO THE TOR. INSTEAD, drunk and furious, she stamped about the meadow, unwilling to go home, or back to The Jumble, or into Haven. Her legs grew heavier and her eyes felt sticky. Eventually she found a solitary kaedo growing in the meadow beyond the port, curled herself into a ball amidst its roots, and fell asleep.

She woke the next morning when somebody kicked her lightly in the ribs. Her clothing was heavy with dew and the morning light hurt her eyes. She squinted and was gently kicked again.

"Off adventuring," said a light, amused voice overhead. "Getting into shape for dashing about the wilderness. It's wonderful," the voice continued, "the lengths people will go to to get in shape for something."

"Go to hell," Quilla said, and sat up. Something pounded in her skull, behind her eyes, and her muscles were stiff. She drew her legs up, put her arms over her knees, and tried to bury her head in the confusion of limbs. "What time is it?" she mumbled.

"Kor'al, or thereabouts." Something gurgled.

Quilla looked up cautiously. Tatha stood slightly to one side, the baby cradled on her hip, and Belshazar sat at her feet, his tongue lolling happily. Quilla closed her eyes again.

"It's not right," she said thickly, "to make fun of a dying woman."

"Bullshit," Tatha said. "You're not dying, you're just hung-over and feeling sorry for yourself."

Something landed on Quilla's shoulders; Tatha's jacket, she discovered.

"Go on," the Theresan said. "Dry yourself off, you're sopping. Here."

She handed Quilla a hotflask. Quilla put it to her lips, smelling the hot, sweet tea, and took a tentative sip. After a moment's consideration, her stomach decided that she could keep it. Tatha squatted beside her and took the flask back.

"I take it that this is not a normal occurrence," Tatha said. "Or I'm sure I'd have heard about it. How do you feel?"

"Rotten." Quilla paused and pulled the jacket more tightly about her shoulders. "Foolish."

"You don't look dignified, in any event. I assume that this had something to do with the Betes trip."

"How did you know about that?" Quilla looked up again. It wasn't as painful, this time.

"I was at the Tor last night, talking to Decca and Hart. And by now, I assume that all Haven knows about it."

"Probably." Quilla held her hand out for the flask. Tatha gave it to her. "It's unimportant."

"Of course. Only unimportant things drive people to get drunk in The Jumble and go to sleep in the meadow. It's when they behave rationally that you've got to watch out." Tatha put the baby down. He crowed and wriggled his arms and legs, scooting along the ground, then raised himself on knees and hands, tottered a moment, and fell backwards to sit down. He looked at Tatha triumphantly. Belshazar came over to him, nosed him, and flopped on the ground, looking like an unkempt rug.

"Hell," Quilla said suddenly. "Did someone send you looking for me?"

"No. I run in the meadow every morning. You happen

"Your own circle," Beriant said quietly and without warmth. "I told you that you would have to choose."

Palen gestured unhappily, turned abruptly, and left The Meeting. The yard before The Meeting was deserted. She hurried through it and paused at the mouth of the nearest corridor. Around her, The Jumble glistened with paint and rang with voices. To take Quilla's place, now, would be to give up The Jumble and her kasirene life entirely, for she would be irrevocably aligning herself with a new tribe. And that new tribe held nothing for her, save the bitterness of Quilla's shouts the night before, and the memory of the good times. And, she reminded herself, the well-being of the Kennerins in toto, and the strength of Haven. She wrapped her arms around herself, suddenly cold, and knew that she did not know what to do.

In her room, she looked about, selected a strong walking staff, and filled her pouch with enough dried food for three days. She had not walked at length without Quilla's company since she was a pup; it would feel strange, now, to trek alone, but she knew that if she remained near Haven the temptation to tell Quilla of the council's decision would be too strong. So she would go away and come back once Quilla was safely out of the way. It was not, she told herself, a decision of any sort. That one awaited her on her return.

She hesitated, then added a large, leather-skinned jug of kaea to her pouch, grasped her staff firmly, and headed south.

A THICK, UNCOMFORTABLE SILENCE SETTLED over Tor Kennerin, through which the family walked on tiptoe, fearing to set off another explosion. Spider, awakening each morning before dawn, sat in his bed and sampled emotions. Decca, already awake, breakfasted alone in the cool kitchen and went down the hill to the barn, her mind ordering tasks in her head. Jared had moved in with Dene Beletes for the duration; Quilla noted the absence of her children sourly and did not comment. The other adult reactions were scattered between exasperation, expectation, and apprehension, save for Mish, who was so angry that she could barely think at all. Jason Hart, still locked in his room, had nightmares; Andrus had none. Hart, in his dreams, turned into an archbishop, a transmutation which so surprised him that he woke up.

Then Alin woke and Spider, sighing, assumed his mental blocks for the day. She still refused to talk and Spider had finally had to hide within his own mind, blocking everything in order to block Alin's unceasing pleas and tirades. It felt strange and uncomfortable to deal with his family thus, as though he were, truly, just another one of them. He made his bed, dressed, and wandered downstairs to the kitchen.

"Let's get out of here," Meya said as he came in. The scent of fresh bread and frying meat filled the air. "Let's get the kids together and go away for the day—maybe down to the stream. If I have to stay in this house for another hour I'm going to start screaming."

"You'll want lunch then," Mim said over her shoulder. One of the kasir cooks went into the pantry. Spider went to gather the children.

Jason Hart still refused to leave his room; Spider had counseled that they leave him be, and his parents, reluctantly, assented. Spider found himself thinking of his cousin as an insect in a chrysalis and wished that he could probe his mind during the day. What indications he could see were interesting and inconclusive. Beneath his temper and cruel curiosity Jason Hart had a tough, inquiring intellect: Tabor, who monitored the children's education, said that Jason Hart had spent the past two days calling up books from the library computer on subjects ranging from poetry and musical theory to astrogation and calculus. Today, when Spider entered his room carrying his breakfast, he noted that Jason Hart was reading sociology. Curious, he lowered his blocks marginally, but Alin's clamor raised them up again. Jason Hart, as expected, declined the invitation to the outing.

Andrus, bubbling with enthusiasm, insisted on carrying the lunch basket. Alin fisted her hand in Spider's shirt, her face screwed in a permanent scowl, but Meya's shoulders relaxed the moment they left the Tor.

Just within the line of the forest the stream fattened into a small pool surrounded by trees and a strip of mossy soil. Alin stopped scowling, pulled her clothes off, and sat in the water, splashing. Spider and Meya sat on the bank where they could keep an eye on the children. After a while Meya lay back, put her arm over her face and went to sleep. A small group of kasirene pups came around the bend in the river and the two groups began playing together, shouting in the sunlight. Spider leaned against a tree trunk and cautiously opened his mind again, but Alin was still haranguing him. He resisted the urge to think something nasty at her and went through the contents of the lunch basket, looking for a snack.

"You threw that rock at me!" a kasir yelled. Spider jumped up and walked to the edge of the pool.

"I did not," Andrus said indignantly. "That rock was in the water already, you should look at things before you splash."

"Was not!"

"Was!"

"Wait a minute," Spider said. He kicked his shoes off and walked into the pool. "Andrus, did you?"

"No," the boy said, and his lower lip quivered.

Spider looked at the kasir, who held one injured hand with three others. "You're Velet, aren't you? Dahl's pouch-child? I've seen you in school. Where was the rock?"

"How should I know? He threw it."

Spider turned to Alin suddenly. "You're going to shut up a minute," he said grimly. "I need to think clear."

She scowled again, then jumped when Spider repeated his order more forcefully in her mind. She nodded reluctantly and waded up the bank to Meya, who sat watching things, her head to one side. Spider turned back to Velet.

"Okay. Where were you standing?"

The kasir released a hand to point. Spider waded over and peered through the water.

"There is a rock here," he said, "but it's pretty far under. And it's in the shade. Perhaps you scooped more deeply than you thought and hit the rock by accident."

"I didn't hit any rock; that albiana threw it at me. And

how would you know anyway? No matter what he said, you'd believe him. All you albiana are alike, you take what you want, you say what you want, you think you're always right, and you're not." Velet glared. "You're a bunch of liars and thieves and we're going to get you, just wait and see if we don't."

Spider blinked, astonished, as the kasirene pups disappeared into the woods. Spider stood in midstream looking after them, then turned to Meya and spread his hands.

"I didn't, really," Andrus said. Spider nodded absently.

"I know you didn't. Meya?"

She shrugged and pulled towels out of the basket. "I can't make sense of that at all," she said. "Lunch?"

On the way home, Spider dropped behind to walk beside Meya. "What do you think they meant by all that?" he said.

She looked at him. "I don't know. I was going to ask you."

"I can't read them," Spider said quietly. "There was, I think, something going on there, other than the yelling, but I can't read them at all."

Meya put her hand on his shoulder. "I wouldn't worry about it. Children say things they don't mean when they're angry."

"Children?" Spider said, and grinned.

∾

SPIDER TOOK THE CHILDREN IN THROUGH THE kitchen, where they could scrub themselves in the big sinks. Meya straightened her shoulders and marched in the front door.

The house was silent. Tabor, in the living room going over the accounts with Mim, looked up and shrugged in response to Meya's raised eyebrow.

"Quilla's upstairs packing," he said. "Mish is up on the

roof walk being furious and not talking to anyone. I've spent the afternoon trying not to breathe."

Mim slapped the receipts together, stood, and stuffed the papers into her pocket. "Damned fools," she muttered. "Fish for dinner," she told Meya on the way out, and Meya grinned. Mim's opinions on the doings of the family Kennerin tended to take concrete form: both Mish and Quilla hated fish. Meya came into the living room and sat on the far side of the couch from Tabor.

"You bearing up okay?" she said.

"Oh, God." Tabor put his hand over his eyes. "I would dearly love to put one of them on an airship going west and the other on an airship going east, and hope never to see either of them again. Why can't this family be boring? What's wrong with some good, old-fashioned, honest monotony for a change?"

"You probably wouldn't like that, either."

"I'd love it," Tabor said fervently. "I pray for it, I long for it, I yearn for it. Let there be boredom! Let there be evenings of absolute silence because nobody has anything to say. Let there be yawns and scratches! Let there be peace!"

He stood, grabbed his cane, and marched to the door. "If anyone asks, tell them I'm at Kohl's getting drunk. If I'm not back by suppertime, it means I'm dining on sausage. If I'm not back by bedtime, it means I'm sleeping it off. And if I'm not back tomorrow, it means I've absconded with Chiba's damned balloon—and a pox on all their houses." He stomped out of the house.

Meya put her head against the arm of the couch, stretched her legs toward the empty fireplace, and considered going down to Kohl's herself. Then she remembered that Ozchan was working late tonight, Hart was in Haven, and some adult had to be at home to keep the bloodshed to a minimum. Sighing, she stood and went to see if there was anything she could do in the kitchen.

Tatha, coming up the hill that afternoon with Tabor's mended receiver, sampled the tension and invited both Quilla and Jason Hart to dinner. Jason Hart considered briefly, nodded, and went back to his bookreels; Quilla's grumbled assent included three complaints about her family, two about Palen, and one speculation about the weather. Tatha, smiling, went back down the hill and stopped off at Kohl's to order a catered dinner, then spent the rest of the day in her workshop.

"No complaints tonight," she ordered when Quilla and Jason Hart appeared at her door, half an hour before sunset. Quilla looked dubious but Tatha filled the house with light conversation, until even Jason Hart, digging into his meatless vegetable pie, giggled and began tentatively to joke.

"Kohl's?" Quilla said, after her first bite of pie, and Tatha nodded.

"I hate cooking," she said. "I can do it if I have to. But I don't do it very well. It's easier to mend Mertika's ovens every so often and eat my payment. And sometimes I catch things in the meadow; Mertika keeps one and cooks the other for me. It keeps me in shape and Mertika in coneys."

Quilla nodded and sipped her wine. "I wondered about that, your running. Sometimes I can see you from the Tor in the mornings, just faintly. I wondered why you do it."

"Custom. On Santa Theresa, a child's coming of age is marked by a hunt, a solitary one. The child leaves home in midwinter and doesn't come home until a kill's been made. Eventually Daren will make his midwinter hunt, but I can't train him for it unless I'm in shape myself." She looked across the table at Jason Hart. "Killing is often a rite of passage."

"For predators," he said.

"Yes." She extended her claws a little and looked down at them. "But it's not the killing itself, you know. It's an understanding of what that killing means."

"The life isn't sacred?" Jason Hart said.

"That life is sacred. And that life is process; that something cannot be understood unless you understand its opposite."

"The kasirene believe that," Quilla said. "They embody it in a circle; every kasirene dwelling has one."

"We have hunts, the kasirene have circles," Tatha said. She retracted her claws and reached for her wine. "I'd imagine that each world symbolizes its philosophies differently—we'd probably be quite baffled at some customs."

Jason Hart put his fork down. "On Gardenia," he said, "they put their dead in heavy metal cylinders, and once a year they take the cylinders out and parade them around the town. On Nueva Azteca it's against the law to invert any pyramid-shaped object. The fisherfolk on Kanē burn all their boats once a year, and wear mourning for them. On Chabad, everyone spends the longest day of the year outside, cursing the sun. It's so cold on Helmsholm that the dead are set on their feet in long buildings, with candles in their hands, facing the equator. When the buildings are full, the doors are sealed and the buildings are burned down. People getting married on Mbue shave all their hair off before the ceremony, heads, crotch, limbs, everything. On Tai Ping, yellow is worn only by old people who have more than ten living descendants. One month every year on Augustine, everyone wears gray paint on their faces. On Briggs Landing, men and women have to wear totally different kinds of clothes. It's against the law to sing in public on Alta Morena. The plains people of Kush bow three times to the mountains every morning when they wake up. On Tabac, you can't wear your hair long unless you've had a child. On Jarawak, every house has a pet reptilian, and if the reptilian dies, the house is torn down." Jason Hart shrugged. "I could go on," he said, and took a bite of pie.

Quilla looked across at Tatha and raised her eyebrows.

"Quod erat demonstrandum," Tatha said seriously. "Jason Hart? Have you finished your rite of passage?"

"I guess so," he said dubiously.

Quilla laughed. "I haven't," she said. "I sometimes think that life is one continuous rite of passage. At least it is for me."

Tatha, smiling, turned the conversation to other channels. After dinner, while they sat in the living room, she excused herself and left the room. When she returned she carried a folding knife. Belshazar trailed into the room after her and looked suspiciously at Jason Hart, but when the boy raised his hand in an offer to pet, the shaggy crossed the room and flopped down, putting his head in Jason Hart's lap. Tatha handed the knife to Quilla.

"We use these for hunting back home," she said, "but I've modified it some. The design's ancient." She flipped out the blades one by one and demonstrated their uses, then closed the knife and handed it to Quilla. "I thought it might come in handy for you."

"A gift?" Quilla said.

Tatha smiled. "More in the nature of a bribe. I'd like a copy of the map that you and Chiba will make."

"Oh." Quilla turned the knife over in her hand. "Unlike Mish, you're assuming that we'll be coming back."

"No complaints," Tatha said, reminding her. "The knife is yours in any event."

"Thanks." Quilla put the knife in her belt pouch. "Sure, you can have a copy of the map. You didn't have to make this for me."

"I wanted to."

The two women smiled at each other, then Quilla rose and put her hand on Jason Hart's head.

"I'm to leave at dawn tomorrow," she said, stretching. "Time to go home."

Tatha watched them moving up the street and, satisfied, went to bed.

BY THE TIME MISH ROSE THE NEXT MORNING, in the pale light before dawn, Quilla had already left. Mish stuck her head into the room Quilla shared with Tabor and, seeing only one lump under the covers, marched up to the bed. She shook Tabor roughly until he opened his eyes.

"Where is she?" Mish demanded.

Tabor looked at the empty side of the bed and shrugged. "Gone," he said, and lay back.

Mish shook him again. "When?"

"I don't know," Tabor said, annoyed. "Lemme go back to sleep."

"Did she go to bed last night?"

Tabor pulled the covers over his head. Mish gave him a look of disgust and left the room. She paused on the landing halfway down the stairs and looked out the window. The sky lightened and she squinted, trying to make out the shape of Chiba's ship on the distant pad. Then she turned abruptly and climbed to the roof walk.

The airship was gone. She looked toward the east in

time to see the tail of the ship suddenly outlined by the rising sun. She snorted, unimpressed, and marched down to the kitchen.

"Who's home?" she demanded of Mim as she marched up to the stove and grabbed the teakettle. The housekeeper frowned and counted on her fingers.

"You. Tabor, Decca, Meya, Ozchan, Hart, Spider. The kids." When she said "the kids" she opened her hands fully and wriggled all her fingers. Mish poured a cup of tea, nodded, and took the cup upstairs.

She shook Decca, waited grimly while Decca yawned, sat, and pushed tangled hair from her face, then handed her the tea.

"Barn first," Mish said. "I want the sap rotated. And we'll need the empty curing vats. Then check with me."

Decca shook her head. "The new vats are out, we did that last week. The second crew's set to rotate them this morning. But Kambala's report mentioned leaf-spot in the hill orchard, I want to check that out. And I want to supervise the weighing this afternoon, it's been done twice and each time they come up with different figures." She swung her legs out of the bed. "What time is it anyway?"

"When did you start running things?"

"This morning," Decca said evenly, and stood. "I've been watching things for months, Mish. And who do you think was taking care of things while you and Quilla were trying to slit each other's throats?"

"Don't exaggerate," Mish muttered, and left the room.

She paused in the hallway, trying to order the chores of the day in her head, saw the door of Quilla's room, and got mad again. She marched downstairs to her office and slammed the door. Mim had already put a pot of tea and a plate of breakfast buns on the desk. Mish poured a cup of tea and sat, pulled some reports into order in front of her, neatened them, pushed them aside, tapped the commiter, and pulled out the Parallax file. She had agreed to go to Althing Green in two months, to speak before the Joint Session: there would be work to do in preparation. The file sat centered on her desk; she glared at it, stood, sat, stood again and went to the cabinet, opened some drawers and closed them, came back to her desk and discovered that her tea was cold. She opened the window and emptied the cup into the flowerbed. She paused, her hand on the windowsill, to watch Decca tie her hair back

as she strode down the hillside toward the barn. The air
smelled of moist earth and, faintly, of curing *Zimania* sap.
Mish pressed her lips together and closed the window.

Children clattered into the hallway, amid the sound of
falling bookreels and the rustle of lunch sacks. Spider ordered them into position and out they marched, a phalanx
of imaginary space warriors off to do battle in the dreaded
intergalactic wastes of Haven schoolhouse. Mish heard the
distinctive triple-tapping as Tabor descended the stairs.
Meya shouted at the base of the stairs and Ozchan, talking to Alin, came down. Alin was silent. Hart's voice
made unpleasant comments about breakfast; Ozchan
laughed; Mim yelled at the cooks. No one came into the
office.

She took her cup, marched into the dining room, and
sat amid the sudden silence.

"All right," she said irritably, reaching for a muffin.
"I'm a terrible bitch and I'm sorry for it. I think."

Everyone looked in different directions save for Meya,
who glanced at her mother dubiously and handed her the
jam.

She left the door of the office open during the morning,
finished making notes on Parallax, then heard reports from
the crewchiefs. Tatha came by to pick up a broken regulator and accepted Mish's invitation to lunch. They sat together in the dining room, talking over their plates about
Parallax. Mish couldn't keep her mind on the subject and
agreed vacantly with everything Tatha said until the
Theresan dropped the subject.

In the afternoon Mish went into Haven to talk with the
council. Jared sat in the back of the room, listening as the
agenda for the next week's town meeting was formed.
When the meeting was over he walked back up the hill
with his grandmother. Alin was asleep under the halaea,
her head on Spider's lap. Spider looked at Mish, shook
his head, and shrugged. Mish and Jared went inside.

The next day, after dinner, the kasirene came.

Mish's sense of dislocation disappeared as she watched
the four kasirene file solemnly into the room. The presence
of Beriant precluded a merely social visit; the presence of
Altemet made the call an official one. Puti, her face carefully blank, stood behind the elder, and Palen walked
across the room to the window so that she stood between

the Kennerins and the kasirene, and off to the side. Mish caught her eye and raised an eyebrow inquiringly, but Palen looked down at the floor and kept her violet eyes hooded.

Beriant looked around the room, counting Kennerins.

"Quilla, Jes, Hart, the children," he said, naming the missing ones. "We need Hart."

"He's in his lab," Meya said. Palen immediately left the room. The kasirene stood silently until she returned with Hart. Hart paused at the door, looking at the kasirene with uneasy distaste, and went to stand by Meya. Palen returned to the window and stared at the floor again.

Altemet leaned on his cane. "This is very strange," he said. "Were you kasirene, we could do it traditionally, but there are too many things you would not understand. And if this had to do with your laws, we would also have a tradition to follow. But we're caught in the middle, and forced to informality."

"You know we'll listen to whatever you have to tell us," Mish said. "Is something wrong?"

Altemet glanced at Beriant, who took his hands from his pouch and announced that the kasirene wanted to try Hart for murder. The Kennerins looked at him, bewildered, but Mish turned to Hart.

"Again?" she said. He shook his head vehemently. She looked back at the kasirene. "I think we can discuss this in my office."

"No," Altemet said firmly. "Were you kasirene, this would be done before the entire tribe. Because you're terrans, it must be done before the entire family."

"What possible good would it do?" Mish demanded. "That happened years back, there's no need to bring it up again."

"There was never any resolution," Beriant said. "So the crime continues."

"Mish?" Meya said. "What are you talking about?"

Mish ignored her. "Then let it be a private resolution," she said to Altemet. "Come, we've always tried to join our traditions, we've always respected each other's customs. Surely now—"

"We could have brought this before the entire town," Beriant said. "That would have been cleaving to our own traditions and disregarding yours. We've not done this."

"Hart?" Meya said. He put his hand on her shoulder.

Mish looked at Beriant. "We understand each other, then," she said slowly, trying to hide her anger. "We follow your dictates, or you take this before the entire island."

Beriant bowed his head in acknowledgment. Mish stood, turned to Hart, and spread her hands.

"I'd like to know what in hell is going on," Meya said.

"I'll have to tell her now," Hart said, speaking over her head to the kasirene. His voice shook. "They'll all have to know. Isn't that punishment enough?"

Beriant shook his head.

"There is a difference between knowledge and resolution," Altemet said. "All Kennerins are summoned to this calling, from the oldest to the youngest, without exception." He paused. "Without exception," he repeated, and Mish spun around.

"Quilla's gone," she said. "You could have waited until she came back, you could have spoken before she left. There's no way to call her back—you know we can't fulfill your requirements."

"That is not necessary," Altemet said. "Palen tor-Altemet, Quilla's blood-sister, today renounced her tribe so that she could take Quilla's place in your family."

Palen refused to look up. Altemet named a time and place for the calling, seven days hence. Then he, Beriant, and Puti bowed and left the room.

Mish lowered herself into a chair and folded her hands in her lap. Hart pulled his hand from Meya's and walked to the fireplace. He turned abruptly and stared at Palen.

"And I suppose you're here to make sure everything is done your way," he said bitterly.

Palen raised her head and looked at him. "I could not make them change the dates," she said evenly. "Nor could I make them change the requirements. I chose to take Quilla's place because I had to."

"You could have told us before she left," Mish said angrily, and Palen spread her hands.

"I couldn't," the kasir replied. "I am—I was kasirene."

Mish looked at her. "And when this is over? When Quilla returns?"

"It's a permanent renunciation," Palen said. "I can't go back."

"Oh, my dear," Mish said. "Will it never stop?"

"Will someone kindly tell me what in hell is going on?" Meya shouted. Ozchan, beside her, crossed his arms and nodded. Hart caught his breath and ran out of the room. Mish spread her hands, helplessly, and began to cry.

"I'll tell you," said a voice at the door. Mish looked up through her tears and saw Spider.

Spider said:

Hart was seven when the refugees came from NewHome, and he hated them. They changed his world, his home, his family—he felt terrified of them and convinced that they had stolen his life. He never learned to accept them, and the fear and hatred grew.

He wanted them to leave Aerie. And, being only seven, he decided to burn them off the planet. First he set fire to the doctor's house, but no one connected his hatred to the burning. Later he tried to set fire to the schoolhouse, and he was caught.

Kalor Gren, who lived near the school, was a biochemist on NewHome, before the purges. He was bitter, and violent, and alcoholic. He caught Hart, put out the fire, and threatened to expose Hart's arson unless Hart did as the old man wanted. Hart, terrified, agreed.

The old man wanted a pupil, an assistant, someone to help him pretend that he still had a calling, that he retained his skills. His hatreds were even deeper than Hart's, and he taught them to Hart, along with biochemistry.

Gren taught Hart to hate the kasirene, to see them as inferior, as no better than shaggies or drayclones. To see them as, at best, interesting meat for experiments. And because Hart could not embody his hatred of the refugees, he accepted hatred of the kasirene as a substitute.

Hart learned, soon reached the limits of Gren's knowledge, and continued on his own. Gren became his assistant. They worked with hoppers, with fourbirds, once with a shaggy that they caught during a cold winter. Hart encouraged Gren to drink. Gren encouraged Hart to kill.

When Hart was seventeen, he began experimenting with kasirene. The young at first, easily taken during the first weeks out of pouch. Later he desired an artificial womb and, unable to afford one from off-planet, he and

Gren captured a young kasirene female, put her in coma, and hooked up her body to life-machines.

There were eight deaths.

Old Laur learned of it accidentally and did not believe what she had seen. But she told Quilla and Doctor Hoku, and the three of them broke into Hart's laboratory and confronted him there. Gren was shipped to a distant planet. Hart was sent to Kroeber. Jason and Mish and Quilla filled in the basement laboratory. Laur died. Jason died. Hoku died. Soon the only ones who knew were Hart, and Mish, and Quilla, and the kasirene. And me.

And now, you.

"Hart did that?" Meya said. Ozchan put his arm around her. Spider looked from them to Palen.

"What do you feel, Spider?" she said, her voice almost a whisper.

"I can't judge him," Spider replied, whispering himself. "I don't like it, and I wish I didn't know about it, and I wish it hadn't happened. But I can't judge, Palen. I love him."

Mish stood suddenly. "I'll call Jes," she said, and walked quickly out of the room.

"You could have told us," Decca said. No one responded, and after a moment they left the room, not talking, not looking at each other. Spider remained, watching the dying fire.

"Can you read me?" Palen said.

Spider shook his head.

"Spider. One of those pups was mine."

"Then why are you here?" he said angrily. "Why aren't you back in the village with the rest of them planning this?"

Palen sighed and came to stand near the fire. "I'm lost, Spider. I'm not a kasirene, I'm not a terran. I can only follow what I love." She paused. "I can't judge either. I don't want to."

Spider looked at her mutely, his eyes filled with tears. When she opened her arms he ran into them and clung to her, trying to smother his sobs.

THE KASIRENE WERE BREWING SOMETHING, of this Tatha was sure. The population of The Jumble increased, but fewer kasirene were to be seen drinking beer at Kohl's, and this despite the fact that caraem season opened in only two weeks and feelings for the teams were already running high. For the first time, the village of Hoku on To'an Betes was fielding its own team, and this alone led to great pounding on tables, gesturing with beer mugs, and rash oratory. But the kasirene kept their surprising silence and withdrew quietly from the social life of Haven. Tatha was puzzled, but did not intend to be puzzled for long.

She varied her morning routines to run in the meadow that skirted The Jumble, and watched the number of kasirene steadily increase. The kasirene ignored her. On the second day she discovered a new path leading from The Jumble into the forest, and an evening's quiet exploration led her along the path to a large clearing two kilometers from Haven. A firepit was half dug in the center of the clearing, surrounded by a mounded dais built of soil. The circle of life with the sun at its center, Tatha thought, remembering her few talks with Palen about kasirene cosmology. The presence of the prime kasirene symbol in the clearing denoted an event of some importance.

Palen took up unexplained residence at the Tor. She worked around the barn or in the fields, but never ventured into Haven and never went near The Jumble. Other kasirene seemed to avoid her. Following a passing suspicion, Tatha entered the vacant comshack at the port one evening and determined that a priority call had been made to Jes. Jes brought his shuttle into the port a few days later, and came alone. Quilla did not come back—from this Tatha deduced that the airship had left Hoku

253

by the time the calling started; she knew that the airship did not carry a comunit. Whatever was taking place, then, would take place in Quilla's absence. Tatha wondered whether this was deliberate, accidental, or unavoidable.

Two days after Jes' arrival the firepit and dais in the clearing were finished, and the day after that the dais was covered with a layer of halaea and kaedo branches, woven together in a complex, concentric pattern. Enough wood for a huge fire was laid in the firepit and torch poles were stuck into the ground in the area around the dais. The Kennerins stopped appearing in Haven.

That night Tatha left Daren with her neighbors, who were used to the Theresan's nocturnal ramblings and cheerfully put Daren to bed beside their daughter. Tatha dressed in a dark, all-covering clingsuit, bound and hooded her hair, and darkened her face. She skirted Haven and entered the woods at a point half a kilometer away from the new kasirene path.

She assumed that the land-dwelling kasirene would not expect visitors to arrive through the trees; once within the woods, she swung herself up a great-trunked halaea and out along a branch, transferred to another branch on a kaedo, skirted an area where the trees thinned slightly, and paused to take bearings. Movement on the ground ahead of her betrayed the presence of a sentry. She bypassed him carefully and continued climbing, swinging, jumping, crawling, until she arrived undetected at the large branching kaedo she had picked as her observation point. Kasirene entered the clearing and one by one the torches blazed to life, although the firepit remained dark. Tatha double-checked the angles of light and shadow, draped herself comfortably in the fork of two thick branches, and prepared to wait.

Within half an hour the clearing was full. Shortly after that the Kennerins appeared. Tatha leaned forward. Mish, walking in the protective circle of Jes' arm. Tabor and the twins. Meya and Ozchan, with Andrus and Jason Hart walking between them. Spider carrying Alin, who looked about unhappily and buried her face in his neck. Hart walked alone, his hands stuffed into his pockets, and he looked stubbornly at the ground. Palen brought up the rear. Tatha remembered that Palen was Quilla's blood-sister; all the Kennerins, therefore, were present, despite Quilla's absence. Tatha frowned and leaned back against the branch while the Kennerins mounted the dais and grouped themselves to the right of the fire.

The kasirene were totally silent. Spider whispered something to Alin and handed her to Meya. The girl clung to her mother's shoulders and followed her cousin with hungry eyes. Spider touched Hart's side lightly. Hart looked at him, then hugged him abruptly and kept him within the circle of his arms. A contingent of kasirene mounted the dais, light flared from the firepit, and the kasirene tensed.

In her short time on Aerie, Tatha had acquired a firm though rudimentary grasp of Kasiri. But the opening ceremonies, to her annoyance, eluded her completely. One of the kasirene moved to stand near the Kennerins and began translating from the ceremonial language to modern Kasiri. The invocation seemed a formality; the old kasir recited blood-ties for the loose family groups gathered in the clearing. All the lines of ancestry ended, one to three generations back, with a death. Grappling quickly with the kasirene dates, Tatha realized that all the deaths took place in the same three-month period. The Kennerins stood silently, looking at each other or around the clearing. Only Hart looked downwards, and retained his grip on Spider. Spider put his arm around his father's waist and watched the old kasir, his expression troubled.

The old kasir stopped speaking and leaned heavily on his staff. A younger kasir came forward and began speaking in modern Kasiri. Tatha frowned and leaned forward, wondering if she understood correctly. But Hart pulled away from Spider and put his hands in his pockets; his back was so tense that Tatha could see the sharp angle of his shoulderblades under the fabric of his shirt. Tatha's eyes widened as the indictments continued. When the young kasir finished, the old one said something indistinct to Mish. She shook her head. Hart took his hands from his pockets and looked at the old kasir.

"It's true," he said clearly, in Kasiri. "All of it. My family punished me in their way, but this didn't satisfy you. I understand that." He paused. "I could plead my youth, or my fears, or my repentance, but it wouldn't change what happened." He paused again, and this time he seemed to be addressing his family as well. "I am not the man I was. I cannot unmake the past, much as I may want to, much as I may hate that past. This, too, doesn't change what happened. I am guilty. I can say nothing in my defense. I only ask that you remember that I am not the man I was."

Tatha moved against the branch while the kasirene shifted and murmured. The kasirene on the dais conferred quietly and the Kennerins watched them. Then the old one rapped with his staff and silence fell. He recapped the indictment against Hart, echoed Hart's own statement, and paused to look at Hart. Hart returned the look gravely.

"Kasirene do not take life," the old kasir said. "But it is fitting that the punishment come from the crime, so that a balance is achieved. You took our children from us, Hart Kennerin. We shall therefore take your child from you."

Hart shouted wordlessly and grabbed Spider, while the other Kennerins objected furiously and the children began to cry. The old kasir beat on the dais until the Kennerins shut up.

"You misunderstand," he said. "I said that kasirene do not take life."

"*I* did those things," Hart said harshly. "Those were *my* crimes. You can't punish my son for my sins."

"We're not punishing your son, we are punishing you. You say that you feel remorse for what you did, and this we accept. You say that your opinions about us have changed, and this we accept. You gave yourself to us for judgment, and this, too, is as it must be."

"Myself," Hart said. "Myself. Not my son."

"Do you think," said the elder, "that you are more grieved than we were for our children? We would take your son to raise among us. He will be well fed and well sheltered, and in time he may be loved. He will be raised the way our pups are raised, but he will not be raised by you."

"Give me a year," Hart said desperately. "I'll bring you another child, another son of mine. Just give me a year—"

"No."

"And if I refuse? If I take Spider and leave Aerie?"

"Then we will tell the other terrans of your crime, and the kasirene will withdraw fom To'an Cault and To'an Betes," the elder said calmly.

"You'd destroy Aerie," Mish said with amazement.

The elder bowed to her in what seemed sad acknowledgment.

"I have spoken the decision of my people," the elder said. "Let us now hear the decision of yours."

Hart turned with Spider still in his arms, and looked at his family. Tatha stretched her arms slowly to ease the cramp. The Kennerins looked at Hart with sympathy or horror, but remained silent. Then Hart knelt and turned Spider in his arms until they faced each other. Spider's face was streaked with tears.

"Help me," he said in Standard. "Spider, help me. I don't know what to do."

Spider looked over his father's shoulder at his family. "Can't you tell me anything?" he said finally, pleading. Mish turned away. Spider looked at the kasirene. He's only a child, Tatha thought suddenly. He should not have to choose.

Spider put his arms quickly around his father's neck and kissed him, and as quickly slid out of his arms and walked to the kasirene. He stood with his back to his family. His shoulders shook. A kasir put a hand on his arm but Spider shook the hand off, refusing comfort.

The elder beat three times on the dais. "It is done," he said, and rapped thrice again. In silence, the kasirene turned and left the clearing. Mish put her arms around Hart, but he pushed her aside and ran from the clearing, disappearing through the trees away from Haven. The kasirene on the dais surrounded Spider and moved away, and after a time the Kennerins, too, left the clearing. Tatha's muscles felt stiff as she swung through the trees to the meadow. She paused, frowning, then ran swiftly through the meadow to her house. She stripped away the dark suit, scrubbed the blacking from her face, and knocked on her neighbor's door, explaining that she had decided to spend the night at home after all. With Daren in her arms she ran through the black meadow until the lights of Haven disappeared beyond the shoulder of the hill. Both moons were down and she had trouble locating the path that ran from Havensport to the Tor. When she finally found it she walked along it until she reached a place where some bushes shouldered up to the path. She walked around them and sat down, facing in the direction of the Tor. Daren gurgled in his sleep. Tatha bent over him and, finally, allowed herself to weep for Spider and his lost father, for Hart and his lost son.

The shuttle in the port, from one of the few non-Aerie-Kennerin ships that serviced the planet, was due to take off twenty minutes before dawn. The crew would not know the Kennerins and would not, therefore, wonder at the sudden, precipitous departure of the family's younger son. So Tatha had determined that Hart would determine, and she did not even bother to feel satisfaction when she saw him coming along the path that led to the port. She waited until he came within a meter of her hiding place before rising to stand before him, arms folded.

Hart looked at her blankly and kept walking. As he passed, she put her hand on his arm and swung him around.

"No," she said.

Hart shook her hand from his arm. "Leave me alone."

"Getting on that shuttle," she said calmly, still holding his arm, "is a guaranteed way of hurting Spider."

"You don't know what you're talking about," Hart said angrily. "Let me go."

"I know very well. I was there last night, watching."

Hart looked at her with pure hatred. "Then you've even less reason to stop me." He tried to yank his arm away. "Get out of my way!"

"You're not getting on that shuttle, Hart. Even if I have to break both your legs."

"I can't stay," he said wildly. "Knowing Spider is somewhere on this island, on this world, not knowing how he is or what he's doing or whether he's well or ill or—*I can't stay!*"

"Do you think it would be any better anywhere else? If he did need you, you'd never even know about it."

"What good could I do for him? What would they let me do for him? Meya won't talk to me, Jes won't, Mish looks at me as though I were—were—" He stopped, unable to find a word sufficiently repulsive.

"That's too bad. They'll get over it, they need you here. I need you here. Have you forgotten about Parallax?"

"Fuck Parallax," Hart shouted.

Tatha dropped his arm. "I don't think you're capable of fucking anything," she said scornfully.

Hart clenched his teeth and swung his pack from his

shoulder, bringing it around in a swift arc toward Tatha's stomach. She dodged it, wrenched it from his hands, and when Hart launched himself at her she grasped his arm, flipped him over her back, spun him around, and held him pinned belly-down against the ground. She sat on his back, holding his arm firmly twisted against his shoulder-blades.

"Of all the Kennerins," she said conversationally, "you're the last one I'd have expected to wallow in self-pity. Don't bother wriggling, I can keep you like this all day, if need be. But you're not getting on that shuttle." She bent her head. "You'll have to curse a bit more distinctly, I can't understand you."

Hart stopped twisting but she didn't relax her grasp. He turned his head and rested his cheek on the dirt.

"If you heard all of that last night," he said finally, "I'd think you'd love to see me leave Aerie. Or perhaps you like the idea of butchering kasirene pups."

"No. The kasirene may think they've come up with a punishment to pay for those dead children, but I don't."

"Then let me go!"

"I need you here. I can't fight Parallax alone. You're miserable. Good, you should be. You're angry, good again. If I can turn your anger against Parallax, then you'll be some help. Then, maybe, you can really begin some sort of reparations. But running away? No, Hart. That's insufficient pain, and I think you've done too much insufficient pain already."

Hart's reply was lost in the building rumble from the pad, and the bright needle of the shuttle pierced the sky above them. Tatha released Hart's arm and rolled off him. He turned slowly and lay on his back, watching the shuttle disappear against the pale dawn sky.

Tatha walked around the bush and came back with his pack and Daren, bundled in blankets. She dropped the pack on Hart's stomach.

"Rise ye now and go forth," she said, her voice compassionate. "For dawn has come, bright with the song of sparrows in the wind. And the song of the sparrows is pain, pain. Get up, Hart. It's time to go home."

Hart rose slowly and, dangling the pack from his hand, trudged up the path to the Tor.

QUILLA STOOD ON THE RIM OF THE GONDOLA, her hands raised to grip the taut lines running from the nose of the airbody to the top of the gondola. She grinned down at Chiba. He scowled at her and returned to his notebook. She stretched her body into the wind. Sixty meters below, the choppy water of Betes Strait gnashed at the cliffs of To'an Cault's eastern shoreline: Quilla lifted one foot from the relative safety of the gondola lip and placed it on a bottom guyline.

"You're going to kill yourself," Chiba said. Quilla ignored him. She had developed this trick a month ago on Betes' east shore, during a spell of light, constant winds, and gradually increased her skill until now she felt confident riding the changing winds of To'an Cault's cliffs. Suspended on wires between heaven and ocean, she felt part of the wind, part of the wild, world-spanning ride of the clouds; became something more than, yet intrinsicially Quilla, casting a defiant, ecstatic shadow on the waves below. She took her other foot from the gondola lip and placed it, too, on the line.

"I'm going to angle up," Chiba said. "Get down from there."

"I can manage it." Quilla felt the wind lift her words and blow them back to Chiba.

"Perhaps. But if you fall, you'll fall on me." Quilla grinned again, hearing the scowl in his voice, and edged back onto the gondola lip. Then she released the upper lines, spun about, and landed in the gondola before Chiba could finish his gasp of alarm. He stared at her, his mouth working, until her high spirits infected him and he laughed in spite of himself.

"You're crazy," he said finally.

Quilla cheerfully agreed with him and made her way to the gondola's stern, where her weight would help tilt

260

the airship's nose toward the sky. In addition to their scanty remaining supplies, they carried a cargo of cloth from Hoku, a box of geological samples from Betes' east coast, and two fine, horned hoppers, one for the Kennerins, who prized them for their meat, and one for the kasirene, who prized them for their horns and hide. Quilla hoped that the hoppers would square her accounts with Mish and Palen both. She had bagged both animals cleanly that morning, outside of Hoku, and this evening she hoped to dine on one in the comforts of her own home, free from the increasing cold of the wind and free also, she hoped, of Mish's accusatory silences and even more accusatory shouts.

In another four hours, given steady winds, the trip would be over. She did not regret its end, as she had regretted nothing save the manner of its beginning. For two and a half months she and Chiba had followed the ragged white line of Betes' east coast, fighting capricious winds, exploring, mapping, learning. Chiba proved a hard master, and was grudgingly proud of her new skills. The airship nosed up the sides of the cliffs, while she and Chiba played the lines, using their bodies to shift, countershift, urge, and delay the forward and lateral movements of the airship. They needed no words save for an occasional grunt, a twist of the head or elbow, to indicate commands, advice, actions. She could, and had, flown the ship by herself, but Chiba remained the ship's master and Quilla did not grudge him his position. She had been given what she needed, and her sense of accomplishment and arrival filled her with wild glee as the ship crested the cliffs and slid down the slope of dense forest toward Haven.

Their homecoming was satisfyingly loud. Mertika served up gallons of beer and platters of sausage, and amid the jollity Quilla kept glancing at the tavern door, waiting for her family to arrive. The evening wore on and still no Kennerins appeared. Quilla stopped drinking and grew quiet. Chiba did not notice. When Palen finally appeared at the door Quilla whooped with relief and wriggled through the crowd to throw her arms around the kasir.

"It took you long enough," Quilla said, disentangling herself from the hug. "Where's everybody else? Is Mish still mad at me? Wait until you see what I've brought—"

"I think you'd better come home now," Palen said. "You seem to have drunk quite enough."

"Funny how beer will do that to you, after almost three months without." Quilla dove through the crowd again, rescued her pack, and led Palen around the side of the inn to where the two hoppers lay by the corner of the porch, carefully and unnecessarily guarded by a band of children and pups. Quilla paid them with bright pebbles from Betes' east coast, which they received with awe and took to show their familes.

"I missed you," Quilla said as she shouldered one hopper and Palen the other. "God, I missed all of you, but not so much that I wish I hadn't gone. Palen! Wait until you see Shosei's sketches, but they don't begin to come close. It was astonishing! Is everyone all right? Mish isn't still mad at me, is she?"

"Mish left for Althing Green three weeks ago."

"Sweet Mother, I'd totally forgotten. Oh, hell. What about Tabor and the kids, are they here or did they go down to the Cault? If they did, they should be back by now. Sweet Mother, I'm chattering, don't mind it, it's just that I'm high on having someone to talk to who isn't me or Shosei. Well? What's been happening? How is everyone? What's going on?"

They were halfway up the hill, well away from Haven's lights. Palen stopped and put the hopper down. "I think we'd better talk," she said.

When Palen finished talking, Quilla shouted, "You could have told me before—I'll talk to you later." She left pack and hopper on the trail and ran toward the Tor. A light burned in the living room, but seeing a fainter light in Hart's laboratory, she veered away from the porch, sprinted through the garden, and yanked open the door. Hart looked up from a microscope and, seeing Quilla, straightened and waited for her, his hands at his sides. Quilla took a deep breath, suddenly uncertain. She came into the lab, closing the door behind her.

"I just got in," she said. "Palen told me."

Hart nodded, expressionless. Quilla came around the table and stopped a few steps away from him.

"Hart?" she said, slightly trilling the "r" as she'd done when she was a child. The corners of his lips moved down and he turned away from her.

"You couldn't have done anything," he said. "It didn't matter—it's not your fault."

"I wasn't asking for forgiveness," she said. Hart put his hands on the table but didn't look at her. "Have they been very rough with you?"

He tightened his fingers and turned his head.

"Oh, Hart, we're a stupid, dray-headed lot."

He moved his shoulders. "You want to know the worst of it, Quil? The absolute damned worst of it? The only people who've bothered to be decent are the kasirene, and Tatha. The kasirene bring me news of him, they come up with stuff for the kitchen or to talk work with Decca, and they stick their heads in here afterwards and tell me how he's doing, where he is, they bring me messages from him. The *kasirene*, Quil! And Palen—oh, Mother, that's the worst of the lot."

"What's Palen done?" Quilla said dangerously. Hart looked up at her.

"Aside from saving our asses? Did she tell you that she took your place?"

"She said something about that," Quilla said. "It didn't seem important."

"It is, to Palen. To us. If she hadn't, they'd have had me up before everyone, in Haven town hall. So she took your place. We didn't ask her to, she decided it herself."

"Wonderful," Quilla said. "If she'd had the sense to tell me before I left, she wouldn't have had to."

"Quilla, shut up," Hart said wearily. "Palen gave up her people to do that. She had to renounce the kasirene, and she can't go back." He paused. "It frightens me, it makes me ashamed of myself. She should hate me more than anyone—but she comes by every evening. To drink, to talk. She tells me how the kasirene raise their pups, and where they go when they wander, and what they talk about, and how the world looks to them—just so that I can know what's happening to Spider, so that I can understand and share things with him. Quilla! Meya won't even let me talk to Alin, and I'm her doctor!"

Quilla touched the moisture on his cheek and gathered him into her arms, whispering the words of comfort that she'd whispered years and lives ago, during their childhoods. Hart finally wept.

Eventually he pulled himself away from her and smiled shakily. "You'd think we were both kids again."

"Sometimes it's useful to be kids again," Quilla replied. They helped each other off the floor and drank from the brandy bottle.

"I suppose I owe Palen an apology," Quilla said.

"She'll be in the Tor—she lives here now. They'll all be up there—some big conference. You ought to be there too, I suppose."

"More bad news?" Quilla said from the sink. She took a palmful of water and rubbed it over her face. "I don't think it would faze me, after all of this."

"It might."

Quilla dried her face and took another swallow of brandy. "Okay, let's go then."

"No, you go on. I've work to do."

"Bullshit," she said. Hart grimaced.

"Going in there is like walking into winter. I don't want to face it. You go on, Quil, I'll be all right."

"You can't hide out here for the rest of your life," she said, crossing her arms. "And it's about time they stopped forcing you to it. Wash your face or I'll wash it for you, but I'm not going into the Tor unless you come with me."

"Sweet Mother, you're a bossy bitch."

Quilla looked stony. Reluctantly, Hart scrubbed at his face and followed her out of the laboratory. She took his hand as they rounded the corner of the house and he squeezed her fingers.

"Can you tell me what's going on?" she said. "I hate walking into dens without knowing what kind of animal's inside."

"Sure," Hart said. "But you're not going to like it."

"Oh?"

"We've a new neighbor. Someone's bought NewHome System."

"NewHome? There's nothing there, the star went nova —there's no planets, just a lot of junk. Who in hell would want a worthless nonsystem like that?"

"Parallax," Hart said, and opened the door of the house.

SPIDER

THE TRIP DOWN THE SAVANNAH WAS SWIFT
and without incident. We left The Jumble in the early
morning, a group of seven adult kasirene, all of them unfamiliar, and I, toting the small pack of clothing that
Palen had brought in the night from the Tor. I wasn't
thinking very much. We walked through the yard by The
Meeting in the paleness just before dawn and entered Havenswood where it swings down to cloak the hilly country
between Haven and Betes Strait. I think the kasirene
chose the path deliberately, to make sure that we would
not be stopped going through Haven or by the port, but I
didn't think about it then, merely walked through the forest as the light clarified, amid the screams and songs of
fourbirds.

South of the port the kasirene swung inland and we
reached the broad savannah. They increased their pace—
I had trouble keeping up with them. Their strong legs covered the distance without trouble and, seemingly, without
tiring. I trudged along, still in shock, and kept moving
even after my legs felt hot and heavy. Eventually one of
the older kasirene scooped me up and carried me part of
the distance. After that I spent half of each day walking
and half riding, until my legs grew stronger. We traveled
the eastern edge of the savannah along the foothills that
bordered the coast, and day by day the mountains of
Cault Tereth grew larger ahead of us. On the twelfth day
the group joined another small set of travelers, this one
with children, and after that the pace slackened. We
turned eastward through a pass in the hills.

The numbness wore off as we moved closer to the coast,
and was replaced with a terrible homesickness. The hills
were colored their usual late-summer brown, rolling and
folding in on themselves, dotted with occasional solitary
trees; their eastern slopes, facing the Strait, were generally

thickly fleeced in dark scrub and the sky was an even, unending blue. I had never been through these hills before and slid into a terrible and profound loneliness. I tried touching each kasir in the group with my mind, but they were opaque to me; I could barely tell that they existed. I hadn't realized, even during those days when I'd closed myself to Alin, that this was the way most people spent their lives, locked inside their own skulls. The thought crystallized my loneliness. I focused all my energy and tried to reach Alin, but when I touched her she shrieked and clutched at me—she still wasn't speaking, was barely responding to the world at all—and I wrenched away from her, screaming that she should learn to talk. I couldn't know if it had done any good or not, but I didn't try reaching her again.

The pass decanted us through high, white cliffs onto a brown, rock-strewn strip of land surrounding a small bay. A tribe of kasirene fisherfolk lived near the water's edge, their village tucked into the foot of the cliffs and their slim boats drawn far up the dun-colored beach. We spent a week there, fishing, foraging, passing the evenings deep in talk and song. Or, at any rate, the kasirene talked and sang, and were unfailingly kind to me despite my continued silence. They set me and the other children to cleaning each day's catch. I quickly learned how to gut and clean the fish with a few strokes of the knife and did it with only half my attention. Seabirds fell down the curve of the air, intent on theft, and were driven away with rocks and insults. Near dusk one of the fisher pups came to collect my pile of fishguts—they were added to a large heap of others on the beach and the pups hid behind a pile of rocks, grinning and nudging each other and peering around the stones. I stood back and watched them until one noticed me, pushed her companions aside, and insisted that I join them. After a moment's hesitation, I did.

The seabirds circled overhead, suspicious, and made raucous noises at each other, then swooped to the pile of guts. They squabbled and fought, filling the air with hideous noises and the frantic beating of their gray and white wings. Two rose, each attached to an end of scrap, and fluttered angrily at each other until a third one dove between them and escaped with the entire piece. The pups howled with laughter. Birds flew from the huddle and made off with whatever morsels they had won, hotly pursued by those less agile or fortunate. Within a few minutes the beach was clean of guts and of birds, save for one old bird who pecked without much hope at the sand and ruffled his four wings unhappily. The pups, chattering and shoving, collected the fish they'd put aside for themselves, built a small fire on the beach, and roasted the fish over it. It tasted strange and smoky, but I ate everything I was given, and afterwards I curled into the sand a bit away from the rest of them. The evening grew chilly. Stars thickened overhead but both moons were down. I did some figures and finally spotted the light of the processing plant, one of the brighter stars. Then I did some more figures, and tried to remember lines of poetry—anything to fill my head.

"Are you planning to sleep out here?" someone said in Kasiri. I sat up and turned around. The kasir squatting near me was the one who'd made space for me earlier, behind the rocks. I shook my head.

"You do know how to talk, don't you?" she said.

I shrugged.

"Oh, I don't really care. Melet says I talk enough for any three, so I suppose I can talk for both of us. That's where we're going, you know. Over to Melet. She used to be on Betes, but she's on a different to'an now, I don't know which one. She travels." The kasir laughed. "We all travel, but Melet travels more than most. It makes her awful hard to catch up with. I'm Kaën."

"Spider," I said. My mouth felt dry.

"There, I knew you could talk," she said with satisfaction. "Come on, if we don't find room in a hut we'll have to spend the night on the beach. That's okay for me, but you look pretty cold. What does Spider mean?"

"It's Standard for talaete," I said, naming the Aerie equivalent. I'd never seen a real spider. Kaën laughed and stood.

"Strange name. It sounds better in Standard, though. I don't speak Standard very well, I only spent half a year in Haven. Could you teach me?"

"If you want," I said. I followed Kaën up the beach. The firepit had been covered with sand, and the other pups were gone.

"Here," Kaën said. She took my hands and put them against the piled sand. The warmth felt good.

The huts were full. Kaën, motioning me to be quiet, snuck into one. I sat down and tried not to shiver, but it was cold. Something rustled in the hut, then Kaën came pelting back out again, holding a blanket and pursued by Kasiri curses. We ran back to the beach.

She smoothed the sand over the firepit, tested it with her hand, and spread the blanket over it.

"There," she said. "That should keep you warm."

"What about you?"

"I've got fur." She stretched out beside the pile of warm sand. "And if I get cold, I'll crawl in. Okay?"

"Okay," I said, and pulled the ends of the blanket around me. I wriggled until the sand shifted to fit all my bumps. Kaën fell asleep immediately and I turned over and looked at her. She was taller than I, which meant that she had to be my own age or perhaps a little younger. I wondered if she'd been instructed to make friends with me. It didn't matter, really, but it felt scary, not being able to read the people around me, to know what their motivations were—it made me feel helpless, and that frightened me. I turned on my back, hastily, and constructed a wall against the fear, like the wall I'd made against homesickness, or loneliness. Eventually, I thought, I'd have a wall all the way around me, and nothing would ever hurt me again.

THE KASIRENE BOATS WERE LONG, SLENDER hulls; arches of wood connected the hulls, on either side, to outriggers. They were made of a deep, greeny-brown wood, polished until it gleamed, and they bobbed and nodded in the small waves of the bay. They were going to take us, Kaën said, to To'an Betes. I asked if the smudge of land visible across the water was Betes. She didn't know. The fishers went through us, directing us in pairs to the boats. Kaën and I were put in one of the smaller

boats, to Kaën's vocal disgust. I stowed my pack under
the plank seat in the middle of the hull while Kaën fiddled in her pouch, rearranging things. There were hatches
set into the deck and I looked down into dark, deep holds,
empty now. The sun rose beyond the Strait and the waves
sparkled. Four fishers climbed into the boat with us and
another pushed us away from the shore; the boat dipped
and steadied and green water flashed under and over the
fisher's paddles.

I'd not been in a boat before and found that I liked
it. The fishers called to each other as the arms of the bay
reached toward us; seabirds followed us into the Strait
itself. I turned to look back at the bay, the inward clasp
of its wooded arms, and the white marching cliffs. The
water grew choppier; I held more tightly to the seat.
Kaën began to sing. The fishers stowed their paddles and
ran a sail up the single mast. The boat shivered and flew.

The smudge of land I'd seen from the bay was the long
northern arm of To'an ba Cault. Shoals extended from it
into the dark waters. The sail rattled down, weighted
ropes were thrown over the sides of the boats, and the
fishers spread their nets. By midmorning Kaën and I were
busy pulling lines, wading through flopping seas of wet
fish, and trying not to get in the way. We chased fish into
the two large holds; Kaën, with four arms to use, did
better than I. One of the fishers laughed at my efforts to
keep a grip on the sliding fish. I ignored him. Later he
passed me a bottle of warm water, still laughing, and
told me that I had done well. The sun glared off the
water. I wiped sweat from my face and went back
to work. By midafternoon the boats were on their way
again, aimed toward Betes' shore.

To'an Betes reaches a mountainous, twisting peninsula
toward Cault and we skirted that peninsula, moving through
the Strait between To'an ba Cault and Betes. I watched
the two coasts slip by, ba Cault gentle and golden, Betes
fiercely toothed and dense with trees and cliffs. The high
ridge of the peninsula was purple with distance and pur-
pled further as the sun dropped behind us; ba Cault re-
ceded. Kaën said that we would avoid the Strait between
Betes and To'an Galae, for the fishers said that it was
treacherous. Instead we'd skirt the southern edge of Galae,
but that was for tomorrow. We swooped toward a narrow
beach under the cliffs of Betes' southern shore and spent

an uncomfortable night on the rocks. The next morning the
fishers flooded the holds with fresh seawater and we
skimmed Galae, turned north, and approached a wide,
comfortable bay on Betes' south shore. Here the mountains had made a concession to the shore, and grassy plain
stretched from the edge of the bay into the heartland of
Betes. I stood in the boat to look at it, holding to the
mast, wondering if this was to be the end of the journey.
But Kaën said that we'd days of travel left yet, and I sat
again.

A group of kasirene and terrans from Hoku was waiting on the beach. Beyond them a line of drays and carts
stretched into the grassy plain. The kasirene didn't seem
to be keeping any guard on me, and Kaën, seeing someone she knew, ran off to talk. I walked toward the group
of humans, expecting to be stopped, but nobody called
out to me.

"Traveling with the kasirene?" one said to me. He
shoved a tub of fish into the cart and pulled wet sacking
over it.

"Yes," I said.

"Your business, I guess. Wouldn't do it myself." He
had a rough brown face and a line of silver over his forehead; he rubbed his hand across his face, wiping away
sweat, and left more silvery fishscales along his cheeks.
"Hey, you one of the Kennerins?"

I nodded. "Could you deliver a message for me? I
mean, if you could take it into Hoku and give it to somebody who's going over to Haven?"

"I can have it commed," he offered, looking at me
curiously, but I shook my head.

The kasirene hadn't said anything about letters, but
they'd treated me fairly—they deserved to be asked. I
found one of the adults from the travel group and waited
until she had finished her business, them asked her my
question.

"Sure," she said. "But I don't have anything to write
on, or with. You'll have to find that for yourself."

That presented no problem. I went among the terrans
until I found somebody to give me a sheet of paper and
somebody else to lend me a pen. While the fish were
appraised, argued over, bought, and loaded into the carts,
I sat on a rock and wrote a letter to my father.

I told him that I missed him, and described the trip

south along the savannah, and the fisher's camp, and the crossing of the Strait. I told him about Kaën and the pups' teasing of the seabirds. I told him that I'd been treated kindly and fed well, that I was safe and healthy. I told him that I didn't know where we were going. I told him the truth about everything except the way I felt. Then I folded the letter, sealed it with a drop of sap that I picked from a bush on the beach, and took the letter to the rough-faced man. He grunted and put the letter in his pocket. The group from Hoku left with their carts, and after another night spent on the beach the traveling group left the fishers and moved north and east, avoiding the plain on which Hoku sat.

I opened my mind to the village that night, but no one in Hoku was thinking about the Kennerins. Someone dreamed about Shosei Chiba's balloon, but Quilla did not figure in the dream. I spent most of the night awake, trying to sample all the minds in Hoku without lowering my own walls—a form of leave-taking, I guess. There might be some scattered farmholds outside of Hoku, but I doubted that we'd go near them; this was to be my last taste of my fellow terrans for an indefinite time. After a while my walls started to weaken, so I closed my mind to Hoku but still couldn't sleep.

I stumbled along beside Kaën the next day, tripping on things. The forest on Betes was thicker and less traveled than the forests back home. Kaën chattered and sang and ignored my silence, but that night, as the evening fire was banked and the kasirene settled around it to sleep, she touched my shoulder, put a hand over her mouth, and nodded toward the edge of the clearing. I followed her into the woods.

Away from the clearing the woods seemed menacing. Kaedos and halaeas were rare here; this forest was a mixture of needled black conifers and climbing, ropy vines that rose from a fern-covered floor and drove their roots into the rough bark of the trees. The vines were pale and naked until they reached the treetops, and then exploded into thick masses of serrated leaves. The forest seemed a silent, fatal fight between the trees and the vines for sunlight and air, and when a branch creaked loudly I jumped a bit and walked closer to Kaën.

"Tree-ghouls," she whispered, and wrapped two of her arms around one of mine.

"That's just a story," I whispered back. I felt pleased that she was as scared as I. "I'd be more worried about shaggies."

"They don't come this far south, this time of year," she said. "I think."

"You hope."

We were walking so close together that we bumped into each other and into the trees and vines, but I had no intention of letting go of Kaën, and her grip on me didn't loosen at all.

"Where are we going?" I asked finally.

She glanced at me, her violet eyes round and luminous. "I thought you'd never ask. It's a bit farther."

"But what is it?"

"Hush. You'll see."

The air lightened ahead, a creeping white radiance that seemed even more menacing than the dark forest. But she pulled me along until the trees thinned and I saw another clearing. The whiteness came from moonlight pouring through the clearing. Kaën stopped just within the line of trees. I peered around her arms.

"It's more gone than last time," she said, her voice still low. "Over toward the middle, behind that bush. Can you see the bricks?"

I squinted and finally saw a pile of something bleached in the moonlight.

"What is it?"

"Come on, I'll show you."

We picked our way through bushes and ferns. The angular pile became the broken remains of a chimney. I made out the vestiges of walls extending from it in a rough rectangle.

"It's a house," I said, surprised, and dropped Kaën's arm to walk forward. She grabbed my shoulder and held me back.

"There might be something there," she said, sounding definitely scared.

"Nothing but stones and bushes," I said with more confidence than I felt. "Come on."

She followed me reluctantly. I walked around the walls, poking at the bushes, and found a shard of glass. Kaën shrugged her lower arms and kept her upper hands fastened tightly on my shoulders. I didn't want to tell her to stop, but I was convinced that nothing here would

hurt us. I stepped over the broken walls into the interior
of the ruined house and Kaën, after a moment's hesitation during which her arms were stretched uncomfortably before her, followed me in.

"It's an albiana house," she offered. "We don't build
things like this."

I nodded. "Old, though. Probably from just after the
time the refugees came."

"Melet says that some albiana came over the first winter, that they went up and down Betes measuring things
and taking notes. Maybe they made this."

"It's possible," I said, frowning at the crumbled fireplace. "Some of them stayed four or five months, and
they'd have needed a place—but why here?"

Kaën shrugged. "Why do albiana do anything?" She
took her hands off my shoulders and put them all in her
pouch.

I touched a brick. "Maybe my grandfather made this,"
I said. "Jason. He came over with that first group, and he
knew how to build things." The thought excited me. I
moved away from Kaën and started poking in the ruins.
She took her hands out of her pouch and tangled all her
arms over her belly, watching me.

Under the grass and weeds, there were treasures. I
filled my arms with them, and cleared the top of a pile
of stones. "Look," I said to her, and she came over to
watch me lay out a broken knife, the handle of a mug, a
rusted spoon, and a bent nail. "Maybe my grandfather
used these things. See, that's where the door was, over
there. And there must have been windows, but it's sort
of hard to tell now, with the walls mostly down. The fireplace was pretty big, you can tell that. I wonder what
sort of roof they had? Nothing too permanent, maybe
sod. See how the logs for the walls aren't really finished?
They made the house quickly, just chopped down some
trees and notched the ends to fit together. And the fireplace isn't bricks, it's shaped stone. That must have taken
work—why did they do that? I wonder what they used
for mortar. Lady, Kaën, that must have been some adventure, to come all the way over here in a handmade
boat, in winter, and explore the island, and build the
house." I put the junk into my pockets. "I wish they'd
left more. Maybe, when I get back home . . ." I stopped,
remembering, and looked at the fireplace again.

Kaën untangled her hands, looking nervous, and reached for me.

"Come on," she said. "We'd better get back before they find that we're gone, and get mad."

I jerked my hand away from her and marched toward the edge of the clearing, then paused to look back at the jumble of logs and stone. Kaën caught up and looked at me, her head tilted to the side. I told myself that it wasn't her fault, she hadn't broken all my carefully made walls —I had. I should have known what I'd get into, I should have refused to come with her, or, having come, refused to get excited. But it wasn't Kaën's fault. I put my hands in my pockets and felt the stuff I'd found, and just before we reached the kasirene camp, I caught up with Kaën and touched her lower shoulder. She turned and looked at me uneasily.

"Why did you take me there?" I said.

She shrugged. "You looked—lonely. I'd be lonely too, if I had to live with the albiana. So I thought you might —well, it was the only albiana thing I could think of that you could see. I thought it might make you feel better." She kicked at the duff with her big feet. "I'm sorry."

I automatically shook my head, and remembered another thing I'd forgotten. That you can tell another person's feelings without reading their minds; that you can watch expressions, gestures, you can listen to the meanings beyond the words or silences. I hadn't much practice doing that; Kaën was better at it than I, and better at it with someone not of her race. I felt ashamed of myself and dug into my pocket until I found the rusted spoon.

"Would you like this?" I said, offering it to her. She looked at me quizzically, then nodded and put the spoon in her pouch. I hugged her tightly and we crept into the camp to find our blankets. That night I had no trouble sleeping at all.

"Who's Melet?" I asked her the next day. We had dropped to the rear of the group, ostensibly to keep our eyes open for any pelberries that might remain on the vines. The forest had thinned and changed and the sun was bright. We found some pel but ate them immediately; Kaën's pouch and my basket remained empty.

"Melet? She's the teacher. Oh, she's even older than Altemet, back on Cault. I think she's older than anything.

But she's not sotty, you can't get away with anything around her. I've tried. She's taught everybody—except the albiana, of course. You'll be her first albiana. That's why they sent me to Haven, to come back with you. But Melet's moved again, somewhere east of here so we'll have to take another boat. That's what Temel told me last night, and I guess he'd know. Anyway, we'll go to her if we reach the shore on time. They say that winter's coming early this year and if we don't make it, we'll have to spend winter on Betes 'cause nobody's going to want to make the crossing in bad weather."

I considered this speech for a moment. If Kaën had come to Haven half a year past, it meant the kasirene had been planning on taking me for at least that long. I filed this away for a while. "Has Melet really taught everybody? Is she the only teacher? What does she teach?"

"Well, not *every*body," Kaën admitted. "But most folk, especially on these to'anet. She's not the only teacher, but she's the best. What does she teach? Oh, everything. Currents, and star patterns, and how to tell the weather, and where to find medicines and how to make them and use them, and she knows all the sagas, all the way back. And she knows about making dyes, and boats and gardens and —oh, all sorts of things. But she's pretty strict."

"Do you like her?"

Kaën stared at me. "Like her? I don't know. She's the teacher."

I had a quick vision of a tiny, prune-faced kasirene carrying a halaea switch. Kaën found another patch of pel and we stopped to eat them.

"Are we all going to stay with her?"

"Us younger ones, sure. The older ones are just wandering. Some of them might stay, but I don't think so. She's not going to have too much room, now that she's moved."

"Where to?"

"To'an Tebetet, east of here."

I frowned, trying to recall Chiba's maps. To'an Tebetet was a small squirt of an island, about fifty kilometers off Betes' southeastern shore. Tebetet meant birdshit.

And I didn't have to read minds to know why we'd been told Melet's location now and not earlier. We'd see no more terrans on our trip; it was now safe to tell me. I took some of the Kaën's pel and ate them. No use getting mad at her—she probably hadn't known before last night either. But I couldn't resist asking another question.

"If she was on Betes before, why did she move to a forsaken place like Tebetet? That doesn't make much sense."

Kaën looked at me and spit out a seed. "She moved because of you, Spider. Surely you know that."

I shrugged and didn't speak again. When we found more pel I put them all in my basket and didn't eat a single one.

Another week passed before we reached To'an Betes' southeastern shore. The good weather held and the kasirene, after a deal of consultation and argument, decided it would be safe to make the crossing. The local fisher tribe agreed and one bright morning, an hour after dawn, the outriggers were floated into the calm waters of the bay. Kaën, four adults, and I stepped into the middle boat. I turned my back to the sea and the rising sun and watched the coastline of To'an Betes until it slid beneath the waves. When the last smudge of land was gone I turned to face east. I put my hand in my pocket and closed my fingers around the knife that might have been Jason's, and reached my other hand for one of Kaën's.

Part Four

CHECKMATE
1245–1246 new time

"We are not interested in the possibilities of defeat."

Victoria I of England
December 1899

"THOSE FUCKERS ARE PLANNING TO INVADE us!" a voice cried, and the town meeting exploded. Quilla waited patiently until the shouting had peaked, then beat furiously on the gong behind the podium. Tatha closed her eyes.

The Aerites, packed tightly into the cavernous hall, had listened patiently while Keloret outlined the twenty-three-year history of Aerie's dealings with Parallax; listened sympathetically to Sandro's story of the destruction of his family and loss of his homeworld; listened with growing anger to Tatha's spare description of Parallax's attempt to take over Gensco Station. When Quilla, taking over the microphone again, told the meeting that Parallax had bought the remains of NewHome System, the Aerites had drawn the obvious conclusion.

Tatha resisted the urge to put her hands over her ears. Instead she looked around the crowded hall while the shouting slowly abated. Ved Hirem was on his feet, waving his cane threateningly and demanding to be heard. His daughter Pixie, sitting beside him, put her large hand on his shoulder and gently forced him into his seat. Tatha watched Pixie covertly. She towered above Ved, her thick body muscled with work in the fields and her hair, cropped short, framed the broad, placid planes of her face. Tatha prodded her memory and it obliged with a brief note. Pixie Hirem, friend of Meya's, co-manager of the eastern belt of truck farms, raiser of the special breed of running drays that Hart had created. Also rumored to be the true author of Ved Hirem's *Codified Customs of Aerie,* although her name did not appear on the book. Now Pixie addressed a few words to her father. Ved slumped sullenly and closed his mouth. Tatha looked away from them toward the group of kasirene in the far corner of the room.

That in itself was unusual; generally the kasirene were scattered evenly through the audience, although, because of their size, they tended to stay toward the back of the room. Tatha saw Beriant standing at the front of the group, his head bent as he listened to another kasir. Palen was not in the room, nor was Tatha surprised by her absence. Manuel Hetch, in his wheelchair, sat in the aisle near the dais, alternately tugging at his chin and frowning terrifically. Tham sat beside him, a grandchild on each knee; since giving up space Tham had taken up drinking and even now, presumably sober, his hands trembled. Cas Hevant the weaver and her son Koyu, Perri the carpenter, Medi Lount the sculptor, Mertika Kohl sitting to the side and watching Hart; Simit, Dahl, Tapir, and the rows upon rows of Aerites, most from Haven but some from Hoku. And all expressing opinions at, thank the Lady, decreasing volume while the gong shouted and shook on its chains. Tatha looked at the podium as the meeting came to order again. Quilla pressed her hands over her wild hair, caught Tatha's glance, and rolled her eyes before leaning to the microphone again.

"There are a few more things to say before we open the meeting to discussions," she said. "As Keloret mentioned, Parallax's growth is finally beginning to worry the Federation. Mish has gone to Althing Green, hoping to get some Federation support for us."

"Fat chance," someone said. Quilla nodded.

"Fat chance indeed. She's been notified of the Parallax purchase and thinks that it may help her make her case, but neither she nor anyone else expects the Federation to help. Parallax hasn't broken any Federation laws, as far as we can tell—it's inconclusive, but it is one thing being done. We've also been keeping an eye on the Z-line market. After the first price drop, Parallax has kept pretty even with us. It's cut into our profits some but not enough to do immediate damage—we believe that they want to keep some pressure on us, but that they won't try to get us through bankruptcy. On the other hand, it remains a possibility. Security at the processing plant has been tripled—again, we expect no difficulty, but we're not positive. And Jes tells us that security for the shipping line has been strengthened both in space and on planet." Quilla paused. "Aerie-Kennerin is a fairshared company.

We up here are your board of directors—you voted us
into office and we run things with your consent and your
advice. We need that advice now, and will continue to
need it for as long as this crisis continues. If you can see
any areas where danger might come, any ways of protecting ourselves, tell us. One at a time, please. If everyone's quiet we can all hear. Ahmed?"

Tatha listened and watched as Quilla fielded questions and dissected suggestions. The Theresan had no
faith in governance by committee and even less in governance by popular meeting, but acknowledged Aerie's
customs. Some of the suggestions surprised her, while
others she anticipated. The suggestion that A-K ships be
armed was one she had foreseen, and she listened as
Sandro gave a succinct description of the disruption it
would cause, and Meya added a coda about the cost. Also
as predicted, someone suggested a patrol of the system,
using tausloops and sensors. Quilla, hands braced on the
podium, suggested that Sandro head the patrol; Jes was
needed by the shipping line and could not be spared.
There were no objections. Someone suggested raiding
NewHome System and blowing Parallax out of it—a dis-
ciple of Ved Hirem's, no doubt. This advice was dealt
with quickly and savagely by Hart. The idea of setting
up a screening procedure at Eagle Grab was both new
and good. Tatha herself suggested a militia; when the
Aerites roared their approval, Quilla appointed Tatha to
head it, as they had both planned. Tatha requested that
all able-bodied and interested parties of both races gather
at Havensport after the meeting. Meya carefully explained why she didn't think a rationing system was necessary. Hart was scathing on the subject of Federation aid.
Eventually, on a tide of anger and resolution, the meeting
ended. Aerites crowded the dais to talk with the board
or stood about in clumps, arguing. Sandro moved through
the room, gathering together anyone with space-time.
Hetch, in his wheelchair, preceded him, calling out names.
The kasirene surrounding Beriant left as soon as the meeting was over. Tatha stretched, looking at the jostling
crowd, put her hand on the sill of the window behind the
dais, and vaulted out of the Town Hall. She climbed over
a fence into someone's vegetable patch, skirted the house,
and came out onto the street. People still poured from the

hall, talking loudly. Tatha swung away from them toward Havensport.

Pixie Hirem was already at the port, lounging in the shade by the wall of the comshack. She nodded and straightened as Tatha came over to her. Tatha looked up at Pixie and grinned.

"I was hoping you'd show up," the Theresan said.

"Wouldn't 'expecting' be more accurate? I saw you watching me during the meeting and thought it might be because of something like this."

"That, too," Tatha agreed. She turned as groups of terrans and kasirene straggled on to the field and came toward the comshack.

"You know about the weapons at town hall, left over from NewHome?" Pixie said.

Tatha nodded without looking at her. "I've already had them transferred down here."

Pixie laughed shortly. "Expecting. I have the feeling, Menet, that this is going to be an interesting experience."

Tatha did not take her eyes from the approaching Aerites. "That," she said wryly, "is an understatement." And went forward to meet her ragged troops.

THE SKY HAD BEEN STEADILY CLOUDING SINCE the day of the town meeting two weeks ago, but so far the rains held off. Decca looked at the sky appraisingly, took a raincloak from the closet in the hall, and draped it over her arm. Just in case, she told herself, and decided not to take boots.

The harvest was finally in and the fields lay either stubbled or already turned over, waiting for the winter crops. Jared was out with his assistants, sampling the soil and taking what Decca called "bug counts" in the *Zimania* plantations. Jared ignored her. They'd grown apart in the past three years and Decca didn't know whether this sep-

arateness was a question of age or of differing expectations. She knew that Jared had a friend in the village with
whom he spent more nights than he spent at home, but
they never discussed their sex lives as, increasingly, they
discussed very little that wasn't concerned with daily activities. Even the shared communication that had been
theirs throughout their childhood had fallen away. Decca
wondered if Hart could explain it, but she hesitated to
ask her uncle, wrapped as he was in his own sorrow for
Spider's loss. Halfway down the hill she suddenly wondered if Hart wanted anything from Haven. She back-
tracked until she reached his laboratory.

Hart and Tatha sat in a corner of the lab, drinking tea
and talking. The Theresan's brown suit was slightly dirty.
Decca felt guilty. She hadn't appeared for training that
morning and knew that she'd have to listen to one of
Tatha's scathing lectures on the subject.

Tatha looked at Decca and raised her eyebrows, sipping from the chipped cup while Decca explained her er-
rand. Hart frowned and rummaged through a pile of
papers on his desk.

"Um, nothing really," Hart said. "I could use some
graph stock, if Ahmed's got any. And maybe—no, that's
it." He smiled at her.

"Okay." She made a note on her list. "About how
much?"

"Five hundred sheets? A thousand—no, that's a lot to
carry. Make it five hundred."

Decca folded the list and put it in her pocket. Hart
touched her raincape.

"Think it's going to rain?"

"I don't know." She turned to go. Tatha put down her
cup.

"Hold on, I'll walk with you." Decca waited uncomfortably while Tatha and Hart exchanged a few more words,
and kept her silence as Tatha strode beside her down the
hill.

"One more absence and you're out," Tatha said after a
while. "You know that."

Decca nodded, looking at the brown grass.

"It's not that you're indispensable," Tatha continued.
"I don't even expect to see action at all, when it comes to
it. But you might find some practice in self-defense use-

ful." Tatha whistled suddenly and kept walking. "Of course, it's up to you. But reliability is a virtue."

"I know. One of the work crews spotted a leak in the barn roof, and we spent most of the morning fixing it."

"Fair enough. Next time have the courtesy to let me know."

Belshazar bounded through the grass and ran in circles around them, baying enthusiastically. Tatha whistled again and the shaggy obediently followed at her heels.

"Spider tried to train that beast for years, and it never worked," Decca said. "I don't understand how you did it, and so quickly."

Tatha grinned. "One predator to another. You might want to look in at the port before you go back home, Chiba's down there and I think he has the maps ready."

Decca nodded. Tatha cut away from her across the hill, heading for The Jumble. The sky darkened a bit. Decca swung the raincloak over her shoulders and strode into Haven.

"Think it's going to rain, um?" Ahmed said, and produced a flat box of graph stock. "Tell Hart that I always have enough in reserve, all he has to do is ask for it."

"Will do," Decca said. She put the stock into her pack and walked out of the store.

"Might rain, right?" said the kasir greengrocer. "Well, it won't spoil the kavish any, you might as well take it with you. Tell Mim I'll send up someone with the staple stuff later on, okay?"

"Sure," Decca said. She packed the round white globes into her pack beside the graph stock.

"Expecting to get wet, are you?" Ved Hirem cackled from his post on the porch at Kohl's.

"You're probably right," the fishmonger said. "But I'll have the kid take the stuff up to the Tor. Mim wanted a couple of bluebellies, didn't she? Fresh today. Well, I suppose we'll have an early winter after all."

The seventh time someone on the street said the word "rain" at her, Decca stuffed the cloak into the pack and stomped down to the port.

One of Jes' tausloops filled a corner of the port, the only one, so far, that he'd been able to send. Beyond it Chiba's airship moved against its tether. Chiba scrambled over its sides. Below him Decca saw the unmistakable figure of Dene Beletes, leaning back and waving her cane emphatically. Lengthening her pace, she strode toward them.

"Right on the nose," Dene shouted, "but slanted back. No, more than that, get it good and tight. That's better. No, not those lines, the ones on the other side."

Chiba, his leg wrapped around a line, rolled his eyes and reached. Decca came around the side of the ship to stand beside Dene.

"What's going on?" she said.

"Good, get up there and give Chiba a hand," Dene said. "Where's that—and take that thing off your back. I put it down here somewhere . . ." Dene bent and rummaged in a box by her feet while Decca slid the pack from her shoulders and leaned it against the box. Dene held out a group of fabric-covered, triangular sails, joined at one corner. Decca spread them open until they looked like the widely spaced petals of an airflower.

"Close it up," Dene said. "Go on, he's almost ready for them."

"What are they?" Decca said, but Dene waved her cane impatiently. Decca vaulted into the gondola and shinnied up a net of wires until she reached Chiba. The airship swooped downward abruptly. They held on tightly until it stabilized, its nose pointed toward the pad.

Decca took the sails from her belt and handed them to Chiba.

"If I didn't know that she makes the damnedest things work," Chiba muttered, "I'd think she was crazy." He inspected the sails. "Here, hold on to the small mast, will you? Just steady it—there, that's good." He slipped the joining rod of the sails over the notched end of the mast, bent the larger mast through the pierced corners in the middle of the arrangement, and hooked it down tightly. A series of fine wires ran through the larger mast. He pulled a laserpencil from his back pocket and soldered them into place. Decca released the small mast when he told her to and looked down at Dene. Sandro had joined her. He stood with his hands on his hips, staring upward.

"What's it supposed to do?" Decca said to Chiba.

"Just watch," he replied. "And don't laugh too hard, or you'll tip the entire ship over."

He fanned the sails open and hooked the far edges together, then, motioning for Decca to move her head back, he took his hands away from the sails. They quivered for a moment and began to spin in the wind like a small, brightly colored propeller.

"A windmill?" Decca guessed.

"Yep. If it works it'll supplement the batteries and give me a spare recharger in emergencies. Or so Dene says."

"I'm coming aboard," Dene shouted. Decca tightened her grip on the lines. The ground swooped away, the buildings of the port rushed by, and she stared at the sky. Blinking, she looked around the windmill at Chiba.

"This is riding in an airship?"

"Only when Dene's around," he said. "Hold on, she's moving again."

The nose slid toward the pad again. "Why don't you deflate the bag?" Decca demanded.

"Dene says that we've got to make sure the lines lie right," Chiba said. "Oh, brother." The ship quivered. Decca thought briefly about her stomach and decided to ignore it.

"Hold the vanes," Dene shouted. Chiba slowed and stopped the windmill with his hand and, at Dene's second shout, released them again. They built up speed.

"If I have to repair them myself," Chiba told Decca, "I'll deflate the bag first. Otherwise I won't be able to do it at all, but don't tell Dene that."

"Shosei!" Dene bellowed. "Come down here and check the leads on your way. Something must be loose." —

"Should I stay?" Decca said. Chiba nodded.

"Don't get your hair caught in the vanes." He started down the side of the airship. Decca put her hand to her hair, then grabbed a line as the airship tilted even further on its nose. Sandro shouted, Chiba yelled, and the ship swung back to sit on its tail. Decca clung to the nose, eyes closed, and cursed.

"You could have moved back, damn it," Chiba shouted.

"The hell I could, all the crap you carry in here," Dene shouted back. "Sandro? You hold on back there. Decca, you all right?"

"I'm going to lose my breakfast," she yelled.

"Not on my airship! Sandro, back off, let it nose down."

Decca braced herself, but the nose swung down gradually until the ship lay centered again. It quivered as Dene and Chiba moved through the gondola.

"Decca?" Sandro's voice shouted. "You doing okay?"

"Yeah. I guess so. Where are you?"

"Dangling from the back like a tail. Are you two maniacs done yet?"

"Nope," Dene said. "Decca, hold the vanes."

Decca cautiously detached one hand from the lines, grabbed the vanes, and held them still. A fine, light rain began to fall and the breeze whipped her hair into her face. She tried spitting it from her mouth.

"Got it!" Chiba yelled. "Now how's it read?"

"Spot on," Dene said. "Okay, Decca, let it go."

She released the vanes and tucked a handful of her hair into the collar of her shirt. The rain thickened. Eventually Dene proclaimed herself satisfied. Decca held on tightly while Chiba climbed out of the gondola.

"How do I get down?" she called to him.

"Jump," Dene suggested. Decca looked at the ground far below and shook her head.

"Decca?" Sandro yelled. "Hold on tight."

She clamped her hands around the wires and closed her eyes. The airship quivered and its nose dipped toward the pad again.

"Okay, kick your legs free," Sandro said from below her. She wriggled until her legs dangled and Sandro's hands clasped her ankles. Hand over hand, he pulled her down until she half-sat on his shoulder. At his signal she released the lines. The airship's nose leaped skyward as she and Sandro fell back onto the pad. Instinctively she tucked her shoulders in and rolled heels over head, ending in a crosslegged squat. Sandro finished his roll at the same time and shook his head, looking down at his clothes.

"*Hijo de la gran puta*," he said sorrowfully as he tried to brush muck and oil from his shirt. Decca rose carefully and shook her head. The ground steadied after a moment. Dene and Chiba were back in the gondola, arguing about something. Decca retrieved her pack and came back to Sandro, who was still trying to clean his clothes. The rain let up marginally.

"That's not going to do any good," she said. "Is there a place we can clean up?"

"In the sloop, I guess," Sandro said. He twisted around to look at his backside. "*Mierda*," he muttered. Decca followed him across the pad to the tausloop.

Sandro rummaged through the storage racks until he found two clean suits and tossed one to Decca. She had already stripped; when he saw her he turned red and whipped around to face the control panel, and she laughed and took the suit into the clensor with her. When she came out Sandro was closeted in his cabin. She shrugged, finished seaming the suit, and rummaged about in the galley while he used the clensor. When he came out she handed him some hot tea and continued poking about the sloop, peering into things.

"It's the only one Jes can spare right now," Sandro said. "Even that wouldn't be so bad, we have enough fuel to keep it up continuously if we want, but I can't find another qualified pilot on planet. Oh, there's a few folk with some experience, but not much. Hetch can't take it up, and as for Tham. . ." Sandro made an expressive gesture and sipped his tea. "Does that suit fit okay?"

"It's a bit tight, but it'll do." Decca sat in the copilot's web and looked at him. "So what are you doing about this space patrol?" She grinned. "Tri-Captain Delta Three, zap, pow."

Sandro didn't laugh. "Just make do, I guess. I wanted to do this, I just didn't expect that it would be this—boring." He sounded unhappy. Decca looked away from him to the ports above the control bank. The rain picked up again—she could barely make out the bulk of Chiba's balloon through the grayness. Then the gray darkened and the world outside the bridge disappeared.

"Do you miss your home much?" she said, not looking at him.

"Home? I don't know." He moved in his web and put his feet on the ledge below the control panel. "Aerie's my home now. Sure, I'm still angry about Marquez Landing, I'd still like to run Parallax out of business. But even if I did, and that's not too likely, I'd come back here."

"I'm glad," she said, and Sandro returned her smile.

"Want some more tea?" he said. She nodded and followed him into the galley. His hair was still damp and curled tightly about his face.

"Sandro? What's likely to happen now?"

He shrugged without turning around. "Sometimes I wish Ved was right, I wish we could blast them out of space. I wish we could do *something*. But Tatha says that when they make a move, it's likely to be nonmilitary, something that we can't fight with ships and weapons, and she's probably right. I just can't see what it could be, and that worries me."

"Then why the militia?"

"Because Tatha's not one to leave any gap unattended," he said over his shoulder. "Sometimes she frightens me."

Decca nodded, watching his shoulders, and when he had his hands free for a moment she touched his arm. He jumped nervously.

"Do I frighten you, too?" she said.

Sandro flushed. "Have some tea," he muttered.

"I don't want any. It's raining and I'm feeling strange and a little lonely and a bit apprehensive and I'd much rather be held."

Sandro's ears turned red and he gestured helplessly. Decca turned abruptly and went to the bridge, where she started digging her raincape out of her pack.

"Please," Sandro said miserably, following her. "I've offended you, I didn't mean to."

"It doesn't matter," she muttered. The filthy pack splattered muddy oil over her clean suit. Sandro knelt beside her and pulled it away.

"You do frighten me," he said. When she looked at him he looked away. "I can deal with things in space, that's one thing," he said. "But here it's different, I'm not used to it—I don't know what is correct."

"I didn't ask you to be correct," she said. "This isn't the Courts of Althing Green. There's no rule book here. I'm sorry that I asked you to do something you didn't want to do. Please give me my pack."

"But I do want you," Sandro said. "I always have, but I'm afraid of offending you."

"You won't," she said.

With the greatest possible formality Sandro put his arms around her shoulders and she put her head against his neck. They knelt like that for a while, awkwardly, until Decca started to giggle. Sandro pulled back and looked at her, bewildered.

"This is the silliest damn thing," she said, laughing. After a moment, Sandro started to laugh too, and they both fell back on the deck, arms around each other, giggling. Decca put her hands on his cheeks, bent her head, and kissed him.

"Well?" she said.

"Oh," he said. He tangled his fingers in her pale hair and pulled her mouth down to his again.

PALEN ROCKED BACK ON HER TAIL AND wiped the rain from her face. The hut should have been finished, but one thing or another always seemed to get in her way—now the rains had come and the roof still wasn't in place. She cursed without much enthusiasm and leaned forward to grab the ragged end of solar sheeting and trim it to size.

Beyond the patter and splat of rain in the yard, she heard music from the Tor's main house; flutes, mostly, and the sounds of Decca's jeverah. Interesting smells had been floating from the kitchen all afternoon. Years-End was a few days away, and Palen was determined to have her hut finished by then. The sheeting, seamed along one edge of the panel, fluttered out of her hands in a gust of wind. She threw her hammer in the mud with disgust and kicked angrily. A wedge of wet earth flew onto the damp plasticrete sides of the hut.

"Can I help?" someone said in Kasiri.

Palen turned quickly. Puti, dressed in a huge water-cape and a wide-brimmed hat, stood at the edge of the kitchen garden, her hands politely extended. Palen picked up the hammer and put it in her pouch.

"It's not necessary," she replied, letting the awkward pause continue for a moment while she debated discourtesy. "Why are you up here?"

Puti came forward. "I wanted to talk with you. You don't come down to The Jumble anymore, and I—" She shrugged. The watercape shivered massively. "I just wanted to talk with you."

"I didn't think any of you were talking to me anymore," Palen said bluntly.

"You're the one who chose that, not us," Puti said. "Changing tribes doesn't mean banishment, you know.

292

You're welcome in The Jumble. If we can talk with Hart, we can certainly talk with you."

Palen grunted with disbelief. "All right. Let me get this panel up and we'll have a dry place—after a fashion."

Puti caught the flapping end of the sheet and pulled it into place. Palen looked at her, pulled the hammer from her pouch, and tacked the sheet into place before taking the seamer and setting the panel permanently. Puti stuck her head into the hut.

"Looks solid," she said.

"Go on in," Palen replied grumpily. Puti stood within the hut's doorway and took off watercape and hat, shaking them and hanging them, for want of a better place, on a stud projecting from the eaves. Palen collected her tools, dumped them in the hut, and hung her own cape and hat beside Puti's.

"This is rather fine," Puti said, looking about the hut. "From the outside it looks like a travel hut."

"It's permanent." Palen took a leather pouch of kaea and offered it to Puti, who sipped and offered it back. "I'll get a fire going when the chimney's finished—it's not cast yet."

"No matter," Puti said. She waited for a moment. When Palen still didn't offer, she sat beside the firepit and looked up.

"We didn't used to be enemies," Puti said.

"You helped Beriant," Palen replied, sitting opposite Puti. "That's an act of friendship?"

"I thought he was right. Even you thought he was right, Palen. It finished the circle."

Palen didn't reply. Puti sighed. "You're not making this any easier."

"Making what any easier? You're the one who wants to talk, not me." Palen looked out the uncovered doorway. "Besides, I have work to do."

"All right. Here's something to think about while you're working." Puti, without asking, reached for the kaea and took a sip. "We all thought things had finished with Hart's Calling, and they should have been. But Beriant's unwilling to leave things there. He's been talking to some of the younger ones, and he's been trying to talk Altemet into holding another Calling."

"About Hart?" Palen said, interested despite herself. "He can't. That's closed."

"About this Parallax business. He's claiming that they're no worse than the Kennerins—no, wait a bit. Listen. He says that the Kennerins marched in and took Aerie just the way Parallax is planning to do, and in his way he's quite right. We didn't sell this planet to anyone, some albiana agency did, without consulting us first. The fact that the people who bought it—who bought *us*—were decent folk is irrelevant, he says. He says that they've disrupted our lives, that they've stolen our lands, that they've forced us to live their way instead of our own."

"That's nonsense," Palen said. "They haven't forced anyone to do anything. If Beriant doesn't like living on To'an Cault, he can move to Ako, or To'an Elt—he can move to Eriant, for all I care, and I wish he would."

"A lot of us do, but that doesn't seem to help. A lot of folk are listening to him, Palen."

"So he's shaggyhowling. Let him." Palen reached for the kaea. A drip began at the far end of the hut, over where the sleeping platform would go. She rummaged about in her toolbox for the sealer and, standing on the box itself, she sealed the leak. Puti watched in silence, her hands in her pockets. The hut smelled unpleasantly of damp 'crete and sheeting, and Palen wrinkled her nose. "I'll have to find some fenet to burn in here, get the smell out. Working with albiana materials has got drawbacks."

Puti smiled. "That's one of Beriant's points. Another is that we'd be better off making some arrangement with Parallax and getting rid of the Kennerins altogether."

Palen turned to her, astonished. "You're not serious."

"He is. He says that Parallax will need someone to run things once they take over, and that it might as well be us. He says that if we help them with the takeover, we'll be able to dictate our own terms to them. That *we'll* be running Aerie, and Parallax could provide support services, could run the processing plant and all of that." Puti shrugged. "He says that we'd be able to manage a kasirene life-style while still taking advantage of albiana technology, that we'd run the plantations just enough to get what we wanted from outside. Some people think it's a good idea."

Palen remembered the tools in her hands and bent to put them away. "What's he planning to do with the albiana already here?"

"He hasn't said, yet, but the implications are pretty clear."

Palen thought for a moment. "So he's not got total support yet, correct? He won't make any plans or suggestions that are totally outrageous until he has a majority behind him. He must be pretty close to one already, to have gone as far as he has. And when he feels that he has everything going his way, he'll propose—what? Evicting all the albana, with Parallax's help? He wouldn't dare propose anything more violent and he couldn't suggest letting them stay, if he's pleading for an entirely kasirene world."

For the first time, Puti relaxed. "Yes," she said. "I told them that you'd get it."

"Is anyone bothering to counteract this?"

"Some of us. A few, we're pretty scattered. Face it, Palen, most of us have never bothered to think about the way things have happened here—we've always tended to take things as they come and cope with them as best we can. Living in the circle. And on many things, Beriant's right. Albana did move in on us, without our permission. Granted it was the Kennerins, but it could just as easily have been the sort of folk that had NewHome originally, and you know what they did to their indigenes. Beriant makes a pretty good case, and just because he's loud doesn't mean that there's not something behind it." Puti stood and stretched. "The point is, it's not what happened that matters, it's what's happening now, and what's likely to happen in the future. We can go one way or another."

Palen stretched her tail, then rocked back and forth on it. "Has he spoken to anyone from Parallax?"

"We don't know. It could just be Beriant making wind, or it could be something he's actually got in motion—we just don't know. And if Parallax is planning something, I don't imagine that they'll have much trouble finding the disaffected folk around here."

Palen reached for the kaea but changed her mind. "Are you going to tell the Kennerins?"

"We don't know."

"Are you making plans to stop Beriant?"

"We haven't yet—we don't know what to do."

"Then what do you want me for?"

Puti squatted on the far side of the firepit. "Because, whether you believe it or not, you're respected in The Jumble. A lot of folk admired what you did for the Kennerins, regardless of whether they approved of Hart. The more Beriant shouts, the better you look. Of all the kasirene, you've been closest to the Kennerins. You are believed, you think straight, and you can help us work out some kind of plan, some way of coping with things."

"You want a leader?" Palen said with disbelief. "Why not ask Altemet? Or is he on Beriant's side of the circle?"

"He's not. But he's the elder and he can't take obvious sides, not until everything's been set out clearly. And he's old, Palen. He's not likely to be around much longer." Puti paused. "We did ask him. He's the one who suggested coming to you."

Palen frowned and rocked forward smoothly until she stood.

"I'll have to think on this," she said. Puti rose.

"We expect that. Will you—let us know your answer soon?"

Palen gestured an assent and bowed. Puti, returning the courtesy, wrapped herself in cape and hat and walked through the mud of the Tor's back garden. Palen watched her go, put on her own cape and hat, and went back to working on her hut.

THE YEARSEND CELEBRATION BEGAN ON THE evening of tian'Bel Eiret Tapan, the day of the winter solstice, continued well into the night of va'Paet Eiret Meir, the first day of the new year, and it seemed that nobody slept. The houses around Market Square had opened their doors, and partygoers trooped from one place to another, trailing mud and raucousness with them. Kohl's dispensed free beer and sausages; Mertika, flushed and laughing, sat at a table on the porch, well out of the rain, and refused to work at all, letting her guests help themselves. The kitchen was a mess. Shosei Chiba, sitting in one end of it protecting his keg of beer, grinned and

burped and insisted on explaining his detailed map of
Aerie, pinned to the kitchen wall, to whoever walked in
the door.

It was easy to tell who'd been at Perri's; these folk
came in covered from head to foot with sawdust, for Perri
traditionally filled his workshop with the stuff and took all
the chairs out. Tatha and Daren, wandering into the kitchen
in search of something to eat, looked like perambulating
piles of shavings, the little one trailing the big one. Behind them, Belshazar braced all his legs and shook himself again and again but could not get rid of the stuff.
Chiba gasped with laughter until Tatha, glaring, picked
him up, marched him through the rain to Perri's, rolled
him thoroughly in the sawdust, and brought him back. A
dozen people, terran and kasirene, followed her into
Mertika's kitchen and followed her out again, laughing,
when Mertika chased them all away. Daren had fallen
asleep against Belshazar's side and Tatha made sure that
both were secure in one of the upstairs rooms before striding into the square again, trailing sawdust.

Sandro and Decca, coming out of Cas Hevant's, saw
Tatha and her followers huddled in consultation on the
porch of the town hall and scampered through the rain to
join them. Bottles and occasional snatches of melody
passed between them. The rain had washed most of the
sawdust from Tatha's body and she grinned with amiable
malice as Decca came up.

"Got your jeverah?" she said. Decca, nodding, noticed
Jared, flute in hand, grinning at her from the far side of
the group. A couple of kasirene had brought peneketas,
the five-stringed kasirene guitars which sounded, to unini-
tiates, like fish in agony. Pixie Hirem's coat bulged with
the outline of a drum. Tatha, with a flourish, produced a
baton and the group tiptoed to Ved Hirem's front window.

"What are we doing?" Decca whispered to her brother.

"You know the one about the scholar and the hog?" he
said. Decca nodded, eyes wide. It was one of the dirtiest
songs ever to come from the beerhalls of Kroeber. "Okay,
just play it and don't try to sing along." Jared grinned and
put his flute to his lips, and on Tatha's signal the ensemble
burst into noise.

Tatha had stolen a copy of Ved's traditional Beginning
Day speech and adapted it to fit a medley of the best-
known bawdy songs in the Federation. Windows and

doors flew open up and down Market Square and Tatha's lilting voice rode over the noise, singing the overblown glories of Aerie with severe seriousness. She'd left the choruses as in the originals. When Ved appeared, apoplectic with fury, she made him a sweeping bow and presented him with a copy of the song, words and music, before leading her raggedy orchestra banging and howling through the square.

Quilla, coming up from Havensport with a com readout secure in her pocket, heard them and cringed. She dodged through side streets until she reached the back door of Hetch's and banged on it. Tabor opened the door and ushered her inside.

"That crazy Theresan's got every Aerite on planet howling like a shaggy," she said. "And if I heard the lyrics right, someone had better go placate Ved."

Tabor shrugged. "Ved can placate himself," he said and kissed her. "What was all the urgency about?"

"Com from Mish. I wanted a hard copy." She kissed Hetch as she entered the living room, accepted a beer, and collapsed into a chair. Meya, kneeling by the fireplace, slid a log into the flames and stood, brushing her knees.

"What did it say?"

"What we expected. The Federation is aware of the Parallax situation, has taken it under consideration, and thanks us for our concern. Shit." Quilla sipped her beer. "Mish thinks that, if she stays for another few days, they'll agree to send an observer back with her."

"What good's that going to do?" Hetch demanded. "Do they want a ringside seat on catastrophe?"

"Speaking of which," Tabor said mildly from his seat by the window, and was interrupted by a clamorous banging on the front door. Quilla rose and let Ved Hirem in out of the rain.

"I'll file suit!" the lawyer shouted, pounding on the floor with his cane. Water dripped down his nose. Ved shook his head sharply and glared around the room. "I want restitution for this surreptitious and felonious entrance, *furandi animus,* abetted by that furacious and alien burgator, to the sole intent of a secret and heinous abstraction and obliquitous abridgement of my property, *alia enorma.* Not to mention—"

"Gotta go," Meya said hastily, and pulled her watercape

over her shoulders. "Promised Ozchan I'd drop in at the hospital." She sprinted out of the house.

"Rapacious and iniquitous—" Ved howled. Meya pulled the hood of her cape over her brow, slowed down, and shoved her hands into her pockets. Tatha's band must have found a home to let them in, for the streets were relatively quiet. The Jumble was unusually dark; Meya wondered if Palen had spent the evening there, as the kasir had said she would. Meya hoped so—Palen's disengagement from her own people worried Meya, but she did not feel that she could bring the subject up.

At the top of the rise, the lights of the hospital glowed through the rain. Meya walked faster, hoping that Ozchan wasn't busy tonight. Perhaps, finally, he'd agree to let his staff handle most of the problems and come into Haven with her. She wasn't very optimistic.

The hospital was quiet. Someone in a treatment room was busy being nauseated and moaning; someone else, blind drunk, staggered about the waiting room, bumping into things and trying to sing. Miri Kazan came out of the treatment room and slapped a hypogun against the drunk's arm. The drunk smiled seraphically and collapsed into Miri's arms.

"Give me a hand," Miri suggested. Meya picked up the drunk's feet, and together they got him into a bed. Miri turned his head sideways, moved her hands over his body, and snapped the restraining slats into place. Meya pushed hair from the man's face and frowned, recognizing Tham Hecate.

"He's on schedule," Miri said. "One of his wives will be here in the morning to get him—I wish he'd listen to Ozchan and cut down on the drinking. Ozchan's in his office, I think."

Meya nodded and went out of the room. The corridors of the hospital smelled of antiseptic and flowers, and bright murals decorated the walls. She smiled at them as she passed, stopping to look at the details of a new scene. Ozchan's office door was open. She stopped and looked in, watching the movements of his hands as he wrote in a slim book. He looked up suddenly, saw her, and smiled.

"Is it that late already?" he said, coming around the desk. Meya lifted her face for his kiss.

"It's even later," he said. "Things seem quiet tonight."

"They'll liven up toward dawn, they always do." He

brushed damp hair from her forehead. "Still raining hard?"

"Yes." She slid her arms around his waist and clasped her hands, leaning back a little to look at him. "Come into Haven with me?"

"Meya, I—"

"Come on. Miri's here and you've some other people on duty, don't you? You can come back at dawn if you want." She smiled at him cheerfully. "I'll even promise to make sure you don't get drunk."

Ozchan looked at her dubiously, pulled her head against his chest, and put his arms around her. "Sometimes I have trouble figuring out who you are," he said into her hair. She tensed slightly in his arms. "I'm afraid of trusting you."

She closed her eyes, listening to his heartbeat, and didn't answer.

"Meya?"

"It's okay. I guess I deserved that." She pulled away from him and went to the window. It faced away from Haven, and the sky was dark with rain. "Is it time to talk about it?"

"I suppose." Ozchan closed the door and leaned against it, looking across the room at her. "Do you want to?"

"No. Yes. It's been a long time." She glanced at him quickly. "I'm not going to apologize for Alin, if that's what you want."

He moved his shoulders against the door. "You don't have to. She's my daughter. I love her. But—"

"And I've apologized before for doing it that way." She crossed the room restlessly. "Why don't the apologies work, then? I fucked up, I know. I thought a lot about what I wanted—I just didn't think enough about the price." They looked at each other across the room. "If this is the price," she said softly, "it's too high."

"If you'd known about this," he said carefully, "would you not have done it?" He paused. "Would you not have had Alin?"

"I'd have had her. I'd just have done it differently. Oh, it doesn't matter, does it? I love her. I have nightmares, sometimes, that she'll be taken away from me, like Spider. And I love you, but you've already been taken away from me—or you took yourself away, or I forced

you to go away." She sat abruptly and put her hands over
her face. "I want it all," she muttered rebelliously. "I want
all of it and all of the time and I don't want it to change
unless I let it and—why are you laughing?" she demanded, jumping out of the chair.

"You sound like Meya," he said through his laughter.
"You sound like me."

She looked at him uncertainly. "You're making fun
of me."

"Yes." He wiped his eyes. "Of both of us."

"I don't think it's very funny."

"Of course it is." He came around the desk and put
his hands on her shoulders, still chuckling. "All of it all
of the time forever and ever and I get to run it all, any-
whichway I want to. With the children, with our jobs,
with each other—for every evening that I spend here,
you spend one at your desk at the Tor, or in the town
hall, doing your own stuff." He tipped his head back.
"Mememememememe," he caroled. "Both of us. We're
hopeless."

A smile grew at the corners of her mouth. "I guess we
are."

"Of course we are. That's probably, by now, the only
way that we are alike anymore."

"And what do you propose we do about that?" she
said, the smile deepening.

"Ummmm—how about going into Haven and getting
drunk, to begin with? You can get plastered for both of
us."

"Oh, no. If I get plastered, you have to get plastered
too."

"Mememememe," Ozchan said. Meya laughed and
watched him get his watercloak out of the closet. He
left a series of instructions with Miri, checked on his two
patients, and followed Meya out of the hospital. She
pulled at his cloak until it covered both of them and,
arms around each other, they caroled "mememememe"
together as they walked into town.

Hart came into Mertika's just as Tatha's group was
losing all but the most dedicated of singers. The songs
had moved from the ridiculous through the bawdy to the
sad. Mertika, curled on a couch in the public room,

shifted and patted a cushion. Hart sat beside her and shook his head when offered a beer.

"How long has this been going on," he said, waving his hand toward the fireplace. Tatha sat crosslegged on a table, strumming a peneketa which she'd tuned to sound vaguely like a terran lute. She swayed gently as she sang, an expression of serene content on her face, and Hart suspected her of being very drunk. On the floor beside her Sandro and Decca sat with their arms around each other, and across from them Jared lay with his head in the lap of Koyu Hevant, the weaver's son.

"If you mean the singing, since just before sunset. You've heard what they did with Ved's speech?" Mertika laughed. "If you mean Jared and Koyu, for the past five months. I think they're planning to live together as soon as they find an empty house. As for Sandro and Decca, that's relatively recent, but I don't think they've done anything serious yet." Piko, Mertika's day manager, came backwards into the room, balancing three pitchers of beer, and turned, grinning, to say something toward the couch. He stopped when he saw Hart, and put the pitchers down on the table, glowering. He went out onto the porch. "And if you mean Piko, it just started again. You've been away for a while, love."

"I know." Hart stretched his arms along the back of the couch. "I'm sorry."

"Hush," she said, closing her eyes.

Tatha had been humming lightly under her breath, and now Sandro said, "I know that one." Tatha looked at him benignly and nodded.

> "El remanso del aire," they sang,
> "bajo la rama del eco.
> El remanso del agua
> bajo fronda de luceros.
> El remanso de tu boca
> bajo espesura de besos."

Mertika, watching Sandro sing, whispered, "But I have the feeling that they're planning something serious now." Hart called her a snoop and kissed her.

"My uncle taught that to me," Sandro said. Decca put her head in his lap.

"It's old," Tatha murmured. Sandro glanced at her.

"Yes, I remember. Prewar terran lit."

She looked at him over the peneketa. "Jes?" she guessed.

"He was rather sarcastic on the subject."

She smiled and began the song about the spacer and the three-sexed alien, and everyone woke up. Meya and Ozchan came in as the room rang with the last line.

"*. . . and then the spacer, baffled, said, I don't know where to put it!*"

"We had a version of that on Solon," the doctor said. He proceeded to sing it. When he was finished, Tatha stretched, put down her instrument, and wandered into the kitchen in search of tea. Meya stood by the oven, poking at something with a fork.

"It'll be another ten minutes yet," Tatha said helpfully. "What kind of observer?"

Meya put the fork down and looked at her, annoyed. "Don't tell me you're another mindreader," she said. Tatha shook her head as she shook the kettle. She filled it at the sink and put it on the stove.

"No. My awesome standing army has orders to let me know the minute anything having to do with Parallax comes through the port." Tatha looked at Meya. "Surely you know that."

"I suspected it. I guess it makes sense." Meya put her hand on the oven door again, but Tatha shook her head.

"Give it time, my flower," she said. "In time even the tides come to fruition, in time the turtle learns to sing, in the passing of hours is the blossoming of all possibilities, even meat pies." The kettle shrieked. "Or tea." She busied herself with the teapot.

Sandro and Decca came through the kitchen on their way to the back door. Decca waved but Sandro turned bright red and followed Decca into the rain.

"So that's the reason she forgot the maps," Tatha said and, ignoring Meya's raised eyebrows, went back into the common room.

Meya glanced at the clock on the kitchen wall and stood at the doorway for a moment. Sandro and Decca had disappeared, the rain had lightened a bit, and so had the sky. She looked at it and blinked, then went inside again.

"Happy new year," she announced, and everyone crowded onto the porch to see the sunrise. The houses along the square spilled people into the rain. As the sun cleared the top of Havenswood, the people cheered and hugged each other.

"And so, on the eve of war, the people danced," Tatha murmured. Ozchan, beside her, smiled.

"And so, on the eve of victory, the people danced," he amended.

"Victory, Dr. M'Kale?"

"What else?" he smiled at her. It's far too early to start thinking of defeat."

Tatha turned to watch the people. She shook her head. "You may possibly be right, Ozchan. I don't know why or how, but it's just tentatively possible that you may be right."

Pale light filtered through the window, disclosing the outlines of Daren and Belshazar where they lay heaped comfortably together in the middle of the bed. Tatha separated child from shaggy and Daren muttered sleepily as she balanced him on her hip. He put his face against her neck and slept again.

She met Hart on the landing as she came down the steps. He was humming the chorus from the song about the scholar and the hog, and he moved aside, smiling, to let her pass.

"You're cheerful," she said, pausing to look at him. The corners of her mouth tilted upwards. "Get some good news?"

"Yes. There's going to be a Choosing."

Tatha raised her eyebrows. "Explain."

Hart grinned. "Palen came up to tell me last night. It's something the kasirene do, after the pups have finished their year with a teacher. They hold a Choosing, and each pup gets to choose where it will go for the next year—it's like a rite of passage, sort of. After the Choosing, they're considered adults. And Spider's going to be in the Choosing this year. He'll be able to do anything he pleases. He'll be able to come home."

Tatha's smile grew. She leaned forward and kissed Hart quickly on the lips. "I'm pleased for you," she said, feeling warm. "That's a nice way to begin a new year."

Hart laughed and continued up the stairs, taking them two at a time. Still smiling, Tatha descended to the hallway, where Mertika glared at her and ignored her greeting. Shrugging it off, Tatha rearranged Daren on her hip, whistled for Belshazar, and went home.

TWICE A WEEK SANDRO TOOK THE TAUSLOOP, *Blind Chance,* up for a survey of Eagle System. He and Hetch agreed that a visual survey was probably useless, but they'd had sensors installed on the sloop, and sensors operated in the processing station and at Eagle Grab; Sandro claimed that if anything was picked up, he could at least go out and take a look. It was more for his own peace of mind than for anything else, Hetch told Quilla, and they let him do it.

Generally his absences lasted only a day, or two at the very most, as he skipped about the system investigating every stray bleep and bump that the sensors put through. Most of them were innocuous, the rest were ghosts, but Sandro enjoyed the trips and even more, Quilla told Jared, enjoyed the idea of playing Tri-Captain Delta Three, off on his own. She made comparisons between Sandro and young Jes. Jared laughed and repeated her comments to Decca, who didn't think they were funny at all.

It was during one of Sandro's absences, one that had lasted two days already, that Mish returned from Althing Green. Quilla was off at Hoku and expected back that evening, so Meya, Decca, and Jared made up the welcoming party at the port. The shuttle settled with what seemed more than normal gentleness, the hatch swung open, and tiny, white-haired Mish appeared. A reverential spacer held each of her elbows, and she glared at them as they guided her down the ramp.

"You'd think I was an old woman," she said indignantly as they released her to Meya's care.

"The tauCaptain said to take care of you, Quia Mish," one of the spacers said apologetically. "If anything happened to you—"

"I know. My dray-headed son would probably flay you alive." She kissed Meya briefly. "I brought us back a present," she said, her lips quirking. "The Federation, in its august concern for its citizens, has sent us an observer. A Galactic Security General Investigator, under Section Forty-nine, subsection twelve twenty-four, paragraph nineteen, subparagraph twelve, 'observation of erratic installations.'" Mish made a face. "They were kind enough to stretch the meaning of the section to include us, and don't think they didn't remind me of it."

"Okay," Jared said, peering at the empty hatch. "Where is it?"

"In there," Mish said shortly. "Asleep."

Jared raised his eyebrows, and together he, Decca, and Meya walked up the ramp and into the shuttle. The crew was busy off-loading cargo; one of them waved a hand at the bridge when Jared asked him where the observer was. Mish followed them, her arms crossed.

The bridge was deserted, save for what seemed a small, relaxed lump in one of the passenger webs. Mish marched them around to the front of the web, reached inside, and shook it.

The lump stirred, a blanket slipped off, and Jared stared at a small, rotund leprechaun with white hair, a skull cap, two side curls, and benign green eyes. The leprechaun smiled and began fumbling with the clasps of the webbing.

"Children," Mish said, "allow me to introduce you to Galactic Security General Investigator Colonel Heschel Zimmerman. Colonel, my daughter Meya, my grandchildren Jared and Decca."

"Uh, welcome to Aerie, colonel," Jared said. "Sir."

Colonel Zimmerman freed himself from the webbing and stood, put his hands along his belt, and smiled up at the assembled Kennerins.

"Shalom," said the colonel. "Is there something, perhaps, to eat?"

Someone had had the sense to send for one of the town's few aircars. They loaded the colonel, Mish, and Meya into it, and Jared and Decca stood at the port,

watching them leave. The colonel had already, by means
of flattering questions, ascertained that Jared and Decca
were not Meya's children, that Quilla was expected back
from Hoku, that Tabor was home, that Ozchan ran the
hospital (he didn't seem impressed), and that Meya's
three children were in school. As they left, he was extract-
ing information about Hart. Decca shook her head and
turned to Jared.

"I have the feeling that there's more to Colonel Zimmerman than a skullcap and an appetite," she said. He
nodded, thinking that no matter how much there was or
wasn't to Colonel Zimmerman, it wasn't likely to do the
Kennerins much good. The shuttle finished off-loading
and departed.

Standing behind the thick barrier wall, Jared looked at
his sister while the donkey engines of the shuttle rose to
a shriek and the shuttle rose to the sky. She faced the barrier, her eyes unfocused. Jared suddenly wondered what
she was thinking, then just as suddenly wondered why
he didn't know. He knew they'd been drifting apart
since their return from Kroeber, but he'd been busy:
busy with chemical analyses, with Hart's various new
strains of wheat or gillifruit or karel, busy most of all
with Koyu Hevant. He knew that Decca had been unhappy, frustrated, angry, and that lately she'd seemed
more content, once she was actually working. But other
than that, her mind was closed to him. The silent bond
had severed, and he hadn't noticed.

Now he touched her shoulder tentatively. She gave him
a small smile and followed him around the barrier. The
shuttle was a brief silver glint in the sky. Pixie Hirem
came out of the comshack and walked toward them.

"Are you going back to the Tor?" he said.

"I don't know. I'd imagine that Meya and Quilla can
keep him occupied for awhile—rather, that he'll keep
them occupied." She paused, still looking in the direction
of the shuttle's flight. "What I should do is go back to
the barn," she said absently. "There's stuff to do—have
you and Hart finished with that catalyst yet?"

"Haven't had time," Jared replied. "It's on the list,
though."

She looked at him. "On the list isn't good enough. I
need it by Eiret Bols at the latest . . . we simply haven't

the time to make new sap barrels, and if we can't clean the old ones with that new stuff you promised us—"

"I said it's on the list," Jared said, more sharply than he'd intended. "We've a lot of other things to do, you know. It won't take much time, once I can get to it."

"Hah. It would take less time if you'd take Koyu's head out of your lap, and yours out of his."

Pixie reached the barrier, raised her eyebrows, and turned her back to them. She crossed her arms and stared intently at the empty field.

Jared stiffened. "You've no right to say that. Koyu doesn't interfere with my work."

"You promised the catalyst by the end of Eiret Tapan— that was two weeks ago. I don't know what you think is more bloody important, but if I don't have those sap barrels ready by spring, we're going to have to ditch one hell of a lot of sap. And I'll leave *you* to explain that to Mish—I'm not going to, because it won't be my fault."

Jared felt his temper fraying and grimly held it together. "Decca, what's got into you? You've changed—"

"*I've—*"

"Wait. I mean, I know we're not as close as we were, but that's no reason, I mean I just don't understand why you're snapping at me. I'm sorry about the fucking catalyst, okay? I've been running field analyses so we'll know what to rotate to where, and if we're going to have the winter fields in within the next two weeks, I'll have to have them ready. You can understand that, can't you?"

Decca crossed her arms and looked angrily at him. "Just because I'm your sister doesn't mean that you can put my requests last and not think that I won't mind it. I have to have that stuff, and soon. Sure, get your damned field analyses done, and then you can work on some private project of Hart's, and then maybe you can fly off to Hoku, and the Lady only knows what all else. But remember that I didn't ask you for a personal favor, I requested something vital, something to keep this damned circus going."

"Decca—"

"I'm plantation manager, damn it. You'd have had the stuff ready by now if it was someone else, wouldn't you? All right, from now on in you treat me as though I were someone else. It's damned hard enough getting things done around here without having to cope with you, too."

Decca turned abruptly and stalked away from the port, her hands jammed into her pockets. Jared looked after her with bewilderment, then turned to Pixie.

"What in the hell?" he said.

Pixie shrugged and pushed herself away from the barrier. "She's been having problems with the Aerites, not being taken seriously, that sort of thing. You'd be annoyed, too, if everytime you ordered something, your workers checked it out with Quilla first."

"No damned reason to take it out on me," Jared muttered.

"Perhaps not. Also, Sandro's been overdue for almost a day now. She's worried."

Jared looked at her. "So? He's often gone for two days at a stretch."

"Not without checking in. Come on." Pixie led the way to the comshack. After a moment's hesitation, Jared followed.

"What can you tell me about that little tub your grandmother brought home?" Pixie said.

Jared took his hands out of his pockets. "Nothing much. He's the official observer that Althing Green promised us, he seems pleasant enough, I guess. Mish told me that he spent the entire trip from Althing Green reading the Parallax files and asking questions. I don't know anything else about him, except he likes to eat. Or says he does."

"Tatha's gone up to the Tor," Pixie remarked. Jared grinned. "Yeah. Did you know that Ved's called her to council?"

"Because of the song? He'll never make a case of it," Jared said positively as they entered the comshack.

Hetch spun his chair around from the commiter and stared at them.

"He's not answering," the old man said. "I've tried every band and I can't pick up anything."

Pixie looked at him, then strode to the tracking screen.

"He's on it," Hetch said as she punched directions into the bank. "The ship's on it." He slapped the commiter angrily. "The ship's up there, but that damned brat isn't answering. Someone's going to have to go up there and fetch him."

"Maybe he's just too busy to check in," Jared suggested, and was not surprised when Hetch shook his head.

"*Blind Chance* is drifting—I've punched out the tracking record, she hasn't burned anything since early this morning. Something's wrong, Pixie."

She pulled at her short hair, frowning. "Could he be hurt?"

"Perhaps. The record shows a smooth flight away from Aerie, some nosing around in the second quadrant, some sort of blip, then the blip disappeared and *Blind Chance* drifted—hell," he shouted. "Can't we get something more sensitive in here? He could have run into anything, and unless it was the size of To'an Cault we wouldn't see it. Is that extra shuttle still in?"

"The old one? Yes, but you're in no condition to pilot it." Pixie pushed Hetch's chair away from the commiter and sat before it. "You get on home, Hetch. You're worked up enough as it is. I'll call Tatha."

"She's no spacer," Hetch said, outraged. Pixie looked at him over her shoulder.

"Neither are you, Manny," she said quietly.

Hetch swore and rammed the chair out of the com-shack.

"Go with him," Pixie said. "It's a long, dry run into Haven, for him."

"You could have been a bit more tactful," Jared said, turning to the door, and did not wait for her answer.

It started drizzling again by the time they were halfway to Haven. Jared took his cloak off and covered Hetch with it, but the old man continued to ignore him. He sat with his fingers white around the control knobs of the chair. Jared could not tell whether it was from pain, or annoyance, or both. Cold water gathered in Jared's long hair and dripped down his back. He put his hands through his belt and hunched his shoulders, and wondered what else would go wrong that day.

Hetch insisted that Jared leave him alone when they reached Hetch's house and, after seeing him safely up the ramp, Jared started to walk toward Kohl's. He stopped halfway there, suddenly suspicious, and traced his steps back down the street.

The door was closed and the curtains in the front of the house were drawn. Jared thought for a moment, then went down a side street, through two backyards, and entered Hetch's house through the back door. The kitchen was dark and silent. He paused, head cocked, and heard sound from the living room. He took his shoes off before walking down the short corridor and stopping behind the open door, where Hetch couldn't see him.

The old man was busy with his commiter, steadily cursing under his breath. "I want to talk to your father," he said precisely, then cursed again. "Can I talk with your Daddy?" His voice was angrily patient. "All right, then let me talk to your mother. What? I don't care which mother, any of them. The nearest one. All right. Hello? Who the hell are you? Well, I don't want to talk to you, I want to talk to your mother. No, I'm not going to tell you a story right now, I want to talk to your *mother*." Hetch resumed cursing, then stopped. "Which one is this? Yes, of course it's me, who in hell did you expect it was? Where's Tham? What? I don't give a fuck, tell him to get to the phone. Then wake him the hell up!"

Jared put his hands over his eyes and thought a number of quick, angry prayers. Tham Hecate lived with his three wives, seven children, and innumerable bottles of alcohol on the far side of Haven, and from Hetch's abusive end of the conversation it was obvious that Tham was in the middle of a good, roaring drunk. But Tham had been one of the best pilots to work for Aerie-Kennerin, before he decided that he had enough common stock to live on. Or, to be more accurate, to drink on. Hetch's stream of invective continued in full spate. Jared realized that he intended to take the old shuttle up, under Tham's piloting, and rescue Sandro himself. Jared shook his head. Hetch confirmed plans to meet at the port in an hour and broke the connection.

"You can come out of there," he called peevishly. "You'll catch a cramp, hiding behind doors."

Jared came into the room and glared at him. "You're not supposed to go into space, you know that. And Tham's probably so drunk that he couldn't find the shuttle in midday with both eyes open."

"Shipdreck," Hetch said. "I trained Tham. He could fly that shuttle sober, drunk, or dead." .

"Let Tatha take care of it—" Jared began, and Hetch slapped angrily at the arms of his chair.

"She runs the militia, Sandro and I run the patrol. She's no spacer, either—and I'm a bit sick of everyone believing that she can run the world and perform miracles at the same time, with her eyes closed."

"All right then," Jared said, perforce following Hetch as

the old man maneuvered his chair into the hallway. "Call processing, they've got pilots—"

"It'll take too long, they're four times as far from Sandro as we are." Hetch stopped the chair before a locked door and fumbled in his pocket. He handed a key to Jared.

"Open it," he said. When Jared did so, the captain guided the chair through the door. The room was lined with shelves and cupboards; Hetch pointed to one and Jared opened it. Under Hetch's direction, he found and lifted out a Barre harness in a dusty wrap. Hetch strapped it around his thick middle, tested the controls, and turned it on. The space around him distorted and when he moved his mouth, Jared couldn't hear him. Hetch turned the harness off.

"Fetch the other one," he said. "You're going with us."

"Hetch—"

"You listen," the old man said angrily. "Regulations say you have to report any disabled ship, and the cause for disability, and every damned thing else. Any of your processing pilots will make that report, because Jes told them that if they didn't he'd have their asses. All right. He can't kick me out, and he can't kick Tham out. Or you. He wouldn't dare. So we're going up and you're coming with us. We need at least one able body," he concluded with grim humor. Jared lifted out the second harness.

"What's wrong with making a report?"

Hetch looked at him, exasperated, and didn't bother to reply.

Tham reeled onto the port, arriving, as Hetch had instructed, through the meadow to the back entrance of the hangar. He fell into the pilot's web in the shuttle and immediately sobered. Hetch rode in the copilot's web, and Jared unhappily took the third web, off to the side where he wouldn't get in the way. Tham ran through the checkout silently, nodding to himself, then flipped a toggle. The huge doors of the hangar swung open slowly. With a minimum of fuss Tham guided the shuttle from the hangar, flung it down the short runway, and into the winter clouds. Looking back from the sideport, Jared could see Pixie and some other people spill from the comshack. Clouds obscured the port and Jared sat back in the webbing, trying to be fatalistic.

Hetch activated a scanning bank and located the blip of *Blind Chance,* turned to an auxiliary bank, and poked at the facings. A screen obliged with a series of numbers and letters. Tham, looking at them, nodded and returned his attention to the control bank. The small bridge reeked of alcohol.

"She's moving pretty fast," Hetch said, more to himself than to anyone else. "She won't accelerate—unless there's someone conscious on board. Tham?"

Tham shrugged and let his fingers dance over the panel. The shuttle hummed slightly as it took a new heading. Peering over Hetch's shoulder, Jared saw nothing but space.

"Get some rest," Hetch said. "It'll be another hour yet."

Jared took a deep breath. "I think," he said, "you'd better tell me what you want me to do. I'm not a spacer, Hetch."

"True. Also, you're not a cripple or an alcoholic." Hetch turned the web around to face Jared. The old captain's face was gray with pain, but his eyes were clear and hard. "When we reach *Blind Chance,* someone's going to have to get into her, kill the drives, and bring Sandro back. I can't do it, and Tham can't do it."

"But I don't know anything about drives, or ships," Jared protested.

"You won't need to." Hetch turned to the control panel again. Jared's stomach knotted. He massaged his midriff with his fingers and carefully went through his centering and calming exercises. They didn't seem to help.

Blind Chance tore through space at almost twice the shuttle's top speed, but the intercept course Hetch had plotted brought the shuttle right up to the sloop. Tham took his hands from the board and let Hetch slide the shuttle into the sloop's field, engage the grapples, and cut the shuttle's drives. A dense silence fell.

Jared pulled on a Barre harness and tied an extra one to his belt, while Hetch repeated, for the third time, what he wanted Jared to do. Hetch tapped the small transceiver he held in his palm; the sound of his fingers made a faint staccato sound in Jared's Barre field. Jared double-checked the equipment dangling from his belt, touched his chin nervously, and went into the air lock.

The tough, flexible lines of the grapples ran between

the shuttle and *Blind Chance*. Jared flexed his hands, looking at them, then looked beyond them to the curve of the sloop's hull. The two ships seemed motionless in space. He reached for a line, hooked his safety line to it, and swung, hand over hand, along the curved grapples. He felt naked, clothed only in his ordinary worksuit, encased in the invisible field of the Barre suit; halfway across he was suddenly convinced that the suit was about to disintegrate and he clung to the lines, breathing deeply, while his pulse thundered in his ears.

"Easy now," Hetch's voice said. "Happens to everyone, first time. Just breathe deep. The suit's fine, don't worry about it. Take it easy, Jared. Now ease up a bit, don't use up all your air. Got it? Slowly. Keep moving along, you'll feel better in the sloop. One hand at a time, and again, and again. Good. Good."

The emergency airlock, outlined in dark metal, appeared against the sloop's hull. Jared moved closer until the field of his suit covered the lock, and pressed the plates. The lock irised open. Jared slid inside, closed the lock, and stood still, breathing steadily, until the interior hatch opened and he stepped into the cargo hold. Following Hetch's calm directions, Jared tested the air. When the green plate on the sensor glowed, he deactivated the suit and leaned against the hull for a moment. Then he left the hold and followed Hetch's directions until he reached the bridge hatch.

The hatch was sealed tight and a red warning beacon flashed monotonously around its periphery. Jared put his hand out and the warning current stung his palm. He cursed and put his hand in his mouth.

"Hetch, I don't like this," he said, and for the first time wondered about Sandro. Unwillingly, he remembered all the scare stories he'd heard about accidents in space. Hetch's curses, as Jared described the sealed hatch, didn't make him feel any more optimistic.

The second-line emergency seal lay behind a seam in the curved hull of the companionway, activated by a panel hidden beneath a grid. Jared broke the grid and pressed the panel; sheets of metal plunged inward from the corridor's sides, floor, and ceiling, locking together. Their edges glowed, a sullen red. Jared backed away from them uneasily, then, following Hetch's directions, found the controls for the bridge hatch and deactivated the seal. He jumped back as the hatch irised open, and when nothing happened, he ventured nervously into the bridge.

It was chaos. A ragged gash punctured the hull near the back of the bridge; the torn metal hunk which created it had plunged through the bridge and now lay embedded in the far wall, shrouded in the webbing of the navigator's seat. The bridge looked as though it had been struck by a windstorm, the lights on the control panel pulsed frantically, and Sandro slumped in the pilot's web, surrounded by the distortion of a Barre field. Jared moved quickly across the bridge and bent over Sandro until their fields merged. Sandro's breathing was shallow and his skin cold; an ugly purple bruise spread over the side of his face.

"He's alive," Jared said, and felt Hetch's relief in the old man's silence. He located the master switch on the control panel and pushed it down. The ship died quietly, the drives whining into silence. Kneeling beside the webbing, Jared ran his hands over Sandro's body. Nothing felt broken or out of place and, muttering a quick prayer, Jared slung Sandro over his shoulder and picked his way out of the bridge. Sandro muttered something in Spanish as Jared opened and resealed the last barrier.

Once in the emergency airlock, Jared put Sandro on the deck and carefully hooked a safety line between Sandro's belt and his own. Sandro curled into a foetal ball and floated around Jared as they moved between the ships, and Jared was too worried about the safety line to let his earlier fears reappear. He pushed Sandro into the airlock and crammed himself in after. Tham waited until they both cycled through before activating the donkey engines and angling the joined ships back toward Aerie.

The shuttle was too small to have a sickbay, but did have a portable biostat bolted to a shelf in the cargo hold. Jared brought it to the bridge and ran it over Sandro's body. Sandro was badly concussed and needed immediate treatment, but was otherwise uninjured. Tham beamed a call to Aerie and Hetch listened in silence as Jared described the condition of the bridge to him. The biostat, on monitor mode, hummed quietly.

"Could a meteor have done that?" Jared said. "I thought that a sloop's fields could cope with that sort of thing."

Hetch gestured and turned away.

When they finally reached Pigeon, the smaller of Aerie's moons, Tham orbited it at increasing speed, then cut the grapples and watched as *Blind Chance* continued orbiting.

"It'll decay fairly soon," Tham said. "You'll need to get someone up here pretty quick."

Hetch kept his silence and Tham angled the shuttle into Havensport.

❧

SANDRO OPENED HIS EYES AND LOOKED around the room. His head ached fearfully and when he put his hand to it he felt the sleek thickness of bandages over his forehead.

"Ay, mierda," he muttered. The door opened. Decca came in, followed by Miri Kazan, the hospital's chief resident.

"Welcome back," Decca said. She kissed him and held his hand while Miri gave him a quick, thorough examination.

"My head hurts," he said to the doctor. She nodded.

"I'd be worried if it didn't. I'll have something given to you, but there's people to see you, first." She pulled the sheet up around his shoulders again. "You'll feel better in a week and then we'll see about letting you out."

"A week!" Sandro said, and tried to sit up. His head objected. He lay down again and groaned.

"A week," Miri repeated. "You've a skull like a metal safe, but you managed to bang it up pretty well anyway. Keep flat, it'll hurt less that way. I'll call the Tor," she said to Decca, and left the room.

Decca pulled a chair to the bedside and sat, still holding Sandro's hand. He squeezed her fingers lightly.

"How much can you remember?" she said.

"Up to when something big hit the sloop." He paused. "Who brought me down? Is Jes home?"

"No. Hetch and Tham went up for you, and took Jared."

Sandro jerked, closed his eyes, and groaned again. "Hetch isn't supposed to go up," he said. *"Virgen Santissima,* can't they give me anything for this damned head?"

"Patience," Decca said, and kissed him again. "You're breaking my hand."

Sandro relaxed his grip marginally. "You want to know what happened?"

"Best wait until everyone else gets here, then you won't have to repeat it." She paused. "Lady, Sandro, I was so afraid that you were gone for good."

"Mi corazon, I would never leave you for good," he said with deliberate humor. Decca put her forehead against his hand and he dozed.

Voices woke him up. Quilla stood by his bed, talking to Tatha, while Mish argued with somebody by the door.

"Oh, all right," Mish finally said, exasperated. "We're just checking up on a friend, but if you insist—"

"Please, Quia Mish. Let's just say that I'm doing my job, okay?"

Mish didn't reply. Sandro turned his head and tried to see the door, but Quilla stood in his way. His head still hurt, but not as badly as before.

"Can someone crank me up?" he said. Decca rose from the foot of the bed and touched a button. The head of the bed tilted marginally, and Sandro looked at the small, innocuous man who stood in the doorway, his thumbs hooked under the belt of his plain blue suit. He smiled at Sandro.

"I'm pleased that you're feeling better," he said politely. "Dr. M'Kale has expressed great respect for the quality of your skull."

"He should," Tatha said rudely. "I suspect it of being solid bone from the eyebrows up. Are you going to tell us what happened?"

"Where's Hetch?" Sandro said.

"He couldn't make it," Quilla replied. She sat at the foot of the bed opposite Decca. "You went up to check on something the sensors picked up?"

"Yeah. I figured it was probably a ghost, or a stray hunk of something—most of the pickups are nothing more than that. But I wanted to check it out." He paused. "It's in an area where we usually don't have much of anything.

I had a bit of trouble finding it, it wasn't very big." He paused again. "I guess I was sort of expecting something like that, but it surprised me anyway."

"Go on," Mish said quietly.

"It was a grabstation. A small one, but big enough for a full cruiser. It wasn't marked, but it was transmitting— if it hadn't been, I doubt if I'd have found it. A scoutship was coming through. The scout had Parallax markings."

Tatha nodded slowly, not at all surprised, but the little man's eyebrows rose over his green eyes.

Quilla said, "A Parallax grabstation. In Eagle System."

"Not anymore," Sandro said. "I blew it out of space, ship and all. A piece of it hit *Blind Chance,* and . . ." His voice trailed off. Mish had closed her eyes, Quilla held her head in her hands, and Tatha made a sharp gesture and said something flatly in a strange language.

"Sandro," she said, "I think we'd better introduce you to Galactic Security General Inspector Colonel Heschel Zimmerman."

"Oh," Sandro said. "Oh, *mierda de un puñetero podrido.*"

"Exactly," Tatha said.

Little Colonel Zimmerman suddenly didn't look innocuous at all.

COLONEL ZIMMERMAN SPENT TWO HOURS IN the comshack, sending and receiving collect codings from Althing Green, before requesting that someone go up to *Blind Chance* and bring back the bridge crystals. Tham went up with a spacer borrowed from a visiting A-K ship, and when he returned the colonel took the crystals and locked himself into Mish's office with them. He sent out occasional orders for cold juice and platters of snacks, and Mim, in a desperate effort to make a good impression, turned the kitchen upside down for two days as she created increasingly elegant treats. The platters always returned empty, with note of praise and thanks, but the colonel remained secluded and the Kennerins' apprehensions mounted.

"I still don't see how we could be liable for anything," Pixie said one evening, while the family and some friends sat in the living room, sipping wine and listening to the rain on the windows. "Parallax put in the grabstation, and that's against Federation regulations. And since the station was Parallax's, then we're not liable for destroying it, because we didn't destroy Federation property."

"They'll be upset because Sandro slagged it, instead of just reporting it," Meya said. "Besides, what can they do to us?"

"Logically, nothing," Pixie said. She tapped the huge book in her lap. "I've tried to figure every possible thing that they could object to, any regulations that we may have violated—but you know as well as I do that if they're really pissed at us, they can find anything to slap us with."

Quilla started to say something, stopped, and looked toward the doorway. Everyone instantly quieted, but after a while she shook her head.

"False alarm," she said ruefully. "I wish he'd get the hell out of there and tell us what's going on. The suspense is terrible."

A silence fell. Quilla went back to mending a harness, Meya to making lists, Tabor to decorating the wooden flute he'd been working on, winters, for the past two years. When the door slammed they all jerked upright, but it was only Ozchan coming in from the hospital. He said something to Mim as he took off his waterclothes, and came into the room rubbing his hands to warm them.

"I'm letting Sandro out tomorrow," he said to the room at large, and Quilla nodded.

"Good. Maybe we'll see something of Decca, for a change. Have you eaten?"

"Yes, at Kohl's." He turned around in front of the fire to warm his backside and looked speculatively at Pixie. "Where's Tatha?"

Pixie gestured with her large hands. "I don't know. She was pretty angry after that interview with Sandro. She hasn't been around much since then. Oh, sure, she spends most of the day training people, taking care of militia stuff, then she disappears."

Mish frowned and put her hands in her lap. "I wish I knew what's going on in her head," she muttered. "I don't like this. Jes has never trusted her."

"She talks a lot to Hart," Jared said.

"Is that supposed to comfort me?" Mish said sarcastically.

Jared turned toward the fire again, and the door of Mish's office opened and closed. Colonel Zimmerman, looking rumpled, came into the living room and smiled.

"Mim has been making me fat," he said, taking a chair near the fire. Everyone looked at him. "It's not *that* bad," he said. He pulled a sheaf of papers from his pocket and looked through them.

"We've had quite enough tension about this already," Mish said tartly. "We don't want to watch you shuffling papers, we want to watch you saying something."

"I'm sorry," the colonel said. "I wasn't being theatrical. It's a sticky problem, mostly because it comes in two parts and the Federation's never had to cope with either part before." He sat back and held up one finger. "First, a non-Federation grabstation in Federation territory. That's not illegal on the surface, if only because it's not specifically stated to be illegal. It simply hasn't been possible, before, for a private group to gather enough money to build one. You know that they barely maintain themselves —its the cargo fees and taxes that generate Federation revenues. So while a private grabstation is not illegal in the letter of the law, it is undoubtedly illegal in the spirit of the law. Do you follow me?"

Pixie nodded. "But if you're going to make a complaint against Parallax, it has to be in terms of the law as written."

"Correct." The colonel stood and helped himself to a glass of wine. When he sat again, he held up two fingers. "The second part of the problem has to do with Quia Marquez blowing the station up. If the station were Federation property, of course it would be an offense. As it is, we simply don't know. The bridge crystals, by the way, show quite conclusively that it was a Parallax ship coming through. I've played them over a number of times, and there's no mistaking it. Of course, Quia Marquez did not bother to challenge or warn the ship, he simply said a number of things which, I'm sure, he would be quite un-willing to translate from Spanish, and cut loose. Parallax could have a civil case against Quia Marquez, and against Aerie-Kennerin as abettors, and the case might hold up, if they wanted to pursue it. But the fact that they'd planted a grabstation in someone else's system, a perhaps illegal station, might count strongly enough against them so they'd be unwilling to take the matter to court."

"They've bothered us before," Mish said.

"Yes, and it could serve to prove harassment, but noth-ing more. There's nothing illegal about trying to buy an-other company."

"And what they did to Marquez Landing?" Quilla said.

"That, too, is not illegal. Oh, I know it was immoral, but whether something is right or wrong does not neces-sarily imply legality or illegality. I've checked into that, by the way. Did you know that your young Quia Marquez has a history of short temper?"

"I wouldn't be surprised," Quilla said. "When he first came to Aerie, he wanted us to mount a jihad against Parallax, in revenge for what they did on Marquez Land-ing."

"He took the first step himself," the colonel said. "He killed the Parallax transfer agent in Ciudad Garcia, that's why he left the planet."

Mish looked at him gravely. "I assume that this is the truth."

"I'll give you the file, if you like. Parallax has a price on his head. I don't think he knows that."

"He will soon," Quilla said. She put her feet on a table. "Can we get back to the main subject? What is the Feder-ation going to do to us?"

"Right now, nothing," the colonel said. "They're aware of the problem, and my report created quite a lot of noise on Althing Green. Aerie is not the first entity to make complaint of Parallax, but is the first to show this sort of invasion. So, while the council debates the problem, noth-ing will be done to Aerie. It's possible that nothing will ever be done—although the incident by itself makes Aerie the aggressor, Parallax's history and the presence of the clandestine grab seem to point accusation at Parallax. I think you can relax for a while—the council's not likely to make a decision for a few months, at the earliest."

"And in the meantime, all we have to worry about is Parallax," Mish said. "How very comforting."

"Perhaps." The colonel smiled. "At least you can worry about them from a distance. My orders are to leave tomorrow for NewHome and observe Parallax firsthand. You don't suppose," he added wistfully, "that I could take Mim? I thought not. Well, perhaps she can find something for me to nibble on in the kitchen, and maybe even something to take along tomorrow." The colonel rose. "The council has sent a patrol ship for me, they should be in tomorrow by noon." He paused at the door. "I suspect that I will be back on Aerie at some point. I'll try to let you know."

"Thank you," Mish said formally.

Smiling, the colonel left the room. Mish sighed and moved her feet on the footstool, and Ozchan came around to rub her shoulders.

"He's far too pleasant for our own good," Quilla said, and stood. "I suppose someone had better go down and tell Decca."

"About?" Ozchan said, not looking up.

"Sandro, of course." Quilla looked around the room. "I suppose I'm it."

"Correct." Mish grunted and turned her head sideways. "It won't make any difference, but by all means tell her. You'd best tell Sandro while you're about it, and be ready to refuse his resignation. If he didn't want to tell us about it himself—"

"It means he's ashamed of it. Mother save us from young men with senses of honor."

Meya stood abruptly and walked over to the window. "Do you think it's not something to be ashamed of? Killing someone?"

Mish straightened and Ozchan removed his hands. Meya stared at the curtains, her back to the room.

"Of course it is," Mish said calmly. "I continue to pay for my deaths. You pay for yours. We think we committed our separate murders for a just cause, defending ourselves, defending the people that we love. It doesn't change the fact of murder. But we accept the burden and go on, we don't make grand gestures, we don't fuck up the rest of our lives, and the lives around us. One sin is enough. I'm not sure that Sandro would see it that way."

Meya gestured helplessly and walked out of the room.

Mish looked at her family, her face hard. "Sandro may feel as guilty as he wishes, but I don't want him to go. We need him here. Decca seems to have chosen him. He's not to leave Aerie, Quilla. Do you understand?"

"Yes." Quilla turned and left the room. Ozchan gave Mish's hair a sharp tug.

"You're growing up to be a vicious old hag," he said, and kissed the top of her head before going upstairs. Mish glared at everyone else until the room emptied, then sat before the dying fire, feeling grumpy and thinking about Ozchan's words. She wondered if Jason would recognize her anymore. After a while she banked the fire and went upstairs. All the doors along the corridor were closed, and she walked slowly, letting her fingers rest on the wood of each door. When she came to her own room she paused, reluctant, before she pushed open the door and went in.

Decca and Sandro were still awake. Quilla knocked at the door of the hospital room and, when Decca called, went in. Decca sat at the foot of the cot by the wall and Sandro, in the high hospital bed, leaned back against the pillows. Strands of curly brown hair poked out of the bandages. They both looked surprised to see her. Decca crossed to sit on the bed beside Sandro and hold his hand. They watched, wide-eyed and silent, as Quilla wandered about the room and thought of what to say.

Eventually she sat on the cot, put her big, calloused hands between her knees, and told it as a story. She told the story of Mish's journey to NewHome and the death of the NewHome soldiers; she told them of Hart's murder of the kasirene pups, she told them of the time someone had tried to murder crippled Jason, and Meya had pulped the man's head with a bed rail. Decca knew the stories, but Sandro listened in silence, his attention entirely on Quilla's face. When she finished talking, he looked down at Decca's hand, turning it over between his. Decca looked at her mother, hurt and bewildered, and let the silence grow.

"Why did you tell me all that?" Sandro said finally. Quilla didn't answer. He glanced at Decca, then released her hand and put his own under the blankets. It didn't take him very long to tell them about the death of the agent on Marquez Landing, and when he finished he stared stubbornly at the bump made by his knees under the covers. Decca looked at her mother and parted her lips, but Quilla shook her head quickly.

"There's a price on your head," Quilla said to Sandro. He looked at her quickly. "It's a Parallax thing, and I don't know how much it is. After your recent escapade, they may increase it."

Sandro thrust out his lower lip, mostly, Quilla guessed, to keep it from trembling.

"You knew," he said.

Quilla nodded. "Colonel Zimmerman told us tonight."

"You will, of course, accept my resignation."

"We'll do no such thing. Although I do find it interesting," she said, "that you offer it now, when we know about the death on Marquez Landing. Why didn't you offer it after you destroyed the grab and that scout ship?"

"But that was entirely different," Sandro said, spreading his hands. "That was an act of war."

"Irrelevant. You've no idea how many people you killed. Two? Five? Twelve? What makes you think it was any less an act of murder than what you did on Marquez Landing?" Quilla crossed her arms and looked at him. "You ended an unknown number of entirely unknown lives, people you didn't know, who had done you no harm—"

"But they were coming to disrupt us, they might have been carrying weapons, they might have attacked us—"

"First, that's not proven. Second, even if it's true, it remains irrelevant. To kill another sapient creature is to murder. The details may vary, but the central fact remains. You committed an act of murder on Marquez Landing, and you committed multiple murder in Eagle System."

"Quilla," Decca said, pleading, but Quilla shook her head. Sandro's face was white.

"If you feel that way," he said shakily, "then why don't you want me to leave?"

"We need you. Decca loves you. We're not pure, I've told you that."

"Then what am I to do?" he cried.

"I don't know. You will have to deal with your own conscience in your own way. We won't punish you for the deaths at the grab, and neither will we punish you for the death on Marquez Landing, although I assume that, should Parallax get its hands on you—". She gestured and stood. Decca and Sandro, each at one end of the high bed, looked at her in confused misery. She suddenly gathered them into her arms and hugged them tightly.

"Get some sleep," she muttered. "Ozchan's letting you out tomorrow, and Mim's got a room ready for you at the Tor." Quilla paused. "A room for both of you. No more nonsense about resigning. And go to sleep." She released them and left the room quickly. It was cold outside, and dawn only a few hours away. She thought about the work waiting for her in the morning, cursed wearily, and trudged through Haven toward the Tor.

The colonel had not expected a farewell committee, and didn't get one. What he did find, arriving at HavensPort half an hour before his shuttle was due to appear, was Tatha drilling her militia in the rain and Hart sitting on the bench in front of the comshack, in the shapeless protection of a watercloak. The colonel deposited his luggage in the shack, confirmed that his shuttle had cleared Eagle Grab and was on its way in, and went outside again. Hart moved over on the bench. The colonel pulled the hood of his borrowed watercloak over his brow and sat.

The militia was wet and filthy and in no mood to respond genially to Tatha's light, sarcastic voice. She had them practicing holds and falls; Zimmerman could hear their grunts of effort and the solid thwack of bodies hitting the pavement through the constant patter of the rain.

"She should train them on grass," he said as a large, solid-looking woman cartwheeled over Tatha's twisting body and landed on a shoulder. The woman sat and rubbed her shoulder, frowning, and Tatha stood over her, hands on hips.

"She does, sometimes," Hart said. "She says that you're rarely given a choice of surfaces when fighting, so she trains them on every surface she can find. Even the town hall, when it's empty. They've broken five benches already."

The large woman stood and grappled with Tatha, and this time the Theresan sailed through the air, to land on bent foot and arm and spring upright. The two women stood in the rain talking, then Tatha moved toward another group.

"She also says," Hart remarked, "that if we are invaded, all this won't do a damned bit of good, but it will help them run away faster." He paused. "Are we going to be invaded, colonel?"

"No." Zimmerman felt water creeping into his shoes. He drew his feet up on the bench and pulled the watercloak over them, wrapping his hands around his knees. "Parallax knows I'm coming, so they won't try planting another grab, I think. And they won't dare bring a force in through the Federation grab." He shook his head, scattering drops of water. "The council is debating a censure, and if they've any sense they'll actually do it. I suppose a slap on the wrist is better than nothing at all."

"And are they likely to do anything more definite? If our reading is correct, and I think it is, Parallax is becoming a threat to the Federation itself."

"I know that," the colonel said unhappily. "They're beginning to learn that. But the very structure of the Federation ties its hands. It controls grabs and communications, it stays away from intrasector or intrasystem politics. It maintains time regs, collects tolls and fees—it was set up as a regulatory body, Quia Hart. Parallax has found a way around those regulations. If the Federation intends to do anything concrete, it will have to revise its entire structure. And as you might imagine, that's not the easiest thing for a monster to do."

"If they wait much longer, they won't have a chance," Hart said.

The colonel gestured under his watercloak. Tatha and a thin young man were standing back to back in the center of the pad, holding off the rest of the militia with their hands and arms and knees and feet. The young man went down, but not before they had fought their way to a fence. Tatha held them off but she visibly tired. Then the warning horns blared, and the militia turned and walked off the field to the barriers. Tatha shook herself and followed them.

"That was timed to a nicety," the colonel said, standing. Hart followed him into the comshack. In the distance, the sound of a shuttle hummed and grew under the sound of rain.

"It would be interesting," Hart said quietly, "to know what's going on over in NewHome System."

The colonel grunted noncommittally.

"For example, it would be interesting to know if they've installed a permanent base, or a manufactory, of if they're just lurking around amid the debris waiting for something."

Zimmerman smiled. "I'm an observer for Galactic Security, Quia Hart. I may have personal prejudices, but I try not to take them to work with me. I'm not a spy, for either side."

Hart grinned. "It was worth a try," he said. "How long do you expect to be gone?"

"I don't know. I may come back to Aerie, I may go on to Althing Green. You'll be notified, one way or another."

The shuttle rolled to a stop beside the comshack and a hatch cracked open. Colonel Zimmerman took off the borrowed watercloak and handed it to Hart, shouldered his luggage, and ran through the rain. Glancing back from the shuttle's hatch, he saw Hart standing in the door of the shack. Hart raised his hand in farewell. Colonel Zimmerman hesitated, then waved back and went in out of the rain.

"I DON'T SEE WHY WE SHOULD LISTEN TO YOU," one of the younger kasirene said. "You're blood-sister to them, you chose them over us, when you come down to it."

Palen sighed and put three hands in her lap. She used the fourth to gesture with. "I've tried to explain that to you. Are you upset when someone chooses a Betes tribe rather than a Cault tribe? Or if someone moves from the tribe here to the one in Cault Tereth?"

"That's different. That's moving amid your own people. You moved away from us. You—repudiated us."

"The word you're looking for," Palen said gently, "is traitor. I'm not one." She looked around at the others gathered in the flame-lit room. Puti lounged against a corner, not saying anything. It was she who had suggested this meeting, overriding Palen's doubts, and she who had gathered a group of not yet committed kasirene to come hear Palen's side. Palen looked at the young, earnest faces and took a deep breath.

"Aside from Hart's crimes," she said, "can you give me another example of albiana disregard for us? And I don't mean the fights children get into at school, I mean something substantive."

"Beriant says," one of them said, and paused.

"Go on."

"Beriant says that they stole Aerie from us. That they bought it from some albiana agency, that we were never consulted."

"That's only partially true," Palen said. "When Jason and Mish came here, they had bought the planet from an albiana group. But they were not told about us beforehand. They were as surprised as we were." She reached for a cup of tea and balanced it between two of her hands. "They made themselves a small house where the Tor is now, and they learned Kasiri. When they knew enough, Jason and Mish came to the village and explained the situation to us. Jason said that if we didn't want them here, they would go away, find another place to live. We debated it for three days and decided that they could stay." She looked around at them. "Ask Altemet. He was young then, but he was there for the debate, and for the vote." She drained the cup. One of the young ones leaned forward and filled the cup again.

"What else does Beriant say?"

"Well, there's the business about the refugees."

Palen made a gesture of surprise. "You would fault an act of charity?"

"But they didn't like us," said the one who had filled her cup. He fiddled with the lid of the teapot. "When Haven caught fire a couple of times, they wanted to blame us."

"That's perfectly true," Palen said. "And the Kennerins prevented them from doing that. Do they hate us now?"

The young ones were silent. Palen looked at Puti, who shrugged marginally. Palen sighed.

"There is nothing they have which we cannot have," Palen told them. "If we wish to attend their schools, we can do so. If we wish to become merchants in their towns,

we can do so. We can live in The Jumble or we can live
in the albiana part of town, it is our own choice. Of the
three teachers at Haven School, two are kasirene. Five
kasirene ship out with Jes Kennerin, and he says that
there is room for more. We have share-right, and we can
vote, if we register."

"But all of that is doing things the albiana way," one of
them pointed out. "That's living things their way, rather
than our own."

"That's beside the point. We are not forced to live here.
We are not forced to attend their schools, or be part of
albiana lives. They have one to'an and part of another;
we have every to'an on Aerie to chose from. They will not
challenge our choices. Nor do they retract privileges if we
do not wish to live beside them. Can any of you prove
that this is not so?" Palen rose and stretched. "I am told
that Beriant would like to see Parallax running this
planet," she remarked. "I find that incredible. Beriant is
not as stupid as that, is he?"

"I don't see what's stupid about it," the teapot kasir
said. "Parallax would let us run Aerie ourselves, and
they'd keep other albiana off the planet. They'd take the
Zimania sap that we gathered and sell it for us; we'd have
the best of it both ways, our own planet but with albiana
technology if we needed it."

"You were at the town meeting. You heard Sandro
Marquez's story, and Tatha's . . ."

"Albiana fighting with albiana," one said as they all
stood. "That has little to do with us. No one's ever said a
word about Parallax damaging indigenes."

"They'd need us," another said. "We'd run the plantations for them."

"Lizardshit," Palen said contemptuously. "They'd ship
people in from Marquez Landing. It's easier to deal with
people you already own. Or is Beriant planning to let
Parallax own the kasirene, too?"

"Beriant is working for our liberation," one said. Palen
took a sharp breath and clenched her hands, willing her
anger to subside.

"I doubt it," she said finally. "It's difficult to fight rhet-
oric with common sense, and I know that it doesn't ring
as well as Beriant's statements. But we've a habit of being
slow to judgment, and that's all I can really ask of you.
Think about what we've discussed tonight. Apply some

flat-footed kasirene logic. Take your time before you make a decision. Can I ask that of you?"

They shuffled and looked at each other. One gestured sharply. "Yes. It makes sense."

As the other young ones, agreeing, trooped from Puti's room, Palen sat by the fire and put her head in her her hands. "I need some kaea," she said.

"You drink too much," Puti said, and gave her a cup of tea. Palen glared at the tea and drank it.

"Do you think that Beriant's actually been in contact with Parallax?" Palen said. "Or is this all just planning for the arrival of the savior?"

Puti gestured. "I don't know. He could be, he sounds very convincing about what they will and won't do."

"Could there be a Parallax agent on Aerie?"

"I don't know," Puti said, and turned her head, listening. Palen, too, caught the minute sound from the sleeping alcove. Puti went to the alcove, pushed the curtains back, and picked up Alin Kennerin, bringing her to the fire. Alin looked at Palen sleepily and put her face against Puti's flat chest. Puti held the girl with two arms, using the other two to brace herself against the cushions.

"Meya thought that living here might help her," Puti said slowly, looking at the sleepy child. "She can read the other terrans, but since Spider couldn't read the kasirene, Meya figured that Alin couldn't, either. And that maybe, being around people that she couldn't read, she'd be forced to talk."

Palen reached over and touched Alin's curly black hair. "Was she right?"

"Yes and no. She can't read us, any more than Spider could. But she's been here twelve days and shows no sign of talking."

"Another of Hart's tragic children," Palen said quietly. She rose. "No, stay down. I'll find my way out. Any news of Spider?"

"Not since Eiret Tapan," Puti said. "The weather's been pretty rough around Tebetet. He's safe with Melet."

Palen put her hands in her pouch. "If any one of us can be said to be safe anywhere," she said, and left the room.

Puti's room was in a far, upper corner of The Jumble, accessible by a series of broad, flat steps on one side, and a covered suspended walkway on the other. Palen looked

at the walkway speculatively, then went down the stairs;
she had never lost her fear of heights and was not, she
thought, going to lose it at her advanced age. The steps
ended at a second-level balcony, and Palen walked along
it. Kagret had a new dissertation on the walls, this one
concerning the wrongs done him by the local fisher tribe.
Kagret sold fish in the market and was always complaining about one thing or another, usually in High Kasiri,
with flourishes. The current effort was one of his better
harangues; Palen flicked on her light stick and read it,
her lips twitching, before continuing down the balcony to
another flight of stairs. Reaching ground level, she sighed
and unclenched her hands. The Jumble was quiet and
dark and she put her big feet down carefully, not making
noise. When she reached the opening onto Tor Street she
paused, her hands on the gate frame. She didn't want to
go to the Tor, she wanted to stay in The Jumble; wanted,
she thought wryly, to go home. She thought of Alin,
sprawled in sleep across Puti's lap, and thought about
Spider. On a shelf in her hut behind the Tor she still
had the tiny grass maze that Spider had given to her. She
wished, suddenly, that she had given him something in
return.

The streets of Haven, too, were quiet. Palen passed
the darkened fronts of houses and the darkened fronts
of stores. Kohl's still had a light on, upstairs, but as Palen
walked through Market Square the light went off. Mertika
going to sleep, now that her night's work was over. Palen
wondered if Hart was upstairs, in Mertika's bed. They
made a strange couple; round, laughing, earthy Mertika,
surrounded by beer suds and the smell of sausages and
meat pies, and Hart, slender, intense, dark, and terrifying. He slept in his laboratory now, in a cot he had
crammed into a corner amid the boxes and tables and
banks of equipment. Some nights Palen woke to the
sound of his weeping, a terrible, dry grief without pause
or change, and on those nights she lay stiffly in her sleeping alcove, telling herself that he deserved his pain, that
he had inflicted worse pain himself. And despite that, it
took all her fortitude not to creep into his laboratory and
comfort him as she would a pup, until he fell asleep.

The lights were still on in the small house that Jared
and Koyu Hevant shared. Palen walked by silently. She
knew, from kitchen gossip, that Jared and Koyu had

spoken to Hart about creating a child for them, and she knew that one of the mechanical wombs in Hart's laboratory held the developing fetus that was partially Jared's and partially his lover's. Another of Hart's children, she thought, and that thought led back to Spider, and to Alin, and to the meeting in Puti's room that night.

"Albiana fighting with albiana," one of them had said. "No one's ever said a word about Parallax damaging indigenes."

That had to be false, Palen thought. We may not have heard about it, but it can't be so. She paused at the place where Tor Street crossed the stream and began its climb up the slope. It was not a question she could ask the Kennerins, who still knew nothing of Beriant's actions in The Jumble, and would, she. hoped, never learn. But there had to be some way of learning whether Parallax had taken over planets with native sapients on them, and what the results had been. Chewing thoughtfully on her lip, Palen hurried up the road to the Tor.

"Sure, if you want to," Quilla said, surprised, and crossed the cluttered office to a cabinet. Palen kept her arms deliberately relaxed.

"It's everybody's problem," she said to Quilla's back. "Albiana, kasirene—what affects one affects the other. Besides, I'm curious."

"Since when is that news?" Quilla pulled a huge folder from the cabinet and glanced through it. "You're sure you just want the history?"

"To begin with," Palen said. "It will give me some idea of the basics, and I can go through the other papers later."

Quilla handed over the thick file. "It's the only copy I've got left," she said. "Don't spill kaea over it."

Palen decided not to make a rude remark and left the room. She put the folder in her pouch. The sharp edges bumped against her skin, hurting her. She put a couple of hands in her pouch to hold the folder and trudged through the rain and the kitchen garden to her hut.

Compared to most kasirene traveling huts, Palen's was an exemplar of luxury. Quilla had insisted on the solar panels and the heating system that kept the floor comfortable, and Meya provided the thick quilts that covered the platform in the sleeping alcove, and the matching curtain that hid the alcove from sight. To Palen's surprise, Hart provided a chair for terran visitors and a high table at which Palen could sit comfortably. Jared, working alone, designed and built a kasirene-tailored bathroom. Most of the cushions were Decca's contribution. Tabor's gift was not visible, but was, perhaps, the best of them all, for he had quietly arranged a permanent place for Palen at the Kennerin table and the Kennerin hearth. The thick pile of cushions in the Kennerin living room was Tabor's idea, as was the kasirene stool at the dinner table. The Kennerins appeared to take Palen's change of tribe as seriously as she did, and she could not find it in herself to tell them that their efforts, although greatly appreciated, nonetheless did not fill the gap. She was a comfortable stranger at the Tor, but a stranger still.

Now she shook herself before entering the hut, shedding the water from the drizzle outside. She spread the open folder over the table and looked at it, pulling her lip. She reached for the kaea, changed her mind, and filled the kettle with water. Part of the firepit was covered with a grill; she poked at the embers under the grill, added some twigs, and put the kettle over the fire while her other hands were busy scooping dried leaves into the teapot. The domestic chores calmed her, each slipping neatly into place, and when the tea was brewed she poured some into a large stone mug and took it to the table.

The search through the file was frustrating. True, the papers traced the growth of Parallax, but all too often the list of planet names and company names was just that, a list, with nothing to tell her of the details of conquest. Slips of paper bearing Mish's handwriting, or Quilla's, occasionally expanded the story somewhat, adding details garnered from here or there, but they were all stories of albiana fighting other albiana, and that didn't suit Palen's purpose at all.

She was still at it, squinting uncomfortably at the unfamiliar Standard script and on her third pot of tea and fifth trip to the bathroom, when Hart knocked on the door frame and, in answer to her shout, stuck his head into the hut.

"It's dinnertime," he said. "Are you eating?"

Palen looked out, surprised, and saw that it was dark.

She weighted the scattered papers with teapot, empty cup, and a few decorative stones before following Hart into the drizzle.

"What are you reading?" he said, walking on the narrow stone path between the muddy rows of the garden. Palen splashed through the mud beside him, enjoying the feel of it between her toes.

"About Parallax," she said and noted his look of surprise. "If we're going to fight them, I figured that I should at least know about them."

Hart nodded and stopped at the kitchen door to take off his watercloak and his boots and hang them on pegs. Palen waited until he was inside before shaking herself and sloshing her feet in the large pan of water that Mim kept by the door for the use of the kasirene. She dried her feet and walked into the kitchen.

"Damnation," Mim yelled. "Get out of my kitchen!"

"But I washed," Palen protested, lifting her feet in turn for Mim's inspection.

"That's not what I mean. Out!" The housekeeper flapped her apron angrily, and Palen retreated from the kitchen. In the dining room, Jason Hart and Andrus set the table, under Tabor's directions.

"Fold the napkins," Tabor was saying. "Don't just drop them. Oh, hello, Palen, what was that all about?"

Palen shrugged. "I don't know. She's never kicked me out of the kitchen before."

Andrus, eyes wide, started to say something and his brother leaned over the table and pushed him hard. "*Fold* the napkins," Jason Hart said angrily. "Boy, are you a treffik."

Andrus tried to look sullen but he kept glancing up at Palen and grinning. Palen rolled her eyes and went into the living room.

"He's marginally better," Ozchan was saying gloomily. "And there's really nothing I can do for him in the hospital, so I had to let him go home. I've sent Josh over there to care for him, he's a good nurse for the old man, won't let him get away with anything. And either Miri or I drop in twice a day." Ozchan waved a greeting to Palen and went on talking to Mish. "But I can't do anything else for him, Mish. He's a stubborn old bastard and you know it. Should I have tied him down?"

"No," Mish said. She looked down at her hands, folded

in her lap. "No, that would kill him faster than—how long, Ozchan?"

The doctor's mouth twitched down at the corners. "I don't know. If he stays down, obeys orders, maybe six months. Maybe more. He's an old man, Mish. And a spacer's life is not an easy one."

"Yes, I know. He's such a part of our lives . . ." She stood abruptly. "Palen. Would you like a drink?"

Palen shook her head. "No, thanks. Mim's kicked me out of the kitchen and the children are back there giggling. What's going on?"

"Who knows?" Mish said. "Since when have I been able to figure out my family? Have you heard that Jes has come back?"

Palen shook her head again and crossed to the pile of cushions. "When?"

"This afternoon, unexpectedly. And he's brought Taine back."

"Taine?" Palen frowned. "The preacher's wife?"

"If you can call her that," Quilla said from the hallway. She looked tired, and when Palen scooted over on the cushions, she dropped down beside her and let her shoulders slump. "I've spent a goodly part of the afternoon talking with her—or trying to. I think Jes is right, Mish. I think she's unsynched."

Mish raised her eyebrows and handed Quilla a glass of liquor. Quilla sipped it.

"She says her name is Beryl, won't answer to Taine. But she's Taine, all right. You can see it a mile off, despite the web scarring. Jes is trying to talk her into going to Hoku to see Kayman but I don't know if she will."

"Then why'd she come down?" Ozchan demanded. "She knows that Kayman's been falling apart without her, doesn't she? And what about the kids?"

Quilla shrugged and put her head against Palen's shoulder. "She says she came down to see Hetch, to say good-bye. And, frankly, I don't think it's a good idea to send her to Hoku. If Kayman feels unhappy without her, he'll be stunned by what she's become." Quilla offered her glass to Palen, who shook her head. "You'll see her at dinner," she said.

Palen muttered a Kasiri curse. "It's going to be another Kennerin family dinner," she said without enthusiasm. "Mim chasing people out of the kitchen for no good reason, the kids sniggering amid the cutlery, stray schizos from the stars—is Tatha coming up?" she asked hopefully, and sighed when Mish shook her head.

Jason Hart marched to the hallway, stood at the bottom of the stairs, and beat furiously on a pan with a spoon. Everyone jumped.

"Dinner's ready," Jason Hart howled. He marched back into the dining room.

"Is he going to make a habit of this?" Palen demanded as they trooped out of the living room.

"He'd better not," Meya said, coming down the stairs. "One more of those and I'll have his hide. Jason Hart!" She stormed into the dining room.

They were seated by the time Jes and Beryl came into the room. Palen watched Beryl curiously. She remembered Taine, the auburn-haired beauty who had come with the original NewHome refugees, and made an unhappy accommodation to her new life. Taine Alendreu's family, on NewHome, had been rich, cultured, and politically unpopular, and the girl came to Aerie expecting another version of the same thing. She hadn't found it. When she disappeared from Aerie it was assumed that she'd gone to one of the wealthy planets, perhaps even to Althing Green. She had still been lovely enough to forge a new life for herself in the Federation's cultured, decadent heartland.

Palen could see only the faintest glimmers of Taine in the woman who sat next to Jes and nodded uncomfortably at the family. Slim, tough, her face laced with web-scarring—she'd be in her mid-forties by now and was still, when her face relaxed, achingly beautiful. Palen wondered if someone had commed Olet in Hoku to tell him that his wife was back. Andrus stuck his head into the room, counted carefully, and popped back into the kitchen. Mish rolled her eyes and looked suspicious, and Tabor smiled.

Mim's surprise was borne into the room by Jason Hart and Andrus; a steaming haunch of hopper, garnished with lacy greens and filling the room with a rich, savory aroma.

"Sweet Mother," Mish said reverently. "Where did you get it?"

Mim put her hands under the apron and surveyed the table.

"It's not what you think it is," she announced, and shook her head when they demanded clarification. "Eat it first." She produced a knife and fork and sliced into the roast.

It was delicious, and tasted only faintly like hopper. Better than hopper. Conversation at the table halted, to be replaced with the rattle of cutlery and appreciative noises. Mim nodded and served herself last.

"Hart made it," she said when everyone had eaten, and Hart looked surprised.

"From Cault Eiret?" he said. "Then this must be one of the first."

"It is the first," Mim said with satisfaction. "They won't reach the market until tomorrow."

"Hart?" Mish said, in her you-had-better-tell-me voice.

"Oh, I thought I told you about that. The rangers weren't happy with the cattle—the terran stock doesn't really adapt too well, and hoppers simply couldn't be domesticated. I made a cross between the two—it's basically hopper, but grows faster, gets fatter, and is easily domesticated. I just didn't think they'd have enough to market already."

Mish looked vaguely uncomfortable. She'd never approved of Hart's laboratory, and now she looked dubiously at her son.

"It tastes okay," she said tentatively. Quilla laughed.

"You should go into competition with the Enchanter Labs," Tabor said. Hart shook his head.

"I'd prefer to stay here." Hart looked quickly toward the place at the table where Spider had traditionally sat, and which was now occupied by Palen. The kasir saw the unwilling pain in Hart's glance and put her fork slowly down on the table.

By fen'al the next day, having skipped both breakfast and lunch, Palen finished with the Parallax file and was no nearer a solution than she'd been before. She carefully squared the edges of the file and put it aside, then looked at the list of planet names she had laboriously copied onto a sheet of paper. They represented those planets about which nothing save the name appeared in the record, and there were forty-seven of them; she pulled at her lip while she put the file and the list in her pouch.

The rain had taken a brief intermission. Grey clouds scooted overhead, breaking occasionally to show paler clouds above, and the light itself seemed liquid and diffuse. She pulled her watercloak over her shoulders and waded through the mud to the Tor.

The house was silent. Palen opened the door of the warming oven and pulled out five meat buns. She wrapped four in a towel and put them in her pouch and munched on the fifth as she went through the dining room into the hallway and down the hall to Quilla's office. It, too, was empty. She put the Parallax file atop the desk and looked longingly at the computer terminal. The temptation was great, but she knew that the terminal logged all uses and she did not want the Kennerins to know, yet, of her quest. Sighing, she left the Tor and walked down the paved and muddy path to Haven.

From the beginning it had been obvious that the best place to locate the library and the public computer was at the schoolhouse, where the children, who used both most often, would have ready access to them. As Palen approached the schoolhouse the recess gong rang and children poured from the main doors of the building onto the playing field. Palen stopped to watch them. A caraem game was set up in one corner of the field—the terran and kasirene players shouted and leaped for the ball while observers on the sidelines howled advice and imprecations. Elsewhere a mixed group formed a huddled circle, playing the stick game. Jason Hart sat on the steps with Kerelet. His hands moved with the force of his argument. Kerelet nodded, bent forward, and drew something quickly in the dirt. Jason Hart frowned at it. Palen walked around the edge of the yard and to the steps.

"I'd like to use the library," Palen said when the proper formalities had been exchanged. Kerelet looked surprised.

"First door to the right," he said, and paused. "You know how to use the computer?"

"Of course," Palen said, insulted. She went inside. The schoolhouse creaked and footsteps ran along a corridor upstairs. Palen remembered the original schoolhouse, a one-room building with a reluctant heater in one corner and Simit pacing the rows of desks, his scar still a livid reminder of the deathcamp on NewHome from which Jason Kennerin has rescued him. Over the years the scar had faded, the school expanded to a solid two-story building with its own solar-powered heating system, and Jason had died. Palen shook her head. Some things didn't change, though.. The school was still cold in the winter, when the sun rarely broke through the cloud cover to bathe the panels; wood fires burned in round-bellied stoves at the corner of each room, and the scent of burning kaedo wood filled the building. Palen pushed open the door of the library and went in.

There were four terminals in the room. Taped to the side of each one, for the benefit of the younger students, were directions for the terminals' use. Palen pulled the list and the remaining meat buns from her pouch and sat at the terminal farthest from the door. Step one, step two, step three—she was more used to working in the fields or in the orchards than she was used to working the knobs and keyboard of the terminal, and she kept making mistakes. She bit into a bun, annoyed, and tried again.

Eventually she got it right: general search mode, all relevant entries regardless of original classification, run in Standard. She poked in the name of the first planet on the list, then the second, then the third.

The entries were basically identical. Astronomical locations, both tau coordinates and real space coordinates. Date of entry into the Federation, or date of first contact. Political structure. Major exports, if any; major imports, if any. Occasionally a piece of information would cause Palen to cross a name off her list: this one a terraformed planet; this one a first-evolution planet; this one a lifeless ball rich in ores. By jev'al, the school closed for the day and the sun already set, she had narrowed the list to twenty-nine names, and the computer could give her no further information on those planets. She rocked back on the stool, an uncomfortably small thing built for pups, not adults, and stared at the terminal's blank gray face.

There had to be some way of tracking down those twenty-nine planets, but there was no way she could find the information on Aerie. Palen pulled on her lip, rose, and grimaced, surprised at the stiffness of her muscles. She stretched and rubbed, frowning at her list, bent forward, and tapped the keyboard again.

Query: Information sources.
Response: Library databanks.
Query: Further information sources.
Response: Define nature of inquiry.
Query: Individual planetary history.
Response: Federation Register, Vol. I-29, Code 457-
　　B169.
　　Grabstation Register, 1244 edition, Code 996Z733.
　　A Brief History of the Galactic Federation, ed.
　　　Kobert & Haimes, 1239, Code 4659920.
　　A Child's Guide to History, ed Franz & abTiko,
　　　1243, Code 845X215.
Query: Halt. Most complete source, individual plane-
　　tary history, accessible Aerie.
Response: Council Record, Althing Green, public ac-
　　cess channel A-1492, Code 801, accessible Havens-
　　port terminal.
Query: Cost.
Response: 95 fremarks/minute.

"Shit," Palen said, and blanked the screen.

"Problems?" someone said at the door. Palen turned
quickly. Jason Hart stood with his hands in his pockets,
his head to one side.

"Why aren't you home?" Palen said. "It's dinnertime."

"I wanted to work here for a bit." Jason Hart came into the library and put some papers down by one of the
terminals. "Can I help you with something?"

Palen sat on the stool and looked at him. "Perhaps,"
she said slowly. "Jason Hart? How are you at keeping
secrets?"

"Depends on the secret," he replied. He turned a chair
around and sat in it, facing her.

Palen considered him, frowning slightly. He'd changed
considerably since his day with Spider at the slaughterhouse, but the change could not, she thought, be charted
with exactitude. He'd become quieter, certainly; and certainly he no longer tormented small animals or other children. He spent much of his time in the schoolhouse or in
his room at the Tor, surrounded by bookreels, charts, and
small instruments, and increasingly she thought that he
reminded her of someone, but the connection evaded her.
Silent, self-involved child; even his laughter had a serious

ring to it. She nodded suddenly and reached for her list of planets.

"I need to find out about these," she said, handing the list to him. "I need their histories, from first contact. But the library here doesn't have them, and I'll have to query the council records on Althing Green."

"Expensive," Jason Hart murmured, looking down the list.

"And I don't want it generally known that I'm doing this."

He looked up for a moment, shrugged, and looked at the list again. "Can you afford it?"

Palen grimaced. "Barely."

"What kind of information do you want hidden?"

Palen didn't reply. She stood and crossed to the window. The library faced away from Haven, and the darkness above Havenswood was illuminated by a few bright stars.

"If I'm going to help you, I'll have to know," Jason Hart said. He put the list down and tapped the keyboard of his terminal. "You don't have to be specific, but—"

"All right," Palen said abruptly. "I need to know whether Parallax has ever taken over a world with native sapients, and if so, how the natives were treated."

Jason Hart thought a moment and nodded. "We can do it. Request a general dump on all the planets on your list. Some might have the information you want, others won't. A general dump will carry so much information that no one, looking through it, should be able to guess what you're really after." He paused, frowning. "We'd better do it under my name. I can cite curiosity."

"And payment?"

Jason Hart grinned. "Transfer the funds to a Market-Port account, under a code number. Send in the request through the MarketPort channel, it shouldn't be too hard. Route Aerie to MarketPort, to Althing Green, to Market-Port, to Aerie again. I'll pick it up at the comshack; if we code it private we shouldn't have any trouble. I've done it before, researching stuff, so no one will think it odd. Okay?"

Palen nodded. "I can have the funds ready for transfer in a day or two."

"No trouble, just let me know." Jason Hart folded the

list and slipped it into his pocket. "If you can ever tell me what it's all about, I'd be interested."

Palen gestured her assent and crossed to the door. "Jason Hart? Thanks."

"Sure," he said, already bent over his terminal. Palen hesitated at the door frame, watching him, and the connection was suddenly apparent. He reminded her of Hart. She shuddered, quickly, and slid out into the rain.

❧

JES WAS UP WELL BEFORE DAWN. HE PUT ON A heavy jacket, filled its pockets with cold muffins left over from dinner, and slid a hotflask into his back pocket before wrapping himself in a watercloak and walking down the hill toward the meadow. The sky had decided to drizzle again, a constant, unpleasant mist that immediately soaked into things. He pushed his hood back and let the water run down the planes of his face. He missed this, in space; the feel of weather, of water falling to its own rhythms, the scent and push of the wind. The world was barely visible and he knew he had reached the stream only because of its sound over the rocks. Crossing the low bridge, he turned right and walked through the truck gardens, skirting Haven until he reached HavensPort road. He walked through the low hills to the meadow by the port, squinted, then struck off through the grass. He found the solitary kaedo and leaned against its trunk under the shelter of its broad leaves. The sky lightened marginally. He sipped tea from the hotflask and waited.

He heard Tatha whistling long before he saw her, and Belshazar the shaggy reached him first. The beast cavorted out of the mist, flopped on its back, and wriggled enthusiastically. Jes squatted and rubbed Belshazar's pale belly. Six shaggy legs thrashed ecstatically.

"How comforting to be so immediately loved," Tatha said. "You're up early."

Jes rose and brushed his hands against his watercloak. "I wanted to talk with you."

"That seems to be the new national sport. Talking with Tatha." She pulled Daren from her watercloak and set him on the ground. Belshazar immediately leaped to his feet and stood beside the child, and Daren, standing, tangled his fingers in the shaggy's long fur. "Why didn't you wait until after training this morning?"

"I wanted some privacy."

She put her hands on her hips and looked at him. "Did you? It's a pity, then. At dawn I run, tauCaptain. You're welcome to run with me, but run I shall. Exercise of the tongue can wait." She stripped off the watercloak and the suit underneath it; her silver fur darkened to gray in the rain. "Belshazar, stay put," she said, tossing her clothing over a limb of the kaedo. "Coming, tauCaptain?"

She was gone before he could reply. He squinted after her, cursing, then flung his own watercloak and jacket atop her clothes and followed her into the meadow. The sky paled even more. He could see her ahead of him and to the side; her muscles bunched and smoothed, rippling the wet gray fur. She swung her head to look at him, grinned, and kept running. Jes sprinted until they ran side by side.

"Tatha," he said. She pulled ahead of him. He clenched his teeth and caught up with her.

Midway across the meadow he began to feel proud of himself, glad that the increased hours in the ship's gym had paid off. Three quarters of the way across his breath started to come heavy and his chest tightened. Tatha glanced at him and he pushed his body to keep pace, determined not to lose her. His pants were soaked and slapped at his legs, and sweat poured down his forehead and into his eyes. He didn't want to break pace to wipe it away. Tatha pulled ahead again. He clenched his hands and ran.

The meadow washed up against flanks of forest. Tatha stopped and leaned against a tree, breathing deeply. Jes put his back to the trunk beside her, trying not to pant.

"Clothes slow you down," she said after a while. "Especially when they're wet."

He looked at her and angrily peeled his clothes off. The air felt icy on his damp skin.

"Keep your shoes on," she said, and set off again. He threw his clothes into an untidy heap at the foot of the tree and followed her.

Midway back the band in his chest loosened suddenly and his body settled into an easy rhythm, legs pumping, arms swinging. The ribbon around his hair came loose; he shook the hair from his face and kept running, breathing deeply. The world seemed fresh and made for running, and his body fresh-made for running in it. The kaedo loomed up through the mist. He turned off on his own and began a wide arc through the grass. Tatha paced him. She grinned at him, running at his side, and they veered back to the tree and fell into the grass at its foot. Jes' heart beat strongly and his skin tingled. He raised his arms overhead, stretched, and laughed.

"Not bad," he said, his voice ripe with satisfaction.

Tatha's eyes gleamed. The sun was fully up and the dark leaves of the kaedo glistened wetly above them. Daren rushed around the tree and threw himself in Tatha's lap.

"Feel like fetching your clothing?" she said, smiling.

"Oh, shit," Jes began sitting up. Tatha dropped Daren onto his chest. Jes grabbed at the child. By the time he sat up, Tatha was a brief silver blur moving through the gray of mist and the gray of grass.

"Wanna see," Daren demanded. Jes swung the child onto his shoulders. Daren grabbed a handful of Jes' hair and bounced gleefully.

"Cut that out," Jes said, reaching up with his free hand. Daren hooked his claws into the kaedo branch overhead, pulled himself all the way up, and refused cheerfully to come down. Jes cursed and climbed halfway up the tree, the damp bark rough and unpleasant against his skin. He pried Daren from the branch and came down, to find Tatha calmly retying her hair. His clothing lay at her feet.

He put Daren down and reached for his pants. Tatha stood balanced on the balls of her feet, tightening and relaxing the muscles of her legs, and breathing so easily that her breasts barely moved. Jes pulled on the unpleasant wet pants.

"Having been properly chastened, I'll go," he said.

"Don't. You said you wanted to talk to me."

"After that demonstration, what could I possibly say to you?" he said sarcastically.

She took his arm and pulled him around to face her. "Perhaps nothing. Jes, I've been running like this every morning since you first brought me to Aerie. Theresans are tailored for running, it's the way we're put together. You can't do everything perfectly the first time."

"I know that," he said, looking away from her. "I'm not fond of making a fool of myself."

"Did you? I didn't notice."

Daren had already worked himself free of his clothing and stood beside his mother, bouncing on his toes. At Tatha's nod, Belshazar flopped down beside Jes and put all his paws atop each other. He rested his chin on the ground and his eyes never left Daren. Jes sat beside him reluctantly.

Tatha said something in an alien language and Daren dashed off, running around the base of the tree. Tatha circled the trunk, watching her son, and Jes watched her. She called something again, and while Daren watched she ran a few steps, pivoted, and ran back. The maneuver was so fluid that Jes could not see where she began the turn. Daren tried it, fell, stood up, tried it again, fell again, stood, and flapped his arms in disgust.

Tatha did the turn again, very slowly. Jes saw her begin the turn as her foot came down, and she was already pivoting when her other leg began its forward step. He itched to try it himself but remained seated beside the shaggy as Daren practiced the move, increasing his speed. Belshazar nudged Jes' hand, and he absently scratched behind the shaggy's floppy ears. Daren moved with surprising ease; made for it, Jes thought, and felt bereft. Tatha said something, and Daren laughed and threw his arms around her legs, hugging her, before dropping into the grass beside the shaggy. Tatha glanced at the sky, bundled Daren's clothes, and handed them to him. She knelt to gather her own clothes together.

"You wanted to talk to me?" she said.

Jes stood and tried to put his hands in his pockets. They were too wet to go in.

"I brought Beryl down with me," he said, and Tatha nodded. "She says she wants to say good-bye to Hetch, but—you've met Kayman Olet, haven't you?"

Tatha nodded and stood, her clothes bundled under her arm. "You want to know whether he should be called?" She smiled when Jes nodded. "Such serious business for a trip before dawn," she said. "Yes, I think you should. She won't like it, and he won't like it, but some illusions are best shattered."

Jes moved his shoulders uncomfortably. "He's still in love with her. I wouldn't want him hurt."

"He will be, whatever you do. He has his children and his rather easygoing god, he'll manage. Will she?"

"Beryl? She can take anything."

Tatha raised her eyebrows and shrugged. "Will you run with us back to the port?"

He was about to refuse when he saw the sparkle of warmth in her eyes. He stripped and knotted his clothes together. Tatha whistled and Belshazar rose and shook himself, scattering water into the mist. Daren shrieked, turned and ran toward the port. Belshazar ranged ahead of him and Tatha, with Jes at her side, jogged behind. It was crazy, he thought, running naked in the middle of winter through the rain, but the grass felt fine brushing his thighs, and the air was sweet and clean. Daren yelled and leaped ahead of them, dancing through the meadow, and the shaggy replied with a long, complicated whistle that modulated into high, joyful yelps. Tatha threw her head back and laughed, spreading her arms as she ran, and Jes laughed with her. Daren ran through a gap in the low fence surrounding the port, but Belshazar leaped over it, and Tatha followed him. Jes recklessly did likewise and landed breathlessly beside her. She looked at him, and turned quickly to help Daren dress. Jes stopped laughing and reached slowly for his own pants and shirt. By the time he had finished, Tatha too was dressed.

"Thanks for slowing down for me," he muttered.

She stepped in front of him and put her hands on his shoulders. "We're built like this," she said quietly. "It's no better and no worse. Just different." She paused. "You can do things we can't. Our faces are hidden, and yours are open. You can ride your feelings on your cheeks and lips."

"That's a good thing?" Jes said sarcastically.

"Yes." Tatha kissed his mouth quickly, swung Daren up to her hip, and trotted down the road toward Haven.

Jes, watching her leave, stood at the edge of the meadow and slowly put his hand to his lips.

"Very pretty," Beryl said. "Charming. Idyllic. Does she know?"

Jes whipped around to face her. She had the hood of a watercloak pulled well over her face and he could not read her expression.

"Beryl," he said angrily.

"Quite a comedy, isn't it?" she continued, oblivious. "Kayman wants me and I want you and you want Tatha. Who does she want, do you suppose? Aside, of course, from herself." She laughed unpleasantly. "And then there's Sandro, but I think he's settled on your niece, so that takes him out of the running. Chancy, for a while there, with Sandro in love with everybody at the same time. And Hetch. All he wants is space; a simple request, you'd think, except that nobody loves him enough to give it to him."

Jes slapped her jaw. She jerked back, put her hand to her face, and shook her head.

"I'm sorry," she said quietly. "I'm sorry."

"That may not be enough. You've no right to speculate about other people's business, and you're wrong anyway."

"I'm not," she said. "I knew what you felt for Tatha the minute you stopped refusing to go to bed with me." Jes looked at her blankly. She gestured and turned away from him. "I've commed Kayman, he'll be here by this afternoon. He won't bring the children and he won't ask me to stay. If nothing else, he's a man who keeps his promises."

Jes closed his eyes, bewildered. "Who are you now?" he whispered, and she laughed again.

"I don't know, tauCaptain. I don't even care. You'd best get home before you chill."

She walked away from him, up the road to Haven. He shivered suddenly, cold through to the bone.

Hetch lay on a makeshift bed in his living room, listening to Beryl's account of a race between *Rabbit* and a competing merchant ship. Jes stood in the hall listening: the old man's voice sounded strange and weak, and Jes closed his eyes tight and waited until the emotion drained from him. Then, fixing a smile on his face, he went into the room.

It was hard to believe that Hetch had ever been fat. He barely made a ridge under the blanket and his hands were brittle discolored claws resting at his sides. Jes' smile disappeared. Hetch, seeing it, gestured briefly.

"Beryl tells me that you whipped Cello's ass over in Greengate Sector," Hetch said. "About time."

Jes nodded. Beryl stood, looking at her chrono. "I've got to get going," she said. "See you later, Hetch."

"Sure. Thanks."

She pressed his hand, looked at Jes, and left the room. Jes pulled the chair closer to the bed and sat.

"I know," Hetch said irritably. "I look like a month old corpse, and I feel worse. No, don't bother being polite about it. I can't even take a shit by myself anymore."

"I heard what you did for Sandro," Jes said.

"Yeah." Hetch picked at the blankets with his fingers. "Someone had to."

"But you knew it would—"

"Yeah. Should I have left him up there?" He moved sharply. "I may be falling apart, but I'm not crazy, Jes. Is my life worth more than his? I'm dying anyway."

"Hetch, please."

"It's a wonderful event," the old man said, ignoring him. "Pity the brain doesn't go first, but then I suppose I'd miss the full impact of it. It's sort of like watching the seals blow, when you know there's not a damned thing you can do about it except watch and count minutes. First the cargo holds go, then the front line seals, and you watch it coming closer to the bridge, and wonder if you should take notes." He paused and looked at Jes. "Trouble is, after a while it gets damned monotonous. You know what's going to happen already, and what in hell's the use of hanging around unless there's a surprise up the line?"

"Ozchan—"

"No. No surprises, Jes. Course has been plotted, and it's in the bank. Nothing to do except watch."

Jes put his head in his hands, and felt Hetch's gnarled hand rest on his hair.

"It hurts too much, Jessie. I can't even give a damn about anything outside of this room." Hetch paused again. "I had the universe, once. Now my universe is this thing lying in the bed. Hell of a note."

Jes raised his head and caught Hetch's hand in his own. "You know what you're asking of me?"

"Yeah."

"Mother, Hetch. How can I do that?"

Hetch smiled. "Easy. In the hope that someday, some-one might do the same thing for you."

Jes swore and stood. He put his hands against the win-dowsill and leaned his forehead against the glass. "I don't know," he whispered.

"I taught you, Jes. You've still got stuff to learn."

Jes turned. "We leave in three days."

"Fine. Come see me again, Jes. And call that fool nurse on the way out. I think I need to shit again."

&

WITH GREAT AND TENTATIVE POLITENESS ON both sides, Beryl and Kayman Olet had agreed to meet on neutral territory, neither in Haven nor at the port. Now, surveying the place they had chosen, Kayman wondered if they had not, perhaps, been a little too concerned with the niceties of the situation; the cemetery was, by any measure, a strange place in which to meet one's estranged spouse. He put the basket from Kohl's atop old Doctor Hoku's gravestone and strolled nervously between the graves, staring at the markers and wondering what he would say.

At first she seemed totally familiar, the swing of her walk, the tilt of her head as she climbed Cemetery Road. He hurried to meet her, then slowed and stopped, unsure of himself. She was dressed in a plain yellow coversuit, with the Aerie-Kennerin logo stitched to one shoulder, and her hair was bound tightly into a club at the nape of her neck. She paused a few yards away and looked at him, letting him note the webbing of scars on her face, the de-tached gleam in her eyes, before moving beyond him into the cemetery. He followed her uncertainly.

"Manny Hetch is dying," she said, looking down at the basket.

Kayman cleared his throat. "So I've been told. It's—unfortunate."

"It's hideous," she said, and did not continue. Kayman wondered if she wanted him to say something more about Captain Hetch, but he couldn't think of anything to add. She touched the basket with the toe of her boot.

"How are the children?"

"Well. You've received their letters?"

"Yes. I'm afraid I don't write as often as I should. Did you tell them that I'd be here?"

"No." Kayman passed his hand over his head. "You said you didn't want to see them, so I thought . . ."

"Yes. I know. Maybe next time." She glanced at him. "You always did that, with your hand. I remember that very clearly."

He put his hand in his pocket. "Would you like something to eat?"

"Not—yes, thank you."

They sat on opposite sides of the gravestone and he pulled meat pies, a small loaf of bread, and a flask of wine from the basket. She watched him soberly and did not offer to help. The food tasted flat, and he had to choke it down, but she ate it readily and licked her fingers.

"It's very good," she said. "Did you make it yourself?"

"No, I bought it all from Kohl's this morning. I just got in from Hoku last night."

"That's right," she said. "I keep forgetting that you live on Betes now. How is it?"

"Pleasant."

The dreadful silence descended again. He brushed crumbs from his hands and wondered desperately what he was doing.

"It's been a long time," he said finally. She looked up at him quickly and nodded, averting her eyes. "I don't know what to call you," he continued. "I'm not sure what your name is."

"Beryl," she said quietly. "My name is Beryl."

"Oh," he said. "Why Beryl?"

She smiled. "It's a gemstone, from Terra. When it's pure it has no color at all—it's the impurities that give it tone. It seemed appropriate."

He bit his lip. "You're not Taine at all, then."

"I don't know." She toyed with the wine flask. "It's like

remembering a dream, or remembering a holo. The name's familiar, but it's not me. Your face is familiar, but you don't feel like a part of my life. I can remember some things, stray things—the way you rub your head with your hand, that sort of thing. But they don't seem real to me. I can accept the memories, now. I mean, I believe that I was married to you, that I have children. That I lived on this planet at one time. But I believe all of that on faith."

Kayman watched her hands as she turned the wine flask between them. She had always seemed exotic to him, strange and mysterious; now she was so mysterious as to baffle him entirely. He remembered his optimistic hope that she'd return to Hoku with him, return to his house and his bed, and realized just how futile that hope had been. She wasn't Taine; she wasn't even someone he could begin to understand. He felt suddenly desolate; he hadn't realized how strong his hope was until it disappeared.

"Kayman Olet," she said, and he looked at her miserably. She leaned over the grave and took his hand. "I can't be Taine for you. It's taken me years to learn to be Beryl, to learn to be whatever I am. Including parts of what I used to be, but that was someone else, in a different life, a different place. But, if you'd like, I can be Beryl for you. I can be a friend, a spacer. If you'd like."

"It seems the best of a bad bargain," he said. She dropped his hand and sat back.

"It's the only bargain you're likely to get," she said coldly, and folded her arms across her breasts.

"I'm sorry."

"Oh, Sweet Mother!" She jumped up and paced about the grave, looking at him angrily. "I remember that, all too well. Can't you manage anything other than a cringing apology? Can't you yell back, for a change?"

"No," he said simply. "I'm not comfortable yelling back and I never have been. You always did the yelling, remember?"

"That wasn't me," she shouted. She dropped to her knees and leaned toward him. "Listen, if we're going to have any kind of contact at all, you're going to have to remember that I'm not your wife. That I never was your wife. That I'm somebody else, I'm Beryl, I'm a spacejock. Yes, I've been crazy, and yes, I may have been your wife at some point, but that was somebody else in my head. I can't go back there, I don't want to go back there. It's been a damned hard fight even to become what I am now, and I'm only here today because Sandro nagged me into it. Either you live with that, or we call the whole thing off, just forget the entire business. It's your choice, Olet."

He straightened his shoulders abruptly. "Then I choose not to," he said with dignity. "I can't accept you as a friend, you're not the sort of person that I'd generally be friendly with. If you want to be Beryl, then you can be Beryl without me."

She rocked back on her heels. "All right," she said after a moment. The anger was gone from her voice. "And the children?"

"They can make their own decisions about it. If you wish to see them, let me know the next time you're on Aerie and I'll send them to Haven to see you." He paused. "Do you really care about them at all?"

She gestured. "I don't know. I've become used to their holos, aboard ship. I like their letters. I'm—fond of them."

"Fond. It's better, I suppose, than nothing." He stood and extended his hand. "Good-bye, then."

She rose slowly, looked at his hand, and took it gingerly. Then she left. Kayman gathered the remains of the meal back into the basket, brushed crumbs off the headstone, and glanced around once before following Beryl down the hill. Perhaps, he thought suddenly, the graveyard had been singularly appropriate after all, and realized, with peaceable surprise, that he felt good.

"AGAIN," TATHA SAID WEARILY.

Hart put his hand over his eyes and slumped lower in the chair. The fire hissed and crackled, and rain beat furiously on the roof.

"Armed aggression," he said.

"Out. Zimmerman will prevent it, as long as he's in NewHome System."

"Surreptitious aggression."

"Out. The colonel indicated that GalSec would be monitoring Eagle and NewHome for any illegal transmissions."

"Embargo."

"Out. We have our own plantations, our own processing plant, our own shipping network, our own wholesale warehouses on MarketPort, our own distribution channels."

"Undercutting our prices."

"Possible, but no sign of it yet. Even if it happened, we'd survive."

"Voting control."

"Ah." Tatha refilled Hart's glass and looked into the brandy in her own glass. Belshazar padded in from Daren's room and flopped at her feet before the fireplace. "We come back to that again. Common stock is available to anyone, but common stock can't vote. Voting shares go to Aerie-born terrans at the age of sixteen; immigrant terrans after three years' residence; any kasirene over the age of sixteen. One voting share per citizen, regardless of the amount of common stock owned. Anyone moving permanently from Eagle System automatically loses her or his voting share." She paused. "Parallax can't send in five thousand new Aerie citizens, it would be too obvious and we'd put a stop to it. They can't buy voting shares. And they're not about to convert a majority of Aerites to their own philosophy—we know too damned much about them already." Tatha reached down absently to scratch Belshazar behind the ears. "It's in there somewhere, but I'm damned if I can figure it out."

Hart grunted his assent. "My brain's in circles," he said.

"It's the damned waiting." Tatha stood and walked to the window. Hart watched her. Her silver hair hung straight to her waist, and when she turned her eyes looked very blue in the firelight. "What do you hear from Spider?" she said.

Hart turned to look into the fire. "Nothing. Palen says that it's hard to communicate this time of year, the seas are impassable."

"Does it get any easier?" Tatha said.

Hart shook his head. Tatha paced across the room, opened the door to Daren's room, and looked in. Belshazar loped into the boy's room, and Tatha closed the door. Distant thunder rattled. She put her fists in the

pockets of her suit and stalked across the living room
again.

"I hate the rain," she said, and Hart looked at her,
surprised. She faced the window and her shoulders were
tense.

"Why?"

"It dissolves things," she said. Hart stood up and joined
her at the window. "It softens edges. Lines get indistinct,
and it's so easy to step from one side to another, and not
even know you've done it."

Hart glanced at her. Her face looked like a mask. She
made an abrupt gesture and pulled the curtains closed,
walked back to the fireplace, picked up her glass, and
looked into it.

"One would wish," she said finally, "at least for some
new *casus triste*, something a bit more original, perhaps.
Something individual. You'd think," she said bitterly, "that
I could arrange something as simple as that. I've a reputation to maintain, after all."

"Is this therapy?" Hart said, putting his shoulders
against the wall. She turned toward him, looking surprised.

"Therapy? For whom?"

"Me. Perhaps a not-so-subtle reminder that I'm not the
only one around with sorrows."

"Don't be an ass," she said sharply, and refilled her
glass. "Do I have a reputation for altruism? It's illegiti-
mate, I assure you. As long as your problems don't make
problems for me, I don't care what you're going through.
Tempus vincit omnia, my friend." Thunder rattled again
and she turned her head toward the window. "Go away,
Hart. I want to be alone tonight."

He pushed himself away from the wall.

"I'm sorry, Lady Fangs. Sometimes my perceptions end
at the end of my nose. And sometimes I do need remind-
ers." He picked up his glass and sank into the chair.
"Which one of us, do you think, is pricklier than the
other?"

Tatha laughed shortly. "I don't know your history and
you don't know mine." She looked at him, amused, and
continued pacing. "Shall we agree to misunderstand each
other, then?"

Hart nodded, barely smiling. "Do you really want me
to go?"

"Why shouldn't you?"

"It's raining," he said, stretching his legs. "You're twitchy. I don't like wet skies either. It's a long walk home. And I'm not fond of complications."

"Um." She paused at the window and pushed the curtain aside. "That's an interesting list." The curtain fell into place and she paced back across the room. Hart balanced his glass between his fingers and watched her tilt the bottle toward her own, newly empty glass. Then he stood, walked to her, and took the bottle from her. She watched him speculatively as he rested his hands on her hips.

"No promises," she said.

"Agreed." He kissed her. Her fur felt warm and soft against the corners of his mouth, and after a while he moved his head and ran his parted lips over her cheek. She put her arms around him and he felt the small prickings of her claws over his shoulderblades. Her body was warm and taut against his and when she took her shirt off her nipples were erect and silvery pink in the firelight. He kissed them and ran his lips over her body, exploring the nap of her fur, the unexpected roundness over the hard planes of her muscles. She lay on the thick rug before the fireplace, still tense, and with his fingers he traced the gilding of the fire along her thighs, taking his time, watching silver fur and golden reflection and the dark copper of his fingers making patterns together. She reached for him, but he caught her hands and shook his head, smiling. "Let me be greedy," he said, and bent to follow the pattern of her body with his mouth. The fur between her legs was thick and soft, and she gasped when he put his mouth to her; her hips arched and she murmured something in an alien tongue. Her fingers tangled in his long hair. He explored her leisurely, feeling the throb of her pulse against his lips, and when at last he slid into her she took him to his hilt and caressed him deeply, her wide blue eyes watching him, her body moving to the rhythm of his own. He shivered at the movement of her fur along his belly and hips and buttocks, and as he fled toward release she held him tightly and rocked him, emptying him. He lay across her, still shaking, and felt her claws trace arabesques on the skin of his back.

Water rattled angrily on the windows. He raised himself on his elbows and looked at her curiously.

"You didn't," he said. She shook her head, smiling.

"I rarely do. Can you reach the brandy?"

He had to slip out of her to reach it. She turned on her side and took the glass from him, sipping and watching him over the rim of the glass. "Does it bother you?" she said.

"Yes." He took the glass and drank. "I'd like to pleasure you."

"You have. There are many pleasures to this. Orgasm is the best, but it doesn't nullify the others." She reached forward and ran the pads of her fingers along his side. "You've a lovely body, Hart."

"Obviously not lovely enough."

"Don't be foolish," she said, turning onto her stomach and propping her chin on her hands. The silver of her hair was lighter than the silver of her fur. He filled his hand with it and let it slide between his fingers.

"Reciprocity," he said lightly, and was grateful when she laughed and put her head in his lap, turning over to face him. He followed the curve of her jaw with his fingers. "I don't like feeling inadequate."

"Were you? I didn't notice." She paused. "You're not responsible for my body, Hart. I don't feel cheated."

"I do."

"That's your problem," she said, and smiled again. "It's more comfortable in bed."

He knelt to bank the fire while she collected their clothing and threw it over a chair. She picked up the lamp and took it with them into the bedroom. The bed was a thick, soft mat covered with quilts. Hart slid into it while she checked on Daren in the next room, and when she blew out the lamp and lay beside him, he turned on his side and curled his body around hers. She took his hand and tucked it between her breasts, and Hart put his face against her hair and fell asleep.

When he woke the next morning she had already left. He found clean towels in the bathroom and showered slowly, surprised that the water stung his back. He peered over his shoulder when he was dry and saw nothing, then rummaged through the closet until he found a mirror. Covering the mirror was a note in Tatha's distinctive, thick-stroked script: "Sorry about that." He peeled the note off and inspected the network of fine scratches on his back. They were light and shallow, and would, he thought, be gone in a day or so. He found his clothes still thrown

over the chair in the living room and found a pot of tea
set to warm in the oven. It was dark and bitter but he
finished a cup of it, rinsed the cup, turned off the oven,
and went outside.

The rain had stopped, but the sky was still clouded
over. Tatha would have finished her run by now, he
thought, and briefly considered going to the port to watch
the militia train. His stomach rumbled, and instead he
headed up the road toward Kohl's, anticipating a plate of
hot sausages. He tried to consider aspects of Aerie's vulnerability, but the memory of Tatha's body kept intruding
and he moved his shoulders, feeling the tingle of scratches.
He thought, suddenly, of something Jason Hart had said
one evening, that on Nubar, in Dalmanite Sector, when
someone falls in love that person is put to bed and the
doctors are called. The victim is treated with fruit juices
mixed with honey, and comforting warmed stones wrapped
in blankets, and is fed an invalid's diet of soft foods and
many liquids until the affliction is passed. Hart smiled; no
fear of that here. Haven was awake, people on their way
to their jobs nodded at Hart in the street, and Shosei
Chiba sat on the porch at Kohl's, taking advantage of the
unexpected dry weather to eat his breakfast in the fresh
air. Hart sat beside him and seamed his jacket all the way
up.

"Pleasant change, isn't it?" Hart said, nodding at the
skies.

"Hart," Chiba began, and was interrupted by Mertika.
She came out of the common room, slammed a plate of
sausages and a cup of tea on the table in front of Hart,
and marched inside again. Hart raised his eyebrows.

"Sorry," Chiba said. "I didn't have time to warn you."

"Sweet Mother, what was that all about?"

Chiba looked uncomfortable. "Well, she knows where
you spent last night. She's not too happy about it."

Hart cursed. "I never promised monogamy to her. And
she sleeps around."

"Since when does common sense have anything to do
with it?" Chiba said. He sipped at his tea. "You'd best eat
before your sausages get cold."

Hart poked at them. "Maybe I should go in and talk to
her," he muttered, then pushed his chair back abruptly.
"The hell with her," he said, stormed down the porch
steps, and disappeared in the direction of the Tor. Chiba

watched him go, speared Hart's sausages, and put them on his own plate. Mertika came back outside, saw that Hart was gone, and flopped into the empty chair beside Chiba.

"Goddamned gutless bastard," she said. Her eyes were red and her nose was pink and shiny. She took one of Chiba's sausages and ate it with her fingers.

"Why don't you go to bed?" Chiba said. "You've been up all night, you've got to get some rest."

"And why don't you go fuck a lizard?" she said. She put her head in her hands. "Oh, Mother, Shosei, I'm sorry. I'm in a foul mood."

He didn't reply to that. The sausages were getting cold.

"Damned Kennerins," she said, both angry and weary. "Think they've got everything by the short ones, think they always know what's going on and what to do about it. Hell, they can barely tell what's going on inside themselves."

"Oh, really, Mertika. I don't think that Hart's—"

"Hart's the least of it. Okay, I'll admit I've never been fond of that Theresan, wish Jes had never brought her home, but that doesn't stop me from watching what's going on."

"And?"

"And I'd like to know," Mertika said angrily, "why she spends most of her afternoons in The Jumble, just to begin with. And how come the comshack's now run entirely by her people, that damned militia she's put together? And why that militia can carry weapons, and nobody else can. And why, when she shows up here, she spends the night nursing one beer and soliciting people's opinions. She's killed someone, you know."

Chiba looked surprised.

"It's the truth," Mertika insisted. "In Priory, where Jes found her. She killed someone for no real reason."

"And where did you hear about that?" Chiba said around a bite of sausage.

"Here and there. I don't trust her, and I don't know why the Kennerins trust her, and I don't like any of it, not one damned bit."

"So do something about it," Chiba said. "Go tell the Kennerins. I think you're wrong, but if it's bothering you this much, the least you can do is tell Mish."

"Maybe," Mertika said, frowning. She stood and collected the empty plates and cups. "I want to think about it some more, though."

"Do," Chiba suggested. "I think you'll find that you're mistaken."

Mertika looked at him and took the plates inside.

PALEN WAITED UNCOMFORTABLY IN THE WET grass just beyond the brow of the hill while Jason Hart went down to the comshack to pick up the reports he'd ordered. It seemed to take an unholy length of time. She fidgeted, wondering when the rain would start again. Eventually Jason Hart came over the hill, his arms full of papers, and Palen stood and took most of them from him.

"Any trouble?" she said.

"No. I told them these were from a scholastic aid outfit on Althing Green, cheap study materials." He grinned. "And they believed me, of course." He fell in place beside her, taking two steps for each one of hers. Palen wanted to sit on the hillside and read them all, immediately, but forced herself to walk sedately along the path through the hills, across the stream, up the path beside the barn, and around to her hut in back of the Tor. Once there, she and the boy spread the reports over the high table. Jason Hart looked at them curiously.

"Oh, hell," Palen said. "Sit down, you might as well know. I obviously can't do all of this without some help from the albiana."

Jason Hart touched the piled papers. "You don't have to," he said. "Maybe you shouldn't."

"Why?"

The boy shrugged. "Things are pretty complicated," he said, looking at the papers. "I can handle part of it, the stuff I have to handle, but—" He gestured. "It's pretty scary. And I don't have Spider to talk with anymore."

"Of course," Palen said. "I must be getting soft in the head. Go on, Jason Hart. Thanks for helping."

He looked relieved and went to the door of the hut. "If there's something else I can do . . ."

Palen smiled. "I'll let you know." The door closed and she turned to the papers, pulled the stool up to the table, and sat.

Five hours later the papers were in a number of piles: the very small pile of papers that, she thought, had some relevance to her search, the large pile that did not treat of her problem at all, and the huge pile of papers she had not yet looked at. Her head hurt and her eyes felt gritty. The rain was still holding off and the air, when she stuck her head out of the hut, smelled damp and loamy. She closed the door of the hut, locked it, and went down the hill toward the barn.

A mixed and muddy group of workers sat just within the large sliding doors, eating lunch and talking about the weather.

"Should be the last big one of the season," a terran said, and looked up at Palen. "What do you think?"

"About what? Oh, storms. Maybe. But we'll have a to'an full of drizzle for another four or five weeks anyway, we always do." She clasped all of her hands behind her back and peered into the barn. "Quilla around?"

"Up at the Tor," one of the terrans said. "She'll be back by the end of lunch—hell, we're not going to get muddy by ourselves, that's for damned sure."

Palen grunted and looked at the work schedule tacked on the notice board. There were only two fields left to do, and after that planting was scheduled to begin. She thought about the weather, shrugged, and went out of the barn. The sky looked darker, brewing toward a giant of a storm. She walked toward the stand of trees that surrounded the hot tub, changed her mind halfway there, circled the brow of the hill, and walked into the *Zimania* orchards. The dark black-green of the leaves looked ominous and she touched them with her fingertips. They're the cause of it all, she thought suddenly. Not the terrans, not the Kennerins. If Beriant had any sense, he'd burn the plantations and get rid of the entire problem. But she knew he wouldn't, if only because he appreciated too well the good things that the plantations brought, the fremarks, the purchased technology, the comforts and conveniences. She thought about Beriant living as the kasirene had before the Kennerins, migrating casually from to'an to to'an, bartering with the fishers, lucky to have a piece of hopper on occasion. Not a bad life but not one, she thought, that Beriant would appreciate. A wind moved through the orchard and the leaves rubbed against each other, whispering. Palen put her hands in her pouch and went back up the hill to the Tor.

When Hart stuck his head in the hut at dinnertime she shook her head and went back to her papers. Eventually Tapir came out with a tray, slid it in the door, made an unpleasant comment about people who make extra work for other people, and went away again. Palen lit another lamp and stretched. Her eyes felt abused and she knew her progress was laughably slow; she wished she'd spent time in the schoolhouse, rather than the fields. The stew in the bowl smelled wonderful. She ate it with one hand, turning papers over with the other, and was so engrossed by the time she finished eating that she pushed the tray aside, forgetting to return it to the kitchen, and kept working.

She woke up when someone shook one of her shoulders roughly, and she raised her head and looked blearily at Quilla. Quilla folded her arms and glared.

"Mother, just leave it to a mush-brained kassie. Are you taking up scholarship in your dotage? And is that all you had to eat today?"

"What time is it?" Palen said, sitting up. She'd fallen asleep over the table, and her back and arms hurt.

"Too damned late. When you didn't come in after dinner, I thought I'd make sure you were all right."

Palen grunted and pushed away from the table. The piles of papers lay all around the hut, and she looked from them to Quilla.

"I didn't read them," Quilla said. "Jason Hart says that you offered to help him do some sociology research, although I can't see what good you'll do him. Damnation, Palen, are you trying to run yourself into the ground? Look at your eyes—you're a wreck. Come on, get to bed."

The hut was lit by a brief, harsh light, and thunder boomed overhead. "More threats," Quilla said. "It's been burping up there all night, but no rain yet." Quilla hugged

Palen, quick and hard, and pushed a pile of papers off the platform in the sleeping alcove. "Come on, you four-armed idiot. I've got enough to worry about without having to worry about you, too."

Palen smiled, plodded away from the table, and fell onto the platform. She groaned and pulled a pillow under her head.

Quilla cursed and poked Palen's side. "Move over," she said. Palen looked at her, surprised, but Quilla was busy pulling her shirt over her head. She dropped it on the floor, wriggled out of her pants, and crawled into bed beside Palen.

"What brings this on?" Palen said fuzzily.

"I missed you." Quilla lay on her back and put her arms under her head. "We haven't spent time together since Spider went away. I'm restless. I've not been very good to you lately. And it's too damned wet to go walking." She reached over and turned off the lamp.

"And?" Palen said.

"And I guess I'm worried. Scared."

"We all are," the kasir muttered. She turned on her side and opened her arms, and Quilla curled up against her body. Palen put her face against Quilla's frizzy hair.

"Go to sleep, alter ego," Quilla said indistinctly. Palen smiled and closed her eyes.

The storm jabbered and shouted and boomed around the hut. Palen bit into a piece of fruit and, once again, read the report. There wasn't much to it, but it was enough. She stood suddenly, put the report in her pouch, grabbed her watercloak, and plunged into the storm.

It was raining so hard that she could barely see the Tor, and twice she slipped from the stone path and barely caught her balance. She hung her watercloak on the peg by the kitchen door, sloshed her feet in the pan of water and dried them quickly, and went into the kitchen. It was dark and empty. She wondered what time it was. The dining room too was deserted, as was the living room, but hearing noises in Mish's office, she plodded down the hall and opened the door.

Mish stood by the window, her back to the room. She turned as Palen entered.

"Oh," she said, and turned to the window again. Palen

frowned and came around the desk to stand beside her. Mish turned her face away.

"Mish? Something wrong?"

Mish shook her head. Palen shuffled uncomfortably.

"I've got to talk with Jes," the kasir said. Mish jerked and moved away from the window.

"He's gone." She looked up at Palen. Her face was streaked with tears. "They've all gone, Jes and Sandro and Tham and Beryl and—and Hetch." She put her hands on the desk, and her shoulders shook. Palen bit her lip.

"And they didn't even let me say good-bye to him," Mish cried. "All these years, from the very first, and now when it comes to it, when it has to happen—why can't I ever say good-bye, Palen? Why didn't Jason wait for me, or Hetch, or—" She sobbed angrily and hit the desk with her fists. Palen picked Mish up in her arms and sat on the edge of the desk. Mish put her face against Palen's chest and wept, while Palen, helplessly, rocked her and murmured soothing nonsense and stared blankly out of the window into the rain.

THAM AND BERYL HAD RIGGED THE FLOAT-bed in the shuttle where the luggage rack normally went, and Hetch, seeing it, grimaced and let them slide him into it. Jes appeared with the hypo and Hetch eyed it suspiciously.

"It won't put me to sleep, will it?" he demanded.

Jes shook his head. "It'll block your nerves for an hour, enough to get us out of the atmosphere. You shouldn't need it after that."

Hetch shrugged and Jes laid the hypo against the old man's skinny arm. After a moment Hetch blinked.

"Damned strange feeling," he said. "I feel like a talking head."

"You look like one," Tham said, dropping into one of

the webs. Sandro, in the copilot's web, looked over at him, his lips pinched down hard, and ran another check of the control panel. Tham was stone sober and his hands shook as he engaged the clasps of the webbing. Jes checked to make sure that Beryl was webbed in before dropping into his own webbing and engaging the board.

"Give me a screen," Hetch said. Jes activated the screen above the floatbed. Hetch watched it silently.

"Can you get us up in this?" Sandro said quietly, watching the ports. They were dark and the storm pounded against the shuttle's sides. Jes didn't bother to reply. He waited for confirmation of clearance from the comshack, fired the shuttle, and slid it smoothly down the brief runway, lifting at the runway's end more through memory and hunch than anything else. The shuttle's engines thrummed. They fled through areas of turbulence and punched into the clear sky above the clouds.

"Hetch?" Jes said.

"Doing fine," the old man replied. Jes angled the shuttle more sharply and increased thrust. The sky blackened and they were out of the layer of atmosphere and homing in on the spangled struts and planes of *Rabbit*.

Greaves was waiting in the shuttle bay and went into the shuttle when Jes cracked the hatch. "Captain," he said, nodding at Hetch, and bent to help Beryl and Sandro lift the floatbed and move it through *Rabbit*'s corridors and up to the bridge. Tham followed; he put his hand on the edge of the floatbed but when he saw Beryl looking at it he put both hands in his pockets. Beryl and Greaves bolted the floatbed into place. Hetch grimaced.

"I need another of those," he said. Jes brought the hypo. Hetch touched his arm when he'd finished.

"Jessie?"

"It's all right," Jes muttered, turning away. Beryl and Greaves went down to the engine room and climbed into their suits, and Jes guided *Rabbit* out of orbit and toward Eagle Grab.

Sandro went down to the engine room and stood by the control bank, watching Beryl and Greaves move in the opacity of the drive suits. His mind felt heavy and he looked up at Beryl, wondering what had happened between her and Kayman. Then, as instructed, he passed through the engine room and into the lifer bays. The first lifeship was prepared, the webs removed, and thick struts bolted in to hold the floatbed when the time came. Sandro flicked the comunit and contacted the bridge.

"It's set, captain," he said. Jes acknowledged and broke contact. Sandro wandered back into the engine room, passed through the gym, and without willing it, found himself back in the bridge. Jes, in his web, leaned stiffly toward the board; Tham had disappeared.

"Sandro," Hetch said. "Come over here." Sandro walked to the floatbed and rested his hand on its lip. Hetch looked as tiny as a child.

"Silence is driving me spacy," the old man said. "I want to tell you a story." He cocked his head and smiled. "Humor me?"

Sandro smiled back. "Do I have a choice?"

"Nope. Listen. I had some friends, once. Good people, honest, hardworking. They ran into a bit of trouble, mostly their own faults—took on more than they could handle. Well, I won't pretend that I couldn't see a bit of profit involved for myself if I helped them out—I was running my own line back then, one ship, scraping by." He gestured with one emaciated claw. "Hell, you know how it is. Anyway, I've got a deal of respect for the law. Most of the time. Now, I'm not saying that I'm any sort of Ved Hirem, but I don't go breaking the laws. Bending them a bit sometimes, maybe, but not breaking them."

Sandro grinned. Hetch's smuggling exploits were favorite stories in Aerie-Kennerin crewrooms. "Of course not," Sandro said.

"Smartass. Anyway, I'd heard of a bunch of people off t'other side of the Federation, had a bit too much of something that my friends didn't have any of, and it struck me that, well, maybe I could even things out a bit. Considering the special circumstances and all of that. So I scooted old *Folly* over there and looked around." Hetch closed his eyes. "Sure was a pretty place, and busy too, everyone always running around up to something. And careful with what they had. Now, I'm not saying they were out and out paranoid, but they were cautious. Caution's a good thing, understand. Up to a point. I figured that maybe they'd appreciate a little loosening up, a bit of excitement. For their own good, generally. So I had Merkit go out and bust up a bar. You never met her, did you? Too bad—best drive jockey I ever had, big, tough-assed, black-toothed lady, sweet as cream most of the time. Anyway, Merkit went out and stirred up some interest t'other side of the port, and I got myself and Tham into one of the warehouses and poked around some. Found the stuff sitting in a locked room—well, the room started out locked. They had sacks and sacks of the stuff, and I only needed but one, so one's all I took. Got it back to *Folly*, stowed it nice and safe, then went and bailed Merkit out of stir. She was a bit roughed up, but she'd done damage herself—never did see Merkit get the worst of it in a fight. Of course, the locals discovered that used-to-be-locked room, and made an unholy fuss, searched all the ships in port before they'd let us leave." Hetch snorted. "Never have met a knocker who can find his own ass in a taushgroup, let alone a sack of seeds. So we scooted on out of there and back to Aerie, and there you have it." Hetch paused and looked at Sandro. "What do you think of that?"

Sandro shoved his hands under his belt and shrugged unhappily. "I don't know," he said. He looked at Hetch, then glanced across the bridge to Jes' stiff back, and beyond him to the screens. Aerie floated on one of them, blue and brown and white and misted over with white clouds. Sandro watched it for a moment, and when he turned back to Hetch he smiled. He bent over the floatbed and kissed the old man's cheek.

"Thanks, I guess," Sandro said, and walked out of the bridge. He wandered back to the gym, hooked his leg around one of the struts, and wrapped his arms around his knees. Aerie, and Decca, and Mim chasing him out of the kitchen. Hetch lying in the floatbed. That ancient theft of seeds seemed distant and petty. Sandro curled himself into a tighter ball and tried not to cry.

When the time came, Jes alone did what was necessary. He hitched the floatbed to Greaves' tooldrone and guided it down the corridors, through the engine room, and to the lifer bay. Hetch watched him silently as Jes bolted the floatbed into place, swung the control panel over it, and clipped the three hypos into place. The last one was banded with red and orange, and he touched it unhappily.

"Selfish, I guess," he muttered. "I don't want to see you go." He slammed his hand on the panel. "I feel like your executioner."

"Dreck," Hetch said. He put his fingers on the controls. "You'd prefer to see me go slowly?"

"I'd prefer not to see you go at all."

"That's not an option, Jes. Come here."

Jes stood over the floatbed. Hetch pulled his head down and kissed his mouth, then pushed him away.

"Get out," the old man said, and grinned suddenly. "Bet I can beat your time."

Jes tried to say something, turned, and left the bay, locking the hatches behind him. When he reached the bridge, the lights of Eagle Grab shone close and clear and steady, and the readylight on the control panel glowed green.

"She's open," he said into the microphone, and heard Hetch acknowledge. The configuration of lights on the panel blinked and shifted. Sandro came in and stood behind him, staring at the screen. The lifeship drifted away from *Rabbit*, banked, and angled toward the curving maw of Eagle Grab.

Tham stood up, put his shaking hands in his armpits, and looked over Sandro's shoulder. As the lifeship approached the grab, Jes heard Beryl and Greaves walk quietly into the bridge. The small lifer drifted into the coil and lights began to dance over its surface. Sandro muttered something in Spanish; it sounded like a prayer. The ship flared briefly and disappeared into tau. Jes stood abruptly, walked away from the control panel, and froze.

He didn't know he was trembling until Greaves put his arms around him. Then Sandro came, and Beryl, and Tham, and they stood holding each other, silently, for a long time.

WHEN BERYL CAME BACK IN THE SHUTTLE AF-
ter leaving Sandro and Tham at Havensport, she had a
message for Jes tucked into her pocket. She handed it to
him, shrugging, and disappeared into the engine room. Jes
shoved the note in his pocket and, as *Rabbit* approached
Eagle Grab, he commed ahead to Tarne, in Terra End, to
make sure that his borrowed Second was waiting for him.
Not having Sandro along was an inconvenience, but, he
thought angrily, Sandro would be no damned use to him
now anyway, always itching to be back on Aerie fighting
the forces of evil and screwing Decca. Jes slammed toggles
on the control panel furiously and let the fury push him
through Eagle Grab and into tau, masking his memory of
Hetch slipping through the coils to find his own chosen
death.

He didn't remember the note until they were sliding
through Terra End, and then only because it fell out of
his pocket while he was bundling his suit to toss it into the
laundry chute. He picked up the note and opened it, read
it, and cursed.

So Palen wanted a Griswold native, did she? What in
hell for? The note didn't say, and Jes was tempted to ignore it. But the request nagged at him. Finally he asked
the computer for a readout on Griswold. His eyebrows
rose as he read the screen. He wondered whether Palen
was doing this on her own or whether she worked with
his family's knowledge. It didn't matter, ultimately, and
Jes thoughtfully tapped his teeth with her note, then
started studying Aerie-Kennerin trade routes. There were
a number of locations in the Federation that seemed to
draw the displaced, and with a few minor changes he
could arrange to have A-K ships hit all of them. He
leaned forward, programmed an A-K private message
band, composed a directive, beamed it out, and sat back
in his webbing. He didn't stop to realize it, but for the first
time in months his thoughts were entirely on his work.

Part
Five

TRANSFOR-MATIONS

1246 new time

"There is no man so good who, were he to submit all his thoughts and actions to the laws, would not deserve hanging ten times in his life."

—Michel Eyquem de Montaigne
Essays, book III, chapter 9
1595

WHEN PARALLAX FINALLY MADE A MOVE, IT was in so prosaic and unexpected a manner that it took everyone by surprise. A full merchant ship, its lateral vanes severed and dangling, appeared at Eagle Grab and requested emergency entrance. Mish and Quilla, rousted from their respective beds, stumbled down to Havensport to find Tatha already there, bent over the commiter while Pixie Hirem kept the captain busy with damage reports.

"It's solid," Tatha told them with quiet anger. "He admits he's Parallax, ship, registry, crew, the whole everything. The emergency appears to be real, there's no way we can turn him away. And he's got Colonel Zimmerman on board."

"What?"

Tatha nodded. "He says he was transporting Zimmerman back to Althing Green, that they'd just left New-Home when the vanes broke. And further that Parallax maintains no repair facilities in NewHome, and we were the closest grab." Tatha glared across the room. "It stinks. It sounds planned. It's what happened to Jes, remember, when he came to Priory? Those fuckers are playing games with us."

"If it was faked, Zimmerman would know, wouldn't he?" Mish said, and Tatha nodded. "All right. Let's talk to Zimmerman."

"It's your planet, lady," Tatha said, and crossed her arms. Mish walked over to the commiter and signaled to Pixie.

". . . yes, I understand," Pixie said looking up. "Just a moment, the boss is here. Hold on, captain." Pixie punched a hold line. "Emilio Barranca, tauCaptain, of the Parallax merchant ship *Mi Estancia*."

"Lady Mother. Sandro's going to love that." Mish slid into Pixie's seat and opened the line again.

"This is Mish Kennerin, chairman of the board of Aerie-Kennerin, tauCaptain. You've an emergency?"

Barranca's thin face smiled at her. "Quia Kennerin, I am told that it is night for you, and I apologize for wakening you. But your operator said that she could not authorize my entry, and in an emergency—"

"Yes, of course." Mish paused. "I am told that you have Colonel Zimmerman aboard?"

"Indeed. It is unfortunate that this emergency interrupted the colonel's trip."

"I want to speak to him."

Barranca made an apologetic gesture. "The colonel is asleep, Quia. Perhaps, by the time we reach your planet—"

"Then wake him up," Mish said. "I'll wait."

Barranca smiled. "As you wish," he said, and turned to issue a command. Mish looked up at Quilla, who was standing outside of camera range. Quilla raised her eyebrows. Tatha crossed her arms more tightly and looked disgusted. Mish leaned away from the commiter and pressed her thumb on the audio-mute switch.

"Get Sandro down here," she said. "And I want someone to com Jes as soon as this Barranca's off the line. Tatha, pick some people to go up with Sandro. He shouldn't go alone—Mother knows what kind of mess he'd get into."

Quilla reached for the Aerie line and began calling around. Tatha nodded. "I'll call them as soon as Quilla's off the line," she said. "But, Mish—"

Mish waved her silent and turned back to the commiter. Colonel Zimmerman's sleepy face filled the screen.

"Quia Mish," he said, and hid a yawn behind his hand. "I didn't expect to be back in Eagle System quite this soon."

"The tauCaptain tells me that there's been an accident," Mish said. "Can you confirm that?"

The colonel shrugged. "If there was, I slept through it." He leaned off-screen slightly, talking to someone, then looked at Mish again. "They seem to have lost a lateral vane or something like that. Are we still in tau?"

Mish nodded. "Let me talk to Barranca again," she said. When the tauCaptain's face appeared on the screen she tapped her fingers against the commiter panel and frowned.

"Very well, tauCaptain. Come through the grab and wait there, we'll send someone up to pilot you down here. We don't have a pit, but we can probably patch you together enough to get you to a full shop somewhere."

"We are most grateful," Barranca said. "But it is not necessary to send a pilot, I'm sure that we can find Aerie on our own."

"I'm sure you can, too," Mish said. "But we're sending a pilot up anyway. And we'll be tracking you."

"Quia Kennerin," Barranca said, laughing and spreading his hands. "I run a merchant ship, merely that. Without any cargo this time, too. What possible harm can we do you?"

"What an interesting question, tauCaptain. I'm sure we'll all be considering it seriously." She broke the connection and swiveled the seat around to face Quilla and Tatha.

"Sandro's on his way down," Quilla said. "I've called the port crew, they should be working on the sloop now."

Tatha slid into the seat before the Aerie line. "I'll com Dahl, Teloret, and Paeven. Three should be sufficient."

"Why all kasirene?" Mish said. Tatha grinned over her shoulder.

"Because, with any luck, they should scare the piss out of tauCaptain Barranca. And Paeven can handle Sandro. And they've all shipped with Jes, at one time or another." She turned to the line and began punching numbers. Quilla coded into the A-K private band and sent a call to Jes. The comshack buzzed with the click of codings and the murmur of voices. Mish watched Quilla and Tatha, shook her head abruptly, and turned to Pixie Hirem.

"Empty buildings," Mish said. Pixie raised her eyebrows.

"Empty buildings. We'll need some place to put them when they get here, and I'm damned if I'll let them into Haven, or the Tor. What's available?"

Pixie touched her finger to her throat and nodded abruptly. "There's a warehouse at the end of the port. It's full of empty sap barrels, but they can be moved. Plenty of space between it and anything else, and we can hack down the bushes around it, if you want to make it really isolated."

"Can we see it from here?" Mish demanded. "Okay, do it."

Sandro came in, looking sleepy. His shirt was half opened and he glared at Quilla.

"You could have waited half an hour," he said.

Quilla shrugged. Decca came in, looking equally grumpy. She went over to Tatha, ignoring her mother, and peered over the Theresan's shoulder. Tatha turned around, dropping the microphone on the ledge.

"They're on the way," she said. "Sandro, you'd best check the tracker. They should be through the grab by now."

Sandro dropped into a seat and pushed buttons. The screen wavered and columns of symbols marched up its face. Sandro frowned at them. "Yeah, they're through. And waiting in designated freespace. Hell, Mish, let's just slag the bastards."

"Zimmerman's on board," Mish said. "You're to go up in *Blind Chance* and bring them in, and I don't want anything strange out of you, understand?"

Sandro grimaced and turned to the screen again. Three kasirene came into the hut and Tatha took them into a corner to issue instructions. Sandro cocked his head to hear her as he continued monitoring the screen.

"We can leave them on the ship," he said suddenly. "Park it off beyond Pigeon and send up a repair crew."

"Send down a repair crew," Quilla said. "From Processing, we don't have anyone here who can do it." She ran her hands through her hair. "That's not a bad idea, Mish. Any reason why they can't stay on board?"

"I don't know. Sandro?"

"If it's just a lateral vane, there's no reason at all to bring them down," he said. "I'll tow them in and set them in orbit on Pigeon's dark side—just as easy, and who wants them peering at us?"

"Do it," Mish said. "Pixie, get that warehouse ready anyway, just in case. Tatha, you'll have to arrange for a guard, to be on the safe side." Mish paused, frowning. "Try to be ready for anything," she muttered, and turned to Sandro again. "Try to get Zimmerman off that ship, can you? But only if he wants to come."

Quilla smiled. "Tell him Mim's cooking something special. He'll come."

"And Sandro," Tatha said, looking over at him. "I'll be monitoring an open band. It may be a great strain, but be polite."

"Chinge a la madre," Sandro said.

"Y chinge a la tuya," Tatha replied. Sandro glared and walked out of the comshack. The three kasirene crew followed him. After a moment the shack rattled with the sound of engines roaring and fading as Sandro ran through the preflight checks. Mish sat at the commiter and contacted *Mi Estancia.*

"Captain Barranca," she said, and waited until the tauCaptain appeared on the screen. "We've sent up a sloop to bring you in. Is your ship stable?"

"I think so," the tauCaptain said, but he looked worried. "We've been running checks, I think we're secure. We'll let you know."

"Fine. Someone will be monitoring from here until you're brought in. Any trouble, let us know." She cut short the tauCaptain's expressions of thanks and leaned back in her chair, rubbing her eyes. Pixie left the shack and Quilla held the door open and looked out. *Blind Chance* roared down the runway and into the sky.

"Mish?" Quilla said. "Come take a look."

Mish stood, putting her hands flat on the ledge to push herself upright, and walked to the door. Her back ached and she rubbed at her neck. "What?" she said, peering toward the runway.

"No, over there," Quilla said. Mish followed her gesture toward the east. The sun rose over Havenswood. Mish blinked, wondering why it looked strange.

"No clouds," Quilla said. "Another few weeks and it will be spring."

Mish leaned back against the door frame. "A few more storms first, though. It's too early for real spring."

"Just drizzles," Quilla replied. "Summer before you know it, and Chiba will be off again."

Mish smiled suddenly. "That's right. Planting and harvest and Chiba off playing explorer and the damned irrigation systems finished in the Hoku fields, with luck —all we have to do is kill the dragon between now and then."

Quilla laughed and put her arm around her mother's shoulders. "Lo, the eternal optimist," she said. Tatha came out of the shack, looked at them, and shook her head.

"One of you had better call a meeting in Haven," she said.

Quilla groaned. "I'll do it. Mish, why don't you get
some sleep? Sandro shouldn't be back until tomorrow at
the earliest."

"Unless, of course, he gives into temptation and blows
Barranca to hell anyway."

Tatha stretched, then extended her claws and looked
at them. "He won't," she said. Mish looked at the sharp
silver claws extended from the silver fur, began to say
something, thought better of it, and turned away, feeling
suddenly exhausted.

♒

IT WAS QUITE TRUE THAT TATHA SPENT MOST
of her afternoons in The Jumble. Originally she came to
recruit kasirene for her militia, later to visit with the re-
cruits, and eventually simply slipped into the kasirene
section for no good reason at all. She liked the atmosphere, she claimed, and found herself more comfortable
with the kasirene than she did with the edgy terran Aerites. Besides, she had taught the kasirene to play the stone
game, and the game pleased her.

It involved five black stones and four white ones, each
stone of a different size but all shaped into rough rec-
tangles. The stones were shaken and thrown on the floor
and the winner was the player whose fallen stones fell
most consistently into one of a number of patterns having
to do with color, placement, and the arrangement of the
sizes of the stones. Tatha played well and usually won.
But lately Beriant had increased his skills until they were
closely matched, and their games continued far into the
evening, to the accompanyment of kasirene kibitzing and
kasirene drink. Tatha was willing to play as long as there
was anyone left to play with, and more evenings than
not either she or Beriant would challenge the other to
just one more round, and one more after that, until the
other players and watchers had drifted off to bed, leaving

the Theresan and the kasir facing each other over the round throwing area, lit by a small fire, companionably passing kaea between them and making rude remarks on the other's skills coupled with outrageous boasts about their own. It was because of Beriant that Tatha eventually learned Spider's location. She tossed the stones from one hand to another, frowning at them, then shrugged and threw them into the light. The two players bent over them, considering their configuration.

"I told you I'd win this round," Tatha said, scooping the pile of fremarks from the betting slab and adding them to the pile by her side. "I was there that night, you know."

"What night?" Beriant reached for the kaea jug and took a swallow. "Another round?"

"Sure. The night you forced Hart to the Calling, the night Spider went away."

Beriant made a skeptical gesture. "I doubt it. We had guards posted."

"Not in the trees, you didn't. My throw, I believe, and I also believe I'll have a sip of that, while you've got it out."

Beriant passed the jug to her.

"The trouble with kasirene," Tatha continued after drinking, "is that you're too damned soft. If someone had done what Hart did to my people . . ." She shrugged and considered the stones, rubbing her thumb across them. "You're sure you want me to have *all* your money?"

Beriant added another fremark to the pile. Tatha matched his bet and threw the stones. She peered at them triumphantly. "Top that!" she said with satisfaction, and sat back. Beriant gathered the stones together, cupped all four hands around them, and lifted his hands to his mouth. He whispered something into his hands.

"Won't do you a bit of good," Tatha said. "They're Theresan stones, they know the language of their home. Are you going to hatch them or throw them?"

Beriant looked at her over his hands. "In my own good time," he said. "What would you have done, if you'd been us?"

"About Hart? Something more emphatic, I think. We don't take kindly to xenophobia on Santa Theresa."

Beriant threw the stones. One teetered on a corner while they held their breaths, and when it finally fell over

Beriant grinned and scooped up the fremarks. Tatha cursed.

"Sheer luck," she said. "Try doing that a second time."

"My pleasure." Beriant smoothed the throwing area with one hand. "You have indigenes on Santa Theresa?"

"We have us, which is probably worse. What Hart did to you is nothing compared to what the furless ones did to Santa Theresa, when they rediscovered us." She hefted the jug of kaea, frowning, and sipped from it. "If you think they treat indigenes badly, you should see how they treat their own inventions. 'Mutants,' they called us. It took an act of the Federation before we were recognized as terrans, and even that didn't do us much good."

Beriant looked across at her, interested. "Bloodshed?"

"Not after the Federation edict. No, just simple things. Like refusing to ship our goods, refusing to give us jobs, refusing to set up trading stations within the system— Santa Theresa might as well be isolated on the rim, instead of near the center of things. At least," she said bitterly, "they don't hunt us for sport anymore."

"Then why do you live among them?"

"For good and sufficient reason," she said, waving her arm. "And also because I didn't have a choice. Are you ever going to throw those things?"

Beriant grunted and threw the stones. Tatha looked at them and crowed.

"You want to up the bet, my pouched and luckless friend? Let it never be said that I refused to take advantage of a downed opponent."

"Not a bad toss," the kasir murmured. "You'll need a double wing to top it. Sure." He tossed two fremarks on the pile. Tatha added two, and one further. Beriant looked at her speculatively and anted up. "What's the Standard term for that?"

"Um? For what?"

"For thinking that you can beat that perfectly good throw?"

"Hubris, I think." She picked up the stones and murmured to them in Theresan. "Oh, the pride that births the fall, the very swing and center of catastrophe, the worst possible sin of all possible sins, and getting more heinous each year, I do believe. Well, my pitted pretties? Well, then?" She pretended to listen to the stones. Beriant laughed.

"More shit than a fourbird," he said. "What would you have done about Hart?"

She shrugged and tossed the stones from hand to hand, looking at them.

"Well, then, what did the Theresans do? When the terrans rediscovered you? You talked about being hunted."

"We're just as terran as they are, and don't forget it," Tatha said, all trace of humor gone. "At first we didn't believe it, we'd see them coming and just walk up to them —it didn't seem possible that they'd want to kill us."

"And afterwards?"

"We hunted them." She threw the stones, leaned over them, and cursed. "Damn the luck. A draw." She pushed the stones toward him.

Beriant left them there. "You hunted them?"

Tatha straightened. "What else? Let them kill us all? Give them our planet and go into hiding, to be picked off one by one? We had no idea whether we'd get help or not; as far as we knew, it was a war we had to fight by ourselves." She gestured toward the window. "You call this winter, and you call this cold. On Santa Theresa this could be summer, except that it wouldn't rain every day. We grew to a hard planet, my friend. And we grew hard to match it—we had to or we'd have died out centuries back. Of course we hunted them. We're not animals."

Beriant's lower hands carefully piled the stones together, white in one pile and black in another, in order of size. "Was it a total decision? To fight back? Or were there people who didn't want to?"

"There always are. Counseling to beg to this Federation the furless ones talked about. Insisting that, given time, the furless ones would realize that we're the same damned species that they are, worse luck. People with brains," she said with precise sarcasm, "tend to use them, and tend to hold their own opinions. Only animals act totally on instinct." She downed another slug of the kaea and slammed the jug to the floor. "Are you or are you not going to throw those damned stones?"

Beriant picked them up, shook them perfunctorily, and threw them. Tatha glanced at the configuration, grunted, and scooped the stones into her own hands.

"Did you persuade them differently? The ones who didn't want to fight?"

"Eventually. It wasn't that hard. We worked on their

leader, the one they looked up to, until he saw what he had to see. After that it was easy. Always is, you know. The native agitator, the member of the pack, is always the most effective persuader. And the most effective spy." She threw the stones and glared at them. "Mine," she said. "And by the smallest margin I've ever seen."

Beriant inspected the stones himself. He shrugged and pushed the fremarks toward Tatha.

"Someone told me about the rite of passage Theresans have," Beriant said. "Sending a child into the wilderness to make a kill."

Tatha, busy counting her money, nodded.

"I presume that your son will do that, when he's reached the proper age."

"Of course. He's a Theresan."

"And who will you set him to hunt?"

Tatha straightened quickly and glared at him. "Animals, Beriant. Not terrans, furless or otherwise. Not kasirene. Animals." She stuffed the fremarks into her belt pouch, rose, and stretched. The fire had burned down to a bare red glow in the firepit and the lamps flickered. Outside, the rain sang.

"Again tomorrow night?" Beriant said.

Tatha's lips twitched. "Are you that eager to lose money?"

"Eager to win it back," he said, and walked with her to the door. "After sunset?"

"You're on." She nodded good-night, put her hands in her pockets, and walked down the wooden balcony, her lips pursed in a silent whistle. As she came to the corner she looked back. Beriant, as she had expected, was still at his door, watching her. She lifted a hand in mocking salute and strolled out of The Jumble and home.

A week later, just before Barranca's ship requested emergency entry to Eagle System, Beriant disappeared from The Jumble. Tatha, hearing the news from the other kasirene with whom she gambled, shrugged and threw the stones.

"I suppose he ran out of money," she said, leaning forward to inspect her throw. "Not surprising, the way he throws it around. Not that I'm complaining, mind." She dropped a fremark on the pile and smiled around the circle. "I'll lay another one on that throw, my friends. Are any of you still in?"

A few more fremarks clattered onto the pile. Tatha continued joking and drinking and mostly winning, while the evening wore on.

"It's not the money," a kasir said eventually, after someone had commented on Beriant's playing style. "He's been planning this trip for months, I think, without telling any of us. And now the weather's finally calmed down, so he can make the trip."

"To Tebetet?" Tatha said idly. "Well, it's about time, too. Another round, friends? I feel like taking advantage of the poor and unsuspecting tonight."

The kasirene laughed and added their antes to Tatha's own, and the game continued.

❧

SPIDER PULLED HIS KNEES UP UNDER HIS CHIN and wondered if he'd ever be warm again. The cold afternoon rain slanted through the worn trees beyond the cave mouth, and over the wind's howling Spider heard the crash of surf. He'd become inured to the sound, especially during that last big storm, when it seemed that all of To'an Tebetet would, at last, be eaten by the sea. But Melet said that the weather was clearing and that they could expect some supplies from Betes soon. Spider was grateful. Their winter diet had been dried fish and dried fruits, boiled with water to make a thick stew which appeared at every meal, a nutritious but profoundly monotonous diet. Melet recommended that they use mealtimes to practice their imaginations, but try as he might Spider could not pretend that the stew was anything other than itself. Kaën claimed that she could make the stew taste like hopper roast, or fresh pel—Spider was convinced that she was lying.

Melet also said that this small storm was a good excuse

to practice patience, and Spider had chosen the damp, cold cave mouth for his meditations. It was warmer inside the warren of caves that Melet had chosen for their winter home, but he craved solitude and, as Kaën pointed out, no one was crazy enough to sit with Spider in the rain.

It was near the middle of Pel ke'Biant, and planting time came soon. He closed his eyes and saw the fields outside Haven, both those near the town and those south of Havensport; saw the ripe black upturned furrows waiting for seed, saw the irrigation ditches with their locks opening and water from the stream moving through the fields, soaking into the loam. Saw terrans and kasirene standing together, talking, gesturing, the kasirene pouches filled with seeds, the terrans shouldering their own seed bags and moving through the field while silver flakes drifted from their hands into the waiting furrows. Spider, with his eyes closed, watched the seeds descending.

He'd asked Melet about it, back when they had chosen scenes for meditation. He knew that Haven's fields had not been seeded by hand for at least fifteen years, not since the seeders had been purchased at considerable expense and brought to Haven amid celebrations. But he told the teacher, the vision seemed fuzzy when he pictured the seeders; he could not smell the loam, or feel the breeze. Melet nodded gravely. "See what is most complete to you," she said. "And that in itself is a good subject for meditation, Spider. Why should you wish to see what is no longer, rather than what is?"

The answer to that, he thought at the time, was quite simple. That which was included seeders, and separations, and Spider himself sitting on a pimple of land thrust into the ocean beyond the Betes shore, in winter, far from home. Better to contemplate that which was not, better to contemplate a world, even if only mythological, in which the tensions and miseries of Spider's life were not to be imagined, and had no place. And so he lost himself in the vision of spring, working his way deeper into the sensations of his particular mythology, while the basis for the myth quietly changed. At the beginning of winter, he had watched the terrans plow and seed and irrigate. Now, as he moved more deeply into his vision, he entered the soul of the kasirene, feeling the easy, competent swing of four arms, the weight and shuffle of seeds resting within and against the skin on his belly, the warmth of the pale spring sun on the fur of his shoulders and back. And slid from the kasirene body to the body of a seed, lifted, drifting, at rest in the damp fertility of the soil; covered, watered, a stirring within as roots worked into the loam, the draw of sunlight waiting overhead. He followed the path of the roots, moving from root to soil, soil to water, water to rock, rock to mountain, mountain to cloud, to rain, to water, and into the sea, where the double pull of the two moons created in him a complex and comforting pull of tides. And spilled on the beach of To'an Tebetet as the foam of a wave, to sink into sand, and sand to rock, and rock to cave, and cave to dim sunlight to Spider, eyes closed, arms wrapped around knees, part and parcel of the entirety of his world. He opened his eyes slowly. The rain had become a soft drizzle, and the winds abated. Kaën stood leaning against the rocks at the cave mouth, waiting patiently.

"I'm back," he said stretching.

"Did you have a good journey?" She smiled as Spider nodded. "Melet wants us to go down to the landing. She says someone's coming, although I can't figure out how she knows. Come on."

Spider followed her into the small valley. "They must have set out during the storm," he said. "That's foolish."

Kaën laughed at him. "The storm blew over three hours ago, dummy. You've been gone a long time."

Spider shrugged, having become used to the plasticity of time on To'an Tebetet. The valley dropped and its walls narrowed until he and Kaën followed a narrow ravine through the low hills and to the beach. An outrigger, sails taut in the wind, skimmed toward them over the brow of the sea.

"With any luck, it's food," Kaën said, looking at the boat hungrily. "One more fish and fruit stew and I'll swim to Betes, just see if I don't."

Spider giggled. "Roast of hopper, um? Fresh, ripe pel. You were so lyrical that I almost believed you and that nonsense about tasting anything in fish stew."

Kaën put her shoulders back and stared down her blunt snout at him. "You didn't even try."

"I didn't have to," he said. "The best you can hope to do is pretend that you can't taste anything anyway. It's better than lying." He swayed to avoid her swinging hand. "Look, they're almost here."

As the outrigger approached the beach some kasirene leaped out of it, put their hands on the outriggers, and pulled the boat up to the sand. Spider and Kaën splashed out to help them and Kaën leaped with the waves to peer into the main hull of the boat.

"Coneys," she moaned to Spider. "A hopper. Baskets of vegetables. A sack of grain. I think there's even some beer there." She leaped again and settled beside Spider with a contented sigh. "There is."

"Are you going to talk or help?" one of the visiting kasirene demanded. The two students set to work. The outrigger was pulled high onto the beach, well above the tide lines. Spider wiped his hand across his face and accepted the basket that one of the visitors handed him.

"Hello, Spider," the kasir said. Spider blinked stupidly before the words made sense. They'd been spoken in Standard, and he had ceased even thinking in Standard months ago. "Do you remember me?"

Spider shook his head. "I'm sorry," he said in Kasiri. "Should I?"

"Not really," the kasir said, dropping into Kasiri himself. "My name's Beriant."

Spider paused. "Yes, of course. I remember you now. The warren's up this path."

Kaën was well up the path, a string of coneys bouncing over her shoulders. Spider followed Beriant along the ravine, lost in conflicting emotions.

When you can't figure out what you're feeling, Melet said, arrange not to feel at all until things have calmed a bit. Spider tried but it was hard work. He ran a few steps to catch up with Beriant.

"How are my family?" he said when he reached the kasir. Beriant looked sideways and down at him.

"They're well."

"Did they send any messages?"

"There wasn't time," Beriant said. "I left Haven rather unexpectedly."

Spider nodded and dropped behind again, thinking about that. It didn't sound right and he couldn't figure out why. Then he looked into the basket at the pale green peapods and his mouth suddenly watered.

An enormous argument sprang up and filled the entire

warren, having to do with who got to cook dinner that
night. Eventually Melet settled the quarrel by picking
two students, who looked at the others triumphantly and
disappeared into the cooking cave, talking about recipes.
The hopper was spitted and set to roasting over a fire and
under a wooden roof. Spider took his turn at the spit,
watching the juices drip, hissing, into the coals. He wanted
to reach out and steal a sliver of the meat but Melet sat
nearby, talking with the visitors and watching the hopper,
and he didn't dare.

"The one from Haven bribed them to come over,"
Kaën told him as they lined up with the other twenty-sev-
en students before dinner. "They weren't planning to come
over for another two weeks, and they're still pretty grumpy,
afraid that there will be another storm tomorrow and
they'll be stranded here." She snorted. "Serve them right,
let them live off fish stew for a while, see if they like it."

"Why was he so anxious?" Spider said, trying to look
over the shoulder of the kasir in front of him. Kasirene
jostled around the serving ledges and he couldn't see the
pots of food. His stomach rumbled. "Has he said?"

Kaën gestured. "Dunno. Maybe he's told Melet, but if
he did, she's not telling anyone. Damn it, you idiots,
hurry it up! We'll die of starvation at this rate."

The kasirene at the front of the line called back insults, which Kaën ignored. She put some of her hands in
her pouch and looked martyred. "My stomach's going to
shrivel," she said. "It's going to turn into the size of a pel
seed and disappear. *I'm* going to turn into a pel seed
and disappear." She clasped her free hand to her forehead.
"Tragedy!" she cried. "Dead of starvation in the midst
of plenty."

Laughing, the students loaded their plates and took
them into the main cave to eat. Kaën and Spider sat together, silent, wolfing down the hot hopper meat and the
crisp, steamed vegetables. They tasted heavenly. Eventually Spider looked up from his empty plate and saw
that Beriant was sitting a scant meter away, picking
through the mound of food before him. Beriant saw him
looking and smiled.

"Want some of mine? I'm full."

"No," Spider said. "Thank you."

"Yes, please," Kaën said. "Don't be a fool," she whispered as she passed Spider. She exchanged plates with Beriant and settled, smiling, to her second dinner.

"Kaën's got a pit for a stomach," Spider said to Beriant. "The more she puts into it, the more she wants."

Beriant laughed but Kaën was too busy eating to do more than glare at Spider and make an obscene gesture with a free hand. Spider stuck his tongue out at her and grinned. Beriant stood and looked at his plate.

"Where does this go?" he said. Spider jumped up.

"Over here. I'll show you." He led the way to the baskets and deposited his plate in one and his cup in another, then showed Beriant where the basins were. They stood beside each other, washing their hands. Spider was not surprised when Beriant said that he'd appreciate a tour of the valley while the sun was still up. As they left the main cave Spider saw Melet watching them, expressionless. He moved his shoulders uncomfortably and led Beriant up the passages to the cave mouth.

The visitors left the next day. Spider did not go down to the beach to see them off but watched from the lip of the valley, seeing beach, surf, and ocean framed in the deep green "V" of the ravine. When the outrigger floated beyond the line of surf and the students turned to come back to the valley, Spider went into the warren and waited, sitting crosslegged beside Melet's door. She didn't seem surprised to see him there and gestured for him to follow her into the room.

"I am troubled," Spider said, after bowing formally to her and seating himself on a cushion. Melet's room had a firepit built under a natural chimney in the rock. She busied herself laying a fire in the pit, the twigs and branches placed in curved rows to form a circle within the circle of stones. She paused when she had done. Spider leaned forward and removed one of the branches, breaking the regularity of the circle. Melet nodded and sat back on her own cushions, leaving the fire unlit.

Spider put his palms against each end of the branch and held it horizontally in front of him, staring at it. He ran his fingertips over the fresh cuts on the branch.

"It's Beriant," he said to the branch, and looked up at Melet. "He wants something from me, but I don't know what it is. And I don't feel right around him."

Melet nodded. "He came to ask me questions about

history," she said calmly. "It seemed a long way to come
for answers that Altemet could have told him in Haven."

"That's part of it," Spider said. "That feeling that
he'd come all this way for no solid reason. Except I think
that he did have a solid reason, only I don't know what it
is." He put the branch in his lap and folded his hands.
"He asked a lot of questions about the warren, and the
valley, and how the winter had been for us, but I don't
think he really listened to the answers."

"The answers in what you said, or in how you said it?"

Spider gestured. "I don't know. He asked me about the
Choosing—well, he didn't ask me right out, he couldn't.
But he kept leading up to it and backing down again."
Spider looked up at Melet. "Why would he do that?"

"Curious, perhaps. Wanting to know what you'd
choose, when the time came."

Spider's eyes widened. "Mother," he said softly. "Why
does he even wonder? Isn't it obvious?"

"Is it?" Melet leaned forward to nudge a twig into more
precise alignment. "One can assume that you'll chose your
own family, although it's not the usual pattern for a kasir
to choose the original family group first off. Or one can
assume that, after spending the winter with us, you may
choose to stay with me for a while longer. Although after
this winter," she said, eyes smiling, "I'd doubt your sanity
if you did. Or you could choose to travel with Kaën for a
while, or to live near Hoku, or down in Cault Tereth, or
even in The Jumble. Or in Haven or Hoku themselves,
with the terrans. Or to spend a year by yourself." She
gestured lightly. "There are an infinite number of choices,
Spider. That's why it's not proper to ask after a person's
choice before the Choosing, or to question it afterwards.
It's a private decision. Which doesn't, unfortunately, mean
that folk don't try to influence a Choosing, one way or
another. Between now and Biant Tapan, if things follow
their normal course, we should be inundated with fishers
and farmers and rangers and everything, extolling the
virtues of their tribes. At least they generally bring food."

Spider returned her smile and looked down at the
branch again. "It never crossed my mind," he said quietly.
"That someone would doubt my choice, I mean. Or even
that I had a choice."

"Because you're the only terran here? That's a false
distinction, Spider. You're one student amid many stu-

dents and whether you are kasirene or terran makes no difference whatsoever. You'll be courted by the tribes just as much as the others, and your decision will be yours alone, just as much as the others."

"I don't think Beriant was pitching The Jumble to me," Spider said slowly. "He talked a lot about being a kasir, about the kasirene generally. I think he was pitching an entire race to me, not just a tribe."

"It's possible." Melet took the branch from him and laid it sideways across the others, keeping the circle broken. "You'll have to think about it, Spider. I think your decision will be harder won, and more costly, than that of any of the others."

Spider grimaced, stood, and bowed. "Thank you," he said, and Melet bowed back to him. As he left the room, he glanced back to see her apply a flame to the fire and hold out all her hands to its warmth.

AFFIXING THE TOW LINES TO *MI ESTANCIA*, should have been simple. She was a class-21 merchant ship, with the distinctive forward struts that gave 21's the nickname "Bugeater." Jes had been longing for a Bugeater for years, but his fleet of 14/b's was more than adequate, and A-K didn't see fit to authorize the huge expenditure that a 21 would entail. Sandro guided *Blind Chance* along the ship's massive sides, studying the mountainous cargo holds, the flat, broad expanses of the drive housings, and the complex curves of the stabilizers. The lateral vanes were in sorry shape, floating at odd angles from the main body of the thrusters and connected only by thick strands of cable. Sandro eyed them unhappily and contacted tauCaptain Barranca.

"I'm going to tie down those vanes," he said when Barranca appeared on the screen. "I don't trust the cables."

"Surely they are sufficient," Barranca said. "I've never had trouble there before, they've always held fast."

"Really?" Sandro said. "You lose vanes, often, captain? I'm going to tie them down anyway. If they fall free they'll be a hazard to navigation, and besides, we can't replace them. We've never had to work on a Bugeater before."

"As you wish, Second," Barranca said, stressing Sandro's title. Sandro snapped the commiter off, sent a grapple line to hook into the vane housing on the Bugeater, and left Paeven at the controls while he and the other crew climbed into their Barre harnesses.

He had seen Bugeaters before, parked in orbit around MarketPort and other main trading stations, but he'd never fully appreciated the size of them. *Blind Chance* could have fit into any one of the thruster housings and *Rabbit* would have found any of the cargo holds more than spacious.

"It's not a ship, it's a damned planet," Dahl muttered in Kasiri, and Sandro agreed with him. They hooked onto the grapple line and pushed away from *Blind Chance*'s hatch. Halfway to the vanes, Sandro turned his head to watch *Blind Chance* dwindle. Dahl and Teloret swung from the line behind him: suspended from Teloret's harness was a line to a cable spool, and Dahl had a couple of hands wrapped around the line leading to a large toolbox. Sandro twisted around to land on the Bugeater's skin feet first. The magnetic soles of his boots engaged and he transferred his safety line to one of the convenience rungs built into the ship's hull before moving forward to explore the damage.

"Come look at this," one of the kasirene said. Sandro skirted the huge gash in the hull where the vane had ripped out and made his way to Teloret. The kasir knelt on the hull, a small plate open before him. Sandro bent down until their fields merged.

"Repair records?" he said, surprised, and Teloret nodded.

"But this is the kicker," Teloret said, letting his finger drift down the series of notations. "These vanes haven't been tested or restabilized in over seven years." He rocked back on his tail and turned to look at Sandro. "Carelessness?"

"Maybe." He frowned. "I wish we had time to check

the other records, the ones for the dorsal vanes—maybe they'll have time during repairs. Let's get this over with."

They strung lines to each vane and warped the vanes down to the hull, fixing them tightly in place. Sandro had never been in space with kasirene before, and by the end of the job he found himself envying their balance and, most of all, the competent coordination of their four hands. Finished, they reattached their safety lines to the grapple from *Blind Chance* and Paeven reeled them in.

"Barranca's pretty pissed that I left the video off," she told Sandro as he stripped and headed for the clensor.

"Good," he said. His skin felt sticky with sweat. He changed into a fresh suit and slid into his web on the bridge. The vanes were holding fast. He skimmed over *Mi Estancia* to the front struts, where he sent out grapples on either side of the tausloop to the struts. He tested them and, satisfied, contacted Barranca again.

"I want you to hook into my board," Sandro said. "We'll need a small thrust from you to get this thing going, and I want control of it."

"Out of the question," Barranca said flatly. "I do not relinquish control of my ship to anyone."

Sandro set his teeth, exasperated. "TauCaptain, have you ever been towed before? No? It's standard procedure to let the towing vessel control both boards, especially when it's towing something the size of your tub. If you give me too much thrust, you'll flatten me. Too little, and the lines will shatter, or my engines will overload. Now hook in so that we can get going."

Barranca folded his arms and looked stubborn. "I will not relinquish my command, *Second*. And that's final."

"Great. Then I won't tow you and *that's* final. *Cabezon.*"

"What?" Barranca said, outraged. "I outrank you, Second."

"Not on my ship, or in my company, you don't. You're not in NewHome System, tauCaptain. I personally don't give a shit if you sit up here and rot."

Barranca started cursing in Spanish. Sandro flicked off his commiter and turned to face his crew, his arms crossed.

"So?" Dahl said.

"He'll give in," Sandro muttered. "The bastard will

have to." He jumped from his web and paced the bridge while the three kasirene looked on phlegmatically.

"He's signaling," Paeven said from the board. Sandro went back to his web and flicked on the commiter. A new face greeted him.

"I'm Second Arista Blake," she said. "We're open to your board, Second."

Sandro glanced at the smaller readout screen and nodded. "Very well. I'm going to give it three minutes of thrust to get going, then cut your engines again. We won't need them until we near Aerie, and then they'll be on reverse."

"That's clear," she said, nodding. "Anytime you're ready."

Sandro double-checked the screen and fed instructions to the sloop's computer. The sloop's engines dropped pitch and a deep thrumming ran the length of the ship. Sandro kept his attention on the screen. *Mi Estancia*'s donkeys had kicked to life and were warming, and the telltales he'd planted on the lateral vanes showed a clear, steady green. He reached overhead and flicked the toggles for the large thrusters in the sloop, readying them to take the load when the initial thrust was over.

"Count," he muttered. Paeven began the steady count, in time with the flashing lights on the screen.

". . . two . . . one . . . now," she said, and *Mi Estancia* leapt toward them suddenly, with too much power to have been generated by the donkeys. *Blind Chance* seemed to plummet backward toward the Bug-eater and the grapple lines snapped. Sandro slapped the board, engaging the large thrusters, and twisted the tausloop over the Bugeater's bridge with barely enough margin. *Mi Estancia*'s thrusters kicked off abruptly and she drifted on momentum.

"Damage," Sandro yelled.

"Grapple housing's off on port side, still on starboard but both grapple lines are gone. Integrity's stable and solid. Some stress on the donkeys before they kicked off. Paeven's broken her arm, and I caught my tail in something."

Sandro looked around. Paeven was cradling one arm with the others, and Dahl was bent over, inspecting Teloret's tail. "It's not fatal," Dahl said calmly. Sandro pounded on the commiter.

"Was that your idea of a welcome to the system?" Barranca demanded angrily, before Sandro had a chance to speak.

"My idea! You dog-headed idiot, you threw the main engines!"

"Impossible. Your computer must have mishandled the connection. I'm holding you directly responsible, Second. We still haven't assessed damage."

"There's not a damned thing wrong with the connection," Sandro said angrily, and saw Paeven lift her head from the readout bank and nod. Her eyes were half closed with pain.

"That can be determined later," Barranca said. "We've sustained injuries through your negligence, my crew's in sorry shape, and so are the seals, it seems. What do you intend to do about that?"

"Get Zimmerman," Paeven whispered. Sandro nodded and repeated the request to Barranca. The tauCaptain swore and turned to yell at someone, then kept his back to the video, obviously listening to damage reports. Zimmerman appeared on the screen. A bruise covered one side of his head.

"Can you get their bridge crystal?" Sandro said, and Zimmerman held up a small blue lockbox.

"Already have it. I'll need yours, too."

Sandro guided the video until it was pointed at the crystal housing.

"Okay," the colonel said. "The seals aren't broken. Now put a second seal on it and I'll collect it when you get us to Aerie."

Sandro obligingly doublesealed the housing and repositioned the video. "What's the damage report over there?"

Zimmerman looked to the right. "Second? Blake can give you a report, I really don't know it all. Someone said something about the seals."

"Which ones?"

"Outer hatch seals," Second Blake said, coming into view. She, too, looked battered. "We've lost some sensors, so we'll have to send someone out to check them. We've got one concussion, a broken leg, and what may be some broken ribs. We need a medic."

"Doesn't Barranca have citations?" Sandro said, raising his eyebrows as Blake shook his head.

"We usually travel with a medic, Second. Bugeaters generally do, we've got a lot of crew."

"And you didn't this time." Sandro swore. "We've no sickbay on the sloop."

"Presumably you've doctors on Aerie," Barranca said, turning around and glaring. "Or doesn't Aerite hospitality extend that far?"

Sandro clenched his teeth to keep from swearing. "All right, tauCaptain. We're going to reattach the grapples. If anyone in your ship so much as sneezes at the control board, I'm going to cut you loose and let you rot, understood?"

Barranca ignored him. Swearing, Sandro began the long job of reattaching the grapples.

Three days later the merchant ship and the tausloop limped into a darkside orbit around Pigeon. Sandro had patched *Mi Estancia* through to Haven hospital and under Ozchan's instructions and Second Arista Blake's care, the injured aboard the Bugeater were in stable condition. Sandro released the grapples and swung *Blind Chance* over the main emergency hatch on *Mi Estancia*'s hull. The hatch seals had steadily deteriorated on the flight to Aerie; there was no possibility of leaving the Bugeater's crew in their ship. The evacuation tube snaked out from the Bugeater's hatch. Sandro connected it solidly to the sloop's airlock and cautiously opened the lock, double-checking integrities. He and the four kasirene were armed and stood by the airlock as *MiEstancia*'s crew and passengers came through the tube. Barranca was a thin, tall man with pale flawless skin and dark brown eyes and hair, and he seemed to have suffered no injury at all. He looked down at Sandro and did not bother to offer the proper formalities. Second Arista Blake walked favoring her right leg. One crew member was carried aboard on a stretcher held by two others, and Zimmerman came last, holding his pack. The bruise over the side of his face was purple and yellow, and he smiled and touched it with gentle fingers.

"It hurts worse than it looks," he told Sandro, then looked beyond him into the open cargo hold where *Blind Chance*'s crew were stowing the new arrivals. "Brilliant," he murmured. "Who thought of that?"

Sandro turned and looked. The officers and crew of

Mi Estancia were staring at the kasirene in frightened awe; even Barranca looked small and subdued beside them.

"Tatha's idea," Sandro said turning to close the airlocks. When he came into the bridge, Zimmerman had already broken the seals on the crystal housing and had the crystal locked into the box with that of *Mi Estancia*. Sandro replaced the crystal with a fresh one.

"But it wasn't my doing," he said. Zimmerman shrugged and dropped into an auxiliary web.

"Let's get down," the colonel said. "I'm hungry."

Ozchan and Miri were waiting at the port with two large cargo wagons and the entire militia. Quilla stood beside Tatha and watched as the shuttle's hatch opened and the militia helped put the crews of both ships into the wagons.

"Look rather harmless, don't they?" Tatha remarked. "Not like the type to damage their own ship."

"You think Sandro did it?" Quilla said.

"I don't know. He might have, he's got a slippery temper. I'd imagine that Zimmerman will let us know, in good time." Tatha walked away to supervise the last load into the cart and Quilla looked after her, frowning. Then she went to find Sandro and rode beside him to the hospital.

"About the vanes?" Sandro said. "I don't know. We found the repairs record and they hadn't been touched in seven years—that's a hell of a long time to go without an overhaul. They could have blown by themselves."

"Or maybe Parallax keeps a huge ship around in deliberately bad condition, on the chance that they might need it?" Quilla shook her head. "I don't know what to think, Sandro. Except that we've got to get them patched up and out of here as fast as we can. I wish we hadn't had to bring them down."

"No choice," Sandro said. "Even if they'd had a medic, or even if we'd been able to send them one, there's no telling how long the hatch seals would last."

Quilla looked at him. "Could that have been deliberate?"

"The seals?" He spread his hands. "I don't know. I just don't know."

Ozchan kept the concussion and the broken leg in the

hospital and sent the rest, patched up, back to the port where Mish had arranged housing for them. Quilla rode with Tatha and Barranca in one of the wagons. The tau-Captain looked at the flashgun casually strapped to Tatha's waist and elevated his eyebrows.

"Dear Lord," he said mildly. "I don't believe those have been made in over a century."

"They're still effective, though," Tatha remarked. Her hands rested lightly on the wagon's controls. "Remarkably lucky, aren't you, tauCaptain?"

"Why do you say that?"

"Of all your ship's complement, you alone aren't injured. A stroke of luck, that." Tatha glanced at him and smiled. "One would almost suspect that you were expecting it. I had an aunt," she continued, oblivious to his glowering, "who expected things. Strange and misfortunate woman. She always knew when something was going to fall down, or pop up, or whatever. Called them premonitions, she did, but they didn't help her in the long run. Oh, but the rest of us disliked her. She always managed to look so cool about things, nothing ever caught her by surprise. Spent a good deal of effort on her dignity, my aunt did, and what with expecting things, she generally got through things with more dignity than anyone else did." Tatha sighed. "Didn't expect her own death, though. Terrible. Had a bad heart and it caught up with her in the lavatory, it did. Auntie didn't come in to dinner and we went looking for her, found her on the stool with her skirts up around her armpits and the most astonished look on her face."

Quilla looked at Tatha suspiciously but the Theresan's expression was entirely serious. Barranca merely looked stupified.

"Course, it's pretty cold, winters on Santa Theresa," Tatha continued blandly. "Poor woman had frozen in that dreadful position. My uncle had to smuggle her down to the kitchens and stuff her in an oven before she loosened enough to lay her out properly. Scandal of the entire province, it was." Tatha shook her head. "Just goes to show that expecting things isn't always useful, is it? Here we are, tauCaptain, the Abode of Charity. And I do believe there's a welcoming delegation, too."

Quilla squinted as they approached the distant warehouse. Mish stood by the door, arms crossed, with Pixie

Hirem looming behind her. Jared and Palen stood on the other side of the opened door, and as the wagon approached the warehouse Ved Hirem stumped around the corner of the building and went up to Mish, waving his cane. For all his self-proclaimed gout, Quilla thought, the old man could get up quite a head of steam. Tatha swung the wagon to a stop in front of the warehouse and jumped down.

"Good morning, judge," she said to Hirem, and went around the back of the wagon to drop the gate. Quilla slid off the high front seat and waited while Barranca clambered down.

"We are expected to stay in this?" he demanded, waving his arm at the warehouse.

"Temporary accommodations," Mish said, reaching up to pat her white hair into place. "We don't have a hotel, tauCaptain, and all our housing's taken up. I'm sure you won't mind." She led the way into the warehouse. Five cots lined the side of the warehouse, surrounding a table set with a number of rickety chairs. In a corner, pipes and plaster indicated where a lavatory had been hastily assembled, and a small wood-burning stove stood against the far wall beside a tiny cooling unit and a cabinet. Barranca and his crew stared around the warehouse. The tauCaptain's face darkened.

"It seems a minimal hospitality," he said finally, his voice tight. "To be carted around in a farm wagon, and given lodging in a warehouse—"

"It really is the best we could do," Mish said, shrugging. "I'm sure you understand, tauCaptain. We're not a cosmopolitan planet, and it's not every day that we find a crippled ship on our hands. And you must remember that you were not invited."

Quilla dropped back to stand beside Ved while Mish explained that meals would be brought in, and introduced the tauCaptain and his crew to the militia troops who would both guard and serve them.

"What are you doing here?" Quilla whispered to Ved. He glared up at her.

"I mean to let them know who they've tangled with," he whispered back angrily. He tapped the pocket of his jacket. "Give them fair warning."

A silvery arm slipped around Ved's side and quickly extracted a packet of papers from his jacket. Ved whipped around and Quilla saw Tatha calmly paging through the papers.

"Why it's a new speech," the Theresan said mildly. Ved snatched the papers back. "What a wonderful scheme, judge. You can bore them to death for us." She grinned and walked away, whistling the chorus from the song about the scholar and the hog. Ved shook with anger.

"That damned, insolent, insufferable tabby," he sputtered. Quilla put her hand on his arm. Barranca was looking at them curiously and Ved controlled his temper. Tatha leaned against the wall by the door, talking with Pixie.

"I want to beam a message to my company," Barranca was saying. His Second had dropped to sit on one of the cots, looking very tired. The other crewmember, Nataste, stood beside Barranca and looked longingly at the lavatory.

"That's fine," Mish said. "Just write down the message and we'll have it transmitted immediately. Pixie?"

Pixie produced paper and pens, put them on the table, and stepped back.

"I'd prefer to send it myself," Barranca said.

"Well, that's understandable," Mish assured him. "But our commiter's out of commission, and we've been using a patch job—it's simply impossible to operate unless you know the equipment. Even I can't do it." She smiled at him. "As soon as you finish the message, just hand it to one of the guards and we'll transmit it as soon as possible. And in the meantime, now that you're settled in, we'd like to welcome you properly." Quilla recognized the unholy gleam in her eye. "Ved?" Mish said sweetly.

Ved stumped forward, looking inflated. Mish dropped back to stand beside Quilla.

"Did you ask him to do this?" Quilla whispered. Her mother shook her head.

"He just showed up, but what the hell."

Tatha had slipped out of the room. Barranca, with the look of a man meeting a surprising and unpleasant doom, sat at the table. Ved rustled his papers and launched into his oration—if anything, it was even more florid than his usual speech. The Kennerins slid quietly toward the door, and Pixie, her lips twitching, let them out. Behind them, Ved continued to orate the history and virtues of Aerie, in detail. And at length.

MEYA PUT HER HEAD IN HER HANDS AND sighed, rubbing her eyelids with the balls of her thumbs. Ozchan had called from the hospital hours earlier to tell her of the conditions of both crews; later Quilla called from the port, detailing the disposition of the Parallax crew and the last-minute arrangements made for their keeping. Other than those two brief interruptions, Meya had spent the day in her office, laboring over a seemingly unending pile of paperwork. Dovetailing Pixie's duty rosters with Mertika's cooking schedules; arranging for a town meeting soon after the arrival of the delegation now traveling from Hoku, and sending out notices of both events. Justifying the absence of certain on-duty militia with the planting schedules. Requisitioning a repair crew from processing and having to argue at length with the processing manager about the schedules of the plant's own repairs and maintenance. Trying to figure justifiable costs for the Parallax repairs, and how much they could reasonably charge Parallax—the temptation to demand an exorbitant repair bill and keep the ship in Eagle System until the bill was paid intruded on her every so often, and she resolutely pushed it away. Above all, the Kennerins must be reasonable. Their possible Federation support, Zimmerman had emphasized before his trip to NewHome, rested with their appearance of vulnerability and with their open rationality. Zimmerman himself, eating snacks brought in from the kitchen, sat in Quilla's office next door busy composing a report to his superiors on Althing Green; on occasion Meya could hear him muttering phrases to himself, indistinct litanies drifting through the walls as the colonel sought the proper cadences for his sentences.

Meya lifted her head. The sun was almost down and her office was dusky. She flicked on a lamp, stared at the pile of yet unfinished work, pushed it aside, and stood wearily. It would have to wait. The lunch Mim had prepared stood untouched and cold on the tray atop a cabinet, and Meya picked it up and took it into the kitchen. Mim looked at her accusingly and started to say something, but Meya put her hand on the housekeeper's shoulder and shook her head.

"I know, I know. I'll starve to death and get scurvy and all sorts of other terrors. I'm tired, Mim. Where are the children?"

Mim put the tray down on the counter. "The boys are upstairs studying. Alin's with Tatha, in the playroom."

Meya, surprised, nodded her thanks and turned to go. Mim stopped her and pressed a warm fritter into her hand.

"Go on," the housekeeper said. "Eat it. Dinner will be ready soon."

Meya nodded and took the fritter with her, but could not work up any appetite. She put the fritter in her pocket and went upstairs to the large playroom.

The room, in the new wing, had been built specifically for the children, far away from the bedrooms of the house. In it were collected the toys of two generations of Kennerins, blocks and books and dolls and toy spaceships, boxes of discarded clothes for costumes, the remains of a multitude of projects, some completed, some unfinished, some long discarded and inhabiting the corners of the room in disorderly piles. The windows of the playroom faced west. As Meya entered the last thin rays of sunlight illuminated Alin and Daren sitting together on the floor, making a complicated house of blocks and sticks and pebbles, while Tatha sat in a windowseat, her forearms resting on her upraised knees, watching the children somberly. Meya paused in the doorway, listening to Daren's slurred, childish patter and watching Alin's mobile but still silent face. Alin's silence didn't disturb the Theresan child at all, and the two often spent afternoons together, contentedly playing or fighting or napping in corners of the room. Sensing her presence, Alin looked toward the door and smiled, and Daren crowed a swift, liquid greeting before returning to the construction. Tatha moved over on the windowseat, making room for Meya.

"They're all locked in?" Meya said, sitting beside the Theresan and watching the children.

"Barranca and his mobile crew? Yes." Tatha paused.

"Pixie left some guards at the hospital, to watch the two that Ozchan admitted. He's not terribly happy about it."

"As long as they don't get in the way," Meya muttered, putting her shoulders back. "Lady, I'm tired."

Tatha grunted an assent. "Meya, I've a favor to ask of you."

Meya looked at her. "Anything, of course. After what you've done for us—"

Tatha gestured impatiently. "I've done very little for you, you've done most of it for yourselves. Nonetheless . . ." She paused and looked at the children. "I'd like to leave Daren here, if I could. With Barranca down, and not knowing what to expect, or when things might happen —my place is pretty near the port. I'd feel safer if you'd let him stay here."

Meya started to say something, but Tatha cut her off. "Of course, I'll pay for his keep, fremarks or work, whichever you prefer, and—"

"Don't be absurd," Meya said curtly. "Of course Daren can stay with us, and payment is out of the question. If nothing else, he's companionship for Alin. You know how fond we are of him."

"Yes," Tatha said, and smiled fully for the first time. She took Meya's hand and pressed it. "I'm grateful for it, so much so that I can't find the right words for it. I'll go fetch his things."

"Don't worry about it tonight," Meya replied. "He can fit in some of the stuff Alin's outgrown, and we can get the rest of his stuff tomorrow. You must be exhausted."

Tatha nodded and stood. She shook her shoulders, loosening them. "Meya, thanks again." Daren stood and ran to her, throwing his arms around her knees. She picked him up. "You're getting heavy," she told him. He grinned and nuzzled his face against her cheek. "You're going to stay with Alin and Meya for a while, okay? It won't be for long, but I'm going to be pretty busy."

"Okay," Daren said. "Play with toys."

"That's right. And you do as Meya and Mim tell you, okay? Just like they were me."

"Sure." He wriggled in her arms. She put him down and he went back to sit beside Alin. Tatha walked to the door.

"Surely you'll stay for dinner," Meya said, standing. Tatha shook her head

"I wish I could, but it's not possible. I've miles to go before I sleep." She blew a kiss toward Meya and went into the hallway. Meya listened to the light sound of her boots fading with distance, then scooped up the two children and carried them, Daren protesting and Alin scowling and wriggling, into the bathroom to scrub their hands and faces. They found the fritter in her pocket and shared it, munching, as they trailed her down the corridor. She rousted her sons from their rooms and sent them to wash, then herded all the children down the stairs to the dining room.

Mish, looking wonderfully pleased with herself, sat down at the head of the table and rubbed her hands.

"Oh, we'll keep them entertained all right," she said. "Ved's arrival today was a stroke of brilliance, whoever suggested it. Tomorrow Simit's going to deliver his lecture on the foundations of Federation law, and that evening I've arranged to have the kasirene band from Kohl's come down to keep them occupied. Then I think I'll let them have a vid; we've still got a load of those dreadful educational tapes on argiculture, don't we?"

"They're quite informative," Decca said defensively, her fork halfway to her mouth. "They're more interesting than that dreck on soil analysis that Jared keeps around."

"Good, I'd forgotten about that," Mish said. "After agriculture, soil analysis. Then I think I'll ask Perri to come read them that poem he's been working on for the past five years—what, it's seven thousand lines by now? Eight?" Mish giggled. "And by then, I'm sure we'll have thought up some more entertainment for them."

"It sounds to me like cruel and unusual punishment," Colonel Zimmerman said, but his mouth twitched. "I could almost feel pity for Barranca."

"Almost, colonel?" Hart said, leaning forward to pour the wine. "I thought you were inflexibly nonpartisan."

"I am. I just don't like people putting sleeping potions in my drink." The colonel looked at Hart blandly. "I was asleep before we hit NewHome grab, and didn't wake up until Mish asked for me." He picked up his glass of wine. "I'm not usually noted for the ability to sleep four days straight."

"Did that go in your report?" Quilla said. The colonel nodded. "What about the bridge crystals?"

"I haven't had a chance to review them in detail," he said. "I will, at some point soon. Could I have some more of that rabbit?"

"Coney, colonel," Mim said, passing the dish. "An Aerie native."

"Excellent, whatever it is," he said, and applied himself to dinner again. Hart watched him a moment longer, then looked down the length of the table to Mish. She watched the colonel, a small frown creasing the skin between her brows, then picked up her fork and attacked her plate. The children finished eating. Quilla, noticing their squirming, dismissed them. They slid from their seats, swept up plates, cups, and cutlery, and took them into the kitchen before pouring back through the dining room on their way upstairs to the playroom. Daren and Alin ran hand in hand, and Hart watched them, frowning.

"Colonel," he said quietly, when they had done eating, "would you be at all interested in seeing a colonial laboratory?"

The colonel glanced at him, green eyes smiling, and nodded. As soon as the table was cleared they excused themselves and went through the kitchen garden, past Palen's dark hut, to Hart's detached laboratory.

Hart unlocked the door and flicked on the lights, gesturing the colonel to enter. He busied himself with windows and wineglasses while Zimmerman strolled along the rows of benches and equipment, his lips pursed. He stood before the keepers, rocking on the balls of his feet, his thumbs tucked into his belt, and smiled when Hart came up to him.

"I'll admit that most of it baffles me," the colonel said. "But you seem to keep it in rather impressive order."

Hart laughed. "I think you're the first person who's realized that." He leaned forward and tapped one of the sealed doors on the keeper. A sequence of numbers and symbols tumbled over the door plate. "New strain of coney, the beast we had for dinner tonight. The domesticated ones, for some reason, taste awful and are excessively fatty, the wild ones are a bitch to catch and expensive. I'm trying for something in the middle."

"Wouldn't it just be a question of diet?"

"In part. In large part, but there's something further in the diet of the wild ones that we can't duplicate for the domesticated ones, something that reacts with their normal diet in such a way that the muscles are affected." Hart gestured. "I could give you the chemistry of it—"

"I'd rather you didn't, I'm not likely to understand a word of it."

"Anyway, what I've done is created a breed that can synthesize that certain chemical structure themselves— the kasirene identified that missing diet component, by the way—it's a fungus which is totally impossible to raise ourselves." Hart tapped the door again. "Only problem so far is that this particular strain has sharp teeth and is mean as hell. I'll have to work on it some more."

The colonel laughed and followed Hart to a corner of the laboratory. A cot stood against one wall, together with a low chest, a couple of chairs, and a wood-burning stove. Hart had set out a brandy bottle and two glasses on the chest. Zimmerman sniffed his glass appreciatively and sipped.

"Local?" the colonel said. Hart shook his head.

"Imported. Much of what we use is, but nothing that we can't live wtihout."

"I've noticed. You're a remarkably self-sufficient bunch, when you get down to the basics. May I pry? Do you live here?"

"In the lab? Yes." Hart sat.

"Why? There appears to be plenty of room at the Tor."

"Personal choice." Hart waved his glass. "Isn't a mad scientist allowed some eccentricities, colonel? I find the burps of the retorts and the fumes from the alembics greatly comforting, and an inducement to sleep."

The colonel shook his head. "I'm much too fond of the creature comforts, Quia Hart. The wide, deep bed and the overstuffed armchair exert a terrible appeal on me. I hate traveling."

"Hammocks and webs?"

The colonel nodded. "And that dreadful swill that passes for food on a tauship. My dream is to retire to a comfortable apartment above the best restaurant on Althing Green—I have it all picked out. I will laze about in bed until well after sunrise, and sit at a sunny table feasting on delicacies." Zimmerman smiled over the rim of his glass. "Either that or marry a good cook. I don't suppose that I could talk to Mim?"

Hart grinned. "Take Mim away and Aerie will secede from the Federation."

"Lord, no. Not another one." Zimmerman put his feet up. "I take it that you know about that?"

Hart nodded. "Twenty-five since the beginning of the decade, and a total of fifty-nine since Parallax began operations, isn't it?"

"Yes. With a distinct possibility that another three or four are on their way out."

"You must admit that it is tempting," Hart replied. "No Federation support fees for the grabs, no cargo fees, no tariffs, a cheap comsystem, much cheaper than the Federation can supply. Guaranteed markets for exports, without having to face the vampiric taxes that the Federation levies on MarketPort commerce or on other Federation-run trading stations. A large enough inventory of imports, and those, too, cheaper because of the absence of Federation tariffs." Hart paused. "A private security force, and quite effective, from what I hear. The Federation doesn't care what happens to any individual member, as long as it doesn't bend Federation shipping or communication regulations, but Parallax guarantees that any individual member won't be overrun, or taken by force. A cozy nest, colonel. Tempting."

"You're not serious."

"Why not? What, on the face of it, makes secession from the Federation and entry into the Parallax worlds sound less than idyllic? Aside, of course, from loss of personal control, but that's the price you always pay for going home to mommy and daddy."

"Inflexibly nonpartisan," Zimmerman quoted back at him. Hart waved the comment aside.

"We're not talking about Aerie, colonel. We're talking about overall Federation politics and structure. Surely you don't claim inflexible neutrality about that."

"I suppose not." The colonel looked at the cot, and when Hart nodded he put his feet on the edge of the cot and slumped in his chair, balancing his glass on his belly. "All right. There's loss of personal control, for one. Presumably, when one goes home to mommy and daddy, one knows what's going to happen. There's a certain trust. Parallax is nobody's beloved parent."

"That's beside the point. They make certain promises, and they do follow through on them."

"Protection? Accessible markets for imports and exports? It's less open than it sounds. The accessible markets are all within the Parallax scope—members are not allowed to trade with entities outside the Combine unless the goods or services sought are, first, urgently needed and, second, not available among the Parallax worlds. And then the individual member does not do the trading, Parallax does. And sells the results."

"For a reasonable fee?"

"For an exorbitant fee. As far as we can tell, most Parallax members are in debt to the Combine for more than their total worth. And not in debt due to luxuries, Quia Hart. You know that Parallax took over Gates a number of years back?"

"The medical planet? I'd heard."

Zimmerman made a rude noise and reached for the brandy bottle. "It's not legal, on a Parallax world, to run a medical school, nor is it legal to run an unlicensed medical facility—licensed by Parallax, of course. Nor is it legal for anyone to practice medicine who has not been licensed by Parallax and Gates. All health services are provided by *paterfamilias* Parallax."

Hart frowned. "At how much?"

"For a hospital, a quarter of the planet's yearly profits. And that's just the physical facility, Quia. It doesn't count physicians and support staff, equipment, medical supplies, drugs . . . tauCaptain Barranca has the necessary medical citation on his Certificate, without it he wouldn't be allowed through a Federation grab. The citation is twenty-seven years old, and there are no update citations on it. The reason a Parallax Bugeater travels with a medic on board is that Parallax demands it. The price for noncompliance, save in certain cases, is suspension of trade routes. And the price for a medic, Quia Hart, is an eighth of profits. Per run. That's true of the hospital, too, by the way. It's not a quarter of yearly profits to set up the hospital, it's a quarter yearly for as long as the facility exists on the planet." Zimmerman smiled suddenly. "A while back, Parallax hired the Enchanter labs to produce a certain drug. It's useful on high-density planets, combats certain gravity related conditions. Works quite well, too. Parallax bought the patent from Enchanter, and guess how you can get the drug?"

"By joining Parallax."

Zimmerman gestured with the brandy bottle and put it back on the cabinet. "What other examples would you like? The medical thing is the most impressive, but it's not the only one. Or the biggest one." The colonel sipped morosely at his brandy. Hart looked around the laboratory, listening in the silence to the small, comforting noises of his equipment.

"The last we checked," he said quietly, after a while, "there were four hundred seventy-eight members of the Federation." The colonel nodded. "And three hundred twenty-one Parallax members."

"Three twenty-two. Marquez Landing seceded last month."

"Mother above, Zimmerman, what in hell is the Federation doing about all of this? Sitting on its hands? Sitting in a corner shitting in terror?"

"Basically," the colonel said unhappily. He dropped his feet from the cot, stood, and wandered over to one of the lab tables. "We're hamstrung by our own structure. The Federation was deliberately designed as a regulatory agency, you know that. As little interference as possible in the member worlds, while smoothing and speeding intramember communications, shipping, all of that. Sounds wonderful, doesn't it? Then Parallax comes along and just walks around the outside—God, the Federation never expected that anything would get big enough to do that. It just didn't seem possible. That grabstation that your young Second Marquez blew up, that tiny grabstation, that spit-stop, cost as much as your entire processing plant. How could the Federation ever expect that any one entity would get big enough to be able to afford that? And to absorb its loss, too, without even quivering. Time and time again—and then it comes down on a planet like yours, a small company—you can't hope to fight them off, and we *can't* step in, not without breaking every regulation we've ever promulgated." Zimmerman turned his head away and cursed at length.

"It seems then," Hart said carefully, "that your only hope is to revise the structure of the Federation. Give it some teeth. And do it before Parallax gets any larger—

the Federation still has the edge on them now. Another three, four years, and . . ." Hart shrugged expressively.

"It's been considered. It's being considered." Zimmerman looked at the brandy bottle. "There's a faction that wants, not just a revision, but an entire change. Scrap the Federation entirely, and use the bones to build something new. They call it the Union of All Worlds. Total control of tau, not just of grabstations and comnets. Intrasector regulations, not just intersector regulations. Something approaching a standing army, God help us. Something approaching martial law—for the duration, they say, but emergency durations have this nasty historical habit of extending indefinitely. Then there's the faction that seems to believe that if we lodge enough formal protests, Parallax will pay attention to the squawking and behave itself." He made an expressive gesture. "Not to mention those whose constituent worlds are so damned far away from Parallax influence that they don't even believe that it's a menace. And there's the Relinquishment folk, and the Mother Terrans, who want to return total control to Terra—my God, the idea of a Federation-wide version of the Four Hundred Families!" Zimmerman changed his mind, grabbed the bottle, and filled his glass. "Well, congratulations, Quia Hart. You've managed to get me both loaded and loquacious, and madder than hell." He dropped back into his chair. "Fuck," the colonel said with emphasis.

"Althing Green must be an interesting place, these days," Hart murmured.

"Althing Green is a madhouse."

"Um." A small bell rang. Hart wandered over to the keeper, did something with the controls, watched it for a moment, and wandered back. He stood beside Zimmerman, staring at the dark interior of the wood stove. "What about a holding action?"

"Pardon?"

"It seems to me," Hart said slowly, "that the main problem right now is time. Parallax is growing too fast, almost geometrically, and the Federation is faced with doing something immediately and is so flustered that it can't think of anything to do at all."

"Reasonable analysis," Zimmerman said gloomily. "Kinder than I'd put it."

Hart laughed. "I do believe that's the first time anyone's

ever accused me of excessive kindness, colonel." He dropped into his seat and leaned toward the colonel, putting his elbows on his knees. "What if some of the regulations were, oh, not changed, but redefined slightly?"

Zimmerman looked at him, interested. "For example?"

"Tau. If the Federation redefined travel regulations so that the Federation controlled tau itself, and not just its own grabstations, then it would automatically be in a position to control, or at least regulate, all Parallax grabstations and comnets. Parallax isn't yet big enough to make a definite break with the Federation, and it would, I think, take it some time to decide on a course of action. If the Federation redefined control, declared a moratorium on any new grab construction or grab changes, and initiated a total inventory of existing grabstations and nets—" Hart gestured. "You'd gain time to make a rational decision, greater knowledge of the exact extent of Parallax holdings and operations . . ."

"And, if the 'redefinition' came through quickly enough, Aerie, too, would have time, either to evade Parallax, or to attempt a better defense."

"Exactly." Hart leaned back and looked at Zimmerman. "There's another thing that the Federation might consider, too. Some control of monopolies."

Zimmerman raised his eyebrows. "What immediate good would that do?"

"None, right now. But it makes more sense than nonsense like creating a standing army, and it's Parallax's specialty. That's why they want us, of course. Once they have both Aerie and Marquez Landing, they have Z-line production tied up tight. If the Federation limited and controlled moves like that—"

"I see your point. It's a novel idea."

"It's not novel at all, colonel. It's an historical solution, and I'm sure that there's someone on Althing Green trying to talk about it right now, and drowned in the general lamentations. But the tau control idea—"

"Yes." The colonel stood. "Is there someone on duty at the comshack?"

"Yes, but you can use the unit in Quilla's office. Less of a walk."

Zimmerman nodded and walked toward the door. "An interesting evening, Quia Hart. I thank you for it."

Hart smiled and opened the door. "Did they provide evenings of equal interest in NewHome, colonel?"

Zimmerman grinned. "Inflexibly nonpartisan," he said, and stepped into the night. Hart watched him until the small colonel had entered the kitchen door, then closed the laboratory door and, satisfied, went to bed.

❧

THE WIND BLEW, A STEADY WESTERLY THAT pleased Chiba and pushed the balloon over the southern forests of To'an Betes. The small auxiliary windmill that he and Dene had fastened to the airship's nose spun merrily, recharging the spare batteries. Tatha, lounging against the gondola's nose face upward, watched the blur of the windmill's vanes. She had buttoned up her jacket against the chill wind and knotted her hair at the nape of her neck. Some strands blew loose and whipped around her face, and she raised her hands and tucked them under the collar of her jacket.

"You're supposed to look down," Chiba told her, making his way to the nose of the gondola.

"Oh, I will. In time. That small line on the port side is working loose."

Chiba slid beside her and glanced up. "Damn. It should last the day, though."

"Um." Tatha twisted around to lie on her belly. The coast of Betes appeared ahead, a tangled mess of forest, cliff, small beaches, and fanged rocks jutting from the ocean. The water was gray and busy with whitecaps. "Are you sure we're headed in the right direction?"

Chiba looked at her and didn't bother to answer. Tatha grinned and made her way to the gondola's middle, where she rummaged in the food locker and found a strip of dried hopper jerky. She gnawed on it, thinking about the superior quality of kasirene teeth, and watched the coast draw closer.

It hadn't been hard to talk Chiba into taking the trip. The geographer was restless after a winter's enforced idleness and jumped at the chance to take his airship on a four-day trip to the east. He hadn't even bothered to ask why Tatha wanted to visit To'an Tebetet, until the night before, as they sat around a small fire somewhere on the plains south of Hoku. When she said that she wanted to visit Spider, he didn't ask how she knew the child's whereabouts. It wasn't so much lack of curiosity, Tatha mused, as a profound disinterest in anything not directly affecting his precious airship. A trip to Tebetet was enough to excite his interest, and the reasons for the trip were irrelevant. Tatha was both amused and grateful, and didn't bother to ask Chiba not to talk about the trip on their return to Haven. That implicit promise of free speech, and the provisions, were the price she paid for the trip. She paid them willingly.

The coastline of Betes passed under them and dropped behind. Chiba checked his instruments, made a few corrections of their tack, and sat beside Tatha. She offered him a piece of jerky and he worried it with his teeth.

"Dull place, Tebetet," Chiba said, continuing a discussion they had had that morning. "Found it about this time last year, after a tribe on Betes told me that it was there. The thing's so small it didn't even show up on the original orbitals." He rummaged around for a flask of water. "Stony island, a few trees and such in the central valley. I guess someone could raise a small crop there, a garden, if they wanted to put in the work. Bunch of caves. No one there, when I came through last time. Are you sure that's where Spider is?"

Tatha nodded and Chiba moved his shoulders uncomfortably. "Damned nasty place for a kid. Prison?"

"I doubt it," Tatha said, but didn't elaborate. She rechecked the boxes she'd brought aboard. A load of the season's first taefruit, all ripe; stacks of Mim's elaborate filled cookies, carefully wrapped against air and damp; some jugs of various juices; a small jug of The Jumble's best kaea; a new jacket for Spider, larger than the one Hart remembered him having. And some extra trinkets, stuffed into pockets in her backpack. She hoped it would be enough.

"There," Chiba said with satisfaction. Tath stood and

looked over his shoulder. A smudge on the horizon gradually enlarged to become a small, rocky island.

"I don't think we want to go down in the valley itself,"
Tatha said. "Is there a place nearby?"

"Sure, there's a small plain just south of the valley,
half a kilometer or so. It should do." He angled the vanes
and opened the valves slightly. The airship swung
smoothly in the air.

There were boats drawn up on the beach. Figures
leaped and waved along the water's edge. Tatha leaned
over the gondola's side and waved back, grinning, feeling a foolish pleasure at causing such a commotion and
at the glorious silliness of her means of transportation.
Chiba set the airship down on the plain. Tatha swung out
of the gondola to grab the anchoring lines and tie the ship
down. By the time she and Chiba had finished, they were
surrounded, at a respectful distance, by young, saucer-
eyed kasirene. Tatha glanced among them for Spider but
did not see him.

"Well met," she called in Kasiri. "I have here some
boxes, in need of feet to carry them and mouths to eat
their contents."

The young ones grinned at the traditional words and
inched forward. Tatha scrambled into the gondola and
began lifting boxes over the side. The kasirene drew
closer, dividing their attention between the boxes and
Chiba's balloon. He started explaining, in his heavily
accented Kasiri, about the airship, and hands lifted the
boxes. Tatha slipped into her backpack and came out of
the gondola again.

"You're the Theresan," one of the kasirene said. Tatha
glanced at the young face and nodded pleasantly.

"Do I know you? Are you from Haven?"

"Oh, no, not really. I was there for a little while,
then came here with Spider."

"You must be Kaën, then. Spider's written about you to
his father."

"All lies," Kaën said stoutly. "Is that really taefruit?"

"Yes. First of the crop and all ripe, too." They began
walking toward the valley. "And I hope they're not lies.
He said that you've got a runaway tongue and you're
the best pel thief on three to'anet."

"True, then," Kaën said, and grinned. "Spider's back
in the valley, he pulled kitchen duty today. He doesn't

know that you're coming, does he? The place is busting
with people, we've got just about everyone down there,
you'd think they were a flock of seabirds, jabbering all
the time. The Choosing's in a week, did you know that?
I thought so. Have you come to speak to us?"

"Yes. May I talk with Melet first?"

"Of course," Kaën said, looking up at Tatha. "Everyone does."

Tatha heard voices behind her as the kasirene young
plagued Chiba with questions. They reached the rim of
the valley. Chiba caught up with her and grinned, totally
delighted.

"Can we stay an extra day?" he said. "They want rides,
and the wind's right, it ought to hold."

"I don't see why not," Tatha said. "You'll have to ask
Melet's permission first."

"Tribe's chief? Sure, why not?" He dropped back to
talk to his admirers again and Tatha followed Kaën into
the cup of the valley.

"Of course you may speak," Melet said. "Although I'll
admit that I'm baffled at your subject. What tribe do you
speak for?"

"None in particular," Tatha said. She sat opposite
Melet in the kasir's room and the fire in the small pit
before them burned with clear, smokeless flames. "There
are advantages to living either in Haven or Hoku, there
are jobs among the albiana which could use kasirene
hands. TauCaptain Kennerin wants more kasirene in
space, he says that they're among the best crew he has.
We need teachers in the schools. The brewery is expanding, there are student positions at the hospital." Tatha
paused. "Traditionally the kasirene have tended to shy
away from albiana jobs and technology. It may be time
to change that."

Melet folded her hands in her lap and rocked back.
"Perhaps. It is, of course, up to the young ones." The
kasir smiled. "I will admit that I find this wonderfully odd,
that a Theresan should come in a balloon, to speak for
the albiana at a kasirene Choosing."

Tatha smiled back. "I find it passing strange myself."

Melet rocked onto her feet, signaling the end of the
meeting, and Tatha rose.

"I thank you again for the gifts," Melet said as they

walked to the room's round entrance. "The fruit is appreciated, but the pastries are superb."

"Coming to speak for the albana, I thought it only fitting to bring albana gifts." Tatha stopped with her hand on the door's fabric covering. "I have various small gifts for Spider, and a letter from his father. Is it acceptable to give them to him?"

"Of course," Melet said. "And you may tell your airfilled friend that he may take some of my students in that device of his, although why anyone would want to go into the air escapes my reason. I expect everyone back, in one cohesive piece, by suppertime tomorrow."

"Of course." Tatha bowed. "Chiba will not go up at night in any event."

"I'm glad that he exhibits some sense. Flying around with the birds . . ." Melet pretended a shudder, smiled, and bowed Tatha from the room.

Tatha walked up the curving, rocky corridor into the sunlight of the valley. Kaën was right: it was raucous out there. Adult kasirene sat or walked or lounged around the sides of the valley, speaking with great enthusiasm to any young kasirene within the sound of their voices, and they looked at Tatha, as they looked at the other adults, with sharp suspicion. Tatha had no trouble gathering a group of young ones around her. She merely sat on a stone, put her arms around her knees, and within minutes they surrounded her, asking questions. She answered them gravely, talking about the benefits of learning and using albana technology, without wild enthusiasm but without unnecessary reticence, either. The afternoon sun slid down the sky. Chiba appeared from the plain, trailed both by kasirene young and adults. He squatted in the dirt and drew something with a stick, waving his other hand in explanation. Tatha watched him, smiled, and returned to a discussion of electronics with the kasir by her side.

"Of course," Tatha said at last, "one of the benefits of chosing Haven, or Hoku, is that you don't have to make a more detailed choice immediately. You can take your time, explore what's available, try things out until you find something that interests or excites you."

The kasir, deep in thought, nodded and wandered off. Tatha rose and stretched. The sun was a bare half hour from setting and enticing smells rose from the kitchen

caves. She walked over and stood at the entrance, looking
for Spider. Eventually she saw him in a corner, his hands
busy slicing vegetables into a steaming pot; his head was
turned and he was talking with great animation to Kaën.
She watched him for a long time, then turned and wandered back into the valley, rubbing her shoulders. Her
body felt tense and twitchy. On impulse she dropped her
pack beside Chiba, muttered something, and walked to
the ravine that led to the beach. Once away from the
valley she started running, leaping from rock to rock
along the stream that flowed through the ravine. When
she reached the beach she stopped and stripped, tucked
her clothing into the crotch of a tree, and ran down the
beach to a set of low cliffs. She scrambled around their
base for a while, balancing and reaching and jumping,
then trotted back along the beach. She dressed as one of
the moons appeared, and jogged back up the ravine,
keeping again to the rocky stream bed rather than to the
path. When she reached the valley, Spider stood at the
path's mouth, holding a plate in his hands. He handed it
to her and followed her into the valley.

"I thought you were going to break your neck," he said.
"Your supper's still hot, mostly."

"Thanks." She dropped onto a low stone bench and
Spider, at her nod, sat beside her. "You've eaten?"

"Sort of. Half the fun of kitchen duty's getting to taste
things all day. I've been stuffed for hours." He paused.
"We're speaking in Kasiri, aren't we?"

She nodded, her mouth full of food. "Would you rather
speak in Standard?" she said when she'd swallowed.

Spider shook his head, looking down. "Kasiri feels
right to me now. Does that make any sense?"

"Yes." She finished her meal. "Would you like to take
a walk?"

Spider smiled slightly. "That's what Beriant asked,
when he came. Did you know about that?"

"Yes." They put the plate and cup in the baskets,
then wandered up a path along the low hills until the
valley dropped out of sight and the air was silent save
for the rhythmic pulse of the sea. They walked along the
edge of the seacliffs. Tatha watched the light of the moons
across the water, enjoying the quiet. Then, casually, she
began telling him about his family.

Spider listened hungrily, asking endless questions,

soliciting minute details. He shook his head unhappily when Tatha told him that Alin still refused to talk, laughed at the news of Andrus' latest antics, nodded soberly when Tatha described the change that had come over Jason Hart in the past months.

"And my father?" he said at last.

"Misses you," Tatha said. She reached into her pocket. "I've a letter for you."

Spider took the letter eagerly and opened it, then shook his head, frustrated. "I don't have your night vision," he said. Tatha handed him her lightstick and walked away, giving him privacy. When the light flicked off she turned and came back to him.

"Thank you," he said quietly. Tatha dropped to sit beside him on the grass.

"A couple of things more," she said, reaching again into her pockets. She'd transferred things there from the backpack earlier, and now she brought out the gifts. A compact vibra-knife, capable of slicing through almost anything. "But it's got full safeguards," Tatha said, "remember that." A very small holocube. Spider flicked the lightstick and stared into the cube at the faces of his family. They smiled and waved. And, lastly, a small, brown cube of plastic, with a finger plate at one end. Tatha balanced it in her palm and looked at it.

"I don't know if it's strictly legal," she said. "And I didn't mention it to Melet. You'll have to decide whether you want to accept it or not. It's a caller. If you ever need help, if you're ever in trouble, you activate it by pressing the plate with the index finger of your left hand. It will transmit directly to Hart, and acts as a direction finder, too."

Spider looked at it without touching it. "Is it from Hart?"

"Yes. But it was my idea."

He put his hands in his lap and looked at her. His face was indistinct in the darkness. "Hart's letter said that you wanted to talk to me about some things. You know that you can't ask after my choice."

"Yes, and I won't. It's only peripherally about the Choosing." She put the caller down between them and leaned back, folding her arms under her head. "Beriant visited you a while back. He did it at my suggestion." She paused. When Spider didn't say anything, she closed her eyes. "Spider, what do you know about Parallax?"

"About as much as the family. Have things happened since I left?"

"Yes," she said, and told him about Parallax, and Zimmerman, and Sandro, and the kasirene. He listened silently, nodding in the moonlight. She sat up, wrapped her arms around her knees, and told him in detail what she was doing. When she finished, Spider leaned forward, matching her position, and they stared out to sea together.

"How much of this does Hart know?" Spider said.

"Less than you do." She put her cheek on her knees. "He knows, of course, that I've come to see you. He thinks he knows what I'll say to you, but he's wrong." She paused. "It's not a thing that I feel good about. He pretty much collapsed after you left—you know about that?"

"No, but I expected it. What happened?"

"He tried to leave Aerie, and I prevented him. Then he withdrew, moved into his laboratory, had as little to do with anyone as possible. Turned himself off. When Palen learned that you'd be part of the Choosing, he came to life again. He's expecting you to come back. I think he believes that when you do come back, it will be as it was before, that nothing will have changed."

Spider shook his head. "That's impossible. Hasn't anyone told him that?"

"Yes. He doesn't believe it."

Spider glanced at her. "I'm the only one who knows what you're trying to do?"

"Yes."

He returned his gaze to the sea and Tatha let the silence gather.

"My uncle Jes doesn't trust you," Spider said finally. "Are you playing games?"

"Read me, Spider. You know I can't lie in my mind."

Spider shook his head. "I've been very careful not to read you, or Chiba. I haven't read anyone since I came to Melet." He paused. "I don't think I want to read anyone, anymore. It's too easy to miss things that way."

"That's surprising," Tatha said, and turned to look at him. "I'd have thought the opposite."

"No." His head moved sharply. "When I read people," he said slowly, "when I used to—people usually think

what they think very strongly. They believe things. It's
hard not to believe things as completely as they do. But
often they're—not right. Or missing things. Or just not
seeing things. It's easy to believe that you know somebody
because you know what's going on inside their heads. But
how often are you right about what you're thinking yourself? And how often to you realize, later, that you were
wrong?" Tatha looked at him silently. "I won't do it anymore," he said at last. "I'll take what's available on the
outside. It's more fair to other people that way. It's more
fair to myself."

Tatha looked away from him, out to sea. "You aston-
ish me," she said finally.

"Do you think I'm wrong?"

"No. I think you're right. But you've made a decision
that I think I'd never have the courage to make myself.
Did Melet teach you that?"

"No. Melet doesn't teach us what to think. She just
teaches us easier ways to think things."

"You make me feel—inadequate," Tatha said, and
laughed abruptly. "It's not a feeling that I'm used to. Do
you think Melet would take me on as a pupil? After all
of this is over with?"

Spider laughed softly. "Maybe. You'd have to ask her.
After all of this—you haven't answered my questions."

"About games?" She paused. "We're always playing
games, Spider. Generally dangerous ones. And I'm not
saying that to put you off. No, I'm not playing games, at
least not that type. I'm very serious about this. I think it
may be the one chance we've got."

"I think you may be right," Spider said.

Tatha nodded carefully. Spider reached for the caller,
touched it, and put it in his pocket. They stood together
and he looked up at her.

"You didn't come to speak for the albiana after all,
did you?" he said.

"I hope I came to speak for all of us," Tatha said.

"I hope you're right." Spider paused. "I think you are
right. But I have to make my choice by myself."

"I understand that," Tatha said. "I'm sorry if I seemed
to interfere."

Spider smiled at her suddenly and took her hand.
"Come on. There's kaea and singing in the evenings,
you'll not want to miss it."

"No, I wouldn't," Tatha said. They swung down the path together. "Did I tell you, by the way, what we did to Ved Hirem's speech?"

Spider's laughter preceded them all the way to the valley.

TAUCAPTAIN EMILIO BARRANCA WAS HAPPY with neither the quality of life nor the quality of entertainment on Aerie, and let his displeasure be known in no uncertain terms. Pixie, hearing him out, shrugged without replying and doubled the guard around the warehouse, and Barranca paced back and forth, cursing in a multitude of languages. Sandro, pausing outside, translated some of them for Pixie's benefit.

"He says that you in particular are the daughter of a syphilitic iguana and a hydrocephalic tortoise whose main diet is rancid shit," he reported. "While your father is a pinheaded bladder leaking oratorical excrement of the most objectionable kind."

"Interesting idea of genetics he's got," Pixie muttered. "What in hell's an iguana?"

Sandro shrugged. "Why don't you ask him?"

"I've got a better idea. Why don't you tell me something I can call him, instead?"

"Sure," Sandro said, grinning, and thought for a moment. *"Hijo de la mala verga,"* he said finally, with satisfaction. "He's from *Mi Patria,* that should get to him."

"What's it mean?"

When he told her, Pixie laughed, repeated it four times to make sure that she got it right, and wandered inside, trying to keep her face straight. Sandro slipped in after her and lounged against the door.

"When in hell is that repairs team going to get here?" Barranca was shouting. Engine Mate Nazumi Karaen, the one with the concussion, put his pillow over his head, and Crew N'Hoste, the broken leg, sat uncomfortably before the vid, staring morosely at a tape which, with the use of cute cartoon characters, explained the effects of excess alkalinity in the soil. N'Hoste did not look either enthralled or enlightened. Arista Blake was asleep, and Crew Nataste poked through a pile of old bookreels, looking for something, Sandro presumed, that he hadn't read before. There were no windows in the warehouse, but the ventilation ducts, eight meters overhead, were open fully and the scent of Aerie in the spring filled the room.

"I'd imagine that they'll be down as soon as Processing can spare them," Pixie said calmly. "And I might point out that they will not get 'here,' they will get 'there.' To *Mi Estancia.* You'll be advised."

"Advised! That's another thing. Why haven't I heard from my company?"

"Because they haven't replied, tauCaptain."

"You said you sent that com five days ago, when we arrived."

"We did."

Barranca stared at her, obviously disbelieving, and stormed over to the table. "This swill that you feed us is pigshit. I demand something decent to eat."

Pixie raised her eyebrows. "I don't see anything wrong with it," she said. "I've enjoyed it often enough myself."

"But not three meals a day and nothing else!" Barranca shouted. Sandro repressed a smile. Mertika fed them fresh bread and a stew compounded of peas, sausages, and miscellaneous Aerie vegetables, and it was, he thought, quite good. Save that she served it up thrice daily, entirely without variety. No matter how nutritious it was, as an invariable diet it was awful.

"And that music," he continued. "One more night of that music and—and—"

"Yes?" Pixie said, crossing her arms.

Barranca descended into Spanish, ending a long, arm-flailing tirade with *"Hija de la puta madre que te pario!"* to which Pixie, solemn, replied with her line of borrowed Spanish. Barranca lost all control and leaped across the room at her, hands reaching for her throat. Pixie braced to meet him and someone abruptly threw her sideways. A fast-moving figure grabbed Barranca in midflight, twisted, and threw him to the floor with such force that the breath exploded from his body. Pixie looked up to see

Tatha standing over Barranca's prostrate form. The
Theresan's eyes were like ice.

"I think," Tatha said precisely, "that this is just about
enough. Hirem, you'll go back to the duty shack and wait
for me. Hand your keys to Paeven and tell her that she's
to take over the rest of your watch. I expect you to be
there when I arrive. And I don't care how long it is, understand?" Pixie, stiff-faced with fury, picked herself up
from the floor and stalked out as Tatha turned her eyes
toward Sandro. "And as for you, Marquez, if I see your
puerile, witless smirk anywhere around here again, without my express permission *and* written pass, I'll report it
to Jes and have you docked time and wages, understand?
Get out."

"But—" Sandro gestured angrily, and left the warehouse, slamming the door closed behind him. Tatha looked
down at Barranca and nudged his side with her booted
foot.

"If you were under my command," she said unpleasantly, "which, unfortunately, you're not, I'd beat the
living shit out of you. I've spent a fair amount of time
listening to whining, bitching, nagging, and all-around
sore-assing, but you, tauCaptain, take the prize. And
considering the competition on Aerie, that's a considerable accomplishment. Stand up, if you remember how to.
You're both a prisoner and a guest here, but I swear it
solemnly, if I hear one more baseless, self-pitying yaup
out of you, I'll make it impossible for you to open your
mouth for a week. And if you doubt I can do it, try me."

She turned her back to Barranca and stalked down
the length of the warehouse. *Mi Estancia*'s crew watched
her silently. She glanced at the vid, said something contemptuous in a strange language, poked her head into
the lavatory, tried the controls on the stove and the
cooling unit, opened and closed the doors of the cabinet,
and came back to stand above Arista Blake.

"What are they feeding you?" she demanded. When
Blake told her, Tatha grimaced. "I'll see what I can
do about it, but I can't make any promises. I can't do anything about the vid or the bookreels. I'll try to do
something about the entertainment—I take it you object to
kasirene singing?" This question she addressed to Barranca.
He started to open his mouth, snapped his jaw closed, and
nodded. "It takes getting used to," Tatha said. "We'll see.

And there haven't been any coms from Parallax, tau-Captain. Perhaps they've forgotten you exist." She walked to the door.

"Quia preParian," Barranca said, with cautious formality. When Tatha didn't offer to hit him, he took a deep breath and continued. "I want to thank you for your offers in our behalf. We did not expect to be treated this way when we entered your system."

"I don't imagine that you did, tauCaptain," Tatha said, amused. "On the other hand, you should have expected it, considering your history. And Aerie's." She paused. "It must be wonderfully frustrating, to be finally down on Aerie and unable to do a damned thing about it."

Barranca looked at her. She grinned and opened the door. "I suggest you learn to sing, tauCaptain. It's an educational exercise, and passes the time quite pleasantly. You might start with an old one, I think you must have learned it in school. *Paloma Verde, Paloma Azul?* Good night."

She slipped out and double-locked the door, then listened in satisfaction to the silence that filled the warehouse behind her. Barranca, if he had the standard postwar Spanish colony education, would know the song. It was from the war years, and had been used by Spanish planet patriots to advertise their presence and hearten each other in Jerusan's prison ships. Whistling the tune under her breath, Tatha strolled to the duty shack to take care of Pixie Hirem.

JES HAD ALMOST FORGOTTEN PALEN'S RE-quest when, one month out of Tarne, the captain of the A-K taushship *To'an Sebet* beamed him a private band message from all the way across the Federation, in Lei-fan Sector. Jes, called from his cabin, slid into his web, punched the privacy shield, and acknowledged the call.

"We've got it," said Daenet. The kasir's face was fuzzy in the screen. "Although why you want it is totally beyond me. Found it in port sector on Rosten's World, like you said I might."

"Found what?" Jes said, rubbing his eyes.

"The Criswold native, except they call themselves Ska'felet. And this one must be the worst of the lot—at least, I hope so. I've got it on board."

Jes frowned for a moment, recalled Palen's requisition, and nodded. "Okay. What's your route?"

"Nowhere near home, unfortunately." Daenet grimaced. "I've got a hold full of junk to hump around Leifan Sector for a while, then I'll have enough for a run to MarketPort, and then, unless something comes up, we're due for a week at home. You want me just to lug this thing along with us until then?"

"No." Jes ran his fingers over the computer bank, studying the listing of routes. "Listen, you're on Rosten's World now?"

"No, just out of it, approaching the grab."

"Get him over to Clemens, it's in the same sector. Take a detour off your current heading to do it. Tzasz ought to be due there tomorrow—I'll com her to wait for you. Transfer the—what did you call it?"

"Ska'felet. I don't know its name, it won't tell us."

"Well, what is it? I mean, he? It, or he, or she, or what?"

Daenet shrugged. "Captain, if I could tell . . ."

"Hell. Transfer the thing to Tzasz; she'll hump it back to Aerie."

"I could take it myself," Daenet offered without much hope.

"Sorry, captain. Give it to Tzasz. You'll be home soon enough."

"Worth a try anyway." Daenet signed off and Jes sent out a com for Tzasz.

Tzasz, with much arm-waving and pulling of pale blond hair and slapping of broad cheekbones, eventually admitted that it would not throw her schedule hopelessly off-kilter if she stayed an extra day on Clemens. She asked if any special living arrangements had to be made for the Ska'felet and Jes shook his head.

"If it did need any, Daenet would have told me. When do you think you can get it to Aerie?"

"Ummmm . . ." She bent to do something to her own bridge computer. "Another week standard after I pick it up. That's ten days from now. Soon enough?"

"Fine." They exchanged a few civilities before Jes signed off, smiling, and commed Aerie. He left a message with the comoperator at Havensport for Palen and went back to bed. Beryl had already fallen asleep.

The note in Tatha's box at the duty shack was sealed and across its face were scrawled the words "Possible interest." Tatha put it in her pocket and conducted the morning drill. The militia, without her direct orders, had gradually moved down the landing field until now they exercised within earshot of the warehouse in which Barranca and his crew were unhappily immured. If Tatha approved of the move she didn't say so, although the exercises she put them through increased in severity and length. The militia grumbled, but not within her hearing, and Pixie continued to treat her with cool, correct deference. Tatha, bending and twisting in the morning sunlight, ignored the entire business. She heard scraps of singing from inside the warehouse, and identified the chorus of *Paloma Verde, Paloma Azul*. She increased the pace of the exercise. Grunting, yelling, making enough noise for a group at least four times as big, the militia finished the morning work-out breathlessly and staggered off the field. Tatha strolled back to the duty shack, alone, reading the duplicate message from the comshack.

It was dated that morning from *Rabbit*, addressed to Palen, and said that a Ska'felet had been found and was being transported to Havensport, due to arrive on a shuttle from the *Mordecai* eleven days hence, and was signed Jes Kennerin. Tatha read it again, expressionless, and put it back in her pocket.

When she finished working on next week's duty rosters she went back to the comshack and made business for herself there until Palen arrived. She waited while Palen took the original comsheet and read it carefully. The kasir put the sheet in her pouch, frowning, and turned toward the door.

"Going toward Haven?" Tatha said. When Palen nodded the Theresan fell into step beside her.

"The Choosing happens soon, doesn't it?" Tatha said. Palen nodded distractedly. "Tomorrow."

"And how soon after that will we know?"

Palen looked down at her. "Why don't you and Chiba fly over and find out?"

"We've better things to do," Tatha said carelessly.

"Like spending time with Beriant?"

"Chiba doesn't play," Tatha said. They were walking through the low hills, where the road to Haven twisted lazily over the grass. "Would you like to learn? You'd be welcome."

Palen glared at her. "What are you doing, Tatha? What are you up to?"

"Me?" Tatha smiled. "I'm just doing my job, Palen tor-Altemet. But one can't work forever—you should relax on occasion. Come join the game."

"I'm not welcome at Beriant's."

"Nonsense." Tatha swung off the Havensport road toward her own house. "Come try it some night," she called over her shoulder. "You might find it interesting."

Palen watched the Theresan disappear around the corner of the house and touched the sheet in her pouch again. Puti said that the people who congregated in Beriant's room for Tatha's increasingly famous game were the same who came to listen to Palen talk in Puti's room, who asked troubled questions, who asked for solutions which Palen could not give them because she did not have them. She hoped, fervently, that this Ska'felet would arrive in time, and plodded on into town.

The game that night was relatively unattended. Many of the kasirene had traveled to To'an Tebetet to watch the Choosing and help bring home those young who had chosen particular tribes, so by losh'al Tatha and Beriant sat alone over the game circle, tossing and collecting the stones with minimal enthusiasm. Near nem'al, Tatha scooped the stones into her hand, yawned, and reached for the kaea. The jug was empty and she frowned at Beriant.

"The least you could do," she complained, "is keep enough of this stuff on hand. With the fremarks you've won from me the last two nights, you can afford it."

"Sorry, I forgot." Beriant rose and paced around the

room. The firepit was dark with ashes. He blew on the ashes to uncover the embers and laid some twigs on the fire. "I've been worrying about this small town meeting the Kennerins have called."

"Why? They won't do anything, they never do."

"They do enough," the kasir said, and put some branches atop the twigs. He rocked back and muttered curses in Kasiri. *"We* don't do enough, damn it. I can't even get close to those people in the warehouse, the militia keeps it guarded tight as a shaggie's ass day and night."

"Indeed we do, and for good reason. I feel no need to have Barranca sniffing around Haven making trouble. He's a puling, unpleasant, slimy man, and the less seen of him the better. If he's the best Parallax has to offer, I'd hate to see the worst."

Beriant looked at her. "You mean he's—uninspiring?"

"To put it mildly." She rattled the stones in her hand. "You should meet him, Beriant. He'll impress you, but not, I think, the way you want to be impressed."

Beriant, with a great show of unconcern, sat himself across the circle from her and dropped a fremark on the betting slab. "I'm told that the repair crew arrived on his ship today."

"True." Tatha dropped a fremark and shook the stones.

"Any idea how long the repairs will take?"

She shrugged, threw, and cursed. "You've got them bewitched," she said unhappily. "About two, three weeks. Maybe more if the hatch seals are as bad as Sandro says that they are. Your throw."

Beriant paused, then slowly pushed his entire pile of fremarks onto the betting slab. Tatha raised her eyebrows.

"You know I can't match that," she said.

"I'll take a service as a bet," the kasir said. Tatha looked at him. "Let me in to see Barranca. Just once, any way that you please. One meeting, no more."

She looked down at the pile of fremarks. "I could fold."

Beriant smiled. "Do they hunt you for sport, anymore?"

Tatha's mouth twitched. "You've more brains than I gave you credit for," she said. "And I do believe my

luck is changing. Certainly, one visit for your fremarks.
Traditional game, winner takes all. Fair enough?"

"Fair enough," Beriant said, and threw the stones.

The next morning, after drill, Tatha went up to the
Tor and took Daren with her for the day. They ran all
the way into Haven, Tatha sprinting off to the side and
back, or running backwards to urge Daren on. Daren
howled joyfully and Belshazar howled in counterpoint.
The square bustled with people. Aerites from Hoku had
already started to come in for the small meeting and
added their clamor to the usual bustle. It began to re-
semble a fair, Tatha thought, and swung Daren up to
her shoulder. He grabbed her hair in both fists and crowed
with delight.

Most of the Hoku Aerites, not knowing Tatha, looked
at her oddly and got out of her way. She paused at the
booths in the market, collecting business, sampling the
wares. Someone reached up to hand Daren a sweet
while Tatha argued with Cas Hevant over the price of a
length of cloth. Eventually a bargain was struck: the
cloth and the dressmaking to turn it into a gown, in return
for an afternoon of general repair work around Cas'
shop. Tatha arranged a time to come by for the fitting.

"How's Koyu?" she said. Daren had smeared stickiness
in her hair, and she tried to untangle it with her fingers.

"I should know?" Cas spread her hands wide. "He's
off with Jared somewhere south, doing samples. Or that's
what they say they're doing." Cas put her hands on the
countertop, amid the spilled colors of her wares. "Spring
comes, planting's done, and they're off again. Fine set of
parents they'll make."

"They'll settle down," Tatha said. "When's the baby
due?"

"Five weeks. Hart says that we can throw a party at
his lab."

"Sounds good. I'll have to think of a birthing gift."
Tatha swung down the length of stalls, briefly wondering
if Jared and Koyu would, amid all the tensions, find the
tranquility to enjoy their child. The scent of hot spiced
meatsticks floated by. She followed her nose to the stand
and stood munching one. The stand stood near the porch
of Kohl's. Mertika, standing talking on the steps, saw
Tatha, turned quickly, and went inside. Tatha watched

her curiously for a moment and wandered away. Ved
Hirem sat at his usual post near a corner of the porch.
Tatha bowed to him, raising a hand to hold Daren in place
and the old man scowled.

Once home she washed the goo from her hair and finished a few small projects in the workshop. Daren complained of hunger, and it was midafternoon before she
wandered into the duty shack, son and shaggy in tow, to
receive the morning's reports.

Quilla, coming out of the comshack, called to her
and walked rapidly across the pavement.

"Play in the grass?" Daren said.

"Sure." Tatha whistled to Belshazar, and the two
bounded off as Quilla came up. Tatha glanced with interest at the sheet in Quilla's hand. "Heard from Jes?"

"Yes. He wants to finish his route before coming
home since nothing here seems urgent. I told him to."
Quilla paused. "Pixie says that you've authorized recreation time for them." She jerked her head toward the far
warehouse.

"That's right."

"Do you think that's wise?"

Tatha put her hands on her hips. "Two hours a day,
guarded by twice or three times as many of us as of them,
allowed only into the hillside directly behind the warehouse—what do you think they'll possibly be able to do?
Blow up Haven?"

"Of course not. But—"

"They've no possibility of either getting near the comshack or making any kind of commiter themselves.
They've been locked in there for a week already and that
would be enough to drive anyone crazy. Dear Lady,
Quilla, are we going to put ourselves on the same level
as they are?"

Quilla shook her head. "Zimmerman finished review-
ing the bridge crystals."

"And?"

"It's inconclusive. There was a burst to the main engines. It could have come from the *Blind Chance* hookup.
Or it could have come from a manual programming from
Mi Estancia's bridge—the timing would have had to
have been perfect, but it could have been done. On the
other hand, there's no overt command from *Blind*

Chance, but that could have been rigged, too. There's no way of telling."

"Have you tried asking one of them?" Tatha in turn nodded toward the warehouse.

"Why? What good would it do? They're not likely to tell us anything."

"You haven't given them a chance," Tatha pointed out. "One of them might be angry at Barranca or angry at Parallax. Some sympathy, some indication that they're not all believed to be pests, and maybe one of them might have something to tell us." Tatha paused. "The Second, Blake, seems rational. And I'm willing to bet that she's no fan of Barranca's either."

Quilla's mouth twisted down. "Why haven't you done that, if you think it's such a good idea?"

"I've better things to do," Tatha said airily.

"Like gambling all night in The Jumble?"

"Listening to Palen, um? It's an entertaining exercise, Quia Kennerin. You might try it." Tatha whistled shrilly while Quilla winced. Within moments Daren and Belshazar appeared out of the tall meadowgrass and came running across the port. "And if you'll excuse me, I've other better things to do." Tatha waved and walked off, trailing shaggy and son, toward the distant warehouse. Arriving at its door, she turned and watched Quilla trudging halfway up the path to the Tor.

"All quiet?" Tatha said to the guard.

The man shrugged. "Barranca's been sounding off, but that's nothing new." The man unlocked the door.

Tatha nodded, pushed open the door, and went in.

"Voting shares," Barranca said to Beriant, and the kasir nodded. The hollow in which they sat was soft with spring grass. Tatha, sitting above them on the hillside with a long, antiquated, but perfectly maintained Albia-Markins resting across her knees, looked over their heads to the roof of the warehouse and the port beyond it. The other crew members sat or walked about the hillside, guarded by overdiligent militia. Tatha was more worried that the militia would shoot the crew out of sheer nervousness, than that the crew would attempt to escape. Besides, as she had pointed out to them earlier, where would they go? Barranca had made a speech about honorable intentions, which Tatha ignored. Hazy

blue smoke drifted from the far end of the port, where
Blind Chance's donkey engines were being tuned. Pixie
Hirem and Quilla stood together at the door of the duty
shack, looking toward Tatha. The Theresan looked around
again and, satisfied, returned her attention to Barranca
and the kasir.

They sat near each other, bending together to talk, and
bits of their conversation floated up the hill. Tatha listened carefully while watching the hillside. They seemed
convinced that she could not hear them. Not that it
mattered by now, she thought, and shifted the Albia-
Markins on her lap.

". . . register as many as we can," Beriant said. "Then
put up a new board . . ." Barranca nodded enthusiastically. Tatha had been expecting that, and felt a brief
annoyance. Of course Parallax would realize that Aerie's point of most vulnerability would be in the voting
shares, and Barranca would realize that Beriant represented Parallax's only hope of electing a governing
board for Aerie-Kennerin that would be favorable to a
Parallax takeover. Register the disaffected kasirene,
those who had never bothered to register before, those
whose minds had been swayed by Beriant's oratory.
Call a vote of confidence and present candidates for the
board who would be guaranteed of the kasirene vote.
Beriant's followers had been leaving The Jumble for
weeks, going to spread his gospel among the other islands on Aerie, and Tatha did not doubt that they would
find the support they sought. Barranca and Beriant talked
about schedules and Tatha resisted the urge to yawn. The
Choosing on To'an Tebetet would have taken place two
days ago, and she expected news of the Choosing to reach
Haven soon. She wondered how Hart would take it; he
didn't know all of her plans, although he thought he did.
Pixie and Quilla went inside the duty hut and after a moment Sandro came out, squinted into the sunlight, and
crossed to the comshack. Tatha glanced at the sky and
checked her chronometer. She stood and whistled
sharply. Recreation time was at an end.

Beriant stayed in the small hollow, out of sight of the
port. Tatha ignored him. She herded militia and crew
down the hill to the warehouse and ushered the crew
inside. Barranca came in last, and paused when he
reached her.

"Hirem hates you," he said quietly.

"Which one?"

"Both of them."

"Sorry, tauCaptain. Ved hates me. Pixie merely doesn't trust me."

"And Beriant does."

"An interesting life, isn't it?" She gestured with her long rifle, and locked the door behind Barranca. Predictable bastard, she thought, and wished suddenly and fervently that all the games were at an end.

∿

THE SKA'FELET WAS VAGUELY HUMANOID IN appearance, having two stumpy legs, two stumpy arms, and a stumpy middle connecting them. Its head was hairless, lipless, and lidless; when it blinked transparent wings flapped rapidly over pallid eyes, as though it had insects permanently affixed to the sides of its face. Its rubbery, rather greasy-looking skin of a strange, orangish-hue was, Palen discovered when they shook hands, subtly repulsive to the touch. All of this she ascertained when she met the Ska'felet at the port. On the way to The Jumble, taking the long route through the meadow around Haven, she learned that the Ska'felet was morose, self-pitying, uncommunicative, and greedy. It refused to divulge its name, saying that it lacked one, and it refused to divulge its sex, stating that although Ska'felet came in two sexes, it felt that it was the last of its race, and had therefore taken on itself all the attributes of the entire race: sex, language, nationality—everything. Palen grimaced, disgusted, and took it through the night to Puti's room.

The entire universe was in league against the Ska'felet. There were no safe places, no havens, no friends, no neutrals—everyone was an enemy and there was no possibility of friendship, the word had no meaning. The

Ska'felet was exploited wherever it went. It had suffered, and it expected to suffer more. Nothing pleased it, nothing could possibly please it. It told Puti that it didn't care what it ate, everything was equally awful, and it complained bitterly about the soup and flat bread that she produced for it. It refused kaea but drank all the beer in the room, morosely proclaiming that the stuff was swill. It didn't care why it had been brought to Aerie, one place was as bad as another, and it argued acrimoniously over the terms of its services. When it learned what Palen and Puti wanted of it, it put its arms over its lipless mouth and hooted derisively. When it went to use the lavatory it evacuated a messy, smelly substance all over the sink, and when Puti forced it to clean up the sink, it muttered in a sticky, glottal language and did a poor job of clearing away the mess. It spoke Standard worse than poorly and announced that it had neither the time nor the interest to learn the barbaric native tongue. It claimed to be descended from the princes of its planet, said that Palen smelled bad and The Jumble smelled worse and Puti's sleeping alcove, sacrificed to its use, smelled more vilely than all the rest put together, and it went to sleep. It made sloppy wet noises as it slept, presumably its version of snoring. Puti and Palen went out to the walkway, leaned over the railing, and drank kaea.

"It's not going to work," Puti said. "That damned thing is so repulsive that even if folk believe it, they'll think it only got what it deserved. If that."

"It has to work," Palen replied, staring over the edge of the railing and forgetting, temporarily, her fear of heights. "I know it's not lovable—"

"Lovable!" Puti snorted. "It's not even acceptable."

"Just because it's awful," Palen continued stubbornly, "doesn't mean that it hasn't suffered. Injustice can happen to anyone, not just acceptable folk. And not all the survivors of persecution are saints. Besides, we don't have any choice."

"Then you'd better think up some way of making your slimy friend palatable," Puti said. "Or it'll do more good to Beriant's cause than to ours."

"I know." Palen glanced into the room behind them. "I wonder if it would react to threats."

"Find out in the morning," Puti said turning to walk down the balcony.

"Where are you going?"

"If you think I'm going to spend the night in there with that," Puti said, over her left shoulder, "you're crazy. Sleep with it yourself." She walked over the swaying wooden bridge and disappeared. Palen went into the room, opened the door and the windows, pushed all the cushions into one corner, and decided to finish off the kaea, after all.

She was delighted to learn, the next morning, that threats worked beautifully. The Ska'felet was a puling coward, and in return for all the food and drink it could eat (although it averred that it would soon die on such a repulsive diet), and the promise not to break its arms, legs, head, or backbone, nor to injure it physically in any way, and enough fremarks, payable at the end of its employment, to take it anywhere in the system that it wished (although why it should even have to choose one hell over another, it claimed, was beyond its considerable intelligence), it promised to go anywhere that Palen took it and tell the story of its planet's conquest to anyone who would listen. It agreed to give its first performance that evening, demanded something to eat, claimed that it felt sick, and threw up in the lavatory. Puti moved out of her room. Palen took it through two rehearsals that afternoon, trying to prune as much self-pitying rubbish from its story as she could. She found it a new piece of clothing, a considerable length of cloth which it twisted about its body and which had the benefit of hiding most of the Ska'felet from view. It said that the cloth irritated its skin and Palen offered to hit it. It said the cloth was fine.

With an audience, and talking about Parallax, the Ska'felet improved considerably. Its story was both 'simple and terrifying. Griswold had been colonized by a Second Reformation group who had rapidly enslaved the natives and set them to work. Ska'felet died in great numbers and were forbidden the comforts of their original language, their religion, and their culture. Families were forcibly broken apart, entire tribes massacred, and the work went on, and went on, and went on. When Parallax agents infiltrated Griswold and offered freedom to the Ska'felet, the natives eagerly accepted the offer of support and rose against their oppressors. The bloodshed was considerable. A complaint was lodged with the Federation, but by the time the Federation sent someone to investigate, Parallax owned Griswold, the detritus of war and death had been cleaned away, and the Ska-'felet were delighted with their new, free, lives. The Federation observer went away. For five years the Ska-'felet lived happily, reestablishing their traditions, and Parallax left them alone. Then Parallax returned and declared that, from now on, Griswold was a manufacturing planet. The Ska'felet objected. Parallax cleared great tracks of countryside from orbiting ships, using slagbombs, regardless of what or who they killed. The Ska'felet rebelled. They had thrown off their original oppressors, they would throw off these new ones. Parallax Security landed on Griswold, systematically reduced the Ska-'felet population by a full third, and set the rest to building the necessary manufacturing plants. A few Ska'felet managed to escape the planet and make their way to Althing Green, to beg for help. By the time they reached the Green, Parallax had heard of their plan and solved the problem in a very simple way. They killed every Ska'felet remaining on planet; there was nothing to complain to Althing Green about, because there was no one left to rescue.

The Ska'felet, stolid and ugly in the midst of the wondering, gray-furred kasirene, wept gelatinous tears and stopped talking, and the kasirene silently filed from the room. Palen, moved even though she'd heard the story before, leaned back against the cushions and allowed herself to feel relief and optimism. She went again over the itinerary she planned for a trip with the Ska'felet among the to'anet of Aerie. The Ska'felet threw up over the firepit and demanded beer.

When Beriant showed up the next morning, furious, to demand the Ska'felet's expulsion from Aerie, Palen and the alien had already left.

HART WOKE AT DAWN AND WENT INTO THE Tor, to his old room. He bathed and dressed quickly and went back to the kitchen. In the time he'd been upstairs, Mim and the cooks had appeared, and he stood at the door, wanting to smile. Dahl saw him and nodded in greeting.

"He's in The Jumble," the kasir said.

"I know." Hart came into the kitchen and lifted the lid of the teapot. "All I want's a cup of tea. And maybe a meat pie to eat on the way."

"You'll starve," Mim predicted, and looked at him critically. "No, you won't. You're getting tubby anyway."

"I am not," Hart said indignantly. Tapir handed him a meat pie. Hart burned his tongue on the hot tea, put the pie in his pocket, and slipped out of the kitchen. He ate the pie as he walked down the hill, shook the crumbs from his hands, and glanced suspiciously at his waistline. Perhaps he had gained a little weight, after all. He was nearing forty, and one couldn't stay slim forever. He'd watch his diet. He wished he had another pie.

Haven already bustled. Every day saw more people arriving from Betes for the meeting, and the kasirene were registering to vote in record numbers. Mish said that it showed that the kasirene, planetwide, cared about the Kennerins and Aerie's future, but when Hart went to seek Palen's opinion he found that she'd left the Tor and The Jumble. Tatha merely shrugged and did not offer an opinion, and when pressed said a number of light, unpleasant things and went home. She had been increasingly uncommunicative of late, something which puzzled Hart but which, now, he had no time to ponder. He skirted Haven quickly, his heart pounding.

At the entrance to The Jumble he stopped uncertainly and put his hands in his pockets. Like Haven proper, The Jumble buzzed with activity and the walkways and corridors were crowded with kasirene. He looked for a familiar face and, not seeing one, made a gesture of greeting to a strange kasir. The kasir returned the greeting politely.

"I'd like to see Altemet," Hart said in Kasiri. The kasir opened his violet eyes wide.

"I'm not sure I know him—the elder?"

Hart nodded.

"We'll find him," the kasir said confidently. "Come along. He's sure to be around somewhere."

The Jumble seemed far noisier than usual, but strangely so. Furious muted arguments sounded from corners and poured from doors, while other kasirene walked quickly, their faces down, and most of them were frowning. Some went to elaborate lengths to avoid others, and once or twice Hart heard muttered imprecations, directed not at him but at other kasirene, which puzzled him with their emotional intensity. The strange kasir, walking at his side, chattered about his tribe on To'an Ako and stopped to ask others for Altemet's whereabouts. Eventually someone directed them to The Meeting, and again they walked through noisy corridors. The strange kasir grimaced and put one set of hands over his ears. He stopped where the corridor opened into sunlight and gestured toward a small building.

"In there," he said, bowed quickly, and disappeared. Hart ran his hands nervously down the sides of his pants and walked slowly across the dirt yard. He filled his lungs at the round door of the building and walked inside.

"Hart Kennerin," a voice said formally. "Be welcome."

Hart blinked as his eyes adjusted to the gloom. A tiny fire burned in the pit and a number of old kasirene sat around it. Altemet stood. Hart walked to him and bowed deeply.

"I would like to see my son, if it is permitted," he said. He barely prevented his voice from shaking and his lips were dry.

Altemet looked surprised. "From ourselves, no permission is needed. Spider is fully an adult, since the Choosing."

Hart's chest tightened. "Then he could come home, if he wants? He could come back with me now?"

Altemet was silent for a moment before saying, with some confusion, "But he has chosen."

Hart shook his head quickly, refusing to be lost in complexities. "I want to see him. Where is he?"

"I don't know." Altemet bent to talk to one of the other kasirene then straightened slowly, his lower hands on his thighs. "Perhaps in one of the kitchens. Come."

Hart bowed to the others and followed Altemet from The Meeting. They entered The Jumble again and Hart kept his eyes down, ignoring the press of kasirene and trying to ignore the sick worry in his stomach. He still couldn't read kasirene expressions, he told himself. Altemet did *not* look at him with pity. And surely Spider would want to see him, would want to come home. He couldn't have changed that much in less than a year. Of course Spider would—

Spider was not in the common kitchen. Altemet talked at length with someone and, beckoning to Hart again, went into a side corridor. Hart followed, trying not to think.

Altemet put his hand on Hart's shoulder. Hart looked up to see an outer door of The Jumble before them. In the sunlight beyond the door a mob of kasirene pups and terran children tumbled through the dust, intent on a complicated game. Hart moved up to stand beside the kasir and, tentatively, called Spider's name in his mind.

The flow of the game did not falter. Hart called again and let the name fade from his mind. Across the heads of the children he saw a group of older children and kasirene gathered under a tree. Spider, seated in their midst, was arguing a point, waving his hands as he talked. Hart couldn't hear his voice over the noise in the yard.

"Go on," Altemet said, pushing his shoulder, and turned to reenter The Jumble. Hart stifled the urge to call the old kasir back. He took his hands from his pockets, flexed his fingers, and wet his lips again. Spider continued arguing. Hart slowly walked around the edge of the yard and leaned against a tree some meters from Spider's group, watching his son. They continued to talk rapidly in Kasiri, and Hart ignored the words.

Spider had grown in the winter and his skin was deeply tanned. His eyes seemed sharper and more blue against the darkness of his skin, and his voice had deepened. His hair, long and shaggy, was tied carelessly at the nape of his neck. He looked sleek and muscled. He'd be fifteen this year, and Hart wondered suddenly if his son was still a virgin. Spider, intent on his argument, did not notice him. Hart's chest hurt.

One of the kasirene saw Hart, leaned forward, and touched Spider's arm. Spider turned and saw his father. The group fell silent and in the silence Spider stood, gestured to his companions, and walked toward Hart. Hart put his hands in his pockets.

"Hello," Spider said in Kasiri. Hart could not read his expression. If Spider were reading the chaos in his mind, the boy did not show it.

"I'm glad you're back," Hart said in Kasiri, hating the inadequacy of the words. "Would you like to take a walk?"

Spider smiled quickly. "I seem to hold most conversations on my feet," he said. "Of course. Just a moment." He spoke briefly to his companions before returning to Hart. They walked out of the yard and into the meadow. Hart turned north, skirting the edge of The Jumble. They walked in silence and Hart, possessed of a formless terror, felt as though the universe contracted until it held nothing but himself and the silent, mysterious boy at his side. He ached to put his arms around Spider. He stumbled and Spider touched his arm. Hart spun to face him.

"Haven't you read me?" Hart cried, his voice cracking. Spider dropped his hand and stepped back.

"No."

Hart closed his eyes. "I'm afraid," he whispered. "I don't know what to say to you." He looked at Spider bleakly. "Help me. Read me."

Spider shook his head. "That's an evasion," he said. "It doesn't help."

Hart looked at him with angry confusion. Spider began walking again. The land sloped ahead of them, leading to the cemetery.

"Reading was an invasion," Spider said slowly, not looking at his father. "Of whomever I was reading, and of me, too. The more I read people, the less I listened to them. And the more they let me read them, the less they said to me." He glanced at Hart quickly. "I became a convenience, I became a—a doorway, or a tree. Something you don't have to pay attention to. An object. Not Spider."

"I never did that to you," Hart said. "Did I?"

Spider shook his head. "I'm talking generally. Or trying to."

"Then talk in Standard. I don't understand."

Spider gestured and rubbed his eyes. "How can you know what you're thinking," he said haltingly, as though translating into a foreign tongue, "if you don't put it into words? How do you know what you feel for me if you can't . . . articulate it? And how can I know? Thoughts get muddy, they settle into tracks and don't have to change because you don't have to think about them anymore—you never have to tell me things, so you never have to tell yourself. And I came to expect things in tracks, so even if there was a change I wouldn't see it. The more I depended on reading things, the less I grew."

Hart felt baffled. He clasped his hands behind his back and twisted his fingers together. "Is that what the kasirene taught you?"

"No. I can't read the kasirene. When I couldn't depend on reading the people around me, I had to start listening to them, and watching them. They said nothing about it. I taught myself."

Hart glanced at him. Spider walked in the sunlight, his black hair gleaming, tilted blue eyes, dark face, and Hart felt as though he unexpectedly confronted his younger self, a self who had taken a different turn in the road so strange, so outside Hart's experience, that Hart could not even perceive the landscape from which his son spoke, could barely comprehend his words. Shaken, Hart twisted his hands together and sought a way to change the subject, but could not find one.

"Reading is a talent," Hart began. Spider gestured abruptly.

"It's a curse," he said. Hart was surprised at the emotion in his voice. "It's a fraud, it's a burden."

"But—"

"Can Alin talk yet?" Spider demanded.

"That has nothing to do with it."

"That has everything to do with it." Spider spun around to face his father and his eyes were hard. "We're cripples—every damned one of us is a cripple. Alin and I with this—this fraudulent talent, Quilla lusting after stars and adventures, Meya so lost she doesn't know what she wants, Jes still trying to find a princess—" he was shouting in Kasiri. He stopped abruptly and put his hands in his armpits.

"And me?" Hart said quietly.

Spider took a deep breath. "And you. Trying to live your life through me, so you won't have to live the life you made yourself," he said with terrible gentleness.

Hart gasped and turned away, fighting with himself. Spider waited silently. After a long time, when Hart felt the threat of tears recede, he gestured and they continued walking.

"I'm sorry I lost my temper," Hart said finally, looking at the grass and the scattered, tight buds of airflowers. "It's your choice, of course. I accept that, and I'll support you, if—if you want my support. Or need it."

"Thank you," Spider murmured in Kasiri. They intersected the path leading up to the cemetery, and without speaking they both turned onto it and walked uphill. Halfway up, Spider paused to look out at Haven.

"I don't think I've ever seen Haven this full," he said. Hart smiled.

"There's the meeting, you know. About Parallax. It seems that everyone's decided to come for that." Hart pointed. "We're going to have to hold it in Market Square, we won't all fit into the town hall. Can you see the bleachers they're making? And the dais?"

"Barely. I took a look at them last night, after we came in." Spider shook his head. "It's going to be sticky."

"I don't think so. Everything seems under control." Hart felt his shoulders relaxing. "Spider? When are you coming home?"

Spider spread his hands. "I *am* home."

"I mean to the Tor. Mim has your room ready, and—" He stopped, looking at his son's face. His stomach went cold.

"But I've chosen," Spider said. He looked at his father. "Didn't you know?"

"I know about Choosing," Hart said. "I assumed that you—chose us."

"No. They didn't tell you. I chose the kasirene, Hart. I've already come home."

"The . . ."

"One of the wandering tribes. I'll be in Haven for another week or two, then we head up to Cault Eiret, probably. Then back to Betes, and eventually to To'an Peles. It should be winter by then, and we'll winter there. I don't know where we'll go after that." He paused. "Hart?"

Hart couldn't talk. He gestured helplessly while his son's face blurred, and he sat abruptly. Spider turned away.

"I'm sorry," he muttered. "I thought you'd have been told—I thought the grapevine—"

"We're not," Hart said, and had to stop for a moment. "We're not, the kasirene aren't talking to us, much, anymore." He shook his head violently. "Palen's not here—they've done it," he cried suddenly. "They've taken you from me, they've—"

"No," Spider said forcefully. He raised his hands. "They didn't make me choose anything. I chose it myself."

"Or so you think," Hart said bitterly. Spider swore in Kasiri and walked down the hill.

"Spider!" Hart shouted, and the boy broke into a run. Hart couldn't see him any more. He put his hands over his face and took deep, painful breaths. When he thought he could, he stood slowly and walked through a dead silence to his father's grave.

❧

"NOTHING," ZIMMERMAN SAID TO QUILLA AS he slid into a seat beside her. Market Square was filling rapidly and Quilla turned her face from the already crowded bleachers to look at the colonel.

"Are they even considering it?" she said.

"Sure. They consider everything. There's a motion before the council to expand control to include all of tau, but so far nothing's being done. It's not scheduled for hearing yet."

Quilla made a face and peered over the crowd again.

Some children had clambered up the roof of Kohl's and sat along the edge of the porch roof, their feet dangling. Someone from Tatha's militia yelled at them to come down, and they ignored her. Vendors moved through the people, selling beer and hot meatsticks and juices and buns stuffed with sauced coney, and Quilla noticed the colonel eyeing them longingly. She grinned. Zimmerman, stuck up on the dais with the Kennerins and the board members, would just have to wait.

Hart pulled his chair behind the others and sat in it morosely, staring across the square to where Tatha stood with Pixie and her watch commanders, keeping an eye on the square. His expression made Quilla shiver suddenly; she hadn't seen such undisguised hatred in his face since he was a child. She looked away before Hart caught her glance. The news of Spider's choice had traveled through Haven quickly, and Quilla suddenly wondered whether Tatha had a hand in that, too. She wished, again, for Palen's presence, advice, and comfort.

Tatha had refused to rescind her orders concerning exercise for the crew of *Mi Estancia*. In itself that would not have been upsetting, but Quilla had heard rumors that Barranca used the exercise time to meet secretly with outsiders—the rumors hadn't identified anyone clearly, nor had they said that Tatha condoned or even knew about the meetings, but Quilla suspected that Tatha knew damned well about the meetings. It would have been very much unlike the Theresan not to know—if the rumors were true.

An argument broke out at the end of the square. Quilla stood to get a better look. One group of kasirene seemed to be feuding with another group; Quilla could see Spider's dark head among the loudest group. A couple of kasirene militia tried to separate the factions and the noise level grew alarmingly. Then Tatha strolled between the two groups and the shouting stopped. One group moved toward the right; the others, including Spider, made their way toward the head of the crowd. Quilla sat back, frowning.

The dais started to fill. Jes, newly arrived, sat beside Meya and looked around impatiently until he saw Tatha, then relaxed against the chair and kept his attention on the Theresan. Decca and Jared helped Mish onto the platform before disappearing into the crowd. Chairs scraped back and forth as people arranged themselves: Simit, Keloret, Perri, Dorlet, and Metenet, who, with Quilla and Mish, comprised the Aerie-Kennerin Board of Directors; Jes representing the shipping line, Gaeva from Hoku, Meya as head of the economic council; Hart and Zimmerman as guests of the directors. Quilla thought about the board as the time for the meeting drew closer. Evenly divided between terrans and kasirene, the board had served Aerie well in the past two years and Quilla hoped that in view of present circumstances, they would be confirmed in their offices during the upcoming elections, scheduled to take place within the month. This time, at least the population had not voted Ved Hirem to office, a fact which gave Quilla relief and Ved a constant topic for complaint. She looked through the crowd for the old man and found him firmly planted in an armchair directly in front of the dais. He must have been there all morning, Quilla realized, dragging his chair into place well before anybody arrived. He looked unwell. Quilla looked around for Pixie and could not find her.

Pixie wasn't very happy with Tatha either. Quilla leaned across Mish to talk with Teloret about the agenda and pushed worry about Tatha from her mind. There was a lot of business to cover.

The people had come to hear about Parallax and let the normal business of the meeting pass with surprisingly little argument. Perri, with wood shavings still clinging to his beard, read the report on Parallax to a suddenly quiet square: there was nothing to vote on here, just unpleasant information to ingest. Folk stared curiously at Zimmerman, who stared longingly at a vendor's hotbox of meatsticks. But when Mish called for new business, not expecting any, the kasirene group at the front of the crowd rose together, Spider obvious among them. One kasir strode forward. Quilla recognized Beriant, and sat back, surprised.

Beriant gained the microphone and, without preamble, introduced seven kasirene as candidates for membership of the board, presenting them as an entire board. No one even had a chance to raise the bylaw which stated that two members of the board must be Kennerins; Beriant already had a bylaw amendment drawn up removing the Kennerin provision. And he had, further, a resolution which would force the Kennerin family to

sell Aerie to the new board of directors, a resolution
which, he pointed out, was perfectly legal under the by-
laws of Aerie-Kennerin. Spider, sitting silently in the
midst of Beriant's proposed board, kept his shoulders
back and his eyes straight before him, lending his implicit
support to Beriant's position. Hart closed his eyes. Before
Beriant had finished, the square resounded with shouts.

"Parallax," Mish said. Quilla shrugged angrily.

"Of course, who else? It'll never pass."

"You think not?" Hart leaned forward, his voice tight
with fury. "Why are all the kasirene registering?"

"Mother of stars," Quilla said, and felt sick.

THE MILITIA WAS KEPT BUSY ALL THAT
night, breaking up fights. Quilla, listening from an office
at the town hall, put her head in her hands and wanted
to weep. It was crazy, all of it, the entire planet had
gone insane. Aerites didn't fight with one another; the
two races had, save for some tension at the very beginning, merged well; Haven had never even needed a po-
lice force. Now the streets were dismal with broken
windows and broken arms; kasirene walked in groups
to protect themselves from terrans, and terrans did the
same for protection against the kasirene, regardless of
political positions.

Zimmerman, standing at a window, winced and
dropped the curtain as a rock clattered against the outside of the building. Quilla raised her head and reached
for the teapot. It was cold. She pushed it away and,
sighing, turned a page of *Codified Customs of Aerie*. The
book seemed to offer no help at all.

Meya came into the room and sat heavily. "Four thousand, seven hundred ninety-five," she said.

"What?" said the colonel.

"Registered terrans on Aerie. Another six hundred

fifty-two on various A-K ships, but a third of those are kasirene. Call it a total of just over five thousand terrans, five thousand no-votes guaranteed."

"Not guaranteed," Quilla said closing the book. "Remember the lands-right people, they'll vote for the resolution to take ownership."

"And won't vote for the kasirene board? Impossible," Meya said. "Beriant's tied all three together, board, ownership, and ousting us from the board. Someone delivered a copy of the entire resolution just after the meeting."

"Spider."

"Yes," Meya said unhappily. "And that's the bad part of the news."

"What's the worse?"

"Just under six thousand registered kasirene, and there have been new registrations at between twelve and fifteen daily."

Someone screamed outside, and footsteps pounded along the street. Zimmerman peeked through a space in the curtains.

"The militia's out there," he said and came across the room to stand by Meya's chair. "Where's your mother?"

"Home, with Hart. Ozchan didn't think that he should be left alone."

Zimmerman nodded and seamed his jacket closed, turning toward the door.

"Where are you going?" Meya said, surprised. The colonel looked at her over his shoulder.

"Up to the Tor. It's late and I'm hungry."

"You're not serious. You don't want to go out into that." Meya nodded her head toward the window. "There's some food downstairs somewhere, and we can make up beds here."

"Nonsense." The colonel paused and smiled slightly. "It's not the first war zone I'll have walked through." He went out the door. They listened to his footsteps on the stairs.

"Not all the kasirene will vote for Beriant's plan," Quilla said suddenly. "People like Palen, Keloret, Altemet, Puti, the ones who live here, or in Hoku—"

"We can't count on it. Remember that the kasirene board members disappeared into The Jumble as soon as the meeting was over."

Quilla shook her head. "I don't believe it," she said, believing it, and went back to the book. After a while Meya left the room. Quilla pushed the book away and listened to the sounds of the night.

Hart, wrapped in a dark cloak, stood at the Weaver Street entrance to The Jumble and pressed his back hard against a doorway. Ahead of him The Jumble was dark and full of noise; behind, he could hear shouts and the sounds of splintering wood from Market Square. Two kasirene stood just inside The Jumble, arguing in low voices, and Hart wondered if he could move away from the doorway without being noticed. The kasirene turned abruptly and went back into The Jumble. After a cautious moment, Hart followed them.

He wished, for the first time, that he had spent more time in the kasirene section; now he followed sounds and occasional lights, barely avoiding detection and peering about for a glimpse of Spider. Eventually he reached the clear area in front of The Meeting. Spider stood in a group of kasirene across the dirt forum; a large pack lay at his feet. Hart inched around the area, keeping his eyes on his son. Spider talked and gestured. One of the kasirene squatted suddenly, drew something in the dirt, and gestured. Spider nodded and picked up his pack, and within a minute the group marched away from The Jumble toward the east. Hart bit his lip and followed.

The group stopped within the first line of trees.

"Please come out," someone said in Kasiri. "We know you're following us."

Hart hesitated and stepped into the light. Spider looked at him and nodded once. He handed his pack to one of the kasirene.

"Hold this, Kaën," he said quietly. "I'll be right back." He approached his father and stood before him, his hands resting on his hips. "What do you want?"

"To help you come home now," Hart said. "You can do it now, can't you? I mean, that charade in the square, it's over with. They can't force you to stay."

Spider shook his head. "No, Hart. I told you, I've made my choice."

"You don't have to abide by it," Hart said, pleading. "You were forced into it, weren't you? Listen, we can leave Aerie, they can't touch you then. I understand what you've been through, I don't hold it against you. But you can leave now, you don't have to put up with it anymore."

Spider sighed and put his hands on his father's shoulders. "Hart. Listen to me. I haven't been forced into anything—I'm doing what I think is right. There's nothing to rescue me from, don't you understand that?"

Hart knocked his hands away. "You're my son, damn it. You'll do as I tell you to."

"No. If you won't be reasonable, there's no need to discuss it further."

"Reasonable! Sweet Mother!" He grabbed Spider's shirt and shook the boy. "I will not allow this!" he said harshly. Spider twisted sharply, breaking Hart's hold. He slid his leg between Hart's and tumbled his father to the ground.

"Let me be," Spider said angrily. "I don't care whether you like it or not—I've made my choice and I'll stick with it. I don't care what you believe."

Hart stared up at him. "Who made you?" he said, his voice a harsh whisper. Spider gestured and walked back to the kasirene.

"Who made you do it?" Hart yelled after him. Ignoring him, Spider shouldered his pack and followed the kasirene into the woods.

Hart sat and took a deep, angry breath. The sounds from Haven and The Jumble seemed distant and fierce. He pushed them away from his consciousness and, controlling his anger, began laying logical, vengeful plans.

By the time Zimmerman reached the Tor, Mish was sitting in the living room before a small fire and her face, in the dim light, looked old and tired. But when she turned to look at him, her eyes glinted.

"Bad down there?" she said.

"Yes."

"I won't let it happen," she said, her voice hard. The colonel looked at her, surprised. She poked at the fire with a long stick. "Jason and I built this world, we fought for it, we shaped it, and I won't let it be taken away. I'll see them in hell first, I'll break every damned one of them."

"The kasirene?"

"Of course not. Parallax. There's food in the kitchen."

The colonel paused, trying to find something to say, then turned and walked through the dark dining room to the kitchen. A ready light glowed over one of the ovens. He opened the door to find a covered dish. As he removed it he heard pounding on the front door.

Mish reached it before he did and he grabbed her arm. "Don't open it," he said. "If they were family they'd let themselves in. You don't know who's out there."

She jerked her arm away. "I've never hidden on my planet before, and I'm not going to start now." She pulled the door open.

Kasirene forms filled the doorway. Zimmerman stepped back quickly. Mish opened the door all the way and looked up at them.

"Altemet," she said. "Come in." The kasirene filed into the hall and from the hall to the living room, while Mish snapped lights on and Zimmerman stood with his back against a wall, wishing for the first time in years that he carried a weapon. The kasirene refused to sit. The colonel recognized Altemet, the old one, but could not recognize the others and realized, unhappily, that they all looked alike to him.

"We've come to offer our resignations," one of them said to Mish. Two others nodded. Mish seated herself before the fire and put her hands in her lap.

"Why?"

"I think it's obvious," another one began. "With Beriant's proposal—"

"Do you support it?" Mish demanded.

"Of course not," one said, and the other agreed.

"We'll try to work against it, but we feel that our positions would be—awkward. Being on the board."

Mish shook her head. "Sit down, please. You're making my neck hurt. If you resign from the board, you'll be giving the impression that you do support Beriant. And you really will turn this nonsense into a racial conflict, which I don't think it is."

Altemet arranged himself on some cushions. "I told them so," he said.

"We felt that we had to make the offer."

Zimmerman relaxed his shoulders slightly. Mish, in the midst of the huge kasirene, looked entirely calm.

"If you believe," she said carefully, "that Aerie-Kennerin runs well the way things are, if you believe that we've made a good life here for everyone, then the best thing you can do is keep your official positions and talk to everyone you can. Argue with them. Make your case. Try to sway them. We can't do that, not if Beriant's drawn racial lines, and he has. But you can. You can do it for all of us, for everyone on this planet." She paused. "You know that Parallax is in back of this?"

Altemet gestured. "Beriant is not saying that, but it must be true. He talks about support from outside, and since I don't think he means the Federation, Parallax is all that's left." The kasir paused. "I assume that the Parallax crew is being guarded through all of this."

"Yes. Tatha went down after the meeting, she's commanding the guard herself."

The kasirene looked at each other and Zimmerman's shoulders tightened again.

"Perhaps," Mish was saying, "Tatha herself could help us. She spends a fair amount of time in The Jumble and seems to be on good terms with the kasirene. Do you think that folk would listen if she talked?" Mish looked at them and frowned, then stared at one kasir. "Puti, what is it?"

"She does spend time in The Jumble," Puti said, looking down at her lap. Her hands were tangled together. "She spends most of her time there gambling. With Beriant."

Mish stared at her and her lips moved.

"She also went to To'an Tebetet, ten days before Spider's Choosing," Puti said. "Some people say she's taken money from Beriant to do things for him. And Beriant has met with Barranca, he was seen."

"During the exercise time," Mish said. Puti nodded. Mish stood abruptly. "Jes is down at the port, he went to check on his shuttle. And if Tatha's—" She went rapidly toward the door.

"Don't." One of the kasirene jumped up. "I'll go."

"Nonsense, Gaeva. You're from Hoku, you don't know the way." Mish tried to push the kasir aside but Gaeva carefully picked her up and carried her back to the chair. "I'll go," the kasir repeated, and left the room. Zimmerman quietly moved forward and took a chair where he could see them all. The colonel cleared his throat and they all looked at him.

"I assume," he said, "that this Beriant business has

been going on for quite a while, and that you knew about it." They nodded. "Why didn't you tell the terrans?"

"We didn't think it would go far," Altemet said to him. The old kasir moved uncomfortably among his cushions. "Beriant's been spouting off for years. He had a small following, generally young people, but not too many. And when it started to get larger, when his influence grew, we thought that we could control it, and him." Altemet gestured. "Obviously, we couldn't. We're trying to counteract him."

"Will you succeed?" Mish said.

"I don't know." Altemet looked at Puti, and she told them about Palen's research, about the arrival of the Ska'felet, and about the journey Palen had undertaken, towing the repulsive alien about the planet, talking to kasirene.

"We're not sure how much good it's done," Puti said. "Beriant hasn't formally announced that he's looking to Parallax for help, but if we can tie them together obviously, openly—"

"You can," Mish said. "Through Tatha." She stood and moved toward the door.

"You're not going out," Zimmerman said, standing. She looked at him.

"No. I'm going to my office and I'm going to locate Pixie Hirem. Tatha's just been relieved of command. I want her locked up until we find out just how much damage she's done."

"And then?"

"I think that's our business, colonel," Mish said. She walked out of the room. Zimmerman turned to the kasirene, and one by one they looked away from him.

IT WAS STILL LIGHT WHEN JES ARRIVED AT Havensport, and he went immediately to the shuttle. It was secure in its dock and locked tight. He let himself in, slipped into the pilot's web, and tapped the board for a total readout. Only when he had run it through twice, the second time with backup details, was he satisfied —the shuttle could, if necessary, leave at a moment's notice. He closed the board and locked up behind him, tugged at his mustache and looked across at *Blind Chance,* then up at the sky. There was another hour, at least, until sunset. He glanced across the port to the far warehouse where a few figures lounged about the door. Tatha would be in there, he thought, and hesitated a moment longer before walking to *Blind Chance* and boarding. He didn't want to see the Theresan anyway.

The Theresan, however, wanted to see him. When he finished the check of *Blind Chance* and was satisfied that the sloop, too, was fully fueled and spaceworthy, he locked the main hatch and found one of Tatha's militia waiting at the bottom of the ramp. The man touched a finger to his collar in salute as Jes descended.

"Commander wants to see you," he said. Jes nodded and followed him across the port. Dusk settled and he heard loud noises from Haven. The man lifted his head briefly, then touched his Albia-Markins and kept walking.

Tatha sat at the table in a corner of the warehouse, surrounded by the crew of *Mi Estancia.* A pile of rectangular black and white stones littered the table before them. She looked up as she scooped the stones into her hands, saw Jes, and nodded.

"In a moment," she called, and bent her head over her hands. Jes came closer. Tatha shook the stones and threw them across the table, and everyone bent forward. Then Tatha crowed and reached for a pile of fremarks. The people around her looked variously amused and surprised, save for one man, who looked very angry. Tatha pushed her chair away from the table and stood.

"TauCaptain Jes Kennerin," she said, waving her arm, "this is tauCaptain Emilio Barranca of the Parallax merchant ship *Mi Estancia*, Second Arista Blake, Engine Mate Nazumi Karaen, Crew N'Hoste, Crew Nataste. I'm sure you're all delighted to know each other, you've so little in common."

"I would like a chance to win that back," Barranca said, ignoring Jes and waving his hand at Tatha's bulging hip pouch. She shook her head.

"Perhaps tomorrow, tauCaptain. Or the day after. We'll be seeing a fair amount of each other before you leave Aerie. Jes, I want to talk with you."

Barranca continued to ignore him, while the other crew bent to the game again. Tatha exchanged a few words with the armed guards at the door and led Jes outside.

"What did you think of Barranca's complexion?" Tatha asked, as though not interested. They walked side by side away from the warehouse.

"His complexion? I don't see what that has—"

"Humor me, tauCaptain." Something much like a gunshot sounded distantly. They both stopped and looked in the deepening gloom toward Haven. "We don't have much time," Tatha said. "His face, tauCaptain."

Jes frowned. "He seemed—handsome enough, I guess."

"Not the right answer. You're trained to see details, and sometimes you actually do. Think, Jes."

"His skin is very smooth," Jes said, and stopped suddenly. "Very smooth."

"Exactly." She lifted her hands and examined her claws. "No webscarring at all. Which means?"

"Either that he's very new to a spacer's life, or that he's never been down to the pit engines. I can't really see a tauCaptain never going into the engines."

"That's because I don't think he's a tauCaptain, tauCaptain. No webscarring, no signs of recognition when I mention various spacer terms, minimal medical knowledge."

"Parallax doesn't encourage that. Ozchan said that his Certificate has the initial citation."

"And that's all, no updates, nothing further. Even if

Parallax doesn't require that, the Federation does, a new citation for every two tau-years." She stopped, midway between the warehouse and the sloop, and they faced each other. "I think that Blake's the tauCaptain, that Barranca's a Parallax agent, that they were deliberately sent here in that disintegrating ship to infiltrate Aerie, that they brought Zimmerman along in hopes that his presence would provide a wedge to get them into the Tor or into Haven. Barranca's met with Beriant and Beriant's supporters. Doing his job."

"But why haven't you told Mish or Quilla?"

"Because it's irrelevant now. What is relevant is that Barranca has further orders. He doesn't have them on him, but from things that he's said I think they do exist somewhere, either in the computer banks on *Mi Estancia* or even, possibly, in NewHome. We have to get them."

Jes stepped away from her. "Why?"

Tatha sighed impatiently. More noise came from Haven. "I think Parallax is running way ahead of schedule, much faster than they expected to. Mostly because of the kasirene, but still—and if we have some knowledge of their eventual plans, I think that we can convince the kasirene to repudiate them, too. I think that knowledge can be found in Barranca's further orders. We must have them, Jes. And we must have them immediately."

"And what do you want me to do?"

"Take me up to *Mi Estancia*. If necessary, take me to NewHome System." She smiled, her teeth bright in the dusky-grayness of her face. "And I promise that this time, I won't even think of asking you to kill someone."

Jes hesitated. The port was completely dark, save for the bank of lights that bathed the warehouse walls with light and a small, yellowish light glowing in the comshack. Over the hill, something in Aerie was burning—its dull red glow stained the dark sky.

"God's love, Kennerin," Tatha said urgently, "we haven't any time at all. Will you or won't you?"

Still he hesitated. "Are you running away?" he said suddenly. "Are you trying to leave, just when things get tough?"

"Am I—" Tatha said, bewildered. "Daren's up the hill with your family. If I were running away, do you think I'd leave him behind?"

"He wouldn't be harmed."

"That's irrelevant, you pigheaded idiot. He wouldn't be with *me*, do you understand?" She took a deep breath. "I do very few things for other people, tauCaptain. I do many things for myself. But I do all things for Daren. If you think for a moment that I'm working for the salvation of this backwash mudball for your sake, you'd better forget it. I'm doing this because I want Daren to grow up here, and if it means having to save your stinking asses for you, then I'll do it. Are we going or not?"

Jes remembered Daren and Tatha chasing each other around the base of a kaedo in the light rain. "We're going," he said quickly, without stopping to examine his decision. "We'll take the *Chance*—if we have to go to NewHome, she'll be better than the shuttle." He paused. "Anything special you want to bring along?"

Tatha nodded to the Albia-Markins slung across her shoulders and raised her clawed hands slightly. "I think I'm prepared, tauCaptain," she said. Jes led the way, almost running, toward the tausloop.

When Gaeva arrived at the port she had to dive behind a wall as protection against the roar of the sloop's engines. *Blind Chance* skimmed down the runway, a silver shadow in the night, and angled smoothly into the sky. Gaeva picked herself off, brushed dirt from her fur, and hurried to the warehouse.

Pixie arrived half an hour later to discover that Barranca and his crew were under a heavy guard, and had been all day and all evening; that *Blind Chance* was missing, and that both Tatha and Jes had disappeared. It could not be determined whether Tatha had or had not forced the tauCaptain to take her away, but one of the guards remembered that the Theresan was armed with an Albia-Markins rifle and the tauCaptain was not armed at all. Barranca seemed as puzzled by these events as did the Aerites. Pixie dashed to the comshack and opened a line to the repairs crew ship servicing *Mi Estancia*.

"That's totally impossible," the crew boss said angrily, obviously awakened from a sound sleep. "You've no idea how big this thing is—it's a monster, Commander Hirem. We couldn't possibly guard every millimeter of it. And even if we could," the crew boss went on, overriding Pixie's objections, "we couldn't. We had to excise all the seals today, there's no atmosphere in there. We'd have to take the entire repairs crew and outfit them in Barre harnesses. First, we don't have enough harnesses, and second, I'm not going to jeopardize my crew or my job by running the Barre suits dry, just to guard a hunk of tin. Besides, they can't take it anywhere. We disconnected the main drive engines before we started the tune-up; this Bugeater isn't going anywhere for a while."

"Tune-up?" Pixie said, baffled. "You're tuning it up? You're just supposed to slap some repairs on and get the thing out of our system."

The crew boss shrugged. "So? It doesn't take any extra time. Mish Kennerin okayed it, said to add it to the bill. And I don't like doing half-ass jobs, commander. If I'm going to fix something, I'm going to fix it right. And fixing it right includes letting my crew get a solid night's sleep, is that understood?"

Pixie cursed. "All right. But would you at least let me know if anything happens up there? If you notice anyone or anything?"

"Sweet Mother," the boss said, exasperated. "I'd do that in any event. Do you think I'm dumb as a knocker?" The screen went blank. Pixie sat back, shook her shoulders to loosen them, and reached for an Aerie line. She wasn't surprised when one of her people turned from the tracking screen to say that the sensors had been tampered with and they could not pick up any trace of *Blind Chance* at all. Pixie had expected that.

DECCA LAY IN THE LARGE BED, LISTENING TO the sounds of incoherent shouting in the streets outside, and put her arms around Sandro.

"You're not going out into that," she repeated. He turned angrily in her arms. She refused to let him go. "The sloop's fine, nobody's said anything about fighting at the port."

"But Jes will—"

"Please," she said. Her voice caught. "If I can't go home—" She started crying.

Surprised, Sandro turned awkwardly and put his arms around her. She buried her face in his neck, weeping as helplessly as a child. He murmured comforts in Spanish and felt like crying himself.

They'd arrived at Hetch's house, where Sandro now lived alone, just after the meeting finished, and he had spent the majority of the evening refusing to let her go home. The increasing noise finally convinced her, despite all her brave and angry plans to march through the streets of her town, up her road, across her stream, and to her house. At first the house had seemed a safe refuge, especially after Decca called Tor, town hall, and hospital to assure herself that everyone else was safe. Now the house seemed terribly isolated, a vulnerable hiding place set amid dark and suddenly dangerous streets. Sandro murmured endearments into Decca's pale hair; the fabric of her jacket felt rough under his hands.

"It's all falling apart," she said through her tears. "My home, everything—it's going away."

"Not yet," Sandro murmured, holding her close. "Not yet." He remember gaunt faces on Marquez Landing, remembered the two times they'd had to expand the fence around the graveyard and the one time they'd not even bothered, just knocked the fence down and planted the dead in an unmarked field. Remembered his brother staggering into the house, holding a faceless body that Sandro would not, at first, believe to be that of his father.

"Not here," he said. "I swear it won't happen here."

Decca shook her head against his chest. Her sobs lessened as she coughed and cried herself to sleep. Sandro rested his cheek against her hair and listened to the increasing insanity outside. He didn't want to go out into it, carrying sword and buckler, to defend the good and true and right. He wanted to lie in bed with Decca, grateful for her sleep, and to ponder things. Going out and demolishing kasirene would do no good; neither would going out and demolishing terrans. The solution did not lay in violence, he thought; not in shining swords and impossible ideals. One foot at a time, do what must be done. Carefully, slowly, logically, dispassionately; all the things he was not good at. But there were others who were, others who knew the problem more deeply than he, who were more likely than he to generate the proper, realistic solutions. He would find these others and put himself under their direction, accept their wisdom and try to acquire some of his own. He nodded, neither pleased nor displeased with the decision, and looked down at Decca's fair head. She wriggled against him. He said her name until she woke up.

"We have to get married," he said.

"Married?" She sat up and pushed hair from her face. "Why?"

"Because of that." He gestured toward the window as a particularly loud noise shattered the stillness. They heard the sound of voices shouting. "Because these are dangerous and unsettled times. What if you're pregnant?"

"What if I am?"

He sat up against the headboard and looked at her. Her face was silhouetted against the moonslit window. "Given a choice, I'd rather you were my widow than I your dead lover."

"Oh, don't be foolish." She turned to lean against the headboard beside him. "You're not going to die and neither am I." Someone fired a shot directly under their window, and they clung to each other. "No, don't get up. If they think nobody's here—"

"They'll come inside," Sandro said trying to push her away.

"No. They're fighting out there, but not looting. Not the Aerites, not the kasirene. Stay here. You're more likely to get hurt running around than you are staying put."

There were no further noises outside. Sandro let Decca tug him back to bed.

"If I marry you," she said suddenly, "I'll have conditions."

"Oh? Such as?"

"Such as, if we're married, you're not to go rushing into trouble. You're not to go rescuing maidens in distress, and all that other nonsense. You're not to go blowing up grabstations for no reason whatsoever. You're to behave like a rational, reasonable adult."

Sandro thought for a moment about content and form. "I have to do what I think is right," Sandro said finally, and Decca nodded.

"Of course. We all do. But there are ways of doing

things reasonably and ways of doing things foolishly. If we get married, I'm not going to spend all my time worrying about you getting into some dumb scrape. The universe is dangerous enough without going out looking for it."

"I don't like being nagged."

"You won't be. You might be yelled at a lot, but it won't be nagging." She touched his hand with her fingertips. "The Kennerins don't spawn mush-minded women, Sandro."

"I know," he said gloomily. "Are there other conditions?"

"Yes. You'll have some too, I imagine. But for now, that's the main one. I want to marry you, Sandro. Not your corpse."

He shuddered, and she grabbed his hand.

"I'm sorry," she said. "I didn't mean it that way." She paused. "You can say no, if you want to."

"Why should I?" He stopped to listen to the sound of wood being splintered somewhere nearby. "You think there will be time tomorrow?"

"Time for what?"

"To get married, of course."

Decca was silent for a minute. "I don't see why not," she said calmly. "Things should be quieter tomorrow, and I'd imagine it will be safe enough."

Sandro licked his lips. "Do you think, maybe, you could pretend some enthusiasm for it?"

"Oh, Sandro," she said, turned to him, and started crying again. And Sandro, dispensing with dignity, started to cry himself.

∿

TRAVELING WITH THE SKA'FELET WAS ALmost impossible. It complained about walking and complained about sailing; it complained about the routes they took during the day and complained about the places they slept at night. The weather, the food, the shelters, and the clothing offended it deeply, and Palen stopped counting the number of times that she felt the need to drown the damned thing, or fling it over a cliff, or simply take its repulsive body and pound it flat.

But the alien fulfilled the terms of its contract, punctiliously if not with courtesy. And as time passed and islands fell away behind it, the Ska'felet developed an interest in what it was doing, and would sit up all night around a kasirene fire while Palen translated, answering questions and countering objections with an increasing passion which, generally, caused it to salivate. It sprayed its opinions damply about the room, and Palen, watching, hugged herself and muttered silent prayers.

It was the Ska'felet who pointed out that, with the Kennerins off the board, the terrans would soon leave Aerie, for they would see kasirene control as a threat against themselves—which was what, Palen pointed out, Beriant expected. With the terrans gone, who was to ship the sap to processing, and from processing to the markets? Not the kasirene—there were not enough kasirene in the space fleet and not enough ships converted to kasirene body structure. And that left only Parallax. The Ska'felet would reiterate its planet's history, growing more and more animated, and the argument would last far into the night. The next morning Palen and the Ska'felet would be on their way again, leaving behind a muttering kasirene village or tribe. Some kasirene, convinced by the Ska'felet's oratory or Palen's comments, wanted to come with them, but Palen pointed out that she needed to move quickly and could not guarantee to feed any additonal travelers. She suggested that instead the kasirene go to Haven and register to vote, if they had not done so already, and that they take time, on their trip to To'an Cault, to speak with any other kasirene that they met, to spread the word of the Ska'felet's experiences and Palen's theories and predictions.

The further they journeyed from the Cault-Betes islands, the easier it was to convince the tribes of their position. Most of these kasirene had never left their own islands and the presence of terrans on Aerie affected them not at all, which pleased them. But the Ska'felet and Palen convinced them that, under Parallax, their distant islands would be invaded, that no land on Aerie would be allowed to exist without its burden of *Zimania*

plantations, overseers, and workers. "You'd be safe on
Eiret or Eriant," she told them, and her listeners frowned,
thinking about the frozen northern and southern wastes.

She sometimes wondered if she was doing any good
at all. Sitting amidships in a fisher tribe's outrigger, tossing over the waves while the Ska'felet groaned and vomited into the sea, she thought about Haven, about what
life might be like without the Kennerins; thought about
the kasirene she sent to The Jumble to be exposed to
Beriant's continued, polished harangues. There had not
been a day of complete rest, or a night without arguments
and discussions, since leaving The Jumble two weeks before, and she had covered the islands with astonishing
speed. On To'an Ako she stood on the westernmost shore
of the westernmost outlying island and realized that it
was time to go back. To'an Elt and To'an Peles remained
unvisited; the strange, morose kasirene who inhabited ba
Eiret and ba Eriant would not leave their islands until
winter, and would not come to vote in any event.

Turning east, she and the Ska'felet began the return
journey, trying to find tribes they had missed on the outward trip. And now Palen learned that she and her alien
were not the only missionaries traveling the islands; Beriant's followers had sent emissaries. Large groups of
kasirene moved toward To'an Cault, each group fervently holding to its own idea of the future. Sometimes,
meeting, they argued and fought. Palen listened, sickened, to accounts of quick battles among the tribes. The
traditional kasirene method of dealing with conflict was
to go away; there were enough islands for everyone and
to fight was to break the circle. Palen cursed Beriant,
realizing that she, too, contributed to the chaos. She stood
suddenly and poured dirt over the fire in the circle. The
Ska'felet looked at her, surprised, and forgot to complain.

"We've lost the center," Palen said bitterly. "Now we
spin without guidance. We are lost, whatever we do."

The Ska'felet had the sense to remain silent. But the
next day, when they found a new tribe, Palen pursued
her arguments with as much force and conviction as she
had before, and so they traveled eastward, while the
center of belief slid away.

The day after the meeting, Haven was unnaturally si-

lent and the streets were deserted. The damage was far
less than Mish had feared; a few windows broken, a few
walls torn down—the main damage had been to the
temporary bleachers and dais in Market Square, some of
which had been burned, and the tables and chairs on
Kohl's wide front porch were splintered. The damage
to the participants had been equally light. Ozchan reported two broken arms, some number of bruises, split
lips, scraped knuckles, sore muscles—Aerites, not ac-
customed to fighting, tended to do it poorly. The spiritual
damage was far more extensive and harder to assess.

Mish, accompanied by Colonel Zimmerman and Tabor,
walked through Haven. A few Aerites worked outside
their houses or shops, cleaning up the debris; most of
them stayed inside. The school was dark and deserted.
Mertika and her day manager roamed the square, collecting the remains of their furniture and stacking it beside the beerhall.

"It will make firewood," Mertika said wearily, pushing
hair from her forehead. "Something should be done
about those, though." She nodded toward the tattered
bleachers. "They'll make firewood, too."

Mish stared at the bleachers, shocked, and although
she tried to tell herself that the Aerites would not set fire
to their own town, she knew that Mertika might be right.
After the previous night, no assumption could remain
unquestioned.

Spring planting was not yet completed, but the fields
stood empty. Mish looked at them in rising anger and
stormed back through Haven to the Town Hall. Ignoring
Quilla and Meya, she climbed to the third floor of the
building and jerked at the bell rope. The discordant jangle of the warning bell filled the valley. Meya came upstairs, looked oddly at her mother, and put her hands on
the rope. She continued ringing the bell while Mish
marched out of the town hall and back to Market Square.

She stood on the ruined dais while the square filled
with distrustful Aerites. Many of them were rudely
armed, carrying sticks or clubs or hoes. The militia
calmly confiscated scythes and knives. The kasirene
gathered to the left and the terrans to the right, and
Mish, seeing the division, pressed her lips together tightly
and waited for the bell to stop ringing. Dene Beletes sent
her assistants scurrying about the periphery of the square,

and as the bell subsided she handed Mish a microphone.

"It won't work very well," the engineer said. "But it shouldn't electrocute you."

Mish took the microphone, nodded, and flicked it on. She didn't mention the night before, or the meeting: she told them that the fields needed planting, that the already planted fields needed cultivation, that there were hundreds of collecting buckets to attach to the *Zimania* and dozens more to double-check; that school was open, that preparations had to be made for regular market day, on the morrow. That there was work to be done. Altemet and the kasirene board members moved to stand in the gap between the two races, and after a moment the terran board members, and some others, came to stand beside them. Gradually, with some muttering, the Aerites of both races moved off to the business of the day. Mish looked at the bleachers and settled her shoulders, then asked for volunteers. Terrans and kasirene together, under her direction, worked not to tear the bleachers down but to rebuild them.

"Haven shall not burn," Mish said stubbornly, into the microphone. The words became a muttered catch-phrase, said as people worked in town or fields or plantations. To say it and to hear an agreement was to find a friend —with distrust the kasirene and terrans worked awkwardly together, tenuously bound by four words.

"Haven is not necessary," Beriant said, hearing Mish's words. If his supporters agreed they did not say so in public. Beriant's statement had little circulation, but he shrugged it off as he went among the constantly arriving kasirene, speaking his case.

To his surprise, a large number of them refused to listen.

For a moment, coming in out of the dark with Koyu at his side, Jared thought the living room at the Tor looked no different than before. Some yellow-globed lamps glowed, augmenting the more ruddy light from the fireplace. Mish sat in her chair near the flames, her hands in her lap; Colonel Zimmerman sat on the footstool in front of her, talking. Mish smiled and stirred the fire with a poker. Meya and Ozcha sat together on the couch, their three children filling their laps; Dahl turned from the liquor cabinet to offer a glass to Kayman Olet. The

preacher took it and offered it in turn to Mim. Quilla,
Decca, and Tabor gathered by the window, and Sandro,
standing alone in a corner, moved from one foot to another and wrung his hands behind his back. Jared was
willing to bet that his shirt was damp with sweat. Smiling, he and Koyu crossed the room to stand on either
side of the nervous Second.

"A preacher?" Jared said. Sandro nodded nervously.
"It seemed—well, more fitting. Traditional." He licked
his lips nervously and refused a glass of wine. "I'll get
drunk and make a fool of myself," he muttered. "I'm
going to make a fool of myself anyway."

"I doubt it," Koyu said. "You know the usual marriage, don't you? You just tell people that you're married,
and sometimes you register it in the town hall, but you
don't have to." Koyu smiled and waved around the
room. "This is almost ceremonial. I'm impressed."

"Well, back home this would be shocking," Sandro replied. "Back home, you get married in the cathedral in
Ciudad Garcia, with two priests and a choir and flowers
and everything, and you can't see the bride for a month
beforehand, and you have to memorize all sorts of stuff
that goes on forever and you have to say it in front of
everyone in the middle of the cathedral with everyone
looking at you and waiting for you to make a mistake."
He grinned suddenly and took the wine after all. "And
there are some old folk who remember weddings not
for who married whom, but for who messed up the words,
or what went wrong, or what should have been done, or
—*Jesus y Maria*, at least I don't have to go through
that."

Jared looked across the room toward Decca and
stopped smiling. She was wearing the dress that Sandro
had given Quilla, and looked lovely and strange and
even more distant from him than before.

"Does she still hate me?" he said without thinking, and
flushed quickly. "I'm sorry, Sandro. That's a hell of a
thing to say at someone's wedding."

"I don't think she hates you," Sandro said, looking
confused. "Why should she—she's never said anything—"

"It's not important," Jared said, feeling Koyu's reprov-
ing look. "We had an argument, and—" Koyu stepped
on his foot.

"My dearly beloved," Koyu said, "has a wonderful habit of being entirely dense sometimes. Of course there's nothing wrong between Jared and Decca, just, well you know how it is with siblings. These things always blow over."

"Of course," Sandro said, relieved. "I used to argue with my brother all the time, it wasn't anything to worry about."

Hart came in and went over to Decca. He looked trim and energetic, but his face looked like a mask. He kissed her forehead and they stood talking together for a moment while Quilla and Tabor found places to sit. Then Kayman Olet drifted over to the fireplace and Decca came casually to the center of the room. Sandro wiped his hands down the seams of his pants and joined her, and the room quieted. Jared watched the preacher curiously.

Olet had come to Haven for the election, bringing his children with him. This was the first time Jared had seen him in over two years, and Jared was surprised in the changes he saw. The pinched look had fled from Olet's face, leaving behind a tinge of sadness and a look of peace; his eyes were serene and the incipient hollows of his cheeks were gone. His pleasant voice was mild and assured. He talked about unsettled times and the value of hope; he talked about accepting change and the ties of love that make acceptance easier. He talked about the immutability of the seasons, talked about continuity, and talked about inevitability. Jared remembered that Olet was said to have met his wife just before Hetch's death, and while Jared did not know what they'd discussed, he thought, now, that the discussion had brought Olet peace. Beryl would stay in space, leading her chosen life, and Olet had been made free to choose himself. He appeared to have chosen a peaceful resignation, and Jared was suddenly profoundly grateful. He reached over to hold Koyu's hand as Decca and Sandro said their quiet, personal things to each other, then they kissed and the room was filled with happy laughter. The chaos below the hill, in Haven, was forgotten.

Mim passed around delicacies and Dahl passed around the wine. Zimmerman, balancing a plate on his knee and a glass in his hand, chattered with Mish. She took bites from the food on his plate. As soon as Quilla

and Tabor were finished kissing Decca and Sandro, she
stood up and hugged them both tightly.

"Don't be silly, I never cry at anything," she said, her
eyes bright, and surrendered them to the rest of the family. Jared watched from his corner, feeling left out. Koyu,
after looking at him sideways, marched over to the couple and stood talking with them a moment before Decca
smiled and kissed him. Jared stared miserably into his
wineglass.

"Well?"

He looked up. Decca stood before him, her hands on
her hips and a scowl on her face.

"Aren't you going to say anything?" she demanded.
"Or did you just come up here to drink?"

"I didn't," he said angrily. "If you didn't want me to
come, you should have told me so."

She made an exasperated noise. "You, Jared Grif
Kennerin, are damn near as stubborn and infuriating as
—as—"

"You are," Jared supplied. "You look lovely. I'm very
happy for you. I hope you're married a thousand years
and have half a hundred children, all of them with sweet
tempers."

You are a totally impossible prig, a voice said in his
mind, with such tones of love and impatience that he
blinked.

Decca?

This time she looked surprised. He felt the sudden
disorientation of her mind. Then she smiled as an echoing smile touched his own lips. They fell into each other's
arms, laughing.

"I'm glad that's over with," Quilla said, holding out
two glasses of wine. Decca put one arm around her
brother and the other around Sandro. Jared looked at
them, then raised his head to smile at Koyu across the
room. The world seemed safe again.

Emilio Barranca, according to Pixie, didn't seem affected by the goings-on in Haven one way or another. He
took his exercise with the rest of his crew, wrote at
length on the paper supplied to him by the guards, and
spent the evenings playing the stone game. Each day Pixie
gave him a report on the repairs of the Bugeater and
each day he ritually complained about the length of time

it was taking. When told about Tatha's seeming defection, he shrugged.

"I never trusted her," he declared. "Besides, she stole stuff from me." Pixie doubted that. Barranca spent the evening in quiet conversation with his crew, and Pixie doubled the guard.

Barranca treated the kasirene in the militia with courtesy, but disparaged them when they were out of sight. Pixie made sure that the kasirene overheard some of his comments, but couldn't tell whether it did any good or not. And Colonel Zimmerman came down to the comshack twice daily, to send urgent messages to Althing Green. He always emerged looking sour, and one afternoon three days after the meeting he came out of the shack looking disgusted.

"I'm not to com on Federation expense anymore," he said to Pixie. "They say I'm wasting fremarks. They've pulled my com account."

Pixie frowned. "Mish subscribes to the Green reports. You can look at them."

"There's a difference between watching and lobbying," Zimmerman said, and went away. But he was back the next morning, and the morning after, using his own personal account to pay for his expensive coms. Pixie reported this to Mish, who frowned.

"I can use my own funds anyway I want to," Zimmerman said at dinner that night.

"Inflexible neutrality," Hart muttered, without humor. The colonel ignored him.

Hart refused to go into Haven but made numerous trips to Havensport. He was there when the repairs boss on *Mi Estancia* reported, the day after *Blind Chance*'s departure from Aerie that someone had been through the bridge and officers' quarters during the night, but nothing seemed to be missing. Hart was also in the comshack the next day when something unidentified left Eagle System through the garb. He nodded to himself, expressionless, and said nothing.

Speculations about Tatha's role in Aerie's current crisis were common at the Tor, and more evidence mounted against her. Hart declined to participate, keeping to himself his knowledge of Tatha's plans, refusing to divulge the information that might, at the least, serve to cast her actions in a different light, or serve to provide for her the

benefit of the doubt. He did not doubt that she had acted
to good ends, or that she was not in league, in any way,
with either Beriant or Parallax. But she had taken his
son from him and for this he would not forgive her.
When she returned to Aerie, if she returned to Aerie, he
would exact his revenge; nothing she had done or could
do would keep him from it. His revenge would be a
public one: only he could corroborate the things that
Tatha might say in her defense, without his backing her
statements would be no more than unsupported allega-
tions. And he would not provide that backing. Let the
Aerites punish her as they saw fit—they might even,
in the long run, be right.

She had betrayed him, he thought with sudden clarity,
lifting his head from a microscope. Betraying him, who
else might she betray?

THE FLIGHT TO *MI ESTANCIA* HAD BEEN SIM-
ple, and only the hours of waiting alone in *Blind Chance*
while Tatha explored the empty Bugeater were hard. Jes
paced the bridge restlessly, keeping an eye on the scanner
banks and trying to visualize Tatha's progress through
the large ship. Two hours, three hours—he had approached *Mi Estancia* during a time when, he knew, the
repairs crew would be aboard their own vessel and
asleep, but time was running short and Tatha had still not
returned. He wondered if the repairs crew had left a
guard on the ship. He wondered if the guard was dead.

One of the scanners blipped quietly; something was
coming up the grapple line. Jes punched up a visual and
saw Tatha, globed in the shimmer of a Barre suit, moving
along the line toward the sloop's airlock. He watched her
for a moment; she seemed calm and uninjured, and her
close-fitting brown coversuit was neat; her lips moved,

their corners curved slightly upward. She was still singing when she came through the airlock.

"Did you get what you wanted?" Jes said.

Tatha unclasped the last straps of the Barre harness and folded it neatly. "No. Not entirely." She glanced at Jes. "Are you eager for a jump into adventure, tauCaptain? A little skulking in a dangerous place? It shouldn't be too unsettling, you've been there before." She slid into the navigator's web and popped something into the crystal housing.

Jes stood behind the pilot's web, his fingers tangled in its lines. "Are you sure we have to go? Do you know what's there?"

"Yes and perhaps. Come now, where's your sense of adventure? You can play Tri-Captain Delta Three this time, if you want. I'll be the Contestor and together, my love, we'll conquer galaxies." She looked up at him, smiling. "It's getting late, Kennerin. I don't think I was spotted on the Bugeater, but I don't think it's wise to wait around for confirmation." She spun the web around to face the controls and locked it in place. As Jes slid into his own webbing, she began humming quietly.

The grapples slid into their housings and *Blind Chance* drifted away from the dark bulk of the Bugeater. He coaxed a minimal thrust from the donkey engines and watched the screens as the skin of the Parallax ship passed by, valleys and hills and planes, as big as a small island. Tatha sang to herself, her eyes closed, and Jes slid the pit engines into engagement and banked away from Aerie. He felt slightly disoriented and glanced at the Theresan, expecting her to be wearing a sling.

"Singing," Jes said, "the Tri-Captain sped into battle, confident of the outcome. Only justice could ultimately prevail, for even the legions of evil can not conquer the Truth."

Tatha laughed, surprised and delighted. "But you're the Tri-Captain, tauCaptain, remember? I am but your humble and loyal servitor, ready as always to return a quip, hold back the enemy, or provide covering fire while you do battle with the archvillain."

"I think you've confused our roles." Jes fixed the course to Eagle Grab in the computer and opened the locks of his webbing. "I gave up being the Tri-Captain years ago, being unsuited for the role."

"And I am? Defender of the faith? Protector of the innocent? Champion of purity?" She shook her head, still amused. "It's a gray universe, Jes, and you keep trying to make it either all white or all black. These slides between being a devil and being an angel are making me dizzy. I wish you wouldn't do them."

"I don't," he muttered. "I just keep trying to figure out who you are."

"Perhaps if you watched more and thought less, you'd be more successful," she said, and went into his cabin. Jes morosely contemplated the control panel. When she came back to the bridge she was wearing a Parallax uniform shirt over her bodysuit.

"Stole it from Barranca," she said comfortably, sitting in the web again. "Think it becomes me?"

"No." He eyed it suspiciously. "I still don't understand what you're up to, or why you're doing all of this."

She grimaced. "I told you. How many times do you want me to repeat? You keep checking my story, waiting for me to make a mistake, as though you think I'm lying. Do you?"

"I don't know. I want to believe you, but—"

She leaned toward him, cupped his chin in her palm, and forced him to face her. "I've never lied to you, Jessie," she said calmly. "I told you that I wanted a home, and that's true. I told you that I'd found one, and that's true. I told you that I'm fighting for Aerie because I want to stay there, to raise Daren there, to make my life there. That's all true. I can't go home again, and I'm no longer sure that I want to—there's enough and more than enough for me where I am. And if I must fight to keep it, I'll fight." She smiled suddenly. "Theresans are used to fighting for their homes."

She dropped her hand. Jes continued to face her, searching for something beyond her silver fur and blue eyes. "More than enough?" he repeated. "You have a home—do you have a family?"

"I have Daren."

He shook his head. She turned away from him and looked at the screens. "Possibilities and realities, Jes. Why do we always argue?"

"You told me, once, that you could read emotions in our faces."

"When I want to. Sometimes I don't want to."

He turned away then and silence filled the bridge. The grab approached, and he beamed a request signal and warmed the Cohen-Albrecht Effect Drives. Tatha watched him in silence. He slipped *Blind Chance* into the coils, killed the pit engines, and opened the effect drives just as the disorientation of the transition faded. The sloop skipped out of the grab and into tau.

"You make it look like dancing," Tatha said. Jes turned away from the unexpected compliment.

"Practice," he replied. He programmed the computer for NewHome Grab and stood up. "Four hours," he said. Tatha nodded. When he returned to the bridge she was singing again. He stood by the companionway, listening, then went into his cabin quietly and came out with his flute. He put it to his lips and fingered it silently for a moment, before sliding into her melody. She turned, surprised, and finished the song, but he took the melody and spun variations on it, filling the bridge with music. He took the flute from his lips and looked at her and she turned away from him.

"Can you read emotions in my face?" she said. He came across the bridge quickly and squatted beside her, looking into her eyes. Finally he took a deep breath and rocked back.

"Do you?" he said.

"I don't know." She paused and tilted her head slightly. "I'm willing to give it a chance."

He started to say something, but she put her fingers against his lips. "This will sound odd, coming from me," she whispered, "but you talk too much."

He drew back sharply, saw the gleam in her eyes, and laughed. They kissed quickly, almost tentatively, and when Jes dropped into his web again he realized that he was not feeling the overwhelming thrill that he had, before, associated with love. Instead he was filled with a deep and solid certainty, a sense of an infinity of time and occasion. He didn't yet know who Tatha was, and to some extent he didn't really want to know, not entirely, not immediately. Not all the questions would be answered, and this seemed more than right. He smiled at her, feeling his shoulders relaxing against the lace of the webbing, and watched the easy curve of her lips as she smiled back.

"Teach me that song," he said. "Teach me the words, and what they mean."

Tatha closed her eyes, still smiling, and sang. *"Western wind, when wilt thou blow . . ."*

Half an hour from NewHome Grab the computer chimed, interrupting the music. Jes slid his flute under his belt and leaned to the board. He beamed the grab request, and Tatha nodded.

"Good," she said, and reached overhead to flip on one of the commiter transmitters. Jes glanced up curiously. When he looked down she held a small stunner pointed at his stomach.

"No," he said.

"I'm sorry," she said. Her voice sounded contrite. "I'm not going to kill you, but I don't need you for a while." She paused, then said, "Jessie—"

He lunged toward the gun and she pulled the trigger.

After the first moment of blinding shock there was no pain; his body simply ceased to belong to him. He slumped onto the deck. Tatha picked him up and shoved him into the navigator's web. She strapped him in and turned his head so that he could watch her.

"Comfortable, tauCaptain?" she said, not smiling. She slid into the pilot's web and reviewed the control board briefly, then sent out a series of silent pulses on the commiter. The go-light winked and she slid the ship into the approach. She handled the sloop competently—Jes decided that she wasn't going to kill them both. He wasn't sure that it made him feel any better. As she slowly jockeyed the ship into the grab's coils, she started humming a new tune. Jes could not close his eyes, and only his paralysis kept him from weeping.

Blind Chance jerked as they came out of the coils. Tatha grimaced and finished closing down the effect drives. "Perhaps you'll teach me how to do that more gracefully, someday," she said. The commiter squawked. She flipped it on and a man's face appeared on the screen. The collar of his shirt was decorated with Parallax insignia.

"Menet preParian?" the man said. "We've been expecting you."

Jes woke for the fourth time and his body ached. He raised his one free arm and touched his forehead gingerly—his arm was bound at the elbow and he could only reach his face with his fingertips. Tatha had left him enough leeway with that one arm to reach the pile of watertubes and meatsticks on the nearby table and convey them to his mouth. His right arm was enmeshed in the tight cocoon of ropes that she'd bound around him after dragging him from the bridge to his cabin. Calmly, thoroughly, she then dumped him into his hammock and pulled the ends of it around his body, sealing them together beneath him.

"The stunner's effects should fade in an hour or so," she said. Her hand rested lightly on his shoulder but he could not feel it. "Jes, I've—" She shrugged. "Perhaps you'll turn into a butterfly," she said as she left the cabin, locking the door behind her. Over the past two days, Jes had generated any number of scathing replies to that, but she wasn't there to hear them.

The sloop was eerily silent, its engines down, and he could hear the slight hum of the life-support systems spilling fresh air into the cabin and evacuating the stale air. Lying still, he tightened and loosened his muscles, trying to keep his circulation going. She'd bound him well, but not so tight as to cut into his flesh or impede the flow of blood. He was in no mood to feel grateful. At least Parallax hadn't searched the sloop.

Parallax. They'd known that she was coming, knew her name, were waiting for her just beyond the grab's freespace. Jes had seen the image of a fully armed cruiser on the sloop's vision screens before Tatha dragged him into the cabin. She said, as she bound him, that she hoped to be gone for no more than three days; as far as he could tell, two of those days were past and she showed no signs of returning. And all of Jes' efforts had not brought him one knot closer to freedom.

A dull, metallic sound filled the sloop, Jes stopped squirming in the hammock and listened intently. A bang, a clatter, a thud, another bang, and footsteps in the companionway. The door opened and Tatha stuck her head into the cabin. She looked weary.

"Good," she said, looking at him, and went away, leaving the door open. He pressed his lips together and clenched his hands in rage. *Blind Chance* hummed to life. He heard Tatha's voice from the bridge. The donkey engines kicked on. The vibrations increased slightly as the sloop picked up speed, and half an hour later they cut off. The effect drives thrummed; Jes felt the disorientation of the grab transition. Then the effect drives came fully to life, and shortly after that Tatha came into the cabin again.

She stood at the doorway looking at him. He stared at her with silent hatred.

"There are four crystals in the housing," she said conversationally. "Will you make sure Zimmerman gets them immediately?"

When he didn't reply she lifted the stunner from her belt and carefully emptied its charge before putting it in a niche on the wall and clamping it down. She took off and folded the Barre harness and put it away, then stripped slowly, carefully folding her clothes and putting them in the clothes niche. She held out the Parallax uniform shirt, frowned at it, and dropped it in the disposer. Then, naked, she walked to the hammock and looked down at Jes.

"I've programmed a flight to Eagle System," she said. "Nobody's following us." She looked as though she wanted to say something else, gestured quickly, and unseamed the ends of the hammock. A deft pass with her claws split the ropes that bound him, and without saying anything further she walked out of the cabin. Jes lay still, waiting. When she didn't return he clambered slowly from the hammock and stood, watching the door and rubbing his arms and legs. He felt sore and stiff, and his rage grew.

She was standing at the back of the bridge, looking at one of the vision screens, and didn't turn when he entered. Nor did she defend herself when he spun her around and hit her, and hit her again, and a third time. Her lack of resistance infuriated him; he dragged her to her feet and hit her again until she lay half slumped against the bulkhead and looked up at him. Blood dribbled from a corner of her mouth.

"I'm sure you're enjoying this as much as I am," she said, her voice tight. "But don't you think it's time to get it over with?"

He jerked her to her feet and clipped her jaw hard, then caught her limp body as she fell. He sat on the hard deck, cradling her in his arms, lost in confusion and a sorrow too deep for weeping.

A WEEK BEFORE THE ELECTION PALEN AP-
peared in The Jumble with the Ska'felet, and the rift in
the kasirene sector became entirely public. Market
Square, every night, was the scene of loud debate;
Beriant and his supporters yelled at Palen, the Ska'felet,
and their contingent, who yelled back. Most of the kasirene were now quite willing to believe that Beriant had
the support of Barranca and Parallax, but they were not
convinced that this support was a bad thing and they
pointed again and again to the lack of any concrete evidence that Parallax meant to harm the kasirene. The
Ska'felet's experiences were waved aside as having happened far away and to an entirely different planet, under
very different circumstances. Some accused it outright of
lying, but others believed. Beriant insisted that Barranca
be questioned, and when he was led into Market Square
one evening, he calmly confirmed Beriant's claim of
Parallax support, and assured the kasirene of Parallax's goodwill and respect. Palen felt sick.

"He's lying," she muttered. The Ska'felet made a gesture of disgust.

"Of course he's lying," it said. "But you can't prove it,
and neither can I. It's too hot here, I want to go away."

Palen ignored it. The next day she tried to talk with
Hart, but he refused to speak to her about Barranca.

"Where's Spider?" Hart demanded. Palen spread her
hands.

"I don't know. He may be in The Jumble, but I doubt
it. I think he went south. What are we going to do about
Beriant and Barranca, Hart? There must be some way to
prove that Barranca's lying."

"I don't care," Hart said walking away.

"I don't know," Quilla said later, after she and Palen
had discussed the problem fruitlessly for hours. "There's

473

nothing on him here, we've searched his gear. No instructions, nothing that would prove our point at all. He's clean."

"He could have left stuff on his ship."

"I doubt it. I've had it checked out, and there seems to be nothing up there either."

Palen frowned. "That's where Jes and Tatha went first, isn't it? What is Tatha looking for?"

"I don't know," Quilla said, exasperated. "For all I know, she's going to lead an armada of Parallax ships into Eagle System."

"With Jes along? I doubt it."

"She could have forced him to it." Quilla turned away. "He may not even be alive. He hates her."

Palen shook her head but could think of nothing convincing to say. And the debates continued.

On the day before the election, Jes and Tatha came back.

∾

"WE WENT UP TO *MI ESTANCIA*," JES SAID ANgrily, sitting in the Tor's living room. Tatha, bound and guarded, sat in an armchair across from him, contemplating her boot tips; aside from asking about Daren she had not uttered a word since Jes marched her off *Blind Chance* and delivered her to Pixie Hirem. And before that, surrounded by Kennerins in the sloop's bridge, she had spoken only to remind Jes about the bridge crystals. Her silence angered and baffled him. He stared at her, but she would not meet his eyes.

"That was the night you left?" Quilla said. Jes nodded. He outlined their actions from *Mi Estancia* through tau to NewHome, omitting only the understanding that he and Tatha had reached about themselves, and that he omitted only because he was still not entirely convinced that she'd been lying.

"And without warning she hit me with the stunner. There was a Parallax cruiser waiting just beyond New-Home Grab's freespace. They were expecting her."

"How could they?" Mish demanded. "Tatha?"

Tatha only smiled at her boots and refused to speak. Pixie, standing beside her, raised a hand, but Mish shook her head. Jes looked at the faces in the room: Palen balancing before the fireplace, Quilla sitting on a low stool, knees and elbows angular, face heavy with concentration, Mish burning with cold fury. Only Tatha seemed relaxed, oblivious of Pixie's angry presence behind her. Jes shook his head.

"She may have signaled them from tau somehow, or when we were coming through the grab. She knows enough about the workings of a sloop to manage that— and more. She brought the sloop out of the grab and right up to the cruiser, tied me into my hammock, and disappeared for two days." He looked at Tatha again, trying to read her expression. "It doesn't make sense. She hid me, and I don't know why—they'd have been more than happy to have me as a prisoner, she could have used me that way. And she didn't need me to get back to Aerie —she didn't need me to leave Aerie, for that matter."

"The sloop was locked," Pixie said. Jes shook his head impatiently.

"Sure, but that wouldn't have stopped her. That's a specialty of hers, locks."

Tatha smiled at her boots and remained silent. Hart came into the room and sat by the door, looking at Tatha with an expression which Jes could not read.

"Two days?" Mish said.

"Yeah. She'd left food and water that I could reach, but I couldn't get free."

"I can believe that," Pixie said looking at the top of Tatha's head with distaste. "She's good at teaching knots, but so far she hasn't taught anyone how to get out of them."

Hart smiled maliciously.

"When she came back, we cut loose from the cruiser and headed toward the grab. When we got into tau, she let me have the sloop back."

Zimmerman, looking disheveled, came into the room as Hart said, "And like a good boy, you brought her right back here. Without trying to find out what she'd been up to."

Tatha grinned. "The tauCaptain behaved in an exemplary fashion," she said, speaking across the room to the colonel. "He beat the shit out of me and locked me up, and kept me there until we came through Eagle Grab. Then he tied me into the navigator's web and kept a stunner on me until we were about to land, and then he used it. Mildly, I might add. For which I am most deeply thankful."

Jes started to say something, but she ignored him. "I presume, colonel, that you did your job and searched the sloop. Do you have the crystals?"

"There weren't any," Colonel Zimmerman said, staring at her. "The housing was smashed and the crystals gone. I suppose you have an explanation for that?"

All traces of laughter left Tatha's face, and she looked at Jes. "Did you—?"

"No, I left when you did. You'd have seen me."

She shook her head. "There were a lot of people in the bridge. I couldn't move. Anyone could have taken them."

Hart shrugged negligently and stood. "Why all the speculation? Obviously she took them herself, perhaps before she let Jes free her. Search her." He put his hands in his pockets and smiled at Tatha unpleasantly. "Or she could have slipped them to someone at the port, she's sure to have accomplices. Search Barranca's quarters." He met Tatha's glance, and his smile broadened further.

"Barranca's no friend of hers," Pixie said. "He says she stole something of his—he's made threats."

"She stole his shirt," Jes said, and Pixie shook her head, frowning.

"Search her house, then," Hart said. "I don't see that it's important, though. Interesting, as a piece of history, but I can't see that they would change anything. I think we know as much as we need to."

Jes frowned and looked at Tatha, but she was staring at her boots again, and her face was a calm, silvery mask.

They put her in a room at the Tor, a hastily converted closet with one door and no windows. Pixie left someone to guard the door, ignoring Hart's suggestion that they keep the Theresan tied up, as well. Meya insisted that they let her see Daren, and she spent an hour with the child, chattering with him in Standard and in Theresan. Daren ignored the guard, seemingly thinking him part of another of the odd things that his mother was always doing, and talked about the adventures he and Alin had concocted during the past few weeks. Tatha was content to hold him on her lap and let him talk until Meya came to take him away.

At dinnertime one of the guards brought in a tray. Zimmerman followed him into the room and perched on a corner of the bed while Tatha attacked the food.

"I'm glad to see that all this hasn't affected your appetite," the colonel said.

"I've not eaten in two days," Tatha said shortly, and finished her meal. She pushed the plate away and cradled the glass of red wine between her palms. "You're here to ask questions."

"I am." The colonel stood and put his hands along his belt. The room was barely big enough for the cot, the chair, and the small table. "I want to know what happened. Your version."

"Find the crystals," she said. "Anything that I tell you will be useless unless you have them."

"You didn't take them?"

"Why should I? Run from Aerie, taking Jes along—and I can't prove that he went of his own free will, not without his corroboration—"

"He says that you talked him into coming with you, under false pretenses."

"I expected that. Then commit an act of mutiny, or piracy, whichever you prefer. Go to NewHome and confer with the enemy. Leave with their permission. Come back to Aerie, presumably with further instructions from Parallax. It all makes sense so far, presuming that I'm a spy, or under Parallax pay or influence." She sipped her wine. "That being the case, why keep Kennerin alive?"

"If you killed him, you'd never get away with anything you tried to do."

"True. Why take him in the first place? I can fly a sloop on my own, if I have to. And locks are no problem, Jes can testify to that."

"As a hostage? As proof of your good intentions to Parallax?"

"Then why hide him?"

"Change of heart?"

Tatha looked at him and the colonel spread his hands. "It was a suggestion," he said.

"I'm not a fool, Zimmerman. Presuming that I had dark motives, that I did all these things, that I fucked things up—then why come back to Aerie? What possible reason would there be for that? I'd be walking into —just what I walked into."

The colonel leaned against a wall and looked at her. "So tell me," he suggested. "Why?"

"Find the crystals," she said, and finished the wine. She put the glass on the tray with the empty plate. "Go away, Zimmerman. All this evil plotting, is exhausting. We villains need our sleep."

The colonel gestured and the guard picked up the tray.

"They searched your house and shop this afternoon, and didn't find them."

"I didn't take them. Someone did, after I left the sloop. Find the crystals, Zimmerman. Until you do, nothing I can say will be of any use at all. To myself or to Aerie."

Frowning, the colonel followed the guard out of the room. Tatha heard the locks shoot home, then stretched out on the bed, put her arms behind her head, and carefully arranged her thoughts.

In the far wing of the house, Daren waited until the rooms around him were quiet, slipped out of bed, crossed the toy-strewn floor, and clambered onto Alin's bed. She woke grumpily, stared at him, and sat, her face puzzled. Daren caught both of her hands and stared back at her, his face screwed up in concentration. For a long time they sat like that, each crosslegged, before Alin pulled her hands away, burrowed under the covers, and closed her eyes. Daren watched her for a moment and went back to bed.

"I don't see any need to hide it," Beriant said. He looked across the firepit to where Palen sat with the Ska'felet. "Of course I met with Barranca. Any reasonable leader, proposing a revolution, looks toward the future. With the terrans off Aerie, or powerless, we'll need some outside help, something to guarantee our freedom and our markets. Parallax can provide both. They have a security force which will see to it that the terrans don't try to reclaim Aerie for themselves, and they can provide us with a very extensive trade network. In addition," Beriant said, raising his voice to shout over the increasing muttering of the crowd, "in addition, I have Parallax's personal assurance of good will."

"Empty words," Puti said loudly. "The Ska'felet had assurances too."

"The Ska'felet, being by nature stupid, shiftless, and easily excited, led a rebellion against Parallax. They deserved what they got."

The Ska'felet leaped to its feet and shouted angrily. Beriant crossed his arms and smiled, letting the alien rant on. Palen pulled the alien down and told it to shut up.

"You've all heard this—thing," Beriant said. "Palen's dragged it all over the to'anet. You've heard its story, but more importantly, you've seen it, you've heard its constant complaints, its whining. This crier of doom, this poor, suffering, mistreated Ska'felet claims to be representative of its race." Beriant paused. "Is it any surprise that Parallax lost its temper? And can you possibly claim to see any resemblance at all between kasirene and this miserable thing? If you do then go with the terrans, for you are no better than they are."

"May I interrupt your harangue?" Palen said, getting to her feet. She looked around the crowded room. "We are taught not to be deceived by appearances. You have not traveled with Ska'felet, as I have. I can assure you that it is far more unpleasant to live with it, than it is to listen to it for an evening. However, is there some immutable law which says that the victim of injustice must always be appealing? That oppression automatically confers good manners, or stoicism, or a pleasant appearance? We have whiners among us, we have complainers, we have self-inflated fools. Would you have all kasirene judged by the unpleasant minority? Would you have our history disregarded, our sufferings denigrated, because some of the sufferers are repulsive idiots? We are not yet as corrupt as that, although I think there are some who would wish on us that sort of corruption." She glanced at Beriant. "Some among us offer you unsubstantiated promises; I have offered you substantiated fact. Beriant has made Parallax appear to be a champion of justice, a protector of indigenes—the Ska'felet has told you that it is not. Beriant has waved aside the stories of such as Sandro Marquez, saying that what happened to terrans does not affect us. But it does —it shows that Parallax champions only itself, and protects only itself. Parallax is not interested in the tensions between terrans and indigenes, Parallax is not interested in racial politics. It is interested in expansion, in making a profit, in collecting worlds. If Parallax takes over Aerie, through Beriant's misguided efforts or otherwise, you will see every to'an turned into a *Zimania* plantation, you will see an end to kasirene wanderings, you will see enforced housing in constructed towns. And you will not see Aerie run by the kasirene—you will see Aerie run by Parallax managers and worked by kasirene, you will see the kasirene enslaved. And that, ultimately, is your choice. Freedom and cooperation under the old order, or enslavement under the new."

"You can't prove that," Beriant shouted, leaping to his feet. "I have the assurances from Parallax, I have them here, written down, signed by Barranca, to be confirmed after we have won the election. You have suppositions, and nothing more. You're painting false pictures. Argue facts, Palen tor-Altemet. But you will not fool the kasirene with specious, inflammatory nonsense. Prove your contentions!"

"Proof is coming," Palen lied calmly. "Proof will arrive before the voting starts tomorrow. Depend on it." She sat again, her expression confident, and looked at the faces surrounding the firepit. Beriant looked suspicious, but Puti, knowing the truth, kept her face down and her eyes closed.

"It's too hot in here," the Ska'felet said. Palen resisted the urge to strangle it.

Zimmerman was sleeping soundly when Mish came into his room and shook his shoulder roughly. She turned on the bed-side light as he peered at her and rubbed his eyes.

"You've got a com," she said before he could speak. "It's a double-security message, and it's down at the port. They called up a few minutes ago."

The colonel's eyes widened. He leaped out of the bed and grabbed for his pants. "Can you get me a flitter?" he said over his shoulder. "An aircar, anything?"

"No. I've called down to the barn, they're bringing you a running dray."

Zimmerman paused, his hand on the seam of his shirt. "I can't—I've never ridden one before."

"You'll ride one tonight, or walk. There's nothing else." Mish smiled. "It knows the way to the port, colonel. All you have to do is climb aboard and hold on."

It wasn't quite that simple. The dray was patient and did indeed know the way to the port, but Zimmerman clung to the reins and the pommel, unable to blend with the dray's six-legged gait. Once down the hill the dray moved onto the thin, moonlit path running along the edge of the stream and began to canter. The colonel jounced unhappily and tried to get the dray to slow down. It ignored him. As they reached the port, someone whistled sharply and the dray turned and jounced over to the comshack, where it stopped and put its nose in Pixie's hand. She helped Zimmerman slide from the saddle.

"You'll never be a rider, colonel," she told him.

"I never want to be," he said, and limped into the comshack. Ten minutes later, he commed Mish at the Tor.

"They've scheduled the voting," he said. "It will begin ten hours from now, standard."

Mish nodded and looked at him out of the vid. "How long until they've finished?"

"Five hours. Sometimes a bit more. I may stay down here, in case something further comes through."

Mish closed the connection and the colonel went outside. The night was clear and cool. Pixie stood by the dray, her large hand on the animal's neck.

"I'm not going right back," Zimmerman said. Pixie nodded and called, and someone came around from the duty shack, took the dray, and led it away. In the distance a light shone before the door to the warehouse, and a guard leaned against the wall.

"He's been strange," Pixie said, following the colonel's glance. "He doesn't seem excited about the election at all, as though he already knows what's going to happen. But ever since Tatha and Jes got back, he's been furious. Says that she stole something of his before she left, and he wants it back." Pixie paused. "The stuff he says about her—"

"Oh?"

"Sandro translates, sometimes. For a head-stuffed idiot, he has a great imagination."

The colonel frowned. "Pixie? What do you think of all of this?"

"You mean Tatha?" Pixie shrugged. "I don't know, colonel. I can't figure her out, and I don't intend to try; everytime I think I know what she's up to, she comes up with something different." The big woman paused. "You remember how my father showed up when Barranca first arrived? He hates Tatha, has ever since that night when she stole his speech and put it to music. And he doesn't hide it, not to anyone. He didn't bother to hide it to Barranca either."

"So?"

"We couldn't figure out how Ved knew that Barranca was here—to make it on time, he'd have had to start out from Haven before the ship landed. He said that someone had called him, someone he didn't know, and told him to come down to the port. Kumbe was on comshack duty that day, and Tatha was in the shack when Sandro commed in to let us know that they were coming. Kumbe says that Tatha made a few calls after that and he thinks that one of them was to Ved." Pixie shook her head. "Now why, in the name of the Mother, would Tatha make sure that Ved came down? Why would she want someone who hates her to talk with the Parallax crew? She had to know that he'd spout off about her—she even left the warehouse before he was done, to give him a chance to do that. I can't figure it out."

Zimmerman frowned and stared at the warehouse, then turned and looked down the field toward *Blind Chance*. "Are you sure that she even had a good reason?" he said.

"Yes. If there's one thing I'm sure about, when it comes to Tatha, it's that she never does anything without a good reason. I'm just damned if I can figure out what it is."

"You're not alone," the colonel replied, and went back into the comshack.

❧

MIM HAD LOCKED THEM INTO THE PLAY-room and Jason Hart was furious. What might be the most important event in the history of Aerie was taking place not more than a kilometer away and he was not even allowed to watch. His temper, carefully kept in check for so many months, shattered entirely and he kicked savagely at the door, screaming. The door withstood his assault. When Andrus tried to pull him away he hit his younger brother in the stomach and marched to the window, where he looked at the two-story drop to the ground with rage.

Alin and Daren were quiet, sitting in a corner of the room holding hands. Jason Hart ignored them. It was only when Andrus began to argue with Daren that Jason Hart turned to them, their voices disrupting the fine, clean lines of his anger.

"I think she's sick," Andrus insisted when Jason Hart stormed over to them. "She hasn't moved all morning."

"She's okay," Daren insisted. "Leave her alone, she's okay."

Jason Hart was going to hit both of them when he saw Alin's face and he dropped to his knees before her, more in curiosity than in apprehension. Her eyes were open, staring straight before her, and they did not respond when he passed his hand before her face, nor did she startle when he clapped his hands loudly by her ear. Only the bare rise and fall of her chest indicated that she was breathing. But when he tried to lift her hand she pulled away from him sharply and continued her listless sitting.

"How long's she been like that?" he said to Andrus.

"All morning," his brother said. "We should call Mim."

"Leave her alone," Daren said angrily, pushing between the brothers to separate them from their sister. "She's—" he waved his silver hands, groping for words. "She's busy somewhere else. When she's done, she'll come back. Leave her alone."

"Has she done this before?" Jason Hart said. Daren nodded but Jason Hart didn't believe him. Alin was given to trances, but he'd never seen her in one as deep as this. "Where's she gone?"

Daren shrugged and, sitting, took one of Alin's hands. She let him; her hand lay limp between his. "She'll be back," Daren repeated. Jason Hart looked at the window and paced around the room, searching for anything that could be used as a rope. He tore through discarded toys and costumes, cursed, gathered some of the costumes to him, and sat crosslegged on the floor, ripping them along their seams and tying them together to form a rope.

Alin came back with a frightening rush of activity. She leaped to her feet, uttering one of her wordless cries, and flung herself across the room. She grabbed Jason Hart's arms and stared into his face urgently, while her lips shaped themselves around silent words. Jason Hart yelled and pushed her away.

"What's got into her?" he demanded. She grabbed him around the waist. Her nose was bright red, and her eyes were wet.

"She wants something," Daren said.

"I can see that, dummy." Jason Hart stopped suddenly and looked down at her. "You're watching something, aren't you?" Alin nodded furiously. "The election speeches? In Haven?" She shook her head, black hair whipping around her face. "Something else? The port?" Again she shook her head vehemently. "The Tor?" This time she nodded, her face excited. Jason Hart thought quickly about who could be in the Tor, and suddenly Alin grabbed his arm. He frowned, trying to reconstruct his thoughts. She pulled away with a look of disgust and stalked across the room. She stopped halfway to Daren, who was looking at her in puzzlement.

"Tatha?" Jason Hart called. Alin shook her head

without looking at him. She began pacing the sides of the room, looking at the piles of toys.

"Mim? Quilla? Mish? Meya? Ozchan? Tabor?" Andrus called out, enjoying the game. Alin ignored him. She began collecting things and piled them in front of Jason Hart. Battered bookreels, an ancient set of drums, a tattered stuffed animal—old things, toys so old that Jason Hart could not remember a time when they had not been present. He looked at them, baffled, and shook his head. Alin exploded with frustration. She kicked the toys aside and grabbed her older brother, beating him with her fists as though trying to batter her thoughts into him. He caught her hands and held her easily while she squirmed and wept silently.

"Alin! Alin, listen to me. Hush. Calm down. Alin, is it important? Yes? Does it have to do with the election? And something more?" She began pulling him toward the window. He pulled her back. "You want me to go outside? Okay, there's something you want me to do? What?"

She looked at him, hopelessly, and her shoulders drooped. Contrite, Jason Hart hugged her. "Alin, I could spend all day playing guessing games. But this is important, isn't it? Really?" He held her at arm's length. "Then you're going to have to tell me. You're going to have to speak to me, Alin. I can't read your mind."

She broke away from him, ran to a corner, and huddled, her shoulders shaking. Jason Hart shrugged.

"I can't do a thing," he told the others. He returned to his rope-making. He estimated that he almost had enough to reach from the window to the ground and began dragging a large toy chest toward the window, where it would serve as an anchor for one end of the rope. He tied the rope around the toy chest and pulled at it, section by section, testing the knots. He retied a few of them, opened the window, and stuck his head out. Alin screamed. He ignored her. He fed the rope carefully out the window.

"Hart."

"Andrus, stop playing guess games," he said without turning around.

"I'm not," Andrus whispered, from a different side of the room. Jason Hart pulled his head back from the window and turned around quickly. Alin sat in her corner, hair straggling over her face, looking at him.

"Hart," she said. "Labba rie. Keesper." The words sounded tentative in her mouth, and she lisped. "Some crystals in keesper. Take them to—" She stopped and closed her eyes for a moment. "To sinna, siminen . . ."

"Zimmerman," Jason Hart said, and she nodded. He came across the room and knelt in front of her. She crouched on her hands and knees, staring at him through her tangled hair. "Alin, do you mean that Hart took those crystals? And they're in the keeper? And it has something to do with the election?" He put out his hand to still her wild nodding. "You're not making this up, are you?"

In answer she bit his hand. He swore and put the side of his hand to his lips. "Now," she said.

"Where in the keeper are they?"

She stared at him, stood suddenly, and marched to the box of building blocks. She pulled blocks out and arranged them on the floor in seven rows of eight blocks each, grabbed Jason Hart's arm, and dragged him around until he was on an eight-block side. She removed a block, third from the top, fourth in from the right-hand side, and put the block in his hand.

"Now," she said again. He looked from the block in his hand to his sister and to the blocks on the floor, then ran to the window. He swung half out, grabbing the rope, and looked in at her.

"If you're playing games with me, I'll beat the hell out of you," he said. Alin just looked at him, her hands at her sides, and he shinnied down the rope. He dove into the bushes near the house, looked back and cursed. The ragged, knotted costumes hung from the window like a flag. Alin's face appeared at the sill and the rope shivered and moved upward. Jason Hart sent her a silent, heartfelt thanks and crept around the side of the house toward his uncle's laboratory.

There were some people in the kitchen, probably Mim and one of her friends, but otherwise the house seemed deserted. Palen's hut was closed and dark, and he kept it between himself and the Tor as he circled toward the outbuilding which housed the laboratory. There was a window at the back of the building; by climbing halfway up a neighboring tree, Jason Hart saw that the window opened into a storeroom. He slid down the tree, hooked his fingers over the outer sill of the window, and pulled himself up. The window was locked; beyond it he saw boxes and barrels stacked carefully against the wall, and the closed door that led to the rest of the laboratory. His arms started aching. He dropped onto the ground and rubbed his shoulders, frowning as he thought. Then he crept around to the front of the building, listening carefully. The laboratory was silent. He dashed around the corner and tried the front door, but it, too, was locked. He went around to the back and stared at the window again. He'd have to break it.

He found a rock and a stout stick and threw the rock through the window. The sound of glass shattering and falling seemed hideously loud, but after a while, when no one came out of the back of the Tor, he reached up and used the stick to knock aside the ragged shards that remained along the bottom of the window. He took off his shirt, wrapped it around his hands, and jumped toward the sill.

One small sliver of glass cut his palm, but within a moment he was into the storeroom. He sucked at the cut and looked around, went to the door, and put his ear to it. He heard the usual humming of the laboratory and nothing else. He turned the knob and the door swung open. The laboratory was deserted.

The keeper that Alin had indicated was locked tight. Jason Hart wasted a few moments trying to pry the door open, then ransacked his uncle's desk until he found a set of master keys. He tried them one by one on the door. Eventually it clicked open and he reached inside.

There were four crystals, not the two he'd expected, and they were carefully wrapped in a small piece of soft material. Jason Hart touched them curiously before thrusting them into his pocket and scooting back through the broken window. Leaving the lab, he looked back at the shattered window and felt proud of himself. The pride lasted until he rounded the corner of the Tor and realized that he didn't know where the colonel was. He ran back to the bushes under the playroom window. Alin was waiting for him, and as soon as he came in sight, she put her hands flat on the windowsill and moved them diagonally outward, quickly. He shook his head. She made the gesture again, put her arms up level with her shoulders and stretched out at either side, and swayed back and forth. Jason Hart shook his head, bewildered, and stopped, abruptly. Alin was nodding before he'd framed the words in his head. The colonel was at the port.

This time he didn't worry about concealment—even if Mim saw him, she'd never catch him. He sped down the slope, tried to take the stream with one jump and almost made it, ignored his sopping shoes and continued running. The path curved and twisted up the side of the hill. He took shortcuts, scrambling through the dirt and airflowers and checking constantly to make sure that the crystals were safe in his pocket. Arriving at the port, he ran past the warehouse where Barranca and the crew were being held. One of the guards shouted at him but he didn't slow down. Heart and feet pounding, he rounded a corner of a warehouse and burst into the door of the comshack. The colonel jumped up from a commiter and stared at him.

Jason Hart pulled the crystals from his pocket, put them on the commiter's narrow counter, and discovered that he was panting too hard to talk. He grabbed Zimmerman's uniform sleeve urgently.

"From the sloop," he gasped. The colonel scooped the crystals into his palms.

"You're sure?"

Jason Hart nodded and fell into a chair.

"Where were they?"

"Hart's lab."

The colonel handed him a glass of water and popped one of the crystals into a reader. He stopped, looking from the commiter to the reader and back again, then reached for a piece of paper.

"I can't leave here," he muttered as he wrote. "Can you run some more?"

"Sure," Jason Hart said, and finished the water. The colonel scribbled furiously, folded the paper, and handed it to Jason Hart.

"Take this to Mish, and make damned sure that she reads it." The boy nodded. Zimmerman looked at him seriously and put his hands on Jason Hart's shoulder. "Young man, the future of Aerie and of your family may rest on what you do in the next half hour. I want you to run, and to run hard. I want you to get to your grandmother, no matter who tries to stop you. And I want you to make sure that she reads my message immediately, no matter what she's doing when you reach her. Is that clear?" Jason Hart bobbed his head. Zimmerman ripped the insignia off the breast of his uniform and pressed it into Jason Hart's hand. "If anyone tries to stop you, show them this and tell them that you're my courier. And if they try to detain you, get away from them—you'll know how. Understood?"

"Yes, sir," Jason Hart said, eyes shining. He clenched one hand around the insignia and the other around the message, and dashed out of the comshack.

There were, to his disappointment, no people on the Havensport Road at all, but as he neared Haven he heard the sound of the crowd in Market Square, and over it the tinny sound of a voice coming over amplifiers. He cut off Havensport Road near the hospital and sped up Townsend Street to Weaver Street. The corner where Weaver, Village Street, and Carpenters Row came together seemed populated, and he immediately cut alongside a house and through a series of back yards. He passed behind the town hall, which seemed empty, then went down backyards paralleling the upper end of Tor Road until he neared the square. The noise increased. He came quietly around a house and saw, as he'd hoped, that he'd come out just behind the dais. But militia stood between the dais and the edge of the square, and Jason Hart circled the square until he was behind Kohl's. He rounded the beerhall and pressed himself into the crowd. They ignored him.

One of Beriant's proposed board members was speaking passionately. Jason Hart registered scraps of the speech as he inched his way forward. Around him people muttered and cursed, but let him through. Pixie stood to the left of the dais and, thinking swiftly, Jason Hart worked his way to her and put his foot on the steps behind her. Her hand descended to grab his shoulder.

"Where do you think—what are you doing here?" she demanded. He opened his fist. She plucked the damp, crumpled piece of material from his hand and spread it open as he talked.

"I'm a special courier for Colonel Zimmerman," Jason Hart said, trying not to sound aware of his elevated status. "I've a report for Mish. The colonel says its urgent."

"What report?" Pixie said, releasing him. He bolted up the stairs. He dashed around behind the chairs and grabbed his grandmother's arm. She turned, startled.

"It's from the colonel," Jason Hart said before she had a chance to speak. "It's important, you've got to read it right now."

The speaker turned to frown at them. Mish said "Hush" and pulled Jason Hart down until he crouched beside her chair. She took the twisted paper from him and urged it flat.

"You're a pretty messy messenger," she muttered. Jason Hart looked down at his torn, stained clothing. He didn't even remember getting dirty, but thought that his tatters were badges of honor. Mish finished reading the note, looked at him, and pulled his face down close to hers. "Do you know what's in this?"

He shook his head.

"You brought the crystals to Zimmerman? Hush, you can tell me about it later. Get Pixie for me, tell her to come around the back. And be casual about it this time."

He nodded, hopped off the back of the dais, and scurried around to where the tall militia commander guarded her set of steps.

"Mish wants you," Jason Hart said. "And give me back the colonel's badge, he gave it to me."

"I ought to wallop you," Pixie said. She signaled to a guard to replace her and followed Jason Hart around the dais. She conferred hurriedly with Mish, then picked Jason Hart up and swung him onto the dais. Mish was bending over to talk to one of the terran board members, and Pixie hurried away. Jason Hart put his arms around his knees and looked out at the crowd, thinking quick thoughts of gratitude toward Alin. He hoped she was listening in.

When the kasir finished talking Mish stood and took the microphone.

"I know that we said, when we started, that we would try to make this expeditious," she said. "But there are a lot of unresolved matters, and we *must* consider them. The futures of this company, of this planet, and of ourselves are in the balance, and we do ourselves an injustice if we do not consider all ramifications of the questions before us. I think you agree." The mutter from both sides of the crowd showed that they did. "Very well. So far, we have heard from Beriant and from each member of his proposed board, and we have heard from all members of the current board. However, we wish to put forth a nonboard speaker, much as Beriant was a nonboard speaker, to talk about some aspects of this question that we've not touched on before. We think it only fair, and I think that again that you will agree." The crowd noise this time was not quite so enthusiastic. "Aerites, please listen carefully to a man who has been on this planet longer than almost anyone else present, a man whose devotion to our world is total and beyond question. Ved Hirem."

"Objection!" Beriant howled as the crowd shouted. "Hirem's an old windbag and anything he says will be totally irrelevant to this meeting."

"Not at all," Mish said calmly. "And if being a windbag is a disqualification, Quia Beriant . . ." she let the statement trail off to general laughter. Ved Hirem latched onto the microphone and began orating. Mish, looking satisfied, returned to her chair.

"What did you do that for?" Jason Hart whispered.

"It's called a filibuster," Mish said. "I'm buying time, Jason." She stopped, surprised. "I've never called you that." She looked at him and put her tiny hand along his jawline. "Maybe it's time I started. Anyway, I'm buying time for us, and for Zimmerman, and, with luck, for Aerie."

Jason Hart looked beyond her to the lawyer. Judge Hirem was already in full swing, calling down metaphors and similes and ringing phrases extemporaneously, pounding his cane or waving his arm for emphasis. "How long can he keep that up?"

"Forever," Mish said confidently. She unfolded Zimmerman's note and read it again. Jason Hart crossed his legs, put his chin on his fist, and began analyzing the positions of the crowd.

THREE HOURS LATER, AS VED'S ORATORICAL talents were beginning to flag, Colonel Zimmerman scrambled up the dais and looked around. A portable reader sat at Mish's feet, and the crew of *Mi Estancia* sat, surrounded by guards, to the left of the stage. Beyond them, Tatha lounged in a chair, her arms behind ber back and her eyes closed. A separate guard stood over her. The colonel nodded at Mish and tapped Ved's shoulder.

"I'll take over now," he said, gently pushing the old man aside. The crowd woke up and rustled as he pulled the microphone down to his lips. He put his hand over his pocket and waited for the murmur to die down.

"I am Colonel Heschel Zimmerman, of the Federation," he told them. "Many of you know me already. I have two things tell you, and I don't know which is the more important. An hour ago, the council on Althing Green voted to expand Federation control to include control of tau. All ships currently in tau have been ordered to the nearest grabstations, and a moratorium of two weeks has been declared on all tau travel while the Federation conducts a census and implements new regulations." He looked down at Barranca. "The New-Home Grab has been closed. I have an authenticated message from Althing Green, confirming the vote and the closure. Aerie will not be invaded."

"Objection," Beriant said. "That was never a possibility—the colonel is rabble-rousing."

"Not so," Zimmerman said. "Give me your patience, and I will prove otherwise."

Beriant stared down at Barranca, who shrugged and spread his hands, the picture of baffled innocence. The colonel brought the reader to the microphone and produced a crystal from his pocket. He glanced over his shoulder in time to see Pixie Hirem move to stand behind Hart and put her hand on his shoulder.

"I have been given four crystals," Zimmerman told the Aerites. "Together they constitute an interesting story, but one in particular is relevant now. It begins with a series of codings which prove it to have been recorded in NewHome System, aboard the Parallax cruiser *Griffin*, seven days ago. I've run all the necessary checks and the codings are authentic." He slid the crystal into the reader. "One voice is that of Tatha preParian. The second belongs to Adair Husman, a general in the so-called Parallax Security Force. Listen."

Thin, clear voices filled the square. Zimmerman stepped back from the reader and looked around. Hart sat motionless under Pixie's hand, pale with fury. The ring of guards had tightened around the Parallax crew, and Tatha listened with her head cocked to the side, as though the recording were new to her, too. But when Zimmerman caught her glance, her lips twitched and she nodded slowly.

"You've come from—Barranca, then? How much did he tell you?"

"Not much. He's under a pretty tight guard and we didn't have a lot of time to talk. He said that you'd fill me in, once you confirmed the crystal from his Certificate."

"No problem there. Why did he send you?"

"Who else was there? The terrans on planet are not trustworthy, and the kasirene—"

"God, if only we didn't have to depend on a bunch of dumb-ass natives."

"No help for it. He wants you to know that things are moving faster than he anticipated. The natives vote within a week, and he needs instructions both ways."

"It would be nice if we could get them to do our work for us," the Parallax general said, and proceeded to outline that work. If the kasirene voted for Parallax, all terrans were to be expelled from Aerie, either shipped out or killed, whichever was easier, and the job was to be done within a month. Then Parallax would move its managers in; it was not anticipated that the kasirene would present any insuperable problems.

"*And if they object—after all, they were promised certain things.*"

"*Let them object. We have a surplus of workers, we can replace them.*"

"*Fair enough. And if the vote goes against Parallax?*"

The general laughed. "*Menet preParian, why do you think I'm sitting out here, in the middle of nothing, in a full battle cruiser? Either you or Barranca will have to com me, one way or the other—the vote takes place in a week?*"

"*Ten days Aerie.*"

"*Fine. If I haven't received word in twelve days Aerie, I'll come through regardless. Tell Barranca that.*"

"Damned lies," Barranca shouted as Zimmerman bent to the reader, and Beriant said "I don't believe it." The colonel shrugged, advanced the crystal, and stepped back again.

"*. . . going. I'll see that Barranca gets the message. By the way, general, you might pick a better agent next time. Barranca doesn't even look like a tauCaptain.*"

"*Barranca's a fool, but we needed someone on short notice and he was the best available. Face it, Menet preParian, Aerie's a mudball. The directors want it so we'll get it for them, but it's not worth more than one cruiser and one third-rate agent. Has he fucked up?*"

"*A bit. Some of the terrans are suspicious. No webscarring, no tau knowledge, he doesn't even have the lingo. Is the Certificate forged?*"

"*No, it's his. He went through a paper course, we like to keep things straight, and it's easier to get a Certificate legally than it is to forge one. But I wouldn't trust him to pilot his hand to his ass.*"

Tatha's recorded laughter filled the square and stopped abruptly as Zimmerman fiddled with the reader again. The square was silent.

"*. . . necessarily. We'll take it from there.*"

"*You probably won't need to. Just to satisfy my curiosity, general, what will you do if the vote goes against you? You come through to Eagle System, then what?*"

"*Follow standard procedure. It will be easier on Aerie, with most everyone on one island. If they won't give in quietly, we'll slag the island. There are others.*"

"*Kasirene and all?*"

"Why not? We don't need them."

Zimmerman turned the reader off and took the microphone. "Would you like to hear more?" he said mildly.

One of the proposed kasirene board members leaned forward. "Colonel Zimmerman? Can you swear, as an officer of the Federation, to the authenticity of that crystal?"

"I can."

"And you're satisfied that Parallax's position, as spoken by that general, is their true position?"

"I am."

The kasir thought a moment, and rose. "I withdraw from this election," he said, and walked off the dais. After a moment of hesitation three others followed him. Beriant watched them go, his expression blank.

Mish rose slowly and took the microphone.

"My friends," she said wearily, "I think it's time to vote."

"I WANT TO GO HOME," TATHA SAID, MUCH later. She moved her arms wearily, still rubbing at the places where the ropes had held her. Hart started to say something and closed his mouth. Behind him, Pixie kept her light grip on his shoulder and one hand rested on the stunner thrust under her belt. Tatha looked at him calmly.

"He'd made his choice before I even reached Tebetet," she said, her voice flat. Hart refused to respond. He hadn't said a word since Zimmerman mounted the dais that afternoon, simply continued to look at Tatha with cold, unwavering hatred. Mish made a small noise. Tatha went to her and knelt beside her.

"Mish, I swear I don't think he knew what he was doing," Tatha said quietly. "I don't think he stopped to realize the consequences—he wanted to hurt me, and didn't think beyond that."

"Do you think that makes it any easier?" Mish said. She folded her hands in her lap and stared across the room at Hart. Her eyes were red. "I won't cover this up —we've tried to protect him too many times already. Stealing those crystals was a Federation offense."

"I've told you that I won't insist on taking him," Zimmerman said.

"Then what am I to do with him?" Mish cried, spreading her hands. "Slap his wrists and tell him not to do it again? Have him put in stasis? Damn it, Hart, *listen to me!*" But Hart sat as though deaf, staring at Tatha.

"Send him to Solon," Ozchan said. "Let them re-structure him."

Mish made a gesture of negation. Tatha climbed to her feet. "I don't think you have a choice," she said. "It's that, or let the Federation put him in stasis." She rested her hand on Mish's head for a moment, then turned to pick up Daren, who was asleep on the couch. Jes saw her stagger as she rose. He took the child from her, nodded to his silent family, and followed Tatha out of the room.

There were only a few lights glowing in Haven, and the town was quiet. Votes were still being counted in the town hall, but no one doubted the outcome. Yet, Jes thought, Mish had been right about the deeper scars —it would take a long time for Aerie to heal, and it would never be the same again. Daren grumbled something in his sleep and Jes shifted the boy in his arms. Tatha, head bent and hands in her pockets, did not look up.

She had taken a monstrous gamble, and almost lost. Listening to her earlier in the evening, Jes understood the game she had played and understood its necessity, but it continued to appall him. It made sense to force a confrontation between Aerie and Parallax at the very beginning, while Aerie's sense of outrage was still fresh. It made sense to bring Beriant and Parallax together immediately, if only so that the Parallax assault could be predicted and, with luck, controlled. It made sense to strengthen Beriant's position, so that Parallax, convinced that the ploy would work, would not try any other schemes. All she had asked of Spider was that he sit with Beriant's group when the kasir's first nomination was made, and this he had done, lending his implicit support, as a Kennerin, to Beriant's position. It made sense to let Barranca know that Tatha was not entirely liked on Aerie—Ved had started that process for her, and her own increasing coldness to Pixie and the rest of the militia had completed the task. Both the Parallax agent and the kasirene leader were convinced that they controlled her, and this was what she wanted. She had engineered Aerie to the brink of crisis. It had almost toppled.

He now understood the trip to NewHome, and that awed him even more than the rest. She stole the identity crystal from Barranca's Certificate; she used that crystal to open the private information computer in Barranca's cabin aboard *Mi Estancia* and from there she took the crystal showing the location of the Parallax ship in New-Home. Coming through NewHome Grab, she used that second crystal to identify herself to the cruiser, convincing them that she was a messenger from Barranca. The third crystal held the record of her conversations aboard the cruiser, a record which, had Parallax discovered it, would have meant her death. And the fourth crystal was simply the bridge crystal from *Blind Chance*, holding within its faceted memory the memory of the other three, and the record of the trip.

Jes had been taken along solely in order to thrash her and throw her in the brig until their return to Havensport. To serve as an excuse to Parallax, should she need one, for not transmitting her messages immediately to Barranca; proof to Aerie that Jes had been dragged along against his will, and had fought his kidnapper to submission; insurance that, once back on To'an Cault, she would be clapped into detention and guarded closely, for by now Barranca would know that she was not working for his side, and Beriant would suspect it. She depended on the crystals to prove her innocence and alert the Aerites, and to prove to Zimmerman that an illegal assault on Aerie was being planned by Parallax, an assault which even without the new legislation on tau would have constituted a Federation offense. If things had worked the way she'd planned, she'd be kept safe from Beriant and Barranca, Aerie would have been alerted, and Zimmerman would call in Federation cruisers to protect the system. What she had not planned on was the extent of Hart's sense of betrayal.

Tatha turned onto Field Road and skirted the town, still walking in silence. Jes followed. The Spiral glowed overhead, one fat moon centered in it and the other one sliding westward along the curve of night sky. Airflowers filled the air with sweetness and a few nightbirds, investigating the planted fields, flapped and warbled. Tatha's boots were silent on the packed clay of the road. Looking up, Jes picked out the light of the processing plant and, after that, the light of *Rabbit*. The Federation's moratorium—he'd be stuck on Aerie for a fortnight, and the prospect did not displease him.

Someone had tried to neaten Tatha's house, without much success. The results of the search lay about the floor; hangings ripped from the walls, furniture upended or pulled apart, even the ashes of the fireplace raked onto the rugs. The contents of a dozen drawers covered tables, chairs, and floors. Tatha stood in the ravaged living room, looking about blankly. Jes walked around her and opened the door to Daren's room. The bed was still intact. He put the sleeping child on it, found a blanket under a broken chair, and spread it over the boy. Daren flipped over, pulled the blankets up to his chin, and snored.

Tatha hadn't moved, save to light one lamp and turn off her lightstick. The yellow glow gilded her face and hair. Jes walked behind her and, tentatively, put his hands on her shoulders. She didn't move.

"We'll get it put back together tomorrow," he said quietly. "It's not as bad as it looks."

She didn't respond and her shoulders under his hands were hard with tension. He looked over her shoulder at the empty fireplace, licked his lips, and began, softly, to sing the song he had first heard in the echoing repairs bay on Gensco Station, the song which had followed him for three years and to which, in surrender, he had finally learned the words.

"Western wind," he sang, *"when wilt thou blow*
The small rain down can rain?
Christ, that my love were in my arms,
And I in my bed again."

Tatha turned swiftly in his arms, buried her face in his neck, and wept.

1